WITCH'S BITE

STEPHANIE FOXE

STEEL FOX MEDIA LLC

COPYRIGHT

Witch's Bite
All rights reserved.

No parts of this publication may be reproduced, stored in a retrieval system, or transmitted in any form or by any means, electronic, mechanical, photocopying, recording, or otherwise, without the prior written permission of the copyright owner.
This book is sold subject to the condition that it shall not, by way of trade or otherwise, be lent, resold, hired out, or otherwise circulated without the publisher's prior consent in any form of binding or cover other than that in which it is published and without a similar condition including this condition being imposed on the subsequent purchaser. Under no circumstances may any part of this book be photocopied for resale.
This is a work of fiction. Any similarity between the characters and situations within its pages and places or persons, living or dead, is unintentional and coincidental. All inquiries can be sent to info@steelfoxmedia.com.

Print ISBN *9781950310012*

Copyright © 2017 Stephanie Foxe
Cover © Steel Fox Media LLC

The Witch's Bite Series (along with the plot / characters / situations / worlds) are Copyright (c) 2017-18 Stephanie Foxe and Steel Fox Media LLC

Dreams do come true.

CONTENTS

Part I
BORROWED MAGIC

Chapter 1	3
Chapter 2	17
Chapter 3	23
Chapter 4	33
Chapter 5	47
Chapter 6	61
Chapter 7	69
Chapter 8	77
Chapter 9	87

Part II
PRICE OF MAGIC

Chapter 1	95
Chapter 2	103
Chapter 3	113
Chapter 4	119
Chapter 5	131
Chapter 6	139
Chapter 7	151
Chapter 8	159
Chapter 9	165
Chapter 10	169
Chapter 11	175
Chapter 12	191
Chapter 13	203
Chapter 14	209
Chapter 15	215
Chapter 16	225
Chapter 17	233
Chapter 18	243

Chapter 19   251
Chapter 20   261

Part III
BLOOD MAGIC
Chapter 1   269
Chapter 2   275
Chapter 3   285
Chapter 4   293
Chapter 5   305
Chapter 6   313
Chapter 7   323
Chapter 8   333
Chapter 9   339
Chapter 10   351
Chapter 11   359
Chapter 12   365
Chapter 13   377
Chapter 14   387
Chapter 15   395
Chapter 16   403
Chapter 17   413
Chapter 18   421
Chapter 19   427
Chapter 20   435
Chapter 21   445
Chapter 22   449
Chapter 23   459
Chapter 24   469
Chapter 25   477
Chapter 26   487
Chapter 27   501
Chapter 28   511
Chapter 29   519
Chapter 30   531

Part IV
FORBIDDEN MAGIC

Prologue	537
Chapter 1	541
Chapter 2	547
Chapter 3	557
Chapter 4	567
Chapter 5	581
Chapter 6	595
Chapter 7	601
Chapter 8	607
Chapter 9	613
Chapter 10	621
Chapter 11	637
Chapter 12	645
Chapter 13	653
Chapter 14	657
Chapter 15	665
Chapter 16	673
Chapter 17	685
Chapter 18	693
Chapter 19	699
Chapter 20	707
Chapter 21	719
Chapter 22	725
Chapter 23	731
Chapter 24	741
Chapter 25	749
Chapter 26	753
Chapter 27	759
Chapter 28	769
Chapter 29	773
Chapter 30	777
Chapter 31	781
Chapter 32	785
Chapter 33	787
A Big Thank You	791
Make a Difference	793
Follow me	795
More by Stephanie Foxe	797

PART I
BORROWED MAGIC

CHAPTER 1

I'm the only healer in two hundred miles that would let a vampire dump a half-dead snack off on my doorstep. I'm also the weakest healer in over two hundred miles, my magical talent is in brewing potions and salves, but I can keep a necker alive if a vampire gets a little overzealous.

Which is why I'm opening the door to a half-dead woman who's bleeding out slowly on my front porch. Her neck is torn in two narrow strips from where they dragged a vampire off of her.

I drop to my knees and put my hand over her heart to take her pulse. It's beating, but thready, and her skin is cold. I grab my X-ACTO knife from right inside the doorway and cut off her top. The poor girl isn't even wearing a bra. Glancing down at her clothes I realize that makes sense; she isn't exactly dressed for church, and any bra would have shown in that shirt.

I run my hands slowly and firmly down her torso, increasing blood production and warming her. Her heart beat regains some confidence as my magic wraps around it. It's moving under my skin like I've pulled it inside me.

I hook my hands under her arms and drag her inside. She's

fairly light, so I take a deep breath, then haul her torso up onto the table. Her legs go up next, then I roll her onto her back, but give up on trying to get her on there straight. I could use some help just for this part.

The emergency supplies are all laid out. The IV, scissors, gauze, and cleaning supplies. The IV bag is already hanging from the stand, ready to go. I don't bother with gloves, but I do grab an alcohol wipe and scrub down her arm. The healing goes much smoother the sooner I can get fluids into the injured person.

A vein is easy to find, thankfully, and I slip the needle in carefully. This part has always made my stomach churn. I wish I could heal without all of this, but I'm simply too weak to rely on magic alone.

Now that the IV is started I can continue healing. Her body is sucking up the fluids like a sponge as I push my magic through her, encouraging her body to replenish the blood she lost. They had gotten her to me just in time. She had been very close to beyond my ability to help. I suspect she was fed on by several vampires; there are bites in various places on her torso. If she had already lost quite a bit of blood; having a young vampire lose control while feeding was very risky. The past six months worth of practice I have had pay off for her, maybe working for the vampires isn't a total waste.

I had been contacted by a vampire about six months ago when I was a little desperate for money, working as a waitress doesn't pay quite enough to live off of, and offered a job. The job was simple; I would do house calls to keep the humans they fed on healthy and help them recover more quickly so the vampires could drink from them more often. The vampires bring them to me if there is ever an 'unfortunate incident', which is a professional sounding term for somebody losing control and nearly draining a necker. In return, I'm paid a decent salary, definitely more than I could get paid for my mediocre healing anywhere else.

Healers are rare, good healers even more so, and you almost

can't find a healer that'd stoop to help vampire leftovers. We can get a bit snooty since we're a rare breed. Of course, I'm so far at the bottom of the barrel I'm barely even recognized as a healer. I've never been able to earn money from healing before. That's enough to take the snootiness out of anyone.

The vampires also aren't as terrible as I expected. They seem to take care of the people they feed on very well; I think they care about them, possibly even love some of them. It's more of a balanced relationship than I had imagined. I should know better than to buy into stereotypes.

I measure out a small amount of my most used salve. It will heal the nasty tears on her neck in a matter of days.

"Who the fuck are you?" The girl slurs as she tries to slide off the table. They always wake up faster than I want them to. I think the magic is stimulating.

"Nope, get back on the table, I'm not done yet," I say as I grab her arm. She pulls against my grip with a shaking arm.

"You can't tell me what to do, bitch," she says as she leans forward to try to bite me.

I do not understand why they always try to bite; it's like they forget they're the food and not the vampires. I smack her across the face, hard, and she jerks back, looking at me with wide eyes that are a little more awake.

"Sit the fuck down. Whoever you were playing with almost killed you. I'm in charge of fixing you. If you give me trouble, they will kick your ass," I snap, pointing at a sign hanging on the wall behind me.

It's a simple sign, something I requested after the first few gave me trouble since they were waking up in a strange place with no idea who I was. It says COOPERATE OR BE PUNISHED. Beneath the words are the clan's sigil and the clan leader's signature.

The girl's eyes go wide, and she slumps back down on the table.

"Sorry, lady."

"Drink this," I say, handing her a small vial. "It's gonna be disgusting but don't you dare spit any of it out. It's expensive."

The girl pinches her nose and chokes it down, cursing me and the vampires as soon as she can get a breath. "What the hell was that?"

"Something to replenish your iron and blood levels. You'll probably have a headache until it wears off in a few days, and you'll have a hard time getting drunk."

"I'm supposed to go to a party tonight!"

"Guess you can be the designated driver," I say with a shrug. "Lay down."

She complies, still grumbling about her party. I push her chin to the side and spread the salve on the bites. She yelps and the skin twitches as the area reddens.

She reaches up to scratch it, and I bat her hand away.

"It itches!"

"I know, it's going to itch until it's healed, but if you scratch it, you'll tear it open and then no one is going to want to bite your ugly neck."

She sticks her hands under her arms, looking mutinous, but still complying. I grab one more potion off my desk and hand it to her.

"If you are going to let someone feed on you again within the next 72 hours, take this about an hour before."

She slips it into her pocket, but the pout doesn't leave her face. I toss a plain white t-shirt at her as well, and she pulls it on. My phone buzzes, it's a text from the chauffeur service the vampires arranged.

"Your ride is here, you can leave through that door," I say pointing at the door behind her. I made sure to set up this room so that no one would have to walk through my house to get out. The neckers had a tendency to take things when you weren't looking. After my third patient, a six-foot-tall man had stolen my flip flops I made some changes.

I rub a hand down my face, I'm tired, but healing always gets my adrenaline going. There's no chance I'll fall back asleep now, which is fine since there's order that I need to deliver, I glance at the time again, today. I have just enough time to make it and deliver it before lunch.

I've been brewing since I was five; so I could make any of these potions in my sleep. The process is cathartic these days. Brewing has always given me a sense of control. It's measured, predictable, and reliable. Water boils at the same temperature every time. A bat eye, dandelion petals, and a pinch of fool's gold always brews into a simple blood replenishing potion.

Mr. Bronson, god rest his soul, had never understood that. He thought the brewing was what got me in with a bad crowd, but it was what had kept me from really losing myself. It was helping me get my feet back on the ground now too.

I wipe a drop of sweat from my forehead and lean over to crank up the window unit. This old rental house doesn't seem to have any insulation left, and Texas is hot as Satan's balls in the summer. If I didn't have the contract with the vampires, I'd be moving into one of the little apartments in town instead of renewing the lease on this place, but I need the privacy.

Soon enough I forget about the heat and vampires and even Mr. Bronson's voice in the back of my head telling me I ought not do the devil's work. I've been working on this acne salve for two weeks. Each stage has to sit undisturbed in the cauldron for thirty-six hours. Then I had to wait for it to settle into the right consistency. It's been stubborn, to say the least.

I lift the lid from the cauldron and poke at the translucent, rosy substance. It's slick and about the same thickness as lard.

"Finally," I lean down and give it a quick sniff too. It smells like rose and marshmallow.

I scoop it into little plastic tubs, wipe off any drips, and slap the labels that Maybelle printed for me on them. It says 'Carter's Brews' in a swirly blue font over a shiny, silver background. It's a little girly for me, but she said it was great marketing and since Maybelle runs the most successful business in town, I took her advice without arguing.

The next brew is a quicker one; there is no need to rest it. It actually works best the faster I can get it bottled. It's been one of the best sellers which suits me just fine. The centering brew is simple and cheap to make. It was one of my mother's best sellers, but that's to be expected in a big town. I wasn't sure how it would do here. Apparently, even out in the country, people want the pinpoint focus and energy the potion provides. They're willing to deal with the minor headache it causes, and I can't blame them. As far as side effects that's not half bad.

The cauldron I need isn't where it should be. I turn in a circle, scanning the room, then remember the one I need is still sitting by the sink. I'd left a potion too long the other day and have been scrubbing goo off it since.

The cauldron is sparkling, polished steel. I bought it two months ago when the previous one fell apart. The magic puts quite a bit of stress on the metal.

I twist the knob on the stove and the burner flares to life. Before the metal of the cauldron gets too hot, I dip my finger in the saltwater solution I keep next to the stove and trace a spiral from the middle of the cauldron up and around the sides to the top edge.

The ingredients for the brew are all lined up on the shelf behind the stove. I set a plain, clear crystal the size of a pea in the very center of the spiral and pour essence of mint over the top. The mint obediently settles into the lines I drew in the bottom of the cauldron, slowly creeping up the sides as though it's trying to escape the heat.

I pull a bottle of cheap Prosecco out of the mini fridge and pour it straight into the cauldron. Something bubbly to give them pep while the mint makes them sharp. It hisses up immediately begins to boil.

I pick out a few wasp wings and crumple them in my hand as I grab my sturdy, old wooden stirring rod. They drop into the cauldron, and I stir quickly. Right, right, left, right, right, left. I continue until the rhythm feels natural and mindless.

The mint, still clinging to the sides of the cauldron, begins to glow green as the brew tugs at it. I pass my hand over the cauldron, my fingers wiggling and scattering bright sparks into the bubbling liquid.

"There we go," I whisper as the brew begins to spin on its own. I lift the stirring rod out of it, and roiling liquid begins to spin faster and faster until it suddenly stills in a flash of green tinted light. "One down, six to go."

The hours pass quickly as I fill little glass vials with my potions, then start another batch. One of these days I'll be able to afford a bigger cauldron.

I'm a sweaty, tired mess by the time I'm done. The workroom is scattered with ingredients, and I need to wash out this cauldron, but I'm actually running out of time to get to town.

I double check my order list and make sure everything is packed up and ready to put in the car, then head into the central part of the house to take a quick shower. I can't show up to Maybelle's looking like a hobo.

A country song twangs out of my speakers as I pull into town. I wouldn't have been caught dead listening to country music before I moved here, but it's become something of a guilty pleasure. The songs make me nostalgic for a peaceful small town life I've never had.

Maybelle's General Store is the most prominent store on Main Street. The sides of the building facing the road are glass all the way around and lit up day and night with antique styled lanterns that always stay polished to brilliance. Nobody can walk by without slowing down to look inside.

She has everything from clothes to kitchenware to potions. Upstairs is a cafe with a balcony that overlooks the street. I can smell the pies from down the street near the service entrance where I'm parking.

Johnny is at my trunk before I can get out of my car. That man has a sixth sense for deliveries.

"Hey Johnny, how's it hanging?"

"Little to the left," he says with a cackle as he grabs the first box of potions out of my trunk. Johnny is missing a few teeth and has spent so much time under the sun that he's darker than even Mr. Brunson was. Johnny's wrinkles are more like craters, even though I suspect he's only about sixty. He moves too fast to be any older. I follow him inside and set my box down on a table in the storeroom, the little vials all clinking together.

"Is that who I think it is?" Maybelle comes out of her office in a whirl of color. She's wearing a ruffled pink skirt with an exquisite yellow blouse. A teal headscarf is holding her curly red hair out of her face, which is covered in freckles and brightened by a wide smile. She's even older than Johnny, but nobody would dare mention it.

"My sweet Olivia, I have not seen you in a full week!" She says as she sweeps me into a hug, bending me side to side. I hug back as well as I can. "Have you been avoiding me?"

"Not at all," I laugh as I pull away. "I've just been a little busy this week."

"Busy with that good-for-nothing boy," she says, flicking the tip of my nose before she sashays over to my box of potions and inspects a few.

"He's not that bad. Besides, we aren't even dating. We're just getting to know each other."

"You are having sex with him, and you are thinking about a

future with him before you've even gotten him to say he's your boyfriend. You know that's backward."

I shrug and look at the floor. She's old-fashioned, and it never does much good to argue with her. It had been over a year since I'd gotten laid. Tyler was easy on the eyes and had that good ol' boy feel about him. He opened the door and paid for our dates and always made sure I came first.

"It's good enough for now Maybelle."

She tisks at me but drops it. "I have a new business proposition for you since you're here."

I perk up immediately. "What is it?"

"I bought a little storefront down the street a few months ago. I think I want to turn it into an apothecary. What would you think about supplying me with more medicinal brews?"

Medicinal brews cost five to ten times as much as other brews. They're tricky to brew, tricky enough that people won't buy them from anyone other than a healer's guild shop. Unless they're stupid. I can brew them, but I'd never be able to sell them on my own. Maybelle however—people would buy it from her.

"I think I would like to do that very much," I say, hoping she can't tell there's a lump in my throat. If I had a contract like that it would change everything. I wouldn't have to work for the vampires. I would be able to afford a rent house that wasn't a hundred years old with rats living under the porch.

Maybelle nods at me with a twinkle in her eye.

"I have contractors coming tomorrow to start building it out. I'll let you know when I'll need some brews. You better give me your best work girly."

"You know I don't do anything else."

She nods proudly. "You coming upstairs for some pie?"

"Not today," I say standing up straight and smoothing down my shirt. "Apparently I need to go visit Gerard."

"Alright, well you don't be a stranger. I better see you again in a few days."

"I promise I'll come by," I say, pecking her on the cheek and heading towards the door.

"If you don't I'll send Johnny to grab you. Don't think I won't!"

"Wouldn't doubt it for a second!" I say as I slip back out into the heat.

I climb into my car and let out a sigh. I'm ecstatic about the business opportunity, but medicinal brews mean specialty ingredients. And specialty ingredients mean Gerard. And Gerard is creepy. There's no use putting it off though.

A quick five-minute drive brings me to Gerard's warehouse. It's the polar opposite of Maybelle's place. His office is in a rickety metal storefront with one window that is boarded up with weathered plywood. The door is always locked, and the sign on the door reads closed. I've never been sure how he makes a living since I've never seen another person here.

I take a deep breath and rap out three loud knocks on the thick metal door, wait three seconds, then one more. I step back from the door and settle in for a wait. He always makes me wait at least five minutes, which is why I jump when the door immediately swings inward.

Gerard is in the doorway, eyes wide and bloodshot. His white t-shirt is stained, and he is sweatier than usual.

"Get inside," he whispers hoarsely, scuttling backward out of the sunlight.

I leap inside to get in before he pulls the door shut on me. It's almost pitch black, so I pull out my phone and use the light from the screen to follow him back to his makeshift office, stepping around moldy pallets and trash. There's also a dead rat, but that's better than the live one that ran across my foot the last time I was here. Gerard is practically jogging, and he keeps scratching at his arms.

"Everything okay Gerard?" I ask as I jog to catch up.

He stops and whips around. "Better watch your back, Olivia.

There's trouble in town and none of the powers that be are going to do a thing about it. They don't listen to reason."

"What kind of trouble?"

"The bad kind," he says as he steps into his office.

Cryptic as always. The man's impossible to have a coherent conversation with. I put my phone back in my pocket, the ambient glow of eight computer screens is enough to see by. This whole room is a spiderweb of wires across the walls and ceiling. There's a pile of empty ramen containers in one corner and a big water jug next to a black rolling chair that leans to the left. He tosses me a notepad and then a pen which I barely manage to catch.

I write down my order, mentally running through the ingredients for the new brews I'll need to make. Some of them I haven't made in years, but the recipes are ingrained in me. A few minutes pass, then I hand the notepad back, three pages filled out front and back. He flips through it eagerly.

"These are new," he says squinting at me. "Who do you think you're gonna get to buy healing brews from a girl with a felony on her record?"

"Can you get it all for me or not? I think I'll need to be brewing within a month," I ask, trying not to bristle at his question. There's no way I could do this without Maybelle, but I don't need Gerard of all people reminding me of past mistakes. He's always known things about me he shouldn't.

He squints at me for a moment longer, then nods.

I take that as my cue to leave and start picking my way back through the warehouse.

Right before I reach the door, he yells across the empty space. "Try not to die!"

I open the door and step back into the sunlight, blinking. I have goosebumps despite the heat.

Rudie's is the best bar in town, and also boasts the best hamburger and curly fries in three counties, possibly even the nation. They open at eleven am, except on Sundays when they don't open until two pm and have a dedicated lunch crowd. Every time I've had the money to spare I end up here for lunch.

My stomach growls as I walk inside and the delicious aroma of fried food hits me. It's glorious. Chevy is behind the bar handing over a beer to Fred, one of the regulars. Chevy waves at me before moving down the bar to take the next order. Susan waves too, pointing at a free table in the corner. I nod and take a seat with my back to the wall. It takes a minute before she can make it over to me, stopping at a few tables to accept a request for more water or sweet tea.

"Hey darling, the usual?"

"Yes, ma'am," I say with a grin. It's been almost two weeks since I've been in for a burger and I've been craving them.

"You got it," she says before bustling away.

The door to my right tinkles and I glance up, a smile springing to my face when I see Tyler walk in. The smile turns brittle when I spot Joanna, the blonde bimbo town slut, hanging off his side. She isn't interested unless the guy has a girlfriend or a wife. I've never been sure if it's daddy issues or if she's just mean. He's got his hand on her ass.

He doesn't see me until he gets a solid five steps in. My face is going blank like it does when I get mad. He stops in his tracks, and Joanna trips over his feet. She finally catches on to where he is looking and rolls her eyes.

"Come oooon Tyler. Let's get lunch."

"Just give me a second to talk to Liv, alright?"

Joanna sticks her bottom lip out like a five-year-old and blinks her eyes up at him. "But I'm hungry baby. You wore me out this morning."

So that's why he hadn't responded to my texts since yesterday afternoon.

"I'll be just a minute," he says as he finally gets his arm out of her grip.

She huffs and shoves him. "Fine, go talk to that stupid bitch, but I'm not hanging around waiting for you to talk to some other girl."

She throws a glare my direction and stomps out.

I lean back in my chair as Tyler approaches, rubbing his hand across the back of his neck.

"Hey Liv," he says, looking at me with a half smile.

I stare him down, a hundred useless things running through my mind, like the last time I saw that smile and how his hands felt on my ass.

"Look, we hadn't talked about being exclusive or anything."

I don't say anything; there's no point. We hadn't 'defined the relationship' or whatever, but he'd started talking about taking me to meet his family in a few weeks because they were having a barbecue. It had felt like we were dating. Then again, any guy I chose was almost guaranteed to be an asshole. It was a family curse.

"I must have thought it was implied when you told me no one else had ever made you feel this way and you didn't even want to look at another girl."

"Come on Liv; we were in the middle of, you know," he says, waggling his eyebrows and glancing around like he's embarrassed to say the word sex in public. "That doesn't count for anything."

"Tyler," I say carefully, leaning forward onto my elbows. "Fuck off and let me enjoy my burger."

Susan walks up with perfect timing and sets my burger down with way more force than necessary, bouncing a couple of curly fries off onto the table. I rescue them and shove them all in my mouth at once.

"See ya some other day Tyler," Susan says with her arms crossed and a thicker accent than usual.

"Whatever," he says before storming out of the door he came in.

"I'm gonna bring you a milkshake sweetie."

"No, that's okay Susan, I'll just—"

"No objections allowed. It's on the house, Chevy will insist on it."

She walks away before I can object again, not that I really want to argue. Their milkshakes are great, and I could use some chocolate.

I take a bite of my burger, but it doesn't taste quite as good as it usually does when I'm not trying not to cry in public.

CHAPTER 2

Mr. Muffins is staring at me from the hallway when I slam the front door behind me.

"Don't look at me like that," I mutter as I stalk into the kitchen. The tequila is in the same cupboard as my glasses. I grab the bottle and take a swig before dropping heavily into a chair at the little two-person table crammed into the space between the kitchen and the living room. I had texted Patrick before I left Rudie's and he still hasn't responded yet. He wasn't a Tyler fan, so I'm sure he'll be excited.

My laptop dings with a new email. It's the deposit from the vampires for the healing I did this morning. I take another drink of tequila and open my account to check the balance. One thousand twenty-two dollars and sixty-five cents. It's the most money I've had in the bank at one time, by legal means at least, but if I can supply the apothecary for Maybelle, this'll be nothing. I'll have thousands.

I grin as I take another drink. Fuck Tyler. This is a celebration.

My resolve lasts for about thirty minutes. My phone rings, a sickeningly romantic country song blaring out of the tinny speak-

17

ers, Tyler's number flashing on the screen. I reject the call and take a drink, sliding my phone away from me across the table.

I move to the living room and turn on the tv scrolling through the static and news channels trying to find something decent, but all that's on is romantic comedies and telenovelas.

My phone rings again, and I stand up on the couch, taking another, longer, drink from the bottle.

"Muffins! I just thought of a new game! Every time he calls, I drink. You think I'll survive the night?"

Muffins meows and twitches her tail disapprovingly.

Two hours later I'm face down on the bathroom floor since it's the coldest place in the house and the room is spinning even though I'm lying still.

"Men are stupid, Muffins," I roll over to find she is facing the door licking her stomach. "Oh my god are you even listening to me? You know what, you're stupid too."

Muffins stops licking and swishes her tail.

"You heard me," I mutter before sitting up to take another swig from the bottle. My stomach rolls and I grimace as I grab the edge of the toilet.

"I think I drank too much," I moan. "Fucking Tyler and his fucking phone calls."

Muffins crawls into my lap, her claws pricking through my jeans.

"Ow ow ow!"

She rubs her face against my chin as the tears start. I hug her close and just feel sorry for myself.

"This why I keep you around you know," I whisper into her fur.

I blink one eye open, then hear the banging again. I try to sit up quickly, my first thought is that someone is trying to break in, but my head objects strongly to quick movements, and I end up on hands and knees. I'm still in the bathroom, and my mouth tastes like something crawled inside it and died.

"Police, open up! We know you're in there!"

What the fuck. I get my feet underneath me and find my phone. It's almost two pm. I don't have any messages from the vampires, so no one died on my porch last night. I rub my eyes then lean over and take a quick drink from the tap so I can talk a little easier.

I look like shit. My hair is falling out of the ponytail I had it in, and my eyeliner is smudged down my cheek. Whatever.

They bang on my front door again.

"Alright! I'm coming! I'm coming!" I yell, despite my headache.

I jerk the door open, and I'm immediately blinded by the late afternoon sun. I keep all the blinds down in the house, so it's always nice and dark.

There are two men, and one of them flashes me a badge that looks official.

"Whatever, just come inside, it's too damn bright out here," I say opening the door wider and retreating back towards the living room.

The men walk inside. The one that showed me his badge is tall, most likely ripped underneath his clothes, and has a military haircut. He looks me over and raises a thick brow. The other guy I've seen around town before. He's a little shorter, more wiry, and has almost white blonde hair.

"Olivia Carter?"

"The one and only," I say sitting down on the couch. "What do you need?"

"I'm Detective Jason Martinez, and this is Detective Alexander Novak," the taller one says. "Do you know Jessica Johnson?"

"Um," I say, going through people I've met recently in my head. "No, that name doesn't sound familiar at all."

"Do you recognize this woman?" Novak asks, stepping across the living room to shove a picture in my face. There's a young woman with blonde hair and a freshly healed bite on her neck spread out naked on the grass. Her skin is paper white, she's been drained.

I sigh, of course I recognize her.

"Yeah, I recognize her. Just didn't know her name. Early yesterday morning, around four-thirty, she got dropped off. I healed her and sent her away."

Martinez grabs the two chairs from the table and sets them in the living room across from me.

He and Novak sit down.

"Did you see her after that?" Martinez asks sitting down in the chair on the left.

"Nope."

"Are you sure she was alive when she left your house?" Novak asks.

So it's going to be like that. I lean back and cross my arms. "She was definitely alive when she was dropped off on my doorstep and was definitely alive when she walked out the door."

"Take us through what happened from the beginning," Martinez says, pulling out a notepad. Novak has his hands on his knees, one finger tapping restlessly.

"I got a text, just said 'dropping off.' I threw on some clothes, got a few things together, heard them drop her on the front porch. Got out there and fixed her up no problem. Called a car for her and she left."

I was already skirting the line of confidentiality; I definitely wasn't going to tell them she was almost dead. I also wasn't going to let them know I went through the same routine at least twice a month. It had gotten more frequent recently too, but some of the neckers weren't hurt all that bad. It was more like the vampires were getting used to the idea that they could keep their toys in better shape.

"You said 'they' dropped her off, who was it?" Jason asked.

"I don't know, I never see them."

"Why don't you see them? Ask questions about what happened to your patients?" Novak asks, sitting up slightly.

"No need to, it would be a waste of my time. It's always an issue of blood loss, and that's something I can fix easily. If it's beyond my skill level, I'd just call 911 for an ambulance."

"And that's something you've had to do," Martinez pauses, flipping back a page, "three times?"

"Yes."

"Where was she going?" Novak asks.

"I don't know, and I didn't ask because it's none of my business."

"How often do the vampires send people to your door for healing?" Martinez asks as he writes something down in his notepad.

"That's confidential."

Martinez looks up, a frown tugging at his lips.

"Do you want to be charged for impeding an ongoing investigation?" Novak asks, moving his arm so that his sleeve slips upward just enough to show me the coven symbol tattooed on his wrist.

The coven was backing the investigation then, which meant there was something bigger going on than one death. I look at the tense line of Novak's shoulders. Maybe something big enough to spook Gerard.

It's early, and I'm too hungover, for these kinds of threats. Covens are always butting into investigations involving paranormals and getting heavy-handed when it isn't necessary. The council lives and breathes public relations, and every coven wants to be on their good side. Humans can fuck up all they want, but if a paranormal is caught being evil, all hell breaks loose.

"No, but legally you have to have a warrant before I can divulge confidential client information. I'm not getting sued by the vampires. Just come back with a warrant, and I'll tell you whatever you want to know."

"You were the last person to see her alive, are you sure you don't want to help us, Miss Carter?" Novak asks. He's getting heavy handed with his threats now.

"I'll help you find your way out, how about that?" I say standing and pointing at the front door. "I'm sure you have my phone number somewhere, give me a call when you get a warrant, and we can chat all you want."

They both stand reluctantly. Novak's face has gone red from irritation. I briefly wonder how he survives summers in Texas with skin that pale.

Novak heads out the door immediately, but Martinez takes a moment to set his card down on the table.

"In case you change your mind."

"Sure," I say moving the card towards the center of the table. I can throw it away after he leaves.

He opens the door but stops in the doorway, with the sun behind him I can't see his face.

"Why do you work for the vampires? Even when they aren't breaking the law, all they do is hurt people. They prey on the weak."

"For the money," I say. It's a simple answer that isn't really a lie, it's not the whole truth, but I can feel the accusation in his question. He doesn't deserve the truth from me, not when he's come to my house and accused me of murder.

He stays in the doorway for another breath, like I might add onto what I just said, then turns and walks out to his partner who is staring daggers at me from their car.

CHAPTER 3

"You will be at the clanhouse in fifteen minutes, or we will find you and drag you there," Emilio hisses into the phone.

Emilio is always so dramatic, he buys into the Victorian, goth vampire persona.

"Oh calm the fuck down, I'm already on my way. I'll be there in five minutes."

Emilio hangs up without responding. I drop my phone into my lap and sigh. I don't want this to fall apart, but I also don't want to get murdered by paranoid vampires. My cross is hung around my neck, I rubbed myself down with holy water right before I left, and I have a few nasty potions on hand just in case.

I've had a lot of time to think after the detectives had left, and I don't like any of the things I've come up with. I doubt anyone hates me enough, much less knows me well enough, to frame me for Jessica's murder. It doesn't make sense for the vampires to have her healed and then kill her either. Not that it was impossible, they could be really damn confusing sometimes.

There was a chance, small though it was, that the coven was

involved. They haven't given me any trouble since I moved into town though. They had made it clear I wasn't welcome in their coven, but that hadn't exactly been big news. Covens didn't accept fuckups.

I don't really know any of the weres in this town. I've seen them around but the alpha, whoever they are, keeps everyone in line and out of the public eye.

No, whatever was going on had to be about the vampires. Maybe whoever had gotten pulled off Jessica that night had gone back for the rest the next night when they woke up. They could get fixated like that sometimes. My shoulder aches just thinking about it.

I turn down the long driveway. The house looms over the yard like an old ghost. The vampires had bought a plantation style house fifty or sixty years ago. The inside is modernized, but the outside is all overgrown vines and boarded up windows. It looks like it's haunted.

I park by one of their sleek black limos and climb out as the sun sets on the horizon. The door is already swinging open. Emilio is hovering in the shadows watching me.

"Good morning, Emilio," I say quietly as I walk inside.

He slams the door shut behind me and looks down his nose as he adjusts his lace cuffs. He speaks with a slight hiss, "You know it issn't morning, and you know that joke iss never funny."

I look behind me but don't see Patrick creeping up. I frown, this is typically when he pops up to tell Emilio his sense of humor is dead or something like that. Which is why Patrick is my favorite. He had scared me the first few times I was here; he thought it was hilarious to sneak up behind me and try to get me to scream. He had finally succeeded the third time he tried. He had broken down laughing so hard he cried. I had ended up on the floor with him, laughing harder than I had in years. We've been best buds ever since. He's the only vampire I'd ever go to a bar with, and he's the only one other than Javier and Emilio with my cell number.

"Where's Patrick?"

"Javier is eager to speak with you, follow me," Emilio says, completely ignoring my question, as usual.

The house is always dark inside. The only lighting is soft, blue-tinted LEDs built into the baseboards every few feet. At first the darkness it put me on edge, but since I've been coming every two weeks for six months, I've gotten used to it. Patrick explained that it really was more for comfort anyhow, it just had the added effect of scaring newcomers. Blood tastes better when it's pumping faster, apparently.

Actual light is coming from under the door to Javier's room though. He uses his bedroom as an office.

Emilio knocks once, then pulls the door open, waving me inside.

Javier is lanky, but always well groomed unlike some of his clan. He's wearing a crisp, white button-down shirt, unbuttoned and hung loosely, over black slacks. His dark skin is dampened by his ghostly pallor causing a stark contrast to his black hair. He is standing in front of his window with the thick, red curtains tied back so he can watch the moon rise.

He turns around, looking me up and down with relish.

"You cut your hair," he comments.

My hand goes to it automatically. It had been down almost to my waist, I cut it to my shoulders about a week ago, and I'm still getting used to it.

"It's hot outside," I say with a shrug.

He pushes out his bottom lip in a pout. "It's still lovely, but I did always hope to see all that hair fanned out on my pillow."

I roll my eyes. "The police came to my house today, the necker you dropped off the night before last ended up dead."

He sits back on the window ledge. "So I heard. What did you tell the police?"

"That I fixed her up, she left alive, and that if they wanted to know more, they had to come back with a warrant."

Javier chuckles, a deep sound that always makes my skin crawl. "How did they take that?"

"One of the detectives is a witch, he flashed his coven mark," I say with a shrug. "I'm guessing they will come back with a warrant if they can."

Javier stands and grabbed an envelope from the bookshelf to his left and tosses it at me. I catch it just before it hits my face and scowl at him.

"What's this?"

"Your six-month bonus, we always want our employees to feel appreciated," Javier says spreading his arms wide and grinning with a mouth full of teeth that are unnaturally sharp.

So, it was encouragement to keep my mouth shut, possibly even if there was a warrant. The smile, however, is a threat.

"Always good to be appreciated, Javier," I say as I slip the envelope into my back pocket. "I'll let you know if they contact me again."

"Please do, you will have our protection if they harass you of course."

I nod my head politely and move towards the door before I pause. "Do you have any idea what might have Gerard spooked?"

Javier's jaw twitches. "No, I didn't realize he was spooked. Did he say something to you?"

"He just suggested that I try not to die."

"Death isn't so bad," Javier says with a wink.

"See you next week for check-ups," I say as I slip out the door. He knows something. Familiar anger is bubbling up in my stomach. Secrets always end up getting the peons hurt, and lord knows I'm definitely a peon.

I flip through the contents of the envelope as I walk down the hall to Patrick's room, five hundred, not bad. I knock on Patrick's door. When there's no answer I try the handle, it's unlocked. The door swings open soundlessly, and I flick on the lights. The room is empty, but nothing is out of place. The sheets on the bed are rumpled, and there's a blood stain on the pillow. All normal for Patrick, he's a messy eater. The only thing that's odd is that he isn't here.

I turn the light off and shut the door behind me, unease settling over me.

It's ten pm, and I've called Patrick's cell about eight times. When I find him, I'm going to kick his ass. It's been about a week since I've heard from him. I thought maybe he was mad at me for that comment I made about how he's been kind of slutty lately, which I meant as a joke, but he took personally for some reason. The longest he's ever gone without talking to me before this is maybe two days, it's gone beyond weird at this point.

I can't sit at the house anymore. There's a small chance that if he's just out wandering around that he'll be in town tonight. He loves Rudie's, there's always a ton of humans there to mess with, and girls that want to feel a little dangerous by flirting with a vampire. It's somewhere to start at least.

I grab my best jeans out of my closet and pull them on. I don't have much in the way of boobs, no more than a handful, but I make up for it in ass. The jeans definitely show that off to good advantage. I grab a silky, dark red blouse too. It's low cut, and one of only two nice shirts I have.

I never know what to do with my hair, so it just hangs straight around my face. I touch up my eyeliner and mascara and shrug at the mirror. It'll do for tonight.

The drive into town feels like it takes twice as long as usual. I have the music cranked up loud, my fingers tapping out an unsteady rhythm on the steering wheel. The parking lot is filling up when I pull in; I have to park towards the back where the lights just barely reach.

I walk in through the back entrance and head towards the bar.

The music is loud, country music still, they don't switch to hip-hop until after midnight. There's a big group of guys in the corner, eyes glued to the tv watching some kind of MMA fight. The bar itself is three people deep waiting for drinks. Chevy is back there with the other bartenders, including a girl I don't recognize that must be new.

I wind my way through the crowd and get in line. The thought of alcohol makes my stomach churn, but I need at least a beer, so I'm not standing around without anything in my hands. I finally make it up to the bar after a few minutes, and Chevy nods in greeting.

"What can I get you?" He shouts over the music.

"Beer, you got anything new in?"

"I've got a new pecan porter."

"I'll try that. Hey, have you seen Patrick around since last night?"

"Nope, but if I see him, I'll tell him you're looking for him," he says as he grabs a glass, spinning it twice before filling it to the brim with the dark, foamy liquid.

"Thanks, Chevy."

He waits for me to taste it before he goes to help the next person. I take a long drink, my eyes shutting on their own. It's sweet and a little nutty and wonderfully refreshing. I'm definitely going to have to order this again. I give Chevy a thumbs up.

There aren't any tables open, so I push back through the crowd and find an empty space along the wall where I can watch for Patrick.

Most of the faces look familiar, some because I've healed them and others just because they're always at Rudie's. One of the familiar ones is attached to a girl named Dawn. She looks like she's already a little drunk as she stumbles towards me with a distraught look on her face.

"Olivia," she says as she grabs my arm, making my porter splash over onto my knuckles. I push her back gently, but firmly.

"Don't spill my beer, Dawn."

"Oh sorry," she says, her face screwing up and her lip trembling.

"Look, it's okay, what'd you want?" I really don't want her to start crying. She can go for hours once she gets started.

"You seen Britney around? Like with the vampires or whatever?"

"You know I don't talk about what I do or don't see with the vampires."

She sighs and smears the back of her hand across her nose, sniffling. "I know it's just she's been missing for a few days, and I'm worried, okay?"

Another missing person. I believe in a lot of things. That people are inherently evil; Maybelle is an exception to that rule, and that curly fries are the best fries. One thing I don't believe in is coincidences.

"How long has she been missing?"

"Since like two weeks ago. She was supposed to come hang last week, like, she promised. She wanted to get together with Bryan, and she wouldn't just not show up, you know?"

"Maybe she found herself a vampire or something?" I say, trying to reassure her even though in my gut I know she's right to be worried.

"I guess," Dawn attempts a smile.

A hand waving frantically catches my attention. Tyler is pushing his way through the crowd headed straight for me.

"I gotta go. I hope you find your friend," I say, chugging down the rest of my porter and shoving the empty glass in Dawn's hand. She looks confused and almost drops it. I'll look for Patrick some other night.

I'm two steps from the door when a hand closes around my arm. I turn around to snap at Tyler, but the person grabbing me is a woman. Her nails press into my skin, and her ruby red lips are twisted into a sneer.

"Why don't we walk together?" she asks.

I glance at her wrist, it has the same coven mark as the detective. Shit.

"Nah, you can go ahead without me," I say as I attempt to tug my arm out of her grip.

A large, bald man steps up behind her, jacket parted just enough to show me a gun. The gun is probably the least scary thing he has.

I can go with them now while we're in at least a semi-public place, or I can give them the slip and have them show up at my house for a much more tense conversation later. I might be able to hold them off there, but I'm not sure I want to bet my life on it.

I catch Chevy's eye at the bar; he's cleaning a glass very slowly, watching what's going down. At least someone will know where to point the police if I disappear tonight.

"Fine, lead the way."

The woman tightens her grip on my arm and drags me out the door. The bald man follows close behind. Her heeled boots clunk heavily against the wood of the patio, a few people look up as we pass, but they're too absorbed in their own conversations to notice the tension.

"So, are y'all here to recruit me for your coven? Heard about how awesome I was and just couldn't wait?" I ask as we pass the first row of cars and the lights from the bar fade.

Scarlett, the nickname seems fitting, rolls her eyes. The prick of her nails on my skin makes me itch to do something stupid, but I know it's not worth it.

We stop in front of a black car with tinted windows and my heartbeat kicks into overdrive.

"Get in," Baldy rumbles from behind me.

I twist and yank my arm, stepping away from Scarlett.

"I'm not getting in that car. If you two want to talk, you can do it here."

Leaving the bar was a courtesy to Chevy, and if I'm honest,

bought me some time to think. I know deep down in my soul that if I get in that car, I'll disappear permanently.

Scarlett snaps her fingers, and a flame wraps around her fingers and down her hand.

"Get in the car, or I'll make you," she says with a smile, her eyes glinting red from the light of the flame. Fire witches always think they're hot shit. Most of them have no idea how to use the magic to its fullest potential.

I pull a thin vial out of my back pocket.

"I guarantee your coven doesn't have an antidote for this," I say as I wiggle it in their faces. "Whatever message you have for me can be given to me right here, right now."

Baldy is watching the vial, his hand twitching like he thinks he might be fast enough to grab it before I can break it.

I put a little pressure on the vial, just enough for the glass to give a little.

Baldy's jaw tenses and he glances at Scarlett. She purses her lips and sighs, extinguishing the flame.

"You need to tell the police that Javier is the one draining the girls that have been disappearing," Scarlett says. "You can tell them you were just too afraid to come forward before."

Girls. How many have disappeared? Jessica. Britney. I haven't been paying attention to the news lately.

"Do you have proof Javier is the one draining them?" I say, hoping my concern doesn't show on my face. Javier would never risk his little kingdom just to drain some neckers.

"No, but that doesn't matter, and you know it. Javier is responsible for every vampire in this district," Scarlett says, her voice snapping in irritation.

"So you want to pin it on him and what? Just hope the murders stop?"

"The vampires got sloppy and killed them, Carter, there's nothing more to it than that. This needs to be settled quickly and quietly, you know the rules."

"Is the council already looking into this?"

"No," Baldy says, stepping a little closer to me. "And this will be resolved before they do. This district has a perfect record, and we will not allow the vampires to mar that."

Gerard's warning is ringing in my ears. He said that trouble had come to town, but the vampires have been here for over a hundred years. Something else is going on.

"You've got a witch in the damn police, why do you need me to lie?"

"He still needs evidence!" Scarlett shouts. "We have to work through the human's legal system, as you well know."

"You are not leaving here tonight until you give us your word that you will do as instructed. You will call Detective Novak tomorrow morning at eight am and let him know that you do have information and that you'd like to speak with him right away. If you do not cooperate, you will face punishment by the coven," Baldy says in an even tone.

By punishment he means death. Covens are fucking overbearing.

"Like hell, I will," I say throwing the vial onto the ground. I'm already running, eyes screwed tightly shut, as it explodes in a flash of light and a boom that rattles everything around us. Through the ringing in my ears, I can hear car alarms going off. I open my eyes and pull another vial out of my pocket, this one is a little nastier, and I hope I don't have to use it.

CHAPTER 4

I crouch down behind a row of cars, running as fast I can in such an awkward position. I can hear Scarlett screeching something, but Baldy is silent. He scares me a little more, especially since I don't know what he can do.

I stop by a big truck and crouch behind one of the tires. I can see my car, but it's in a different row. I'll have to go out into the open. I should have brought another flash-bang potion.

There is the distinct crunch of gravel behind me. I run without even looking and hear the footsteps speed up behind me. I skid to a stop behind my car and turn and throw the second vial. I don't want to be too close when it breaks.

Baldy is directly in its path, his skin a mottled, dark gray. I grin, impervs are always more caught off guard by this kind of potion. They tend to think they're actually invincible. The vial breaks on his chest as he barrels towards me.

I don't even see Scarlett until the bright light of a fireball comes hurtling towards me from behind Baldy. Baldy clutches his chest, his mouth gaping uselessly as he falls to his knees. The fireball fizzles out of existence, and Scarlett hits her knees behind him, her mouth open in a silent scream.

I yank my car door open and jump inside. The two seconds it takes to turn the car on and get it in reverse feel like a century. I only have five more seconds before they get their oxygen back. I back out, car swinging a foot from Baldy's head.

My tires spin and kick up gravel as I shift into first. Scarlett's indignant scream is the only warning I get before a fireball engulfs my car from back to front. Bathing the thing in a fire resistance potion was a pain in my ass, but I don't regret a second of it now. The fire is still hot enough that it probably singed the paint, but I'll worry about that later.

I pull out onto the main road, my tires screeching on the pavement. I make a beeline for my house. Since I didn't actually injure anyone, the coven probably won't show up at my home in force to kill me tonight. They seem to want me alive for now at least.

My knuckles are white on the steering wheel. I'm already starting to shake. I hate this feeling after a fight when my body doesn't realize the danger has passed.

I glance at the rearview mirror every few seconds. The roads outside of town are always empty. It would be noticeable if someone followed me.

The house looks perfectly innocent as I drive up the driveway. The light in the kitchen is still on, and there are no black cars waiting for me. I step out of the vehicle hesitantly, every sense on high alert.

I crack open the back door and listen carefully for the telltale creak of the floor, or a breath. I step inside and shut the door behind me, turning the lock.

Something touches my leg, and I scream, throwing the lights on as I scramble for a potion on the workbench.

Muffins stares up at me, not pleased with the ruckus I just made at all.

"You fucking, stupid, worthless cat. Trying to kill me," I gasp out as I slide to the floor. "Swear to god I'll take you to the pound if you ever do that again."

She meows and walks away with her tail held high.

I rub my hands briskly over my face and stand up. With the adrenaline fading, I'd like nothing more than to just go to bed, but I'm alone, and I can't risk letting the coven walk up to my house and murder me in my sleep.

Mr. Brunson wouldn't approve of what I'm about to do. Honestly, my mother wouldn't either.

"There's a balance Livvy, especially with brewing. You give yourself a high, be prepared for the low."

I slam my copper cauldron down on the stove and light the fire. The pot needs to be nice and hot for what I'm about to brew. Everything about this potion is extreme. I'm lucky I have most of the ingredients on hand for it. I'll have to substitute stinging nettle for a scorpion tail, but it'll do.

I grab my packet of peppers out of the fridge. I had them special ordered from South Carolina a few months ago and carefully dried them. Next is the ginseng, tequila, three cubes of ice, and a scorpion tail. The last item takes me a moment to decide.

I run my hand carefully over the drawer of crystals. A pink danburite practically jumps into my hand. It feels bright and ready, it's perfect.

I crush everything separately and set the ingredients in order on the counter. The cauldron is radiating heat. The tequila hits it first and sizzles loudly. I quickly add the rest of the ingredients, the crystal going in last.

I grab my crystal stirring rod and plunge it into the brew. It begins to glow red and grows hot in my hand. Magic beats in my chest as my heart speeds up and I'm breathing like I've just run a marathon. A bright red spark jumps from my chest into the fire under the cauldron, then another, and another, until the fire is burning hotter than it should be able to.

The ingredients dissolve into a black liquid that just barely covers the bottom of the cauldron. Just as it starts to smoke, I lean over the cauldron and take a long, deep breath. The smoke twists up, curling into my nostrils and burning its way down into my lungs. It hurts like hell and my eyes water. I grit my teeth against the urge to scream as energy rushes through me, this brew is strong as hell.

I'm finally able to exhale. I turn off the fire underneath the cauldron as I pant, sweat dripping down my forehead. I've never felt so awake, the next eighteen or so hours should be fun.

I go into the living room and turn on the window unit, cranking the temperature down to sixty-eight degrees. My silky shirt is stuck to me from all the sweating I did between running for my life and brewing a super hot potion. I brace my hands on the window sill and let the cold air pour down shirt. It feels like heaven.

Jessica. Britney. Patrick.

All missing. The girls are dead, which doesn't reassure me about how safe Patrick might be. I have to consider that he has lost control, but the idea of it is ludicrous to me. Patrick is well fed and other than a perverse enjoyment of startling people, a sincerely nice guy. The timing doesn't look great though.

I have no idea if anyone turned up dead before Jessica. I chew at my thumbnail and stare at the detective's card on my dining room table. I hadn't thrown it away after all. He would probably know if there are any other connected disappearances, but I can hardly call him at two am and ask.

Maybelle might know if anyone has disappeared even if she doesn't know about the investigation. I should be able to connect the dots myself. So far it's been neckers. The coven seems to be out on the list of suspects; they're too angry about the potential for bad press. Covens tend to be a lot more subtle about their killing anyhow; the police would never find a body.

My hands are shaking, but with unspent energy instead of lack of adrenaline. I can't talk to Maybelle until seven or eight tomorrow; there's no point pacing my living room worrying about Patrick. I jog back to my workroom. I might as well brew some things I haven't had a reason to brew in ages. Whatever happens next, I want to be armed to the teeth.

I've been sitting outside Maybelle's cafe for twenty minutes when Johnny arrives to open the front door. I've been smelling food baking for almost an hour, and I'm starving.

"The hell you doing out here so early?" He asks as he strolls up. He stops when he's in front of me, his smile dropping into a frown. "Girl, you high on something?"

I smooth my hair down; I'm sweating again. I'd changed clothes, but I think I forgot to brush out my hair.

"Not really, just didn't sleep last night," I say, forcing my face into a smile that has to look even more uncomfortable than it feels.

Johnny shakes his head. "Maybelle don't like you treating yourself like that. You know I don't either. You get in here and have a glass of water, then we're going to have a chat."

He goes over straight back to the kitchen, knowing I'll follow. The cooks nod in greeting, but they're fully focused on getting ready to open. A couple of the waiters are yawning and pulling on their aprons already.

Johnny pauses to pour a glass of water for me and a cup of coffee for himself before continuing back to Maybelle's office. He points at the chair in front of her desk. I sit down and take a long drink of water.

"What did you take?" He asks, his tone steady, as if he's trying to reassure me I can't shock him. If I were to close my eyes, I could imagine Mr. Brunson standing there instead with his cowboy hat, and his thumbs tucked into his gun belt.

"Just a no-sleep potion," I say, bouncing my leg up and down nervously. "It's not a drug, magic or otherwise, it's just a brew that keeps you up for fifteen to twenty hours depending on how strong you make it."

"Now why in the hell would you need to take something like that?"

"I had a run-in with the local coven last night. They were asking me to do something I couldn't do, and I didn't feel safe sleeping last night."

"Why didn't you go to the police?"

I laugh, and it gets away from me. The no-sleep potion can do that, take your emotions to extremes you don't intend. I'm cackling, tears streaming down my face, and Johnny is starting to look concerned.

"I'm sorry," I gasp, wiping away the tears. "It's just that I always forget how human you are, Johnny."

"What's that supposed to mean?" He asks with narrowed eyes, the wrinkles in his forehead deepening.

"Witches and vampires and weres, we have to keep up appearances and look like we are operating under human law, but that's not really how it works. Some witch goes to the police to report a coven is being mean to her? She'd disappear before anyone even had a chance to follow up. Besides, some of the police are part of the coven. My complaint would never make it to anyone that could help and I'd just look weak."

"You know Maybelle would protect you if you needed it."

"I'm doing alright on my own so far. I know I look a little crazy today, but I'm okay, I promise."

He looks skeptical but doesn't push the issue. "Well, you come get breakfast and stay here for today, alright? And you better be ready to talk to Maybelle when she gets in, she should be here around lunchtime."

"Breakfast sounds good, and I need to talk to Maybelle anyhow."

I stop in the employee bathroom and lock the door behind me. My reflection looks at me blearily from the mirror, and I freeze, no wonder Johnny was concerned. Makeup is smeared down my cheeks, and my eyes are bloodshot. My hair is tangled and windblown from leaning into the window unit trying to get cooled off last night.

I rinse my face off in the sink and run my fingers through my hair as well as I can. I still don't look great, but I look more like I'm hungover instead of like I've been on a bender for three days.

The cafe is already half full when I get back to the front. I find a table in the corner and sit down. A waiter, Kevin something, hands me a menu then rushes off again. My stomach growls hungrily. I'd forgotten how much this brew increases my appetite.

I'm ready to order when Kevin gets back, and if he's judging me for how much I order it doesn't show on his face. Good man.

I dig my phone out of my pocket and send a couple of texts to Patrick, just in case, and text Emilio as well. No matter what I find out today from Maybelle, I need to talk to Javier again. With the coven threatening me I want some assurances that the vampires will have my back since I'm sticking my neck out for them.

A shadow falls over my table, and I look up, surprised my food is out already. Detective Jason Martinez stands over me instead. He's wearing a black t-shirt that stretches in a real flattering manner over his biceps and a pair of light wash jeans that I really need to see from the back. I realize I'm staring when he clears his throat, and my eyes jump back up to his face.

"You're up early," he says with a smirk,

I roll my eyes. "I don't always sleep until two in the afternoon, you just caught me on a bad day."

"Why was it a bad day?"

I immediately bristle. They're always on duty, even when they're not. "My sorta boyfriend was sorta fucking someone else."

He purses his lips but doesn't bother apologizing for asking. He just pulls out the chair across from me and sits down. "Anyone sitting here?"

"You apparently," I say with a raised brow.

Kevin shows up right then, three plates of food balanced on a tray. He sets them all down in front of me.

"Oh, you were expecting someone?" Martinez asks, moving to scoot back his chair.

"No," I say before I think better of it. I pull the plates in a little closer, Martinez is eyeing my biscuits and gravy, and I am not sharing.

"Would you like to order anything, sir?" Kevin asks politely. I'm going to have to tip Kevin well.

"Um, sure," Martinez says. "Biscuits and gravy with a side of bacon."

I knew it. I grab my fork and take a quick bite, I'm not waiting for him to get his food.

Kevin hurries away, and Martinez watches me eat my first plate of food in silence.

"So, are you on something?" He asks carefully.

I sigh and roll my eyes, slamming down my fork. "Everyone needs to stop asking me that, it's going to give me a complex."

He waits, like that wasn't really an answer.

"I'm not high," I say as I butter a piece of toast. "Did you want something in particular? Or just to watch me eat?"

"I didn't really have a plan when I saw you, actually. Watching you eat is pretty mesmerizing so far though," he says with a slow smile that has a heat to it I didn't expect to see from him. Maybe my staring earlier put some thoughts in his head.

His food is delivered, and we eat in silence for a few minutes. I stare at his arms flexing as he cuts through his biscuits and gravy. He stares at me, probably looking down my shirt. I put a large piece of bacon in my mouth, then lick my lips. His eyes follow my tongue, and I have to chew faster to keep from smiling. He grins and looks down at his plate.

Last night I didn't think there was any chance I could ask him about the other missing girl, but the universe has seen fit to deliver him to my table. Maybe it's a sign.

"You heard anything about a girl named Britney going missing? She would have been in Jessica's crowd kind of."

He leans back and wipes his mouth, the flirtatious look in his eye falls away, he almost looks guilty now. "Britney Davidson, twenty-five-year-old white female, her body was found at four am this morning. The preliminary cause of death is blood loss due to a vampire bite."

Shit. That confirms what I suspected. I poke at the last half of my waffle, my appetite is suddenly gone.

"Why did you ask me about her?"

"Last night one of her friends, Dawn, asked if I'd seen her. I hadn't, by the way," I say, flicking my eyes to his to make sure he understands my meaning. "The way Dawn was talking made me think she'd probably disappeared like Jessica."

"Britney was actually killed first. A full week before Jessica as best we can tell. Are you sure you didn't see Britney around a week ago? Anywhere?"

"I'm sure," I say, leaning back and crossing my arms.

"Why are you trying so hard to protect the vampires?" He asks, leaning forward, his brows knit together as he searches my face.

"I'm not trying to protect anybody."

"They prey on these girls, you understand that right? They use them until they end up anemic and then toss them out. They end up addicted to drugs and turning tricks on the street corners, it's not right."

"You really hate vampires, don't you?" I ask, tilting my head to the side.

"No, I don't. I just don't trust them."

I scoff. "Right. You don't hate the monsters that prey on the weak, you just don't trust them."

"Why do you work with them?"

"I already told you, the money."

"You could join the local coven if you need money."

"Are you fucking kidding me?"

"Excuse me?" His brows climb up his forehead, and he tightens his grip on his glass.

"Join the coven? I really thought you were in on it, that you knew what your partner was up to, but you are actually completely oblivious."

"What are you talking about?"

I lean forward, resting my chin in my hand. "Why don't ask your partner why two people from his coven strong-armed me out of Rudie's last night. Ask why they threatened to kill me and tried to force me to call Novak and pin these murders on the vampires. They asked me to lie. The bitchy one with the red lipstick burned the hell out of my car too."

Martinez is staring at me with narrowed eyes. "I don't believe you."

"That doesn't surprise me," I say leaning back in my chair. "Now, fuck off."

He stands up, his chair sliding back loudly. "If you have information we need, come to the station and talk or next time I'll have to drag you there."

"Oh, onto threats already. I thought you were playing the good cop."

He throws a twenty down on the table then marches out of the restaurant. He falters when he walks past my car. I know it still smells like smoke and the paint on the rear is peeling off and streaked with burn marks.

I have to wait another two hours for Maybelle to show up at the cafe. She frets and repeats everything Johnny already said after she arrived. She doesn't know of anyone else missing and hasn't seen anything out of the ordinary. I don't stay long; I'm not in the mood to have her fluttering around worrying about me right now. She keeps asking questions I don't want to answer.

I sit in my car out front for a few minutes, weighing my options. I could get supplies to make another no-sleep brew, and I might have to, but first I want to talk to Gerard. Maybe he'll be less cryptic today.

Gerard's place looks the same as it always does from the street. I sit in my car for a few minutes regardless, just in case someone was following me, but no one else pulls onto the street. With a sigh, I climb out of my car.

I knock on the door and stumble forward when it swings open then swings right back shut. The latch on the door is busted. I pull out my phone and turn on the flashlight, then pull a vial out of my pocket.

I kick the door, and it swings all the way open this time and stays that way. With one last glance behind me, I step inside. The light from my phone only reaches so far, so I shine it in a wide circle around me. There's the usual trash, but no people as far as I can see.

I walk through the debris slowly, turning around to check behind me every few steps. I feel watched in here.

"Gerard, you here?" I shout. My voice seems to die in the big warehouse.

I finally make it back to his office. The door is wide open. The room is empty.

I pull up to the vampire's house a full hour before they'll be awake. The nervous energy I've felt all day is fading, and fast. I chug the last of my coffee, but I know it isn't going to stop the crash that's coming.

I climb out of my car and sit on the porch facing the door. The white paint by my hand is peeling slightly. I pick at it absently and lean my head back against the porch railing. I wonder if they find me passed out and sweaty out here after sunset if they'll bring me inside.

I don't have anywhere else to go. I won't put Maybelle at risk by hiding out at her place. I don't think the coven would go after a pillar of the community like her, but covens can be unpredictable. I've always hoped that Javier might offer some measure of protection since I'm an employee, but I've never tested how far that protection goes before.

I send a text to Patrick, even though I know he won't see it; he's probably dead like those girls. I miss that little prankster. He would have brought me inside and made sure I didn't die if he'd been here.

My eyes slip shut against my will. The front door opens, and I force them back open.

"Get in here," Emilio hisses.

I struggle to my feet, my body protesting the sudden movement, and hurry inside. I didn't know they could wake up before the sun had set at all. I had heard rumors about some of the older ones, but Emilio?

He slams the door shut behind me and pushes me towards the stairs. I'm stumbling, my feet not quite wanting to work.

"What's wrong with you?" He asks, irritation plain in his voice.

"Haven't slept in a while, I'm crashing. Stupid brewing and its need for balance." My words are slurred by a yawn that makes my eyes water.

Emilio throws open the door to Javier's room, and half waves half pushes me inside. It's pitch black in a way I didn't think was even possible during the middle of the day.

"Olivia, why do you smell like spice and exhaustion?"

"Morning, Javier. Could you turn on a light? This is kind of creepy."

A lamp flicks on in the corner casting just enough light that I can see around the room now. Javier is still sitting in bed wearing an old-fashioned, white nightshirt.

"Olivia," he prompts when I just stand and stare.

"I took a no-sleep potion, and I'm crashing."

"I heard all of that. Why?"

"The coven threatened me last night. They want me to go to the police and lie and say you've been killing those missing girls."

Javier steps out of bed, his movements smooth and menacing as his mouth curls into a snarl. "And did you?"

"No, you haven't been killing anyone, and I'm not in the habit of lying to the police," I stifle another yawn. "Or doing what a coven tells me."

He's standing in front of me in the time it takes to blink. My hair flutters around my face from the displaced air.

"Did they hurt you?" He asks, a growl bleeding into his voice.

"No, I didn't give them a chance. My car will need new paint though." He puts a hand on my shoulder to steady me, and I realize I've swayed forward.

"Come sit down." He pulls me to the bed with an arm around my shoulders. My legs are shaking, and my vision is blurring.

"Where is Patrick?"

"Don't worry about him right now," Javier murmurs as he sits me down on the edge of the bed.

"No." I shove at his hands. "Where is he? You know." I hit him in the chest, but it's so weak it's almost a pat. "Is he dead?"

Tears well up in my eyes. I don't want to cry in front of Javier, but the brew is taking its price, and I feel like I'm watching everything from outside my body.

"I don't know where he is Olivia, I need you to find him."

I'm laying on my back, but I don't know how I got here. Javier is sitting next to me looking down at me, his eyes are so black. I think he is touching my face.

"I can't find him. I can't find anybody." The tears are sliding out of my eyes and down my cheeks. I can't stop them. I can't ever prevent anything terrible from happening.

"I have faith in you."

CHAPTER 5

It's pitch black, but I'm floating on a cloud. There's something cold here though, it's touching my hair. I blink and try to sit up, then everything comes rushing back to me.

"Fuck," I croak. My mouth feels like it's full of cotton and my throat is sore.

"If you'd like," Javier says with laughter in his voice.

"Lights, Javier," I push his hand away and sit up, glad to find that I'm still wearing all my clothes.

He steps out of bed and turns on the lamp. I have to blink against the light, but at least I can see him now.

"How long did I sleep?"

"All night and all day. The sun just set again." He holds out a glass of water. I take it and chug it and immediately want another. I make a mental note to never use that brew again. I should have come here sooner.

"Mind if I use your bathroom?"

"Not at all, I had Emilio get you a change of clothes. They're on the vanity."

Javier's bathroom is—striking. That's really the best word for it.

The floor is black marble, and the walls are blood red. An ornate chandelier hangs from the ceiling casting a dim, but warm light throughout the room. A jacuzzi tub sits underneath a window framed with black, velvet curtains.

The shower is the centerpiece of the whole thing though. There are no doors. The edges curve out of the wall giving way to glass in the front. The left side juts out just a little farther providing a way into the shower. It's big enough to fit about eight people comfortably, just enough for a really decent orgy. There are ten total showerheads, five at the normal height and five at waist level. They are solid gold too.

A change of clothes is waiting for me on the counter as promised. It's not even horrendously immodest either. There's a black shirt that looks like it will be too tight and a pair of black jeans. Emilio even got me some panties, good man. A soft leather jacket with silver rivets on the shoulder is hanging from a towel hook. There's no way I'm wearing that in this heat, but I'll definitely take it.

I turn on the closest showerhead and dump my clothes in a pile on the floor. The water is instantly hot and feels amazing as it washes away the anxious sweat of the last of the forty-eight hours.

Javier has lightly scented shampoo and conditioner that somehow smells like a spring morning. I think I've smelled this on Patrick before, which makes me wonder if Patrick has been in here. I frown, something about Patrick and Javier together seems incestuous.

Patrick would give me such shit for being in this situation today. He always said Javier wanted a taste, but wouldn't ask because I worked for him. I'd have said no even if he had asked, so it was better that he hadn't.

Thinking of Patrick spurs me to move a little faster. I need answers, I should have come to Javier sooner, as soon as I was worried about Patrick. I can only hope that my hesitation hasn't cost Patrick his life.

I look like some kind of vampire groupie once I get the clothes on, especially with my dark hair, which looks black when wet. All I need is some eyeliner and studded collar. I lay the jacket carefully over my arm and walk back out into the bedroom. Javier has changed since I last saw him, he's wearing his usual white shirt, buttoned and tucked in this time, and black slacks. He is reading a book in the armchair by the window.

"Did you have a good shower?"

"It was fine," I say, wanting to cut him off before he gets started with more nonsense. "Where is Patrick?"

"As I said last night, I don't actually know," Javier says, shutting the book. "I want you to find him. I've exhausted all my other options."

"If you can't find him what makes you think I can?"

"You're a very resourceful young woman."

I close my eyes for a moment to keep my frustration from overwhelming me. No one other than my long-dead mother should have any idea what I can do, but this conversation is skirting uncomfortably close to implications that scare me.

"How long has Patrick been missing? He stopped responding to my texts about a week ago."

"It has been eight days since Patrick was last seen. A week before that, Emily went missing."

My heart kicks into overdrive. Emily is one of Javier's newer vampires, which means there are two missing vampires. Two dead girls. If Emily went missing two weeks ago, that would be a week before Britney was most likely killed. More than long enough for a vampire to go from in control, to starving. Most vampires would lose control after just four days without a drop of blood. The question is, who would want to do that? Who would go to the trouble of framing the vampires?

"Anyone else missing?"

"No, and no one is permitted to leave the grounds until this is resolved. Patrick left without permission, he thought he could find

Emily on his own. He didn't seem to trust that I was doing everything I could to look for her," Javier throws his book across the room in a sudden movement that makes me take a step back. "I do not want my last words to him to be in anger."

"I don't know how to find Patrick. I think whatever has happened to him is connected to the missing girls the cops have been questioning me about. They were both drained by vampires, but I have no idea where to start."

"I need you to do something," Javier says, his fingers curling over the handles of the armchair. "You are a witch, not some helpless human. Find a way."

"I can't find him, I'm not in a coven, I can't just cast a spell like that."

"Find a way!" Javier shouts. "I have people searching for him, but his scent is gone. Erased. I don't know if he is alive or dead or if someone is hurting him. I have failed him just like I have failed Emily."

He puts his hand over his mouth for a moment, staring at the floor.

"If you do not find your friend, who will? The police will pin the murders on him or me if we go to them, and the coven would rather kill us all than help."

I have that sick feeling in the pit of my stomach again. I know what happens next. I search, and I search, and there is nothing. No clues. No one to help, or even care. I can't go through that again.

I have something now that I didn't have then. It's stupid to consider, but I couldn't live with myself if I didn't do everything possible to find Patrick just because I was scared someone might find out what I could do.

"I'll give you ten thousand dollars if you can find Patrick and get the police to look elsewhere for these murders."

I look up sharply. "I'll do it, but I'm doing it for Patrick. Keep your money."

Some of the tension bleeds from Javier's shoulders, and he nods.

I turn and walk away. It's time to go find my least favorite coven member. I won't be sorry if I accidentally kill him.

Aaron Hall is an arrogant, sadistic, self-obsessed asshole. He is also a talented witch and the only witch within a hundred miles from the Hamilton lineage. The Hamiltons are an old family that emigrated from Britain just before the American Revolution. Their specialty is finding lost things, a weird branch of mental magic that has all but died out.

Finders are almost as sought after as healers. For Aaron to get traded out to a coven in a smaller town with no real power to speak of means, he fucked up in a big way. Whatever the reason, it makes what I need to do so much easier.

He's part of why I came to this town actually, but the coven leader shot me down before I ever had a chance to ask him for help. I figured out for myself that he wouldn't have helped me regardless; after an incident involving one of the neckers right after I moved here.

Aaron, while a terrible person, is also very predictable. Every weekend he ends up at Full Moon Saloon, the trashy bar at the edge of town with the strip club in the back. He likes girls, feeling like he's the baddest guy in the room, and spending money. Full Moon is more than happy to accommodate all of that. The tricky part will be getting him outside.

The bright blue neon sign set on a pole by the road says 'Full Moo' right now because one of the lights is out. I smirk and park my car behind the bar where there is the least light. It's also fairly close to the back door. I pop the trunk before I get out and pull on the leather jacket, even though it's still hot as balls at eleven pm.

My jacket clinks a little as I move. I'm loaded down with brews just in case I get into some trouble. I grab a little green vial from my pocket and unplug the stopper. Green smoke curls up my nose as I tip it back and swallow the contents. It's minty and sends a chill down my spine that makes me shiver involuntarily.

I shut my eyes for a second and slip back into a version of myself that I don't like to acknowledge ever existed. Desperate. Rash. Stupid. This would have been her stomping grounds if she had lived here. She could work a stripper pole; and did for about six months before things got out of hand and everything changed.

I go around to the front, letting my hips sway as I walk. The windows are all blacked out, but I can hear the bass from outside. The bouncer at the door checks my ID, his face passive as he hands it back and waves me inside.

I push the door open, and I'm almost overwhelmed by the scent of cigarettes and stale beer. The front area is full of tiny, dirty tables. A long bar stretches the length of the room. The place is pretty empty. There are barely-dressed shot girls getting refills for their trays and a few patrons, but that's it. A curtain separates the bar area from the strip club, red lights flash through the gap like a beacon.

I wind my way through the tables to the curtain and push aside with the edge of my arm. It swings back behind me as I duck inside. There is one large raised platform in the center of the room shaped like a cross. There are poles every six or so feet, at least half have a girl gyrating on them in varying stages of undress.

Men stand around the edges dancing along to the music or watching the girls intently. I walk around a lap dance and almost bump into a man twerking very badly.

Loud laughter draws my attention, and I see Aaron climbing up on the platform with a wad of bills sticking out of his hand as he grinds up on one of the strippers. She bends over and pushes her ass back against him as he drops the money down on her. Two friends are cheering him on. Behind them is a table littered with shot glasses and an empty bottle of tequila.

I plaster a smile on my face and stroll in that direction; forcing myself to look around so it's not obvious I'm here for Aaron. An overweight, balding man leers at me. I'm sure they don't get many women in here that aren't employees.

A shot girl almost walks into me.

"You need anything?" She asks, still walking, like she knows I'll say no.

"Actually yes, can you bring me a bottle of tequila? Something good."

"Hundred dollars baby, you want to open a tab?" She says, holding out her hand.

"Nah, just the tequila will do," I dig out my wallet and count out the money. I'm absolutely sending Javier a bill for this.

I find a table a few feet away from the stage, right in the line of sight for Aaron, and sit down. I drape my arms around the back of my chair and stretch my legs out in front of me, looking for all the world like I'm settling in to watch.

The girl on the pole in front of me is pulling off a bird of paradise in spectacular fashion. I'm surprised they have someone this talented in a smaller town like this. A girl that strong and limber could make a good living in a big city.

Aaron stops grinding on the stripper, and I can see the moment he notices me. He elbows one of his friends and nods towards me. His friend says something to him, but Aaron just keeps staring at me.

The shot girl shows back up with the tequila and a stack of glasses. I hand her another few dollars for a tip and pour myself a drink. I look at Aaron and lift the first shot in a toast, holding his gaze as I toss it back.

He licks his lips and shoves one of his friends when they tug on his arm. I look away, pretending to be interested in the stripper again. He'll either come over here or he won't, the invitation was clear. If he doesn't, I'll just have to catch him in the bathroom or something.

It takes ten minutes and another shot before he walks into my line of vision.

"I know you from somewhere," he says, his eyes traveling from my chest to my feet.

"Tequila?" I pick up the bottle and swing it gently from side to side.

"Sure," he says pulling out the other chair, flipping it around, and sitting down. "What's your name?"

"Olivia." A drop of tequila splashes onto my finger as I pour, I lick it off and hand him his glass.

"Aaron," he says as he takes it, his fingers clumsily brushing against mine.

We drink, and he slams his glass down on the table, sucking at his teeth.

"You're a witch aren't you?"

"Got it in one," I say with a slow smile. "Maybe you can even guess why I'm here tonight."

"Hmm," he says, leaning forward a little further. "A witch, hedgewitch I'm guessing, with no coven in a human strip club. You playing trick or treat?"

"Got a regular Sherlock here. No tricks though only treats." I wink and twirl my finger around the edge of my glass.

"I don't know if you were any good the coven would have snatched you up as soon as you got to town."

"Oh please, the coven doesn't want me because I'm not willing to kiss their asses or the council's," I roll my eyes. "If they had the balls, we'd be working together. There's no reason something this profitable should be left to the humans."

"Maybe you're right," he hesitates, tapping his fingers against the table. "Maybe if you give me a treat tonight, and it's good, I can get you some more business."

I lean forward. "Maybe that sounds like a deal."

"Do you have it here?" He asks, glancing at my jacket pocket.

I glance over at one of the bouncers. "No, I'm not stupid enough to bring that stuff in here. I'm not looking to get banned."

"Where is it then?" Aaron asks, his hand twitching impatiently.

"Outside, we can go out the back exit over there."

Aaron stands and starts heading toward the door. I have to scramble to catch up, I didn't expect him to be this eager.

He's halfway into the parking lot before he realizes he doesn't know where to go. I catch up and tug on his arm.

"This way," I have to bite my tongue before I add 'dumbass.' I can't go offending the customer.

I open the trunk and pull a black bag towards me and fish out a fat, glass vial. The brew inside is a shimmery silver, I always thought it was pretty.

"Try this, it's a great ride," I hold it out to him.

"You take some first," he says, crossing his arms and looking down his nose at me like he's caught me out. This shithead obviously knows nothing about brewing.

I uncork it and pour a little out onto my tongue where he can see it. It's cold at first, then warm. It slides down easy and even though I feel absolutely nothing I let my eyes slip shut and shiver.

"Fuck, that's good," I whisper like I can't help it. I open my eyes, wider than normal, and hold it out for him. My breaths are coming in faster just from the adrenaline, it makes it easy to act.

He grabs it and tosses it back like it's a shot. His eyes roll back in his head immediately, and his knees buckle. I catch him awkwardly, he weighs almost twice as much as I do. It's all I can do to tip him towards the trunk and roll his torso in.

He's lying face down with his legs hanging over the edge. I grab the right leg and pull, but his gut is hung up on the latch.

"Should have gotten you to climb in the trunk before I knocked you out," I mutter as I shove his other leg in. He rolls towards the back of the trunk. I hope he'll be easier to get out. I'm ready to be done with this. My heart is racing as what I'm about to do hits me.

I haven't done this intentionally in a decade. Last time, just like every life-changing moment so far, it had made everything worse.

I slam the lid of the trunk shut and hurry around to the driver's side of the car. I'm not driving all the way back to my house. I have everything I need with me, and I know just the place to do some risky magic.

The drive back into town makes me feel like I've actually taken some drugs. My eyes flick between the road and the rearview mirror. Someone could have seen me in the parking lot. I could get pulled over, not that they'd have any reason to search the car, but I'm not sure I could play it cool.

I tap my fingers against the steering wheel. Just a few more miles. I pass car after car and can hardly take a breath. The lights fade behind me, and I finally turn down into a less busy area.

The street in front of Gerard's warehouse is deserted as usual. I park my car directly in front of the door and trot back to the trunk. Aaron is still out cold. I lean in and get a good grip under his shoulder, pulling him out with short tugs.

His hair is sticking up my nose as I give one last yank and he comes completely out of the trunk, his legs hitting the ground with a thud. I barely stay standing as his weight threatens to pull me down. One careful backward step at a time, I drag him to the door.

I fumble for the door handle with one hand and lose my grip on Aaron.

"Dammit."

I drop him and get the door open, then grab his arms and drag him into the filth. I kick a few pallets out of the way, then lay him out in the cleared area. I grab the bag with ropes out of the trunk and tie him up as tight as I can. He won't be going anywhere unless I cut the ropes off of him.

I check my watch, it'll be another few minutes before he starts to wake up, so I have time to kill. I check the warehouse again. Gerard is still gone, and other than the ever-present rats, we're the only living beings in the place.

Aaron's leg twitches, his boots scuffing against the floor. I walk over and stand behind him. The first spasm shakes his body so hard his head bounces off the concrete, probably hard enough to leave a sore spot tomorrow. The second spasm is much lighter, and his eyelids flick open. It takes another minute for awareness to filter in.

He looks around with wide eyes, taking in the flashlight sitting on the stool and the surrounding darkness. His breath kicks up, and he struggles against the ropes binding him.

"Where am I? Who's there?" He shouts, his voice going high pitched at the end.

I walk up behind him, and he tries to shimmy over to his other side to face me, but he's tied too tightly.

"It doesn't matter, you won't remember any of this tomorrow."

He goes still. "Olivia?"

I step around into the light and squat beside him.

"What the fuck are you doing to me, you weird bitch?" He screams at me, the veins in his forehead popping out.

"You have something that I need. It's just your bad luck that you happened to be born into the Hamilton family."

He bares his teeth at me like some kind of animal. "I'm not finding shit for you! You can't make me!"

"I know," I say as I reach my hand out and press it against his bare arm.

He flinches, expecting pain or something else I'm sure. When he doesn't feel anything, and I don't make any other movements he stares at me, his eyes flicking between my face and my hand.

"You'll feel it soon. Let me know when it feels like you're about to die."

He starts to struggle again, but all he can do is wiggle and curse. For a witch, he's strangely vulnerable. I know what it's like to live without offensive magic at my fingertips, but I make do with my brews. Aaron is too used to having a coven at his back, but the only protection they really offer is scaring your opponent.

As soon as someone is willing to risk the consequences, you're dead.

"Stop it! What are you doing! Stop, stop, stop," he pants. He's starting to feel it for real then. My mother described it as being emptied and turned inside out all at the same time. The pain is secondary to the panicked knowledge that you're losing something. She had thought I was somehow sucking out her soul.

The power is running up my arm and pooling in my chest. It's like I'm slipping into a warm bath after being cold for a long time. A pang of hunger stirs in me, and I wonder why I don't do this more often, but that's an answer in and of itself. Addictions are tricky things.

"Why are you taking it?" Aaron sobs. Big, wet tears are sliding down his cheeks, and he is trembling from head to toe.

"I need to find my friend," I whisper. I don't know why I have this urge to comfort him, especially since he won't remember it, but I hate watching this. It makes me feel like a monster.

"Don't kill me," he pleads. "I'll find them. I'll do it I swear."

"Shhh, I'm not going to kill you."

His face has gone pale, but the trembling is slowing. I'll have to stop soon, but I want to take as much as I can. I need to be able to use the magic to its full potential, I can't afford for it to be gimped like the healing magic.

His mouth parts and he struggles to breathe, drool dripping out of his mouth and pooling on the concrete. I yank my hand away and fall back onto my butt. I know I haven't taken too much, but I pushed it to the limit. He still isn't moving, and I'm afraid to touch him again too soon even though I know I can't accidentally steal his magic.

I leave him to recover, he'll be like this for a while. The new magic is twitchy inside of me, trying to figure out how it fits in and testing its bounds. The healing magic was instinctual after I took it, so I flex my fingers and feel out what I need to do. Finding magic can't be that much different.

I grab the town map from my bag and lay it out on the floor in the light. My fingers trail over the worn paper. I let my eyes slip shut and let the magic take over. It knows who I'm looking for. Certainty rushes through me and out of my fingertips. It feels completely different from the healing magic, it's so much brighter and hotter. I gasp as the knowledge of Patrick's location hits me. The area my finger covers on the map is large, but I know exactly where he is.

Rudie's. He's at the bar.

It doesn't make sense, but I know Patrick is there. My phone rings and I jump. I grab it out of my back pocket, and Emilio's number flashes on the screen.

"Emilio, I found him," I say in lieu of a greeting.

"Good, but we need you here now. Javier has been severely injured."

"What? How?" My heart drops into my stomach. I want to go find Patrick now, but if Javier dies, I don't even want to think of what might happen to the clan. Or me.

"He was attacked while out searching for Patrick, despite the fact that I told him not to leave. It was stupid. Rash. The mistake of a child, not a two-hundred-year-old clan leader."

"I'll be there as soon as I can, but I have a mostly unconscious witch tied up at Gerard's warehouse. I need someone to remove all trace of me from him and dump him in the parking lot at the Full Moon."

"It will be taken care of, now come."

He hangs up, and I shove my phone in my pocket and scramble for the memory erasing brew. I lift Aaron's head off the floor and tip the potion into his mouth, holding his nose shut so he has to swallow. He goes completely limp, and I shove him off my lap and grab my things, throwing them roughly into the bag before running back out to my car.

My hands are shaking as I shove the keys into the ignition and screech down the street. I hope I have enough power to heal Javier.

I've never had to heal a vampire before, they heal on their own. Whoever hurt him had to know what they were doing, and it must be bad. I'm not even sure if the healing magic will work if the wound was caused by holy water.

I also need backup if I'm going to go get Patrick. Whoever took him overpowered a vampire, and possibly Javier too.

I drive past Maybelle's, and a siren turns on behind me, the lights flashing in my rearview mirror. I'm the only other car on the road.

"Fuck."

I pull out my license and insurance card, texting Emilio as quickly as I can. Every other word is misspelled, but I don't care. I don't like the timing on this.

The officer shines his flashlight into my car, his hand is already on his gun.

"Olivia Carter?"

"Yes." He hasn't even taken my license, how does he already know my name?

"Ma'am, I need you to step out of the car."

I open the car door slowly, my heart pounding. I wasn't speeding, I hadn't done anything worth getting pulled over for. I step out, and he grabs my arm and shoves me around and into the passenger door of the car, slapping the cuffs onto my wrists. I force myself to stay limp and move with him, not fighting a single movement he takes. My driver's license and insurance have fluttered to the ground.

"Olivia Carter, you're under arrest for the murders of Britney Davidson and Jessica Johnson as well as the abduction of Laurel Ramirez."

What the fuck happened while I was sleeping.

CHAPTER 6

The interrogation room is cold, but they, of course, took my jacket. I better get it back, it's growing on me.

I'm still handcuffed, and my legs are chained to the floor as well. I don't know what they think I can do exactly, but they're not taking any chances. Or maybe they're trying to intimidate me. The chains just make them look stupid though.

I've been staring at the mirror-that-isn't-really-a-mirror across from me for about ten minutes. Hopefully, I can catch someone's eye and freak them out, but I'm sure I just look angry. The adrenaline of the arrest wore off, and frustration is taking over. I don't have time for this.

Martinez walks in. His suit is wrinkled, and he has dark circles under his eyes. He tosses a file folder onto the table in front of me and then sits down, taking a sip of coffee from his little styrofoam cup.

"How have you been, Carter? It's been a couple of days since I've seen you."

"I've had better weeks Martinez, but thanks for asking."

"We found some interesting things in your car. Novak isn't sure what most of the brews are. Are you inventing new drugs again?" Martinez's hand tightens around his cup for a moment, and the look he's giving me feels personal. Maybe he feels bad for thinking I'm hot since I'm also a terrible criminal.

"Drugs are so 2013 detective. I brew all sorts of things lately, but they're all legal." Mostly legal. Memory potions are a serious gray area, but there is none of that particular brew left, and what they don't know won't hurt anyone.

"Where have you been since I saw you at the diner?"

"Hmm," I say, tilting my head and pursing my lips. "Sleeping with Javier mostly."

His eyes narrow and his jaw clenches. So he is jealous, interesting.

"For almost twenty-four hours? I guess what they say about vampire stamina is true." His tone is sharp and accusatory. He didn't call me a slut, but it feels like he did.

"I suppose, but when I say sleeping, I mean actually sleeping. I crashed pretty hard that evening and didn't wake up until just after sunset tonight. Javier, the gentleman that he is, made sure I was taken care of."

"So that's what you're going with? Sleeping for twenty-four hours and the only people that can corroborate your alibi are vampires?"

"That's what happened, Martinez. You seem to be under the impression that I'm constantly lying to you when I'm not."

He flips open the folder between us. A picture of Jessica's body sprawled out on the ground is on top. Her face is so, so pale and the vicious bite marks on her neck and thighs are circled in red pen as if I could miss them. He slides that picture to the left revealing a similar picture of Britney, except Britney has started decomposing. It's not a great look for her.

"You've already told me they're dead," I say looking up from the pictures. "Are these pictures just supposed to shock me?"

"Did you know the vampires were going to kill them when you took the girls to them?"

I laugh once, I can't help it. "This is ridiculous."

"Laurel Ramirez, the mayor's daughter, went missing just before sunset today. These girls are already dead, but it's not too late to save Laurel. Where is she? Are the vampires already feeding on her?"

I lean forward, getting as close as the chains will allow. "Martinez, get your head out of your ass and think about who could be doing this. It's not me, and it's not the vampires. And as much as I'd like to pin this on the coven, it's not them either."

"What do you know?"

The door to the interrogation rooms slams open and a woman with steel gray hair pulled back into a neat bun glides in. She's almost six feet tall, with broad shoulders and a square face. Everything about her says she means business.

"You're done questioning my client," she says to Martinez. "Get her out of those cuffs, she's coming with me."

I have no idea who she is, but I lean back and shake my hands at Martinez who is glaring at the woman with a look of open hatred.

The police chief steps in behind the woman, his face red and his jaw tight. "Do as she says Martinez."

Martinez pulls the key out of his pocket and unlocks my hands first. I let the handcuffs fall to the table and resist the urge to rub my wrists even though they ache. He kneels in order to reach the leg cuffs. I lean back and let my eyes trail over him, he looks good down there.

"You won't get away with this," he says as he stands back up, our eyes meeting for a moment.

I follow the woman that is apparently my lawyer out of the police station, relishing in the frustrated eyes that follow me. Novak is standing by the door almost shaking in anger. I flip him the finger as we walk out.

"Please tell me Javier sent you," I say as I jog to catch up with her. She has a long stride.

"Emilio technically, but I do work for Javier," she says as she opens the door to a sleek black car. "Get in, I'll answer questions on the way."

I hurry to comply and slide in on the passenger side. She guns it out of the parking lot.

"What's your name?"

"Lydia Holland. I've been Javier's lawyer almost since I graduated from law school."

"Is Javier still alive?" I have to know.

"Yes, for now. I'm not sure how though." Lydia's voice goes low on the last part, and her hands tighten on the steering wheel.

"So, what are you? A human?" I ask, the question is a little rude, but I don't care right now.

"Yes, Javier has found that useful over the years."

The drive drags, she's driving exactly the speed limit, but it feels so much slower. I tap my fingers against my thigh and try not to sigh out loud. Now is not the time for Lydia to speed despite my impatience.

I throw off my seatbelt as soon as we pull into the driveway and have the door open before the car comes to a stop. The front door swings open as I run up the steps and Emilio leads me through the front of the house to one of the sitting rooms.

Javier is laid out on the rug in the center of the room like a sacrifice. I want to throw up looking at him. There is a stake sticking out of his chest, and he has gaping slices all over his arms interspersed with burns.

"Holy fuck," I whisper.

"Language," Emilio hisses with a glare.

I kneel down beside Javier and put my hands on his face, the only uninjured part of him. He's staring at me silently, and I have to shut my eyes. I can't do this with him watching me like I'm his only hope.

"Patrick is at Rudie's. I don't know why or how or exactly where, but he's there," I say before beginning the healing.

Emilio immediately pulls out his phone and dials someone. I tune out what he's saying and focus on pulling out every bit of healing magic I have. With the new magic swirling around inside of me I feel stronger than normal. I hope it helps.

Javier feels different from a human. The magic burns through him faster and stronger. It's almost like he's flammable and the magic is a spark. I can feel the worst of the wounds slowly closing from the inside out and his skin warming under my hands.

My healing magic is already waning though. I won't be able to heal him completely, not even close. I cling to him, pushing through the fatigue that normally has me stopping. Just a little more. Just a little—

He grabs my arms and shoves me away. I slump back onto the floor, panting. I had pushed a tiny bit farther than I intended. He grabs the stake still buried in his chest, rips it out with a grunt and tosses it across the room. The hole in his chest begins closing slowly.

Another of his vampires, someone I don't recognize, comes into the room with a curvy brunette following closely behind him. Her cheeks are flushed, and she's trembling with excitement. She hurries over to Javier's side and kneels, bending her head to the side to give him easy access to her neck.

Javier sinks his teeth into her neck and the girl moans. I try to look anywhere but at the feeding, however, my eyes keep getting drawn back. Javier is staring at me over her shoulder with a predatory look in his eyes.

"Water?" Lydia has a glass in one hand, the other extended to help me up. I take her hand gratefully and let her pull me to my feet. I take the glass eagerly and gulp it down. The water feels amazing in my throat, I hadn't realized how thirsty I was.

"Thank you."

"No problem, will food help as well?"

"Yes, but I need to talk to Emilio. I need to know how we're going to get Patrick back. He's alive for now, or the magic wouldn't work, but they could be killing him or hurting him. I have to—"

"Olivia," Lydia interrupts. "We can do nothing until Javier finishes feeding, and you need to be at your full strength as well. It will only take a few minutes to eat."

I curl my nails into the palm of my hand. "Fine, but I want to talk to Emilio."

Lydia snaps her fingers at another vampire standing in the corner who immediately runs out of the room, then walks toward the kitchen. I follow with one last glance back at Javier. There is already another human waiting for him to feed on.

Lydia forces an apple on me and watches, hands on hips, until I take a bite. I eat it mechanically because I know that I need it, but I barely taste it.

Emilio sweeps into the room. "The coven refuses to take my call."

I snort. "Too good for everyone else, as usual."

"The wolves, however, are willing to assist," Emilio says, his voice smug.

I look up shocked. "The wolves? They never get involved in anything. Why are they willing to help now?"

"Because I was attacked by humans," Javier says from the doorway. He is standing up straight, but his wounds still aren't fully closed. His skin is flushed from the feeding though, I have no doubt he will recover now. "Humans affiliated with New World Reformation to be exact."

Everyone in the room goes still. NWR is the boogeyman that hides under the bed of every paranormal. A quiet war has been waged against them since before we went public, and it's one that will probably never end. Someone will always hate us, and they will always be there to recruit them and arm them. Paranormals might have power beyond the average human, but our vulnerabilities are just as extreme. Balance, in everything.

"You're sure it was them?" I ask, shoving my hands in my pockets to hide my trembling. I don't want to think about what they're doing to Patrick. They never shy away from hurting people, part of what makes them so scary. They don't just kill, they do everything they can to make us fear them.

"We can't go into this fight with only paranormals. They'll destroy us," I say quietly.

"And who will help us? The police?" Emilio sneers. "Did you forget that they just arrested you and accused you of kidnapping the missing girls?"

"No, but just because it might be difficult to persuade them doesn't mean that we don't need them," I say, stepping forward, my hands clenched into fists.

"Then persuade them, Olivia, if you are so convinced. We will attack Rudie's within the hour, with or without them," Javier says before turning and stalking away.

Emilio glares at me and follows after him.

"I'll make a phone call as well, maybe I can help," Lydia says pulling out her phone.

"Thanks," I say, pulling Martinez's card out of my back pocket and staring at it.

I dial the number before I can second guess what I'm doing. The phone rings once, twice, then three times, then four and I'm almost convinced he just isn't going to answer when I hear a gruff hello.

"Martinez, I have some information for you."

CHAPTER 7

"Information," he bites the word out like a curse word. "After I have been asking for days, after an interrogation in which you refused to help me. Now you want to talk?"

"Yes, you want it or not?"

"I'm not sure. Why should I trust anything you say now?"

I bite the inside of my cheek. I knew this wasn't going to be easy.

"Do you want to know why I work for the vampires? The real reason?"

Martinez is silent for just long enough to make me worry. "Sure."

"My mom disappeared when I was sixteen. The coven we were with kicked me out without a second thought, and I ended up with a bad crowd. I was desperate, and I made bad decisions and did bad things, I'm sure you've seen my record. Chief of Police Howard Brunson found me one night when he was off duty and saved my life. He helped me turn things around. The only problem is, paranormals live by a different set of rules than humans. It's hard for anyone to get a job with a felony on their record, but add in being a witch? You're fucked."

I pause, weighing how much about myself I want to tell him. Talking about myself like this feels like I'm stripping off my actual skin.

"The vampires are much more lenient than any of the other paranormals. After Mr. Brunson died, Javier offered me a job. It was humiliating at first and terrifying. They prey on the weak after all. They're monsters that feed on women then, when their blood isn't good anymore, turn them out on the streets to be drug addicts and whores," I say, echoing what Martinez had told me at breakfast. They were stereotypes I had bought into as well.

"Only that wasn't what was happening. There are some girls like that, but they make those choices despite the help Javier offers them. The majority are in college and doing well. They don't allow any of the neckers to do drugs, or anything else illegal. They protect everyone that is associated with them. I still don't like working for them sometimes, but before Javier offered me this job, I was about to start brewing drugs again. Javier saved me. And that's why I'm still working for them. That's why I wouldn't give into the threats and throw them under the bus for these murders."

"What information do you have?" Martinez asks. I just barely stop myself by letting out a big sigh of relief. I still don't have his promise of help.

"Two vampires are missing, they were taken just like the girls, and I suspect being starved into a loss of control. Javier went to look for them again tonight, and they tried to capture him, he was almost killed. New World Reformation are the ones that have been taking the girls and trying to frame the vampires for the murders."

Martinez barks out a laugh. "NWR, that's a pretty bold claim."

"It's the truth," I say angrily.

"Where are these alleged terrorists?"

"Rudie's."

He doesn't respond, but I hear a muffled conversation like he is holding his hand over the phone and talking to someone else.

"What's going on?" I ask.

"So, what is it that you want? The police to raid the bar to prove there are terrorists hiding out there?"

"Yes."

"We can't do that based on your word any more than we could arrest you tonight off one tip. We'll have to get a search warrant."

I bite the inside of my cheek. I won't let Patrick die because the police can't deal with a little red tape.

"Look, just give me an hour or two. I will be able to get something pushed through, the Mayor is all over us to find his daughter," Martinez says with a sigh.

"They could be dead in an hour."

"Look, Carter, I know you're worried, but I need you to be patient. Don't do anything stupid and let me handle this, alright?"

As usual, I can't rely on anyone else to help. Gerard did say that the powers that be wouldn't be getting involved, I guess he was right.

"Olivia, did you hear me? I need you to promise me you won't do anything stupid."

"Sure thing, Martinez." I slip my phone back into my pocket and go to find the others, my stomach churning.

We're standing behind Rudie's in the tree line that's about fifty feet from the parking lot. It's still muggy outside, I don't have any of my brews since someone took them, and Javier is nervous. I've never seen him nervous before.

"You're sure Patrick is in there?" Javier asks quietly.

"Yes." I can feel Patrick still, like a tug in the center of my belly. It's stronger now that I'm so close to him.

Javier straightens and looks over my shoulder. A woman with

light brown hair cut in a short bob, wearing nothing more than a sports bra and a pair of men's running shorts, is approaching. She must be the local werewolf Alpha. Even though I've been here over six months, I still haven't met any of the weres, that I know of at least. They keep to themselves from what I've been able to gather.

"Ms. Georgia," Javier says, bending at the waist in a deep bow. "I am honored that you are joining us today to hunt a mutual enemy."

"I couldn't leave all the fun to you, now could I?" She asks with a wide grin that turns her face from stern to youthful in an instant. She looks me up and down. "Who's this?"

"Olivia Carter, hedgewitch." I hold out my hand, and she shakes it firmly.

"Georgia Willis, werewolf and Alpha of this pack," she says, extending her hand behind to the group of about ten weres, a mish-mash of people ranging from what looks like a couple around my age to grizzled old men, all watching us closely.

"It's nice to finally meet you," I say.

She inclines her head in agreement then turns to look at Rudie's. The parking lot is mostly empty, and there are lights on inside still, but there is nothing that would indicate it's housing terrorists. Patrick was probably in there the last time I was here. My stomach twists in anger, and I have to look away.

"I always liked this bar, it's a real bummer we're going to tear it down brick by brick and soak the ground with the blood of every soul contained within it," Georgia says, her eyes bright and her teeth already growing into fangs in her mouth.

"Not to take away from your analogy, but not every soul," I say cautiously. "The mayor's daughter and two vampires should be in there as well. They're on our side."

Javier is holding back laughter, but I had to say something. That would be such an awkward mistake.

She laughs, the sound deep and wild, coming up from her belly. "I will not eat your friends."

Javier and Georgia turn around first, and after a moment I too can hear the rumble of a truck coming down the narrow road that runs past the left side of Rudie's back toward town where we parked.

"It's Lydia," Javier says. "I think she has something for you."

I raise a brow but walk back through the trees to meet her. She steps out of her truck with a small black bag that she lifts in my direction.

"I got what I could, but it wasn't everything," she says as I take the bag from her. It's my brews and my jacket. I set the bag on the ground and crouch next to it as I take inventory.

"Thanks, I wasn't happy about losing any of this." I shrug on the jacket and start loading my pockets with brews. "How on earth did you get it?"

"I just walked into the police station and took it, to be honest," she says with a mischievous smile. "If you look like you belong there, most people don't stop to question you."

I feel like I have a chance of making it out of there alive now. I had felt naked without my brews.

Lydia kicks off her heels and pulls a pair of sneakers out of the truck. She pulls out a gun as well that she tucks into the holster she is wearing under her clothes. She pulls out another pistol as well.

"This one is for you," Lydia says, handing me the gun "It has fifteen rounds in the magazine, and one in the chamber, so don't point it at anyone until you're ready to shoot them."

I take the gun hesitantly. I know how to use it, but it's been a long time since I've held one. "Thank you."

Lydia shrugs. "I know you have your magic, but sometimes you just need to shoot someone."

"You coming in there with us?" I ask as I tuck the gun into my waistband on the left side.

"No, I have to stay alive so I can keep you all out of jail once you are finished rescuing Javier's vampires. I will, however, keep an eye out for anyone trying to run away."

I check my watch, we only have three more hours until sunrise.

"Thanks again Lydia," I say with a nod. She waves my thanks away and I jog back over to Javier and Georgia. I can feel Georgia watching me approach, I can almost feel her hunger to get in there and fight. I understand it.

"Do we have a plan, other than kill everyone?" I ask Javier.

"Don't die," he says with a wink, echoing Gerard's advice.

I roll my eyes and pull out the same potion I had used while kidnapping Aaron. I have three vials left, enough for about nine people. "There isn't enough for everyone, choose three vampires and three wolves," I say, nodding at Javier and Georgia in turn. "It should protect us against anything the NWR has that could knock us out or make us lose control."

Javier waves over three of his vampires without hesitation, while Georgia takes a moment longer, whispering with a man that I think is second in command. He jogs off, then returns with three weres. A slender woman with bright eyes, a burly man, and boy that I suspect is barely over eighteen.

I hand a vial to the slender woman and another to one of Javier's vampires. "Everyone get close to the vial and inhale deeply."

Javier and Georgia step in close, our shoulders touching, and I pop the cork out of the vial. The green smoke pours out, curling up into our nostrils. I hear the weres grumbling that it burns.

"I don't recommend breathing in the fumes from anything else I'll be using tonight."

"Noted," Georgia says, rolling her neck in a circle and flexing her hands.

We start toward Rudie's, Javier on my right and Georgia on my left. Behind us is the crunch of bone as the werewolves drop to their hands and knees, their skin morphing into fur, and their teeth lengthening into fangs. The transformation is disgusting to watch, but I glance back nonetheless. I never can keep myself from looking.

As soon as the first wolf is changed, he races ahead, fading into the night as he circles around to the other side of Rudie's. The vampires are nowhere to be seen. They're probably already there, I think I see movement on the roof.

As we walk through the parking lot, the lights go out one by one with the sound of shattering glass. Darkness advances before us like a shroud. The lights inside of Rudie's go out all at once and the darkness is complete.

The back door to Rudie's is unguarded, at least on the outside. Georgia crouches in front of it, waiting for Javier to give her the signal. I grab a brew out of my pocket and the glass vial digs into the palm of my hand as I clench my fingers around it. Javier is directly behind me, almost plastered to my back.

Georgia busts through the door with one well-placed kick.

CHAPTER 8

Georgia takes one step inside before an explosion flings her back and knocks me in Javier. I'd be flying too if he wasn't there to stop me. My ears are ringing and my night vision is almost completely gone.

I throw a brew inside on reflex and hear a guttural scream as it instantly heats the immediate area by two hundred degrees.

Javier is gone, I don't even feel him move, just the sudden absence as I tip backward. I scramble to my feet as howls erupt around me. A huge, red wolf flies past me through the doorway, followed closely by a black wolf.

There is gunfire behind me and above me. Someone screams and I don't know if it's vampire or human. They're fighting on the roof too, possibly in the parking lot. If they're in the parking lot, then they have us surrounded. They must have known we were coming though I have no idea how.

I run inside. The entire place is smokey, I can't even see the bar from here. There's a man laying on the floor directly in front of the doorway, his skin is blistered and red, and his throat has been torn out. A gas mask hangs half off his face. The burn in the back of my throat tells me that they expected this smoke to knock us out. They're in for a surprise.

A door slams open and I can see a glimpse of movement through the smoke. There's a crack and a net flies out and wraps around Georgia. She howls in pain and jerks as the net crackles and sparks. Two wolves charge into the smoke amid the crack of gunfire.

A vampire drops from the ceiling and is immediately struck in the chest by a bullet. The vampire shrieks, clawing at his shirt. A purple flame licks out of the wound and the room fills with the scent of sulfur.

I dive behind the bar and several more wolves rush inside after me. Wood splinters over my head and a wolf yelps in pain, but one of the guns stop. I army crawl toward where I think the shooters are. There is broken glass and the floor is sticky from spilled alcohol. I'm glad I'm wearing the jacket. I grab two brews from my jacket and fling the first over the bar like a grenade. It shatters and I hope it didn't catch any of the wolves, but it won't keep them down for long. I can hear the panicked gasping for a breath they can't take.

An explosion rattles the glass bottles in front of me and makes my ears ring. Then another, and another. I can't even hear myself breathing at this point, just a faint ringing in my ears. The wolves and vampires must be hurting right now. The explosions are worrying. I can't tell where they're occurring. How many of us are dead now?

The smoke is beginning to clear though, so I peek over the bar and see one of the men firing from the corner. I throw the brew directly at him. It breaks over his black armor and begins to eat through it, glowing bright green. He shouts and slaps at the green fire, but all that does is make his hands burn too. I look away as the fire begins to crawl up his neck, but I can't block out the anguished screams.

Javier is dodging two of the men who have dropped their guns.

One is swinging a silver net at him, the other has a long wooden spear sharpened to a point. Georgia is still struggling under the net she was caught in. One of the other wolves tries to pull the net off of her, but yelps in pain as it burns his mouth. There is another wolf dead in front of her. I fumble with the brews in my pocket, trying to find the right one by feel.

Two more men come through the doorway and I twist and fall onto my back, pulling the pistol from my waistband. There's no time to aim. I point and shoot, hitting the one closest to me, but he doesn't go down. He turns his gun on me, his teeth bared and his eyes wide. A wolf hits him from the side, jaws clamping down on the gun and ripping it from his grip.

I jump to my feet to shoot the second man, but a vampire has latched onto him. I finally find the brew I was looking for and throw it at Georgia. The glass shatters over her back and the net begins to melt. She squirms her way out of it and climbs to her feet with an enraged howl.

I leap over the side of the bar and run through the doorway the men had come out of. My gut and my newfound magic are leading me in this direction. We may not be able to win this fight. I have to try to get Patrick while I can.

"Olivia wait!" Javier shouts from behind me. I can't wait, every instinct I have is pressing me to keep going.

The hallway is empty. All I can hear is the wet sound of tearing flesh coming from the bar behind me as my hearing slowly returns. There are only two doors, both closed. The tug in my belly leads me past the first door. I stand in front of the second, hesitating for just a moment before I grab the handle and yank the door open.

Narrow, wooden stairs lead almost straight down. I leave the door open behind me and walk down carefully, both hands on my gun. There is more gunfire overhead, but it's dead silent and dark down here.

The stairs lead down into a tunnel that seems to have been dug right into the ground. It still smells like damp earth down here even though the walls are concrete. There is one dim light dangling from the roof of the tunnel. Patrick is close now, so very close.

The tunnel curves ahead, and there is something is around that turn, I can feel it. I grab a brew with my left hand, my last one, then bring it back up to grip the gun. The ringing in my ears has mostly faded, but I know my hearing still isn't fully back.

I glance behind myself one last time, then peer around the curve in the tunnel. It opens immediately into a circular room that smells like blood and shit. A girl with a blonde pixie cut is dangling from shackles that attach to the ceiling in the center of the room, her hands are purple and swollen. Her head is hanging listlessly and her bruised eyes are shut. She looks like she's still alive though.

A dead vampire, I assume must be Emily, is lying next to the wall behind her. Her face is, for lack of a better word, destroyed. It looks like someone beat it in with a two by four.

I creep forward, one foot in front of the other, my hands shaking slightly as I grip the pistol. I step cautiously into the circular room and Laurel's head shoots up. She sees me and her eyes go wide. She begins screaming and kicking and I lower the gun slightly, but she's looking past me.

The press of a gun to the back of my head is all the warning I get.

"I tried to warn you, Olivia, I had hoped you would listen and let the vampires fight for themselves," Martinez says, his breath tickling my ear. He slides his hand down my arm and rips the pistol from my hand. I manage to hold onto the brew and drop my hand to my side, my fist clenched tightly.

I feel like my heart has fallen out of my chest. Martinez. I hadn't seen that coming at all. If it had been Novak standing here holding a gun to my head, I almost wouldn't have been surprised. Martinez had seemed so earnest.

"Why are you doing this?" I ask, hoping to buy time.

"I believe in the cause," Martinez says. "Walk forward."

He pushes the gun more firmly into my skull and I comply. As I walk further into the room, I see Patrick in my peripheral vision. He is chained to the wall, his arms are stretched taut in each direction and wrapped in silver chains that are burning his skin. His cheeks are gaunt and his eyes are completely red. He's gone feral from the hunger. Chevy is standing next to Patrick, a gun hanging loosely from his hand.

My heart almost stops. Chevy? I had thought he liked me, he had always been so friendly. He was always asking how I was—No. He was always asking about the vampires. Almost every conversation came back to them. A snide comment here or there, asking how business was, seeing if I was having any trouble. He had been fishing for information. Is there no one in this town I can trust?

"This will work just as well. A rabid vampire kills not only the mayor's daughter but his conspirator as well," Chevy says with a grin that is all teeth and spite.

"So that's what you're going with Martinez, killing me too?"

"No, Patrick will kill you, just like he killed those girls."

"You are so full of shit--"

Martinez grabs me by the throat and pulls me flush against him, pressing the gun into my cheek so hard I can feel it grinding against my teeth. "If you had listened, you could have lived. I could have helped you, gotten you a job, maybe even recruited you. You're barely a witch after all. If you stopped using magic, you could live a pure life and be redeemed. You chose this," he says, forcing me to look toward Patrick, whose red eyes are following our every move. His fangs are fully extended and dripping with saliva.

I smell ozone before I hear the crackle of magic.

"Let her go," Novak says as he walks into the room, his gun trained on Martinez. Electrical energy crawls around his free hand, sparking and jumping as he clenches it. Novak's hair is almost standing on end.

"Watch out!" I yell as Chevy raises his gun to shoot Novak.

Novak turns and fires first. A ball of lightning flies towards both Chevy and Martinez. Martinez pushes us both forward out of the way of the magic, then lifts the gun that was pressed into my cheek to shoot Novak.

I grab his arm and slam my elbow back into his jaw. Martinez stumbles back and I throw the brew into his face, dropping down to my knees and covering my head with my arms. The brew explodes in a burst of fire and he shrieks as his skin blisters. A wave of heat passes overhead that I can feel even through my jacket.

More gunfire echoes through the room and I see Novak stumble forward, eyes wide in shock. A red circle is forming on the front of his shirt. He falls to his knees, revealing one of the terrorists behind him. I run for my gun, it's barely ten feet away.

I'm hit from behind and Martinez grabs my hair and jerks me back. I go with the yank, turning and smashing my fist into his jaw. His skin is slick and hot and my fist slides off to the side, taking skin with it, but I can tell it rocks him. I jerk my hair out of his grip and hit him again, forcing him to take a step back.

There's another shot and I feel a hot, sharp pain in my left arm.

"Move again and I'll shoot you in the head!" The man in black shouts from behind me.

Martinez grabs his dropped pistol and shoves me towards Laurel. His eyes are wild with anger and pain. The entire left side of his face is beginning to blister, his eyebrows are gone and his left eye can't seem to open all the way between the burns and the swelling from my elbow strike.

"Grab him," he says pointing at Novak, who's staring at him in both disbelief and hatred.

"You were my partner," Novak says hoarsely as the man in black grabs him under his arms and begins dragging him towards the center of the room.

"You were filth I had to tolerate," Martinez hisses. "Tie them together."

The man in black grabs a thin chain from the side of the room and pushes Novak and me together, back to back. He binds us so tightly together I can hardly breathe.

Laurel is sobbing behind us. I keep looking toward the doorway, hoping to see Georgia or Javier. Surely someone will come for me. Martinez steps up to Laurel and smashes the side of her face with the gun, she goes limp and quiet.

Chevy is bleeding from a wound on his shoulder and his stomach, but he is still standing. Martinez walks over to the door from the tunnel and closes it. The door is solid steel and two heavy bars drop down, reinforcing. My heart sinks into my stomach.

There is another door to the right of Patrick, but it looks like it locks from the other side and is similarly reinforced. I have no idea where it leads. Martinez and the man in black walk toward Chevy.

Novak's head lolls to the side and I grab his wrist, sending my healing magic into him. His wounds are beyond my skill to heal, but maybe I can buy him some time. I can feel him regaining consciousness, but the bleeding isn't slowing fast enough. They must have hit an artery.

Chevy grabs a lever on the wall near Patrick and pulls. The chains fall off and Patrick lunges forward, running straight toward us, concerned only with the smell of blood.

"Patrick, no!" I scream.

Chevy pulls the second lever and a large, round cage falls from the ceiling and slams onto the ground, trapping all four of us inside.

I twist so that Novak is behind me and kick at Patrick as he tries to jump over us and grab Laurel. He turns and hisses at me, no recognition in his face at all. His eyes flick to the wound on my arm and he strikes, his teeth tearing into the muscle. I bite down on the scream and try to yank my arms free, but all I manage to do is bruise myself.

Patrick locks his jaw down tighter and sucks down deep pulls of blood. It burns and aches so much I can hardly stand it.

"You see now, don't you Olivia? They're vicious, soulless, monsters," Martinez says, crouching down by the cage to watch me die.

"The only monster I see here is you," I bite out. Novak is barely hanging onto consciousness, and I don't want to die like this. I grab his limp hand and I begin to pull. The magic rushes into me and I take it greedily. This will speed up his death, but so will letting Patrick eat him.

"Patrick, listen to me," I say, my voice not as steady as I'd like. "I know you're still in there, and I know you're hungry, but--"

Patrick releases my shoulder, and for a brief moment I think maybe he is listening to me, but he pulls Novak forward, shoving me onto my face, and buries his face in Novak's stomach. I pull on Novak's magic faster, I need more. I can feel Novak dying, he's already lost too much blood. I have to take it all now before it's too late.

I have always pulled slowly before, but this time I reach an invisible fist inside of him and rip out every last bit of magic. Novak dies. I feel his soul leave like a whisper, the one thing I couldn't take.

Electricity crackles around me, my hair lifting around my head. The sharp, bitter smell of ozone overtakes my senses.

Martinez is already running towards the door. "Shoot her!"

The man in black lifts his gun towards me and I push the magic at him, uncontrolled. A jagged bolt of pure energy crackles through the air and hits him in the chest. He falls down face first, his body jerking and spasming.

Chevy shoots wildly in our direction. I throw another bolt of lightning at him. It hits the gun more than him and he shouts in pain as the guns falls to the ground. I feel weak already, I've used too much magic, too fast. There's no stopping now though.

I grit my teeth and hurl another bolt of electricity at Chevy. As it hits him, I realize that Martinez is running out of the other door.

"No!" I shriek, but he pulls the door shut behind him. I hear the bars slam into place as I struggle uselessly against my bonds again.

He's gone and Novak is dead. Patrick is sucking at the wound on his stomach still, practically bathing in the blood. He's going to hate himself for this, I hope he doesn't remember it. I also hope I can stop him before he kills the rest of us.

CHAPTER 9

I gather the last of my strength and reach back, grabbing Patrick's bony wrist. He jerks when I begin electrocuting him and tries to pull away, but I refuse to let go. I send more magic into him and he grabs my hurt arm with his free hand, digging into the wound. I scream in pain but don't stop.

He bites down on my forearm and I push everything left into him, enough that I'm worried I might kill both of us. His eyes roll back in his head and he finally falls, his teeth ripping my skin on the way out. Blood drips freely from the wound.

I feel like I'm floating now. I'm so tired and everything hurts. I close my eyes to rest, just for a second, when I hear banging on the door I had come in earlier. I think I might have been hearing it for a while.

A strange dent appears on the inside of the door, then another. The door rattles with each impact, the metal straining against the hinges and the frame. Another hit and I realize they aren't dents, they're the opposite. Something is coming through the other side.

There is a loud crack and the concrete around the door begins to give way. Two more hits and the entire door falls down flat in a cloud of dust. Georgia, now in wolf form, and Javier lunge into the room, looking around for anyone else.

"We're alone," I croak out. "Martinez—got away."

Javier runs over to the cage and tries to lift it, but hisses and jerks away when he touches it.

"How do we open it?"

"Lever. Wall."

The cage lifts slowly towards the ceiling and Georgia slides underneath, changing back into her human form as she does. She watches Patrick warily as she yanks apart the chains holding Novak and myself. She pulls me out from underneath Novak. Patrick grunts and holds his meal closer as it shifts, growling irritably at us for disturbing him. He's still not fully conscious. His muscles are spasming randomly.

Javier crouches next to Patrick, smoothing a hand down the side of his face and whispering in his ear. He bites his own wrist and presses a few drops into Patrick's mouth, who latches on eagerly.

Georgia picks up Novak and moves him a short distance away, closing his eyes and folding his hands across his chest respectfully. Laurel is still hanging unconscious behind us, so Georgia moves to get her down next. Javier crouches beside me, his face unreadable.

"Is Patrick okay?" I ask.

"He will be," Javier says, helping me sit up. "Olivia, drink from me. It will help you heal."

"I don't need--"

"You are exhausted magically and physically, please let me help you."

He presses his wrist to my mouth, and I let him. I'm too tired to fight, and some instinct inside of me knows it will help. As soon as the blood hits my tongue, I want to clamp down and suck. I can feel the magic that runs through him, keeping him alive. I could take it, all of it, so easily.

I shove his wrist away. "I'll be fine."

He stares at me, brows pinched together, then finally sighs and helps me stand "You will stay with the clan for tonight at least, we don't know if NWR might try to retaliate. We can't be sure we got them all."

"We didn't get them all. One got away," I say, tears burning at the back of my eyes. I refuse to let them fall. Javier has already seen me cry once.

"Who?"

"Detective Jason Martinez."

The rest of the police are already outside once Javier carries me back upstairs. The mayor is there too, and he sobs as he holds his daughter. She's still unconscious, but the paramedics are saying she'll live.

I get a lot of questions and answer them all the same way. Detective Novak was able, despite his terrible wounds, to kill two of their men and render Patrick unconscious before he died. I did my best to heal him and keep him alive, but it wasn't enough. The words taste like ash in my mouth, especially since I'm the one that killed him.

They load me into one of the ambulances, one of the wolves goes with me at Javier's insistence. As soon as the painkillers hit my bloodstream, I don't care what they do with me.

I manage two hours of sleep after we get back. I still feel dirty, the nurses cleaned most of the blood off of me, but I didn't get a proper shower. Javier had insisted I stay in his room, I didn't bother arguing. Before I had fallen asleep, he had paced the room, asking every few minutes how I was feeling, if I needed anything. I think he wanted the comfort of someone else there as much as I do. He's dead asleep now, curled up under the covers like a little boy. I smooth his hair back and tuck the covers a little tighter around him. I wish I could do the same for Patrick.

The bath fills up quickly with almost too hot water. It feels amazing as I step in. I have to keep my right arm out of the water, but I manage to bathe awkwardly with my left hand. It helps, but I know I still won't be able to sleep.

I change into the fresh pajamas Javier had laid out for me and slip downstairs to the kitchen. Lydia is pouring herself a cup of coffee. She's wearing a fluffy pink robe over a long nightshirt with a picture of a cat on it. She still holds herself like she's in the courtroom though, and the combination is odd.

"Want one?" She asks quietly.

"Yeah, that'd be great."

She grabs another mug and fills it with coffee. I add cream and three scoops of sugar, then follow her out onto the back porch. We sit down on the porch swing and I curl my feet up underneath me.

Javier keeps a really beautiful garden out back. The back of the house looks out down a sloping hill. Javier had a maze of hedges built that covers most of the backyard, but right in front of the porch is a colorful array of flowers that are all pointed toward the sun, drinking up the rays.

"How are you feeling?" Lydia asks as she pushes off the floor with her toe, swinging us backward.

"A little crazy. Worried about Patrick. Scared," I admit.

"Patrick is going to be okay, he'll recover," Lydia says, blowing across her mug before taking a sip.

"But he won't be the same. They hurt him, and even though it was unwillingly, he still killed some people."

"You killed some people too, from what I heard. You both will recover from that. Patrick is resilient, I'm not sure how much you know about his history, but this won't be enough to break him."

I take a drink to avoid answering. I know it won't break him, but I dread seeing him without the twinkle in his eye. "I expected to get questioned by the police again before I left the hospital."

"I was able to get them to wait. You'll have to submit an official statement tomorrow, but I'll be with you, and you'll be rested.

There's no reason they can't wait. It's clear what happened, they found all the proof they need."

"How many were killed? Of our people." I can't help but ask, even though my stomach is a tight knot of worry as I wait for the answer.

"Too many. You were right about the slaughter. But less than could have been," she says with a long, slow exhale. "Javier and Georgia are smart. They were able to minimize the casualties."

"What now?" I ask. My hands are shaking, my body thinks I still need to be fighting for my life.

"Just another day, Olivia. There's no point in worrying about tomorrow."

"If you say so," I say with a snort, leaning my head back and shutting my eyes. A breeze blows across the porch and some of the tension leaves my shoulders.

Lydia's phone rings and she pulls it out of the pocket of her robe. She pinches her brows together as she looks at the screen, but answers it anyhow.

"Lydia Holland, how can I help you?"

Lydia pauses, her back straightening as the other person talks. "A representative from the council? Coming here?"

I look up sharply. I was sure the council knew about what had happened here, but it had been handled. Why would they be interfering now?

Lydia turns to me, eyes wide, the phone still pressed to her ear. "What do they want with Olivia?"

Fuck.

PART II
PRICE OF MAGIC

CHAPTER 1

Four vampires. Three werewolves. That's how many died that night. Avoidable deaths.

That's all I can think about as I stare at the detective across from me who is waiting for an answer to a question he has already asked twice. He's going through everything that happened for the third time, and it's starting to feel like an interrogation.

"You stated that Detective Alexander Novak was able to kill Chevy before succumbing to his wounds?" he repeats, his brows pinched together as he looks down at me over his glasses like I might be too stupid to understand what he just asked.

"Yes," I answer, again. I have to bite the inside of my cheek to keep from adding a 'for the last fucking time'. My hands clench into tight fists where they are tucked under my arms.

Lydia glances at me and shifts to sit up straighter. "This interview has gone on long enough. If you have any other questions, you can refer to my client's written statement. After all, she's a victim here, not a suspect in a murder investigation."

I should be. But I'm not stupid enough to say that aloud, though I wonder what they'd do if I did tell them. It's possible they wouldn't even believe me. No one should be able to do what I can do; it's abnormal even for a witch. My mother had made sure I understood from a young age that if anyone ever found out, my life would be over. I'd be killed or used, and I don't like the idea of either.

I want out of this tiny, cold room and out of the police station. There are too many memories that creep up on me in these places.

"Of course, Ms. Holland." Detective Ross says, his mustache bristling as he purses his lips and nods his head. He stands and thanks each of us. His warm hand is a sharp contrast to my frigid one as we shake.

Lydia leads me out of the room. "Do you mind stopping in to say hello to the police chief? He wanted to apologize in person for Martinez."

I sigh but nod. Turning down the chief's goodwill offering would only lead to me looking bitter. I don't want to have to deal with him ever again, but if I do, I'd rather he remember me fondly.

"Let's just make it quick."

I follow Lydia down the narrow, dingy hall. There are office doors every few feet with little brass nameplates. Most of the doors are closed, but a few are open. A woman with a pixie cut is sitting in one office, feet propped up on a chair. She watches as we walk by, eyes narrowed.

The chief's office is at the end of the hall around a corner. The door is shut, but raised voices are clearly audible from where we stand.

"Your coven member interfered in an ongoing investigation. If that witch hadn't gotten involved, an NWR cell would have stayed active in my damn town! For the last time, McGuinness, your coven's petty bullshit feud with the vampires ends now, or I won't have another witch in this department. I'll report you to both councils if I have to."

McGuinness' response is muffled by the door.

Lydia and I share a look. Her brows are raised, and she's smirking. I can't help smiling as well. I've waited my entire life to hear a coven leader get dressed down like this, and it's just as satisfying as I imagined.

McGuinness went out of his way to make sure I understood I would not be joining his coven as soon as I moved into town. It had almost been enough to run me off before my stubbornness kicked in.

The door flies open, and a red-faced man in a suit that barely stretches across his chest comes barreling out, almost running right into me.

At first he just looks annoyed, but then he recognizes me, and his face turns even redder. He bares his teeth at me, brows furrowed and nostrils flaring. He steps forward, his fingers twitching like he's thinking of casting a spell. I uncross my arms and take a step toward him, holding his gaze. He can fucking try, but it'll be the last thing he does.

Novak's magic is buzzing through me. The coven leader has no idea I have it. I want to fry him to a crisp. I feel a spark on the tip of my finger, then Lydia is jerking me back and getting between us. Sound filters back in, and I realize the chief is shouting at McGuinness again, ordering him out.

McGuinness brushes past Lydia and stomps down the hall without a backward glance, taking the smell of fire with him. My breath is coming uncomfortably fast. The Chief and Lydia are both staring at me, the latter with pinched brows and lips pressed tightly together.

"Olivia, are you all right?" Lydia asks.

"I'm fine," I say, clearing my throat and straightening my jacket.

The chief holds out his hand. "Chief of Police Samuel Timmons. It's good to meet you in person, Ms. Carter."

I shake his hand. "Likewise."

"I intended to apologize for the mishandling of the investigation, but it appears I will also need to apologize for the behavior you just witnessed. I would like to make it clear that I will not be party to the coven's obvious prejudice."

"I appreciate that," I say with a tight smile. "Not your fault he's an ass."

"Do you have a moment to sit down?" Timmons asks, waving back toward his office.

"Sure," I agree.

Lydia tugs my arm to get me to follow Timmons into his office.

His desk is oversized and cluttered. There's a bookshelf behind him filled with awards and pictures of his family, but no books.

"Now, we are still looking for Jason Martinez. We don't have any information yet, which isn't surprising considering his connections. I've been in contact with JHAPI and the Vampire Council. From what I hear, there will be a representative from the Vampire Council coming to town to assist JHAPI with the search if he can."

Joint Human and Paranormal Intelligence are involved? They must be serious. That particular organization hasn't actually been around that long, only six years if I remember right. It was formed after the NWR became a more public problem. It was the first cooperative human and paranormal task force created, and it was a surprising success. The councils are always vying for influence over it, of course, but JHAPI has been successful in slowing down the NWR over the years despite that.

"Please keep us updated, Chief Timmons. We, of course, will continue to help in any way we can," Lydia says politely.

Timmons pulls two cards out of his desk and scribbles a number on the back of each. "My personal cell number is on the back. Don't hesitate to contact me if you need anything or have any information."

I stand and tuck the card into my jacket. "Thanks."

"We'll be in touch," Lydia says.

I walk out before he can think of anything else to discuss. I'm halfway down the hall before Lydia makes it out of his office. I can hear her hurrying after me, but I don't slow down until I'm in the parking lot.

I lean back against my car and cross my arms. There's a crisp coolness in the air that wasn't there yesterday. The first hint of fall always comes as a surprise to me. Summer seems endless until I walk outside and it smells different, and a breeze raises goosebumps on my arms.

She comes to a stop in front of me. "Will you reconsider staying at the clanhouse for the rest of the week?"

"No, I need to feed my cat and catch up on brewing," I say as I pull my keys out. "I also don't want another night of Javier hovering over me like some kind of creepy mother hen."

Lydia sighs, but her lips curl up into a smile. She had laughed at me this afternoon after I finally woke up when I had complained. "He means well."

"I know." I gnaw at the inside of my cheek. "How is Patrick?"

"He is not himself yet. Which is why Javier is being so ridiculous. Patrick won't let him hover either."

I roll my eyes. That's the most I've gotten out of her since yesterday morning, and it's not enough.

"You're being vague. Not himself," I mock, throwing up sarcastic finger quotes. "Javier wouldn't let me see him, so something is obviously wrong. Just tell me."

Lydia huffs and shakes her head. "Javier didn't want you to worry, but I suppose that's impossible. Patrick is angry. He has had several outbursts. He almost hurt one of the neckers and did not appreciate the manner in which Javier stopped him. They've been arguing like cats and dogs."

"I want to talk to him."

"Javier has said no visitors since the incident with the necker. He's even having his blood delivered in a cup."

I grimace at the visual. "That's only going to piss Patrick off more. Is he really that out of control?"

"I don't know." Lydia clasps her hands in front her, thumb tapping restlessly against the back of her hand.

I need to see Patrick, but I can't deny the little shiver of fear that accompanies the thought. Especially if he isn't fully back in control. The rational mind has a hard time reconciling that a friend could try to kill you and it is not their fault.

"I'm going to come see him soon, whether Javier likes it or not."

"Just give him one more night, Olivia. I wouldn't ask you that if I didn't think it was best for Patrick too. He's struggling for control right now."

I nod. Lydia's honesty is what I need right now. "Any news on when the council representative is coming? Or why they want to see me specifically?"

"Nothing yet," Lydia sighs. "They won't tell me who they're sending, or when. Javier is preparing for the visit as best he can."

"Do you think I'm in some kind of trouble?"

Lydia taps a finger against her chin, considering.

"Having the council's attention is never a good thing, but I don't think you are in trouble for something you did," she says. "You'll have to be careful, and I know this goes against all your instincts, but please be polite to the representative they send."

I roll my eyes. "I'll be polite if they're polite."

"Olivia, this will not be someone like any of the vampires you've met. They'll be old, and strong, and possibly not willing to deal with any attitude."

"I'll figure it out. Just keep me updated, all right?" I say, crossing my arms. She has no faith in me. I'm not a six-year-old. I can be polite if I need to.

"I'll keep you updated. Oh, that reminds me. Will you still be able to come by for the regular checkups this week?"

"Yes." The return to routine sounds like a nice distraction.

Lydia squeezes my arm gently. "Stay safe, and stay in touch, all right?"

"Sure thing," I say as I slip into my car.

Lydia watches me drive off, her lips one thin line. I must seem worse off than I thought if she's worrying this much.

We spent almost three hours at the police station. The sun is setting now, and since it's a cloudy night, it's magnificent. I roll the windows down and dance my fingers in the brisk wind. Patrick is alive. I'm alive. We won. That should be enough to get this sick feeling out of my stomach.

Yet, all I can think about is how it felt when Novak died. I wasn't even sure it was possible to kill someone just by taking their magic.

I smack the power button on the radio. I have to stop thinking about this; it's not healthy. Avoidance is a much better option. Tequila might work too, but I don't think I have any left.

I sing along with the radio as I drive. Classic rock, then some generic pop when commercials come on. I'm ready to be home. If I can just bury myself in normalcy, maybe I can get this knot of anger in my chest to loosen.

Martinez's face, the skin twisted and burned on one side, seems to be all I can see every time I shut my eyes. That or Laurel Ramirez hanging from the ceiling like a side of meat. Or Patrick with empty eyes and spit dripping from his chin, nothing left but hunger.

I turn down my driveway, finally, and I'm relieved to see everything is as I left it. The kitchen light is on, and the porch is lit up. I park, grab all my things, and hurry to the front door, keys ready. As soon as I open the door, Mr. Muffins is twining between my legs, meowing loudly.

"I know, I know, I'm sorry," I say as I trip my way inside.

She bites my ankle through my pants.

"Ow! Give me a damn second." I dump my keys, gun, and jacket on the table and go to the laundry room to refill her water and food, only to find they're both still half-filled. I turn around and glare at her. She's sitting in the middle of the kitchen, licking her paw.

"Seriously? All that, and you aren't even starving?"

She meows and stalks over to the fridge.

"I see how it is. You miss one day of treats and turn feral," I grumble as I get a can of wet food out of the fridge. Mr. Muffins is aggressively spoiled, and I only have myself to blame.

The can opener is still in the sink from the last time I fed her. I open the can as she paces back and forth behind me.

"Here you go, Princess Butthead," I say as I drop the can on the floor and ruffle the fur on her head. She buries her face in the food and ignores me.

Everything is where I left it, including the pile of dirty clothes in the bathroom and the mess in the workroom. I don't want to deal with any of it. It'll still be here tomorrow anyhow.

There's a knock on the door, and I jump, my heart kicking into overdrive. No one ever visits me. If Javier were having someone dropped off to be healed, I would have gotten a text.

I walk as quietly as I can to the table and grab the gun. I should have just gotten Mr. Muffins and stayed at the clanhouse.

"Olivia?" the person shouts through the door.

I'd know that voice anywhere. It's Patrick.

CHAPTER 2

I run to the door and pull it open, the gun forgotten in my other hand. Patrick is standing on the porch, face gaunt, and the blue eyes that should be sparkling with mischief are instead glassy and bloodshot. His hands are tucked into the pockets of his faded blue jeans, and his mouth is a thin line of worry. His usually artfully tousled brown hair is dull and messy. He looks nothing like himself.

"Hey," he says quietly. "Do you think I could stay with you for a while?"

Lydia's warning is ringing in my head, but I can't stop myself from stepping out onto the porch and throwing my arms around him. He hugs back tightly, his body trembling. We stand there for a long moment. I wait until he stops shaking so much to pull back.

"So, is that a yes?" he asks, his mouth twitching up into a forced smile.

"Always," I say, punching him lightly on the arm. His eye flicks to my forearm, and the bandage covering the bite he inflicted and the area the bullet grazed me. The smile fades into a frown. I grab his hand and drag him inside.

Mr. Muffins leaves her food and trots over to him. Patrick is her favorite; she definitely loves him more than me.

"Hey, pretty girl," he says, leaning down to pick her up. She rubs her head against his jaw and purrs so loudly, it sounds like she's growling.

I lean back against the sink and watch him cuddle my cat. The tension is bleeding out of his shoulders as he whispers sweet nothings to her and scratches behind her ears.

"So did you run away or Javier let you out of solitary confinement?" I ask as I grab an old bottle of whiskey out of the cabinet. I shouldn't drink right now, but I need something to relax. It's been one thing after another.

I look back when he doesn't answer. He has his face buried in Muffin's fur, and his shoulders are tight once again. He turns away and walks into the living room, plopping down on the couch.

I sigh and pour too much whiskey into my glass. He can make this as difficult as he wants, but I'm getting answers.

He doesn't scoot away when I sit down shoulder-to-shoulder with him on the couch.

"Seriously, Patrick? You don't have to explain everything, but I need to know if Javier is going to come bust down my door looking for you," I say, nudging his shoulder and reaching over to smooth my fingers through Muffin's fur.

"He won't be looking for me. I've left the clan," Patrick says quietly, his voice monotone.

My hand stills, and I look at him with wide eyes. Leaving a clan isn't something you do lightly; it's like disowning your family.

"What—why?" I stutter over my words.

"Javier is a selfish, idiotic asshole," Patrick says, eyes flashing. "I will not serve someone who doesn't care about their clan members. It's his fault Emily is dead."

I take a deep breath, then drain my glass. This is a mess, and whatever he and Javier are fighting about seems like it might have been coming for a while. I've never seen Patrick this angry.

"Are you okay?" I ask quietly.

"Not really," he says, staring blankly at his knees.

"Do you have people you can feed on? I can round up some girls if I need to. They know me."

"I'll be fine. I have some neckers that like me. I fed before I came here." His eyes stray to my bandaged arm again.

"It wasn't your fault."

"I wish that made me feel better."

My heart sinks into my stomach, heavy as a stone. I knew it would be like this, and I hate that I can't fix it.

"They were beating me, and she provoked them. She got under Martinez's skin to distract him, and he took a baseball bat to her head. It just split open and..." He stops talking, his voice catching. "She did it to save me. It's my fault she died. I was weak, and I was begging for them to stop and let me feed, and she couldn't stand to watch it anymore."

I pull him into a hug, and he buries his face in my neck as sobs wrack his body. I can't stop the tears that slip out of my eyes.

There's a bright light shining in my eyes. I blink and roll over, and my stomach jerks as I fall. I flail against the blanket I'm tangled in, and my shin hits something hard.

"Ow, fuck." I look around groggily and realize I'm now on the living room floor. I was on the couch before I rolled off it like an idiot.

Patrick. I jerk upright and look around. He's not in the living room, but I don't remember him leaving either.

I disentangle myself and stumble toward my bedroom. The blinds are tightly drawn, and the closet door is shut. I breathe a sigh of relief.

I tiptoe over, even though I know I couldn't wake him now if I tried, and crack open the door. Patrick is curled up in the back corner of the closet with his head on one of my pillows and my fluffy blanket pulled up to his chin. Mr. Muffins is curled up by his head, also fast asleep.

I must have fallen asleep last night after he started watching that show he loves so much. It's a stupid kids' show, but he loves it. He hadn't even cracked a smile last night, but he had stopped sobbing, so I was calling it a win.

He looks peaceful now. I lean down and tuck the blanket a little closer around him. My phone vibrates. I pull it out and see an email notification for a delivered shipment. I frown; what did I order?

"The warehouse?" I mumble as I read the address.

Oh, of course. It seems like I placed the order with Gerard months ago, but it's been less than a week. I shove my phone back in my pocket and slip out of the closet, closing the door carefully behind me. I wanted to talk to Maybelle, so this is just another reason to head into town. It's also almost four pm. I've been on the vampire sleeping schedule since before the attack.

I take a quick shower and braid my wet hair to keep it out of my face. I grab jeans, boots, and a flannel shirt out of the closet, just because it's starting to feel like fall. Mr. Muffins meows at me for disturbing her.

I grab my jacket and make sure I have the right potions in the pockets. Novak's magic is still settling into place inside of me, but I don't feel like I can rely on it yet. The brews make me feel safer. The gun is still sitting on the table, and I almost leave it, but I grab it, just in case. I'll have to leave it in the glovebox since I can't get any kind of carry permit with my record.

Stepping outside doesn't disappoint. It's not cool enough to see my breath, but I do get a chill when the breeze picks up. The paint on the rear of my car is peeling badly now. I really should get it fixed. Maybe I'll be able to afford it once I start selling the medicinal brews.

I climb inside, tuck the gun in the glovebox, and head toward town with the windows down and the radio turned up loud. Leaving Patrick alone makes me nervous, but he's as safe there as he is anywhere else. If the NWR wanted to attack, they're more likely to hit the clanhouse directly anyhow. I shift in my seat and try to push the 'what if's out of my mind.

I don't have to drive past Rudie's to get to the cafe, but I do anyhow. The whole thing is starting to feel like a bad dream, and I need to see that it's real. I park along the street and climb out of my car. Police tape lines the entire area, flickering in the breeze.

The parking lot is empty. Most of the windows have been busted out. It looks like something out of a ghost town or dystopian novel. The sign isn't lit up, and the faint smell of smoke drifts across the parking lot.

No one had any way of knowing what was underneath it. I didn't know when I was eating my burger and thinking the worst part of my week was going to be seeing Tyler with another girl.

Martinez had seemed so normal. Chevy had too. I don't understand what makes a person build a dungeon under their restaurant and start killing people.

I shake my head and climb back in my car, slamming the door. My tires squeal as I take off, eager to get away from all of this.

I almost pass Maybelle's but decide I want to talk to her before I pick up my delivery. I haven't seen her since everything went to shit. She called twice, and I ignored the calls each time because I just couldn't talk to someone else about what had happened. Hopefully, an in-person explanation will be a good apology.

The lunch rush is in full swing, so I park across the street. A blissful combination of freshly baked bread and cinnamon hits me as I walk through the door. I head upstairs to the cafe and spot Johnny chatting with a couple at one of the tables. He stops mid-sentence when he sees me and hurries over to wrap me in an unexpected hug.

"You had us worried, girlie," he says as I hug him back, slightly overwhelmed by the odor of cigarettes that always clings to him. He releases me and pats my arm, his eyes looking a little wet.

"Sorry, I would have come by sooner, but..." I shrug. "I hadn't even made it home before last night. Is Maybelle around?"

"She is, just head on back. She's in her office."

"Thanks, Johnny."

The loud chatter of the restaurant is replaced by the clank of plates being washed and the cooks shouting over each other as I pass through the door to the kitchen. I dodge a waitress carrying a full tray of food and weave my way back to the offices.

Maybelle's door is half-closed. I knock once as I push it open. She jumps and shoves something in her drawer.

"Sorry, is this a bad time?" I ask, hesitating in the doorway now.

"Don't be ridiculous," she says, coming around her desk with a big smile on her face that doesn't reach her eyes. She's wearing a bright red dress with a sea blue scarf and glittery black flats, but the dress is wrinkled and her hair is in a bun instead of its usual curly chaos. She doesn't have any makeup on either.

She gives me a brief, tight hug, then leans back and pats me on the cheek. "There's been a lot of rumors all over town about what happened in Rudie's. Everybody thought you were dead for a while. Someone was even saying the NWR had wiped out the entire clan."

"They definitely killed some of them. Some of the weres too," I say with a sigh. "We're lucky there weren't that many of the terrorists, or it would have been a massacre."

"Here, sit down," she says, herding me to a folding chair that sits facing her desk. She sits in another one across from me and smooths out her skirt. "Now, I know it's a bit trivial, but I thought it might cheer you up to hear they've already started construction on the apothecary. In a couple of days, you can go and see it if you want."

"Already?" I exclaim, sitting up straighter. "You move fast. I'm glad my ingredients just got delivered. I'll have to start brewing as soon as I can."

"Hopefully, the brewing can be a good distraction for you. I'm sure the next couple of months won't be easy," she says, patting my knee.

"No joke," I sigh. "A representative from the vampire council is coming to town at some unknown point to see me as well. We have no idea what they want."

"To see you?" Maybelle asks, her voice going hard.

"That's what Lydia was told," I say, confused at her sudden change in demeanor.

"You can't trust them, no matter what they tell you or offer you. Stay away from them if you can," Maybelle says through gritted teeth.

"I'll be careful, but aren't they on our side?" I ask taken aback. I've never seen Maybelle angry before, ever.

"No, they're on their own side. They'll do anything they can to gain power. Promise me, Olivia, promise me you won't trust whoever they send. You have to keep your guard up," she says, leaning forward and reaching out to grip my knee tightly.

"Okay, I promise," I say, patting her hand awkwardly.

She raises a brow like she doesn't believe me.

"I really will," I insist.

"All right," she says, shaking her head. "And I don't mean to rush you out, but I have some things I need to finish up on a deadline. Will I see you later this week?" she asks as she stands.

I stand as well, confused. "Um, sure."

"Stay safe, sweetie," she says, pulling me into a brief hug before shooing me out of her office and shutting the door.

I stand in the hallway, dazed by the whole interaction. She's never run me off like that. Why does the vampire council representative have her so flustered?

The expression on Maybelle's face bothers me all the way to the warehouse. I park across the street from Gerard's warehouse and text Lydia for a quick update. I was already worried, but now I'm extra anxious about the visit.

I walk up to the door and realize I don't see the packages outside. Surely, the delivery driver wouldn't have left them inside. I grab the handle and find it's locked.

I frown and step back. I had left it unlocked when I was last here. I tilt my head to the side; I suppose Emilio could have locked it.

I knock loudly three times, wait three seconds, then knock one last time. I hear footsteps inside, and the door swings open, revealing a bleary-eyed but slightly cleaner than normal Gerard.

"You're back," I say dumbly.

"Obviously," he says, squinting at me, then opening the door wider. "It's there."

He points at a pile of boxes just inside the doorway set on a grungy looking pallet.

"Oh, great, thanks," I say, stepping inside and grabbing the first box. He nods and starts back toward his office.

"You could have told me it was the NWR in town," I blurt out. It's been bothering me since I figured out who had taken Patrick.

Gerard stops but doesn't turn around to answer.

"I didn't know who it was," he rasps. "Just had a bad feeling, that was all."

There's no way. Absolutely *no way* Gerard is a Diviner. I can't think what else he might be implying though.

I carry my boxes out to the car, and by the time I'm done, I'm starting to regret the flannel. It's not nearly cool enough outside to be carrying heavy stuff in the afternoon sun without working up a sweat.

I double check that I haven't missed anything inside.

"I'm all done!" I shout across the warehouse. Gerard waves a hand out of his office in acknowledgment.

I climb back into my car and lean my head against the steering wheel. Always more questions than answers. All I want is one calm day. That shouldn't be too much to ask.

My phone rings. It's Lydia.

"Hey," I answer as I start the car and pull out into the street.

"Before Javier wakes up, I just had to ask if Patrick was with you, or if we need to be concerned?" Lydia asks, her voice tired.

"He's with me, and he's fine. I wouldn't rule out being concerned though."

"I know you don't want to hear this, but—"

"Then don't say it," I interrupt.

"Olivia, he's not safe."

"I'll take my chances," I snap.

Lydia is quiet, and I take a deep breath and change the subject. It's too early to be fighting. "You hear anything else about when the council rep is supposed to show up?"

Lydia huffs, annoyed. "No, they don't tend to give much notice, but this is getting ridiculous."

"Figures. I'll talk to you later then."

"Be careful," Lydia says quietly.

I end the call and rub my fingers across my brow. I really can't blame Patrick for being angry with Javier. Things got messy and people got hurt and Patrick isn't thinking straight. Javier is also kind of an ass sometimes. I don't want to be caught in the middle though.

I stop for groceries on the way home. It's been a while since I've had a home cooked meal, and a quick soup sounds great. It takes me less than ten minutes to get in and out, my passenger seat now full of bags.

I park my car in the usual spot in my driveway. The sunset almost fifteen minutes ago, so I know Patrick will be up. Part of me wants to just sit in the car and eat some of the ice cream I got before it melts instead of going inside to face Patrick and everything that has happened.

I sigh and open the door. The sound of shouting makes me freeze, one foot on the ground, halfway out of the car. There's more than one voice. I lean back in to grab my jacket and yank the glovebox open, grabbing the gun as well.

I run toward the house, trying to stay low and keep quiet. There's no sign of another car. The front door is still intact, but it isn't shut all the way. I step onto the porch cautiously, avoiding the creaky parts, and peek in the living room window. The blinds are down, but I can see two figures through the narrow slits. A man is standing over Patrick, whose lip is bleeding.

I stand and kick the door open in one fluid motion, my heart pounding out of my chest. I find the sight on the end of the gun and fire twice, the gunfire cracking loudly inside the house, but all I hit is the wall. The man has disappeared, and I never even saw him move.

I blink rapidly. Did I imagine him? I take a step back, scanning to see where he has vanished to. Patrick is yelling something, but I can't hear him over the ringing in my ears.

I back into a hard chest.

CHAPTER 3

I freeze, but he doesn't move. His chest is cool and I can feel the magic that keeps him alive stirring under his skin. As if I needed any more proof he was a vampire.

"Quite the warm welcome, Ms. Carter. Both your pet and you attacked me without so much as a hello," he says in a lightly accented voice.

I swallow and step away from him, turning around very slowly with the gun lowered. He's at least six feet tall, with a sharp jawline and slightly hollowed cheeks that are softened by dimples. He's smiling, his fangs poking out over his full bottom lip. His thick, wavy auburn hair, which is smoothed back, sharply contrasts his crisp black suit. He's lean, but he's probably ripped under the suit.

"Who the fuck are you, and what are you doing in my house?" I say in measured tones. I should have called someone, or at least texted Lydia, before I walked in here.

"Reilly Walsh," he says, bowing with a flourish. "The representative sent by the esteemed vampire council to investigate the appearance of the NWR in a small, unimportant town in the middle of nowhere."

I edge toward Patrick, who is still sitting on the floor, glaring at Reilly.

Reilly smooths a hand over a wrinkle in his suit jacket and looks between us, raising a brow. "I believe you were told I was coming?"

"Sure, just not your name or when you'd be here or *why* you were coming," I say, finally tucking the gun in my waistband. It's useless against someone like Reilly. "Or that you'd be walking into my house without an invitation and attacking my friend."

Reilly scoffs. "He attacked me. I was well within my rights to kill him."

"Are you kidding me?" I exclaim, taking two large steps forward before Patrick pulls me back.

"Not worth it, Olivia," Patrick whispers into my ear. Normally, I'm the reasonable one and he's the hothead.

My skin is tingling, and I have to pull Novak's magic back sharply. How did he live like this? I seem to be on the verge of accidentally electrocuting someone every time I get mad.

"He has a right to be here; you don't. Get out. You can talk to me at the clanhouse, but you are not staying here."

"As a representative of the council, I have a right to go wherever I need to in the course of my investigation," he snarls, his dimples disappearing along with his smile.

"You are out of your jurisdiction, buddy," I snarl back. "I'm a witch. You don't get to tell me what to do. Now, get out."

"Make. Me," he says, baring his teeth after each word.

I have the same odds of winning the lottery as I do of landing a hit before he kills me. I grind my teeth together, and Patrick tightens his grip on my arm; he obviously has no intention of letting me do anything moronic.

"This is stupid," I say, jerking at my arm until Patrick finally lets go. Reilly watches me, his brows pinched together. "I'm getting my groceries out of the car. If you hurt Patrick while I'm gone, I'll *find* a way to kill you."

I stomp back out the front door, slamming it uselessly behind me. My car door is still open. I slap it shut and walk around to the passenger side to get the bags. I hook them all on my uninjured arm, then turn around and walk into Reilly once again.

"Seriously?" I say, stumbling back against the car. "Personal space. It's a thing."

"You're the one that keeps walking into me. Perhaps try watching where you're going?" he says, those dimples making a reappearance. I want to kick him in the teeth.

"Did you come out here to help me carry in the groceries, or is there something you wanted?"

"I did want to talk, privately," he says as he hops onto the hood of my car and makes himself comfortable.

I set the bags back in the passenger seat and cross my arms. "Well? Get on with it."

"I thought southerners were known for their hospitality?" he pouts. "Maybe it's just this town."

I stare at him. He obviously just likes the sound of his own voice. He's hot, in a rich city boy kind of way with his slick suit and perfect hair. I'm sure girls normally fling themselves at his feet, panties already halfway down their legs. Hell, I would have been one of them if he hadn't come in and attacked Patrick.

"As I said before, I'm here to investigate the incident with the NWR, and most importantly, to make sure none of them are left."

"That's great," I say, though my tone says *I don't care.*

"I also intend to find Martinez, and in a show of good faith, the council is going to work with a witch in order to arrest him and bring him to trial. You were their choice. It'll make a good headline. Witch Gets Justice With Help of Vampire Council," he says, waving his hand through the air. "The journalists will come up with something catchy, I'm sure."

"Awesome, let me know when you find him, and I'll come kill him for you."

"We definitely need to catch him alive. The council was very insistent on that point."

"The council can go fuck themselves."

"Such bold words," Reilly says as he leans back on his hands. "Do you know Aaron Hall?"

"I know of him, why?" There's no way, just absolutely none, that they know what happened, but that doesn't stop my heart from doing a pitter-patter in my chest.

Reilly tilts his head to the side, looking me up and down in a way that should be flirtatious but instead leaves me feeling exposed.

"He's supposed to be a Finder, which would make things simpler. The coven should be trying to get some good PR, so I imagine they'll even lend him out for free."

Of course. He's a Finder. It makes sense for them to ask about him. This is fine.

"No one has any idea where Martinez is. It's not like a Finder can search the entire country for him, what's the point?"

"We'll have him search the local area first, just in case. If we need him to search a larger area later, we'll do so."

"Sounds like you have a well thought out plan–"

"You're going to come with me when I talk to them."

I stare at him, mouth hanging open. "No, I'm not."

"What do you want, Olivia? More than anything?"

"For you to go away and never bother me again," I say, rolling my eyes.

"Not to find your mother?"

He says it so casually, as if it's a trivial matter. Something he can joke about. I clench my hand into a fist to keep the sudden heat of electricity from escaping.

"My mother is dead. Has been for years," I say with gritted teeth.

"Most likely," he agrees pleasantly, as though he can't tell I'm furious. "However, the medical records and death certificate Detective Brunson found were faked."

"What?" I don't want to go through this again. The sick hope already curling in my gut feels like a betrayal. Why is he trying so hard to get my help? As far as he should know, I'm not special.

"He knew that, didn't he tell you?" Reilly asks, tilting his head to the side. "Perhaps he didn't get a chance to before he died. Or perhaps he never intended to; you did get a bit obsessive about finding her when you were younger."

I don't respond. I can't.

"Come with me tomorrow evening to talk to the coven, and I'll tell you what I know about the faked records," Reilly says, hopping off the hood of my car.

"Why do you even want me there?"

"Because I am demanding, unreasonable, and secretive. I'll see you tomorrow just after sundown," Reilly says with a smile before disappearing without a sound.

I stand, stunned, and stare at the spot he just occupied. My mind is spinning as I think back to the day Brunson told me he had found her, and that she was dead. I had no doubt then that he was telling me the truth. Why would he lie about that? And despite what Reilly implied, I have a hard time believing he would. I hate everything about today.

I grab my bags out of the car and walk back inside. Patrick is sitting in the middle of the living room next to what used to be my coffee table. It looks like someone was slammed down on top of it. One of the legs is on the other side of the room.

"Are you hurt?" I ask, dropping the bags on the counter and fishing out my ice cream.

"No, but my pride may never recover," Patrick says as he stands. "I've never seen a vampire move that fast."

"I'm not convinced he isn't teleporting." I find a spoon and take a bite of ice cream.

Patrick stares at his hands, strangely quiet.

"Are you sure he didn't hurt you? Or threaten you?"

He hesitates just long enough to make me worry, then looks up with a smile. "He didn't, it's fine. Don't worry about me."

CHAPTER 4

The blinds are drawn tight, so the room is pitch black. I check my phone. It's only three-thirty in the afternoon. Just enough time to get started on some of the brews for the apothecary before the sun sets.

I groan and rub my eyes. I'm still tired, probably because of the nightmares that keep waking me up every few hours.

I roll out of bed and find my clothes. Mr. Muffins is waiting for her breakfast in the kitchen. She lets me pick her up for once, and I carry her around while I get her food together and refill her water. She's warm and soft and happily purring.

The coffee table, which was broken in Reilly and Patrick's fight last night, is still lying in the middle of the living room. I look at it, then just walk around it. That's a problem for another day.

The bandage on my arm has come half-loose. I pick it off and examine the wound. It's mostly healed. I press my hand on the wound and push the warm, healing magic into it.

It's always odd, healing myself. It turns into a feedback loop almost. It's more tiring than healing anyone else, and harder to focus. I think the sensation and awareness of my body distracts me.

I exhale shakily and raise my hand. There's a light scar, but it's better than it was. I wad the bandage up and throw it away, feeling cleaner in a way, now that it's gone.

My workroom is still a wreck. That is actually a problem for today, so I crack my knuckles and choose a corner to tackle first. The door and windows open up first. I need the fresh air; it still smells vaguely of spice and smoke in here.

The bag that I carried everything in when I kidnapped Aaron is sitting by the door. I dump it out and start putting everything away. I pick up the flashlight, and the map catches my eyes. I reach for it slowly, my fingers tracing the back. She's dead. I know that. I shove it back in the bag and shove the bag in the corner.

One bag of trash, two sets of brewing instruments scrubbed, and a shiny stove, and I'm done. Now it's time to get everything dirty again.

I run through a mental list of the healing potions that might sell best. Headache potions, of course. Potions to keep bad dreams at bay and help someone sleep. I haven't made a Sweet Dreams brew in years.

My fingers trail over the cauldrons, as I think. I get to the cast iron cauldron and pause. The iron is rough under my fingers. It brings back memories I haven't thought about in a long time. When I was younger, my mom would sometimes just make a cider in the cauldron, then share it with the neighbors and tell them it was a good luck brew. They always walked away with a warm belly and their heads held a little higher. It's been a while since I've used this cauldron, and it feels neglected. It seems right to brew the Sweet Dreams potion in it while I'm full of these good memories.

I grunt as I pick it up. The cast iron cauldron is heavy and unwieldy, but the sturdiness is what makes it good for this brew. I light the fire underneath it and turn it down low. This is a potion to brew nice and slow. No rush, no stress.

I open the chest that I keep all my dried plants in and grab a bundle of lavender and the sweet alyssum I picked a couple of weeks ago. It still smells lovely even though the flowers have wilted.

The crystals are a different matter. I open the drawer and look over them, biting my lip as I consider each one. I need something cool and steady.

My hand drifts away from the usual crystals to the little pile of abalone shells in the back of the drawer. I smile as I wrap my fingers around one. The sound of the ocean is soothing, rhythmic, and relaxing. These will be perfect.

I fill the cauldron with water before it gets too hot, then put in a handful of chamomile tea in. The leaves begin a merry dance around the pot, forming swirls within swirls. Next is the lavender. The water deepens to purple as soon as the plant dips under the surface. It breaks apart quickly, and the little buds of lavender join the tea leaves in their hypnotic dance.

The alyssum I warm in my hands first, rolling it between my palms until the scent is bright and new again. The petals unfurl as they hit the water, the bruises disappearing and the wilted petals smoothing out.

I let the ingredients settle in the cauldron as I grab my mortar and pestle. The abalone shells grind up easily, crunching into a sparkling powder that looks like stardust.

I hum a lullaby under my breath; my mom used to sing it to me before I decided I was too old to be tucked into bed. I can't remember all the words now, but they're not important. It's the feeling I need.

I pick up my wooden stirring rod and tap the edge of the cauldron. The petals all sink slowly to the bottom, disappearing in the purple liquid.

I grab a handful of the powdered abalone shells and hold my hand high over the cauldron. I tap the edge again, and the potion chimes, the sound ringing out around the room, as it turns to a milky dark blue.

Little starbursts of light burst out of my hand, igniting the abalone shell with magic as it falls from my hand, catching on some unseen flow of magic that sends it swirling around me. They hover like a cloud of stars, swaying slightly in an unseen breeze.

I dip the rod into the cauldron and stir, slow and steady. The little, twinkling stars begin to move in rhythm with the rod as though they are being pulled along on gossamer threads. Each stir brings a little more into the cauldron. They glint in the potion, dreamy and beautiful. I keep stirring, almost unaware of the passage of time. The light is the room is dimmed, and I feel calm and comforted.

With one last circle, the last of the abalone shell is pulled into the cauldron, and I feel my magic settle into the brew. I lift the rod out and step back with a contented sigh, a warm, floral scent drifting lazily from the cauldron. If only everything could be this simple.

The sun is setting, so it's just a matter of time before Reilly shows up. He had said he would be here promptly after sundown.

I hear Patrick moving around in the closet; he always twitches as he wakes up. I walk into my bedroom and sit on the end of the bed.

Patrick opens the closet door and stares at me, blinking blearily. He looks like his old self for a moment. He has slept over regularly in the past, never in my bed, always in the closet. It's always been an unspoken agreement that I've never thought too hard about. I care about him too much to fuck it up with sex, especially since, while he is attractive, we don't have that spark that always leads to me making dumb decisions.

"Did you sleep well?" I ask, smirking at him.

He rolls his eyes and runs a hand through his hair, trying to smooth out the weird bump on the left side.

"Fantastic, as always." His voice is rough, and he sounds grumpy.

"Reilly is going to be here any minute." I stand back up, unused to this sullen version of Patrick. "Do you need anything? I might be gone most of the night. Will you be going out?"

"I can take care of myself," he says, his hand twitching. "I didn't come here to have you babysit me."

"I'm not trying to babysit you. I'm just making sure my friend is okay," I say, lifting my hands.

"You're treating me like Javier did, like I'm sick or a child," he says, jaw tense and brows pulled tightly together.

"Sorry I asked," I snap, turning and walking out of the room.

Patrick follows me sullenly, then walks straight out the front door. I sit down at the table and put my head in my hands. I hope he doesn't do anything stupid.

I look back down at my phone, my thumb hovering over his name in my text messages. I don't really know what to say to him. I don't know what his problem is, but I don't want him to think I'm angry. I drop my phone back on the table without saying anything. Sometimes it's just better to leave people alone when they've turned into a grumpy asshole.

I'm supposed to have dinner with Lydia after this meeting with the coven. She has some kind of update from Timmons. I needed to go to the liquor store anyhow; I've been out of tequila for far too long. It's going to be a long night too. I'll be headed to the clanhouse after dinner for the checkup.

I stand up and stretch. I'm wearing a T-shirt that says *Resting Witch Face* and a pair of low rise jeans. It's completely inappropriate for everything I'm doing today, my own personal little rebellion.

Mr. Muffins meows loudly, and I turn around to see Reilly crouched down on the floor, engaged in some kind of staring contest with her. I wish she would bite him or something; instead, she purrs when he runs a hand down her back. Traitor.

Mr. Muffins rolls over onto her back and lets Reilly ruffle the fur of her belly.

"Stop petting my cat," I say, feeling further betrayed. "I want to get this over with."

Reilly smirks at me and buries his fingers even deeper in the fluff. She bites him, and he jerks his hand away with a hiss. I smirk; maybe not so much of a traitor after all.

"Even your cat is cranky," Reilly complains. He stands and adjusts his suit. He is dressed just as formally as last night, and I can't help staring. He makes a suit look good. He's even wearing a tie today. "You can drive. I'm sure you know your way to the coven's meeting hall."

"Sure." I grab my things, pulling my jacket on, and head outside without waiting to see if he follows.

He slips into the passenger seat as I am putting the car in drive and looks around with a wrinkled nose.

"It smells odd in here. You should really get your car cleaned."

"I should smear garlic all over the seats," I mutter.

Reilly chuckles at that and rolls down the passenger window. "How long have you lived in this town?"

"I'm sure you already know." I hate small talk on a good day. I have no desire to chat with this asshole.

"True, what I don't know is, why here? You stopped in quite a few towns before you settled down here."

"I got a job offer here. It was just kind of dumb luck, no point in leaving after that."

"You're referring to the contract you have with the local clan?"

"Yes."

Reilly rubs a hand thoughtfully on his chin. "What dumb luck led to you getting a job?"

"What is this? Twenty questions? I'm already helping you."

"Let's do a trade, then. You answer a question, then I do."

I tighten my grip on the steering. He just does not give up. "Fine, but I've already answered one question, so it's my turn to ask."

Reilly waves a hand magnanimously. "Go ahead."

"What did you fuck up to get sent on a low priority assignment in a middle-of-nowhere town like this?"

He doesn't react, which is annoying. I was sure that was it.

"Perhaps this assignment is more important than you realize," he says easily. "I don't make mistakes."

I roll my eyes.

"Now, answer my previous question."

I tap my fingers against the wheel before answering. "I had just gotten a job as a waitress at Maybelle's cafe in town, but it was only part-time, and I was having trouble finding a second job. This girl stumbles in one morning, starts eating breakfast, then passes out. I grabbed her and realized it was blood loss, then kept her alive until the ambulance got there. Turned out she had lied about how many people had fed from her, so the last vampire ended up taking too much. It got back to Javier, and he paid me for it, then offered me a job. So, like I said. Dumb luck. I just happened to be in the right place at the right time."

"Interesting."

I don't like the way he says it, like it really is interesting and now he knows something he shouldn't. A hedgewitch shouldn't be able to heal, but the magic is so weak, it's never aroused suspicion before.

"How long have you worked for the council?"

"Almost ten years, though it seems like far longer."

He doesn't follow up with another question, seemingly content to stare out the window for now. I stay tense as we drive through town. The coven lands are on the north side. It's almost fifty acres, with its own subdivision, as well as several large buildings, including an old church only coven members are permitted to attend.

The old mansion McGuinness lives in is in the center of their little town. Before you can get to that, however, you have to pass through the main gate. I can see it already. The black, wrought iron gate looms over the road, both a sign and a warning. I've never tested the enchantments, but I know there are many. The Ignatius Coven isn't weak even if they are in a remote area.

I come to a stop next to the guard's station and roll down my window.

"Do we have an appointment or what?" I ask as the guard approaches.

"No, I thought a surprise visit would be more fun," Reilly says with a dimpled smile.

The guard leans down to look through the window. "Name?"

"Olivia Carter," I say. Reilly stays silent.

"Do you have an appointment?"

"Nope, but ol' Dermot McGuinness is an old friend. I'm sure he'll want to see me," I say with a straight face.

The guard snorts, then points at Reilly. "What about you?"

"I'm just her security. John Smith if you need a name," he lies smoothly.

The guard steps back, talking to someone through his radio. They argue back and forth for a moment, then the guard waves the gate open. I pull through, surprised they're actually letting me inside.

"You know they're probably planning on killing me or something as soon as we get inside."

"We can only hope they try. I'd probably get a bonus for the PR from that alone," Reilly said, tapping a long finger against his chin. "I've heard McGuinness is a hothead."

"That's a serious understatement."

The main road runs right into the circular driveway in front of the mansion. The lawn is perfectly manicured, with a large fountain spurting water about ten feet in the air in the center of the driveway.

Two ornate pillars stand on each side of the door. The wooden trim around the large double door is carved into two figures, one holding a bundle of herbs, the other with fire in one hand and a lightning bolt in the other. Aris and Izul, the witches that founded the original council a millennia ago.

I park right up front and step out of the car, feeling wonderfully underdressed. The big, wooden door opens when we're halfway there, and Baldy steps outside. He looks rather angry.

"Hey, old friend," I shout with a wave as we approach.

"You are not welcome here, Olivia Carter," he says in his deep voice. His skin is already tinged gray; it's like he doesn't trust me.

"So welcoming, as always," I say with a grin. I'm a little mad that this is fun. Reilly is going to be smug about it later, I just know it. "Where's McGuinness?"

"You will not be seeing McGuinness," Baldy replies, crossing his arms. "You have one chance to leave before we report you to the police for trespassing."

Reilly takes one step forward, and then simply walks past Baldy through the open door. The only evidence he didn't teleport is the rush of wind I feel as he moves. How is he this fast?

"What the fuck are you doing?" Baldy bellows, rushing after Reilly. I jog after them; I definitely want to see it if Reilly beats the shit out of him.

I step through the door as Baldy gets a hand around Reilly's arm. Reilly pivots and smacks him in the chest. Baldy wheezes and flies through the air, past me, and straight into the wall by the door. The sheetrock crumbles under the impact.

Baldy wrenches himself free, his skin now completely gray, and runs full speed back at Reilly. Impervs are impressively dense. Reilly sidesteps the reckless charge and winks at me. Baldy skids to a stop at the base of the staircase that dominates the room. He whips around, preparing to charge again. He is not a fast learner.

"Enough!"

At the top of the staircase is McGuinness, his face as red as ever, and Scarlett on his left. On his right is someone I don't recognize though. She's young but most likely at least eighteen. She has platinum blonde hair and looks like she weighs a hundred pounds soaking wet.

"McGuinness, how lovely to see you," Reilly says, spreading his arms wide as though he's expecting McGuinness to rush forward for a hug.

"Who the hell are you?" McGuinness growls.

"Reilly Walsh, the representative sent by the vampire council to investigate the activities of the terrorist group known as the New World Reformation in relation to the recent incident in your quaint little town."

McGuinness snorts. "That's been handled. The witch council is considering the case closed. Do the vampires have nothing better to do?"

"Case closed? How sloppy," Reilly says, shaking his head in disapproval. "The main conspirator escaped custody. Do the witches have no intention of tracking him down?"

"We'll leave that to JHAPI. What do you want?"

"Aaron Hall," Reilly says simply.

McGuinness laughs. "Then we're both out of luck. That little shit turned up after some kind of bender. Confused, barely able to remember his name."

Oops. Guess I brewed that memory potion a bit too strong. It's not like I could test it beforehand though.

"He hasn't been able to perform even the most basic magic since. His family had me send him home to be examined."

"A witch losing their magic right before it's needed? How convenient," Reilly scoffs. "That's impossible, and we both know it."

"Perhaps you can ask Olivia how it happened?" McGuinness snaps. "She was seen talking to him the night he disappeared."

I snort. "So did he refuse to help me find the missing vampires because he had already lost his magic? Or is he just as much a prick as you are?"

I stare McGuinness down, but my heart is pounding. I'm sure Reilly can hear it. He's going to have questions later, especially since I didn't admit to knowing Aaron. I should never have come here. Reilly is more demon than vampire with his shitty bargains.

"We're done here. You can get out, or I'll have you removed," McGuinness growls, crossing his arms. Scarlett and the blonde girl step forward like eager guard dogs.

Water wraps around the blonde girl's arm like a snake. I twitch when I feel a drop of water hit my cheek.

Reilly steps in front of me, his shoulders hunch slightly, and his posture shifts into something far more menacing.

"Attacking a representative sent by the council violates every treaty we have, McGuinness. Are you sure you want to be *that* coven?" Reilly growls, all pretense of amiability now dropped.

"I am done entertaining the whims of the vampire council. See yourselves out."

McGuinness walks away, but Scarlett takes a step down the stairs. She is eager to fight, as always.

Reilly turns his back on them and offers me his arm. "Alas, a wasted trip."

I slip my arm through his, even though it pains me to take my eyes off the threats. "As usual."

CHAPTER 5

I don't know why he hasn't asked me about meeting with Aaron yet. We're halfway back to town, and he's been acting like nothing is wrong.

"Is there somewhere I can drop you off?" I ask, uncomfortable with the silence. "I'm supposed to have dinner with someone."

"Who?"

"Lydia Holland."

"Ah, Javier Moreno's attorney. Is she a friend, or simply acting as your lawyer?"

"Both," I say, tapping my thumb on the steering wheel.

"I'll join you. I've heard she's a very interesting woman."

"You're not invited."

"Good thing I don't care," he says, flashing those dimples again. "If you'd like to explain why you didn't tell me you had met with Aaron Hall recently, I might be persuaded to reconsider."

I grit my teeth. "There's nothing to explain. The conversation was so unimportant that'd I'd forgotten all about it."

"You are a very bad liar."

"I don't know what you're talking about," I say as I gun it through a light that just turned yellow.

"Where are we having dinner?" Reilly asks.

I sigh. "What difference does it make? You can't eat."

"So hostile," Reilly pouts. "And I could eat something, it would just be disgusting."

I drive just past Maybelle's and park along the street. The main dinner crowd is already filtering out.

"How quaint," Reilly says as he steps out of the car. "Maybelle's Cafe. That's very southern. Do they have chicken fried steak and pies?"

I roll my eyes. "Do you ever shut up?"

He mimes locking his mouth shut and throwing away the key. I bite my tongue to keep from smiling, pivot on my heel, and walk toward the restaurant. He catches up to me almost immediately and even manages to open the door.

I hurry through the store and up the stairs to the cafe. The smell of food is making my mouth water.

Lydia is sitting in a booth in the corner, her nose buried in her phone. She's in a suit as usual, but her steel-gray hair is down and curled nicely. It does nothing to make her look less intimidating.

"He insisted on joining," I say as I plop into the chair across from Lydia.

She looks up, confused, until Reilly sits down next to me.

"Reilly Walsh, council representative," he says, extending his hand across the table. Lydia reacts much better to meeting him than I did and shakes his hand firmly, all trace of surprise gone from her face.

"Welcome to Pecan Grove, Mr. Walsh. How are you enjoying your stay so far?"

"It's been extremely pleasant." He inclines his head with a smile. "Olivia has been kind enough to agree to assist me, as well as drive me around town this evening."

I look at him like he's crazy, and I'm starting to suspect he might actually be.

"Oh, has she?" Lydia says. She smiles at me broadly, but her arched brow says I'm going to get fussed at later. At least Lydia understands he's full of shit too.

"Yeah, it's been a riot." I cross my arms and look around for the waiter. I need food if I'm going to endure this.

He appears right next to the table as though I summoned him. His face is familiar.

"I'm Kevin, and I'll be your waiter this evening. Can I get you started with drinks?"

Ah, of course. He was my waiter the last time I ate here. With Martinez.

"Water, please," Lydia requests with a smile.

Kevin turns to me next, his pen ready.

"Coffee and the biggest chicken fried steak you have, lots of gravy. Also a basket of biscuits."

Kevin smiles as he jots the order down; he must remember me. "Would you like to go ahead and place your food order as well?" he asks, turning back to Lydia.

"Sure," Lydia says, scanning her menu. "The Cowboy Stew."

Kevin nods and takes her menu, then looks at Reilly.

"Nothing, thanks," Reilly says, smiling wide enough to show his fangs.

Kevin the-almost-unflappable pales slightly, takes the other menus, and walks away at a perfectly normal pace even if his shoulders are a bit stiff. Most humans don't think they're scared of vampires until they meet one. Witches and weres are easier to treat just like anyone else, but vampires creep people out.

"So," Reilly says, folding his hands under his chin. "A human lawyer working for vampires and representing a witch. Quite the collection of friends you have."

"I suppose," Lydia says, matching his posture. "What about you? The youngest vampire in your position, though young is an odd word to pin on you. Sired by one of the most powerful clans, and in fact, sired by the vampire most believe will succeed Claudius when he finally turns to dust. I imagine you have much more interesting friends."

Sired by the Sacrum Tenebris Clan leader? Seriously? There were three original vampire clans once paranormals started getting organized. Sacrum Tenebris, Familia de Sangre, and Ānjìng De Sǐwáng. They're all still in power today, in some way. Sacrum Tenebris and Familia de Sangre are two parts of the vampire council. The third is a newer clan that formed around the time Europeans began settling North America.

A cold chill runs down my spine. I've been threatening and being a huge pain in the ass, to someone way out of my league. This guy has the power to make me disappear. It wouldn't even be hard for him.

"You're not wrong." Reilly laughs, his dimple brightening his face and almost distracting from the hint of fangs under his lips. "Still, this town has certainly attracted all types."

"There's more room to do things a little differently out here, where we're unimportant," Lydia agrees with a nod. "That attracts the right sort of person."

"Very differently indeed. Moreno's clan is certainly a shining example of propriety. How long has it been since there was a death? Before the last week, of course."

Lydia's hand tightens around her silverware, still wrapped up in the little paper napkin. "A little over seven months."

I look at Lydia, a little confused. Only seven months? Javier had stressed that they took every care not to kill the neckers that came to them. Surely, they weren't just killing people left and right before I showed up. "It's lovely to see such a high survival rate among the new sires and the clan's resources. Moreno's methods are widely admired, well—by the people that matter at least," Reilly says, leaning back in his chair.

Resources. He says it like they aren't people. It'd be less

insulting for him to call them neckers. And I can't imagine who wouldn't approve of what Javier has done. It's better for everyone.

"Olivia is coming to give the bi-weekly checkups tonight, actually. If you are interested in the process, I'm sure she can go over it with you," Lydia says, her hand still tight on the silverware.

"I needed to speak with Moreno, so the timing is perfect. I am very interested in the process."

Kevin appears with the basket of biscuits, and I eagerly grab one. I need something to do with my hands and mouth before I start asking questions that make me look stupid. Questions I obviously should have asked sooner. I was just so focused on the paycheck.

I shove half a biscuit in my mouth and chew, my cheek puffed out like a squirrel. Reilly looks at me with a grimace distorting his face. I glare at him and take another big bite.

"Timmons sent me an interesting email," Lydia says, turning to me.

I swallow uncomfortably. I should have asked for a water too. "Concerning Martinez?"

"Yep," Lydia said, making her lips pop on the 'p'. "Apparently, the NWR released a video featuring Martinez claiming they were attacked, unprovoked, for defending themselves against a marauding vampire."

I rub my hands over my face. "But there are no clues on where he is, are there?"

"Not yet, at least not any the JHAPI agents are willing to share with us," Lydia says, stealing a biscuit. "If they can narrow down the region, they'll be able to put a Finder on the case. No such luck yet."

Our food and drinks arrive together. The smell makes my mouth water. Kevin's hands only shake a little when he has to lean past Reilly to set my plate in front of me.

"Thanks, Kevin," I say with a smile.

"No problem. Need anything else?"

"I'll take a water," I say, already cutting into my chicken fried steak.

Kevin nods and hurries away. The table is quiet for the next minute or so as I shovel food in my mouth, Reilly watches with horrified fascination, and Lydia looks between us, her brows pinched slightly.

"I understand you intend to help with the investigation?" Lydia asks in-between bites.

"Somewhat. The council wants reassurance the NWR's influence is gone from the town. They are, of course, interested in locating Martinez as well."

My water arrives, and I gulp it down eagerly.

"Olivia has generously offered to assist with the investigation while I'm here and, if any leads on Martinez are found, lend a hand in apprehending him."

Lydia's eyes flick to mine. I shake my head slightly, and she lets it go, for now.

"The clan is willing to help as well. You have Javier's number?"

"I do."

I see Maybelle come up the stairs to the cafe. I catch her eye, and I'm about to wave when she sees Reilly. She freezes, her shoulders tensing. She immediately turns and walks back downstairs. I poke at the last bite of my chicken fried steak. Her hatred for him seems almost personal, though I have no idea how she would have met him before this.

"Can you slide out? I need to use the restroom," I say, poking Reilly's arm, then immediately remembering who he is. He doesn't seem to mind though and slides out of the booth before I have a chance to get unnecessarily nervous.

I slide out as well and start winding my way to the back of the restaurant. I do need to pee, and then I intend to track down Maybelle and see why she's acting so oddly.

I pass by a crowded table, bumping into a chair. I feel a hand on my arm and turn around to tell them to let go before I rip their fingers off, but my words die in my throat.

He's a spitting image of his father. Dark, almost black eyes. His hair is shaved short now, nothing like the long twists he had worn in college.

"Zachary," I swallow. "It's been a while."

"Four years," he says, his jaw clenching and unclenching. His hand is still tight on my arm. "Four years since the day my father died and the girl I called my sister disappeared without a trace. And that's all you have to say? It's been a while?"

I shrug, glancing around like I might be able to find a way to escape. My hands are clammy, and I feel like I might suffocate.

"How's Debra?" I ask like an idiot.

"Where did you go after you left? Back on the streets?" he demands, ignoring my question. His nostrils are flaring, and his teeth are bared like he wants to rip me apart. "Is that what you're doing here? Selling the drugs my dad tried to save you from?"

I rip my arm out of his grip, anger finally overtaking the guilt. "If you just came here to try to make me feel bad, you can fuck off. You never even wanted me there, or do you not remember that?"

"You were part of our family, and we needed you," he says, his voice raising loud enough to attract some odd looks.

"Did you somehow track me down just to come guilt trip me over leaving?" I ask.

Reilly is walking over to us. Fuck.

"No, but when you're name came up in a case connected to the NWR, I volunteered for the task force," he says, pulling his badge out of his pocket. It says JHAPI in bold letters at the top, with his picture underneath.

"Howard Z. Brunson," Reilly reads, leaning over Brunson's shoulder. "Our JHAPI liaison?"

Zachary whips around, startled, and takes in Reilly. "Who are you?"

"Reilly Walsh, council representative," he says, holding out his hand. "I believe we'll be working together at some point."

Zachary shakes his hand but looks like he couldn't care less who Reilly is. He turns back to me. "I've got some follow up questions for you, Olivia. Come to the station tomorrow morning around nine am," he says, immediately turning to walk away.

"No."

My answer stops him in his tracks. He turns back, a muscle in his jaw twitching. "Excuse me?"

"Everything I know is in my statement. I have nothing to add. You can read that and watch the interview. I'm not talking to you," I say, crossing my arms.

"This is not optional," Zachary snaps.

"Am I under arrest?"

He glares.

"I'll take that as a no." I glare right back. He doesn't scare me; never has.

"I've found she responds much better to a delicate sort of bribery," Reilly says, leaning toward Zachary conspiratorially. "She seems to get a bit stubborn if you phrase it as an order. Issues with authority, I think."

"Shut the fuck up," I snap at Reilly. He's not helping.

"Always looking out for yourself first. I guess old habits die hard," Zachary says, his eyes clouded with something more than just anger. He turns and walks away. Half the restaurant is staring at us, the other half are whispering.

"What?" I challenge the room. Everyone is quick to avert their eyes. I stomp off to the bathroom. I need to pee even worse now.

CHAPTER 6

"I must say, I couldn't really see the family resemblance," Reilly comments after five minutes of silence.

I don't respond.

Reilly sighs and shifts around like he's bored. "What exactly did you do to make him hate you so much?"

"I don't want to talk about it," I snap.

Zachary being here is like a slap in the face. I still remember that day like it was yesterday. He had answered the door without even checking to see who it was first.

Seeing the men in uniforms, their faces drawn and eyes red, was all either of us needed to understand what had happened. Debra had walked over from the kitchen, looking to see who it was when neither of us answered.

She had screamed. She had begged, and pleaded, for them to tell her it wasn't true. Zachary had simply crumpled. He sat by the door, face blank, staring at nothing.

And it was all my – no. I couldn't do this again. The past needed to stay in the past.

"How did you end up sired by some big wig vampire?" I ask, needing something to distract me.

Reilly looks at me from the corner of his eye. "A question for a question, remember?"

I grip the steering wheel a little tighter. "You're a real piece of work."

The rest of the drive passes in silence. Reilly's presence is like an itch under my skin. He's always pushing, needling.

I was able to warn Javier that he was coming to the clanhouse before we left the diner. I assume Lydia warned him as well. As I pull into the driveway, I wonder if that was the right choice.

What the fuck?

Javier is standing on the top step in a black suit with a wine colored shirt. Emilio is to his right in full, ridiculous Victorian regalia. The rest of the clan is spread out like a greeting committee, lined up according to their weird little hierarchy as best I can tell. There are odd gaps here and there, and I realize it's for the ones they lost recently. I'm not sure if they're making some kind of statement, or if it's just a ritual. Knowing Javier, it's probably somehow both.

Everyone is dressed well. They look polished, and the front of the house is practically sparkling. It's like they prepped for meeting the Queen or something.

I park in my usual spot and climb out of the car. Reilly follows suit and walks toward Javier without waiting for me to catch up. He's not moving at the insane speeds I've seen him use, but he's moving faster than any human could without sprinting. He makes it look effortless.

"Reilly Walsh, you are welcome here," Javier says with none of his usual flirtatiousness or flair. He bows low, and every single vampire follows suit.

"Your hospitality is accepted," Reilly says. Only then does everyone rise from the bow.

"Please join us inside. I can show you the house," Javier says. "Are you hungry?"

Everyone files in after Javier and Reilly, and I'm left standing in the driveway, forgotten. It's a relief. I was worried Reilly would follow me around like a parasite while I did the checkup.

I walk around to the side entrance I normally use and step inside. This area of the house used to be some kind of servants' quarters I think. There are a few small rooms, all used for storage now, down a long hallway that connects to the kitchen, and a staircase that leads upstairs.

I head upstairs to the usual room and knock once before walking in. All the neckers are already gathered here. Normally I see them more or less one at a time, but judging by the hunted looks on their faces, they're all hiding in here.

"Is everything okay?" I ask. Surely, it's not just Reilly's presence that has them so scared.

"Never been better," Leslie scoffs. She's a skinny brunette who's been here longer than I have. She hated me when I first started; I think she thought I had some special relationship with Javier and was all kinds of jealous. Luckily, she got over that real quick when she realized I wasn't interested. She was a practical sort of person.

"The council representative might come watch part of this, just so you know," I say as I walk over to the chair I always sit in.

The room isn't large. There are two high back chairs arranged in front of a fireplace that's never used and a bookshelf on the opposite wall filled with books in foreign languages. French, I think. There is one narrow window, but it's blacked out like most of the windows in the house. The only other decoration is a bland landscape painting hung above the fireplace.

I sit down, and Leslie takes the initiative to come sit across from me. I've developed a sort of ritual with them. It's intended to put them at ease as much as it is just practical.

Leslie extends her hands, and I meet her halfway, palm to palm. All my healing really requires is skin to skin contact. If it's bad, it's easiest for me to be touching the wound, or at least near it. For this, it doesn't really matter.

"Any dizziness, headaches, or nausea?" I ask as I prod at her with my magic, searching for wounds or blood loss. I heal a bruise on her back and scrape on her knee.

"Nah, I've been good, and taking those brews you gave us like clockwork," Leslie says, puffing out her chest in pride. She's something of a leader among the others, so I'm hoping they're all taking them now.

The constant feedings do put a strain on their bodies. The brews I gave them help with absorption of nutrients and ever so slightly increase the amount of blood their body can recover. If they weren't being fed on regularly, it would probably give them high blood pressure.

"Thanks, Leslie. You're all good," I say with a nod.

She gets up, and the next girl takes her place. More bruises, an unhealed bite mark, slight anemia. It's never bothered me before, but today I can't help wondering what they would be like without my healing. Would they be drawn and anemic? Would the vampires have already asked them to leave?

The next girl sits down. She's a young, pretty thing with dark brown hair and cheekbones that could cut glass. Her full lips and big eyes make her look like a doll. She smiles and holds out shaking hands. She has probably never been healed before.

"It's all right, it won't hurt at all. You'll just feel a little warm, maybe itchy if I heal something," I say, trying to be reassuring. Most humans still don't understand magic, and there is a lingering fear in some communities. People tend to either be fascinated by it or shun it along with those who possess it.

I press my palms to hers and almost flinch as my magic spreads through her. Her back is a mass of bruises, and there are claw marks on her arm I couldn't see under her cardigan. The back of her head is bruised too. She's lucky she doesn't have a concussion.

"What the fuck happened? Why didn't they send you to me?" I demand.

The girl glances back at Leslie before she answers.

"It's no big deal, we knew you were coming today. Javier didn't want to bother you," the girl stutters in a thick southern accent.

"Who hurt you? They shouldn't be losing control like this." I don't want any more vague answers today, this is ridiculous. They should be taking better care of themselves than this. Javier shouldn't have kept her from me.

"It—it doesn't matter. I'm fine, and you can heal me now, right?"

"Just tell me—"

"It was Patrick, all right?" Leslie interrupts. "Javier asked for a volunteer, she stepped up. She got hurt. We just didn't want to upset you. We know you two are friends or whatever."

I shut my eyes for a moment and take a deep breath. They're not really the ones I want to be yelling at. I'm going to have a very blunt conversation the next time I see Javier.

I heal her quickly, the magic leaves me in a rush, and I feel...fine. I should be more tired than this. It wasn't anything extreme, but my healing magic has always been weak and quickly depleted. I took barely any of the magic when I stole it. I refuse to worry about it now though; there's enough going on today already.

The door opens as the girl is standing, and Javier walks in, followed closely by Reilly.

"Olivia performs the checkups here," Javier explains, stepping to the side.

Reilly looks around the room, and at each of the neckers, before settling on me. "Please continue."

Leslie has to shoo the next person to me. It's a young man, another new arrival. He holds his hands out like the others, but they are shaking. I grasp them firmly and smile at him reassuringly.

I don't have to heal him at all. If he has been fed on, it was brief and healed up on its own. He's in perfect condition. I release his hands, and he hurries to the back of the room. Everyone stays still and quiet, waiting to see what the vampires want.

"Any of my clan's servitors would be happy to feed you," Javier says, gesturing broadly at the room.

I look at them, huddled in their groups, and disagree. A few look eager, but more of them look scared. Leslie is one of the eager ones, she's standing a little in front of the others. She's wearing a low cut black shirt that accentuates her best assets. Her blue eyes are taking in Reilly's clothes, his hair, and his easy confidence. I look away and swallow down something that feels like jealousy, which is ridiculous. I'm obviously still upset with the break up with Tyler and not thinking straight.

Reilly walks towards the group, taking his time and looking at each of them in turn. I wonder what he is looking for. A certain smell? Does he want them afraid? Is he looking for someone who will let him do more than feed?

He stops when he gets to Leslie. "What is your name?"

"Leslie," she purrs.

"May I feed from you?" he asks, holding out his hand.

She places her hand in his and nods.

"Please take him to the front room, Leslie," Javier instructs.

Leslie nods and leads him away, her hips sashaying and a proud smile on her face. My stomach twists uncomfortably. It's ridiculous, he's not going to hurt her, and it doesn't matter to me who he feeds from.

Javier clears his throat, and I tear my eyes away from the closed door. "Can I assume Patrick is staying with you?"

"Yes, and he's fine so far. Upset, but fine," I say with a shrug. It's really too bad I can't heal emotional damage.

"Come with me," Javier says, tugging on my elbow. The neckers begin whispering as soon as we step out of the room; I'm sure they have tons of new gossip to dissect.

Javier leads me through the house to his room and waves me inside.

"I wanted a little privacy. Reilly won't be able to hear us from this far away," he says as he closes the door behind us. He doesn't continue though; he simply walks to the window and sighs.

"Javier, out with it," I say, leaning back against the door and crossing my arms.

"You need to convince Patrick to come back here. It's not safe for him to be away from the clan, feeding without supervision. I don't want to have to force him to return," Javier says, his face blank and his posture relaxed.

"He hates you right now," I say quietly.

Javier's face falls, and his hands tighten into fists. "I know."

"He's really not in control?" I ask. I have to know for sure. "He seemed upset yesterday but not violent."

"It comes and goes. I thought the same, and I tried to let him feed from someone directly, but he –" Javier shakes his head. "He threw her across the room and then tried to kill her. I had to stop him, for his own sake, and I hurt him. I should have stopped him from leaving too."

Patrick had left that part out. Perhaps he really was still somewhat feral. A surge of hatred for the NWR, for Martinez, and for Chevy swelled up inside of me. They had no right to hurt any of us like this.

"I can try to talk to him, but he said he had left the clan. That's usually final."

A muscle in Javier's jaw twitches. "Until I accept his renunciation, it means nothing."

"All right." I don't know what to say or do. Javier is not quite what I'd call a friend, and I don't really care to sit around and talk about our feelings.

"So, is Reilly staying here, or can I leave?"

"He said he was staying with you," Javier says. "He also brushed off all my attempts to persuade him to stay here instead."

"He's such a pain in the ass," I grumble.

"Be careful of Reilly Walsh," Javier says, standing back up straight and pulling himself together. "I cannot protect you from him, no matter how fond I am of you or how much I value the work you do for me."

"Fond of me, are you?" I say with a smirk.

Javier winks. "Yes, terribly fond. You're my favorite witch."

I roll my eyes, but I don't really mind it.

"I'll see you again week after next. And just send them to me if they need healing next time," I say, opening the door. "I don't like it when you wait."

"As you wish," Javier says, joining me. He slings his arm around my shoulders as we walk down the hall. I elbow him in the ribs, and he removes the offending appendage.

"I wonder how long he's going to take," I say, glancing at the time on my phone. I want to check on Patrick; I don't like leaving him alone for this long. "Do you think he'd be offended if I just left?"

Javier frowns at me. "Perhaps, don't risk it."

"You're no fun when you're like this, Javier," I say. "I'm going to go wait in the kitchen."

Javier nods and heads over to a necker who has been trying to get his attention.

I head downstairs. Some of the vampires are milling around, whispering among themselves. Ada Talbott, a more senior vampire nods, in my direction, but the others all give me a wide berth. Patrick is the only one who ever attempted friendship. I'm not sure what the others think of me.

I'm not sure what I think of them either. Some of them take after Emilio with their lace and Victorian dress, others just look like the average person on the street. Only a few seem to have gone goth. They keep their fangs extended constantly, which honestly makes them look ridiculous.

I slip into the kitchen and look around. I'm not hungry after that big meal, but I could use a drink. I pull open the fridge and poke around. Water, boring. Lemonade, but that just doesn't sound good right now. Way in the back, I finally find a beer.

"Thank god," I mumble as I pull it out and pop the top off. It's cold and exactly what I needed. I take a long swallow, tilting my head back.

"You make it look delicious."

I cough and sputter, glaring at Reilly, standing across from me in the kitchen.

"That was fast."

"I was feeding, not fucking her," Reilly says, shrugging one shoulder.

I laugh despite myself and shake my head at him, which earns a smile.

"You are ridiculous," I say before taking another long drink. I guess I need to finish this quickly.

Reilly tilts his head. "I don't know that I've ever been described as ridiculous before."

I shrug and take another drink.

"Why aren't you staying at the clanhouse?" I ask, twirling the bottle in my fingers. It's been bothering me since Javier told me.

"I prefer to stay close to my assignment," Reilly says.

Close, right. I wonder if he pulled Leslie in close when he fed or if he just bit, sucked, and walked away.

"Right." I finish my beer and throw the bottle away. As soon as we get out of here, I'm questioning him on what he knows about my mother. I upheld my end of the bargain after all. "Do you need to do some formal goodbye, or can we just leave?"

He chuckles. "We can just leave."

Emilio is at the door like some kind of clairvoyant butler. He opens the door and bows deeply. Reilly doesn't acknowledge him as we walk outside.

Some of the tightness leaves my shoulders as we step out into the cool, night air. It's a relief to know the first visit is over. No one died. No one was horribly insulted.

It's pitch black outside. There's hardly even a moon right now, and the light from the town is just enough to make the stars seem dim. We climb in the car, and I turn it on, the headlights illuminating the front yard. I text Patrick we're headed back, partially to warn him Reilly is still with me, and partially just because I've been worried all evening and want to make sure he's still at my house.

That done, I drop my phone in my lap and pull out of the driveway. The road twists and turns, the trees looming over the road. Reilly is sitting in the passenger seat, alternating between staring at me and out the window.

"So, was your, uh, feeding good?" I ask to fill the silence. If he's going to stare at me, he can at least talk to me.

"It was satisfactory," he says, running a hand through his hair.

"That sounds like what someone says after they eat at restaurant they'll never eat at again," I say, raising a brow.

"Sounds about right." He smirks.

"Do people really taste that different?"

"Yes and no. Blood is blood, but some people taste more robust. I am spoiled in the capitol."

"I guess it makes sense that you'd get all the best neckers there."

"Of course," Reilly says. "It is strange though, the way they beg to be bitten. Most prey run from their predators."

"Can't say I really understand it either," I say, rubbing at my neck. Just the thought of it brings back unwelcome memories and makes me shudder. "I can see being curious, I guess, but the neckers always act like it's the best thing in the world."

"We can make it feel good," Reilly says, leaning toward me. "If you ever find yourself overwhelmed with curiosity, I'd be happy to help."

"Actually, the only thing I'm curious about is what you know about my mother's death," I say, gripping the steering wheel tighter. "I went to the coven with you, that was the deal."

"You waited longer to ask than I expected," Reilly says with a grin. "I thought you were going to ambush me as soon as we walked out of the coven's meeting hall."

"Well, I'm asking now." The whole fiasco at the coven had distracted me, and seeing Zachary again hadn't helped. Reilly doesn't need to know all that though.

"The death certificate was created by someone the council knows to be, let's just say, easily persuaded," Reilly says. "Two months before he died, Brunson requested an internal investigation. It was quickly determined that quite a few death certificates this person had created were faked. The only thing we don't know is who requested that he forge it, or why."

"Can you find out? Can I talk to this guy?"

Reilly doesn't respond. I glance at him, but he focused on staring out the window again.

"Reilly, I want to talk to him," I say with a frown. "I have a right to some answers. She could still be alive."

"You're being followed," Reilly says.

"What?" I check the rearview mirror automatically. There is a car behind me, but I have no idea how long it's been there, and it's fairly far back.

"Whoever it is followed you to the clanhouse, the car was parked down the street. They picked back up as soon as you left."

"Is it NWR? Or someone from the coven?" I demand. "Did you see them?"

Reilly rolls his eyes. "Calm down, I don't think it's either. We can find out for sure though."

"How?"

Reilly turns to me with a shit-eating grin.

CHAPTER 7

"Are there any roads you can turn down coming up?"

"Um, yeah," I say, trying to remember what roads connect to this one. I make this drive so often, I don't pay attention to the roads I don't take. "There are a couple."

"Turn down the next one, then pull off the road and shut the car off. We'll need to get into the tree line as quickly as we can."

The next road is right after a curve in the road. I take the turn sharply, drive over the bridge that runs over a dry creek, and pull off into the grass. There isn't much space between the road and the tree line, so part of the car is still on the narrow shoulder.

I shut the car off and jump out, following Reilly into the trees. He leads me about ten feet past the tree line, then crouches down behind a tree. I squat beside him and watch, my heart racing from the short run.

I see the headlights first; it seems like he stops once he sees my car sitting there. Finally, the car drives past, definitely driving slower than the speed limit, and stops just before the road curves again. It sits there, and whoever is inside doesn't make any moves to get out.

"He's trying to decide if you're still in the car, or if he can risk approaching," Reilly whispers, his lips way too close to my ear for comfort.

"I'm going to go see if I can tell who it is," I whisper back. The trees are thick, and unfortunately so is the underbrush. I pick my way through carefully, stepping over what I can to avoid thorns.

"I can just tell you who it is if you'd like," Reilly says as he follows me.

"If you already know who it is, why are we even doing this?"

"I wanted to make sure."

The car is plain, black, and completely average. It's the kind of car you drive when you're trying not to attract attention, or you're just cheap. I pause. It has government plates. So not the NWR. I get a little closer but still can't see through the tinted windows. Not that I need to. I know it's Zachary.

"It's your biggest fan," Reilly says.

"Why is he following me?" I ask, my nails biting into my palm.

"Based on what he said earlier, I imagine he's trying to catch you selling drugs."

I glare at Reilly. "I'm going to go tell him to fuck off."

Reilly grabs my arms, stopping me before I even get to take a step. "Not tonight. He's on the phone with someone, and he's about to leave."

"If he leaves, I can't kick his ass."

Reilly sighs, and I suspect rolls his eyes, but I can't see clearly enough to tell for sure. "Right now, you have leverage. You know he's following you, but he doesn't know you know. Try to be smart for once and use that your advantage."

"Being straightforward doesn't mean I'm being stupid," I say jerking my arm out of his grip. "Sometimes it's best just to confront people and get it over with."

"Have you ever tried another way?" Reilly asks, doubtful.

Zachary's car starts moving again. He turns around and drives back the way we came.

"Guess I have to now." I stomp back to the car, and Reilly follows.

I'm relieved to see Patrick on the couch when we walk in, but I pause in the kitchen. He's staring at his hands, and they're shaking.

"How could you go back there?" he asks, so quietly I almost can't hear him.

"I do the check-ups on the neckers every other week," I say, taking a cautious step forward. Reilly is standing quietly behind me. "It was a good thing I went too. One of them was pretty banged up."

Patrick's head snaps up.

"It wasn't my fault," he growls. "Is that what Javier said? He's lying!"

His eyes are bloodshot, and his fangs are extended. Fuck.

"Reilly, can you give us a minute? I want to talk to Patrick alone." I don't know what Reilly will do if Patrick attacks him again, and I don't want to find out.

"He's hungry," Reilly says, stepping closer instead of leaving. "How long has it been since you fed last, Patrick? Since you left Javier's?"

"Reilly, just go," I say, shooting him a glare.

Reilly hesitates, staring at me. "Why are you willing to risk your life just to help him?"

"Really not the time," I say, shoving at his chest. He moves this time and walks back to the door.

"If you kill her, I'll make sure you regret it," Reilly says to Patrick before stepping outside and slamming the door shut behind him.

Patrick is still focused on me, his breath coming in short pants.

"Patrick, Javier didn't tell me anything, I—"

"Liar!" he says, unfolding from the couch and taking three

quick steps toward me. "I can smell him all over you. Did he finally get you in bed? I've never been sure why you haven't jumped into bed with him. You'll fuck anyone who looks at you twice. Did you let him feed from you too?"

My face heats, and I want to punch him in the mouth.

"What the fuck is your problem?" I demand, trying to keep from shouting, and failing.

Patrick's hands curl into fists, and he tenses.

"If Javier fed from you, I should be able to," he hisses. He takes another step forward, and his movements are jerky, like he's fighting with himself. I grab a vial of holy water from my jacket pocket and curl my fingers around it. I should have been more prepared for this.

"You're not in control, Patrick, this isn't you."

"No." He laughs, the sound high-pitched and grating. "No, this is me. It's always inside of me, Livvy; you just don't like to see it. You want the jokes and the fun at bars, but I'm always hungry."

He takes another step forward, eyes locking on my neck. "I'll only take a little."

It's a testament to just how malnourished he is that I can dodge the first strike. He rushes at me. I flick the stopper out of the vial and sling the holy water at him. It splashes the arm he holds up to block it, some of it hitting his neck and face. He growls as it burns but lashes out and grabs my arm before I can get another potion out.

Instead of pulling me to him, he shoves. I hit the wall, my head bouncing off the sheetrock, and crowds in close. I shove my free arm in his throat, holding him back, just barely. He's stronger than me; I can't do this forever.

"Patrick!" My voice breaks. "Stop it. You have to stop!"

He's leaning in closer, and my arm is collapsing slowly. I shove again with all my might, and his eyes finally snap up to mine.

He freezes. His hand trembles, and he stops pushing quite so hard on me.

"Livvy," he sobs. "I'm so hungry."

"Let me help you, please," I whisper. "Let me take you back –"

"No!" he shouts, moving away from me so fast, I almost fall forward. "No. I won't go back."

He runs out the front door, leaving it standing open behind him. I run after him, my legs shaking. I almost trip on the porch when Reilly steps into my path.

"Let him go," Reilly says, wrapping an arm around my waist and pulling me flush against his chest.

"No," I struggle against Reilly's grip, but I can't get his arm to budge. "He's going to hurt himself, or someone else. He can't. I can't let him."

"I can stop him."

Reilly finally lets go, and I turn around so I can see his face. "But let me guess, you want something in return?"

"Always," Reilly says without a hint of humor on his face. "Tell me what you were really doing with Aaron Hall the night he disappeared."

I stare at him. I can't lie outright; he'd know. I wonder how close I can get to the truth without betraying secrets that would make my life forfeit. I don't have time to bargain either. Patrick needs to be stopped now.

"I kidnapped him," I say, biting the inside of my cheek nervously. "Drugged him at the strip club and took him to the warehouse and forced him to find Patrick for me. I guess the memory potion fucked his magic up, I don't know. I've never exactly tested it on someone."

He searches my face, looking for some hint of deception.

"Reilly, please," I beg.

"I'll be back tomorrow after sunset," Reilly says before disappearing. I stand on the porch for a moment, feeling lost. I can't see or hear either of them now. I have to hope Reilly keeps up his end of the bargain and doesn't hurt Patrick.

It finally registers that I'm shivering from the cold. I turn and walk back inside, my energy drained, new bruises forming on my arm.

I wish Zachary was here so I could kick his ass and work out some of this pent-up frustration. Having him in town and hearing all this stuff about my mother brings back all the memories of late nights pouring over missing person reports and Jane Does found all across the country. Women with amnesia. Dead bodies, unclaimed.

Brunson and Zachary had been with me through the whole thing. Zachary was the one who had let me grip his hand until it bruised when Brunson told me my mother was dead. Had Brunson known then? Or had he thought he was telling me the truth? If the death certificate had been faked, it could be because someone wanted us to stop searching.

I pause in the living room and realize how big of a mess the house still is. I won't clean it up anytime soon though. My mom would have fussed at me until I cleaned it up if she was here. If she was alive.

I grab the coffee table leg and throw it across the room with an angry shout, then stand there panting. I don't know what I'm waiting for. I should have done this as soon as Reilly told me the records had been faked. I can't help Patrick tonight, but I can do something. I have to know for sure if she's dead or alive.

I rip open the junk drawer in the kitchen and dig until I find it. A map of the entire United States. My hands shake as I unfold it. Partly from hope. Partly from fear.

It's reckless to use a map that covers the entire country. Even the best Finders need a smaller area to search. Aaron Hall was weak, and that means I am too. But I don't care. I have no idea what happens if the person you're looking for is dead either. The Finders never talk about it.

I spread it out on the floor and smooth a hand over the wrinkles until it lays flat. I close my eyes and take a deep breath, searching for the subtle and warm Finding magic. It's there, almost hiding from the electric magic I took from Novak. I pull on it and let it take over.

I stretch my hands out over the map, and the magic moves under my skin, a warm trickle. It spills from my fingertips, and the map shudders and lifts. The certainty I felt as I searched last time isn't there. I don't know if the map is too big or if it simply can't find the dead.

Bright lines of red slip down from my hands like puppet strings and slide across the map, searching and searching. The tendrils crinkle the paper of the map as they slide across it.

The magic grows hot. One of the red lines burns a hole through the map. Then the next and the next. It surges down into the floor, and I try to jerk away and end the magic, but I can't. The magic has crept up my arms and is holding on to me now. I can't stop.

I fall. Light flashes around me. Then absolute darkness. I can feel my arms burning where the magic is curling around them, but I can't move. I can't scream. I can't see.

Memories of my mother come rushing back to me. Her face. Her laugh. The first time we brewed together. Her eyes and mouth wide as she screams the first time I stole her magic. When I didn't know what I was doing. A dusty room with candles all around. Blood and gray ash all around me.

Olivia. Olivia. Olivia. Olivia.

The pleading.

The day she left.

Burning arms. The smell of smoke filling my nose.

CHAPTER 8

I wake up all at once, my breath coming in great, heaving gasps. My vision is blurry. I rub my hand over my eyes and hiss in pain.

My hands are covered in stripes of blisters that swirl all the way up my arms. I sit up, shaking, and look around. The map is ash on the floor, and there are scorch marks all around me.

"Shit," I whisper hoarsely. My throat is raw, as though I've been screaming. I struggle to my feet and try to think. I have a salve for burns. It's in the workroom. I'm exhausted, and so is my magic. There's no way I'll be able to heal myself right now.

I stumble down the hall and through the open door to the workroom. I'm able to nudge the door to the mini fridge open with my foot, but I'm going to have to open the salve with my hands.

I grit my teeth, grab it and twist the lid open as quickly as I can. A blister pops, and my eyes water. I hate the feeling of burns; nothing hurts quite like it.

With shaking fingers, I spread the salve over my hands first. It itches like crazy as the magic seeps into my skin and begins to heal from the inside out. I have to take a break after my hands are covered. I slide down the wall and lean my head against the cool door of the fridge.

I knew she was dead. It was stupid to let Reilly rekindle that hope. I should probably stop all of this right now. Stop looking for a cover-up. Stop looking for her killer. Even thinking it makes me feel like a failure. She would have done anything for me, but I don't have her strength. I fell apart when she disappeared, and every choice I've made since then only seems to lead me farther down the wrong path. Brunson tried to help me, but after he died too, I just ran. I've been barely hanging on ever since.

I turn my hands over and examine the backs. The burns are fading, but the salve can only do so much, and I apparently can't heal this with magic. Red welts wind around each finger and the back of my hands. They reach up my arms, almost to my shoulders. I spread more of the salve over my arms. I have to pause every few seconds, panting against the pain.

Mr. Muffins pads into the room, stopping just inside the doorway.

"Come to judge me?" I ask in a whisper.

She swishes her tail behind her.

"I know, it wasn't my best decision."

It takes effort, but I stand and toss the half-empty tub of salve onto the counter. I need two things today; Zachary to stop stalking me, and apple pie.

I find my phone, and I'm relieved it's not even noon yet. It means I got hardly any sleep, not that passing out from misusing magic really qualifies as sleep. But it also means I have at least seven hours before I have to deal with a single fucking vampire again.

My hand twitches, still trying to heal, and I flex it uncomfortably. I can't walk around with these welts showing. Wearing gloves would raise even more questions than the welts themselves. I hurry back into the workroom. I have a cosmetic salve meant to cover pimples and dark circles under your eyes. If I put on enough, I might be able to hide the marks on my hands.

I rummage through a box meant for Maybelle's and find a small case of them at the bottom. I open it and scoop some out, rubbing it on like lotion. I breathe a sigh of relief when I see that it hides them. Mostly. It's good enough.

It'll only last for about eight hours, so I take the tub with me. I can't have them reappearing and have no way to cover them back up if I don't make it home again in the next eight hours.

I grab a long sleeve shirt out of my closet and pull it on. I'm not going to bother trying to use the cosmetic salve on my arms.

I catch a glimpse of myself in the mirror and decide to put some on my face too. I look like shit. The dark circles under my eyes fade away, along with the bruise on my chin I hadn't even felt until I saw it. There's not much I can do for my hair except put it up in a ponytail.

I pause in the kitchen, my hand on my jacket, then go the cabinet and grab the whiskey out of the cabinet. I unscrew the lid and take a long, deep swallow. I'm tempted just to stay here and finish the bottle. I slam it back in the cabinet. That'll have to be enough to dull the frustration for now.

Now, to deal with Zachary. The pie can be my reward.

The police station is quiet when I walk in. A woman in a uniform sitting at the reception desk looks up when I walk in. She seems to recognize me. I walk up, tugging my sleeves down, just in case a mark is peeking out.

"I need to talk to Special Agent Brunson," I say.

"You're Olivia Carter, right? That witch that got caught up in that NWR business?"

"Yes."

Chief Timmons comes down the hall, a stack of files tucked under his arm.

"Oh, Olivia, I wasn't expecting you today," Timmons says, approaching with a smile on his face. He shakes my hand firmly.

"I'm actually here to see Agent Brunson. We're old friends," I say with a smile.

"He hadn't mentioned that," Timmons says, his brows pinching together.

I shrug. "He's fairly private. Probably just didn't think it was pertinent."

"Ah, understandable. Let me show you to his office. He and his partner have taken over one of our conference rooms for the task force," Timmons says, pointing down the hallway to my right. It's in an area of the police station I haven't seen yet. "I'll walk you there."

"Thanks," I say, the fake smile still plastered to my face. The linoleum floor is dingy, and our shoes squeak with every step until the flooring changes to carpet at a fork in the hallway. We go right, but halfway down the hall Timmons pauses.

"I didn't want to bring it up when you were here last," he says, talking in hushed tones. "But Novak's funeral will be in two days. I'll be sending the details to Lydia. It will be in the morning, so unfortunately, the clan won't be able to attend, but I did want to give you the option."

I'm not sure if it's worse to go to the funeral of a man you killed or avoid it. I swallow and clear my throat, trying to find my voice.

"I'll be there," I say finally.

Timmons pats my shoulder, then continues down the hall at a faster pace. I jog after him.

"By the way, any updates on the search for Martinez?"

"Not yet," he says. "The NWR has always been effective at hiding their members. We did search the entire tunnel. It led to the middle of the woods, but we can't find their trail after that at all.

They treated the area with something that makes the tracking dogs lose their minds. The werewolves won't go near it either."

I shake my head. No one can ever accuse the NWR of doing a half-assed job of things.

The hallway opens up into an open area with six desks arranged in pairs. Each desk faces another in a line down the center of the room.

The conference room isn't hard to find either. There is a large window in the wall that provides a clear view of the room. Zachary is standing at the head of the table next to a woman with long black hair and eyes that look blue even from here. There's a whiteboard behind them with pictures of faces I recognize and notes under each. Martinez, before half of his face was melted off. Chevy. Even Novak.

The woman nudges Zachary as we approach. He stops talking and turns to see who is coming. His jaw tenses as soon as he spots me.

"Brunson, Ms. Carter requested to see you," Timmons says, poking his head into the conference room.

Zachary looks at me, barely keeping his face blank. I cross my arm and stare him down. We can talk in there in front of everyone, but he won't like it.

He says something quiet to the woman, then steps out of the conference room.

"Thank you, Chief Timmons," he says.

"Let me know if you need anything else, Olivia," the Chief says, patting me on the shoulder as he walks away.

Zachary and I stare at each other in middle of the room.

"What do you want?" he asks, crossing his arms to match my posture.

"Just wanted to chat. See if you found anything interesting last night on your little surveillance run."

He scoffs but brushes past me, taking the hint that this should be a private conversation. I follow him down the hall to an office.

He opens the door, and I brush past him. He slams it shut behind us.

"I have a right to investigate everyone connected to the attack. Especially anyone who has a questionable history."

"Oh please," I snap, whirling around to face him. "You just want an excuse to give me shit. Quit trying to make this anything other than you just trying to get some kind of pointless revenge."

"You are so selfish," he says, shoving his finger in my face. "My dad believed in you. He said you wanted to help people, but he was wrong."

"I am helping people!" I say, slapping his hand away. "I'm doing good here, but you don't know any of that because you came here with your mind already made up."

"You abandoned us!" he shouts, a red flush darkening his face further. "You could have saved my mom, but you were gone and I couldn't find you!"

I take a step back, my heart dropping into my stomach. "What are you talking about?"

"Brain tumor. She lived for barely two months after we found out."

The room tilts, and I can't breathe. I had just assumed that if I left, they could just be okay. Debra had always been full of smiles and eager to feed you. She was ageless. I can't imagine her dead. I don't want to.

I try to walk past Zachary; I don't want to be here anymore, but he grabs my arm. His fingers dig into my skin right over a welt, and pain shoots through my arm. I stop and don't try to pull away, but I stare at the floor as I speak.

"I couldn't have saved her Zack." My voice wavers. I have a lump in my throat I can barely talk around. "My healing, it's weak. I can't touch things like cancer or tumors. I wouldn't have been able to—I'm sorry."

I pull my arm away, and his hand drops to his side. I open the door and leave him standing in the office, staring straight ahead.

CHAPTER 9

I sit in my car, hot tears rolling down my cheeks. My arms are aching again, but I can't bring myself to care.

My mom is dead. Brunson is dead. Debra is dead. Patrick is basically feral. And then there's Reilly. The devil incarnate who will no doubt find a way to get me to sell him my soul.

I bash my hand against the steering wheel and shake it like it's the source of all my problems. I hate this. All of it. Life shouldn't be like this, just one tragedy after another.

Still grinding my teeth in frustration, I turn the car on and shift into gear. I'm going to get pie and a bottle of tequila, then go home and drink until I can't remember my name, much less how shitty my life is.

It's still the lunch rush at Maybelle's, so I have to park three blocks away. I wipe away any evidence I've been crying like a little bitch from underneath my eyes, then get out of the car and hurry down the sidewalk.

Maybelle's is crowded as usual, but the line at the counter isn't very long. An old man with a long white beard bumps into my shoulder as he hurries past me. He mumbles an apology, then hurries out of the store. I don't even have the energy to glare at him.

I get behind the last person and check my phone. The only message is from Lydia, and it's informing me she has no updates. I shove it back in my pocket and wait impatiently for the line to move.

It takes less than five minutes, but it feels like longer than that.

"One apple pie, please," I say before the girl at the counter has a chance to ask what I'd like.

"Whole pie?" she confirms, fingers hovering above the register.

"Yep."

"That'll be twenty-five dollars," she says, holding out her hand for my payment. I grab the money out of my wallet and pass it to her.

She puts the money in the register, then walks back to the pie warmer and takes one out. It smells amazing. She sets it in one of Maybelle's pretty fall colored boxes, and then in a bag so it's easier to carry.

"Here you go," she says, passing it across the counter.

"Thanks."

I turn around and almost walk into Georgia.

"Olivia," she says, smiling warmly. "I was hoping to find you here."

"I guess I come here too much," I say with a half-hearted chuckle.

"It has become predictable," she agrees. I'm not sure if she's making a joke or not, so I simply nod.

"I understand that you heal the people the vampires feed on, I have a similar request."

"All right, is someone hurt?" I ask.

"Yes, since the fight with the NWR. We had hoped he would on his own, but there must be silver deep in his wounds we cannot smell. I do not think he will recover without help. Will you heal him? I can pay you whatever is necessary. Name your price."

"I'll do it. And you don't need to pay me; we can just call it a thank you for helping with the fight in the first place," I say, jumping at the chance to help. This is someone I can actually save. If I was in my right mind, I'd just take the money, but I can't. I don't want Zachary to be right about me.

Georgia looks surprised but nods. "All right. I have to run one more errand. Can I meet you back here in twenty minutes? I'll drive you out to the house."

"Sure, sounds good." I wanted to check out the apothecary anyhow. "Here, let me give you my cell number just in case."

She hands over her phone, and I type in my contact information.

"Thank you, Olivia. I will text you as soon as I am done." She walks briskly out of the store.

I grab a plastic fork, then back out. The apothecary is only a few stores down. I reach down into the bag and open the lid to the container the pie is on. It'd be a crime not to eat some while it's still warm.

The first bite is almost orgasmic. The crust is just flaky enough. The apples inside are soft and covered in just the right amount of cinnamony, sugary filling. I hurriedly scoop another bite into my mouth.

For all my skill in brewing, I can't cook anything this good. Debra had tried to teach me and laughed when my pie crust was dry and crumbly. I drop the fork in the bag and smash the lid down on the pie.

I hadn't lied when I told Zachary I wouldn't have been able to save her. Perhaps someone could have, but there's no way they could have afforded it. The waiting lists for those healers are also years long, just like organ transplants. Part of me is relieved I didn't have to watch her die, but I'd rather have had a chance to say goodbye. My fingers tighten on the bag. Who am I kidding? I had the chance; I was just too afraid to go back and face them.

The large coming soon sign hanging from the front of the

apothecary distracts me from my thoughts. The storefront is with thick glass, and 'Maybelle's Apothecary' is etched into the glass in large, looping letters.

I cross the street and peer in the window. It's still empty inside. It looks like the contractors are still putting up sheetrock and building out the back. I still can't believe this is happening. It's something my mother had dreamed of. She wanted to open a little shop with just the two of us, and she was working on getting her guild membership approved before she disappeared. My hands and arms still ache, a physical reminder of the pain of missing her that I'll never be rid of.

My phone buzzes, and I turn away with a sigh. It's a text from Georgia. I'm looking forward to a distraction. Maybe they can eat this stupid pie for me too.

I don't hear anything, not a shout, or even the explosion itself. I'm flying through the air, and I can't see. I hit the ground and slide, asphalt scraping my cheek and chest.

There's smoke. I blink. Sirens. Blink. Someone is shaking me. Blink. Brown eyes and dark hair and a pale hand reaching for me. Blink. Georgia's face over mine. Blink. Blood in my mouth.

CHAPTER 10

I gasp awake, reaching for someone who isn't there. It's dark in my room and dark outside. Javier is leaning over me, his wrist bleeding sluggishly. I can still see my mother's face like an aura in my vision. It's like I looked at the light for too long, and now it's all I can see.

I blink, trying to dispel it. The blood in my mouth distracts me, and I reach for Javier's wrist. I want *more*. I need it.

"Olivia," a sharp voice shocks me into full consciousness. There is an IV strung from my wrist to a pole next to the hospital bed. Fuck. I'm in a hospital.

"What happened?" I croak, wiping my mouth on the back of my hand. It leaves a smear of blood, and I have to fist my hands in the sheets to keep from reaching for him again. He tastes even better than I remember.

"The apothecary was bombed. You were caught in the blast," Javier explains. His face is downcast. I think he feels sorry for me. I'm furious.

"Was it the NWR? Is Martinez back? Do the police have any leads?" I bite out each question, my hands twisting further in the sheets. My entire body aches, and if my face looks how it feels, then it looks like someone tried to scrape half of it off. It would hurt worse if Javier hadn't shared some of his blood. It's an odd thing, the way it helps to heal. It can't really save anyone's life, but if you're a witch, the magic gives you a boost that helps your body heal itself. Most people find it disgusting and not strangely addicting like I do though. My jaw aches for another taste.

"They're assuming it's the NWR, but they have no idea who set the bomb," Javier says.

"Fucking fantastic," I say, shooing Javier out of the way and swinging my legs over the side of the bed. I bat away Javier's hands and yank out the IVs. "Is Georgia okay? I think she was there…it's all fuzzy."

"She found you after the explosion. She's fine," he says, trying to push me back down. "Olivia, they want to keep you overnight."

"No," I snap. "I'm fine. I'll go home and take a couple of potions. I can't pay this hospital bill anyhow."

Javier steps back, his hands held up in surrender. "Come to the clanhouse, at least. It'll be safer for you there."

The door opens, and Patrick steps inside, his eyes wide as he takes in the hospital bed and the IV. The wince he makes when he looks at my face confirms it's about as bad as it feels.

He walks toward me slowly, glancing briefly at Javier but ignoring him for now.

"You look like shit," Patrick says, a smirk on his face that fills me with relief.

"That's what happens when someone tries to blow you up, I guess," I say, grinning at him even though it hurts my cheek.

Neither of us is the type for apologies. Not the traditional kind, at least. I know he means he's sorry, and he knows he's forgiven.

"Let me guess, you're trying to escape the hospital already?" he asks, walking around to the side of my bed opposite Javier.

"You guess right," I say. "Where are my pants?"

Javier crosses his arms. "You can have them when you agree to come to the clanhouse."

"I just want to go home! I need to feed my cat."

"It's not safe," Javier insists,

"Is anywhere safe?" I ask, throwing my hands in the air. "I was in a public place in the middle of the day, and someone set off a fucking bomb."

Javier opens his mouth to retort, but Patrick holds up his hand, stopping him.

"Javier, give us a minute?" Patrick asks.

Javier stares at Patrick over my shoulder, breathing hard, then nods and walks out of the room, slamming the door behind him.

Patrick waits a moment, shifting uncomfortably on his feet. "I'll go back if you go back."

I bite the inside of my cheek. He must be serious if he's actually helping Javier get me back to the clanhouse. It's a sharp change from the night before. I briefly wonder if Reilly is somehow coercing him to do this the same way he got me to go to the coven to look for Aaron Hall. Instantly, I feel guilty for doubting his intentions, but it could actually be the case knowing Reilly.

"If they're setting bombs, I'm not necessarily safer there," I say with a sigh. He's already won the argument, and he knows it.

"Then we might as well die together," Patrick says lightly, grabbing my jeans out of a bag sitting by the window and tossing them at my face. I catch them and roll my eyes.

My legs are shaky as I crawl out of the bed. I need a few of the potions I normally reserve for emergencies with the neckers. I yank my pants on underneath the hospital gown, then drop it on the bed and reach my hand back for a shirt.

"What the fuck happened to your arms?"

I snatch my hand back, trying to hide the welts even though it's too late for that.

"It's nothing, don't worry about it," I say quickly. "Just give me a shirt."

"Those look new. Did someone hurt you?"

I give up on modesty and turn around, hands on my hips. "No one hurt me. Just give me the damn shirt."

"Your boobs aren't going to make me forget my question. What the fuck did you do, Livvy?"

I bite my tongue to keep from yelling at him. I can't explain this without risking both our lives and everything I've worked to build here. My mother had made me swear to never tell anyone, not for any reason. It's the only promise to her I haven't broken yet.

"It was a brewing accident," I lie. "It's embarrassing and doesn't matter, and I don't want to talk about it."

I thrust out my hand again, barely stopping myself from stomping my foot too. Patrick glares at me but hands the shirt over. I slip both arms into the shirt.

There's a perfunctory knock on the door, then Reilly walks in, followed by Georgia and Javier. Reilly's eyebrows shoot up as I hurry to pull the shirt the rest of the way on.

Javier looks between me and Patrick, a muscle twitching in his jaw. Georgia brushes past them both, completely unconcerned. I finish buttoning the shirt before I look at them again.

"I seem to have arrived five minutes too late," Reilly says as he plops down in the only remaining chair. "What did I miss?"

I roll my eyes. "Glad to see you're all right, Georgia."

"I am glad to see the same. I was concerned you were dead when I first saw you," Georgia says matter of factly. "You were twitching."

"That's disturbing," I say, raising a brow. "How is your wolf? I can still heal him tonight if I need to."

Georgia frowns. "You don't look like you're in any shape to heal."

I shrug. "My magic is fine. You said he was getting worse and no good will come from waiting."

"If you are sure," Georgia agrees. Her fingers loosen their grip on the arms of the chair, like she's relieved. "I'll have him brought to your house."

This is why she's my favorite. She doesn't argue or baby me.

"Bring him to the clanhouse, actually," I say.

Javier breathes an audible sigh of relief behind me. I'm not sure what Reilly is thinking, but he doesn't look upset. I would thank him for whatever he did to help Patrick, but considering he took advantage of the situation to try to extort information from me, he can go fuck himself.

"The doctors aren't going to like you leaving like this," Javier says, already hovering. This is why he's my second least favorite. Reilly still holds the title of first.

"They can just try and stop me."

Reilly chuckles, and Javier glares at him. I guess Javier got over the formality from when they first met.

"Who even called all of you?" I ask

"I did," Georgia said. "I didn't know of any family, but I had Lydia's number."

"Lydia is harassing Chief Timmons for answers currently," Javier says, answering my question before I ask it.

"Has anyone heard from Maybelle?" I ask, suddenly worried. It didn't look like anyone was there when I stopped by, but...

"Lydia said she was at the police station," Javier says.

"Does someone have my keys?" I ask, patting at my pockets.

Patrick winces. "About that."

CHAPTER 11

The phone rings and goes to voicemail once again. I sigh and drop my phone in my lap. I was hoping to talk to Maybelle tonight. I'm not sure when I'll make it into town again.

I slouch down in the back seat of Javier's sleek black car, arms crossed, and glare out the window. Reilly is on his way to the police station, and I'm relieved to be rid of him for a little while at least, but I wish I was there with him. I want answers.

"I still can't believe my car is totaled," I mutter.

"The car wasn't that great," Patrick offers.

"It was paid off!" I throw my hands up in the air, exasperated.

"You can use one of mine until you can afford a replacement," Javier says from the front seat.

"Not the point," I grumble as we pull into the driveway. My car is gone, and so is my chance at making a decent living. Maybe I can guilt Javier into giving me a raise. I think I've earned it.

Javier drives past the house to the garage and parks in an open slot. It's practically a parking lot back here, with all of the cars for the vampires and the neckers. Only Javier's cars are in the garage itself though.

Javier's phone rings as we get out of the car, and he hurries into the house. Patrick and I follow. He's tense as we walk in, his nose twitching as he looks around.

There's a vampire, whose name I've forgotten, downstairs. He stares wide-eyed at Patrick, then scurries off. Most likely to share the latest gossip with the other clan members.

Having Patrick back at the clanhouse makes everything feel right. He slings an arm around my shoulders as we walk into the kitchen, his fingers tight. I pat his hand comfortingly. It's always awkward to come back after a dramatic exit.

Georgia won't be here for a little while, and I'm hungry. My chest is starting to ache again, and my cheek is still swollen. I need food. Or a drink.

Patrick hops up on the counter, and I open the door to the freezer and dig out some ice. I wrap it up in a towel and hold it to my cheek.

"You think they have any tequila hidden in here?" I ask, opening a couple of cabinets.

Emilio appears in the doorway. "We do not, but some can be acquired."

"You never get me tequila when I ask for it," Patrick says with a fake pout.

"You have returned," Emilio says. I can't tell if he's pleased by this or not.

Patrick leans forward with a smile. "Did you miss me?"

"No," Emilio frowns, turning a glare on Patrick before looking back at me. "Olivia, Javier instructed me to go to your house and bring you whatever you require. What do you need?"

"You need to bring Mr. Muffins here. I'm not leaving her alone at the house for a week if people are trying to kill me. So, you'll have to grab her food and her kitty litter. Don't forget the canned food in the fridge either, or she'll murder us all in our sleep."

Emilio nods, taking my requests as seriously as I would expect.

"I need all of my medicinal brews. My cauldrons too," I pause.

The apothecary has been destroyed. I don't actually need to brew anything anytime soon. "Just the brews will be good, actually. I guess I'll need a week's worth of clothes too."

"I'll have it within the hour," Emilio says with a short bow before turning and striding away.

"Don't forget bras and panties!" I shout after him.

Patrick snorts.

"Not to kill the mood or anything, but you seem a lot...better today," I say, shifting the ice around on my cheek.

Patrick looks at the floor.

"Reilly fed me," he says quietly.

"You mean he found you someone to feed on?" I ask, confused.

"He did find someone for me to feed on after, but no," Patrick says, shaking his head. "He gave me some of his blood. It's something a stronger vampire can do to help someone regain control, but most won't because it weakens them."

"Javier gave me his blood after the attack, and in the hospital today. He seems fine."

"It's different," Patrick shrugs, his eyes downcast like he's ashamed of what happened. "To bring someone back from the verge of losing control, they have to give a lot more than what you took. Javier wanted to do the same for me before I left, but I wouldn't let him. He isn't powerful enough; it would have half-killed him."

"I've never heard of that before."

"It's not something that's widely talked about," Patrick says, sliding down off the countertop. "Someone just drove up. It's probably Georgia."

I dump the ice out in the sink and head to the front of the house.

Leslie is already at the door, and she opens it and waves the guests inside. Georgia strides in followed by a tall, bearded man. With his shaggy black hair, he looks like he should shift into a bear and not a wolf. He's holding another were, a shirtless boy with black hair who doesn't even look eighteen. I wonder if it's his son. The kid's face is contorted in pain, and his skin is covered with a sheen of sweat.

Georgia looks around, apparently never having been here before. Javier appears at the top of the stairs.

"Leslie, you may take them to the front parlor," he says as he walks downstairs.

She nods and leads the way to the same room I saw Javier laid out in less than a week ago.

"You can just lay him down here." I point to the floor in front of the couch.

The man lays him down, and I'm able to see the wound on his side clearly. It's not very big. It looks like someone stabbed him. Black tendrils are creeping from the edges of the wound toward his heart. I haven't seen a silver-infected wound on a werewolf in person before, but the signs are obvious.

"I appreciate your hospitality, Javier," Georgia says.

Javier nods graciously and stands out of the way near the door. He leaves a few feet of space between him and Patrick.

When I spoke with Georgia before, she hadn't seemed all that worried, but she's standing with her hands in tight fists at her side, and a muscle in her jaw is twitching. Perhaps the werewolf has gotten worse since we last spoke.

"I'll do what I can, but this might be worse than what I can fix," I say, laying my hands on the boy's trembling chest. His eyes are wide, and he looks terrified.

My magic stutters slightly, and for a moment I think I must have damaged it when I tried to find my mom. I take a deep breath, and it smooths out. I can feel the boy's heart, beating fast and hard from a mixture of fear and pain. There are no bruises or cuts other than the unhealed wound.

He feels warmer than a human would, but I think that must be because he's a werewolf. The flecks of silver in the wound are cold spots. I move my hand over it, and the boy jerks. I frown; this shouldn't hurt.

With little jerks, the silver slowly begins to separate and slither out of him. He twitches, and the bearded man presses his shoulders down to hold him still. The silver begins sliding out of the wound and winding up my hands. It makes my skin itch, but that's better than what it was doing to him.

Slowly, I feel the cold spots disappear. The wound still feels odd, like it has gone stale. I press my hand down over the wound as hard as I can, and the boy groans.

"Hold still, David, it's almost over," Georgia says in soothing tones. She crouches down by his head and smooths her hand over his forehead.

I should be tired now. Exhausted, even, but I'm not. It's like the pool of my magic has somehow gotten deeper. It doesn't take a genius to figure out how, though I had no idea stealing different kinds of magic would help like this.

Patrick and Javier have seen me heal before. They've seen me exhausted from pushing past my limits, Javier especially, but I can't leave David like this if I can finish healing him. I push a little farther and feel blood finally begin to seep into the wound. The blood is dripping out onto the carpet now, and it seems to be flushing the wound clean. My jaws ache with something like hunger. I swallow and try to ignore the feeling. This isn't normal. The boy lets out a sigh like he's finally no longer in pain and stops trembling.

With every remnant of the silver gone, my magic is able to knit his flesh together from the inside out. The wound closes and smooths into a red, teardrop-shaped scar.

I move away carefully, and the silver falls from my hands to the carpet. My palms are slick with blood. Patrick is staring at me, brows knit together. "David, how do you feel?" Georgia asks, brushing a stray piece of hair back.

"I'm sorry, Mom," David says, his words slurred. "Didn't mean to be trouble."

I look up, my mouth hanging open. I had no idea she had a son, much less that he was the one hurt.

"He wasn't supposed to be there. He followed us and joined the fight against my wishes." Georgia smiles at me, tight-lipped. "His father, my mate, was killed a couple of years ago while traveling on pack business. The police investigated, but the NWR is good at what they do and good at disappearing their members when they need to. David could not stand to pass up the chance at revenge."

Georgia chuckles, but it is a humorless sound. "I can't blame him; he is his mother's son, after all."

"I'm so sorry, that's awful," I say, a quiet rage settling in my chest. The NWR has hurt so many people, and all for something so pointless.

"Thank you for healing him. I could not have stood losing them both."

I nod. "He still needs to take it easy for a while. There was a lot of silver still in the wound."

"I will make sure he rests," Georgia says as she scoops her son up. The bearded man squeezes Georgia's shoulder briefly, then nods in my direction.

"If he's still like this tomorrow, let me know. He should be back to normal after he sleeps though."

"I will," Georgia says. "He smells right now though. I am no longer worried."

Leslie walks Georgia, and the other werewolves back out. A tense silence settles over the room, and I have the urge to flee and let Patrick and Javier hash out whatever issues they're having.

"Olivia, Emilio, put your things in the room across from Patrick's." Javier pushes off the wall.

"Great," I say, standing up and holding my hands out in front of me so I don't smear the blood on anything else. "Is there an attached bathroom?"

"Yes," Javier says.

"All right, I'm going to go clean up," I say as I hurry out of the room. Neither of them moves to follow. I'm almost to the stairs when Reilly walks in the front door.

"Have you been murdering people without me, Olivia?" Reilly asks, nose twitching. He cocks his head to the side. "Is that from a werewolf?"

"Yeah, one of them still had some silver in him from the fight with the NWR. I healed him; it got a little messy." I hurry upstairs, hopeful Reilly won't follow.

I pause at the door to my room, and Reilly reaches around from behind me to open the door. I jump, then glare at him. So much for him not following me.

"You're welcome," he says, raising a brow and his mouth cocking up into a one-sided smile.

"I'm not thanking you for being creepy," I say as I walk inside.

The room is laid out exactly like Patrick's, though the walls are bare and the bed has a sedate, navy comforter set instead of the colorful one Patrick uses.

I head straight for the bathroom and begin scrubbing at my hands. The blood is already drying and starting to flake. It's under my fingernails too, and that's always a pain to get out.

"There was another bomb," Reilly says as he leans against the door to the bathroom. "It was at the cafe. An employee found the old bag it was in and thought it was odd. They tossed it in the dumpster behind the building, and that dampened the explosion enough that it hardly did any damage."

I stare at Reilly's reflection in the bathroom mirror and swallow uncomfortably. This could have been so much worse. The cafe had been so crowded that day, just like every other day.

"Why would the NWR go after Maybelle like that?"

"Why indeed?" Reilly asks. "That was Special Agent Brunson's first question as well."

"Didn't the NWR already take credit for it?"

Reilly nods.

"They'd take credit for someone they didn't like stepping on a Lego though," he says, shrugging one shoulder and waving his hand dismissively.

"Who would want Maybelle hurt like that? Everyone in this town loves her," I say, turning the water off and facing Reilly.

"Maybelle told the police there was no one who would want to. That she couldn't think of a single person," Reilly says. "She was lying."

"She wouldn't do that," I say sharply. Maybelle has never lied in the time I've known her. She's always been ruthlessly optimistic and cheerful; it's my favorite thing about her.

"And yet, she did," Reilly says, spreading his hands wide.

"How do you know?" I demand, stepping toward him.

"I heard her heartbeat."

I roll my eyes. "Polygraphs are unreliable, and so is your hearing, apparently."

"Go ask her yourself. Perhaps she'll tell you the truth," Reilly says, stepping toward me so he can tower over me.

"She told me not to trust you," I say, pointing an accusing finger at him.

His lips close around the tip of my finger, and I'm too startled to jerk away, even as his tongue flicks across the tip of it, sending a spike of pleasure through me. My lips open slightly, and my breath catches in my throat. He pulls back, his cheeks dimpling in amusement.

"You missed a spot."

I lower my hand, a blush creeping up my neck. "Don't do that."

"Can you think of a good reason Maybelle would warn you not to trust me when she hasn't even met me?" Reilly asks, licking his lips slowly.

"You're with the council, and everyone knows you're power hungry, interfering assholes. There's a reason no one wants to catch the attention of the council."

He walks forward, pushing me back until I'm pressed against the bathroom sink.

"Maybelle is lying, and you need to find out why."

"I'll find out, but it's going to prove she's telling the truth," I say, jutting out my chin stubbornly. He might have distracted me with his little finger sucking stunt, but I'm not that easy to convince. My finger is still tingling though.

"I'd keep chatting, but that has made me hungry," he says with a wink before stepping away and walking back through the bedroom.

I step into the hall with a retort on the tip of my tongue, when I see Emilio with a very angry Mr. Muffins in a cat carrier. Emilio's sleeve is torn and his hair mussed. I've never seen it mussed before.

"Take your cat," he says, thrusting the crate into my hands. "I suspect it is possessed."

He goes into my room with the other bag, a couple of the neckers trail behind him, carrying the rest of my things.

I follow but can't help a glance back. Reilly is waiting at the end of the hall. He winks and smiles at me, cheeks dimpled and not looking nearly guilty enough.

"I do not have enough potions to deal with this," I whisper under my breath as I hurry into my room.

I lean in and inspect my face in the mirror. Thanks to the potions I took before bed, and the healing I did on myself, the bruising and scrapes on my face are mostly gone. The shower washed away the last of the concealing potion on my hands. The welts are still red and tender.

Emilio brought all my medicinal potions to my room last night. I grab the salve and work it into my hands and up my arms. The welts don't fade at all. I'm starting to worry they're going to scar.

Perhaps because they were made by magic, they won't heal like a regular burn. I need to try to brew a stronger version of this salve, or maybe something new.

I press my palm to a welt near my elbow and prod it with my healing magic, then yelp as it shocks me. My palm is unmarked, but it feels warm and achy. I won't try that again anytime soon. I really need to figure out what I've done to myself, and soon.

There's a knock on my door.

"Just a minute!" I shout as I hurry back to the bathroom to pull on my clothes. I'm still sticky from the shower, but I can't let anyone see these welts. It's bad enough Patrick saw them.

Clothes finally on, I hurry to the door and crack it. Lydia is standing in the hallway in a crisp black suit, her hair pulled up into a chignon. I pull the door completely open and step aside to let her in. Mr. Muffins runs out as she walks inside. I hope she pees on Reilly's pillow or something.

"I'm glad you're up," Lydia says briskly. "Special Agents Brunson and Hawking will be here soon to take your statement."

"I don't have to go to the police station this time?" I ask as I walk back to the bathroom to finish getting ready.

"No, I insisted they come to you this time," Lydia says. She tugs the comforter straight, then perches on the end of the bed since there is nowhere else to sit.

"Are they still assuming the NWR is behind this?" I ask as I brush a little mascara on my eyelashes. It makes me look a little more awake.

"Yes and no." Lydia walks over to stand in the doorway. "Did Reilly tell you about the second bomb?"

I nod and turn to face her, leaning against the bathroom counter as I braid my hair.

"They have to investigate the possibility the NWR is, in fact, responsible. But the second bomb they found is making the agents question that."

"Reilly said Maybelle is lying about not knowing who might want to hurt her." I roll my eyes, still irritated about that.

"Did he say why?" Lydia asks, forehead furrowed. "She seemed adamant about finding out who had planted the bombs. She insisted the police provide extra security at the cafe as well."

"Apparently, her heartbeat gave her away," I scoff. "I think he's full of shit."

"It is strange though, for her to be the target," Lydia says thoughtfully. "She has to be hiding something. There's no way she wouldn't realize it if someone hated her enough to set bombs at two of her businesses."

"You'd think," I agree with a sigh. I don't want Reilly to be right. "I'm going to try to call her again."

"All right," Lydia says, looking at her watch. "Make it quick, I think they're already here."

I grab my cell off the dresser and dial Maybelle's number. The phone rings and rings and goes to voicemail again. I end the call and shrug, but I'm getting concerned. It's not like her to ignore me like this. A small part of me is just hurt that she hasn't checked in on me at all. I did almost die.

"Voicemail again."

"After the funeral, I can drive you into town to see her in person. I'm sure she's just caught up with the fallout, probably dealing with insurance," Lydia offers.

"Probably," I agree, shoving my phone in my pocket. "Let's go get this over with."

The house is strangely quiet, with all the vampires, and most of the neckers, asleep. Zachary's voice drifts upstairs, then Leslie's. It seems like she takes over Emilio's job during the day.

I follow Lydia down the stairs. Zachary and his partner are waiting in the foyer. Hawking looks up first, her nose twitching. Zachary doesn't look at me.

"Sorry to keep you two waiting," Lydia says, holding out her hand to Hawking first, then to Zachary.

"No problem at all. Leslie here promised us sandwiches for our troubles," Hawking says with a wide smile, hands on her hips.

She's wearing the usual JHAPI uniform, black slacks and jacket over a white button-down shirt. Her belt buckle draws my eye though. I stare for a moment before it makes sense. It's a pineapple turned sideways. What an odd choice.

"We can sit in the dining room, then." Lydia leads the way. I wave Zachary and Hawking ahead of me and trail after them. Zachary's shoulders are tense as he glances back at me. I look at him impassively even though my stomach is twisting and palms are sweating.

Lydia sits at the head of the table. Hawking takes the chair to her right, and Zachary sits down next to her so I'm forced to walk behind Lydia to sit on the other side of the table.

"All right," Hawking says, pulling out a notepad and a recorder. "Go ahead and start at the beginning when you got into town."

She looks at me expectantly. I take a deep breath and think back to that afternoon.

"I got some pie at Maybelle's, spoke to Georgia. She wanted me to heal one of her people," I say, crossing my arms and leaning back in the chair.

"Georgia?" Hawking asks. "She is the Alpha of the local werewolf pack, correct?"

"Yes."

Hawking motions for me to continue.

"I agreed to heal her packmate, but she still had a couple of errands to run, so I decided to go check on the progress of the apothecary. I don't really remember what happened next," I say with a shrug. "I just remember smoke and sirens, and then I woke up in the hospital."

Hawking nods, biting the end of her pen. "Did you see anyone you didn't recognize at Maybelle's Cafe? Anyone acting nervous?"

"No, but I wasn't really paying attention." I shrug.

"Has anyone sent you threats?"

"Not that I know of. I'm fairly certain Martinez wants me dead, but that's not exactly new information."

She scratches down a few notes. Zachary hasn't said a word since we got in here. He has his notepad out as well, but he hasn't written anything down. He has been glaring at me for the past five minutes though.

Hawking glances at him too and narrows her eyes at him. "Brunson, do you have any other questions?"

"No, I don't."

"All right," she says, tapping her pen against the table once. "I guess we're done, then."

She pushes her chair back and stands. Zachary follows suit.

"I had a question before you leave, actually," I say, standing as well. "Do either of you think this was the NWR?"

"We can't discuss an ongoing—" Zachary begins.

"No," Hawking interrupts. Zachary turns his glare on her, but she ignores him. "I don't, and I intend to find out who is actually behind it."

"Any leads on who it is?" I ask, leaning forward. I'm glad Hawking is willing to talk to me, at least.

"Nothing solid. There's a suspicious person on the security camera, a man with a long white beard. Maybelle Williams is cooperating but somehow being completely useless as well. You know her personally, right?"

"Yes." I nod.

"If you can, get her to be honest with us. We can't help her if she's hiding things from us," Hawking says, tapping her pen against her leg, agitated.

"I'll do what I can," I say, disquiet stirring in my gut. Everyone is saying the same thing, and Maybelle isn't acting like herself.

Hawking nods. "We'll be in touch."

Lydia and I follow them out of the room. Brunson pauses just outside of the doorway. Hawking gives him an odd look, then rolls her eyes and continues on. Lydia follows her.

Brunson grabs my elbow as I go to walk past him as well. "Can I have a word?"

Lydia and Hawking are deep in conversation now, so I nod and lead him to the front living room. I let him shut the door behind us and plop down in one of the chairs.

"Why is there blood on the carpet?" he asks, staring at the spot where David had been lying the day before.

"Vampires." I shrug. Brunson looks between me and the spot, clearly concerned, then shakes his head and leans back against the wall.

"Did you ask me to talk so you could just stare at me?" I ask. I don't want to sit in here with him longer than I have to, and he doesn't seem willing to start whatever conversation it is he wants to have.

Zachary rubs both hands over his face, then finally looks at me. "Why did you leave?"

I bite the inside of my cheek. Why can't he just hate me and avoid me like a normal person?

"Does it even matter? I left. You hate me. Debra probably hated me. It's done."

He groans in frustration. "Maybe I just want to know! You owe me that much."

I lean forward, elbows on my knees and press the palms of my hands into my eyes. "Your dad promised to help me find my mom. He did that, and then he—"

I bite off the word, unsure of how to continue. The paranoia that followed and the worry over the way his tone with me had changed after he had found the information are hard to explain.

"He changed. You didn't see it, but he did. He avoided talking about my mother's disappearance, and her death, after he found her. He got angry with me when I said I wanted to find out who had killed her, said I needed to let it go. Which was the opposite of what he said when he took me in. I saw fear in his eyes, Zachary," I say, a lump forming in my throat. "Then those cops came to the door, and he was dead. I just assumed it was connected. It wasn't logical, and I didn't wait to find out the truth. I couldn't face either of you while I thought I was somehow responsible for his death."

"It wasn't—"

"I know," I interrupt. "Six months after he died, I got drunk and worked up the courage to look at the cause of death. A drunk driver hit him when he stopped to help someone change their tire."

I remember the pictures of Debra and Zachary standing by his casket, overwrought with grief. The lines of men in uniform. The deep, wrenching realization of how much I had failed them. I'm tired, and I want Zachary to leave, but instead he walks over to the chair across from me and sits down.

"A stupid, pointless accident killed the best man I've ever known. And I abandoned his family because I was selfish and self-obsessed. Because I couldn't watch you grieve while I was still grieving myself," I say, my voice cracking on the end.

My lower lip trembles, and I dig my nails into my palm to distract myself. I refuse to cry. Again. I stand abruptly. This will have to be enough for whatever closure Zachary wants.

"I don't know if I can forgive you," Zachary says, eyes tired, face locked in a frown.

"Good," I say firmly. "Don't."

I walk out of the room before he can reply.

CHAPTER 12

It's three a.m., and I can't sleep. The funeral is in five hours, and I'm going to look like the undead. I rub the heel of my hand across my eyes. Every time I try to go back to sleep, all I can see is my mother's face. I didn't even have this problem right after she disappeared. I can also hear the vampires in the hallway, whispering and laughing about whatever it is they gossip about. Between all that and dread for the funeral tomorrow, well today, sleep has been elusive.

Mr. Muffins is currently kneading my stomach, her claws pricking through the blankets. I sit up, dislodging her, and pick her up as I slide out of bed.

"How about we both go get a snack?" I ask.

Mr. Muffins meows and licks my arm. I take it as an affirmative. I'm wearing an old, worn T-shirt and baggy sleep pants with tacos all over them; hopefully, I can avoid running into too many people on my way to the kitchen.

I open my door and check the hallway, but it's empty. I pull the bedroom door shut behind me and readjust Mr. Muffins, smoothing down her fur.

I'm halfway down the hall when I hear a disgustingly flirtatious squeal from the room I'm about to pass, and I can't help myself. I edge toward the door and peek inside. I shouldn't have.

Reilly is with a different girl tonight, a redhead with long, straight hair. She's perched on his lap with her head thrown back in laughter and her arms wrapped around his neck. She whispers something to him as he trails a finger up the side of her neck. I should look away, but a sick curiosity keeps my eyes glued to the spectacle in front of me.

He smooths a hand across her cheek, and she quiets, her head tilting to the side with a breathy moan. She has got to be faking it; no one is that excited before anything is even happening. He leans in slowly, flicking out his fangs at the last moment. They sink in slowly, and she sighs like it feels good, her back arching. Reilly's eyes slip shut as he sucks. I swallow, my throat suddenly dry. Warmth pools in my stomach, and I'm not sure if I'm jealous of the girl, or if I want to be the one sucking her dry. I can almost taste Javier's blood in my mouth. It had made me so *hungry*.

Mr. Muffins meows loudly, clearly ready for her snack, and Reilly's eyes open. He doesn't stop feeding, and I'm frozen to the spot, watching him watching me. He pulls away slightly, licking the puncture points as his arms tighten around the girl and she moans. I finally find my feet and hurry away.

"You are such a bitch," I mutter to Mr. Muffins as I jog down the stairs. Reilly is guaranteed to give me shit for that. I am such an idiot.

A girl I've seen around the house often passes me on the stairs, her eyes flicking between my pants and sleep-rumpled hair. I frown at her, but she doesn't comment.

Thankfully, the kitchen is empty. Then again, it's almost always empty. I don't think the neckers cook very often.

I drop Mr. Muffins on the floor and dig through the cabinets for a bowl. All the dishes are slightly fancy, but I guess Mr. Muffins does deserve the best.

I grab a white and gold china bowl and set it on the ground as Mr. Muffins winds between my legs, purring like a lawnmower.

"You're shameless," I say as I grab the milk from the fridge.

"Shouldn't you be asleep?" Patrick asks, startling me. The jug of milk almost slips through my fingers.

"You need lessons on how to make a sound when you walk so you can stop sneaking up on me," I say as I crouch down and pour the milk into the bowl.

"Where would be the fun in that?" Patrick asks, rolling his shoulders. His eyes are bright, his hair is mussed, and he's practically bouncing on his toes.

"How much did you eat?" I ask, raising a brow.

"So much," Patrick grins. "Reilly suggested I drink more than I usually would, just for the next couple of weeks."

I shake my head, though I can't help smiling. "You're going to be blood-drunk for a week? God help us all."

"Speaking of drunk, Emilio put tequila in the pantry for you."

"He did?" I ask, perking up and heading straight for the pantry, pulling the door open and scanning the shelves. "Where is it?"

Patrick reaches around me and snags it off the top shelf. "You're worse with alcohol than your cat is with her treats."

"I am not!" I object as I unscrew the bottle and take a swig. It burns, but Emilio got some top notch stuff, so it's also smooth as tequila can get.

A couple of neckers walk by the kitchen, whispering when they see us.

"Let's go sit outside," I say, already walking toward the back door. Patrick jogs after me.

We walk out into the back yard, past the weird little garden of night blooming plants, and into the maze of hedges. My breath puffs out in little clouds as we walk.

I take another swig, choosing random directions until I think I might actually be lost. The tequila already has my head feeling fuzzy.

"You sure you should be drinking that much before the funeral?"

I stop and throw a glare over my shoulder. "I think I can decide for myself, thanks."

Patrick raises his hands in front of his chest. "Just making sure."

"You normally encourage bad behavior and decisions. Who even are you?" I plop down on the ground, leaning back against the hedge. The leaves are prickly and cold. I shiver and take another drink to warm up.

"I don't even know anymore," Patrick says, sitting down beside me and resting his head on my shoulder. He looks at the bottle enviously. "I wish I could drink tequila still."

"Ugh, remind me to never become a vampire. If I couldn't have tequila, I'd rather be true dead than undead and immortal."

Patrick snorts.

We sit quietly for a few minutes. I stare up at the sky, spinning the bottle listlessly between my fingers.

"Did I ever tell you why I chose to take the bite?" Patrick asks, picking at the seam of his jeans.

"No." I set the bottle down between my legs. "Why did you?"

"I was sick all the time. Not anything serious, just a cold that would always turn into bronchitis, and sometimes pneumonia. Or the flu. Or whatever might be going around." He shrugs and readjusts his head on my shoulder. "I was just sick and weak and useless."

"And you wanted to be a strong, immortal vampire instead?"

"I suppose," he says, spreading his hands. "I'm not sure exactly what I expected. I definitely thought it would be more glamorous. It might have been, I guess. If the vampire in the city I was living in had accepted my request, it could have been everything I imagined."

"They turned you down?" I take another sip.

"They laughed me out of the clanhouse. Said they didn't need a weak, pathetic human in their clan."

I snort. "Assholes."

"Yeah, we're something," he sighs, slipping his arm through mine. His skin doesn't put off the same heat a human's would. He's useless for staying warm out here.

"How'd you meet Javier, then?"

"I got desperate and started contacting every clan within three hundred miles. Javier invited me here for an interview." Patrick laughs. "It was so strange, but he was dead serious. He made me meet everyone, asked all sorts of intrusive questions, then offered me the bite on the spot. Said it was now or never, and I didn't even hesitate."

"Do you regret it?" I ask, something uncomfortable twisting in my chest as I remember his face twisted in hunger and spit dripping from his chin as he latched onto my arm in that basement. And the night before last, when his hunger almost overtook him again.

He twists so his forehead is resting on my shoulder and wraps his hand around my arm. "This week I have. I never thought it would turn me into a murderer."

"You're not a murderer," I say, almost harshly. "You're not."

He shakes his head, his breath hitching. "You don't know what it's like to kill someone. You can't understand."

I laugh, a humorless sound, and my eyes sting. I squeeze them shut and take another drink.

"Yes, I do."

He lifts his head. "What are you talking about?"

"The first person I killed was a vampire," I whisper as I grab the neck of my shirt and pull it to the side to show him the faint scars I could never get to disappear entirely. "Got obsessed and tried to kill me."

Patrick traces the scar with a cold fingertip and looks at me with tired eyes. "I'm surprised you don't hate us."

"I almost did," I say with a smile. "I was terrified when I started here. Only took the job because I was desperate as hell."

"You said the first person you killed?" he asks quietly. "Have there been more?"

I pull my arm away and stand; I've already said too much. Damn tequila.

"What happened to your neck?" I ask, pointing to the bruise on the side closest to me. His hand goes to it, and he shrugs, looking almost embarrassed.

"I left the clan; coming back wasn't as simple as just walking back in the house."

"Javier didn't hurt you, did he?" I demand, tugging at his hand to get a better look.

"No," he says, taking my wrists in his hands to keep me from pawing at his neck. "It wasn't like that."

"What was it like, then?" I ask, sitting back and taking another drink.

"When a vampire joins a clan, there's a sharing of blood," he says, a blush creeping up his neck. I didn't even know vampires could blush. "Javier and I had to do that again, in the presence of the clan."

I stare at him, brows raised. "You people have the weirdest fucking rules."

"Tell me about it," he says with a harsh laugh.

We go quiet, and the silence makes my skin itch. Sitting and thinking is the last thing I need.

"Let's walk more."

He opens his mouth to argue, then snaps it shut and shakes his head.

"I'll race you to the center."

I grin, wide and manic, then take off at an unsteady sprint.

The room is still spinning from the tequila, and I'm starting to feel like I might barf. Fucking tequila. I stumble towards the dresser, fumbling through the vials Emilio lined up on top of it.

"Where are you?" I ask in a singsong voice. Don't need the blood replenishing potion, don't need the iron supplement potion, don't need the sweet dreams potion.

"There it is!" I exclaim as I find the little purple vial that contains the sobering potion I keep for emergencies. I flick the cork out and down it before I can hesitate.

I gag immediately and have to pinch my nose to swallow it back down. Disgusting doesn't cover it. It's bitter and salty and sour all at the same time. The potion rushes through me, chasing the alcohol out of my bloodstream and back into my stomach, which twists and cramps.

I run for the bathroom and fling the toilet lid open, vomiting three times before I can catch a breath. I'm pretty sure some came out of my nose.

"So gross," I groan. My stomach cramps again, and I vomit up the remaining tequila. With the haze of the alcohol gone, I just feel tired, and stupid.

I get a hand on the sink and pull myself up on shaky legs. Panting, and still nauseous, I brace myself and wait to see if I'm going to vomit again. My stomach cramps once more, but I don't vomit. I turn the water on and rinse my mouth out before grabbing my toothbrush.

It takes a couple of minutes of scrubbing to get the taste out of my mouth. I spit in the sink and make the mistake of looking in the mirror. I'm going to need a shit ton of makeup to make myself look presentable. First, though, I have to take a shower.

The hot water soothes my now sore muscles and eases the last of the cramping in my stomach. I want to linger, but it's already six-thirty, and the funeral is at eight am. I really can't be late, plus I don't think Lydia would wait for me, and I don't have a car anymore.

I sigh and lean my head against the shower wall. Tequila had helped me forget that little piece of information, and I could have done without remembering it. I slap the water off and grab the towel I put on the counter.

Fifteen minutes later, I have my one nice dress laid out. It's a navy blue, a-line dress that belonged to my mom. I smooth out a wrinkle and stare at it. I haven't ever worn it, but I couldn't ever bear to get rid of it. I don't have many of her things left, just an old cauldron I can't even use anymore, and this. I shake off the memories and pull the dress on. It fits like a glove.

I blow dry my hair and twist it up into a bun. Then I slather on the concealer and foundation followed by a little blush to put some color on my cheeks so I don't look like a vampire. Finally, I put on mascara to make myself look awake. It's the closest I can get to reputable looking.

Standing there, looking in the mirror, all I can see is my mother. She looked almost exactly like this every time she went to deal with coven business. The welts striping my arms ruin the image though. The salves haven't been helping at all. I touch one; it's still tender, and I can feel the tingle of magic still running through it. I shove down the worry over what exactly I've done to myself and pull on a long sleeve cardigan to hide them.

My phone buzzes. Lydia is asking if I'm ready, or if she's going to have to come drag me out of bed. I text back that I'm headed down, then grab my purse, stuffed full of potions because you can never be too careful, and a light jacket.

Lydia, who is waiting at the bottom of the stairs, looks perfect, of course. She's wearing a tailored black dress with a string of pearls, her hair in a perfect chignon. The dress softens her broad shoulders, and her makeup makes her look both younger, and more somber than usual.

"I'm glad you had something decent to wear. I almost had Emilio get you something, just in case."

"Oh, ye of little faith," I say, adjusting my skirt as I come to a stop in front of her. I feel awkward in a dress.

Lydia crosses her arms like she's preparing for a fight. "All right, just so you know, the coven is going to be there, and they aren't happy you're attending. Novak's girlfriend, however, is human and insisted that you be permitted to attend. She's been insisting on meeting the witch her boyfriend died to protect."

"Great," I say, going to rub a hand across my face, then thinking better of it. I drop my hand to my side. "I'm not great with comforting people."

"Just tell her he was your hero, and don't crack any jokes. You'll be fine."

"Sure," I say.

Lydia looks unconvinced but heads to the garage regardless. She's driving one of Javier's sleek black cars today. The leather squeaks as I try to find a comfortable position.

We're almost to the cemetery when Lydia interrupts the silence.

"I got an email from Agent Hawking this morning."

"They found something?" I demand, sitting up straighter.

"Perhaps," Lydia shrugs. "It's a very tentative lead, but they think they have Martinez on a security camera at a gas station about fifty miles from here."

I clench my fingers around the strap of my purse. I want to find him so bad, I can taste it. Suddenly, Reilly extorting me into helping doesn't seem so bad.

"That's something."

Lydia nods. "It certainly is."

She turns down the narrow lane that leads through the cemetery. The parking lot is already full of cars with a stream of people walking toward the canopy tent set up over the gravesite.

Lydia parks at the back of the parking lot. I get out and smooth my dress down. I'm not sure how my mother ever sat in it without wrinkling it.

I see a few familiar faces as I walk up. Some I've simply seen around town, others are in pressed blue uniforms. A narrow black strip with the words *nemo me impune lacessit* stretches across their badges. They did the same at Brunson's funeral, from what I saw in the pictures.

"It means 'No one harms me with impunity,'" Lydia says, seeing my stare.

"That's a good motto," I say as we near the canopy. There aren't many seats left open. Novak's family has filled the front row, the police the second and third, and the coven most of the rest. However, there is one face missing I expected to see.

"Wasn't Maybelle supposed to be here?" I whisper as we take a seat in the back corner. The chairs are rickety plastic here in the back, and it squeaks as I sit down.

Lydia glances around discretely, brows pinching together. "She was."

A hush settles over the gathering. The minister steps up to a podium behind the casket and clears his throat.

"We are here today to honor a fallen hero, a dear friend, and a distinguished member of the Ignatius Coven and Pecan Grove Police Department, Alexander Novak. He was not only a police officer, nor was he only a witch, nor was he only a son. Alexander was a part of this community, and a good man who stood ready to defend this town against the greatest threat of our time."

I stare at my hands, clenched tightly together. Novak threatened me. He tampered with evidence at the request of the coven leader. But in the end, he came down into a basement to try and stop his partner, and he died trying to do the right thing.

"We are here today to lay this man to rest surrounded by the community he cared so much for," the minister continues. "Surrounded by the family that loved him, and his fiancée, whose future with him has been cut short. We are all here seeking comfort, which we will find in each other. Each of us mourns the loss of Alexander, and we will continue to mourn. I encourage you to lean on one other."

His fiancée is sobbing audibly now. His mother and father are staring straight ahead, eyes locked on the casket. I shouldn't be allowed here. I shouldn't be sitting at the funeral of a man I killed watching the people who cared about him grieve. It wasn't my fault, really, that he died, but I still sucked him dry and felt his soul slip from his body.

I dig my nails into my palm just to keep myself in my seat. The minister drones on. Lydia nudges me, and I realize I've been tapping my foot. I still and take a deep breath.

Three officers line up to the left, shotguns held at their sides. A fourth officer stands apart from them. He clicks his heels together, standing at attention.

"Firing squad. Attention!" His voice echoes across the space.

The other officers snap to attention as well.

"Ready. Aim. Fire."

The three shots crack through the air simultaneously. I flinch, digging my nails into my palm even deeper.

"Ready. Aim. Fire."

The shots crack again. I force myself to look up.

"Ready. Aim. Fire."

The final shot sounds, the report of gunfire echoing into the distance.

"Present arms."

The officer lifts a trumpet and begins playing taps. As the somber tune carries over the gathering, Novak's mother finally breaks down, tears streaming down her face.

The minister says a few more words, but I don't hear them. Lydia's hand on my arm startles me, and I realize they are finally lowering the casket. She presses the keys to the car into my hand and leans in to whisper in my ear.

"I'll get a ride back to the clanhouse from someone else."

I grip the keys tightly and nod. I'm the first person out of my seat, and it's all I can do to keep from sprinting to the car. I don't see Brunson and Hawking until I'm rushing past them. Zachary's eyes follow me, that same tired look on his face from the last time we spoke. This must be even harder for him than it is for me, yet I'm still the one running away.

CHAPTER 13

I drive exactly the speed limit on the way into town, even though I want to rush. I'm almost desperate to see Maybelle at this point. There are too many unanswered questions, and if I can't do something productive, I think I might go crazy. I could also use some good news about rebuilding the apothecary.

The cafe is almost empty. It's unheard of, and it makes my heart twist in my chest. Even the lights seem dimmer today.

I adjust my dress and wish I had thought to bring a change of clothes. I hadn't really planned for after the funeral though.

"Olivia," a familiar voice says from behind me.

I turn around and click my jaw shut after a moment. I've never seen Gerard out of the warehouse before. He looks even paler in the light, and he doesn't seem to like it based on the angry squint twisting his features.

"Gerard?" I ask dumbly.

He rolls his eyes and huffs. "You aren't normally this stupid. But yes."

I glare at him. "I've never seen you outside the warehouse. It's weird. What do you want?"

"Maybelle has been taken," he says, baring his teeth. "Find her."

I swallow. My mind is running in a million directions. Does he know? Who has taken Maybelle? I curl my hands into fists. I don't know if I could stand it if someone else died.

"Who took her?"

"It doesn't matter," he says, shaking his head. "You find her, and you get her back."

I pull my phone out of my purse. "Is this related to the bombing? Do you know who did it?"

He closes the distance between us in four quick steps, snatching my phone from my hand. I didn't realize he was capable of moving that fast.

"You call no one, and tell no one," he bites out. "If she's still alive, she'll not thank you for ruining her life by involving JHAPI."

"How do you know any of this? And why do you care?" I ask, taken aback by his vehemence.

"Because," he hisses, "she's my sister."

"Your *sister*?" I demand, leaning toward and speaking in a low voice. "Is this some kind of joke?"

"We are private people," Gerard says, crossing his arms. "You can demand all the answers you want after you find her."

"Why do you think she has been taken?" I ask, narrowing my eyes at him.

He thrusts a crumpled note in my face. I snatch it and smooth it out to read it.

What was stolen must be returned. Your sister for the book. You have forty-eight hours.

I look back up at Gerard, my brow furrowed. "What was stolen? A book?"

"It doesn't matter," he says, thrusting a finger at me. "We sold it years ago, and we can't get it back. They will kill her if we don't find her first."

"This is insane," I snap. Of course I'm going to try to Find her, but none of this makes sense. "When did you get this note?"

"Midnight the day of the explosion."

"Shit, so we're already down, what, twenty-four hours?"

He nods.

"You should have asked for help sooner," I say in a barely controlled tone of voice.

"I couldn't get to you without giving everything away. You have been surrounded by the vampires almost constantly since the bombing," he hisses at me. "It would have done neither of us any good."

I brush a stray piece of hair out of my face roughly. "This is insanity."

"It's only a matter of time before they come for you as well. I'm surprised they haven't made the connection already," he says, shaking his head.

"What connection? I apparently don't know anything about Maybelle," I say, waving the note at him.

"That's for her to tell you," he says. He's already backing away.

"Why are you always so damn vague?" I snap. "Just give me a straight answer."

"I know what you are, and what you can do. Find Maybelle, or I tell the vampire," Gerard says evenly. His shoulders are hunched up by his ears, and his hands are curled into fists like he's ready for a fight.

I glare at him, my heart in my throat and the note crumpling in my clenched hand. I clench my teeth to keep from yelling at him or threatening him. I want to find Maybelle even if I do hate him right now.

"Do you have a map?" I grit out.

"At the warehouse," he says, turning and walking away. I lock the car and follow.

Gerard's office is in even more disarray than usual. The chair is knocked over, and one of the computer screens is dangling from the wall, held up only by the cord. I stand in the doorway while he digs through a drawer and pulls out several maps.

"I don't think they've taken her far," he explains as he pulls a map partially open, then tosses it to the side and keeps digging.

"Why do you think that?" I ask, my thumb brushing over the worst of the welts on my hand. I want to itch it, but I know I would regret it.

"They think she still has it. That she has just hidden it somewhere," he says. He opens another map, nods, and brings it to me.

"But she doesn't?" I ask, taking the map with both hands.

"No." Gerard shakes his head wearily. "It would be easier if we did though. These people can't be reasoned with."

"Is it the NWR?"

He laughs, though there is no humor to the sound. "I wish."

"You or Maybelle are going to tell me everything after I find her," I say before I begin. "Especially why you think I might be next."

"If you really want to know," Gerard agrees begrudgingly.

"I do."

I brush past him, dump my purse on the ground, and spread the map out on his desk. It's a map of the county. Just large enough to ensure that I'll find her if she's here, but small enough that there's less chance I'll overexert myself.

The welts on my hand are starting to show through the concealer I put on them, probably because I've rubbed my hands too much today. I curl my fingers under and focus on the map.

The paper is dusty as I smooth my hands over it. I shut my eyes and nudge the Finding magic. It responds almost eagerly. I breathe a sigh of relief and push harder, picturing Maybelle's face in my mind as I search. Red lines wind down from my hands, scattering across the map like a spider web. She's close. Still in the town, but I can't see where yet, I can't—

A wave of pain hits me in the gut, and it feels like the welts are being burned into my skin all over again. My hands twitch on the map as I try to pull the magic back. It won't stop.

Olivia.

I gasp and try to open my eyes, but I can't seem to move. It feels like I'm falling.

Olivia.

I can hear her voice like she's right behind me. The burning pain in my arms doubles, and I think I might be screaming, but I can't hear anything but my own labored breathing and the frantic beating of my heart.

My head and back hit something hard. The air rushes from my lungs. My body shakes as my muscles contract violently.

I can see my mother standing over me, but I can't reach her.

CHAPTER 14

My hand twitches spastically. I can see it from the corner of my eye, but I can't make it stop. I can't seem to move at all.

The cardigan I'm wearing is scorched and falling to pieces on my arm. The welts, now an even darker red and inflamed, show through the gaps.

Another spasm wracks my body, and I grunt in pain, but I'm able to move my fingers. I focus on that, forcing my first finger, and then my second to curl in toward my palm. One by one, I coerce each muscle to move and roll onto my side.

I can't hear anyone in the room. Gerard must have abandoned me like this. I lift my head, the room spins for a moment, then comes back into focus. He's gone, the asshole. I guess he decided since I failed at Finding Maybelle, I wasn't worth fooling with anymore.

I groan and push myself upright and lean back against the wall. It takes a second to catch my breath. I rip the cardigan off and touch the shoulder of the dress tentatively. It's ruined. The welts are much worse as well. And not just that, they've spread.

I brush my hand from my shoulder up my neck and feel the welts stop just above my collarbone. Based on the ache in my chest and side, I think they may have extended there as well.

My phone rings. I stare at my purse and consider just letting it go to voicemail, but as it rings again, I sigh and push myself onto my knees and crawl to my purse.

The caller ID says it's Lydia. I answer and put the phone to my ear.

"Hey, Lydia," I say hoarsely. It hurts to speak.

"Olivia, you need to come to your house," Lydia says, her voice tight.

"Why?" I ask, trying to keep my voice steady despite the pain shooting through my side and the growing headache pounding in the back of my head.

"Your house was broken into," Lydia hesitates before continuing. "Nothing was taken that we can tell, but there has been some damage."

I want to sink into the floor and never get up. My heart twists when I think about what could have happened to Mr. Muffins if I hadn't decided to stay with the vampires.

"How much damage?" I ask finally.

"Slurs on the door and some of the walls. Some things have been broken. Your workroom is the worst. I think the ingredients will be unusable."

"And this was done by…" I trail off. I don't want to say their name. *His* name.

"It does look like something the NWR would do, though there is no evidence Martinez is back."

I look down at my still trembling hands, the red welts darker and inflamed. I have no choice. I can't do this on my own.

"Maybelle has gone missing. She left a note you may want to read before we talk to the police."

"Where are you?" Lydia demands. I can hear her heels snapping against a wood floor.

"The warehouse. Gerard's."

"What—" She cuts herself off. "Stay there, I'm sending someone to get you."

"You can't," I object. "Only you. No one else, not until we talk."

"Olivia, it's been almost five hours since you ran away from the funeral. Special Agent Hawking was already starting to get concerned something had happened to you. There will be questions."

"I'm sure you can help me think up a good excuse." I let my head thunk back against the wall. "I also need a change of clothes."

One of the computer screens flares to life, almost blinding me. I squint into the sudden light and realize it's showing Lydia opening the door.

"Olivia?" Lydia shouts from the front of the warehouse.

"In the back!" I shout back, which sends me into a coughing fit. It's dusty in here, and I desperately need some water.

She shuts the door, and the computer screen goes dark once again. That explains why Gerard was never surprised to see me at least.

Lydia's heels echo loudly as she walks to the back room. I don't bother trying to stand. The door to Gerard's office swings open. Lydia is wearing a low cut red dress with a ruffled skirt and glittery black heels. Her gray hair swings around her face in soft curls.

"What—were you on a date?" I ask, mouth hanging open.

"I'm old, not dead, Olivia," she says, chunking a bag of clothes at my head. I only manage to half-block it and barely keep it from dropping onto the dirty floor.

"Thanks." I dig through the bag, relieved to see a long sleeved shirt. I'd forgotten to specify.

"What the hell happened to you? Are those burns?" Lydia says, concern tinging her voice as she comes closer, crouching down next to me.

"I think they are," I say with a shrug. "Help me up?"

She grasps my hand and pulls me up quickly. My legs tremble, but I don't collapse.

"Olivia," she says, hands on hips. "What is going on?"

I turn away from her and strip my dress off. She gasps as it falls away. My back must look even worse than it feels.

"Magic is temperamental sometimes. I made a mistake the other day that I'm still paying for," I explain as I dig the jeans out of the bag.

"What did you do?" she asks firmly.

I pull the shirt on and tug the sleeves as far down over my hands as I can. If I'm lucky, and if no one looks too carefully, I might be able to get away with it.

"Olivia, don't ignore me," she snaps.

I turn around, suddenly angry. Angry I have to ask for help. Angry Gerard put me in the position. Angry I've made so many stupid decisions in a row.

"They'll kill me, Lydia, or find a way to use me," I snap back. "I don't know which is worse, but I don't want to find out."

"You can trust me—"

"No, I can't," I say, curling my arms around myself. "If I told you, you would have to tell Javier. I know you can't lie to him, and he's your employer anyhow. The only reason you're helping me at all is because he told you to."

Lydia takes a deep breath and looks at me steadily. "That is true, but you are useful to Javier. He would want to protect you."

Her honesty hurts more than it should. *Useful.* That's what I've been reduced to. All of my struggling and pain and all the risks I have taken for Javier can be summed up in one word. I knew all of this, but I guess some childish, fanciful part of me still cared. I should know better by now than to get attached.

"If you want me to keep being useful to Javier, then forget what you saw and don't ask me about it again."

Lydia pinches the bridge of her nose, considering. "Javier may not take no for an answer. What you do after that will be up to you."

I groan aloud and run my fingers through my hair. "Did you know Gerard was Maybelle's brother?"

"What?" Lydia asks, thrown off by the abrupt subject change.

I thrust the note toward her.

"Gerard brought me this and asked for my help Finding her. He didn't want the police involved."

Lydia takes the note, reading it silently. She looks up finally and hands the note back to me. I can see the wheels turning in her head; she knows I shouldn't be able to use that kind of magic. She knows I found Patrick. She probably knows about Aaron Hall lying in this very warehouse last week. I had asked Javier to clean up that mess for me after all. That was sloppy.

"As your lawyer, I have to advise you to take this to the police," she says. "Did you Find her?"

"No, I passed out. Gerard left while I was unconscious."

She turns and paces the small, cleared area in the middle of Gerard's office. "The note said forty-eight hours?"

I nod and tug on the ends of my sleeves again. The material of the shirt feels like sandpaper on the welts, even though it's fairly soft.

"Then you have to tell them," Lydia says, coming to a stop. "We can't risk waiting and trying to find her ourselves."

"She didn't want the police involved."

"Did she tell you that, or did Gerard?" Lydia asks.

I gnaw on the inside of my cheek. "Gerard."

"Can he be trusted? Is he even actually her brother?"

I put my head back in my hands. "I don't know."

I feel utterly lost. I cared about Maybelle, someone else who apparently has secrets. Gerard could be playing me somehow. I have no idea if he's out to get Maybelle or help her. He seemed sincere and desperate when he came to get my help. Well, to force me to help him.

"Come see your house, perhaps that will help you decide," Lydia says, hands on hips.

"Is it that bad?"

"Whatever you think, it's probably worse."

CHAPTER 15

As we approach the house the first thing I can see is the fluorescent red scrawl of *BLOODBAG* and *WHORE* across the front of the house.

"I can see they wanted to keep it subtle," I mutter. Lydia snorts and parks the car behind the police car and the unmarked black car I recognize as Brunson's.

"Just wait 'til you see the inside," she says with a shake of her head.

We climb out of the car, and I take a deep breath to steady the sudden churning in my stomach. I have felt unsettled since we left the warehouse, and the feeling has only gotten worse on the way here.

Brunson meets us on the front porch.

"What happened to you?" he asks, looking me up and down, brows furrowed.

"Nothing, I just changed clothes," I say with a tight-lipped smile.

"There's dirt on your face," he says, pointing at my cheek. I rub at the spot he pointed at with my sleeve.

"Just let me inside. I need to see how bad the workroom is."

He turns and pushes the door open for me. It swings unsteadily on the hinges. The doorknob is more or less dangling from the door, and the latch is completely busted off.

Inside is chaos. Every cabinet has been flung open, the contents strewn across the floor. A jar of cherries is broken in the middle of the kitchen. Sticky red syrup is splashed all over the cabinets like a murder scene. A carton of eggs is upside down in front of the refrigerator. My last bottle of whiskey is broken too. Assholes.

The table is flipped over, one chair is broken, and the other is lying on its side. The couch is ripped open, and the stuffing has been shredded and scattered around the room like snow. I feel numb. It doesn't even look like my house anymore.

I step over a dented can of green beans and walk through the kitchen and living room, absently noting they broke the television as well. The window unit is lying face down on the floor surrounded by glass. There are random holes in the walls. The edges of the carpet have been pulled up in various places.

The workroom door is shut, and I hesitate before I push it open. I should have left it closed. The chest of herbs is upended. Perfectly good ingredients are ground into the floor, wilted and smashed. Two of the cauldrons are fine, but the copper one is dented beyond repair. These were things that touched something inside of me no person ever has. It feels like my heart is lying trampled on the floor.

Every drawer has been pulled open, but one, in particular, catches my eye. It's empty. The crystals are gone.

I hear someone come to a stop in the hall behind me and glance back. It's Hawking; I hadn't even realized she was here.

"They took my crystals," I comment.

"Crystals?"

"Yeah, stuff like azurite or citrine. Everything in that drawer," I say, pointing it out. "Just odd since they didn't take anything else. At least nothing I've noticed so far."

"Any idea what they were looking for so intently?" Hawking asks, crossing her arms and leaning against the door jamb.

"I really don't." I shake my head. "I don't have anything worth all this. The only things of value were in here, and they didn't even take the most expensive things."

"What are the most expensive things?"

"Just the cauldrons, they're solid metal," I say, waving a hand at them. "They're not rare though. Some of the crystals were, I guess, or at least hard to get."

"And who got them for you?"

"Gerard."

Hawking scratches a few notes down. "Got a last name?"

"Not that I know of." I shrug. "He's a little odd. Doesn't like to give out personal information."

"All right, let me know if you see anything else missing," Hawking says before walking back toward the living room.

I nudge a fallen vial with my foot. It's cracked but not completely shattered, which is good considering it's deoxygenation potion. I press the palms of my hands against my eyes as I try to process all the things I'm going to have to replace.

"You smell like fire, and old Chinese food," Reilly says.

I jump and turn around, almost stepping on the vial when I see he is standing right behind me now. He grabs my shoulders and steadies me. I bite down on a wince. I need to get back to the clanhouse soon. The salves I have may not be able to heal these marks, but it does keep them from hurting so much.

"You have got to stop doing that," I say, shrugging his hands away.

"Perhaps when it stop amusing me," he smirks. My eyes stray to his dimples and the curl of hair sticking out from behind his ear.

"Where have you been?" he asks.

I jerk my eyes away from him and look around the room instead.

"At a funeral," I step around him.

"Whoever did this were witches," he says, looking around the room with his hands in his pockets, jacket pushed back. He's wearing his usual suit, but he didn't put on a tie today. The first couple of buttons of his shirt are undone; he looks like he dressed in a rush. "I can smell the magic."

"Of course it smells like magic in here," I say slowly, raising a brow. "I brew here."

"I know what your magic smells like," he says, stalking toward me. "It smells like copper and fire and herbs and blood."

I take a step back, but he's faster. He crowds me against the wall by the door, one hand on either side of my head. His eyes are so blue, they almost glow up this close. My heartbeat is picking up, but I can't claim it's all from fear.

"These people smell strange, like dust and mildew. Their magic is colder as well."

"Are you seriously trying to pin this on the coven?" I ask with a huff. "I know McGuinness hates me, but I don't think he'd go to this much trouble to ruin my day."

Reilly shakes his head. "No, it wasn't the local coven, but it was a coven."

"So, a coven trashed my house, and the NWR blew up the apothecary?" I ask, crossing my arms over my chest to keep the space between us.

"Oh no," he says, taking a step back finally. "The people who trashed your house are the same ones who planted the bomb."

I bite the inside of my cheek. The note left after Maybelle's disappearance definitely didn't seem the like NWR. I'm not sure if that should reassure me or not.

"That would explain Maybelle's disappearance and the note that was left, I guess," I say flatly.

"What note?" Brunson asks, appearing in the doorway.

I pull it out of my back pocket and hand it to him. "Where's Agent Hawking? I only want to have to explain this once."

I slip past Brunson and walk to the living room, where I can hear Hawking and Lydia talking. He and Reilly follow close behind. I grab one of the overturned chairs and right it, then sit down heavily, my legs stretched out in front of me.

"Where did you get this?"

"Gerard gave it to me and demanded I help him find Maybelle," I say, crossing my arms. "He didn't want to get the police involved, but I can't find her on my own."

"What else did he tell you?" Brunson demands.

"He said she was his sister." I look down to avoid the glare Brunson has focused on me.

"Interesting," Reilly says. "Maybelle seems not to have been very forthcoming at all."

"Has Maybelle ever hinted that Gerard was family?" Hawking asks.

"No, not in the slightest. She wasn't even the one to recommend Gerard to me as a supplier for my potion ingredients."

"Who was?" Brunson asks.

"Javier," I say with a shrug. "He said Gerard had gotten him something in the past."

"Any idea what?" Brunson asks, looking between me and Lydia.

"Blood replenishing potions for the people the clan feeds on," Lydia says. "Now Olivia supplies them for us."

"Is it possible they were searching your house for this book as well?"

"I guess, but I have no idea why they would." I shrug. "I'm connected to Maybelle and Gerard, but I've known them both for less than a year."

"So this note was left for Gerard?" Hawking asks, reaching for it. Brunson hands it to her, and she reads it carefully, flipping it over and examining the edges. She sniffs it carefully and grimaces.

"That's what he said." I shrug. It hadn't occurred to me before, but every partnership in JHAPI consists of a human and a paranormal. Hawking must be a werewolf.

"Can you get anything off this other than Olivia and dust?" Hawking asks, handing the note to Reilly.

He takes it and sniffs it carefully, turning the slip of paper over and sniffing that side as well. I press my lips together to keep the sudden urge to laugh under control. It just makes for such a ridiculous image.

"There's some scent I have smelled before but can't place," Reilly says, frowning. "There is a hint of whoever came here as well."

"We should go to Maybelle's house, see if we can find any trace the people who came here," Hawking says to Brunson. "If they're connected, that makes it even less likely the NWR is behind any of this."

"I'll give Olivia a ride and meet you there," Reilly says, striding toward me.

Hawking nods and pulls keys out of her pocket.

"I need to go update Javier," Lydia says. "I'll see you back at the clanhouse, Olivia."

I nod and follow Reilly outside. He is parked behind Lydia, apparently having borrowed one of Javier's sporty red convertibles.

I slide into the passenger seat, the leather squeaking as I try to get comfortable. It still has that new car smell, even though I know Javier bought this right around the time I started working for him. What a waste.

Reilly folds himself into the driver seat, which is pushed back as far as it will go. The car rumbles to life, and Reilly puts it in reverse and whips around. I grab the door handle and glare at him.

"It's not a race," I snap.

"No point in wasting time though." He grins. "It would be convenient to get there before the agents as well."

He doesn't slow down for any of the sharp turns. The car hugs the road, but I always feel uneasy when other people drive. It doesn't help knowing that Reilly could walk away from a wreck that would kill me.

"Why did Gerard think you could find his sister?" Reilly asks.

I grip the door handle tighter. "I found Patrick. I suppose he thought I could do it again."

"But you couldn't?" Reilly asks, turning his head to look at me.

"Watch the road." I reach out and push his chin back forward. His skin is warmer than I expected, much like his mouth was. I swallow and abruptly cut off that line of thinking. "And no, I couldn't."

Not a lie, but I'm sure my heartbeat is giving me away. Maybe he'll just attribute it to some kind of twisted attraction to him.

"You really do smell odd," he says, leaning over to sniff me again.

"Don't do that." I reach out to shove him away, but he takes a sharp turn and I am thrown into his side instead. I might smell odd, but he smells amazing. His cologne is warm and masculine, and I have a sudden urge to bury my face in the curve of his shoulder. I sit up and settle back in my seat instead. Anyone over the age of thirteen shouldn't blush, but I can still feel my cheeks heating up. I hate him so much.

"You're a terrible driver," I complain. "Can you try being a decent driver for a little while?"

"And stop giving you excuses to cuddle with me?" he says with a grin. His stupid dimples make him look innocent, but I know it's all a facade. "You do jump into my arms every chance you get."

"Walking into you because you don't understand personal space is *not* the same thing, asshole," I say, crossing my arms. I flinch when I hit a welt on the side of my arm more forcefully than I intended. My shirt dampens over the spot, and I'm not sure if it a blister popped, or if I'm bleeding. I glance at Reilly from the corner of my eye.

"The answer is yes," he says without looking at me.

"What?"

"I can smell that you are hurt." He downshifts, revving the engine as we take another turn far too fast. "And you will tell me why, eventually."

I huff and turn toward the window. The trees thin out, and we reach the edges of town. My stomach aches less than it did, but the discomfort has been replaced with irritation and worry.

He turns into a subdivision I've never driven through before. It's a little out of the way, but still close to town. Halfway into the subdivision, Reilly pulls into the driveway of a particularly nice house. It's slightly larger than the others and perfectly maintained.

Maybelle's house looks untouched. The door is shut, the blinds drawn, the freshly mowed lawn undisturbed. There are no slurs painted across her perfect, white shutters. It looks like everyone's favorite grandmother's house, just as I expected.

Reilly parks, and we climb out. I tug my sleeves down again, but the ache in my arms is getting worse. I wish I could have put salve on the burns before coming here.

Reilly inhales deeply then in the time it takes me to blink is halfway across the front lawn. I frown and hurry after him.

"Do you smell anything?" I ask.

He ignores me and opens the front door. I follow him inside and see that Maybelle's house is trashed even worse than mine was. Everything that could be ripped apart is.

Reilly turns around slowly, inhaling deeply, his mouth pulled into a frown.

"I should have recognized it on the note," he says, tone irritated.

"Recognized what?"

"The same witches that trashed your house were here," he says, turning to look at me. "But there have also been goblins here."

"Goblins?" I say, confused. "They never leave their cities."

"Apparently, they do."

The door opens behind us.

"Apparently, they do what?" Hawking asks, eager blue eyes

darting between us. She stops, her mouth opening slightly as she inhales. "What is that smell? It's almost reptilian."

"It's proof Maybelle is a liar," Reilly says, his eyes never leaving mine. He smiles, cheeks dimpling.

I turn away, frustration and irritation coursing through me.

CHAPTER 16

*H*e parks right in front of the house, and I shove the car door open, practically jumping out. I'm tired of being trapped in that car with him.

"The smell isn't superficial either. It's part of the house. However long Maybelle has been there, the goblin has been as well," Reilly says as we walk up the steps to the clanhouse. "Hawking agreed."

"There has to be something we're missing. She can't be a goblin," I say, aghast.

"Do you have any other explanations?" he asks, stepping toward me. There isn't even a hint of a smile on his face; he seems almost angry.

"A goblin could have visited her, even lived with her," I say, taking a step back from Reilly.

"Use your head," he says, poking my forehead, "and not your heart."

He presses his finger over my heart a little more gently.

I slap his hand away.

"I am," I snap. "You're just jumping to conclusions. If Maybelle is a goblin, why does she look human?"

"There are Enchanters that have successfully made objects that are capable of disguising someone."

I scoff. "For it to disguise her appearance all day, every day would be an insane amount of magic."

"I have seen more powerful magic used," he says, crossing his arms. "It's not impossible, and it's the simplest explanation."

"And Gerard? He says he's her brother."

Reilly's head tilts to the side. "I need to smell you again."

"I'm sorry, what?"

He doesn't respond, just walks toward me. I shuffle backward and bump into the railing. I reach back to steady myself on instinct, and Reilly presses his hands over mine on the railing. His thighs brush mine as he leans in. He lowers his head, his cheek right next to mine, and breathes deeply.

I'm frozen, my heart beating wildly and crawling up my cheeks. I hate that he's my type and that I can even be considering something like this when Maybelle is missing. My body doesn't care though; it just wants him to lean in closer. It's been way too long since I've gotten laid or had any *alone time*.

"You smell like goblin here, and here," he says, lifting his hand from mine and brushing a finger across my shoulder, and my arm. "Did Gerard touch you?"

"Yes," I mutter. "Fuck."

It's impossible to deny at this point. The only question now is just, why? Why is she hiding here? She's been lying about who and what she is for years, and apparently hiding from some very powerful witches. That isn't something you do on a whim.

"If you want," Reilly says, pulling back just enough to look down at me. His lips are inches away.

It would be so easy to just forget all of this for an hour. Sex is almost better than tequila for dealing with a bad day.

"You all right, Olivia?" Patrick asks from the doorway.

I jump and tug my hand out from under Reilly's. He steps back, and I hurry toward Patrick.

"I'm great, just fine," I say as I walk quickly inside. Reilly chuckles behind me. He's going to be unforgivably smug about that.

Patrick looks between us, shakes his head, and follows me inside. Reilly's phone rings, and he pauses just inside the doorway and answers it.

I get halfway to the kitchen when Patrick's hand closes around my elbow. He drags me to the back door, then pushes me outside.

"What are you doing?" he asks, voice tight with anger.

"Looking for Maybelle," I say, jerking my elbow out of his grip. "What the fuck is your problem?"

"You know you can't trust him," Patrick hisses. "But you were about to stick your tongue down his throat like some kind of horny teenager."

"I was not!" I whisper back heatedly.

"I've been out with you enough to know that look," Patrick sneers. "You can lie to yourself, but don't lie to me."

"You know what? It's none of your business," I say, pushing past him and grabbing the door handle.

"I'm trying to help you," Patrick says, throwing his hands in the air in exasperation.

"Nah, you just think I'm a slut."

I yank the door open and walk back inside, slamming it behind me. I head straight for the kitchen. I need something, anything, to drink. Javier and Lydia walk out of the dining room behind me.

"Olivia, did you find any information on who might have taken Maybelle?" Javier asks.

I stop and turn to face them, tucking my thumbs in my pockets to keep my hands from shaking.

"All we've found are more questions."

"What do you know about goblins?" Reilly asks, walking up behind me. He comes to a stop at my elbow.

"Goblins?" Javier asks, brows furrowed.

"It seems both Maybelle and Gerard are not who they have said they are," Reilly says, slipping his phone back into his pocket.

"Lydia explained that Gerard is claiming to be her brother," Javier says with a nod.

"Both Special Agent Hawking and I smelled the distinct scent of goblins at Maybelle's house. As I was telling Olivia, it's obvious that the person living there is the goblin. There is almost no trace of visitors. It seems Maybelle did not invite people over often."

"Did you find any information on who has taken her?" Lydia asks. "Is it possible she has simply run away?"

"She did not run away," I say vehemently. "You read the note."

"The same witches who were at Olivia's house were at hers," Reilly says.

"And it's not the local coven?" Javier asks.

"No." Reilly shakes his head. "They smelled off. They've been somewhere very old recently."

"None of this makes sense," Lydia says. "I've known Maybelle for years, and while we weren't friends, she was never involved in anything less than reputable."

"It's insane," I say. "She has built so much here, she would never leave it all behind willingly."

"We have another complication as well," Reilly says, looking at me. "I just got off the phone with Agent Brunson. The JHAPI agents have been reviewing security footage for everything within a hundred square miles. Apparently, the day Martinez fled, there was a break in at a veterinarian's office about sixty miles from here. Martinez stole medical supplies, then fled."

My heart constricts painfully. "Do they know where he went from there?"

"Not yet, but it's a start. We know he fled alone and didn't receive help from the NWR right away," Reilly says. "JHAPI is planning a raid on several known NWR locations, they want the council's support."

"Has the council agreed?" Javier asks, his shoulder's tense.

"Not yet, but they will," Reilly says. "Olivia and I will be part of the support team."

"What?" I turn on Reilly, jaw clenched tight.

"I told you when I came here that you would be helping the council apprehend Martinez. That hasn't changed."

"Maybelle has been kidnapped!" I object, my voice raising. "I can't just leave before she is found."

"Then you better hope she's found within the next few days, because we are leaving regardless," Reilly says coolly.

The realization that they aren't going to be able to help her hits me like a punch in the gut. They care about finding Martinez, but not her. I'm going to have to do this myself. Somehow.

The Internet, unsurprisingly, does not have many details on the finer points of using Finding magic, much less what to do when you fuck it up. I lock my phone and roll over and groan into my pillow.

I have about twelve hours left. The police have no leads, no idea who might have taken her, and the only thing we have learned is that we know nothing about Maybelle. That no one does.

I sit up and grab the salve off my nightstand. My arms are aching again. The blisters are all gone now, but sometimes it still feels like the welts are growing. Thankfully, the nausea I've been struggling since the warehouse has been slowly fading over the last hour.

The salve is cold, especially in contrast to the heat the welts are putting off right now. I lift the arm and check my side. One of the welts winds down from the top of my shoulder to my ribcage under my arm.

The only option I have left to find Maybelle is to attempt the Finding magic again. I poke at the welt and wonder how much it will grow if I try again. I'm not even sure where to start, or what went wrong last time.

My stomach jerks suddenly, and I'm on my feet, halfway to the bathroom, when something hits the bedroom window. The tug in my gut wants me to walk toward the window. I press my hand to my stomach and realize this is the magic.

I run to the window and fling the curtains to the side. I yank on the cord, and the blinds fly up. Standing just by a hedge at the edge of the maze, barely concealed, is Gerard. He tosses another rock at the window and waves me down, then ducks back behind the hedge.

I grab a handful of various potions, tuck the gun into my waistband, and run out of the room. It's just past dawn, and everyone else is asleep. Lydia left over an hour ago. I really hope this isn't a trap, but I know Maybelle is out there. I can feel it. The Finding magic had worked somehow, just not like it should have.

I shut the back door behind me quietly, then dart across the yard to the opening of the hedge maze. The early morning sun is obscured behind clouds, and the area is covered in fog.

"Gerard?" I half-whisper, half-shout. There is no response.

I step into the maze and let the tugging sensation guide me. Right turn, left turn, right, right. Gerard appears in front of me, startling me.

"Where is she?" I demand, one hand on the gun behind me, the other wrapped around a potion.

"This way," he whispers. He walks just a few more feet, the pulls a long duffel bag out from under the hedge. My stomach unclenches, and a weird relief spreads through me. It reminds me of what I felt when I found Patrick. He unzips it quickly and pushes the edges away.

Inside is—I don't know what. There is a pile of blood-soaked red curls on the thing's head. The face is swollen and misshapen, a long bulbous nose appears broken, and the skin is mottled blue and purple and green.

"Heal her," Gerard says, staring up at me with wide eyes.

Oh god, it's Maybelle. The realization makes me want to vomit.

"Is she even still alive?" I ask as I kneel next to the bag, my hands hovering over her. I don't know where to begin.

"Yes," he hisses, grabbing my hands and pulling them onto her chest.

Maybelle groans and twitches. I shut my eyes to block out the sight in front of me and let my healing magic sink into her.

There are numerous cuts all over her body, and even more bruises. Her nose is broken, she has lost too much blood, and she is slipping in and out of consciousness. I do what I can to steady her heartbeat and pull her back from the edge of shock, but this is completely beyond my skills. The damage is too extensive.

"Lift her head and give her the red and yellow potions that are in my left pocket," I say to Gerard.

He digs the potions out of my pocket, setting the green one aside. He has to pull the bag farther open and tug her shoulders up in order to rest her head on his lap. He tugs her mouth open, revealing a missing tooth, and pours the first potion down her throat, and then the second. She swallows, her eyes flickering open.

"It will help with the pain and the blood loss," I explain.

Maybelle lets out a sigh, and I can feel the pain potion sweeping through her.

"How did you find her?" I ask.

Gerard squints at me. "The Finding magic, it worked. I saw it on the map before you collapsed and burned the whole thing up."

"Why didn't you tell me? I could have helped!" I demand. I should have recognized the strange feeling in my stomach, the constant disquiet. I wish I had someone who could teach me, but instead I'm left bumbling through all of this on my own.

"She wouldn't have wanted you involved," he says, leaning over her head protectively.

I pull my phone out, one hand still on Maybelle's chest, and dial 911.

"What are you doing?" Gerard demands, grabbing for the phone. I lean out of his reach.

"She's dying," I snap. "I'm barely keeping her alive right now. We have maybe thirty minutes to get her medical attention."

"She's going to hate you for this," Gerard growls.

"At least she'll be alive to do it," I growl back.

"Pecan Grove Police Department, please state your emergency."

CHAPTER 17

"No, for the last time, he just showed up at the clanhouse shortly after dawn and asked me to heal her," I say evenly, though my nails are digging into my palms.

Brunson is using this as an opportunity to work off some pent-up aggression by being an asshole. Hawking isn't here to reign him in like she usually does. He has asked me to repeat my story at least five times. He tried to make me tell him what happened in reverse order, and I barely reined in the impulse to kick him in the shin.

It's been four hours since we got to the hospital, and I haven't had any updates on her condition. We're obviously not related, so I'm not sure if I'll get them at all.

"Did Gerard mention how he had found her?" Brunson asks, leaning in.

"No," I say, holding his gaze. I can only hope Gerard will back up my story, I have no idea what he'll do now that I've gotten the police involved.

"Ms. Carter?" A tall nurse with a deep voice and bright purple scrubs is scanning the waiting room from the doorway.

I stand and walk toward him. "That's me."

"She has woken up," he says with a calming smile. "And she is asking for you."

"Thank god," I say, relieved. "Where is her room?"

"I'll take you there."

"I'm coming with you," Brunson says from behind me.

"I'm afraid you'll have to wait, sir," the nurse says. "She requested to speak with Olivia alone first."

Brunson pulls out his badge, and I roll my eyes. "I'm a JHAPI agent, I have a right to— "

"Miss Maybelle is a victim, not a suspect, and per hospital policy, you will have to wait to talk to her until she is ready," the nurse says firmly, his friendly smile fading into a frown of disapproval.

Brunson bristles but doesn't argue further, shoving his badge back into his pocket with jerky motions.

"Now, it's just down this hall," the nurse says, putting his hand on my shoulder and guiding me out of the waiting room.

The hall is empty except for the occasional nurse slipping from room to room. I hate the open doors because I can't help looking, and each person lying inside looks gray and old with all the tubes sticking out of them. When I was younger, I used to sneak into the hospital and try to heal them all a little bit, but it was never enough, and I was left depleted. My mom put a stop to it as soon as she found out.

The nurse stops in front of a closed door. Maybelle's name is scrawled on the little whiteboard, and her doctor's name underneath.

"She looks rough, but she's not in any pain, all right?" he says, his hand on the door handle.

"All right," I say with a nod.

He pushes the door open, and I step into the dim room. The blinds are drawn, and the only noise is her raspy breaths. I hear the door click shut behind me as I approach the small lump in the bed. She'd be barely four feet tall if she was standing. More than that though, Maybelle always had such a large presence. She seems so diminished here.

I can understand the nurse's warning as well. They cleaned off the blood, and that has only made the cuts more obvious. They crisscross her face and arms, and I imagine they must cover her entire body. I don't understand why anyone would do this to her.

She opens her eyes and squints at me.

"Olivia?"

"Yes." I force myself forward and sit in the chair next to the bed.

"Tell her, Maybelle," Gerard says, materializing out of the shadows.

I jump out of my chair, startled to see him in here.

Maybelle shakes her head, the curls bouncing around her narrow face. The heart monitor blips faster.

"You can tell her, or I will!" Gerard snaps.

"You had no right to force this," Maybelle hisses. "After everything I've done for you."

"I had to! If I hadn't, then we would all have been doomed."

Maybelle scoffs. "You and your premonitions."

"Have I ever been wrong?" Gerard says, baring his teeth back at Maybelle.

"What the hell is going on?" I blurt out finally.

Maybelle goes quiet, still not looking at me.

"Ask her a question, Olivia," Gerard says. "Ask her how she knew your mother."

I stare at Maybelle, eyes wide, my heart in my throat. She isn't speaking, just staring at her hands.

"How—how did you know my mother?" I ask.

A wave of purple magic rolls from her throat to her mouth. Her lips tremble. She sighs heavily and looks up at me. "I knew your mother, years ago."

The magic explains the cuts and bruises all over her body. I feel sick to my stomach; I wouldn't have asked if I had known. She has to answer now, and she has to answer truthfully, or the potion will attack her. It will kill her if she resists too many questions. Whatever the coven that had kidnapped her was asking, she was resisting strongly. No one holds out forever; not many secrets are worth dying to protect.

This explains the missing crystals too. Some of them could have been used to brew a potion like this. I curl my fingers into my palm, hating them for taking something that could be used for good and twisting it like this.

"We weren't friends. More like business partners," she says with a shrug. "She had hired me to procure a few specialty ingredients for her personally, and she was my contact for any work I did for her coven. A couple of years after we started working together, she calls me. Turns out, she's fallen in love with her boyfriend, wants to have a baby with him."

Maybelle shakes her head like she disapproves. "Everybody knows vampires can't have kids, but she's set on it."

She's right. Vampires are undead, kept alive by magic, and can't seem to reproduce. Even if they could, witches can generally only have children with another witch. There's maybe a two percent chance of a successful pregnancy with a human.

"She hired me to find a way. And I did, which, no offense, was the biggest mistake of my life."

My palms begin to sweat, and I can feel Novak's magic getting twitchy inside of me. I should probably sit down, but I'm feeling the urge to run away.

Maybelle picks at the blanket, clearly uncomfortable telling me about any of this.

"I found a way though. For her to have her child. There is an old coven full of some real crazies. They collect magical artifacts, and there were rumors about this spell book that contained the secret to creating a child of a witch and vampire."

I swallow uncomfortably. "Creating something like that would be a bad idea. The vampire and witch councils already hate each other. Something like that would just be a reason to fight."

"Indeed," Maybelle agrees, inclining her head. "Your mother didn't care though. And so, we worked together to steal the book. If she helped, she could use the book to have her baby, and then I would get to sell it and keep all the profits. She agreed."

I want to throw up, but I stare at her instead. I have to hear this; I have to know.

"This coven isn't your normal, run of the mill coven. They're more of a cult, really. They claim to be the guardians of some ancient artifact. No one is really sure what they think they're protecting everyone from, but they hoard power and old magical items. They were the perfect target. We took several things that day, but all they've ever wanted back was that damned book."

Maybelle doesn't continue; simply stares at the floor.

"What happened next?" I ask, knowing the potion will force her to answer. She has to tell me the rest; I can't go the rest of my life wondering. Purple magic crawls up, constricting around her throat.

"It's ugly, Olivia, not the kind of thing you should have to hear about your mother," she says, straining against the tug of the potion.

"Just tell me," I bite out.

She takes a deep breath and looks up again. "They prepared for the spell we found in the book. She had to acquire a few things. Something from each branch of magic, a special brew she made herself, and the stars had to be aligned. As luck would have it, in a few weeks they were. We met in a cabin in the woods to perform the spell."

Maybelle pauses, taking a deep breath, her eyes scanning my face before she continues.

"I waited in another room until I heard her screaming." Maybelle covers her face with her hands for a moment before continuing. "He turned to dust while he was still inside her. Apparently, the magic required a price, one we didn't know about. The book," she shakes her head, "it was not clear. We barely kept in touch after, but I knew the spell worked, and I knew what you were. I went into hiding with my brother, buying both of us a new identity. Gerard watched you throughout the years. He urged me to hire you when you came through town because he insists you are important somehow. And I admit, I have grown fond of you."

Maybelle smiles tremulously for a moment, but the smile falls away at the expression on my face. I stare down at the floor, trying to wrap my head around this. In some ways, it explains everything.

My magic has never been normal. I was born with no magic at all, or so my mother thought until the day after I turned five years old.

I was watching her brew and decided I wanted to be able to brew as well. I had grabbed her arm, and I had *taken*. I can still see her face, the confusion turning to horror, then the scream of pain as I stole her magic. I had stopped as soon as I could, but I was confused, and I was hungry for her magic. She had laid on the floor, unable to move, while I had cried and shaken her shoulders, begging my mom to wake up.

I shake my head, trying to pull myself out of the memories.

"So I'm…" I can't finish the sentence.

"Half-vampire? Yes." She winds her fingers together and shakes her head. "And the people who planted the bombs weren't trying to kill me, they were sending a message. They want to know where the book is. Well, they wanted to."

She pauses, glancing at Gerard, who nods.

"I was not able to fully resist the potion, Olivia, I am sorry," she says quietly.

"What do you mean?" I ask, even though I think I know the answer.

"They know who you are now. They will be coming for you."

"Okay," I say even though it isn't. I run my hands through my hair and pace the small area by the hospital bed. My mind is teeming with questions. I'm not sure I want the answers to all of them, but I feel compelled to ask.

"Who was my father? What was his name?" My mother would never tell me, and now I finally understand why.

"Dominic Bernard," Maybelle says. "I don't remember what clan he was with, but it was not a powerful one."

"The stars will be aligned in the same way again in just a couple of months, but they cannot find the book. I think the cult is desperate," Gerard says. "Leave with us, Olivia. We are going to go into hiding again. We can help keep you away from them."

Running away doesn't sound bad at all. If what I am gets out, and it most likely will with Maybelle under the influence of a truth potion still, I'm screwed. I don't even want to think about how Reilly might react.

"What are you going to tell the JHAPI agents?"

"Nothing," Gerard says. "We're leaving before they will have a chance to question her."

I press the heels of my hands to my eyes. "I need a minute to think. How long do I have, before you leave?"

Gerard shares a look with Maybelle.

"A few hours, at most. We have to leave well before sunset."

I take a step back toward the door. "I'm going to get coffee. I'll be back, just don't— don't leave without me."

"It's not safe for you to go anywhere by yourself," Maybelle objects, but I'm already opening the door and slipping out.

I had always known I was different and that there was something wrong with me. I walk down the hall, fighting the urge to run, barely seeing anything in front of me.

My mother had made such a big deal about me keeping what I could do a secret. I wonder if she ever intended to tell me the truth about what I am.

I slip out of the intensive care unit and hurry toward the elevators. This part of the hospital is busier. The halls are filled with worried families, new parents, and dreary people being pushed along in wheelchairs. I wind my way through them as quickly as I can without breaking out into a jog.

There is, thankfully, no one else waiting for the elevators. I press the button a few times, then watch the floors count steadily up on the left one. I stand a couple of steps back from the doors, arms crossed.

The elevator dings, and the doors open. Hawking steps off, her eyes landing on me immediately.

"Olivia, I was hoping you were still here," Hawking says, "How is she?"

I brush past her without answering and mash the door close button on the elevator without making eye contact.

Her brows pinch together, an expression of pity already forming on her face, and she steps forward.

"Olivia—"

The doors close in her face, and my stomach jerks as the elevator rushes toward the basement parking level. I lean against the wall and cover my face with my hands. I don't know what I should do. Running has always worked for me, sort of.

Zachary's hurt face nags at the back of my head. I had run without a second thought that day, and I've regretted it ever since. I wonder if Patrick would feel as betrayed.

The elevator dings, and the doors slide open. I step into the dimly lit parking garage and pull the keys from my pocket. They hadn't let me ride in the ambulance, so I had borrowed one of Javier's cars.

My footsteps echo loudly as I walk. I'm not sure where I intend on going, but I have to get out of this hospital to think.

I unlock the car and the flicker of the lights illuminate a woman standing near the trunk with her hands clasped. She's about my height, with dark brown hair. The odd part is that she's wearing long white robes.

I stop and stare at her.

"I need you to move, that's my car." My voice seems overly loud in the empty garage.

"Where are you going?" she asks in a girly voice.

"I don't know, just move."

She steps into the light and smiles at me.

"You are special, you know."

"Thanks, I guess," I say, my hand slipping into my jacket pocket for a potion that isn't there. I grit my teeth and sincerely regret my stupidity. I should have just stayed in the room with Gerard and Maybelle.

"You could be trained and given even more magic, Olivia," she says, walking toward me, hands held out to her side as though to show me she isn't holding any weapons. "We could give you anything you wanted."

"I really, really doubt that," I say, taking a step back to keep the space between us. "What the fuck do you want?"

The woman stops, a smile spreading across her face. "We want to help you."

"Help me? Is that why you kidnapped and tortured my friend? Blew up the store we were building together?" I demand, my voice rising with each word.

The smile fades from the woman's face. "She was trying to keep you from your birthright."

I snort. "You know nothing about my birth."

"I know you are the progeny of a vampire and a witch," the woman, says almost worshipfully. "You are a miracle, and you will be our salvation."

"You are insane," I say, taking a step back. "Get away from me and stay away from Maybelle, or I'll hunt you all down and kill you myself."

"You are so stubborn, Olivia. Just like your mother," the woman says with a sigh. She lifts her hand, and wind rushes past my ears, whistling through the parking garage like a freight train.

CHAPTER 18

Just like your mother.

Rage boils up in my chest, and the electric magic snaps down into my fingertips. I lift my hand, intending to annihilate her somehow, but a wall of air hits me and flings me backward.

I hit a Suburban, my head snapping back painfully against the window, but I stay conscious. The wind presses against me, impossibly strong. It tugs at my cheeks and whips my hair around my face.

The woman walks forward, one hand outstretched, not even a hint of effort showing on her face.

"You will come back with us, and you will come to understand your place in all this," she says calmly. "I wish you would come peacefully, but I'm afraid I can't take no for an answer."

"Did you kill my mother?" I ask, struggling to my arms. My voice is barely a whisper over the wind, but I know she heard me. She shakes her head and frowns.

"No, your mother killed herself with her lies," she says, her face twisting into a frown. "We could have found you so much sooner if she hadn't."

Maybelle's bloody face flashes through my mind, and I scream in anger. The pain they must have put my mother through makes me want to kill each and every one of them.

I quit pushing against the wind and simply let set my magic free. A bright orange bolt of lightning darts through the wind. The woman leaps to the side, and the blot strikes where she had been standing, melting the concrete.

I run forward, but another burst of wind hits me from the side. It lifts me from my feet, and I slam down onto the concrete sliding toward another car. Several car alarms go off, the blaring echoing through the parking garage.

I lift my hand from where I'm lying, and the magic surges up from my gut and flies from my fingertips, darting across the space like a lightning bolt. My hair stands on end as the magic strikes twice in quick succession, but the woman leaps out of the way each time.

"You won't hit me, Olivia," the woman says with a tinkling laugh. "But I could teach you how to."

I push myself up into a sitting position, panting as I try to catch my breath. Novak's magic takes so much more out of me than the others.

"Go to hell," I bark at her.

The wind shifts, pushing at me from my left side. I claw at the ground, but there is nothing for me to hold on to. The woman pulls a potion from the pocket of her robe. I don't want to find out what it is.

"Police!" Hawking's voice cuts through the garage, drawing the attention of both of us. She's striding forward, hands held by her sides, fingernails lengthening into claws. "Set the vial down carefully and back away from Olivia."

The woman snorts at Hawking and dismisses her.

"This isn't over."

A growl reverberates the area, followed by the snap of bones as Hawking shifts, her clothes simply ripping off her body as she morphs into a wolf. She howls, a sound that shakes me down to my bones and echoes painfully through the parking garage. It makes me want to run even though I know I'm not the one being hunted.

The witch's face twists into irritation, and she lifts her hand toward Hawking. The wind pushing at me stops suddenly, and I leap at her as Hawking is hit with a rush of wind.

My fist collides with her jaw, shooting pain through my hand. She stumbles back but catches me in the stomach with a kick. The next kick hits my face, and I see stars. My knees hit the floor.

Hawking leaps over me, teeth bared, but the woman is running away. Another push of wind keeps us pinned where we are, sliding slowly away from her. Hawking struggles against it, her head pushed low, but I know there's no point. I'm nauseous and angry and despite my dangerous abilities, unable to kill even one air witch, apparently.

The wind ceases suddenly, and I hear the quick slap of someone running coming from the direction of the elevators. I stay crouched on hands and knees. Hawking licks my face once, then darts off in the direction the woman ran.

Someone kneels next to me, putting their hand on my back. I look up into Brunson's worried face. I jerk away, dislodging his hand, and struggle to my feet.

"Air witch," I gasp. "Go help Hawking."

"Are you okay?"

"I'm fine! Just go!"

Brunson sprints after his partner, gun drawn.

As soon as he gets out of sight, I dash for the elevators. I hit the button several times, but the elevator doesn't open. I give up and run for the stairwell, taking the steps two at a time.

I'm gasping for breath by the time I hit floor three, but I don't stop. My legs burn and my lungs ache, but I make it up the last flight of stairs and burst out of the stairwell. I look around, trying to gain my bearings. A nurse gives me an odd look, but people are frantic in hospitals all the time.

I walk briskly down the hall I think Maybelle's room is in. I scan each door for her name and finally find it. Her door is shut, but I don't bother knocking. I push the door open, then freeze. The room is empty.

"Everything all right?"

I jump, startled, but see it's the same nurse as before, with the purple scrubs.

"Where is she?"

"What are you talking about?" he asks, brows furrowed.

"Maybelle, she's gone," I say, pointing into the room.

He pushes past me and looks into the room. When he turns back, his eyes are wide.

"You said you lost the scent," Brunson argued.

"I did, but if we get Reilly out here, he might be able to catch something I missed," Hawking says, hands on hips, staring Brunson down. "The older vampires can track better than I can. Especially in a well-trafficked area like that."

"I don't think we should involve him this early. I don't trust him," Brunson says, crossing his arms.

Hawking rolls her eyes and huffs. "You don't trust anyone."

"I trust you."

"That took a couple of years," Hawking says, smirking at him, her eyes crinkling around the edges with mirth.

Brunson grins like it's a well-worn conversation, made humorous because of the familiarity.

I rest my elbows on my knees and put my face in my hands. For once, I'm in agreement with Brunson; they should leave Reilly out of it. I'm not about to suggest that though. I also don't think

Maybelle and Gerard were kidnapped again. They just fled and left me behind. I guess I deserve this after doing it to other people so many times.

Hawking comes and plops down in the chair next to me, thumbs hooked around her belt buckle. It's a taco today. I wonder if they're all food-themed. She must keep a collection of them in her car with her extra clothes. I had expected her to have to borrow some hospital scrubs after she had busted out of her clothes with her shift, but she had come back up dressed in another suit, gaudy belt buckle in place.

"Did Maybelle say anything about who had taken her?" Hawking asks.

I lean my head back against the wall.

"She said they were insane."

Hawking barks out a laugh. "I think that's a given."

My phone buzzes. I check it absentmindedly, but the message makes my fingers tighten around my phone.

Meet us behind the Full Moon bar in two hours or we leave without you. Come alone.

"Everything all right?" Hawking asks.

"Yeah, sorry." I try to smile, but I'm sure it looks more like a grimace. "Just Johnny asking how Maybelle is. It'll be hard to break it to him that she's gone again."

Brunson's phone rings, and he answers it and Hawking goes to stand next to him to listen in. I slip my phone back into my pocket and tap my fingers restlessly against my knee.

I could stay. I could help them find the coven that killed my mother and risk everyone finding out what I am, but I don't want to live a life in servitude to the vampire council. Or the witch council. Or be killed by someone afraid I can steal their magic.

There's a chance I can find and kill this coven on my own if I get away now. I have to try that first.

I've found the easiest way to sneak away from someone is to make it look like you aren't sneaking away. Walking anywhere with confidence makes it seem like you belong, and it makes people far less likely to question you.

I stand and walk out. Hawking's eyes follow me, but she stays in the room with Brunson. I have two hours to go back to the clanhouse, get Mr. Muffins and anything that might be useful, and get to Full Moon.

I fling the front door open, startling two of the neckers who were about to open the door themselves. One is the girl Patrick had hurt. She looks much brighter now and gives me a big smile as she steps out of my way.

"Hi, Olivia," she says, her accent slightly less thick now that she isn't nervous.

"Hey…" I realize I don't actually know her name. I don't know most of their names, I've never bothered to ask. It was easier to keep them all at arm's length. I was their healer, not their friend.

"It's Abby," she says with a smirk. "And this is Jackson. He's new too."

The young man next to her extends his hand. He has blond hair and patchy scruff that doesn't suit him. I'm sure that'll be gone in a few days. Emilio has a way of cleaning them all up the first week they're here.

"Nice to meet you, Abby and Jackson," I say, shaking his hand. "I'll see you around."

I start to walk past them, but Abby puts her hand on my arm.

"Could you tell Patrick I'm really not mad next time you see him? He's been avoiding me."

"Sure," I say with a smile that doesn't reach my eyes.

I can't, and the reminder that I'll probably never see Patrick again twists in my gut, but there's nothing I can do about it. I brush past them and race upstairs.

Mr. Muffins looks up when I burst into my room, her tail twitching.

"Time to go," I mutter as I scan the room for the cat cage. It's in the corner under a few dirty towels. I throw the towels on the floor and open the cage door.

Mr. Muffins tenses, butt twitching like she's going to pounce. Her lips curl back, and she hisses at me.

"No," I say, pointing at her sternly. "There is no time for this. We have to leave."

She meows and darts into the bathroom. I run after her and slam the door shut, trapping us both inside. She hates the cat carrier, but I'm not leaving her behind. She can claw me all she wants.

I lunge, arms outstretched, and she jumps into the shower and tries to claw her way up the shower wall. I grab her with two hands, but she somehow twists and gets me with her claws and her teeth at the same time.

"You cranky bitch!" I shout while trying not to squeeze her too hard. Her soft fur makes her slippery, and she's still flailing around, clawing at everything she can reach. I grit my teeth and push the door handle down with my foot, then kick the door open.

I shove her into the cat cage and quickly slam the door shut. She attacks the door once, then curls into the back, growling continuously.

"I know you hate it," I apologize. "But I'm not leaving you behind, okay?"

Her tails whips from side to side, and she hisses at me again.

"Good talk," I say, patting the top of the cage and standing to look around the room. I can get more clothes, all I'm going to take are a few potions. Maybelle may still not be completely healed.

I grab a bag and carefully set the potions inside. I toss a couple of clean shirts in on top as well; they'll work as padding.

The gun Lydia gave me is sitting on the top of the dresser. I consider leaving it, but I may need it. I tuck it into my waistband and pull my shirt over it to hide it.

I hoist the bag onto my shoulder, then pick up Muffin's cage. Her paws poke out the holes in the door, and she meows pitifully.

"I see you have moved on to bargaining. That's not going to work either."

I check my phone. It's been almost an hour since Gerard texted me. I have another hour to get to them.

I peek my head out into the hall, which is empty. I slip out, kicking the door shut behind me with my foot and hurry toward the stairs. I get halfway down when I hear a knock on the door. I freeze, one foot hovering over the next step.

They knock again, louder this time. Leslie comes from the direction of the kitchen and sees me standing on the stairs, staring at the door. She rolls her eyes.

"You could have answered it," she says, hand already turning the doorknob.

"Leslie, wait!"

She pulls the door open.

A man with white hair and a long beard stands on the front porch, his hands clasped in front of him. He's wearing robes. Black ones with long sleeves and strange symbol embroidered on the chest.

"Can I help you?" she asks.

"Are you Olivia Carter?" he asks, smiling serenely.

"No," Leslie says, crossing her arms.

The man lifts his hand and backhands Leslie. She flies backward and lands limp in the middle of the foyer, her head cracking against the wooden floor.

The man steps inside, his eyes going straight toward me. Wind whistles through the open doorway.

CHAPTER 19

I turn and sprint back up the stairs. I don't know where to go, or if there is a way back out from up here, but I can't take two of them. I couldn't even take one of them in the parking garage, and that was with both hands free.

Mr. Muffins is banging around in her cage, partially from me running, but mostly because she's losing her shit. Wind is already whipping up the stairs behind me. I sprint toward my room, no plan other than getting a door between me and them, but the gust catches me around the shoulders and I hit the floor, hard.

The cat cage bounces a foot away, and Mr. Muffins shrieks angrily. The wind stops abruptly, and I scramble toward the cat cage, grabbing it.

A necker bursts out of one of the rooms, hair tousled, wearing yesterday's clothes. I think she's the one I saw Reilly feeding from last time. She opens her mouth to yell at me, but I don't wait for her to speak.

"Run!" I yell at her. "Wake Javier!"

I sprint down the hall, searching frantically for Reilly's room. I have no idea if he's old enough to wake during the day, but I have to try.

I open the door and see him lying in bed, completely unclothed except for a pair of silky boxers that really don't leave much to the imagination. I run to his side, shove Mr. Muffins under the bed, and shake him violently, looking over my shoulder to see if they've found me yet.

"Reilly, wake up, wake up," I whisper harshly.

His eyes twitch, but he doesn't budge. I don't have time to wait for this, and there's only one thing I can think of that might wake him. I pry his mouth open and shove my wrist into it before I can hesitate anymore. His fangs pierce my skin painfully as his jaw clamps down around my wrist.

His eyes fly open, and his hands wrap around my arm. He sucks once, hard, and it makes my knees go weak with a combination of ill-timed pleasure and fear.

"Reilly," I gasp.

He shoves my arm away from him and stares at me, breathing just as hard as I am.

"What are you—"

There's an explosion in the hallway that shakes the entire house.

"Don't make us play hide and seek, Olivia," the woman from the parking garage shouts. "You won't like our technique."

"I don't have time to explain," I say, running toward the door.

Reilly leaps out of bed and follows me, but his movements are slow and stilted.

"I will not be at my usual strength with the sun still up," he says as I put my hand on the doorknob.

"Then just run, get anyone out you can," I say before pulling the door open and stepping out to face this crazy bitch and whoever she has brought with her.

The woman is standing at the end of the hall, a man beside her who looks exactly like her, even down to the length of his hair.

They walk in sync toward me, a wide smile on her face, while his expression stays blank. The walls and carpet are scorched, whatever fire damaged them gone now.

A man with a long white beard walks behind them. A sick feeling tears through me. I recognize him from the cafe. I had forgotten it until now, but he bumped into me. He must have set the bombs.

He's wearing a black robe, which he unbuttons and drops to the floor. Underneath is a sleeveless shirt and strange, loose fitting pants that are tight at the ankle. Magic ripples down his arms, and the muscles twist and bulge. A power type, then.

He runs at me. I take a step back, but I won't be able to dodge this. The door next to me swings open, and Reilly steps out, landing a kick in the man's stomach as he gets close. It stops the man in his tracks, but he grabs Reilly and tosses him back toward the stairs.

He turns back to me, but the woman raises her hand.

"Deal with the vampire, we will handle Olivia."

Reilly struggles to his feet and smiles at the bearded man. "You're weak, old man."

"Strong enough to crush you," the man says in a deep, rumbling voice as he charges at Reilly.

I have no time to see what happens next because the witch gets my attention with a rush of wind that forces me to stumble backward.

"You will be coming with us today, Olivia," the woman says. "I'll give you this one chance to come peacefully."

"Like hell I will," I snap. I'm pretty sure I'm screwed, but I'm not going down without a fight.

The two attacking witches step forward in unison, almost as though they are dancing. The moves seem practiced, or at least familiar.

I pull the gun from my waistband and point it at her, but the woman lifts her hands and moves them like she's conducting an orchestra. Wind pummels me from every direction, and I struggle to keep my footing. The gun is ripped from my hands and flies down the hallway.

I send a single burst of electric magic toward her, but she steps out of the way without any effort. She pushes me back farther and farther until I hit the wall. Nowhere to run, no way to stop her.

The wind ceases, and she stares at me like I'm a specimen to be examined.

"The goblin told us everything," she says, walking toward me as I lean against the wall panting.

"Only because you poisoned her," I sneer.

"We can teach you, Olivia," she says earnestly, like I never spoke. "The power you could wield is amazing. You just have to have the courage to take it."

"You are out of your mind," I say, looking between her and her silent twin.

"Here's your first lesson, dodging an offensive attack."

She doesn't move, but her twin does. He lifts a hand and ball of fire hurtles toward my location. I jump to the side, tucking into a roll. Fire smashes into the spot I was just standing, burning through the sheetrock, then disappearing in a flash.

"You were born for a reason, one you don't understand yet, and one your mother and father had no way of knowing when they performed that spell."

Her twin twitches his hand, and another fireball appears out of nowhere, hurtling toward me faster than the last. I dodge again, but just barely. The smell of singed hair fills my nose.

"You could be faster, Olivia," she taunts.

Her brother lifts his hand, and I brace myself to move, but nothing happens. She smirks. I smell something burning and risk glancing behind me but still see nothing.

A breeze pushes my hair against my neck. I leap away from it on instinct, and a pillar of fire shoots down from the ceiling. The carpet curls up from the sheer heat of the fire that is intense even from a few feet away.

"Bravo, Olivia!" She claps in excitement with a bright smile. "Your potential is undeniable."

Her eyes are bright, and the smile on her face seems genuine.

"Why did you kill my mother? Just for stealing your shitty book?" I ask. The question has been weighing on me since she attacked me in the parking garage.

"I already told you, she killed herself. She told lie after lie before we could even ask her a question. She was dead within minutes, and there was nothing we could do to stop it."

"And you bribed someone to fake a death certificate?" I ask, rage building in my chest, the stolen magic sparking along my whole body.

"Yes, we had to end the searching. The case had gone cold. At the time, we thought the detective searching for her was simply trying to earn a promotion or curry favor with her coven. It was simple enough to end it quietly with a little paperwork."

I lift my hands and shove magic at both of them. Pure white crackling bolts of electricity leap from my hands and shoot across the room. The smell of ozone fills my nose.

The twin lifts his hands, and a wall of flame shoots up between us, blocking the magic I've just cast. The electricity spreads out like a net when it hits the wall of flame. The opposing magics twist together in a shower of sparks and fire. I feel the collision down to my bones; it's almost enough to bring me to my knees.

The flames suddenly grow, leaping around the net of electricity. I feel wind on my face. I push, but I don't think I can outlast them, not with both of them working together. I falter just for a moment, but their magic overwhelms mine in that instant. I'm thrown back, my head bouncing off the floor.

Stars spark across my vision, and I feel like I might throw up, but I struggle onto my knees.

"Perhaps you just need us to raise the stakes," the woman says.

She nods at her brother, and he kicks in the door next to him. My hearts drops into my stomach as I realize whose room that is.

Her twin walks out, dragging a completely unconscious Patrick by his arm.

"Get away from him," I say, my hands curling into fists and my magic surging up inside of me again. I won't let them hurt him. With shaking legs, I rise to my feet.

"Oh, is this one a friend?" the woman asks, tilting her head. "That makes it so much better."

The twin drops Patrick's arm, and they both step away from him.

"Come and get him, Olivia. See if you can save your friend before Logan turns him to ash."

She lifts her hand, and I sprint toward Patrick. Flames are already rushing toward him, and her twin, Logan, has a strange expression on his face bordering on glee. I reach in my pocket and grab the potion I've been saving for the right moment. This is it.

I wrap my hand around Patrick's arm and throw the potion with my other hand. The vial shatters on the floor right in front of the rushing flames which disappear in a pop, fizzling out with no oxygen to fuel them.

I drag Patrick with me, running backward as fast as I can. Oxygen rushes back into the area, and the flames charge toward us once again. I grit my teeth and raise my hands and *push*. I don't hold anything back.

My magic collides with Logan's once again, but I don't falter this time. The woman's magic joins his, battering against the sparking net of electric magic that is barely holding back the flames. Inch by inch, they push forward. I stand over Patrick, who is still dead asleep, and hold my ground. But I know I won't be able to last forever.

I hear a door open and slow steps. I glance back and see it's Javier. He stumbles down the hall, his eyes half-open, using the wall to support him. He stops directly behind me.

My arms are shaking. My magic is draining out of me like a river while Logan only seems to be growing stronger with his sister feeding the flames.

Javier can barely stand. He won't be able to help; he can't even drag Patrick away.

"Javier, feed me," I gasp out. "I need your magic."

He looks at me, eyes widening.

"Please," I beg. "I can't hold much longer."

Javier squares his shoulder, then bites down on his own wrist.

"Drink…Olivia…" he whispers as she reaches around and holds his wrist in front of my mouth.

I sink my teeth into his wrist and drink. I give into the dark, hungry thing inside of me. The part that has ached for more since the first time I stole magic.

The magic that keeps Javier alive is different from a witch's magic. It's cold and forceful, almost sentient. It's very much like the thing inside of me. I want it.

Lydia must have told him about her suspicions. I'll be upset later, but for now I just want to survive. I pull it inside of me, letting the cold magic curl up around the fading electricity inside of me. I take and I take, wishing I could just rip it from him like I did Novak.

Javier shudders and sags against me. I can see the limits of his power fast approaching. I rip my teeth from his arm before I'm tempted to take even more. Blood drips down my chin, and I lick my lips, aching for every drop.

The electric magic is still wavering, almost completely drained from me, but there is another kind of power surging through me now. I send one last push of magic against the wall of flame, then charge forward.

My legs pump faster than they ever have. Wind whistles past my ears, and it seems like everything slows down around me. The flames move like butterfly wings, lazy and slow, as I run straight through them. The fire witch's face doesn't register shock until I'm already in front of him, my fist connecting with his jaw with a crunch.

His eyes roll back in his head as he flies backward, slamming into a door frame with a loud thunk. His sister screeches and turns on me, but I dart to the side of her gust of wind. I kick her knee, bone popping and cracking as it gives way. She falls to the side, and I punch her in the side of the head. Pain shoots through my hand.

She goes down on one knee but punches me in the stomach. I grunt in pain but block the second punch, catching her wrist.

"There's so much you don't understand," she says, looking up at me with wide eyes.

"I don't care," I say, shoving her back and kicking her in the side of the head. She flops to the ground, unconscious.

Javier is dragging himself across the floor, teeth bared, toward Patrick, who is still lying prone in the hallway. Patrick's eyes are twitching, but he still can't wake up.

I spot the gun the air witch had tossed away from me earlier and grab it. The metal is still hot to the touch. I stand over her, thinking of my mother's laugh, and the way she smiled as she taught me to brew with the magic I had stolen from her.

I could reach down and steal this woman's magic. Turn her inside out and take everything. But I don't want any part of her in me alongside my mother's magic. She is filth in comparison.

I pull the trigger. The sound deafens me as the bullet rips through her head. Her body twitches, and stills. I walk over to her brother, his eyes flutter open just in time to widen as I point the gun at him as well. I barely hear this shot, my ears still ringing from the first.

I walk into the hallway, my blood pumping, my anger and my hunger unsatisfied. The slide is locked back on the gun, it's out of bullets. I drop it and walk toward the stairs when I hear a crash.

Reilly flies into the front door, cracking it on impact. He struggles to his feet, but his movements are sluggish. The sun still hasn't set.

The witch runs forward. Reilly's shoulders are slumped, and he's blinking like he can't quite see. I could let the witch kill him. I could just run away.

Instead, I dart downstairs, everything slowing again. The bearded man is running at Reilly. I step into his path and punch him in the chest. I feel his sternum crack. He grunts and coughs, blood splattering my face.

I swing again, but he blocks the punch this time. He's insanely strong. Stronger than me still, but I'm faster. I punch over and over again, driving him backward.

He misses a block, and I wrap my hand around his throat. Summoning the last of the electric magic, I send a surge of it through him. His muscles all contract at once, and he falls to the ground, unconscious.

I stand there, panting and shaking, drained. I can't help looking back at Reilly. He's watching me with a smile on his face.

CHAPTER 20

He rolls up onto his feet, showing little of the previous exhaustion.

"When Patrick told me you had used Finding magic, I thought he was lying, trying to throw me off with some half-baked plan. Lydia though, she I believed."

"What are you talking about?" My mouth feels strange as I talk. Something sharp pricks at the inside of my mouth. I prod it gently with my tongue and find a fang. Smaller than a vampire's, but definitely there.

I dig my nails into my palm to keep from reacting, but I'm sure my heart is going crazy. I can almost hear it.

"The welts on your arm. The way you found Patrick when no one else could, and Aaron Hall turns up unable to cast the simplest of Finding spells." He stalks toward me, the glow of the sun setting in a riot of reds and oranges visible through the windows behind him. "The electric magic that sparks on your fingertips every time you get angry."

I step backward, edging around the bearded man's prone figure.

"The healing magic was the first hint. As soon as I started paying attention, the rest became so, painfully, obvious," Reilly finishes with a smile that makes heat stir in my gut and fear twist in my chest. I am one hundred percent fucked.

"So what now, you're going to drag me to the council? Or are you just going to kill me?" My muscles tense, ready for the slightest move even though I know he's far too fast for me to defend against.

"Not the council, not yet. My sire will meet you first."

Reilly crouches down by the bearded man, takes his head and twists. His necks cracks sickeningly as it breaks.

"Why did you kill him? We could have questioned him—"

"He was a loose end," Reilly says, wiping his hands on his pants as he stands. "You're mine now, Olivia. I don't want anyone else knowing what you can do until I am ready."

"I'm not going anywhere with you," I bite out, my hands shaking at my side. "I'll die first."

It's barely dawn, Reilly could still be weak. I shift on my feet, trying to decide if I can move fast enough to kill him. I blink, and he is pushing me back against the wall, his body warm against mine and face inches away. He wraps his hands around my wrists and holds me still.

"You can't kill me, Olivia," he breathes. "If you try, I'll make sure you regret it."

"I doubt that," I growl at him, struggling against his grip. Javier's power is still pulsing through me, but all my other magic is drained.

Reilly grins, all teeth. "You will cooperate, or I will kill every single member of this clan, down to the last necker."

Over his shoulder, I see Patrick standing on the top of the stairs, tears slipping out of his eyes. He mouths, *I'm sorry*, and slips back down the hallway.

I had hoped I would never live to see this day come. Every

warning my mother gave me is ringing in my head. I can almost see her out of the corner of my eye, saying, *I told you so*. I let people get too close. I let them see too much.

I have to find a way to get away from Reilly, and I will. Even if it means killing him. It will be hard though, especially with the lives of everyone I care about hanging in the balance. Anger at them, and at myself, is swirling through me. I don't know how to feel, but I know I'm not willing to let them die, even if they have betrayed me. I should have run while I could.

Reilly steps away from me, but I stay pressed against the wall.

"Pack enough for a week. We're leaving early. I'll have Javier send the rest of your things to my clanhouse."

Brunson and Hawking burst into the house, guns drawn. They take in the destruction. Leslie's too still body, and the bearded man lying in the foyer.

"There are two more bodies upstairs. They're part of some kind of cult," I say hoarsely.

Hawking holsters her gun and sprints upstairs. Brunson hesitates, eyes flicking between me and Reilly.

"Everything all right?" he asks, finger on the trigger of his gun.

Zachary knows me well, too well I suppose. He senses the tension that Hawking didn't. Reilly looks back at me, and I know there's only one answer I can give that won't result in Zachary's death. I've been wrong a lot recently, but I was right about one thing. Reilly did find a way to steal my soul.

"Everything's fine," I say, gesturing to the chaos around us. "Just peachy."

Brunson huffs out a chuckle. "I see your point."

I can hear Hawking talking upstairs, saying something to Javier in soothing tones. I look up, brows pinched together. I shouldn't be able to hear that. I guess I took more from Javier than just speed and strength.

"Did they say if they had taken Maybelle again?" Brunson asks.

"They didn't," I say, lifting my shoulder in a half-shrug. "She and Gerard ran away. They asked me to go with them, but I couldn't get to them in time."

"You were going to run?" Brunson asks confused. "Why?"

I wrap my arms around myself. "They were obviously targeting me. I just wanted to keep everyone out of harm's way."

"You could have told someone!" Brunson says, voice rising, but not quite to a shout as he shoves his gun back into the holster on his side. "We could have helped you, or even prevented this."

Javier chooses that moment to walk downstairs, followed closely by Hawking. He heads straight for Leslie, ignoring us. He scoops her up, careful to support her head, then turns to Reilly.

"Will you help me turn her?"

The room quiets as we all look to Reilly for his response.

"If I do, she must return to my clan. I will be her sire."

Javier nods, but his face falls. He cared for Leslie, depended on her. I know this is my fault. If I hadn't taken so much, he could have turned her himself.

Reilly walks toward the parlor, motioning for Javier to follow. Hawking, Brunson, and I stay in the foyer. Watching would feel like intruding.

"I need to call this in," Hawking says.

Brunson nods. "Go ahead."

Hawking steps outside, phone to her ear.

Brunson looks at me.

"I know it isn't much comfort right now, but we have solid information on Martinez. We can find the rest of this cult too. We won't let this happen again."

He's so earnest, just like the Zachary I knew growing up.

"Reilly said I'd be helping with some raids. Where are we going first?"

"Arizona."

The land of cactus, desert, and scorpions.

"Sounds great," I mutter, slipping down the wall.

I can still feel Reilly's hands around my wrists, trapping me. I rub at them, but there's no escaping the shit I've gotten myself into. Not this time.

PART III
BLOOD MAGIC

CHAPTER 1

The movers are wearing crisp gray uniforms. They have the truck almost completely packed with boxes. I pull my jacket a little tighter around me; it's chilly this evening.

I'm going to miss this house. It was just a rental, but I had felt like it was home, even if it did have rats under the porch and no central heating or cooling. Having it taken away like this is humiliating. At least I didn't have to pay to fix all the damage. Reilly did that when he broke my lease for me.

I turn and watch the sun disappear in a wash of golds and oranges. It's not quite six pm, according to the clock at least. Daylight Savings Time is such a joke.

The heavy weight of exhaustion that has been bothering me all day dissipates as it sinks below the horizon. Twilight turns to darkness, but I can still see every detail of the trees that surround my house. Javier's magic stirs inside of me with relief.

"Ma'am?" one of the movers asks hesitantly.

I turn around.

"What?" My tone is a little harsh, and the guy looks nervous, a bead of sweat forming on his forehead.

"Mr. Walsh said you would need to select a week's worth of clothes for us to pack separately. Would you mind doing that now?"

I rub my hands over my face so I don't snap at the mover. His heart is hammering loudly in his chest, and it's distracting, though I am relieved to find I don't have any urge to bite him.

"Sure, lead the way," I say, shoving my hands in my jacket pockets.

He walks back inside, leaving the door open behind him.

I follow slowly. I haven't been inside since I came here with Lydia and found the house was trashed. The graffiti on the outside of the house has already been stripped off and repainted. The smell of bleach and other cleaners burn my nose as I step inside.

The cabinets are empty. The mess of food and glass has been cleaned out of the kitchen. The window in the living room is fixed, and a shiny new AC unit has replaced the old one. The couch and broken coffee table are gone.

The mover stands awkwardly in my bedroom door until I follow him into the room. My clothes are all hanging on a rack. Anything that can't be hung is set in neat piles on the bed. A suitcase is lying open on the floor to my left.

I grab things off the rack and throw them in the suitcase. I barely see what I'm grabbing. My skin is crawling with anger, and my gums ache, fangs pricking at the inside of my lips as my control begins to slip.

I want to set it all on fire and run, but I can't. Reilly would wipe out the clan, and he'd probably kill me too when he inevitably tracked me down. I hate him. I hate someone else having this kind of control over me. I wish I didn't care.

My phone buzzes. I glance at the screen; it's Lydia again. I reject the call and shove the phone in my back pocket.

"So, uh, is that everything you'd like?" the mover asks, his voice quaking.

"Yeah, that's it," I say before turning and stomping out of the room.

Reilly had insisted I come here this morning with no explanation, and while I had wanted to refuse just because he had insisted, I had wanted to say goodbye to this place. I'm not sure it's helping though. It doesn't feel like closure; it feels like I'm losing it all over again.

When I get in the car, I'm tempted all over again to just drive off and never look back. Instead, I drive to the clanhouse. I want to see Patrick before I go. I want to know why he betrayed me.

There is a plain white van parked in the driveway I don't recognize. There isn't any writing on the side. I park Javier's car in the garage, then walk around to the front door and knock loudly.

A moment later, the door opens and Emilio steps aside to let me in without a word. His face is paler than usual, and his mouth is locked in a frown. The house is quiet, as if no one is here tonight.

"Good morning, Emilio," I say out of habit.

He doesn't respond. I shove my hands in my pockets.

"Where is Javier?"

"In his room, recovering," Emilio says, casting an accusing glance at me.

"I wasn't trying to hurt him," I say through gritted teeth.

"But you did," Emilio says, whirling around. "You hurt him, and now you have taken Leslie from us. The clan is weak because of you."

I step closer to him, my new fangs popping down as rage and hunger stir in my gut. I can practically smell the magic inside of Emilio. It's less powerful than what I took from Javier, but I still want it.

"None of this is my fault," I growl. "If anything, Javier betrayed me."

Emilio growls back and curls his lips up to reveal his own fangs.

"Javier should never have hired you."

"Enough," a voice rasps from above us. I don't think I would have been able to hear it without vampire magic coursing through me. Javier is standing by the banister, shoulders drooping, and his face gaunt like he's been starved. "Olivia, please come upstairs."

I brush past Emilio, keeping my eyes on him until I'm halfway up the stairs. Javier's knuckles are white where he grips the banister, barely able to support himself. He stares at me, something flickering in his eyes I don't understand.

I offer him my arm. He slips his hand through and clings to my bicep as I help him back to his room. The lights are all off, but a fire is flickering in the fireplace in the corner. I've never seen it used before.

He sits down on his bed, panting slightly from the effort of walking.

"I didn't know it would be this bad," I whisper. "In the past, it hasn't—I haven't done this on purpose very often. I'm sorry."

"Don't apologize. You saved Patrick, again, and defended yourself. I would not have let you take my power if I was unwilling to deal with the consequences," Javier says, attempting a cheeky grin.

I walk over to the chair Javier normally sits in and plop down, resting my elbows on my knees. A heavy silence settles between us. I'm not sure if I want to offer more apologies, or accusations.

"How long have you suspected there was something different about me?" I ask.

"Since the day I heard you healed the necker in the cafe," Javier says hoarsely. "On Lydia's advice, I reported it to the council, which has gained me the status I had been looking for. I sold the idea of hiring you to them by saying it was an experiment."

Javier sighs and crosses one leg over the other.

"The news spread surprisingly quickly, and someone from Reilly's clan contacted me within a couple of weeks of your hire date."

"Good to know I had been sold out from the very beginning," I say, my voice thick with exhaustion.

Javier smiles wanly. "There is a lot I misunderstood about your situation. I don't think I would have done anything differently even if I had known though."

I look up sharply. I expected at least some remorse.

"I know you will not, and cannot, accept this right now," Javier says in a whisper. "But there was no one else who would be able to protect you like they will. This will be for the best in the long run."

"For the best?" I sneer. "That's easy for you to say when you aren't the one being forced to serve the whims of a psychotic vampire."

Javier is silent. His heartbeat is still even and quiet. I hate that he isn't as angry as I am.

"Reilly can protect you."

"He's using me," I hiss at Javier. He has barely any magic left in him, but I still want it. My hands curl into fists, and my gums ache. I could rip it all out and wipe that smug expression off his face.

"You're hungry," Javier muses, the ghost of a smile playing at his lips.

"What?"

"You're craving magic like I crave blood." His eyes search my face. "I've sired dozens of vampires. I know the look."

"You don't know anything about what I'm dealing with," I snap. "No one does."

"Perhaps not," Javier says, leaning further back into the pillows. "But Reilly could help you figure it out. Help you control it."

"Reilly is concerned with only one person, and that is himself." I turn and walk toward the door. I don't want to hear anything else from Javier.

"Patrick left because he didn't agree with my cooperation with Reilly. It's part of why we argued."

I stop, my hand gripped tightly around the doorknob, wanting this part to be true.

"He cares about you, Olivia. Very much."

Mr. Muffins pads out of Javier's bathroom. The door handle

bites into my palm, and my heart clenches with guilt. I had forgotten about her. Hadn't even considered what would happen to her now that I was leaving.

"I'll take care of her, I promise," Javier says.

I open the door and walk into the hall and slam it behind me. Of course I have to leave behind her too.

Patrick is leaning against the wall by the door. His arms are crossed, and he's staring hard at the floor. I take a few steps past him, then pause. I don't know what to say to Patrick either, but I do know it's nothing like the apologies I offered Javier. I'd rather punch Patrick.

"Reilly already knew what you could do," Patrick says as he stares at his feet. "He said I could either help him learn more about you, or he could just go ahead and kill you."

"Then you should have told me," I say, turning halfway back around to face him. "You could have warned me somehow."

"He was always listening, and if you had disappeared, he would have blamed me whether it was my fault or not. He would have destroyed the entire clan. I couldn't risk them all for—" He bites down on his cheek. "I couldn't risk them all."

"I risked everything for you," I say quietly.

Patrick runs his fingers roughly through his hair.

"I'm sorry," he says, taking a step toward me.

"Don't apologize," I snap. "Don't talk to me ever again."

The coven had threatened me and the clan, and I had risked my greatest secret to protect Patrick. I don't understand how easily they gave up. Reilly isn't all-powerful. In their position, I would have found a way. I should run and let the clan deal with the consequences.

I pause at the top of the stairs and glance back at Patrick. He is slumped down on the floor, his head in his hands. I squeeze my eyes shut for a moment, then go to look for Reilly.

CHAPTER 2

There are two strange vampires standing on either side of the door to the parlor with their arms crossed. They are wearing matching expensive black suits with a red sigil sewn into the lapel, but other than that, they are a study in opposites.

The one on the right has sandy blond hair tied back at the nape of his neck and looks like a Viking. His broad shoulders are testing the limits of his suit jacket. The one on the left has intricate tattoos that are barely darker than the skin on his face. There is more ink visible than skin, and the designs are in the negative space. It's striking.

They're both staring at me as I approach. The one on the left sniffs the air, then relaxes slightly.

"Mr. Walsh will be done in a moment, Ms. Carter," he says in a deep voice. There is a hint of an accent, but he speaks well and easily.

I come to a stop a few feet away from them.

"Who are you, and why are you here?" I ask, crossing my arms and looking at the door behind them suspiciously.

"We are Reilly's clanmates. He requested that we care for Leslie while he completes his duties."

"Are you taking her somewhere?"

Tattoo inclines his head. "Yes, but you do not need to worry about your friend. She is our clanmate now, she will not be mistreated."

I scoff. "Sure."

The door cracks open, and Reilly slips out, tugging the sleeve of his dark blue button-down shirt back down over his wrist. His suit jacket is slung over his other arm.

"Olivia, I didn't expect you to be done packing so soon," Reilly says with a satisfied smile, his cheeks dimpling. "I thought you might drag your feet."

"Well, here I am," I say drily. "How is Leslie?"

"She is sleeping as her body adapts to the changes. It will be successful though. I was able to turn her in time," he says as he pulls his jacket back on.

I scuff my boot on the ground and release a breath I didn't realize I was holding. "Good."

Reilly nods toward each of his men. "Take Leslie home."

The Viking claps his hand on Reilly's shoulder. "We will keep the new one safe. Good luck on your travels, brother."

Tattoo and Viking go into the room, and Reilly strides toward me.

"We need to leave now, or we won't make it to Phoenix before sunrise."

"We're driving all the way there tonight?" I ask, falling into step beside him.

"Yes, we need to meet up with the JHAPI agents tomorrow. They won't wait for us if we are late."

As we reach the front door, I notice Patrick hovering at the top of the stairs. I ignore him. The betrayal still stings, even if he does claim he was trying to protect me. I hadn't trusted anyone for so long. It figures that as soon as I do, they all turn out to either be terrorists or liars.

I pull the door shut behind me a little more firmly than necessary. Reilly glances back with a raised brow.

"You're in a great mood," he comments.

I roll my eyes at him.

"Of course I am. Why wouldn't I be? I've always wanted to drive to Arizona with a vampire that is blackmailing me into helping him. It was on my bucket list."

"You have a strangely specific bucket list," Reilly says, ignoring my sarcasm.

I shove my hands in my pockets. "Are we going or what?"

He waves his hand toward a sleek, black sedan parked in the driveway. "After you."

I brush past him and yank the front passenger door open. The seats are leather, and it smells like a new car. I pull the door shut behind me and try to find a comfortable position to sit. I don't know how long the drive to Arizona is. It has to be less than eleven hours, or we'll run into the sunrise. Either way, I'm in for a long night.

He puts the car in drive and speeds out of the driveway. I tighten my seatbelt over my lap. His driving hasn't gotten any better.

"You were a bit harsh toward Javier and Patrick," Reilly comments.

I whip my head around to face him. "Are you kidding me right now?"

Reilly shrugs. "No, simply voicing my opinion."

"On a private conversation you had no right to listen to in the first place," I say with clenched teeth.

"I'm not very concerned with your privacy," he says, smiling.

"Ah, of course not," I mutter. "And it's not harsh to be pissed at a friend for betraying you."

"Javier is your employer, not your friend," Reilly says slowly, as if I'm stupid.

"He was both," I say back just as slowly, mocking him. I worked for Javier, but Reilly wasn't there when Javier was begging me for help. Javier cared about me; it just turned out he cared about himself more. Patrick has no excuses at all.

"You weren't in his clan. He doesn't have any obligation to protect you."

I snort. "I didn't have any obligation either, but when it came down to it, I protected him and helped him."

"That's your problem, Olivia. You do more than you need to for people," he says as he shifts into a lower gear to speed around a semi-truck. "You wouldn't have a felony on your record if you hadn't gone back for that hurt cop when you were first arrested. The council wouldn't have found out about your abnormalities if you hadn't healed that necker in the cafe. Javier was using you from the beginning, but you helped him the with NWR issue. Everyone is always trying to use you, and for all your bluster about not letting anyone control you, you do let them."

"I help my friends. Only you could make that sound like a bad thing," I say, settling back into the seat and crossing my arms.

"I'm not trying to talk you out of it," Reilly says with a shrug. "It makes what I have to do so much easier."

I glare at him. The window is down, and his auburn hair is whipping around his face. He looks completely carefree, and I suppose he is. He's getting his way. I'm the one getting screwed.

"And what exactly is it that you want?" I ask. "If you just wanted to hunt down NWR members, there are easier ways. I'm not that much of an asset."

Reilly turns his head just enough to see my face. "I want to see what you can do."

"There are still easier ways," I mutter.

"This way is more efficient," he says, accelerating again. "Besides, you do best under pressure."

An uncomfortable silence falls. I have to be missing something. If he wants to see what I can do, then he has plans for me beyond this. Or even worse, perhaps his sire does.

"Have you attempted to Find Gerard or Maybelle yet?" Reilly asks.

The welts on my arm ache even thinking about it. "No."

"Why not?"

"There's no point. I don't want to know where they are. You'd just use them against me somehow."

Reilly grins. "I guess I can't argue with that."

"Are you going to try to find them somehow?"

"Not if you tell me what Maybelle told you about your birth."

I pinch the bridge of my nose between my thumb and forefinger and take a deep breath to keep from lashing out.

"If you know so much about me, you can just figure it out yourself."

"What about a trade again? Question for a question," Reilly retorts.

"And why should I believe you won't just lie to me?"

"You can tell now," he says, putting his hand on his chest. "I suspect you'll be able to hear it."

"That's bullshit, and you know it."

"Do you want to test it?"

I sigh in irritation but nod. Maybe if I prove him wrong, he'll shut up about it.

"Ask me a question. Something obvious so you can hear what it sounds like when I tell the truth. Just remember to listen very carefully to my heartbeat."

I tuck my hair behind my ears and cock my head to the side. I think my hearing must not be quite as good as his because I can barely hear it over the rumble of the engine and the tires flying over the road. It's there though, a faint and steady thump, *ba-thump, ba-thump*.

"Is the sky blue?"

"Yes," he says. His heartbeat stays the same.

"Is it currently nighttime?"

"Yes," he says. *Ba-thump. Ba-thump.*

"Are you a werewolf?"

He chuckles. "No."

"Are you an NWR member?"

"Yes," he says. His heartbeat thumps slightly faster and takes a moment to slow back down. There are no other signs he's telling anything but the truth. He isn't sweating or twitching. There's no reason for him to be nervous though.

"This is too easy. How do I know your heartbeat isn't speeding up because you're amused?"

"So you think I'm an NWR member now?" Reilly asks, grinning as his fangs descend.

"That's not what I mean, and you know it."

"Then you'll just have to trust me."

"Of course." I sigh deeply.

"How did your mother conceive you?"

"Magic," I say, waggling my fingers at him.

He sneers at me. "You're not funny."

"I'm hilarious. Did you already know about my parentage before you came to town?"

"No," he says. His heartbeat ticks faster, just slightly, but enough to make my stomach twist. He was toying with me from the beginning and taunting me when he forced me to go to the coven.

"I thought you said you weren't going to lie?" I snap.

"I thought you said you didn't believe my heartbeat could give away a lie?"

I consider opening the car door and throwing myself into a ditch. Death isn't so bad. Probably.

"Why are we doing any of this?"

"My sire saw fit to assign me to get as close to shutting down the NWR as possible. The best way to do that is by using the resources already in place to hunt them down. JHAPI was more than happy to accept my help and yours."

"Do they know what I can do?"

"The team lead does. The others will find out. We don't have the luxury of keeping that a secret in the middle of a fight. I did tell you I needed to see what you can do."

"You don't think they're going to want to lock me up?"

"I wouldn't allow them to."

I scoff. "So you're above the law?"

"Absolutely," he agrees. "So keep that in mind if you decide you think they could help you escape our partnership."

The threat steals away the comfort I had slipped into despite the bickering. It's so easy to forget what Reilly is. He's charming and attractive, but he's not my friend or anything else. He's my jailer. His heartbeat is beating slightly faster, but so is mine. It's strange to be able to hear it. He looks calm, but the thump of his heart betrays his irritation.

I tap my hand impatiently against the counter as Reilly checks in. We'll be in an interior room, of course, since Reilly is a vampire.

Most newer hotels have two types of rooms. They'll have the usual rooms, ones with windows and direct outside access, but they'll also have interior rooms with no windows and doors that very carefully block out the light. Twenty-four-hour check-in is also absolutely necessary. They'll let anyone book the interior rooms, no questions asked, but everyone knows they're meant for the vampires.

Reilly hands over a credit card for the reservation.

"How many keys would you like?" the hotel clerk asks. She's smiling at him and blinking so much, she looks like she might be having a seizure.

"Two keys," he says with a flirtatious smile.

The girl glances at me and frowns. I don't think she had noticed I existed before just now.

"Sure thing," she says, her smile returning.

She activates both the cards and hands them to Reilly, who lifts his suitcase and heads toward the elevators. I trail behind him, annoyed that we have to share a room.

The elevator arrives immediately. There aren't many people up this time of the morning.

"You couldn't have gotten me my own room?" I ask as we step inside.

"It's much easier to keep an eye on you this way," Reilly says, unapologetic.

The elevator opens onto the sixth floor. The room is about halfway down the hall. Reilly slips his key card in and opens the door, waving me inside.

There are two beds at least. It's a nicer hotel than I've ever been in. The walls are painted a nice, neutral shade of gray instead of being plastered with dingy wallpaper. The carpet is plush and looks clean.

I toss my bag on the bed farthest from the door and sit on the end. The room smells like people and old socks. I guess no amount of cleaning can get the scent of the last hundred guests out.

I flop back onto the bed, but that only makes the odors waft up around me. I stand up and pull my shirt up over my nose so I can breathe better-smelling air for a moment.

Reilly raises an eyebrow at me. I cross my arms and glare at him.

"It stinks."

He sniffs the air. "It's usually much worse. You'll get used to it. Just ignore it until then."

I stalk toward the bathroom, muttering unkind things about vampires I hope he is listening to. It has a shower and a clawfoot bathtub I'll definitely be taking advantage of tonight.

I glance at my watch. It's only ten minutes until sunrise now.

Reilly certainly cut our arrival close. He has proved he can be awake during the day, but I doubt he can stand direct sunlight without burning at least a little. I turn to walk back to my bed and realize he's stripping out of his clothes in the middle of the room without any warning whatsoever. He lays his suit jacket, then shirt on the bed neatly. The muscles in his back ripple as he moves. It's mesmerizing. The scars that crisscross his skin are more interesting though. He turns around slowly, but my eyes don't snap back up to his face until I realize he's unbuckling his belt.

"See something you like?" he asks, smirking.

"No," I say, rolling my eyes. My heart is beating fast enough that I can hear it faintly.

"Lie," Reilly whispers.

I walk quickly past him and grab my bag, then retreat into the bathroom. I hate vampires.

I turn the tap in the bathtub on. The water comes out hot, steam rising as it hits the cool tub. The running water drowns out the rustle of clothes and the quick beat of his heart. I might be attracted to Reilly, but I'm not stupid enough to let it go anywhere. I get suckered by shitty men often enough. I'm not going to start something with someone who is literally out to ruin my life.

I dump my clothes on the floor and climb into the hot water. It makes my feet sting, but I don't wait to adjust to the temperature; I just grit my teeth and sit down. After another few minutes, the bathtub is full and the hot water is slowly relaxing my sore muscles. I still have bruises from getting thrown down the hallway several times by the witches that attacked the clanhouse.

More salve would be great, but I don't have what I need to brew it anymore. I tap my fingers against the edge of the tub. Perhaps I can talk Reilly into acquiring it for me under the guise of seeing what I can do, or whatever it is he's after. It's probably not worth it though.

Lethargy steals over me, and my eyelids slip shut. I shake myself and scoot back up, but I want nothing more than to sleep.

Dawn was hard for me yesterday as well. The first couple of hours after sunrise seem to be the worst. It probably doesn't help that I was up half the day and the entire night as well. I grab the soap and scrub my arms down first. As much as I don't want to sleep anywhere near Reilly, I can't afford to exhaust myself. When I get tired, I get stupid, and that's dangerous around him.

I finish bathing and slip down into the water until the only things still sticking out are my eyes and nose. I shut my eyes and listen to myself breathe for a few moments, then sit up, water dripping into my eyes from my hair. I wipe it away and climb out.

It's cold out of the water, so I dry off and redress quickly. I didn't pack any pajamas, so I'll have to sleep in my jeans. I'm not even going to consider the alternative.

I open the door as quietly as I can and peek out. Reilly is lying in bed, perfectly still. He doesn't look up or acknowledge me at all as I pad across the carpet to my bed. I slide between the covers, my legs still slightly damp. I put my back to the door and stare at him. He's facing me as well, his face slack and his breathing slow and even. I wonder, just for a moment, if I could kill him while he slept. His eyes pop open like he can read my mind. I grit my teeth and force myself to shut my own.

CHAPTER 3

I slap my alarm off and curl into a sitting position, my elbows resting on my knees. The sun is still up, but it's going to set in about twenty minutes. I push the heels of my hands into my eyes, then push the covers back and crawl out of bed. I grab my duffel of clothes and head to the bathroom.

I change into my nicest pair of jeans and a flannel shirt. This is as fancy as I can manage for meeting the JHAPI agents today. I wasn't paying that much attention when I was packing. I yawn and rub my hands up and down my face again. I hate this lethargy. I wish I hadn't taken Javier's magic in moments like this, but I didn't really have a choice at the time. I had no idea how it was going to change me.

I dip my hands under the faucet and splash the ice-cold water on my face. It wakes me up a little more, but I won't feel completely myself until the sun sets. I look up into the mirror and freeze, my heart clenching in my chest.

There's someone standing behind me. I stare at her reflection, afraid to move. My mother is dead. I know that. She can't be here.

But she is standing right behind me, staring at me with her finger pressed to her lips like she's quieting me.

The door flies open, the lock splintering. Reilly fills the doorway with his fangs bared and his hands curled into fists. I stumble back, my hands just barely coming up in time to prevent the splintered wood from hitting me in the face.

"What happened?" Reilly demands.

The bathroom is empty other than me. I whirl around and look into the mirror again, but all I see is my own reflection.

"Olivia," Reilly says, his fingers wrapping around my arm. His fangs are still extended, and his grip is too tight. "What is wrong with you?"

I lower my eyes and swallow thickly. "Nothing. I'm fine."

"Liar," he says, his eyes searching for an injury. "Is it the welts hurting again?"

"Just a bad dream, all right?" I say, hurrying past him toward the bathroom. "I'm fine."

"If it was a bad dream, your heart would have been racing when you woke up, not five minutes later," he retorts, following me out of the bathroom.

"Just let it go," I snap as I toss my bag back on the bed.

Reilly rolls his eyes. "You reacted like you were in danger. Something isn't right. You aren't leaving here until you explain what's going on."

"Why do you care?" I ask, hands clenched into fists at my side. "I haven't tried to run away. I'm cooperating. You don't need to know every thought that passes through my head."

"I need to know if you're about to do something stupid so I can talk some sense into you."

I cross my arms, wincing at the sting. "Well, I wasn't about to do anything. So don't worry about it."

Reilly's lip curls up in anger, and he opens his mouth to say something else, but a knock at the door interrupts.

"It's Agent Hawking," Reilly says instead.

I wrench open the door and plaster on a smile. Her suit is slightly rumpled, and her bright blue eyes have bags under them. Her belt buckle is a native Saguaro cactus today.

"Good morning, Hawking," I say with false cheer.

She raises a brow at me. "If you're going to be that perky, I'm going to need coffee immediately."

"Coffee sounds great," I say in a much calmer tone.

"Also, call me Elise," she says. "The whole last name thing annoys me, and we're going to be working together closely."

"Noted," I say.

"You both ready?" Hawking asks, looking at us.

"I have to run an errand before the meeting. I'll see you there," Reilly says dismissively.

I glance back, suspicious. I notice a piece of the door is visible from where we are standing and edge a little to the left to block her view of it. Elise doesn't seem to have noticed though.

Elise nods once, her long hair swinging around her face. "You have the address?"

"Yes," Reilly says.

"All right, let's go get coffee for everyone," Hawking says, patting me on the shoulder.

I follow her out of the room. We walk to the elevators silently, then pause in uncomfortable silence in front of the closed doors. She taps the button and glances at me.

"So, is that a thing?" she asks, twirling her finger between me and the room.

"No," I say sharply before clearing my throat. "Never has been, never will be."

"Is the council just trying to save money on hotel rooms or something?" Hawking asks with a raised brow.

"Something like that," I say as I shove my hands in my pockets.

The skeptical expression stays on her face. I guess she wouldn't make it very far as a JHAPI agent if she couldn't tell those were bullshit answers.

"That's why I'm always stuck in a room with Zachary," she says with a shrug. "He snores so much. I've thought about putting in a request for a new partner just to escape that."

I laugh. "He does snore, and he doesn't think he does, so he won't try to fix it."

The elevator dings, and she steps inside with a groan. "I might smother him one day."

"I'm sure the jury will acquit you," I say solemnly.

The elevator carries us down to the parking garage in the basement, another thing most hotels offer for the vampires. If it can't be in the basement, they always have some kind of completely enclosed parking area.

Elise drives a standard black sedan. I open the door and go to sit down, but there is a pile of paper and old ketchup packets in the passenger seat.

"Oh, just toss all that in the back seat," she says, grabbing a couple of handfuls and throwing them behind her. I scoop up all the rest and move it to the back of the car, which is also a huge mess, before sliding into my seat.

"Have you ever been to Phoenix before?" she asks.

"No, I hadn't ever left Texas before this." I shrug.

"It's too bad we don't have time for sightseeing."

She punches an address into the GPS in the car, then backs out of the spot. It's a weekday, and the traffic is atrocious. Of course, we're trying to get to a meeting at the same time the rest of the city is trying to get home from work.

"Oh, there's a phone for you in the glovebox," Elise says, pointing at it. "It's nothing fancy, but it has the team's numbers already programmed in, and it's what you should use to communicate with us. No texting any friends about our cases from your personal phone, all right?"

"Don't worry, I don't have any friends," I say as I open the glovebox and fish out the phone. It's not a smartphone; just an old-fashioned flip phone. "Wow, I didn't think they even made these anymore. JHAPI makes you share hotel rooms and use antiques?"

Elise snorts and pulls her phone out of her pocket. It's the same as mine. "They're cheap as hell."

"We're paying for the coffee ourselves, aren't we?" I ask.

"You're a fast learner," Elise says with a toothy grin. "I tried to expense it my first week here, and the damn accounting department went on about how coffee is a privilege, not a necessity."

She rolls her eyes dramatically, then punches on the accelerator to make it through a yellow light.

"Coffee is absolutely a necessity, especially when you keep the random hours we do," she says with a sharp nod of her head.

My stomach growls. "Breakfast is also going to be a necessity."

"Oh, don't worry, I never forget breakfast either," she says with a smile.

She turns into a packed parking lot. We have to wait for a car that is backing out, but it snags us a spot right in front of the door to the coffee shop. The amazing scent of sausage and peppers wafts through the air as soon as I open the car door. Right next door to the coffee shop is a Mexican restaurant selling breakfast tacos.

"This place is great, and the tacos are only a dollar, as tacos should be," Elise says as we climb out. "Let's get the food first so we have something to eat while we wait for them to make this huge list of coffee."

"Sounds good to me," I say as I follow her inside.

Elise orders four tacos just for herself. I order two, my mouth already watering. I'm glad they're cheap because I realize I have no idea how much money I have. It's been a while since I checked my bank account, and I don't exactly have a job anymore. I swipe my card with a little sigh. So much for my savings goals.

We don't have to wait long for our orders to be ready. Elise grabs two little white bags from the counter and hands me the smaller one.

It's a brief but chilly walk next door to the coffee shop. I snag us a table while Elise goes to submit our coffee order.

I get out my chorizo and egg taco first and lay out a couple of napkins. The first bite is heaven. It's barely on the right side of greasy, as chorizo tends to be.

Elise plops down in the chair across from me and devours her first taco in three bites. I swallow my second bite and raise a brow at her.

"What? I'm hungry," she says around another mouthful.

I chuckle and shove the last of my taco into my mouth. It takes two napkins to mop up the grease from my knuckles. I'm glad the other taco I got is just potato and egg.

We chew in silence for a bit, but I can see her looking at me, working up to some kind of question. I avoid her gaze as best I can, focusing on my food instead, which I finish far too quickly.

"So, you're working with the vampires," Elise says before taking a big bite of her last taco. She chews slowly, watching my face the whole time. "I was surprised. You and Reilly didn't seem to get along that well."

I shrug, but I wish I could get her to drop this line of questioning.

"Nobody really gets along with their boss. It's no big deal as long as they keep paying me," I lie. If only I was getting paid for this.

The barista calls our name. I drop my crumpled, greasy napkin on the table and hurry over to the counter. Nine cups of coffee in two trays looks right. One of them is just wedged in the center of a tray between the other cups.

Elise wolfs down the rest of her taco, then gathers our trash off the table. We meet at the door, and she leads me back to the car.

Nerves are churning in my stomach. Or perhaps it's just the grease. Either way, I'm not looking forward to sitting at a table of

JHAPI agents. The fact that they'll be finding out what I can do, if not what I am, makes it that much worse. I hate being exposed like this. It's been a secret for so long, and I've never considered what it would be like to tell people the truth.

I tap my foot against the floorboard the entire drive to the local headquarters. The building isn't much to look at. It's not even the tallest building on the block. It is square and beige, with JHAPI in big black letters over the main entrance. Hawking drives past that and around to the back and parks in the employee parking area.

I hand her one of the coffee carriers, and we head inside. The inside is just as dingy as the outside. Beige linoleum and plain white walls. The ceilings are dotted with fluorescent lights that throw a harsh glow over everything.

A few people nod as we walk down the hall, apparently recognizing Elise. She leads me to the desk near the front entrance.

"Sorry, I forgot you need an ID card," Elise says before turning to the young man peering at us from the desk in a crisp blue uniform. "I need a visitor pass for Olivia Carter. She should be on Agent Stocke's list."

"Yes, ma'am," the man says, his fingers flying over the keyboard. He scans his screen for a moment before nodding. "I'll get that printed immediately."

He taps a few more keys and slips a blank card into a little machine on his left.

"Please stand on that X for your picture," he says, pointing at a black X on the floor to my right.

I grimace but step on it and face him. He doesn't wait for me to be ready or give me a countdown; he just snaps the picture.

"All right, that will work," he says, clicking on his computer screen again. The printer whirs, then he pulls the card out and slips it onto a lanyard.

"Please wear this at all times while you're in the building. And try to keep the picture facing out," he says, handing it to me with a smile.

"Sure thing," I say, looking at the ID. The picture is awful. I'm squinting, and I have bags under my eyes.

Elise leans over to look at it and laughs.

"Oh, that is perfect," she says, clapping a hand on my shoulder and pushing me in the direction we need to go.

CHAPTER 4

The meeting room is on the top floor. The far wall is taken up by a large window that overlooks a decent portion of the city. Of course, there's not much to see right now since it's now completely dark outside. The lights of the city aren't as bright as the one I grew up in, but overall I think I like this place. It's not so different.

Elise takes a seat on the side of the table that faces the door. I turn away from the window reluctantly and sit down on her right side.

"I'm surprised we're the first ones here," I comment.

Elise shrugs. "I thought it'd be better to do it this way. Didn't want you to have to walk into a room full of agents."

"That would have been a little intimidating I guess," I say, pulling the stopper out of my coffee and taking a sip. I grimace and suck at my lip; it's still too hot. "Where's Brunson?"

"Doing something for Stocke. He'll be here in a bit." Elise takes a long drink of coffee, then turns to face me. "By the way, I don't think he hates you anymore."

"That's, uh, nice, I guess?" I say hesitantly.

The door swings open without a knock, and a woman with dark skin and a short tapered haircut walks in. She's wearing a crisp black suit that looks both trendy and professional. The suit and white shirt underneath are completely free of wrinkles and fit perfectly.

Walking close behind her is a woman with wavy, reddish-brown hair that drapes over her shoulders. She's wearing a suit as well, but the jacket is unbuttoned and the shirt underneath is silk. She has a long necklace with an amber stone around her neck. She smells like magic.

Something hungry shifts inside of me. I bite down on the inside of my cheek to distract myself. The craving startles me. I've always wanted other people's magic, but never like this. Damn vampire magic is making everything more intense.

"Agent Ivy Andreas," the first woman says, stepping forward with her hand outstretched. I stand and shake it.

"Olivia Carter." Her grip is firm but not overbearing.

"Corinne Davidson," her partner says with a gentle smile. She takes my hand gently and covers it with her other as we shake.

Elise pushes a pair of coffees across the table toward them, which they take gratefully. The two women take the seats across from me and Elise.

Corinne leans back in her chair, a pleasant smile on her face, while Ivy sits with perfect posture. She seems to be the one who takes the lead in their partnership even though she is the human.

"You're the witch the vampire council has brought in, correct?" Ivy asks.

"Yep," I say before taking a long drink of coffee. I didn't sleep well with Reilly so close to me. Elise seems to be in the same boat I'm in, judging by the way she's also sucking down her coffee. Adjusting to a night schedule isn't easy for anyone. I'm surprised the team was willing to do it just to work with the vampires.

"I've never heard of a witch working with the vampire council before," Ivy comments. Her dark brown eyes scan my face for answers.

I shrug. "First time for everything, I guess."

The door opens again, and a tall man with light brown hair walks in. He looks like a clean cut, all-American jock. Skin tanned from spending all his free time outdoors, muscles, and a sharp jawline. I groan internally; guys like this always seem to have a mean streak.

"Dude, I'm serious, football is really nuanced once you start paying attention," the jock says, looking back over his shoulder.

I wonder if he realizes how much of a stereotype he is.

The man behind him chuckles. "I'm still not watching it."

"Andreas, Davidson," the jock says with a big grin. "I had no idea you two were in on this."

An Asian man with a stocky build walks up beside him. His black hair is short on the sides and slightly longer on the top. It's styled neatly, nothing flashy, but the red and orange flash of tattoos that peek out of his collar make it look like fire is crawling up his neck.

"You know I'd never pass up an assignment like this, Cook. Who'd you have to bribe to get something this good?" Ivy asks, leaning back in her chair as she turns toward the two men.

"Bribe? You wound me," Cook says, playfully clutching at his chest. "Brunson requested me and Hu personally."

Ivy snorts. "Of course he did. Good ol' boys club hard at work."

"We're not all that bad to work with," the Asian man objects.

"You're great, Peter," Ivy says with a snort. "This idiot is going to drive me insane before we're done though."

Cook just grins at her insult, unaffected. The two men seem to finally notice me.

"Who do we have here?" Cook asks, sauntering toward the table.

"Olivia Carter," I say without getting up.

The smile falls off his face, and he looks me up and down, appearing unimpressed.

"The one and only Olivia," he says with a sneer. "Brunson didn't mention that you were going to be on the team."

I raise a brow at him but don't ask. It sounds like he knows Brunson well. I have no interest in knowing what Zachary might have told him about me, or why he didn't tell him I was going to be here.

"Peter Hu," his partner says, leaning across the table to shake my hand.

"Nice to meet you, Peter," I say as I stand and shake his hand.

Cook crosses his arms and continues glaring at me until Ivy kicks a chair into his leg.

"Sit down and stop making us look bad," she says sternly.

Cook and Peter sit down next to each other. Peter seems perfectly at ease, obviously not affected by his partner's dislike of me.

"Where is Brunson?" Peter asks Elise.

"He's with Stocke. They should be here soon," she says with a yawn.

The door opens again, and a woman walks in. She has mousy brown hair pulled back into a bun and thick-framed black glasses that are too big for her face. She's wearing a black skirt and a blazer over a white blouse. Her thick heels clunk against the floor as she walks to the head of the table and sets down the stack of files she is carrying.

"Good evening, everyone," she says with a stiff smile. A chorus of responses goes around the table, but no one seems overjoyed to see her.

She walks toward me and stretches out her hand.

"Olivia Carter, I am Agent Staci Young. I'm Agent Stocke's partner."

I stand and shake her hand, already tired of the up and down.

"Nice to meet you," I say with a nod before plopping back down in my chair. She straightens her jacket with a sharp tug on the hem and walks back to the seat next to the head of the table. She sits down and folds her hands in front of her.

"Agent Stocke will be here in a few minutes," she says quietly.

"Thank you, Staci," Corinne says with a warm smile. Staci straightens a little, seeming pleased that someone actually responded.

Cook turns back to Ivy, and everyone chats about unimportant things as we wait. I tilt my head back and stare at the ceiling. I feel out of place here. I've never been on this side of the law before. The thought makes me smile. If only Detective Brunson could see me now. He would have wanted me to join something like this. He loved the idea of humans and paranormals working together to protect both sides. He always said that ignorance breeds fear, and cooperation kills ignorance.

The door opens again, and I hear a familiar voice; Zachary has arrived. The person who walks in first though is a slender woman in her forties with curly blonde hair that is pulled back into a barely contained ponytail. She has a no-nonsense air about her. She walks to the head of the table while Zachary heads to his seat on the other side of Elise with a brief nod in my direction.

"Where is Mr. Walsh?" the woman asks me.

I glance at the empty chair to my right and shrug. "I have no idea. He asked Elise to bring me here and said he would join us later."

She sighs and checks her watch.

"I'm not waiting for him," she decides. She grabs the top file from the stack and flips it open.

"Earlier this month, there was an attack in a small town in Texas where the NWR attempted to frame the local vampire clan for the murders of several humans. The clan and a pack in the area cooperated to take out this cell since the local police department refused to offer support. It was later discovered this was because the department had been infiltrated by the NWR."

She taps a button on the table I hadn't noticed before, and a screen lowers from the ceiling. A face appears on it, one I despise. His smug, handsome features bring back the memory of sitting across from him at the diner. The flirting makes me sick to think about now. He's not so handsome anymore though. There's no way to heal the kind of burns I left him with without magic, which he'd never resort to using.

"Jason Martinez has used a number of aliases over the years, which are listed in his file. He is most likely using another identity at this point, but we are looking for him under all of these names."

Stocke grabs a small black remote control and clicks to the next picture. A map with several red points dotted across the country is displayed.

"This map shows all NWR attacks carried out in the last year."

She clicks the remote again, and the map changes. A large number of the red points turn blue.

"The points marked in blue are all the attacks that Martinez is believed to have been involved with on some level. He appears to be an idea man," Stocke says, spreading her hands. "He has been personally involved with only a quarter of these attacks due to his limited ability to travel previously. Now that he is no longer tied to one location, it is likely that he will become more aggressive with his attacks, and also risk himself in more situations."

She turns back to face her team and crosses her arms, tapping the remote against her bicep.

"We believe the attack in Texas was a test run. They wanted to see if they could manipulate law enforcement and local opinion against the vampire clan. They were mostly successful. The local coven believed the vampires were involved and attempted to help speed along the investigation through unethical and illegal means. If Ms. Carter had not discovered the plot and persuaded the clan to act, it would have succeeded. It was just bad luck for the NWR, and good luck for us, that it turned out how it did."

Agent Stocke nods at the Staci, who stands and passes around the remaining files. One is handed to me as well. I tug the thick file a little closer. The folder is dark brown, and JHAPI's seal is stamped on the front, along with CONFIDENTIAL in bold, red letters.

"Ms. Carter wounded Martinez's pride when she undid his plot. More importantly, however, she took away one of his tools. His face."

Stocke clicks the remote again, and his face appears on the screen again. This picture is blurry, and he appears to be from a security camera in some kind of veterinary office. The left side of his face is blistered and red from the burns I inflicted on him. I can't help the smirk that curls on my lips. I'm glad I left my mark even if I would prefer him dead.

"Martinez had been charming his way around the country. He's going to stand out now. We are working with local police departments and the media to distribute this picture, as well as others. We're going to make him America's most wanted criminal."

Stocke uncrosses her arms and turns the screen off, then sits down. She steeples her fingers and looks around the table. The door opens just as she moves to speak again, and Reilly strolls in.

He is wearing his usual suit. He looks like any other JHAPI agent except for the predatory glint in his eyes and the unnatural grace of his steps. He walks without hurry to the seat next to me.

Cook watches him with narrowed eyes. Even Ivy looks uncomfortable at his entrance. Her shoulders are tense, and she keeps her eyes glued to him.

"Meredith," he says, inclining his head in Agent Stocke's direction.

"Mr. Walsh," Stocke says drily. She turns back to the group, ignoring the interruption. "Martinez is an important target. However, he is not our only target. JHAPI, with the support of the vampire council, intends on taking down NWR once and for all. Whatever resources we need will be provided to us."

Staci sits up and leans forward, an eager look in her eyes.

"Yes, Agent Young, that does mean you can have that cauldron you've been asking for," Stocke says.

I knit my brows together and reassess her. I hadn't even considered that she might be a witch, much less a hedgewitch. I had assumed Agent Stocke was the paranormal in that partnership.

"Taking down the NWR is more than just a difficult task," Ivy says, her posture relaxed once again but her tone slightly disbelieving. "Don't get me wrong, I'm happy to do it, but they've been around longer than this country has in some form or another. We can't stamp out hatred."

"They've never faced opposition like this before. In the past, we have only reacted to their attacks." Stocke taps her finger against the smooth table. "We are going to strike first. We are going to make them fear us."

Cook barks out a laugh. "I like the sound of that."

"So where do we start?" Ivy asks.

"We're going to start here in Phoenix. The files in front of each of you are different cases connected to a local cell, as well as the information we have on their possible location. Agent Davidson, we'll need to start with you. Can you find them?"

Corinne nods, flipping through the file. "I should be able to find one or two."

"Ms. Carter, can you assist her?" Stocke asks, looking at me.

I freeze, my heart racing at her casual question. Everyone turns and looks at me. Zachary pinches his brows together, confused. I don't know what she has told the team, and my instincts can't relax.

I clear my throat and try to ignore the stares of the team.

"I—uh, cannot," I say haltingly.

"She's a hedgewitch, not a Finder," Zachary interjects, looking between us like there must be some confusion.

Stocke smirks and folds her hands in front of her.

"According to Mr. Walsh, that is not actually the case. He

informed me that she was a Finder, a hedgewitch, an electric witch, and a healer." She pauses and looks at each agent in turn. "This is obviously unusual, to say the least. As agents, you are all used to dealing with confidential information. This will be no different. The vampire council is lending us their help, and in return we will not betray on their trust, or Olivia's."

Staci frowns in my direction, adjusting her glasses with a nudge from her finger. She looks disapproving.

Cook scoffs. "A witch that can use more than one time of magic? That's ridiculous. I don't buy it."

"Why is it that you cannot help Agent Davidson if you are a Finder?" Stocke asks, ignoring Cook's comment.

I glance back at Reilly, but he just raises a brow at me. I sigh and pull my sleeve up to reveal the welts that have been getting steadily worse. Corinne gasps, her hand flying to her mouth. Stocke simply looks at the red stripes curiously, her head tilting to the side.

"Damn, did you lose a fight with your curling iron or something?" Cook asks.

"I had a little incident," I say as I shove the sleeve back down. "If I use the Finding magic, it knocks me out for several hours."

"Well, we need to get that fixed. What do you need? Salves?"

"No," Corinne interrupts. "None of that would fix it."

"She's right. I've tried all that," I agree with a shrug.

"I can help her with it, but it will take time," Corinne says, directing her response to Agent Stocke rather than me.

"All right, get it handled and keep me updated. I need to know if someone isn't at a hundred percent. Will it affect your performance in any area other than Finding magic?" Stocke asks me.

"No, I can deal with it like I have been," I say, crossing my arms.

"I still don't buy this," Cook interjects again. "No one has ever heard of a witch that can use more than one branch of magic."

"Until now," Reilly says, speaking for the first time since his greeting to Stocke.

"Why should we believe you?" Cook asks, spreading his hands out and raising a brow at Reilly. "She just said she can't use Finding magic, and she obviously can't heal herself."

"Want me to electrocute you?" I snap at Cook, tired of his attitude. Bright electric magic rushes to my fingertips and singes the table where my hands are pressed, white-knuckled, into it. I don't like being called a liar.

Cook leans back in his seat, pretending he's unconcerned. I know he isn't because I can hear his heart beating angrily from here. His fingers twitch like he wants to go for his gun.

"That won't be necessary," Stocke interrupts. "Please keep your magic under control, Olivia. I was assured you wouldn't put this team at risk."

Cook holds my gaze, his jaw clenched in anger. He hates me, though I have no idea why. He could have at least waited for me to give him a good reason.

"I won't put anyone at risk." I push back into my seat and cross my arms.

Stocke pinches the bridge of her nose, then continues with her explanation.

"The vampire council has been instrumental in making this possible. We will extend the same trust and respect to the consultants they have provided us with, that I expect to receive from them."

Her tone is sharp, chastising both me and Cook. I bite down on the impulse to say 'he started it'. She seems like the type of woman who doesn't care.

"Does anyone have any other questions or concerns?" She scans the room, but no one moves.

"All right, everyone get caught up on the case files you have been provided with. Pass them around, make sure everyone gets a chance to read through each file. Agent Davidson, please try to Find at least one of our targets. Everyone needs to have their go bags ready. We will leave as soon as Davidson gives the word."

"Agent Young, we'll need a full range of the usual brews, and you have my permission to brew anything else you think might be useful while we travel."

"All the standard brews are already prepared," Staci says. "I'll start making a list of other brews that will be useful."

"Excellent," Stocke says, nodding toward Staci. "Agent Andreas, please visit the armory and make sure everyone is appropriately armed. Make sure you include protective body gear and gas masks. I foresee us needing both."

"Does everyone include our consultants?" Ivy asks, nodding her head toward Reilly and me.

"Yes," Stocke says with a nod. "Treat them like full members of the team."

"Noted," Ivy says as she pulls out a notepad and scribbles a few things down.

Everyone scatters, and I open the file that was set in front of me. Martinez's face looks up at me. It's an old picture, he looks young and happy. I have to clench my hand into a fist to keep from scorching the file with the sudden surge of magic that rushes behind my anger.

CHAPTER 5

I'm reading through a third file when Ivy appears at my elbow.

"What's up?" I ask, turning the chair to face her.

"JHAPI agents are trained on a variety of firearms, but I don't know what kind of experience you have. What can you shoot with accuracy?" she asks, her pen poised over her notepad.

"I can use a pistol, and I'm all right with a rifle, but I've shot those less."

"Have you ever shot an AR-15 before?"

"No, just a basic hunting rifle."

"All right, I'll get you a pistol."

"Sounds good to me," I say with a nod.

Reilly walks up behind me. I stand up and move out from between them. I hate it when he stands behind me like that; it feels predatory.

"Would you like a gun or any other weapon?" Ivy directs to Reilly.

"No, that won't be necessary."

"All right, I'll make sure you have what you need, Olivia." She turns and strides from the room, intent on completing the assignment given to her by Stocke.

Corinne is off by herself, unfolding a series of maps on the table we were just gathered around.

"Did your introduction go well?" Reilly asks quietly, having moved closer to me when I wasn't paying attention.

I snort, my eyes straying toward the scorch marks on the table.

"It went fine."

Reilly looks at the marks as well and raises his brow.

"You have a strange definition of fine."

"No one died," I mutter.

"Not yet at least," he says, clapping his hand on my shoulder before striding toward Zachary and Cook.

I walk over to Corinne and stand a few feet away from her next to the table. Hopefully, I can learn something. I've never actually seen a witch Find someone in person. I'm curious how incorrectly I've been using the magic.

She glances at me but doesn't speak as she finishes arranging her maps. Once they are all where she wants them, she takes a step back and looks them over. The maps cover not only the county we are in, but every surrounding county. Each one has smaller maps showing the main roads in the major cities in that county.

"You tried to Find someone who is dead, didn't you?" Corinne asks without looking at me. She speaks softly enough that the others wouldn't be able to hear her.

I tense and bite the inside of my cheek.

"I wasn't sure," I say quietly, glancing at Reilly. "I thought my mother was dead, but then I had reason to believe she wasn't and—well, it doesn't matter."

Corinne smiles gently, her brown eyes soft as they scan my face. "We all do it eventually. The lucky ones have someone with them to help and protect them. You weren't trained, were you?"

I shake my head. She doesn't know the whole story, of course. It's hard to get training when you've stolen someone's magic.

"Not surprising if you've had to hide your abilities. We'll fix that though. Can't have someone on the team with untapped potential."

"I would appreciate it. Do you mind if I watch?" I ask, suddenly unsure if I'm intruding.

"Not at all," Corinne says, sweeping the soft waves hanging around her face up into a ponytail. "I have to search for them one at a time. I'll be looking for this guy first. He was spotted in town a week ago."

She taps her finger against one of the open files. It's a younger guy. It's one of the files I read. He was a chemical engineering student, but his girlfriend dumped him for a witch. He flunked out and fell into a downward spiral that included drug charges and assault. The NWR recruited him while he was in jail.

She cracks her knuckles and extends her hands over the maps. Her shoulders drop as she relaxes all the muscles in her body one by one. Magic hums in the air. For the first time, I can smell it as well as taste it. Her magic is different from anything I've felt before. It's warm, which I expected, but not nearly as hot as my own.

Red lines of magic unfurl from her fingers and twist through the air until they stretch over the entire table. A hush falls over the room, and the group stops talking, all turning to watch her work.

Every welt covering my body responds to the magic. I take a step back, but it doesn't help the dull ache, so I grit my teeth and try to ignore it and the hunger that is growing inside of me with every moment. I don't want to miss any of this.

The magic hovers above the table, each line writhing with eagerness. She extends them down onto the maps in a wave from left to right. The magic grows warmer and brighter as each line digs into the map, searching. A line on the left disappears with a pop that makes me jump. Another follows, then another and another moving in the same direction she lowered them.

Only one tenuous line remains when the pops of magic finally cease. It extends from her left pointer finger to a spot in the city. Corinne walks toward the map, lowering her hand toward the point. The magic grows narrower, but brighter, as though she's focusing in on the person's exact spot.

She pauses and stares off into the distance with unfocused eyes. She exhales slowly and presses her finger to the map. A wave of magic rushes out from her. I shiver in pain and hunger as it brushes past me. Everyone else in the room takes an involuntary step back.

"I Found him," Corinne says, still staring at something no one else can see.

"Can you pinpoint his location?" Stocke asks, flipping through the file.

"I need a more detailed map, but I'll be able to tell you what block they're on. I won't be able to say what building until I get closer," Corinne replies after a moment of consideration.

"All right," Stocke says, scanning the information in the file. "Brunson, get a better map for Corinne and set up surveillance so we can figure out where exactly these people are hiding out. I want everyone ready to go tomorrow evening. We'll go in just after the sun sets if we can."

Everyone scatters, grabbing their things from the table, but Corinne taps my elbow.

"We need to try to fix these as soon as possible. I know they make it impossible for you to use your Finding magic, and I'm not sure what else they might affect as they get worse."

I nod, pressing my hand against my forearm. They still ache just from being around her magic.

"Yeah, fixing this would be great. As soon as we have time."

"Be careful, try to avoid using magic tomorrow if you can, all right?" I nod, and she walks over to see Ivy.

Zachary slips up beside me, startling me slightly.

"So, you can use multiple types of magic?" he asks, his brows furrowed.

Cook is frowning at us from the corner of the room, his arms crossed in front of him. I turn more toward Zachary so I don't have to see him.

"Yes," I say with a tense smile. "But you've known that. The healing magic and the brewing."

"If you had been able to use Finding magic back then, you wouldn't have had such a hard time finding your mom," he says hesitantly.

I grit my teeth and stare at my shoes. I'm not going to offer up information. He needs to either ask his question or leave me alone.

"So, you're just going to stand there? You aren't going explain anything?" he asks, irritation slipping into his voice.

"I'm not sure what you want me to say." I cross my arms and look up at him.

"You got this magic somehow, and recently," Zachary says, mirroring my posture.

"All right," I say with a shrug. "And?"

Zachary looks at me like I've lost my mind and throws his hands in the air. "And? Seriously? That should be impossible. How are you doing it?"

"None of your business," I say. I turn to walk away, but he grabs my arm. I glare at his hand, then at him, and jerk my arm out of his grip. "If you think you *need* more information, go ask Stocke. I don't want to talk about it."

"If you are putting anyone in danger by keeping this secret—"

"Zachary, stop it," I snap, trying to keep my voice quiet, but not doing a great job of it. "I'm not putting anyone in danger, and it's insulting that you think I would. The how and why of what I can do isn't important, and it isn't anyone's business but mine. Stocke wouldn't have allowed me to work with any of you if I was a danger. Use your head."

He takes a step back, his jaw clenched tight. Half the room is watching us, the other half is studiously pretending it's not obvious we're arguing.

"Gerard and Maybelle disappeared. Are you going to try to Find them? To run again?"

I chuckle humorlessly. "No, I'm not."

"That'd be a first," Zachary says, his voice low enough to be a whisper.

Magic sparks at my fingertips again. "I guess Elise was wrong."

"About what?"

"She said you didn't hate me anymore."

I turn on my heel and walk toward Reilly, who is waiting for me by the door. The level of anger that's coursing through me is an overreaction. I know it is. Yet, I still want to rip Zachary apart. My skin is crawling with rage and barely controlled electric magic.

I splash cold water on my face and stare into the sink. I don't want to look in the mirror again, in case she's there. Watching me.

I'm also hungry. The anger and the sparks of magic and being surrounded by so many paranormals today is harder than I expected. I can feel Reilly's presence in the room next door, taunting me. I dig my fingers into the cold porcelain, but my hands won't stop shaking.

"Olivia," Reilly says quietly from behind me. "What the hell is wrong with you?"

A low growl bubbles out of my throat, and my fangs press against my bottom lip as my mouth curls into a snarl.

"Nothing," I rasp.

Reilly moves fast. I shouldn't be able to track it, but the vampire magic is coursing through me like a cold wind. I can't dodge him though, and his hand wraps around my throat as he shoves me against the wall next to the sink.

"Another lie," he snaps in my face.

His eyes are dark and dangerous, and his body is hot against mine. That's not what I want though, even if it is tempting. I want the magic and the blood inside of him.

"You're hungry, aren't you?" he asks, his hand relaxing, but not moving from my throat.

I don't respond. I don't want to admit it. I hate it.

His thumb strokes my pulse point, up, down, up, down, in time with my heartbeat. It's soothing, in an odd way. My breathing slows, and some of the anger fades, curling into a different kind of heat. His thigh is pushed between my legs, and his arm is pressed against my chest. Every point of contact is electric.

"You are going to have to feed, or you are going to lose control," he whispers, his breath skating across my cheek.

"It's not just blood I need," I say, my voice hoarse. "It's magic. I can't get that from some necker."

"How much?" he asks.

"I don't know. Not much, I think. It's never been like this before. It wasn't like this until Javier."

"You're going to feed from me—"

I start to object, but Reilly presses down on my throat and shushes me.

"You will take the absolute minimum you need to maintain control," he says, his face serious, not a dimple in sight.

"Why?" I ask quietly.

"Because I have invested time and money in you, and I need you to keep it together. After tonight, I will find another way. But you are too close to being out of control, and you have to be ready to go tomorrow."

I clench my teeth tightly together but nod. As much as I hate it, he's not wrong.

Reilly lifts his hand from my neck and offers me his wrist. I open my mouth, my gums aching in anticipation of the bite.

I close my teeth and lips around the edge of his wrist. My tongue flicks out, sampling his skin, and I almost moan at the taste. My teeth sink into his flesh like a knife through butter, and hot, sweet blood spills over my tongue. Not just blood though. His magic seeps into me from every point of contact, and the rush from that is almost overwhelming. I want to take it all.

I shove him away as hard as I can, and he stumbles backward, slamming into the bathroom wall. He leans against the wall, breathing just as hard as I am, watching me with a heated gaze.

"Fuck," I say, running my hands through my hair.

"If you want," he says, his cheeks dimpling.

"That line is getting old," I say, rolling my eyes.

"One day, you'll take me up on it." He straightens and adjusts his jacket. "Take a shower and order some room service. I imagine you need human food as well."

"Yeah, I do," I say, pressing a hand to my stomach. It's been quite a while since I had the tacos.

"Don't let it get this bad again," he says, his tone hard.

I look at the floor and bite the inside of my cheek. I can still taste his blood in my mouth.

"I don't intend to."

"I have another errand to run. Don't do anything stupid while I'm gone."

He strides from the room, and I slide down the wall, my legs suddenly weak. I press my hand to my mouth and stare straight ahead, not really seeing anything at all.

CHAPTER 6

"What do we know?" Stocke asks, leaning back in her chair.

Brunson has the remote this time, and he clicks it, pulling up a map on the projector.

"Agent Davidson was able to narrow down the suspect's location to this city block," Zachary says, pointing at the street highlighted in red. "Surveillance was able to confirm that the suspect is there and was seen entering this building."

The slide changes, showing a plain building set back from the street. It looks a little run down and definitely abandoned. A lone figure is walking across the parking lot toward a side entrance.

"There have been four other people observed entering and exiting the building, but we have not been able to identify them," Zachary says.

Commander Benjamin Driver leans forward and clasps his hands. He's an unassuming man with white hair and a soft, round face. He looks like the sort of man who enjoys mowing his lawn and putting up Christmas lights.

"They've all kept their faces hidden," he says, tapping his

thumbs together. "They don't park anywhere near the building, except for one van which drove into the parking lot around seven am this morning."

"So we have no way of knowing how many people might be in that building?" Stocke asks.

"We can estimate five to ten suspects," Driver says, spreading his hands. "But ultimately, that's just a guess."

"Since this is the NWR, we have to assume there will be booby traps and that the suspects will be heavily armed. Commander Driver confirmed for me yesterday that we will have SWAT backup, but that will not make this easy," Stocke says as she looks around the table. "All of you have been on raids before, and you understand the risk we're taking."

I guess you can call the fight that went down at Chevy's bar a raid, but I'm hoping whatever we do tonight will be better organized. And have fewer casualties.

"Now, our goal is to arrest the NWR members, not assassinate them. However, you do what you have to in order to make sure that you, and your team members, come back alive," Stocke says, her tone allowing for no argument. "Brunson, please walk us through the tactical plan."

Zachary stands up and walks to the front of the room. The slide changes to an overhead view of the building. Several points are highlighted, including the street across from the front of the building, and three entrances on the building itself.

"Officers with the City of Phoenix's Homeland Defense Bureau will secure a perimeter around the building. The streets will be blocked here," he points to the main street leading past the building, "and here," he points at the side street east of the building.

He clicks the remote, and the slide changes, zooming in on the building itself.

"We do not have any information on the internal layout of the building; however, we have identified three entrance points which you can see highlighted in red, yellow, and blue. We will have three teams, one for each. Hu and Cook will be Red Team, Davidson and Andreas, you two are Yellow Team, Hawking, Walsh, Carter, and myself will be Blue Team. I have already gone over this with Commander Driver, who is coordinating with the SWAT team for us. They will be with us through the initial entry and attempt to secure the immediate area, and our teams will push into the building."

Stocke turns back around. "Does anyone have any questions?"

The team stays silent.

"The suspects have no idea we are coming, which is a benefit of organizing these raids so quickly. Let's all go downstairs and get prepped. SWAT will be driving us to the location."

Everyone stands and heads out into the hall. We don't all fit on the first elevator, and I end up waiting with Reilly, Cook, and Hu for the second one.

I shift restlessly on my feet. I hate the anticipation of a fight. Everything that can go wrong runs through your mind over and over until you can't see how something terrible won't happen. I follow Reilly onto the elevator and cross my arms tightly over my chest. At least I'm not going into this fight alone.

The elevator carries us down the basement, and I follow the group into the parking garage. There are three armored vehicles lined up, waiting for us.

Ivy gets my attention, and I walk over to her.

"Body armor," she says, handing me a black vest with a patch that reads JHAPI velcroed to the front and back. "And pistol."

The pistol is strapped into a holster attached to a black belt. I take the gun as well, and she hurries over to Agent Stocke. I tuck the gun between my legs and pull the body armor on over my shirt. It's heavier than I expected, and it feels like putting on a new shoe for the first time. It fits, but it definitely needs to be broken in.

Cook steps up beside me.

"You're on Brunson's team," he comments, his voice low, so no one else can hear.

"Yep," I say, popping my lips on the 'p'.

"If you do something to get him hurt or killed, I will bury you," he says, stepping into my personal space.

I hold my ground and look up at him, tilting my head to the side.

"What exactly is it you think I did to him? Or would do to him?"

He laughs in my face. "Don't act like you don't know you broke his heart."

I stare at him, confused, then roll my eyes.

"It's been five years. I've grown up; maybe you should too. I'm here to do a job, not deal with high school drama."

Cook walks away, shaking his head. Whatever his issues are with me, they're going to have to wait until another time. I tighten the belt around my waist and adjust the pistol until it isn't poking me in the stomach.

Reilly is waiting for me by the last vehicle. I tug at the uncomfortable vest one more time, then walk over to join him. Time to get this over with.

The earpiece is too big for my ear canal. Having something in my ear makes my breathing seem louder too, and I can't hear everyone's heartbeats, which makes me feel weirdly off balance. I hadn't realized how quickly I'd come to depend on that for knowing where everyone is in the room. I readjust the body armor again, but there's no making it comfortable.

The gas mask is even worse. It smells like plastic and someone else's sweat. Each puff of my breath makes my face hot and the inside of the mask humid. I tug at the strap on the back of my head and try to adjust where it sits under my chin. All my senses are muffled. I don't know how anyone is expected to fight like this.

Elise's hand appears on my shoulder, and she gives me an irritated look.

"Quit fidgeting," she whispers.

I mouth back *sorry* and try to hold myself still. The waiting is making me nervous though. Storming in without thinking is more my style.

Elise, Zachary, Reilly, and I are entering behind the local SWAT team through a side entrance. The rest of the JHAPI agents, excluding Agent Stocke and Staci, are divided up between two other entrances. The building isn't very large. It's nestled in-between two much larger structures, and it's the kind of place you'd never think twice about.

The front is plain stucco, with minimal windows and no signs. A fairly large parking lot obscures the view of the building from the road. The parking lot is generally used by people who live in the apartments next door and overflow from the roofing business on the other side.

"Red Team is a go," Stocke's voice says in my ear.

The SWAT member in front motions forward, and the two men behind him swing their battering ram against the door, which instantly gives way. In the midst of the splinters of the door, I see the glint of silver.

Two canisters are tossed through the open doorway, gas pouring from the spout. Our group pushes forward, and I follow Elise, my left hand resting lightly on her shoulder while my right hand grips my pistol tightly. I keep my trigger finger carefully indexed. I'm grateful for the night vision the magic I stole from Javier gives me because it is dark as sin inside the building.

My breaths puff loudly inside the mask as I scan the heavy fog of gas for movement. I can barely make out the silhouette of the SWAT member who entered first.

"Two doors to the left. Staircase straight ahead," an unfamiliar male voice sounds in my earpiece.

The team splits up with two of the SWAT members and Zachary peeling off toward the closest door on the left. Three others advance to the door just past it. Reilly stops the second team at the door, crouching down to listen to something the others can't hear.

The gas has cleared just enough since we came in that I can see the staircase that stretches up into pitch black ahead of us. One SWAT member heads toward it, and Elise follows. I hesitate for a moment, then go after Elise.

We reach the top of the staircase and spread out quietly. There are double doors in front of us, and two smaller rooms to the left. One door is half-open, the other is shut. There is a short wall that lines the opening of the staircase.

The SWAT guy approaches the open door cautiously and pushes it all the way open as he enters the room. Elise follows close behind. I'm a few paces behind, my eyes glued to the double doors, all the hairs on my arm standing on end. I'm a beat too slow, and the door slams shut behind them, trapping them inside and me outside.

The double doors fly open, and I lunge for the wall that lines the stairwell. There's a bulky, decorative chrome planter with a fake tree sticking out of it at the corner that I squeeze behind. Bullets fly over my head, and there is muffled shouting in my earpiece, along with more gunfire. I guess the fight is on now.

A man in a mask and camo pants steps around the wall, holding a shotgun, and I lift my pistol and fire three times. The bullets go wide because my hands are shaking, but he falls back.

I scramble backward and take a deep breath as electric magic rushes through me. Right now, they think I'm human. I won't use my magic unless I have to, and definitely not before I can use the element of surprise to my advantage.

The door Elise and the SWAT member went into rattles

violently, like someone was thrown into it. At the same time, gunfire echoes up the stairwell. It finally registers that someone is shouting my name in the earpiece. I tap it three times, the code I was told to let the team know I was still alive but unable to respond.

The men in front of me don't try to advance again, but they do shoot every few seconds to keep me from moving. I tighten my hands around my pistol and try to think. I can stay here for a while, but I don't know if Elise is okay, and I'm not willing to leave her in that room forever. She hasn't shifted, which worries me.

I can't breathe right or see, so I rip the gas mask off. A symphony of smells assaults me. Gunpowder. Blood. Silver. Vomit. The welts on my arms twinge unexpectedly, and I see movement in my reflection in the planter. I lean a little closer and see my mother looking back at me. My heart jumps into overdrive. I cannot be hallucinating right now.

She points behind me and holds up two fingers, then disappears. I push my back up against the planter just in time to see the second door fly open and a man step out, his gun pointed right at me. I shoot first, and my bullets thud into his chest. He falls forward, blood spreading across his shirt, but there's another man behind him. I feel, more than hear, the planter shatter as a bullet strikes near my shoulder.

I push forward onto my knees and fire again. I hit him in the arm and halt his advance. My gun clicks, and I realize the slide is locked back. I drop the magazine and scramble for another, but he's already lifting his gun again.

I pull on the magic inside of me and rush forward faster than any human would be able to move. In the time it takes his heart to beat once, I close the distance between us and my fist collides with his jaw.

He falls, unconscious, and I pivot and lunge for the other door as gunfire explodes from my right. A bullet punches into my body armor, and it feels like I was just hit by a baseball bat, but my momentum carries me through the door.

Elise is hunched in a corner over the SWAT guy who isn't moving. Her lip is bleeding, and she is half-shifted. Her hands are curled into claws, and fur is creeping across her face. There are three men standing in front of her; one is holding some kind of taser, the other two have nightsticks. There is shouting in my earpiece. I rip it out. I need to be able to hear.

Elise lunges forward, taking advantage of the distraction my entrance has caused. She hits the man on the far right, one hand wrapping around the nightstick, the other landing in his stomach.

I lift my hands toward the man with the taser and push out a burst of electrical energy. It crackles across the room like a lightning bolt and strikes him in the chest. He flies backward and hits the sheetrock with a thud.

The other man runs toward me. I slip to the left to avoid his first strike. There is gunfire outside the room, and I vaguely hear what sounds like Zachary shouting from downstairs.

A howl erupts to my right, and out of the corner of my eye I see that Elise has finally shifted. She locks her jaws around the throat of the man she was fighting and twists her head violently. He struggles, his hands clawing at her face.

I drop under another swing and punch upwards, catching the man in the stomach along with a surge of electricity. His body goes tense, and he falls.

I try to stand but find myself unable to. The welts on my arms twist in pain, and my vision swims. Elise runs for the door, pausing to glance back at me. I nod, and she races out.

This cannot be happening. I didn't try to use my Finding magic, so there's no reason the welts should be reacting like this. I push to my feet with a pained grunt and stumble toward the door. My senses are still buzzing on overload. Everything is sharp and clear despite the dim lighting. There are clusters of heartbeats all around the building, all racing with fear and adrenaline.

Olivia, I hear Reilly say, his voice cutting through all the chaos. *Put your fucking earpiece back in.*

I roll my eyes but fumble for it nonetheless.

"Carter here," I say, my voice shaking to an embarrassing extent.

"Olivia, stay put," Brunson responds. "We have them cornered, but if you come out of that room, you may get caught in the crossfire."

"Is Hawking with you?" I ask. "She ran out of here just a moment ago."

There is a pause. "No."

A howl echoes through the building, and I hear Zachary curse. I edge around the corner of the doorway and look outside. The team is advancing up the stairs. The double doors are still wide open, and I can see Elise facing off against three men. She's holding her own against them, but there is a fourth coming up behind her she doesn't seem to have noticed.

"Don't shoot me," I say into the mic before charging out. The welts ache, but I push through the pain and pull on the vampire magic inside of me. I have to be fast.

CHAPTER 7

I sense Reilly coming up the stairs behind me and put on a burst of speed to stay ahead of him. The fourth man lifts his gun. I tackle as he fires, and we both go flying. I reach for the gun as he's trying to turn it towards me, but I'm faster. I squeeze his wrist, and the small bones give way with a crunch. He screams in pain, and the gun falls. There is gunfire behind me as the team enters the room.

The man struggles against my grip. I rear back and punch him hard in the jaw with my left hand. It's an awkward angle, but I'm stronger than I normally would be, and he goes limp.

I flip around, ready for another threat, but the men Elise was fighting are face down on the ground. One of the SWAT members is cuffing two of them. The third appears to be dead.

Reilly steps out of the shadows on the far wall and sets Elise, who is still shifted down. She shakes from snout to tail, then licks his hand gratefully. He must have grabbed her and gotten her out of the way.

Zachary rips out his earpiece and storms toward me, his lips curled into a sneer.

"What the hell were you thinking? I told you to stay put!" he shouts.

I stand upright, even though the movement makes me want to vomit. I desperately need something to dull the pain shooting through the welts.

"He had a gun pointed at Elise. There was no time to wait for you to enter the room," I shout, pointing at the unconscious man behind me.

Zachary clenches his jaw and glances back at Elise, who is limping towards us as she shifts back into human form. Reilly is looking me up and down, his nose twitching as he checks for injuries.

"Stop yelling at her, Zach," Elise says quietly. "I ran in here on my own and shouldn't have. She's right, he would have shot me. The bullet grazed my leg as it is."

Zachary's face changes from angry to worried in an instant. "How bad is it?"

Elise rolls her eyes. "It'll be fine, but it burns. There was silver in that bullet."

"I can fix it," I say, taking a step forward. My knees buckle, and the room spins. I don't realize I'm tipping forward until I face plant into Reilly's chest.

"You're not using any more magic tonight," Reilly says as he swings me up into his arms.

"You're not using any—any magic," I slur. Everything is buzzing, and my vision is foggy.

Elise walks closer and peers down at me.

"You're naked," I comment helpfully.

She raises a brow and looks back up at Reilly. "Is she all right?"

"She'll be fine," Reilly says, but his heartbeat thumps uncertainly.

"Lie," I mutter, slapping my hand against his chest. "He doesn't know."

"Get her out of here. Staci probably has something that will help her," Zachary says. His brows are pinched together in unexpected concern.

Reilly carries me out of the room. I distantly hear Elise shouting for someone to bring her some clothes.

I blink, and we're at the bottom of the stairs. I'm not sure if Reilly moved vampire fast, or if I just passed out for a minute. I can smell the magic inside of him, and if I had any strength left, I'd try to take it.

"You need to feed again, don't you?" he asks.

I nod slowly, my cheek sliding against his rough body armor. "Not gonna lose control, but the vampire magic, I think it took from me while I was using it."

I let go of the magic as much as I can. The sounds fade into the background, and the overbearing scents stop making my nose itch.

Reilly lowers my feet to the ground and helps me stand. I blink and look around. We're outside now by the van. No one else is around, but I can see Agent Stocke talking to Ivy and Commander Driver near the entrance.

"It really is a curse." A laugh bubbles up in my throat, and I bite my lips to try to keep from losing it. "I never thought I'd be made weaker by stealing magic from someone."

"It's not making you weaker," Reilly says. "You just don't have any control. You dump all of your energy into every move."

"I did what I had to—"

"That's not the point I'm trying to make," Reilly interrupts. "You need to be trained. You're using magic you weren't born with. You've never been taught how to control it or channel it. Anyone, even a vampire, can wear themselves out like this. You understood that with your healing magic, why did you think this would be any different?"

I sit down on the edge of the van. "It was easier to feel my limits with that. I also hadn't taken much of the magic. I thought that was why it was so hard to use."

"What you did today was stupid," Reilly chastises. His heart is thumping with annoyance.

"I don't need a lecture," I snap. "You're the one who wanted to test my limits under pressure. Guess we just found out."

"I meant running in after Hawking. I didn't bring you into this to have you get killed because you're reckless."

I stand abruptly. "I wasn't going to watch her die. The risk was minimal anyhow. I took that guy completely by surprise."

"You had no idea who else was in that room, and you could have gotten shot by your own team members," Reilly says, shoving his finger in my face.

I slap it away. "You ran right in after me."

"Because I protect my investments."

Staci rounds the front of the van, then stops at the expression on our faces.

"I was told you needed me?" she asks, adjusting her glasses primly.

"You were told wrong. I'm fine," I say.

"You look like you're about to keel over and die, but if you say so," Staci says with a tight smile before turning and walking away toward Agent Stocke.

"What a bitch," I mutter.

"You're going to feed tonight," Reilly says quietly.

"You offering your wrist up again?" I ask, hunger swirling in my gut.

Reilly crosses his arms. "No, but I have found a volunteer."

"An actual volunteer, or someone who has no idea what they're getting themselves into and has no choice in the matter?" I ask.

"He'll be in the hotel room at five-fifteen a.m. Don't use any more magic before then."

"Fine," I mutter, wrapping my arms around myself.

Reilly stalks off, but Elise comes and finds me after a few minutes.

"Are you going to be all right to join us for dinner? Or an early breakfast, I'm not sure what to call it when you're eating at two a.m.," she asks.

I'm still shaky, and my mind is scattered, but food does sound good. I don't know what else I'll do for the next few hours if I don't join them, so I nod.

"Sure, I'll be fine."

"All right," Elise says, clearly skeptical. "Let's go. I'll drive you."

"It's tradition," Ivy says as she pushes a plate toward me. She's the only person still dressed in her suit. She seems comfortable in it though, like it's just how she prefers to be. "I started it in the Academy, back when I was with the FBI. Eating together, especially after a night like this, helps."

I grab the plate and pile a few pieces of pizza on it. "So, this is meant to be family bonding or something?"

Ivy shrugs. "Sure, but it's practical too. We need to discuss what was found and clean our weapons."

I sit down next to Elise. She's the only person here I am even remotely comfortable with. She's on her fourth piece of pizza already. I guess the shift really does increase a were's appetite.

Everyone else is already settled in. Hu and Corinne are discussing something about an upcoming council summit. I don't pay attention to what the councils get up to, and I don't care to start, so I tune them out.

"How's your leg?" I ask.

Elise shrugs. "I think there's still a speck of silver in there somewhere, but it's healing, so it'll work itself out tonight."

"If it doesn't, let me know. I can get it out," I say, taking a bite of my pizza before it gets cold.

"So you really can heal?" she asks.

"Yeah, nothing like what a real healer could do, but simple stuff like that is easy enough."

"You definitely packed a punch with that electric magic," she says with a short laugh and a shake of her head. "To be honest, I was kind of doubting whether or not you could actually use that kind of magic until I saw it."

"Well, I'm obviously not great with it."

"You moved really damn fast too. Is that some kind of physical magic? It wasn't part of what Stocke mentioned."

Elise has a way of asking not-so-innocent questions out of nowhere. I chew the bite of pizza in my mouth and swallow uncomfortably. Cook is staring at us from across the table, not even pretending not to be listening in.

"Um, yeah. Some kind." I shrug and grab another piece of pepperoni and jalapeño from the box. "I've never tried this combination on pizza before, but whoever ordered this was a genius. I'll never order anything else."

"I am, indeed, a genius," Hu says from the end of the table, toasting me with his own slice of pizza.

Agent Stocke walks in, and the conversation dies down. She's dressed down as well in a long-sleeved blouse and jeans. Her curly blonde hair is out of its bun. She grabs a plate and some pizza, then sits down at the head of the table.

"Tonight, we arrested three members of the NWR. A few were killed instead of being captured," Stocke says before taking a bite of pizza. "The raid didn't go perfectly, but everyone made it home, and no one on our side was seriously injured. Good job."

"Hell yeah," Elise says, lifting her can of soda in a toast. Everyone lifts whatever they're holding, pizza or drink, and sounds their agreement.

"Now, this particular cell seems to be relatively new. From what we found, it seems to confirm they were more of a recruitment center than anything else. We did, however, find bomb-making materials and information on several targets around the city. The suspects who were arrested are being interrogated, but none of them are offering up any information yet," Stocke says.

"Was there any information on their computers?" Hu asks.

Stocke shakes her head. "They were able to destroy the hard drives before we got to them."

"What's next?" Ivy asks.

"We have a flight to catch tomorrow evening. We're headed to Las Vegas," Stocke says.

"Vegas?" Cook asks, perking up.

Stocke nods. "We received a tip that Martinez may be in the city sometime in the next week or two."

"Any other information?" I ask, leaning forward, my heartbeat kicking into overdrive.

Stocke shakes her head. "Not on Martinez. You can look through all the intelligence we have on NWR activity in Las Vegas on the flight."

I hadn't thought there was any chance we might catch him quickly, but if we already know what city he's in, maybe there is hope. I stand to throw my plate away, and Elise hands me her plate as well, leaning back in her seat and patting her stomach in satisfaction.

I throw the trash away but have to pause at the unexpected jolt of pain that runs through my arm at the movement. It's been a couple of days since I've been able to apply the salve to my welts. I need something tonight; this is getting ridiculous.

"You gonna pass out on us again, Carter?" Cook asks from across the room. His tone suggests he hopes I do.

I roll my eyes and walk back to my chair, ignoring the slight dizziness that accompanies the movement.

"It's not a permanent fix, but Staci does have some salves that can help with the pain," Corinne says, her eyes full of concern.

"The traditional salve will help for now, but I need something stronger to really make a difference, and I don't have anything to brew what I need," I say, wiping some grease I had missed off my fingers.

"Can Olivia just borrow Staci's cauldron and brew whatever she needs?" Hu asks as he pops the trigger pin out of his gun.

"No."

"Absolutely not," Staci and I say in unison. I turn and glare at her, and she's frowning at me like it was my idea.

"She's not touching my cauldrons," Staci bites out like the idea disgusts her. I absolutely understand because I wouldn't let another witch near my cauldrons either, but her tone is a little much.

Hu looks at us, clearly amused. "Sorry I suggested it."

"I do have a basic healing salve with me," Staci says, patting her napkin on her mouth before standing and walking over to her briefcase. She unzips it and picks up a blue tub that is neatly labeled. "This should last you a couple of days. I'll make more once we are at our next location."

I walk over and take the tub. Staci looks smug about it, and I'm tempted to throw it back in her face, but this is one of those moments where it's really not worth it to let my pride get in the way.

"Thanks," I say with a flat expression.

"No problem," Staci says with a smile as she walks back to the table.

Once it's clear everyone is done eating, the remaining pizza gets cleared away. We pull out our guns, carefully clearing and checking them before laying them on the table.

Ivy had given me a cleaning kit along with the pistol. I grab it and go through the familiar motions of disassembling the Glock and laying out each piece. The minty smell of the lubricant takes me back five years.

I had spent most Sunday afternoons with Brunson and his

father at the shooting range, always followed by cleaning the guns, then the family dinner. It was their version of church.

I look up to find Zachary staring at me, and I pause, brush in hand. It takes him a moment to turn back to his gun. I'm sure he's reliving the same memories I am. It's bittersweet for me, I have no idea what it means to him anymore.

CHAPTER 8

❧

My hands are trembling as I pack up my gun and cleaning supplies. It's just past five am. I don't have long to get back to the room, and honestly, the feeding can't come soon enough. The pizza helped with some of the dizziness, but I still feel completely drained.

I try to slip out of the room unnoticed, but Corinne follows me into the hallway.

"We need to talk soon, about what's going on," she says quietly.

"I know, there's just nothing I can do about it today. I need to rest," I say, taking another couple of steps toward the elevator so she doesn't think I'm willing to linger.

"Then we talk as soon as we get to Vegas, all right?"

"Sounds like a plan."

The elevator dings and opens. I turn away and hurry inside, punching the button for floor six. Corinne stands in the hallway, watching me as the doors slide shut. I slump back against the wall and put my face in my hands. The welts are hurting more than I want to admit.

The elevator arrives at the sixth floor, and I step out but pause

333

in the hallway. I don't know who I'm going to be meeting tonight, but I don't want to go in there this weak.

I slip out of my jacket and crack open the little container. I can smell the sweet, light scent of aloe and some kind of mint. It's nothing like my healing salve, but as I dip my fingers in the cool cream, I can sense there is magic brewed into it.

The first swipe of the cream cools the welt considerably, but then it and the skin around it start to go numb. I sigh; if she had brewed the healing salve properly, it wouldn't need to numb anything. It would just *heal* it.

I spread it across my hands and up my arms regardless. I can't reach everything without undressing in the hallway, but the pain has already eased considerably. I feel a little cold and a little sticky now, but it's a welcome change from the constant aching.

I pull my jacket back on carefully and shove the tub in the pocket. The room is a short walk down the hall, but far enough for the nerves to settle in. I don't know what I'm going to do if the poor sap Reilly has in there is afraid or begs me not to feed from them.

The door swings open as I'm pulling out my keycard, and Reilly stands in the doorway, arms crossed.

"You're late," he says before sniffing carefully, then frowning. "Why do you smell like you bathed in toothpaste?"

"Because Staci is a shitty hedgewitch," I say, crossing my arms self-consciously.

Reilly raises a brow but steps aside and waves me into the room. I can smell the volunteer as soon as I step in and hear a slow and steady heartbeat. Whoever it is, they're not nervous like I feared. At least not yet.

A man about the same height as Reilly, but with short black hair, is currently leaning against the far wall, watching me. He is a bit pretty for a man, but he holds himself with an easy confidence. He has light hazel eyes that are currently working their way up to my face from my feet and cheekbones that could cut glass. The light stubble across his jaw keeps him from looking too feminine, but he wouldn't be out of place on a catwalk.

"Olivia, it's lovely to meet you," he says, strolling toward me with a predatory smile. "I'm Damien Black."

For someone who's about to be food, he's doing a good job of acting like he's in control of the situation.

"Is that your real name, or did you change it to try to sound like you're in a bad vampire romance novel?" I ask as I reach out to shake the hand he has held out.

His smile falters, but his handshake does not.

"You'll have to blame my mother for that one, perhaps she had bad taste in books."

"Be nice, Olivia," Reilly chastises.

I smile at Damien, but that doesn't seem to help exactly.

"Reilly said you required my assistance, and while I am happy to help," he pauses, his eyes flicking down to my lips, "in any way, what exactly did you have in mind?"

That explains the lack of nerves. I turn to Reilly and cross my arms.

"Seriously?"

Reilly ignores me and looks at Damien. "I'm calling in your debt."

Damien's face pales, and he swallows once. "In what manner?"

"You will allow Olivia to feed from you and take as much as she needs. You will speak of this to no one, not even your sire."

Damien's expression morphs into confusion, his brows knitting together.

"Feed from me? She smells like a witch."

"Your sense of smell must be severely lacking," Reilly says as he slips his hands into his pockets and leans back against the desk. "She's a vampire."

I force my fangs out and smile at him in lieu of further explanations. Damien looks at me carefully, taking in my jeans, wrinkled

T-shirt, pale face, and the small fangs pressing against my lower lip.

"I can hardly object to the attention of a beautiful woman," Damien says with a smile. "Where would you like to feed from?"

He tilts his head to the side in offer.

I snort. "Your wrist is fine."

Damien unbuttons the sleeve of his jacket while holding my gaze. His movements are slow, and his eyes keep straying to my lips. I suspect he might be doing it to wind up Reilly, and oddly, it seems to be working. Reilly's jaw clenches and unclenches slowly as he watches us.

"As requested," Damien says, lifting his now bared wrist in my direction.

I step forward and inhale, breathing in the light scent of leather that clings to Damien. I wrap my hand gently around his forearm and lean in, my mouth practically watering now that he's so close.

There is the slightest tremor in his hand. It's not visible, but I can feel it. It makes my stomach twist. He's afraid of me, of what I might take from him. It must be odd for a vampire to be fed from like this. Then again, anyone would be scared to not have a choice. I know it scares me.

I hesitate, my mouth hovering over his bared skin, as my hunger wars with my conscience. I glance up and see he is staring at me.

"It's all right, Olivia," he says, pushing his wrist toward me.

His heartbeat stays, elevated but steady, and something untwists inside of me. I bite down, and warm blood rushes into my mouth. The magic inside of Damien is stronger than I expected. Whoever he is, he is older and more powerful than Javier. He still isn't as strong as Reilly though. I pull and feel the cold strength pour into me.

Damien gasps, his eyes going wide. He can feel it already then, the strange pull from deep inside that's more than any normal feeding should take. He leans away slightly, but my grip on his wrist is unyielding. I can feel his pulse quickening with each tug on his magic.

The dizziness and pain I've felt since the raid fades away. My senses sharpen, and I can practically smell Damien's fear growing. I can hear people walking through the hall two floors down. I can hear Reilly's heartbeat thumping away in irritation.

I don't need to take any more blood or magic, but I don't want to stop. It feels too good. I hold Damien's gaze, but there is no heat to it anymore. His face is tight, and he keeps glancing at Reilly as if asking when this will be over. I bite down harder, my teeth bruising his skin around my fangs. He should be asking me, not Reilly. I'm the one taking, I'm the one who gets to decide, I'm—

The hunger is overwhelming. Taking magic like this makes it even worse. I have to stop this, or I'll take too much. Reilly blackmailed Damien into this, and I can't leave him vulnerable and drained like I did Javier.

I tear my fangs out of his wrist and press the back of my hand to my lips as I swallow the last of the blood in my mouth. I'm panting like I just ran a mile. I take a step backward so I don't grab Damien again.

"What the hell was that?" Damien asks, breathing almost as hard as I am.

"You can consider the debt paid in full. However, if I find out you have spoken of this to anyone, I will personally put you in a coffin," Reilly says, his arms still crossed.

Damien straightens, trying to force his face back into indifference but failing.

"Business as usual, then," he says.

I step out of his way and sit on the end of my bed.

Damien hurries toward the door, staying as far away from me as he can, and I flop back. The door opens and shuts, and an awkward silence settles between me and Reilly.

My body is buzzing with magic, but mentally, I'm exhausted.

"I don't want to do that again," I say, staring at the ceiling.

"You may have to if you exhaust yourself like that again. You have to maintain control, and you have to recover," Reilly says.

"I know, but I'm not going to take from someone unwilling like that again. I shouldn't have done it this time."

Reilly is silent for a moment. "You need to be practical. It's going to be hard, if not impossible, to find someone willing to let you feed on their magic."

I roll over onto my side, putting my back to him.

"I don't care."

All I can think about is the tremor in Damien's hand. It's the same way my hands shook when I realized Reilly knew what I was and was going to use it against me. I can't do that to someone else.

Reilly sighs deeply but doesn't argue farther. Exhaustion steals over me, and I realize the sun must have just risen. I squeeze my eyes shut and slip into sleep.

CHAPTER 9

For some reason, I had been expecting some kind of private plane, not an economy class ticket on a generic airline. The flight had been noisy, there were two bachelorette parties on board, and there hadn't been any leg room. The plane landed around one a.m., and we took a cab to the hotel, which isn't even on the Strip. The rest of Vegas looks sadly normal compared to the glitz and glam you expect from Sin City.

The hotel we're staying at is nice though, so I can't really complain. I dunk my head under the spray again and rinse out the conditioner. The JHAPI agents are all busy chasing down information on the alleged sighting of Martinez. My only assignment for the evening is to meet with Corinne and work on fixing the effects of my stupidity with the Finding magic.

I shut off the water and climb out. The heat is starting to irritate the welts, so I don't want to linger. I wrap myself up in the oversized towel and reach for the tub of salve but don't pick it up. They are irritated but aren't hurting that badly right now, and I'd like to make sure I can tell if anything changes while I'm with Corinne tonight. I don't want to be numbed at all.

I get ready quickly and without putting in too much effort. My hair goes up in a loose bun, and I wear a loose T-shirt and my most comfortable pair of jeans.

When I walk out of the bathroom, Reilly is sitting in the chair at the desk, waiting for me.

"You're going to see Corinne?" he asks.

"Yes." I wrap my hand around my forearm. "I need to try to fix this."

He nods. "Don't overdo it today."

"I'm not going to," I say in exasperation. "Do you think I'm an idiot? I don't want a repeat of last night."

"Come directly back here when you are done. I expect to see you before sunrise," he says, ignoring my outburst.

"Sure thing, *Dad*," I say sarcastically.

Reilly grins. "I always suspected you had daddy issues."

"Oh, shut up," I snap.

The phone Elise gave me back in Phoenix buzzes once. I flip it open angrily and see a text from Corinne; she's on her way. I'm impressed this old thing can even send and receive texts.

She had insisted on coming to fetch me from my room. I'm starting to think the team has a pact with Reilly to help monitor me twenty-four/seven.

Reilly looks at his watch and stands. "I'll be back in a couple of hours. Don't make me come find you."

I roll my eyes and scoff, pulling on a sock.

"Or you'll be grounded," he says.

I glare at him, but he's grinning, his dimples on full display like they're trying to disguise the fact that he's an asshole.

"I hope you get staked," I mutter.

He clasps his hands over his heart in mock agony.

"So cruel," he says with a laugh as he walks toward the door.

I focus intently on my other sock until I hear him open and close the door. I listen to his footsteps disappear down the hall, then, once he's far enough away, I throw myself back on the bed and curse him soundly.

It takes a few deep breaths, but I pull myself together and sit up. I pull on one shoe, then hear a knock at the door. I go answer it, the other shoe in hand. I peek through the peephole, just to be sure it's Corinne, but when I see it is her, I open the door and wave her inside.

"I'm almost ready," I say in lieu of a hello. "Come on in."

"No problem," Corinne says with her ever-ready smile as she steps through the doorway.

"Do I need to bring anything?" I ask as I sit down and pull on my other shoe.

"No, just yourself and an open mind," she says, looking around the room curiously. My clothes are strewn around my bags and bed. I've always found that when living out of a suitcase, my clothes have a way of ending up all over the place.

"Where are we going anyhow?" I ask.

"The room Ivy and I are staying in," Corinne says. "I just thought the walk would give us a few minutes to chat and get comfortable."

I chuckle. "Okay."

"I know, I'm kind of a hippie," Corinne says with a smile. "My coven is very unorthodox, which is part of why I even ended up in JHAPI. Most covens wouldn't allow it."

"I was surprised to hear there was a Finder on the team. You could be earning a lot more money doing private work."

Corinne nods. "It wouldn't be as fulfilling. I do take the occasional private commission, but most of the work I do outside of JHAPI is charitable. I make enough to pay my bills. I'm not concerned about becoming rich, and my coven is supportive of that."

"Must be nice," I say, standing. "I've never heard of a coven like that."

"You aren't part of a coven are you?"

"Nope." I shake my head decisively. "And I never will be."

Corinne nods without argument.

Most witches lose their shit when I say something like that. Covens are part-protection, part-employment, and part-family. Usually highly dysfunctional families, but witches are still very loyal. Most will stay with the coven they are born into unless they are courted away somehow. Everyone understands moving to a better coven for reasons like money or power, just as long as you don't turn into a coven hopper.

"Are you ready?" she asks.

"Yes." I grab my key card and wallet and follow her out the door. Their room is a floor up, but luckily the elevator doors open as soon as she presses the button.

"So, were you able to Find people from a young age? Or did you discover it on accident somehow?" Corinne asks as we step inside. She fiddles with her necklace, rolling the crystal back and forth between her fingers.

"It's more of a recent, uh, acquisition," I say hesitantly. Stocke didn't explain how I was able to use more than one type of magic, and I'm not eager to get into the details. The elevator doors open, and we head down the hall.

"After the raid, you seemed like you were hurt, and possibly upset?"

"I was just exhausted, magically. The welts started bothering me."

She slips her key card into the door and opens it, waving me inside first. Her room is exactly the same as the one Reilly and I are staying in. There is a simple, black suitcase next to the bed closest to the door, and then two bright red bags next to the other. I assume that must be Corinne's bed.

"You didn't seem upset about being shot at though," she says as she walks over to the desk that sits to the right of the television. She grabs an electric kettle and heads toward the bathroom.

I pace toward her bed and sit down on the edge since there is only one chair, and I'm not sure where else to sit.

"I guess I wasn't, really. I was relieved no one was seriously hurt," I say with a shrug.

"Have you been shot at before?" she asks.

"Yes."

"That's pretty unusual outside of law enforcement." She walks back into the main area and plugs her kettle into an outlet underneath the desk.

"Not as unusual for witches outside of a coven."

"I didn't realize that," she says thoughtfully, finger tapping against her chin. "I don't know that I've ever met a covenless witch before."

"I imagine you haven't," I say with a sharp laugh. "You seem like a nice lady."

She shrugs. "You seem like a nice lady too."

"I suppose I am now. For the most part."

"Did you know that in the past, Finders didn't use maps when working their magic?" Corinne asks, changing the subject abruptly.

"I'd never thought about it. I guess there weren't always maps, definitely not as detailed as we have now, were there?"

"No, and back then, your types of injuries were much more common. Being a Finder was dangerous. They're rare now because so many families lost their sons and daughters to the magic, and their lines ended."

I had studied magical history as a child, but it hadn't interested me at the time, and I don't remember much of it. The kettle beeps behind her, and she pours the hot water into one of the paper cups. She drops in a teabag and stirs a packet of sugar into her tea, then takes a sip to test it. She nods contentedly and sits in the chair behind her, the cup cradled in her hands.

"How did they use it at all without a map?"

"Finding magic, at its most basic level, is trying to guide you to the living thing you are trying to find. It uses whatever tools you provide. A witching rod. A map. Or nothing more than your magic itself. That's the most dangerous way to use it, of course, because the farther away you are from your target, the more of your magic it needs."

"Is that why the rule is to not try to Find someone who you can't guarantee will be on the map in front of you?" I ask.

Corinne nods. "We follow all these safety rules now, and people forget why. I think they're overly limiting, but I also think the only people who should be bending them are advanced users with a deep understanding of magical theory."

"That sounds a lot like people's attitudes toward brewing. Safety first. Don't experiment." I shake my head. "Brewing without experimentation is just— chemistry. It's not even magic anymore."

Corinne laughs. "It somehow doesn't surprise me you think that."

I shrug, unapologetic. She lifts her necklace, and the crystal spins a little, back and forth, from the sudden movement.

"This is actually a sort of witching rod. It's an old pendulum that's been in my family for so long, no one actually knows when it was acquired," she says, her eyes following the movement of the crystal. "I've used it several times in particularly difficult cases. I think it helps me channel my magic, to keep it from getting away from me."

I lean forward to see it better. From a distance, it just looks like any old amber crystal, but I realize it's not that at all.

"Is that carnelian?" I ask.

"Yes," Corinne says with a grin. "I think you may need to get something like this when you can. It can be hard to find something that will work, and there are things you need to learn before you even attempt to use one, but it might help you."

"What do I need to learn first?"

She drops the necklace and leans forward, clasping her hands together. "You are going to Find me."

I raise my brow. "You're right in front of me."

"Exactly," she says, pointing at me. "You won't have to strain your magic at all, and you can practice not only controlling it, but really feeling it. I get the impression that every time you've used it has been in a sort of panic."

I shrug. "You're not wrong."

"One of the ways my mother taught me was by playing hide and seek with me as a child, except I had to use my magic to Find her. It was a simple game, but it worked well. I learned how to listen to my magic."

"I didn't realize it could work with the person right in front of you."

Corinne nods. "It does. Are you willing to try it tonight?"

I hesitate. I don't want to overdo it and have to feed again, but I have to be able to fix this. The welts are only going to get worse if I don't.

"How much magic will this use? I can't overdo it, or I'll be comatose for almost eight hours," I say finally.

"Hardly any. I doubt it will be anything more than uncomfortable. Of course, this is magic; I can't guarantee anything."

"All right, then. Let's do this," I say, standing. I'm worried, and a little scared of how this might go, but that's never stopped me before.

Corinne grins. "First, I'm going to blindfold you and have you put on these earmuffs. Then, I want you to Find me. What you're looking for is that tug in your gut that tells you where I am in relation to you. You'll point left or right, then let go of the magic, and we'll do it again."

She hands me a pair of black earmuffs that smells like it came straight out of her gun cleaning kit, then a fluffy eye mask. I take them and hold them hesitantly.

"How, exactly, do I Find you without a map?"

"I suggest starting by using your hands like a witching rod. You do something similar when using Finding magic with a map. Let them point me out like this room is one big map," Corinne says, spreading her arms wide.

I take a deep breath and mentally shake off the nerves.

"All right, I guess I'll just try it."

Corinne moves to stand directly in front of me. "Remember, once you Find me, just point left or right, then let it go."

I nod, then pull on the eye mask, followed by the earmuffs. I can hear the sound of my own breathing, but nothing else. I shake my hands out, then clasp them tightly together.

The Finding magic is responsive as soon as I tug on it. My arms burn immediately as well, but not bad enough that I'm worried. It's more like what I felt when Corinne was using her magic at that first meeting.

I picture Corinne as she looks right now. Simple green blouse, jeans, and her wavy hair loose around her face. The magic moves through me like a wave and pushes out into the room. It's an odd sensation. In the past, it has been directed toward the map. This makes me feel off-balance, like all of my senses are focused outside of my body.

I squint even though I can't see and try to sort out what exactly I'm sensing. I can feel the shape of the room as the magic searches with invisible fingers. I extend my hands cautiously and feel a pull that grows stronger and stronger to my left. My magic slides around Corinne like water.

There's a flash of an image in my mind. It's of me with my hands outstretched. My lips are turned down into a frown, and my brows are furrowed tightly together. The image disappears as quickly as it arrived, but I'm left trembling and drained.

"Left," I gasp out as I begin pulling the Finding magic back into myself. I rip off the earmuffs and the eye mask and toss them on the bed beside me. My hands are shaking, and the welts are burning enough that I have to grit my teeth to keep from groaning.

"Are you okay?" Corinne asks, hurrying to my side.

"It took too much. I think I saw something—" I stop, struggling for words with the pain coursing through my arms.

"Another hallucination?"

"No," I say, shaking my head fervently. "It wasn't like that at all. I saw me. I think I was seeing what you were seeing."

Corinne sits back on her heels and looks at me with wide eyes.

"You don't do anything by halves, do you?" she asks with a laugh.

I stare at her, wondering if she's lost her mind. "I'm glad you find this funny."

"It's not that," she says, shaking her head fervently. "Your ability to focus is excellent. Perhaps too good. I think it's what got you in trouble when you tried to Find your mother."

"I don't understand."

"You have a lot of power and raw talent, and you can easily hone in on what you are trying to Find. Someone as inexperienced as you shouldn't be able to Find someone who is no longer living, much less get their magic so entangled that they can't undo it. It should just have failed."

I put my head in my hands. "Double-edged sword, then."

"Pretty much," Corinne agrees.

"Do you believe in ghosts?" I ask. It's been bothering me since the first time I saw her, and I figure now is as good a time to ask as any.

"Ghosts?" she asks, tilting her head to the side. "No."

She leans back against the desk and crosses her arms, looking at me critically.

"Are you asking because you have seen what you assume is a ghost?"

I shift on the bed, leaning forward to rest my elbows on my knees.

"I've seen her more than once. My mother," I say quietly. "It's like she's haunting me ever since I tried to Find her."

"Where and when have you seen her?" she asks, tucking her hair behind her ears.

"The first time was in the hotel, the morning we arrived. I saw her in the mirror. The second time was during the raid. I saw her in this chrome planter. She pointed behind me, and that's when I realized someone was sneaking up on me. She saved my life."

"Hmm, that is an interesting manifestation," Corinne says.

"Interesting how?" I ask, twisting my hands together. I want her to respond, to tell me I'm not crazy. Or that I am but she can fix it.

"Well, for one, there's no such thing as ghosts. Superstitious human nonsense. You did find a sort of echo though. It's like you're being haunted by her memory," Corinne says, picking up her tea and taking a long drink. "The magic searched everywhere to find her, and because you cannot let her go, your magic is tied up in making these hallucinations manifest. It's the most basic thing we teach Finders, but of course, you were never taught."

I gnaw at the inside of my cheek. On the one hand, I'm glad I'm not being haunted by the ghost of my mother, but it had felt so real. Part of me doesn't want to give up being able to see her.

"And the warning? Is that just a memory too?"

Corinne shrugs. "A memory, your magic protecting you, perhaps."

Her answer is underwhelming, perhaps because I wanted it to mean something more. I take a deep breath and press the heel of my hands into my eyes for a moment, then look up.

"So what now?"

She sets her tea down and walks over to me, pushing up my sleeve. She traces one of the welts on my arm with a feather-light touch.

"This will never fade until you can untangle your magic and let go."

"Let go of what, exactly?"

"This kind of thing happens when the person using the Finding magic is obsessed with Finding someone. You may have tried to end the spell, but you didn't. You are burning yourself up with the magic, and the only way to stop it is to let go. You have to accept that you will never Find her. That she's gone."

I grit my teeth and dig my nails into my palms.

"I know she's gone. She's dead."

Corinne smiles gently.

"You know it up here," she says, pointing to her head. "But you need to accept it here." She points to her heart.

"It sounds like you're saying I need to just get over the fact that my mom is dead."

"That's not what I'm saying at all," Corinne says sharply, her lips pulling into a frown. "I'm saying that you have to accept that she isn't coming back. It's not something you can do overnight either. Until then, it's just going to be difficult."

"No offense, but I really thought you'd be more helpful than this."

Corinne's frown twists up into a smile. "I hear that a lot. You should have Staci brew you something for those welts."

"I still have enough salve left to last for a few days. I can figure this out before I run out of it," I say, tugging my sleeve back down over my forearm.

Corinne presses her lips together, her face skeptical, but she doesn't argue.

"I should just get some sleep," I say, standing. I head toward the door, wishing I could just be alone for a few hours. Maybe I can hide out in the bathroom for a while.

"I'm sorry, Olivia," Corinne says as I turn the door handle. "For your loss. It's awful, and you'll always miss her."

I pull the door open and walk out without responding. My feet lead me to the elevators, but I hit the button for the first floor. I can't go back to the room yet.

The elevator is empty and carries me swiftly to the ground floor. The sun will be rising soon, and I want to see it. I push through the double doors that lead out of the hotel and step out into the brisk air. The wind is blowing hard, pushing my hair around my face and cooling the hot sting of tears that escaped down my cheeks when I wasn't paying attention.

The buildings here are spaced farther apart in this city than the one I grew up in. They're far enough apart that you can see the sunrise on the horizon between them. They're bathed in reds and golds right now as the sun begins creeping up into the sky.

The vampire magic curls up inside of me like a cat, stealing some of my energy as it goes dormant. The sounds of cars get a little more distant, and the heartbeat of the man hurrying down the sidewalk across the street simply ceases. I feel human for a moment.

With a sigh, I turn to go back inside, but I stop when I see a woman with long brown hair reflected in the hotel door. She's smiling at me, a worn book in her hand. My heart twists all over again, and I realize what Corinne meant. I don't want to stop seeing her.

I yank the door open and stomp inside. It's going to be a long night tomorrow.

CHAPTER 10

The JHAPI office is located on the outskirts of the city. It's a large, square three-story building. The bottom is red brick, while the top two stories are white brick, making it look like someone stacked two different buildings on top of each other. A large archway stands in front of the building. There are three pillars in the archway representing the three tenets of JHAPI. Fidelity, Bravery, and Integrity, something borrowed from the FBI since JHAPI was originally just another department within that organization.

We step out of the car, and I pull my jacket tighter around me. The temperature dropped fast after the sun went down. Reilly's phone rings as he shuts his door.

"Yes?" Reilly asks as he answers it. There is a pause. "No, I don't want her mingling with the rest of the clan yet."

I glance back at him and pull on the vampire magic, hoping to hear the other side of the conversation.

"—control is excellent, and she had requested a little more independence," the caller says. It sounds like it might be the tattooed man I met at Javier's.

"I'm glad to hear it, but I know you understand my reasons for wanting to keep her away from the others," Reilly says, sounding annoyed like this isn't the first time he has had this conversation.

"For how long?" the caller asks.

"At least a couple of weeks more. If she's getting too restless, take her out somewhere; just make sure it's away from the clan."

"Yes, sir," the caller says, resignation clear in his tone.

Reilly hangs up the phone and looks at me.

"Was that about Leslie?" I ask.

"Yes," he says as he starts toward the building. I trot after him.

"Is she all right?"

"Yes," he says again.

"Why won't you let her meet the rest of your clan?"

He stops short, and I almost run into his back. He looks back over his shoulder.

"What did Maybelle tell you about how your mother conceived you?" he asks, his eyes scanning my face for the answer. "A question for a question, Olivia. I've already answered two of yours."

I grit my teeth. He can't ever make anything easy. I brush past him, but his hand on my arm stops me.

"You are going to tell me eventually. I've been asking nicely, but I won't do that forever," he says, voice low and his breath on my ear.

I jerk my arm away. "I hate you."

He laughs like that's the best joke he's heard all week. "You sound like a petulant teenager."

I open my mouth to argue with him, but he simply walks around me and heads toward the entrance. I stay where I am for a moment, equal parts angry and frustrated, before following after him. I really do hate him.

Elise and Zachary reach the front door just before I do. Zachary holds the door open and lets me walk in before him.

"I cannot get used to this schedule," Elise says, pressing the back of her hand to her mouth as she yawns.

"It might be easier if you actually went to bed in the mornings instead of watching TV," Zachary mutters.

Elise rolls her eyes. "It'd be easier if you didn't snore."

Zachary glares at her. "I don't snore."

I laugh and try to turn it into a cough, but Zachary has already turned his glare to me.

"I'm sorry, but you definitely snore," I say, stepping back and raising my hands in apology.

Elise claps me on the back. "This is why I like you. Now, we need to get upstairs, or we're going to be late."

Reilly is already in the elevator. He holds the door open for us, and we all squeeze inside. My stomach lurches as it speeds toward the top floor. It stops just as abruptly as it started, and the doors slide open.

The conference room is directly across from the elevators. It's not as nice as the one in Phoenix. There is only one window, and it's not very big, so the room is stuffier and darker. The rest of the team is already there. We grab empty seats at the end of the table, and Corinne slides coffee in our direction.

Stocke stands and looks around the table, making sure she has everyone's attention.

"One of the reasons we're here in Vegas is because of recent disappearances, now believed to be kidnappings or murders. Vampires from five different clans have gone missing. Each clan has only lost a single member, and each clan leader had reason to believe the vampire might have simply run away. However, per clan law, they were still reported as missing to the vampire council." Stocke pulls up a slide with pictures of five vampires, the dates of their disappearances, and their names next to them. "The disappearances caused alarm; there were too many to be a coincidence. The vampire council forwarded this information to JHAPI to investigate. Because of the increased chatter from the NWR in this area and the sighting of Martinez just last week, the case is believed to be related. We will be investigating this until we find the missing vampires, or find proof it is unrelated to terrorism."

"Have any other paranormals gone missing?" Elise asks.

Stocke nods in Elise's direction, looking pleased with her question. "The other councils have not reported any missing persons. However, I would like you to go in person to the local were packs and ask them. Explain that vampires have gone missing and that we are concerned what the NWR is up to. If nothing else, I'd like them to be extra cautious in the coming weeks."

"Sure thing, Boss. I'd like to take Olivia with me if that's all right," Elise says.

"I have no objections," Stocke says with a nod. "Corinne and Hu, I'd like you to do the same with the local covens."

"We'll get started tomorrow morning, bright and early," Hu says with a grin. Corinne nods in agreement.

"Reilly, would you be able to accompany Ivy to speak to the clans that have had a missing vampire?" Stocke asks, looking toward Reilly at the end of the table.

"Yes." Reilly nods.

"Everyone else will be following up on the Martinez sighting. I want everyone who might have seen him questioned. I want every surveillance tape that might have caught a glimpse of him walking down the street. I want to know who he is talking to, what he is doing, and where he is."

The remaining agents all nod.

"Corinne," Stocke says. "In a couple of days, I'd like you to attempt to Find him. However, we're going to do it by the book and take every safety measure possible. I want to know with certainty that he is close by."

"Yes, ma'am," Corinne says, sitting up straighter. I'm surprised Stocke is being so overly cautious about trying to Find him. I thought it would be one of the first things Corinne did when we got here.

"All right, everyone get to work. Anyone you can't talk to

tonight, find a way to see them tomorrow during the day. I want progress updates, and anything of note should be sent to the entire team immediately."

I spend the entire night with Elise poring over pack member lists for the two packs in the Las Vegas area. The werewolf council has always refused to report their exact numbers, insisting instead on giving ranges in terms of pack size in certain areas. The lists Elise have been cobbled together from personal knowledge of contacts in the area and whatever information the local police have.

Reilly had disappeared after an hour to go visit one of the clans since they're actually awake in the middle of the night. I almost wished I could go with him, just to avoid reading any more reports. Luckily, Elise called it quits well before sunrise.

Elise parks the car, and I rub my eyes, only half-awake.

"Thanks for the ride," I mumble as I open the car door.

"Yeah, no problem," she says with a yawn. "I'll see you tomorrow at ten a.m."

"So early," I whine.

"The rest of the world hasn't adapted to the night shift," Elise says as we walk toward the elevators. "Just be glad we get to sleep at all."

We ride the elevator up to our floor silently and head our separate directions with a short wave goodbye. I hope Reilly isn't back yet. It would be nice to fall asleep without feeling watched.

I finally reach the hotel room and dig the key card out of my back pocket. I slip it into the lock, and the light switches to green with a click. I push open the door and stop on the threshold. Reilly is sitting on his bed, and a girl is sitting on him. Her shirt is stretched down over her shoulder, and his fingers are tangled in her hair, pulling her head sharply to one side to expose her neck.

His tongue trails up across a fresh bite. She shudders and

moans, but he is looking at me. There's no shame or embarrassment in his face, but I can feel mine heating up.

My fingers tighten on the door as a wave of conflicting emotions crash through me. The first is anger. Then jealousy, which only makes me angrier. Then annoyance, and finally exhaustion. I don't want to deal with whatever this is. I'm not sure if he intended to taunt me, or if he just didn't expect me back so soon. He has to feed; I just expected him to do it anywhere but our room.

I take a step back and pull the door shut, then rub my hands over my face. Elise's room has a couch just like mine. Maybe she won't mind if I sleep on it.

I'm barely three steps from the door when it opens again and Reilly shoos the girl out. I keep walking without looking back. His footsteps get louder instead of quieter though, and I can hear his heartbeat speeding up.

"Olivia, where are you going?" he asks as he wraps his hand around my arm.

"Just finding somewhere to sleep," I say, attempting to tug my arm out of his grip.

"Then come back to the room."

"No, you have company," I say, swaying on my feet slightly.

He frowns at me, eyes scanning my face.

"She's gone, and you're exhausted. Come back to the room."

I sigh deeply and run a hand down my face.

"Don't do that again," I say quietly.

"Do what?" he asks.

"Bring your dinner back to the hotel," I say sharply.

"Why does it bother you?"

"It's just gross. You could have at least put a sock on the door. That's common courtesy."

He smirks. "Were you jealous?"

"No," I say, looking up at him in alarm. "No. Absolutely not."

His smirk widens into a smile, and he presses his hand into my lower back.

"Come get some sleep. It won't happen again."

His heartbeat stays steady. He means it.

CHAPTER 11

I haven't been awake at noon in well over a week. It's painfully sunny, and the roads are much busier than they are at night. I yawn and squint as I stare out the window. We've driven about twenty minutes north of the city.

Everything immediately around us is flat, including the shrubs and cactus. Nothing seems capable of growing higher than my knee. The mountains on the horizon look like crumbling mounds of dirt. They aren't regal like the mountains I've always seen in pictures with snow on their peaks and trees climbing up the base. Even the sky seems flat here. There are no clouds, just a washed out blue that fades into white at the horizon.

We round a turn, and the first body of water I've seen since we arrived in Nevada appears. It's bordered by dull green grass that's swaying stiffly in the breeze. We've somehow gotten into the hills I had seen in the distance without me realizing it. The river blinks in and out of view between them as we drive.

Elise slows down, then turns left and drives over a small bridge that crosses the river. The pavement doesn't last long, and the car bumps along a gravel road that is mostly designated by the high fence that springs up along either side of us. A mile away from the main highway, we arrive at the main gate.

On each side of the wrought iron gate are pillars of white stone stacked as high as the fence. In front of each pillar is a statue of a wolf. The one on the left is sitting, staring straight ahead. The expression on its face is creepily life-like. The one on the right is howling, its head thrown back and its eyes shut.

Elise comes to a stop in front of the gate and presses a buzzer. Immediately, the gates swing outward. We drive in slowly, but I can't help glancing back at the wolf on the left after we pass through. I almost expect it to have turned around to watch us somehow.

The road winds through more low hills for a quarter of a mile before it opens up to about twenty acres of flat land, neat lawns, and cookie cutter houses. The road we're on goes down the center of the subdivision. At the end of it is a huge stone house that looks like a castle. A watchtower extends up from the middle of the structure. I wonder if the architect didn't realize how phallic it looked, or if that was the point.

Elise pulls over to the side of the street just before the first house and parks the car. There is a man sitting in a rocking chair on the porch. His hands are folded in his lap like he's relaxed, but I can see the coiled tension in his body. He pushes the chair back and forth in a steady rhythm as he watches us. There is no one else to be seen, but I'm sure they're hiding somewhere.

Elise opens her door, and we both climb out of the car. The man stands up and walks down the front steps, coming to a stop at the edge of the yard. His shoulders are wide, and the muscles in his arms are straining against the fabric of his sleeves, but he walks with an easy grace you don't expect of a bigger man.

I tuck my hands into my pockets and wait for Elise to approach before I walk after her. She stops a few yards from the man, who I assume is the alpha of this pack, and pulls out her badge.

I pull on the vampire magic as well as I can in the middle of the day. It's sluggish, but it does respond. The fact that I can't see anyone else makes me nervous. I don't think this is an ambush, but I'd like to be able to hear and smell everything I can.

There are three more heartbeats in the house behind the pack leader. The scent of werewolf is overwhelmingly strong, like they've marked the place. I can't smell anything else, and I'm regretting being able to smell that at all.

"Pack Leader Miller, I spoke with your secretary yesterday evening about meeting with you. My name is Elise Hawking. I'm an agent with JHAPI."

The man purses his lips and nods. "Yes, you are here to investigate the NWR. I can assure you we aren't harboring any of them."

Elise laughs and puts away her badge. "That's good to know. However, that's not what brought me here today."

"Who is this with you?" Miller asks, looking past her at me.

Elise looks back as well and waves me forward. I come to stand beside her.

"This is Olivia Carter. She is working with JHAPI at the request of the council," Elise says, carefully leaving off *vampire* council, probably hoping he'll assume I'm a witch based on my scent.

Miller looks at me for a long moment, inhaling deeply, then turns back to Elise. "What does bring you here today, if not searching for NWR members on my lands?"

"Missing persons," Elise says.

Miller doesn't seem surprised, or concerned, at her proclamation. "No one is missing."

Lie.

Elise tilts her head. "Five vampires have gone missing. All from different clans, all high flight risks. The only reason anyone noticed is that the clans all reported them missing, and the council noticed the trend. Is it possible that's happening with the local packs?"

Miller shakes his head. "There are only two packs around here. It would be noticed by us."

Not a lie.

"Noticed, but not necessarily reported?" Elise prods.

"My pack will always do its duty to the council," Miller says, his tone going hard.

Not a lie. I hear movement inside the house and glance at the window. The curtain is swaying slightly, like someone just moved it.

Elise pulls her card out of her pocket. "If you do hear or see anything suspicious, please call me. I'd also recommend caution over the next couple of weeks. We're not sure what the NWR is planning, but there has been increased activity in the area."

Miller steps forward and takes the card from Elise, shoving it in his pocket. I'm sure it will be thrown away as soon as we leave.

"Thank you for your time. I hope to hear from you soon," Elise says. She turns and walks straight back to the car, but I take a few steps backward first. I don't want to turn my back on Miller. I don't think he would attack me, not really, but the primal part of my brain recognizes that he's a serious threat.

Miller turns and walks back inside before I even get back to the car. I slip in and slam the door shut.

"He was lying," I say, glaring at the curtain that is swaying again.

"Yes, he was," Elise says, her nostrils flaring in irritation. "He knew we could both tell, and he lied to our faces."

"Why would they do that?" I ask.

"They're telling us to back off. That it's a pack issue and they don't want our dirty, JHAPI help." Elise throws the car into drive and whips the car around. "Stupid, overly traditional, dumb assholes."

"It shouldn't surprise me. I could see a coven doing the same thing," I say with a sigh.

Elise rubs her hands roughly over her mouth. "I get their hesitation, it just frustrates me. JHAPI has done really good work over the last five years, but we could have done so much more if the paranormal community actually trusted us."

"Do you think there's any chance he'll call?" I ask.

Elise shakes her head. "Not really. I just have to try."

The gate opens, and Elise pulls onto the highway.

"That whole thing where everyone was watching us, but no one else was outside was creepy as hell. Just for the record," I say.

Elise laughs. "I guess it is. I've been on the other side before, which takes away a lot of the intimidation factor. I know they have all the kids in there, giggling and daring each other to peek out."

I smile. "That does make it less intimidating."

"You're training with Hu this afternoon, right?" she asks.

I nod. "Yeah, apparently sleep isn't necessary."

"Coffee is all you need," Elise says solemnly. "You'll come to accept that soon."

I shake my head. "Coffee can only help so much."

CHAPTER 12

The gym is in the basement. There are way more fluorescent lights than necessary, filling the whole room with a harsh lighting. There is a rack of weights on the back wall, which is also lined with mirrors. To the right is an MMA style octagon cage, and to the left are five punching bags hung in a row. The floor is wooden, except for two matted areas by the cage and the bags.

Hu is at the punching bags, and he is frighteningly strong. He cuts across the front of the bag and throws a left hook punch. His fist connects with a deep, resounding smack that shakes the bag on the chain. He punches with the other hand, then slides backward with a quick jab. He's a fast and powerful striker. I hope he isn't expecting me to spar with him.

He's wearing a tight black tank that clings to the muscles in his back. I can see more of the tattoo that is always peeking out of his collar. My first impression that it is fire was wrong. It's the tip of a vibrant red and orange wing that disappears into his shirt. He circles around the bag, striking faster and faster, stopping only when he spots me.

"Hey, Olivia," he says, leaving the bag swinging and jogging toward me.

"Hey," I say, mustering a smile. He is helping me in his free time, so I'm going to try to be as pleasant as possible even if I have been forced to get up before the sun has set and I feel like shit.

"I'm glad we found time to do this today," Hu says. "Have you received any training at all for this magic? Or has it always been something you hid?"

"No training," I say uncomfortably.

"All right," he says. "Well, let's get started with this."

Hu jogs over to the corner and drags a training dummy over to the empty area between the punching bags and the door. It's the torso and head of a man, no arms, on a black stand. This sort of dummy is normally used for kicking practice. This particular one looks like it has seen better days. The head is lopsided, and there are random gouges and a stain that looks suspiciously like blood.

"This thing is getting thrown away after today," Hu says, rubbing his hands together. "So I was able to talk them into letting us use it for a little practice."

"What kind of practice, exactly?" I ask.

"I want you to show me an attack. Use your electric magic," Hu says as he walks over to stand beside me.

"Okay, so just…" I gesture at it and make an explosion noise.

"Keep it on the lighter side. I'd just like to see what you know." Hu steps back a few steps behind me and nods in encouragement.

I face the dummy, hands on my hips. I don't really know anything about how to use this type of magic, but I don't want to admit that just yet. The things I have done have been on instinct, and they were effective. Maybe I can do this.

I take a deep breath and let the electric magic buzz through me. The hair on my arms stands on end, and some of the hair on my head floats up like someone rubbed it with a balloon. I lift my hands, and a sparking ball of light and electricity hurtles from my palms toward the dummy.

It hits it with a flash and a sound like thunder that makes me flinch. The center of the dummy is melted and twisted, and the lopsided head is now hanging off the side, connected by one lumpy strip.

I clear my throat and smooth down the flyaway hairs that are still floating around me. I feel staticky. With one final breath, I turn around to face Hu.

He has his chin in his hand, and he is staring at the smoldering remains of the practice dummy. He starts to say something, then shakes his head.

"What?" I ask, crossing my arms and looking back at it self-consciously.

"That was very—powerful," he says haltingly. "I'm glad you didn't actually follow through on your threat to Cook in the meeting room the other day. I'd have ended up scorched too."

I smirk at the mental image of Cook looking like the practice dummy. It's harder to be smug without a head. Or a chest.

"As great as that sounds, I wouldn't have done all that to him," I say, waving a hand at it dismissively.

"Are you sure about that?" Hu asks.

I shrug. "Yes?"

"Show me a light attack," he says, waving at the dummy and stepping back a couple of paces.

I frown. He's being dramatic. I can do a light attack. I just didn't understand how light he wanted that last one to be. It's probably easier than putting all my power into it anyhow.

I lift my hands again and pool the magic in my palms. The electricity streaks across the space, a bolt this time, and slams into the dummy, knocking it backward and splitting the base in half. I drop my hands and swallow uncomfortably.

"OK, so I might have a problem with controlling this," I say as I look down at my still tingling fingers.

"Yes," Hu says, striding toward the wall and grabbing a fire extinguisher. He sprays down the dummy but keeps the extinguisher as he walks over to me. "Let's start with something a lot more basic."

I rub my hands against my sweats and nod in agreement. "Right. Basic."

"When using offensive magic, you have two options. A big, powerful attack," he says, gesturing at the dummy. "Or a precise, focused attack that uses less magic and requires less strength."

He lifts his right arm, and fire snakes down it, leaps from his fingers and cracks in the air right in front of my face like a whip. I stumble backward even though I'm a breath too late to avoid it.

"Way to give me a heart attack," I mutter.

Hu laughs. "Sorry, just thought a demonstration would be more impactful."

"Consider it successful."

He snaps his fingers, and a flame jumps up, then stretches out and curls around his hand in a spiral. He slowly builds the size of the flame until I can feel the heat from where I'm standing.

"This was one of the first exercises my mom taught me," he explains, lifting his arm. "The point of it was to keep my magic small and contained, and going exactly where I want it. Electric magic is a little different in execution, but the same concept applies. What I want you to do is take that wild energy you normally throw at people and contain it in your hand."

"That's it? Just keep a little ball of electricity in my hand?" I ask, crossing my arms.

"That's it," he says with a shrug. "It's simple and something you can practice pretty much anywhere. Once you master that, we'll talk about the next step."

"Okay." I sit down on the floor and cross my legs. Hu comes and sits across from me, keeping the extinguisher within reach.

When I'm brewing, the magic isn't trying to escape or control me like the electric magic does. It's just part of me. I don't remember struggling against it even as a child. Even the healing magic was never this hard to control. I did have to learn quickly not use too much of it, but it was gentle. I always thought of it as a faucet. I could turn the flow up or down, but it wasn't much more complicated than that.

Controlling this magic is like holding a pit bull on a leash. Once I pull on it, it starts pulling on me. It was especially difficult to control at the beginning whenever I got angry. Hell, it's still hard to keep under wraps when I get angry.

"Does your magic respond to your emotions?" I ask, staring at my hands. "I feel like it's always trying to escape when I get angry or frustrated."

"Yes," Hu says with a nod. "When I was younger, it was difficult. However, I had been meditating from a young age, and I knew what to expect. Fire witches are known for their tempers, and some of us use that as an excuse. My mother didn't believe in accepting weakness like that."

"So it is possible to control it?" I ask.

"Yes."

I nod and take a deep breath. If it's just a matter of being more stubborn than the magic, then I've got this. There's no way I'm going to let the magic I stole control me.

The crackling energy is still pounding in my chest, ready to be used. I tug on it, and the magic sparks along my fingertips. I stop thinking about an attack and simply wiggle my fingers, trying to coax the magic to the surface. A bright blue arc leaps up from my palm. I keep pulling on it, and another crackles across my fingers, then my wrist, then another from my thumb.

The magic is unruly, and asking me to contain something like that in the palm of my hand seems impossible. I grit my teeth and pull harder on the magic until my entire arm is crawling with visible electricity. I look like a Tesla coil. My hand starts to shake with the effort of holding back, then the electricity surges. My hair lifts all at once, and the magic that has been crawling up my arm surges and a bolt shoots toward the floor, scorching it.

Hu is spraying the area before I have a chance to blink, and I cough as the cold fog blows up into my face. I let the magic go and scramble backward.

"I see this is going well," Reilly says from behind us.

I stand up and turn around, still dusting the chalky powder off my side. Reilly is wearing a loose-fitting black tank and dark gray sweatpants. I've never seen him dressed down like this before. He almost looks like a normal person. Except for the drool-worthy muscles, that's something you don't see every day.

"It was a good start, actually. If she had gotten it perfectly on her first try, I would have been a little annoyed that it was that easy for her," Hu says with a chuckle.

"I wouldn't have minded," I say, staring at the mess on the floor, and then the mutilated dummy.

Hu shrugs. "Oh, Elise wanted me to invite you out tonight. We're headed to some club on the Strip around eleven."

"She'll kill me if I don't go, won't she?" I ask.

Hu grins. "She wouldn't kill you, but she might kidnap you. She's aggressive about her friends enjoying themselves."

It occurs to me that while a club isn't necessarily my scene, there will be tequila there. I plaster on a smile.

"I'll come. It'll be a nice break."

"Awesome," Hu says.

"And I can clean up all this," I say, gesturing at the mess from the fire extinguisher.

"That's good because I'm actually running late. Ivy is expecting me in a half-hour to go visit another local coven, and I still need to shower. I'll see you tonight." Hu leaves with a wave.

I turn to Reilly, who is staring at the dummy with a grin on his face.

"Anger issues?" he asks.

I roll my eyes. "Can we just move on to the part where you show me how to not exhaust myself and skip the small talk?"

"Your wish is my command," Reilly says with a mock bow.

The electric magic tingles at the edges of my fingertips. It would be so easy just to lose control and throw everything I have at him. The only thing stopping me is knowing he could probably dodge the attack. He's unreasonably fast. Faster than anyone else I've seen.

"You move insanely fast," I say, trying to nudge him to get to the point. "How do you do that?"

"Well, the strength and speed of a vampire are based on two things," Reilly says, rolling his head in a circle as he stretches his arms out in front of him. "Their sire and age."

"Why the sire?" I ask.

"Strength begets strength. The original clans all have different advantages they are known for. Tenebris is known for our speed. Familia de Sangre are known for their strength. Ānjìng De Sĭwán seem almost immune to the sun; even their younger vampires can wake during the day."

"So your sire's strengths are passed down to you?" I ask.

Reilly nods. "And sometimes their weaknesses. The most effective sires have the best control as well."

I wonder if my sire would be my father, or if it would be Javier. Or now that I've fed from Damien and Reilly if I've somehow taken on their talents and weaknesses as well.

"That explains that half. I've always known that older vampires are stronger, but not why. Witches don't gain actual power as they age, skill maybe, but everyone seems to just have the power they were born with, and nothing more," I say.

"The magic that keeps us alive is different. I remember what it felt like when I was first changed," Reilly says, looking off into the distance. "Every day, with every feeding, I could feel it growing. The potential seems endless sometimes. That's part of the hunger as well; you can feel it making you stronger, and that's addictive all on its own."

I press my hand to my stomach. I can understand that. Sometimes, when I was younger, I thought about all the magic I could steal. I wondered if it could make me invincible.

"So if you drained a hundred neckers, would you become crazy powerful?" I ask.

"No." Reilly shakes his head. "There are limits to the speed at which the magic can develop. I can always feel the point at which I'm tipping over from feeding the magic to simply glutting myself. Some can't, and their lack of control always causes problems eventually."

"This is great and all, but how is this supposed to help me not overuse my magic?" I ask, shifting from foot to foot. I've never had much patience for history lessons or lectures. No one ever just gets to the point.

"The less magic you have, the more sparingly you have to use it. If you dump every ounce of your strength into one punch, then you will have nothing left to dodge their counterattack." Reilly moves without warning. My eyes are barely able to follow he is moving so quickly.

I whirl around, but he's already standing right behind me.

"When I put on a burst of speed, in that brief moment I am engaging my strength, or magic if you want to call it that. Standing here now, though, I'm not still pulling on it."

"So it's about little flashes of magic, and not one constant stream of it?" I ask.

"Yes."

"That's not that complicated. I can do that," I say, squaring off with him.

Reilly grins. "It is simple. It is not easy."

"None of this is easy," I say, raising a brow at him. "I just got done trying to make a lightning bolt fit in the palm of my hand."

"That was amusing to watch," Reilly grins, dimples taunting me.

I yank on the magic inside of me and lunge to the left, hoping to get around behind him this time. He matches my movement though, and he is faster. I skid to a stop, then trip over the mat as it bunches up from the force of my momentum. I fly a couple of feet before hitting the ground just outside of the matted area with a grunt. Pain shoots through my elbow, and I roll onto my back.

Reilly is laughing unreservedly. There are actual tears of mirth leaking out of his eyes. I push up to a seated position and try to not look like I'm horribly embarrassed. My cheeks are hot though. It irritates me that there's nothing a person can do to stop blushing. It's the ultimate betrayal by your body.

Reilly finally manages to take a breath without laughing and wipes his eyes. "That was a very dramatic start."

"Whatever," I mutter, glaring at the floor.

"You had the right idea," Reilly says, still grinning. "Stopping gracefully is a learned skill."

"Obviously," I say, standing up and just managing not to wince.

"Think of it more like one big step, rather than running," Reilly suggests. "Try it again."

I shake my arms out, irritated by the bruise on my elbow. Using the magic was easy enough, apparently, the struggle will be keeping my body under control. I don't remember having this issue during the raid. I had just moved on instinct without worrying about showing off.

I take a deep breath and dart across the room, ignoring Reilly, ignoring everything but the feeling of movement. I pull back on the magic right before sliding to a stop this time, and my feet glide smoothly across the mat without bunching it. Without pausing, I repeat the movement and stop right in front of Reilly.

I'm a little closer than I intended, but he doesn't flinch.

"Much better," he says.

I can feel his breath on my face. I take a step back to put some space between us.

"I can see how that would quickly be tiring," I say. I'm not exhausted from those two bursts, but I'm not sure how many I could do. The training I did with Hu and using the vampire magic just then, it's all taking its toll.

"You seem to be understanding the basics," Reilly says, circling around me. I turn with him, not wanting him behind me again. "Let's play tag."

"What?"

He darts away, his shoulder brushing against mine and knocking me off balance as he flies past.

"You're it!" he shouts from across the room.

"What are we, five?" I shout back. I run at him though; I'll be damned if I'm going to make this easy on him.

Reilly moves like he was born for this. He doesn't just run in straight lines. He seems to be able to change directions, no matter how fast he's moving like a damn gazelle. I have to pause every few seconds to conserve my energy, but he doesn't seem to tire. Every time I get close, I realize it's a feint and he twists away and ends up behind me.

Again and again, I just miss him. I'm starting to feel the strain now. If I don't finish this soon, I'll have just chased him around the room for fifteen minutes with nothing to show for it. I charge at him again, and he slips to the left.

Gritting my teeth, I lift my foot to go forward, like I have been, then launch myself blindly backward with the foot still on the ground. My back hits Reilly, and I have a moment of triumph until his arm wraps around my throat. I tuck my chin just in time to keep him from locking the choke in and twist around to jerk my head out of his grip.

We're facing each other now, and he ducks down and pushes forward, his shoulder in my stomach, and wraps his hands around the backs of my knees. He pulls his hands sharply toward him, and since I'm already tipping to the left, my right foot is jerked off the floor and I'm airborne once again.

I hit the ground hard, and Reilly pushes in-between my legs while I'm struggling to catch my breath. I have just enough experience wrestling to know I am terrible at it. I fall back on the only thing that has ever marginally worked. I flail wildly.

My elbow catches his jaw, and I get a foot in the crease of his hip. He seems to be trying to crush me under his weight, and if I couldn't pull on the vampire strength, he would. I grit my teeth and push with my feet and my hands, anywhere I can get leverage, until I'm almost lifting him off me.

Reilly shifts and spins around to my side. His arms move fast and, no matter what I do, it seems to help him. He works his way around to my back, and this time I can't tuck my chin quite well enough. He slowly but surely forces my head backward, and his arm wraps completely around my neck. The hard edge of his forearm chokes me against his bicep, which is unfairly just as solid. I struggle for a moment longer, but vampire magic or no, I need to breathe. I slap at his arm, and he drops me immediately.

I flop onto my stomach, panting. He stays glued to my back for a moment, his hand resting on my waist. My shirt has ridden up from all the wrestling. Two of his fingers brush against my skin in a momentary caress that makes me shudder before he rolls away and lays flat on the floor.

I roll over onto my back as well. I dislike not being able to see where he is and what he's doing. Even less so after he's almost choked me out.

"Where did you learn to fight?" he asks.

"The school of hard knocks," I say, wiping sweat away from my eye with the back of my hand and sitting up. "And the MMA gym Zachary's dad enrolled both of us in after he took me in."

"They didn't teach you very well."

I glare at Reilly, and he grins back, both dimples showing.

"It's been over five years, and I wasn't really interested at the time," I say I as get up to my feet in a huff. I walk over to the bench my water bottle is sitting on and take a few long swallows. "Hell, I'm not interested now. I'm just trying not to die."

"If you master your magic, you won't have to spend as much time up close and personal like this," Reilly says.

"I know that," I say, rolling my eyes.

"Not that rolling around on the floor with you is a bad time," Reilly says from right behind me.

I jump and stumble forward.

"I am seriously going to put a bell on you," I say, trying to wipe away the water I splashed all over my neck. "Personal. Space. It's not that hard."

"I don't think you want personal space," Reilly says as he closes the distance between us again.

This close, it's impossible to look anywhere but directly at him. His cheeks are warm from the exercise. It makes him seem almost human. I don't think I've ever noticed how rich of a brown his eyes are. His hair is a mess, and the muscles in his shoulders are practically begging to be traced with my—

No. I take a step back and stop those thoughts in their tracks.

"Well, I do," I say, but my face is heating up again. "Want personal space."

"Did you forget I can hear a lie?" Reilly whispers, taking another step forward.

"You know what, here's a truth. I am not doing this with you," I say, looking him in the eye.

"You think that is true," he muses, smirking at me. "But last night, you were jealous."

I roll my eyes. "Don't flatter yourself; it wasn't about you."

"You should quit lying to yourself, at the very least," Reilly says before turning and walking away. I watch him go. I can't deny it's a good view.

I put my head in my hands. I'll be glad to get out for a little while tonight and get my mind off all of this crap. Maybe I can even find someone to invite me back to their hotel room, since I obviously can't bring anyone back to mine.

I groan and grab all my stuff. I need a shower. A cold one.

CHAPTER 13

*E*lise answers the door in a tight blue dress that makes her eyes stand out even more. Her makeup is half-done though, so her left eye looks twice the size of her right eye.

"I didn't realize this was going to be a dress kind of place," I say, looking down at the jeans, red shirt, and tall black boots I had put on. I hadn't even packed any dresses.

Elise looks me up and down and purses her lips. "We're about the same size. I've got something that'll work."

She waves me inside and shuts and locks the door behind us, then jogs over to her suitcase. She digs around for a moment before pulling out a black dress.

"Here," she says, tossing it at me. "Try that on."

She walks back into the bathroom, and I strip down. The dress slides on easily, but it's a good thing I didn't have a big dinner. It has long sleeves, which thankfully cover the welts on my arms, but the hem doesn't even make it halfway down my thighs. There are three black mesh strips at the narrowest point of my waist, and another bigger one right where my cleavage should be. The dress is tight enough that it helps push everything into a good position.

Elise pokes her head out of the bathroom. "God, I hate you."

"What?" I ask, confused.

"I think that looks better on you than it does on me," she says with a pout.

I laugh. "I really doubt that, but it does fit all right."

I smooth my fingers through my hair and pull my boots back on, then plop down in the chair in front of the desk. I spin around lazily, and my elbow bumps the files that are spread out on the desk. I catch it before it falls, but a picture that was tucked inside slips out and flutters down to the carpet.

I reach for it and pause halfway there. The bearded man. The memory of Reilly snapping his neck flashes through my mind. I pick it up and stare at it, then glance at the bathroom doorway. Elise is still in there, bemoaning the difficulty of keeping clothes from wrinkling in a suitcase.

Before I can hesitate anymore, I flip through the file. This guy, Demeter Yagislov, apparently, had ties to one of the most powerful covens in the US. Hell, he had ties to the council itself. I close his file and open a couple of others. There is one for each of the three witches who attacked the clanhouse, and a couple I don't even recognize. I didn't know JHAPI was still investigating the attack at the clanhouse.

The woman's words come back to me. She kept claiming I was born for a reason not even my mother had known, which was bullshit. The words unsettled me then though, and they still bother me. What do they know that I don't?

Elise comes out of the bathroom, but I don't bother hiding that I've been snooping.

"I didn't know you were still investigating those crazy ass cult members," I say as she stops in the center of the room.

"I'm not," she says, adjusting her dress. "Zachary is."

I look up, surprised. "What?"

She shrugs. "It's not official either, just his little pet project."

"Why would he do that?" I ask, confused, and a little worried. Does he suspect something?

"That's a good question, Olivia. I ask myself every day. Why do you think he might?" she asks, giving me a knowing look.

"No," I say, dropping the file back on the desk. "That was never a thing."

She laughs. "You're kidding, right?"

I just stare at her.

"Oh my god, so you really didn't know he had a whole thing for you?" she cackles, her eyes watering from laughing so hard.

"Cook said something like that too. Zachary did not have a thing for me. Why does everyone think that? He was like my brother," I say, crossing my arms.

"Dude," Elise says. "He literally told me about the girl he loved who ran away and could never be found when we first became partners. It was a whole thing about trust issues and why he doesn't date."

I open my mouth to refute what she's just said, but if he told her that, I can't exactly argue. I close my mouth and stand up and head toward the door instead. Maybe Zachary was just messing with her.

"This is great. Tonight is going to be so entertaining," Elise says as she follows me out the door.

She catches up when I stop to press the button for the elevator.

"I'm still not sure why we're doing this," I say, my tone grumpy. "Not that I'm going to turn down a chance to drink too much tequila."

"We're in Las Vegas," Elise says, doing jazz hands.

I give her a blank stare. The elevator doors slide open, and we step inside. We head down to the parking garage in silence. My mind is caught in a loop, trying to remember if there was ever some kind of spark between me and Zachary. It never felt like flirting to me; it just felt like family.

We climb in the car, and Elise turns to look at me. "Are you going to brood about what I said all night?"

"What? No. I'm not brooding," I say, crossing my arms.

"Right," she says, turning the car on.

I roll my eyes but can't help the guilty smile that spreads across my face. She laughs at me and pulls out of the parking spot.

We're only about ten minutes from the strip. The club has valet only parking, so we hand over the car keys to a young guy in a blue jacket and get in line.

The bouncers aren't picky. If you're over twenty-one and not wearing a tank top and flip flops, they wave you inside. After a small cover charge, of course.

The club is loud, which isn't surprising. Strobe lights flash around the DJ and stage, highlighting the mass of gyrating bodies. It smells like smoke and old alcohol. Elise grabs my hands and pulls me deeper into the crowd around the bar.

"I think I see them," she shouts over her shoulder.

Hu and Corinne are standing near a table with four chairs. Not enough for everyone, but we're lucky they managed to snag a table at all. Corinne is wearing a tight little black dress that looks great on her. She looks much younger out of the suit.

"What do you want to drink?" Elise asks me.

"Tequila," I say without hesitation. "So much tequila."

She laughs. "You got it."

Elise pushes back toward the bar, leaving me alone with Hu and Corinne.

"Is anyone else coming?"

Hu shrugs, but Corinne nods.

"Zachary should be here shortly, he's riding with Cook. Is Reilly coming tonight?" she asks.

"I have no idea, to be honest." I shrug. I hope he doesn't. It'd be nice to have one night to loosen up and forget about all my adult problems.

We pass a few minutes in silence. It's not worth trying to make much conversation with the volume of music. Elise pushes her way back to the table with eight shots and a pile of limes balanced on a tray.

"Time to get this night started," she says with a grin as she sets it on the table.

I lick my hand and sprinkle the salt on liberally, then glance around the table to see if everyone else is ready. We all lift our shots and clink them together. I knock back the shot and bite down on the lime in a fluid motion. It burns just right. I grab the second shot of tequila and throw it back without waiting for the others. It's time to dance.

I push into the crush of the crowd. The bass is pounding, and I can feel each thump all the way down to my bones. There's not enough room on the dance floor to move without touching someone, so I give in to the flow and stop worrying about it. The energy is high. Everyone has a smile on their face. No one is worried about who they're dancing with. Hands are roaming, people are kissing and grinding against each other.

A hand slides across my lower back, and I glance over my shoulder and see a man with a generically handsome face and dark brown eyes. I move into his touch, and he slips his hand around to my stomach, pulling me in close. The music speeds up, and we move together. Everything floats away as the tequila courses through me and the thrill of dancing erases all the worries that have been bouncing around my brain for weeks.

The guy spins me around and holds me chest to chest against him. His eyes stray to my lips, and I smile in invitation. His hands slide up into my hair, and he leans in, pressing his forehead to mine. The connection isn't electric, but it's enough to have warmth curling through my stomach. It's enough for a Saturday night in Vegas.

His lips press into mine. Our lips part, and the hot slide of his tongue against mine was exactly what I needed. The kiss deepens until we're not even attempting to dance anymore. We're just making out underneath the flashing lights in the midst of a crowd.

His fingers twist in my hair, and I gasp into his mouth. He breaks the kiss and leans in closer to talk into my ear.

"Want to get a drink?" he asks. Even this close, I can barely hear him over the music.

"Sure," I shout back.

He wraps our hands together and leads me toward the bar. He's able to slip into a gap and pulls me up in front of him, leaning into my back.

"What's your poison?" he asks. It's slightly quieter over here, so he doesn't have to shout.

"Tequila, always," I say, leaning my head back to smile up at him.

He gets the bartender's attention and orders two shots.

"What's your name?" he asks.

"Olivia, what's yours?"

"David. What brings you to Vegas?"

"What brings anyone to Vegas?" I ask with a laugh.

"Fair enough."

The bartender slides our shots across the bar. David hands me mine and holds my gaze as we throw them back.

I feel a hand on my elbow and look back to see Elise grinning at me.

"I see you've made a friend," she says.

"Elise, this is David. David, this is Elise," I say.

"Nice to meet you, Elise," David says, extending his hand. Elise shakes it with a smile.

"Oooh, you even found one with manners," she says, nudging me with her elbow. "Everybody is here now. Did you want to come say hi?"

"Umm, sure," I say hesitantly. I really just want to dance more.

The kissing was nice too. "We can come over for a quick drink. If that's all right with you, David?"

David nods without hesitation, one arm still snug around my waist. It takes a couple of minutes, but we each get a vodka soda, then follow Elise back to the table.

Austin is leaning against Corinne's chair, laughing about something with her. Zachary is standing off to the side, nursing a beer and scanning the room like he suspects something fishy is going on.

Corinne spots David behind me and interrupts Austin.

"Who is this?" she asks with a big grin. Her eyes are a little glassy, and I suspect she's had quite a few drinks while I was dancing.

"David, this is everyone. Everyone, this is David," I shout over the music. Most of the group nod in greeting. Austin just stares at David for a moment before looking at me like I'm dirt. His eyes linger for a moment on the neckline of my dress, then he scoffs and turns to Zachary, who is still looking over the crowd intently. I sip my drink and let David snake his arm around my waist again.

There is an awkward tension in the group. I take another drink. I want to finish this and get back to dancing. I didn't come here to stand around. Hu and Corinne seem to be in a good mood, at least. He's had a smile all night, and so has she. I don't think I've ever seen Corinne in a bad mood though.

I finish my drink and set it on the table with the other empty glasses. The table is a bit crowded now.

"Are you done with your drink?" Corinne asks, reaching across the table to grab my hands.

"I am," I say with a smile.

"Let's dance, then!" she exclaims, dragging me forward.

"Ok, hold on." I laugh as I tug my hands away. David follows me around the table, and I let Corinne grab my hands again and lead us to the dance floor.

She bounces, flipping her hair from side to side as a new song comes on. I dance with her, David a constant pressure against my back. We slowly push farther and farther into the crowd.

Someone I don't quite see spins Corinne around, and David takes that moment to turn me as well, capturing my mouth in a kiss. I kiss back, but it doesn't have the same heat as it did earlier.

I pull away. Corinne is laughing next to me, her arms linked around the neck of a girl with blonde hair and full lips. I spin around in David's arms. My lips are starting to feel bruised, and I've either had too much to drink, or he's making me nauseous. I shut my eyes and try to lose myself in the music again.

Someone slides into place in front of me. They're close enough that their legs brush against mine. A hot finger traces the line of mesh along my waist, just above David's arm. The touch makes my stomach clench and my skin heat.

I look up and find dark brown eyes and dimples staring back at me. I grit my teeth. Reilly looks smug, like he thinks he's won something. The room is spinning though, and I don't care what he thinks. I came here to dance, and to forget. He doesn't get to rile me up today.

I lean back into David's chest and grind against him, keeping my eyes locked on Reilly's. The dimples fade, and he clenches his jaw tightly. He steps in closer until I'm sandwiched between the two men. His hands find their way to my waist, and his fingers press into my skin, like he's trying hold onto me. His thumb traces the curve of my ribs.

David tries to tug me away and step backward, but I'm leaning toward Reilly. One hand leaves my waist and comes up to rest on the side of my neck.

David says something behind me, then scoffs when I don't respond. He shoves me forward and disappears back into the crowd. Reilly doesn't let me scoot back away; he holds my hips tight to his as we continue dancing. The music fades into the background. I wrap my hands around his neck. His heart is pounding just as fast as mine.

He leans in, his head just inches from mine. It's just like that moment on the porch. I hate him, but I can't ignore him. I can't ignore the heat spreading through my body either, but it doesn't have to make me weak. I lean in until I see in his eyes that he's sure I'm going to kiss him, then slide past him and push my way through the crush of bodies to get off the dance floor.

Elise isn't at the table anymore, so I turn in a circle, searching for her. Reilly didn't follow me, thank god. I head toward the back of the club and the neon sign that says 'restroom'. The bathroom isn't completely empty, but there at least isn't a line.

One girl is swaying in front of a sink washing her hands. I step up to the other sink and turn on the cold water, scooping up a handful and splashing it on my face and neck. The contrast between my hot cheeks and the cold water is exactly the slap in the face I needed.

The girl teeters out of the bathroom, slamming the door shut behind her. It sounds like she falls back against it before stumbling away. I look up in the mirror and freeze. My mother is standing behind me, finger pressed to her lips just like she had done during the raid.

She looks younger than I remember her being when she left, but I suppose all children think their parents are old. I can't take my eyes off her even though I want to look behind me to see if she's really there.

"What do you want?" I whisper. No matter what Corinne says, it feels like this is her ghost. Like she's haunting me.

My mother holds up a tattered, brown book. As she holds it out toward me, cuts and bruises begin appearing all over her body. Her mouth opens in a silent scream, and tears prick at my eyes as my fingers dig into the porcelain sink. I don't want to watch this, but I can't turn away. The book begins crumbling in her fingers. The pieces are carried away like ash on the wind. She reaches for me, and I turn around, almost expecting her to be standing there, but she's gone. The tingle of magic skates along my arms and pain shoots through the welts as I slide down the wall. I bury my face in my knees and wait for it to pass.

I don't know how to stop this. It's hard to want to, even as horrible as it is. It still feels like I might be able to find something, even if I can't find her.

CHAPTER 14

The electric magic dances across my palm. I can't get it to take on any sort of shape, but I have kept it contained in my hand this time. I close my fingers around it, snuffing it out and glance at my phone. It's two hours until sunset. Reilly is dead asleep in his bed, and I know I won't have many more chances to do this.

I text Zachary to let him know I'm headed over to talk to him. Elise is doing something with Stocke, and odds are Zachary is already awake. I almost brought it up last night when Zachary drove me back to the hotel, but I couldn't get Reilly's face out of my head, and I knew I was too drunk to ask the right questions.

I crawl out of bed and tuck my room key into my pants, then slip out of the room. I'll figure out what to tell Reilly about what I was doing later. I hurry to Zachary and Elise's room and knock twice.

He opens the door and steps back to let me in.

"Is everything all right? Your text sounded kind of urgent."

"Yeah, it's fine. There's just something I need to talk to you about," I say, fidgeting with the bottom of my sleeve. "You've been looking into the cult. The one that attacked the clanhouse."

"Elise told you?" Zachary asks, irritation flashing across his face.

"I saw the files in your room and asked her if she was looking into it. She said you were."

"All right, I have been. Someone needed to," Zachary says.

"I agree. Have you found out much about them? Do you know who they are?"

Zachary sits down and flips open one of the files in question. "They're interesting. They've been around longer than most covens, and they have ties to the witch council. Did you already know that?"

"Nope. I don't know anything about them, unfortunately."

He looks at me like he's looking for the lie. "Why'd you bring this up, then?"

I roll my eyes. "Because I want to know who they are and why they targeted me. Those assholes blew up my future. They ran off Maybelle. And they tried to kill Patrick."

"Is that why you agreed to help the vampires? Because you didn't have any other choice?"

"Well, it certainly wasn't out of the goodness of my heart," I say, sarcasm dripping from my voice.

"Is he forcing you to do this somehow?" Zachary asks, leaning forward. The irritation on his face from earlier has shifted to concern.

I shake my head. "Why are you acting so concerned?"

He throws his hands in the air. "Because I care about you! I shouldn't. I should hate you, but I can't. I still worry."

"Save it for someone who needs it," I say softly. His father always had a big heart for anyone he thought might need help. It's not surprising Zachary has that as well. "I'm fine, and I can take care of myself."

"You don't always have to," he sighs.

"Can you tell me what you know, or not?" I ask.

Zachary runs his hand over his head roughly, then sits up straight and pulls one of the files closer and flips it open.

"Demeter Yagislov, Brittany Gable, and Benjamin Gable were the three witches who attacked the clanhouse. We've been calling them a cult, but that isn't really right. They're more like religious fanatics, but instead of worshipping a particular god, they believe they are in charge of killing one." He pulls a picture out of the file. An old woman with snow-white hair in a bun on top of her head stares out at us with a stern expression on her face that reminds me of a disapproving teacher. She is dressed in black robes like an old school witch. "This is the woman we have tentatively identified as their current leader."

"They want to kill a god?" I ask, confused. As far as I know, there's no such thing.

Zachary nods. "The few texts we have been able to associate with them speak of the Bound God and a prophecy of some kind that centers around the Day of Breaking. It appears they are looking for the key to the prophecy so they can kill this Bound God once and for all, and prevent the apocalypse. They've been keeping him trapped for something like two-thousand years, but it looks like he might break free soon."

The woman who had been at the hospital, and the clanhouse, had kept insisting I was special. Perhaps they wanted to recruit me to fight this alleged god.

I twist my hands together. Zachary doesn't have all the information about what they were looking for, and why they went after Maybelle.

"I want to help you investigate this. There are some things you don't know yet, that are important, but I want you to promise you won't shut me out if I tell you," I say, staring at the floor.

"Dammit, Olivia, why didn't you tell me you had information sooner?" Zachary asks through gritted teeth. "I try to trust you, and every single time it turns out I shouldn't."

I look up at him and catch his gaze.

"Promise me, Zach. They killed my mother. I want to help you catch them, but I need to be part of it."

His eyes go wide, and he stares at me open-mouthed for a second. "They killed your mother? Why?"

"I'll explain all of that. Just—"

"All right, I promise," he interrupts, dropping his hands into his lap. "What the hell do you know?"

"Maybelle knew my mother." I hesitate, trying to decide how much to share. I'm not ready to tell him everything. The circumstances of my birth don't really make much of a difference anyhow. "Maybelle and my mother stole something from these people. Some kind of spellbook which they later sold. The coven questioned Maybelle about who she sold it to."

He's quiet for a moment, and I can see the wheels turning in his head. He saw Maybelle after she had been rescued. He knows what they did to her.

"They killed your mother when they tried to question her?" Zachary asks.

I nod, grateful I didn't have to say it out loud.

"Maybelle knew who I was, but I didn't know who she was until the day she was in the hospital. She told me everything then."

"Do you know why this spellbook is so important to them? Or what's in it?" Zachary asks, pulling the file toward him and taking out a pen.

I shake my head. "I don't know why they want it so badly. Do you have any idea where they are? Or how many of them there are?"

Zachary taps his pen against the desk. "No one knows where their headquarters are, or if they have any. Do you think Maybelle might know?"

I shrug. "She stole something from them once, so I guess she knew where it was. Do you think they would have moved it after something like that?"

"Perhaps," he nods. "And as far as how many there are, I'm just not sure. We don't know what they do, just that they have influence with the witch council. I'm not sure how they've managed that either. I've wondered a few times if the fanaticism was just a front for something else, but the more I look into it, the more sincere they seem in their beliefs."

"Could you, I don't know, subpoena the witch council to give up information on them?" I ask.

Zachary chuckles. "That's not exactly how that works. Though, we might eventually be able to question the council. However, I haven't been able to get a proper investigation opened. It's being blocked."

"Blocked? By who?" I ask, immediately angry.

"I don't know, and neither does Stocke. She was furious when the refusal came down. JHAPI is supposed to be above those kinds of politics, but of course, it isn't."

"So you started your own, off the record, investigation?"

"Yes," he says with a nod. "The refusal was a huge red flag. There's obviously something big going on, and I want to know what it is."

"How far do you think you can get investigating this under the radar?"

"I hope far enough that I can make a case they can't ignore. I'm not sure what I'll do if they continue to try and bury this."

I rub my hands down my face. "I want to find Martinez, but I'd rather be spending my time tracking down these fanatics. I want the people who killed my mother dead."

Zachary looks at me with pity in his face, and I hate it. He always got that look when I talked about her, so I eventually stopped bringing it up. His father had understood better. He had always encouraged me to keep looking for my mother. I run my thumb across a welt, not that finding her turned out to be a good thing.

"This god they want to kill, do you know why they want to kill it? Normally people worship them," I say.

"It's a god of destruction. It hasn't been clear, but they believe he intends to destroy either magic itself, or all paranormals."

"I guess I can see why they'd want to kill him. If he even exists."

Zachary laughs. "And that's a big if. Nothing like that has ever been proven to exist before."

I sit down on the end of the bed. "There are the old stories that witch children all learn. The ancient demons, beings that were made of magic itself. Aris and Izul supposedly led a war against them."

"Aren't those stories debunked as myth? Like the dragons humans supposedly fought in the dark ages?"

I shrug. "No one really believes them anymore, but I know I wished they were true as a child. It all sounded so epic."

"I hope this one doesn't exist," Zachary says, shaking his head. "Especially since it seems like this coven might have trouble containing him this time around."

I tap my thumb against my thigh, an idea forming in my head. "Would it help if I tried to Find one of these people?"

"What?" Zachary asks, sitting up straight. "I thought you couldn't use that magic because of your injury?"

"I'll get better. I've already started working with Corinne. Just answer the question."

"Of course it would help. We couldn't question anyone in an official capacity, but if we end up in the same city, we could do some surveillance. Stocke might even help us. Off the record, of course."

I nod. "Then I'm going to figure out how to Find one of them. Whatever it takes."

Zachary furrows his brows together. "Do not do anything stupid trying to use magic that hurts you. That won't help either of us."

"I know that." I roll my eyes. "I'm not trying to martyr myself, I just need to know that we have a plan besides sit around and hope we figure out who they are."

"You just have a history of acting before thinking."

"I won't try to Find them until I know I can do it, all right?"

He nods once. "All right."

"And one last request, does Reilly already know you're doing this?" I ask.

Zachary shakes his head. "No one knows but Elise and Stocke."

"Let's keep it that way. I don't want him involved in this."

"Are you sure?" Zachary asks. "He could help. He has connections we don't."

"I'm sure," I say with a decisive nod.

"All right." Zachary leans back in his chair. He looks like he wants to ask more questions, but instead he taps his pen once on the desk and turns back to the file.

I pull out my phone and text Staci, pride be damned. I need to dull the pain in these welts so I can practice using my Finding magic again. I pause, my thumb hovering over the keys. I also need to figure out a way to let go of these hallucinations. I shake the thought away. One step at a time.

CHAPTER 15

Staci manages to sound smug even over text. I roll my eyes and shove the phone back in my pocket. Zachary has the files spread all over the desk and both beds. I think I've memorized the faces of every person that might be connected to the coven.

"I need to go see Staci about getting more of this salve. I'll talk to you about this again next time I can get away. But text me if you find anything, all right?" I ask as I walk toward the door.

Zachary nods absently and waves me away. He's chewing on the end of his pen and not really paying attention. I'll have to text him later just in case.

My phone buzzes as I step into the hallway. Reilly's number is flashing on the screen. I sigh and answer it.

"What?" I ask.

"Where are you?" he asks.

"I'm still in the hotel, but I'm on my way to see Staci. I need more of the salve. She said she could brew it and give it to me this morning," I say. It's not a lie exactly. He doesn't need to know I've been somewhere else for two hours.

He's silent for a moment. "Where is she going to be brewing?"

"At the local JHAPI offices."

"I'll drive you over," he says.

"I can get a cab," I say, and it sounds whiny even to my ears.

"I'll meet you in the parking garage." He hangs up, and I slap my phone shut. That's the only thing I like about this old piece of crap. Hanging up is more satisfying when you can slam something.

I head toward the parking garage, muttering to myself the entire way about controlling vampires and bad life choices.

Reilly is leaning against his car when I get there. He's dressed impeccably. I can't help remembering the heat of his body pressed against mine the night before, and how close I came to being an idiot. The fact that I didn't helps me keep my spine straight as I walk up to him. He lets his eyes wander, and I ignore that too.

"You smell like Brunson," he says as I tug on the door handle, which is still locked.

"And?"

"So you saw him sometime recently," Reilly says, raising one brow. "Why?"

"He's my friend, I'll talk to him if I want to," I say, tugging on the door handle again for emphasis.

Reilly sighs, frustrated, but unlocks the car, and we climb in.

"I'm sure you know the annual council summit is in just over a week," Reilly says as he pulls out of the parking spot.

"Uh, sure," I say. "I don't really pay attention to that. I know it happens every year; it just doesn't really affect me." I shrug.

He stops the car and looks at me. "The council summit is the single most important event of the year for every single paranormal. This summit is going to be even more important than normal. Do you have any idea what's going on?"

"No," I say, crossing my arms. "I'm not in a coven. I'll glance at the news to see if any laws change that affect the brews I can sell, but other than that, it just doesn't seem to matter."

Reilly shakes his head, exasperated. "The goblins are moving to create their own council."

"What? Seriously?" I ask, suddenly interested. When all the other paranormals came out of the closet, the goblins chose to stay underground. Everyone knows they exist, but they refused to integrate with humanity. They stay hidden, refuse legal protections, and refuse to submit to any laws protecting humans. It's been a huge source of tension for decades.

"It's going to shift the balance of power within the councils. For the most part, the weres side with the witches on votes," Reilly says. "No one knows who the goblins will side with, if anyone. The votes could end up split, and we don't have any way to resolve that."

"Are the witches going to try to stop them from joining?"

Reilly nods. "They have been. They want them to submit to one of the councils that are already in place. It's one of the things the council will be voting on this time. No one has any idea which way the weres will vote; they've been silent on the topic. Some people think they may be secretly trying to get the goblins to submit to them instead of the witches. Some think they don't want them to have a vote either."

"That's all crazy, but I'm not sure why you're bringing it up now?" I ask.

"We will be attending the Summit. I have to report to the vampire council the status of our attempts to eliminate the NWR."

I dig my nails into my palm. "Are you going to have to report my existence as well?"

"You will be coming to the Summit with me, as my guest. I will introduce you to my sire, of course. He has wanted to meet you for a while. The rest has not yet been decided since your evaluation is not complete."

I pull on my vampire magic and listen very carefully to Reilly's heart. He doesn't seem upset or excited.

"Is there a chance he's going to try to kill me or anything crazy like that?" I ask. I haven't thought about that in a while, the chance that someone might try to put me down. It makes my skin crawl.

"No," Reilly says. Not a lie. "You're more valuable alive."

I huff. Of course, he's still thinking of how I can be most useful. That's all that matters to him.

The rest of the drive to the JHAPI office is silent. I think over everything I found out from Zachary. To be honest, he has very little useful information. Names and faces are a start, but there is no meaningful information on what the coven *does*. With the number of magical items they seem to have access to, I'm starting to wonder if perhaps it's just a front. Maybe they're just the paranormal version of arms dealers. They seem to be rich enough.

I wish I had a way to contact Maybelle or Gerard. If she could just tell me where they stole the spellbook from, it would give me a starting point.

Reilly pulls up near the front door.

"I will be visiting another clan with Ivy this evening. Wait for me to pick you up."

"You've made it clear that you will literally kill everyone I care about if I try to run. I'm not planning on disappearing into the desert," I say through gritted teeth.

"I know you won't," Reilly says. "However, you are still a target for the NWR and the coven that attacked the clanhouse. I'm not risking something happening to you when it's simple enough to keep you protected."

Not a lie. I push my door open and climb out. I hadn't really considered that the coven might still be looking for me. I think about texting Zachary. Perhaps that's something we can take advantage of. I wouldn't mind being used as bait.

The JHAPI building is freezing cold today. They must have forgotten to switch from air conditioning to heat after the sun went down. The building is also mostly deserted since it's almost seven and most people went home two hours ago.

I wander the empty hallways, trying to make sense of Staci's

WITCH'S BITE

directions. All she had said was that the brewing room was near the workout room on the second floor. There are no signs for either of those rooms.

I pass an office with an open door and stop. At first I think the agent is still in the office, but I realize it's the janitor.

"Hey," I say hesitantly.

He looks up and takes one headphone out of his ear. He's a middle-aged man with unruly grey hair and a round face.

"Do you know where the, uh, brewing room is? I'm supposed to meet Agent Young there, but I can't find it."

"Yes," he says with a thick Russian accent. He hurries to the door and points in the direction I just came from. "You go back. Left, then end of hall."

"Thanks, very much," I say, hurrying back in that direction. Sure enough, there is a room at the end of the hall. The only sign on the door simply says Room 102.

I shrug and open it without knocking. Staci looks up, startled, as I walk in. I guess she expected me to be lost for a while.

The smell of bleach and some other unfamiliar chemical assaults my nose, and I grimace. There's no lingering scent of herbs or smoke. The air isn't tinged with magic. It feels like a science laboratory, not a hedgewitch's workroom.

"Do they even use this room?" I ask, still standing with one hand holding open the door. It looks like a laboratory in here too. The walls are stark white with no decoration. The cabinets and countertops are all white as well with shiny silver handles. Glass beakers and flasks are arranged by size in neat rows on a metal shelf.

"Of course. They employ a couple of hedgewitches at this location," Staci says curtly as she lifts a thick book and lays it next to her cauldron. It's the only thing in the room that looks well-used. She turns the thick, stained pages slowly scanning each one for something. She's a quarter of the way through the book when she pauses, humming to herself, and taps next to a line of writing.

"What is that?" I ask.

She looks at me and adjusts her glasses on her nose.

"I thought you were a hedgewitch?" she says with a haughty sniff.

"I am, and no part of brewing requires a book, so..." I gesture at the book and shrug.

She snorts. "Of course you're one of those."

I lean back against the counter and cross my arms.

"One of what, exactly?"

She grabs a canister out of the cabinet.

"A sloppy brewer. No recipe, no consistency, unreliable."

I laugh aloud. "You have got to be kidding me."

She simply sniffs and continues scanning her recipe.

I stare at her, completely aghast. "You have to realize how much more powerful it is. Brewing with a recipe makes the magic stale and weak."

She scoffs and turns to face me.

"Hardly. It makes it controlled, and I'm sure it isn't as fun," she sneers, "but that isn't the point. I know exactly how each brew I give the agents will act. Exactly. How," she says, jabbing her finger against the counter to emphasize each word. "Whatever you do in your personal life may not matter very much, but JHAPI requires a little bit more of its witches."

"It sounds more like they require less," I snap back. "I know exactly how my brews will act too. And I can guarantee they'd be more powerful than yours."

She turns back to her cauldron. "Just keep telling yourself that."

"What is your problem with me, exactly?" I ask, pushing off the counter.

She pulls out a knife and begins roughly chopping some herbs. The pieces are too big; a potion like this needs a finer blend.

"You are a felon," she says as she cuts. "And that's just for the crime they managed to catch you committing."

I roll my eyes. "I was nineteen."

"You're an untested, untrustworthy civilian the team has to carry because of politics. Stocke didn't want you involved, but we had to accept you at the vampire council's insistence."

I bite the inside of my cheek before I reply. "So, you're going to be passive-aggressive every time we have to work together?"

"I'm going to be polite when I have to," she says as she scoops the herbs up and tosses them into the already hot cauldron. "But if you want to be an ass, I can be one right back."

Her hair is slightly frazzled from the heat, and her glasses are sliding down her nose again. She looks like an angry mouse, and I have to press my lips together to keep from laughing at her. I can't completely hide the smile though, and two spots of color form on her cheeks.

She turns back to the cauldron and stirs angrily.

"I'll bring you the salve when it's done. I don't need you in here monitoring my spell work."

I roll my eyes but don't argue about staying. I don't want to watch her massacre this brew any longer than I have to. It's going to be absolutely useless.

"Sure, I'll just wait out in the hall," I say with fake sweetness. "But definitely let me know if you get stuck with your little recipe and need some help."

There is a perfunctory knock on the door, and Ivy steps inside. I'm not surprised she's here so late. She struck me as the workaholic type. The expression on her face makes me pause.

"One of the missing vampires has turned up, but it's a disaster. We need to go now," she says.

Staci flips the burner off, and we both hurry out of the room after Ivy.

CHAPTER 16

The van is already running, Cook behind the wheel, when Staci, Ivy, and myself run into the garage. The door slides open, revealing the rest of the team, minus Zachary. He must still be at the hotel.

We pile in, and Cook speeds away as the door shuts behind me. I'm thrown sideways into Hu's lap. He grunts, his hands tightening around my waist for a moment.

"Sorry," I say as I drag myself over to his other side.

"No worries, Cook is a crazy driver," Hu says with a grin.

Reilly mutters something I can't quite hear across the van from him. I narrow my eyes at him, but he's staring up at the front of the van now, ignoring me.

Stocke leans around from the front passenger seat.

"What we know is that one of the missing vampires, Ryan Johnson, was found a couple of hours ago at a bar known to be frequented by vampires by one of his clanmates. He was brought back to the clanhouse immediately, where they attempted to revive him." Stocke pauses and shakes her head slightly, her curls bouncing. "He immediately killed the human woman they had brought down to feed him. He also killed his clanmate, who was both older and stronger, but another was able to escape the room and lock him inside."

"Has he gone feral, or was this an intentional attack?" Ivy asks.

"That isn't clear. His sire, Lee Vaughan, believes something else is going on but won't say what. He requested help from JHAPI, which is unheard of."

Reilly scratches his chin and leans forward. "Who exactly did Ryan Johnson kill? It's possible Vaughan simply doubts his ability to put this vampire down."

Stocke presses her lips tightly together. "He killed the sire's second."

Reilly stares at her. "Vaughan's second is well over two-hundred years old. There is no way a youngling caught him off guard."

"So this kid somehow overpowered him?" Elise asks. "That would be like a freshly bitten were killing an alpha. That just doesn't happen."

"No, it doesn't," Reilly agrees.

"This is what we're here for. The clan leader wants the vampire put down, and under every law we have, he has the right to request that." Stocke pauses. "However, we have a chance to find out what happened to Ryan. He is the only person that knows who took him, if anyone, and where he has been all this time. If he was somehow made stronger, I want to know why and how."

"You want to capture him," Ivy says.

Stocke nods. "If we can."

"We will need the most powerful tranquilizer you can get your hands on," Reilly says. He glances at me, and I can see the gears turning in his mind. He's excited about this.

"It's already on its way," Stocke says.

"The Sleeping Beauty brew?" Staci asks, her face lighting up. I can't help it; I'm curious to see it as well. It's one of the most tightly regulated brews in existence.

"Yes," Stocke confirms. "They had a double dose on hand in Los Angeles. It will be here in an hour and a half."

"So, we have a vampire that was able to kill someone hundreds of years older. He's going to be insanely fast," I say, leaning around Hu to look at Stocke. "How exactly are we supposed to administer this brew? Ask him nicely to drink it?"

Stocke looks at Reilly.

"Are you serious?" I exclaim. I'm not even sure why I'm upset. I couldn't care less if Reilly gets killed, but it is ridiculous to expect him to go in after this thing by himself.

"I'll help him," Elise says, cracking her knuckles.

"No way," Cook objects from the front seat. "Even shifted, you aren't as fast as a vampire."

"I'm fast enough," Elise argues back. The front of the van descends into a debate over the speed and agility of werewolves versus vampires.

I lean back and cross my arms, staring at Reilly. He's staring right back at me. I pull on my vampire magic and hone in on the beat of his heart.

"I'm going in with you," I whisper. I know he'll hear it.

"You're not fast enough," Reilly back with a shake of his head.

"Like hell I'm not. The sun is down. I can do this."

Reilly stares at me for a moment longer, then smirks, his cheek dimpling.

"If you're that eager, I won't turn down your assistance. It'll be good to test your limits."

I roll my eyes. Every time I get the impulse to help or hate him less, he reminds me that he's an ass.

"Just remember, if you overdo it, you'll have to feed again, and it won't be from me," he warns.

I turn away. I'm probably not ready for this. I've only had one day to focus on training since all of this started, but life doesn't seem to want to wait for a convenient time to test me. I'll just have to deal with it if I do use too much magic.

Elise doesn't stop arguing in favor of werewolves for the rest of the drive. Cook objects the most, to the point that I start to suspect he is just worried about her. I hadn't really paid attention to their interactions before, but it's possible he has a crush on her. Based on her reaction, I think this is the wrong way to go about seducing her. She looks furious.

The van comes to an abrupt stop, and Cook rolls down the window, shouting at someone to come open the gate. He and Stocke talk to someone, showing their badges, and then we are moving again. We don't have to drive far before Cook stops the van again and throws it into park. Ivy slides open the door, and we all pour out.

The clan house is a mix of modern and rustic desert vibes. It's three stories tall with balconies jutting out in unexpected places. The roof is flat, and while there are dozens of windows, they are all blacked out from the inside. I can't tell with what, but it looks like it might be steel of some kind.

I follow Hu toward the front door. Reilly falls into step beside me.

"I can already hear him, can you?" he asks me quietly.

I try to focus my hearing past all the chatter around us, but it's hard to both tune out what's happening around me and listen harder.

"I think I hear someone screaming," I say hesitantly.

Reilly nods.

Two EMTs come out of the building, carrying a stretcher. Whoever is on the stretcher is in a body bag. The absence of their heartbeat between the other two is almost disorienting.

A man with long, white-blond hair stands in the doorway. He's wearing a neat gray suit that happens to be smeared with blood. He waits for us to approach with his hands folded in front of him. His eyes stray to Reilly, and he nods.

"Mr. Vaughan," Agent Stocke says, showing her badge briefly. "I am Agent Stocke, with JHAPI. Can you please tell us what you know?"

"Ryan has gone feral," he says in an even tone. Not a lie. At least he doesn't believe it is one.

"He killed your second. As far as I understand, that shouldn't be possible. Feral vampires are normally sloppier, not stronger," Stocke says, tucking her thumbs into her pockets.

Vaughan looks at her blankly. "Yet, it happened. You have my permission to put Ryan down. Do I need to sign anything, or is my verbal consent enough?"

Vaughan doesn't look like he cares at all. If Javier had been in a situation like this, he would have been fighting to keep his vampire alive. I don't understand how this guy can stand here so calmly and ask for Ryan's death.

"There are some forms we need you to sign," Stocke says, looking back at Staci, who trots back to the van, I assume to grab those forms. "However, we will be attempting to take Ryan alive."

The clan leader furrows his brows, the first moment of emotion I've seen from him. "Why?"

"We want to know where he has been. Our investigation has suggested he was kidnapped. I think it's odd that someone would kidnap a vampire, then drop them off at a local bar. Don't you?" Stocke asks, tilting her head to one side as she scans his face.

Vaughan smooths out his expression once again. "I don't presume to understand anything the NWR does."

"So you know it was the NWR that took him?" she prods.

He shakes his head once. "I simply assumed. I have never heard of anyone else kidnapping paranormals of any kind."

Stocke smiles. "I've never heard of them letting paranormals go. So I'm sure you can understand why this whole thing has piqued my curiosity. Ryan has answers, and I would like the chance to learn them."

"Whatever you think is best," Vaughan says, bowing slightly from the waist.

Staci jogs back up, forms in hand. Stocke flips through them, then takes them to Vaughan and points out each place he needs to sign.

I check the time again. There are still twenty minutes before the brew we need will be here. The entire clan has been sent out of the house. They are gathered in front of the small parking lot next to the garage, watching us.

Reilly appears out of nowhere from behind me and grabs my elbow.

"Come with me," he whispers.

I hurry after him as he heads inside through the front door. I glance back at Agent Stocke and the others, but they aren't paying attention.

It's dark inside the house, but my eyes adjust quickly. Reilly is turning down a hallway just past the winding staircase that dominates the entryway. I stop staring and run to catch up. I don't have to go far though; I almost run into Reilly as soon as I round the corner.

Vaughan looks at me and narrows his eyes. "I asked to speak with you alone."

"She is mine. You can trust her," Reilly says. "What do you want?"

Vaughan sniffs but doesn't object further. "I want Ryan killed."

I flinch and look at Reilly, but he doesn't seem surprised at all.

"Of course," Reilly says. "And he will be, but JHAPI needs a chance to get their answers first."

"If Ryan walks out of here alive, I will be a laughing stock in front of the council and the other clans," Vaughan hisses, his lips curling back over his fangs.

"The council wants to know why and how this happened. You will be repaid for any damage done to your reputation, and you will earn the council's gratefulness," Reilly says, slipping into that tone I only now understand means whoever he is talking to is about to get played. I've certainly heard it often enough.

"Gratefulness? That is a poor currency," Vaughan says, pacing in front of Reilly.

"I can also tell the council that you attempted to interfere with their direct request," Reilly says calmly. "You can accept what you are offered, or you can find out what it means to face their displeasure. The choice is yours."

Vaughan stills and straightens his back. "I want my new member allotment doubled for the next two years to replace what I have lost."

"I will submit your request."

Vaughan clenches his jaw tightly. He has no leverage here, and he's starting to realize that Reilly knows that, and that Reilly will use it ruthlessly.

"However," Reilly says. "I will guarantee it if you let Olivia feed from you, right now."

Vaughan looks at me, his anger shifting to confusion. "What?"

Reilly tilts his head to the side. "You heard me. Take it or leave it."

Vaughan licks his lips, looking at me with interest for the first time. "That does not seem like a fair trade for you. What are you not telling me?"

Reilly smiles. "You know what a feeding involves. There is nothing more to tell."

I take a step back. Why is Reilly doing this? I told him I wasn't going to feed from someone unwilling again.

"No," I say, finally finding my voice. "Absolutely not."

Vaughan looks at Reilly, then at me. "Yes."

Reilly turns to face me. "You heard him, he said yes."

"He doesn't—" I stumble over my thoughts. I'm not sure what to say. He doesn't really understand. He's still being manipulated.

"You don't get to withdraw this offer," Vaughan says, stepping up next to Reilly and glaring at me. "If I'm going to get shit on by the council, I want something out of it."

Reilly looks at me, satisfaction written across his face. He's so sure, as always, that he has the upper hand. There is a constant hunger in me that I do my best to ignore, but it's flaring up now with this easy temptation.

Vaughan jerks off his jacket and drops it on the floor, then pulls his sleeve up. I can't look at him. I stare at Reilly instead, my heart pounding angrily in my chest.

Vaughan holds his wrist out toward me, but I don't move. He glances at Reilly, then lifts his wrist to his own mouth and bites into it. With my senses already enhanced by the vampire magic, it's impossible to ignore the warm, bright scent of blood.

I squeeze my eyes shut but realize that was a mistake when a hand wraps around the back of my head and Vaughan's wet wrist is pressed against my mouth. My fangs descend, and I bite down purely on instinct. Blood pours into my mouth, and my hands wrap around his forearm.

It only takes two long pulls before I realize what I'm doing. I reach for his magic but stop as I brush against it. Vaughan didn't agree to this. I grind my teeth into his wrist as I struggle for control. I want this, I want it so much, but Vaughan didn't understand what he was agreeing to. He might be an awful person, he definitely seems to lack empathy, but I'm not. I refuse to be.

I look back at Reilly, who is watching intently, and pull my magic back into myself. Vaughan's blood is powerful on its own. It's feeding the hunger of the vampire magic within me. Whatever I can take from this alone will have to be enough.

My hands are shaking, and a small, dark part of me keeps insisting I take just a little of the magic. I keep my eyes on Reilly. As long as I focus on him, it's easy to remember that I can't. I swallow one last time, then shove Vaughan's wrist away from me.

I'm still hungry in a way the blood couldn't satisfy, and I

suppose I always will be. If that's the worst thing I have to endure to keep from turning into a devil, then I'll learn to live with it.

I spin on my heel and walk away from them both. The tranquilizer should be here. Reilly and Vaughan can keep playing politics if they want to; I'm done.

CHAPTER 17

I hear the thrum of the helicopter and look over in the direction of the noise, but I don't see it yet.

"I can hear it too," Elise says, coming up to stand next to me. "It's still a couple of minutes out."

"You're determined to go in there with Reilly, aren't you?" I ask. I won't say it aloud and piss her off, but I'm a little worried she isn't fast enough as well.

She nods decisively and rolls her shoulders in a movement that looks more wolf than human. "He's going to need help. I've fought vampires before. Old ones. This is something I can handle."

"I'm going in there too," I say, uncrossing my arms and tapping my fingers against my leg.

She glances at me. "The way you moved in that last raid was different. That's not something a hedgewitch or a Finder or a healer can do."

"Sure isn't," I agree.

"Are you going to explain how you can do it?" Elise asks.

"I'm not supposed to talk about it," I deflect.

Elise rolls her eyes and punches me in the shoulder. "Your super-secret hidden talents better not get us killed."

"They won't," I say, punching her back and letting a little of my vampire strength slip through to make my point. She winces and glares at me.

"You passed out last time," she says, rubbing at the place I punched.

"Not until *after*," I say. "Whatever happens in there is going to be over quickly anyhow. Either we subdue him within a few minutes, or he kills us all."

Elise chuckles. "Such positive thinking."

"Realistic thinking," I correct.

The helicopter finally comes into view. It circles the house once, then chooses a point off the west corner of the house to land.

Staci hurries off toward the helicopter, and Reilly finally walks out of the house. He heads straight for Agent Stocke. Elise and I walk in that direction as well. I can't hear what they're talking about over the noise of the helicopter, but Stocke glances at me, her brows raised, and shakes her head. Reilly says something else, waving his hand through the air. She rolls her eyes but finally nods.

Elise and I approach, and Stocke walks over to me.

"I don't need you dying the first two weeks on the job," Stocke says, arms crossed.

"I'm not suicidal, Agent," I say firmly. "I wouldn't go in there if I didn't think I was going to walk out."

"It's your neck," Stocke says, shaking her head, still looking unconvinced. "I think you have a better chance with three people than one, but I'd be more comfortable sending in Hu if I thought he stood a chance of being able to move out of the way of an attack."

"I can't blame you. Hu is a better offensive magic user than I am," I say with a shrug.

"Every time I turn around, there is something else you can do that should be impossible," Stocke says, looking at me intently. "After this, we are going to sit down, and you are going to tell me exactly what you are capable of, and why, or you and Reilly are off the team. Politics be damned."

I'm taken aback for a moment by her vehemence, but I shouldn't be surprised. She is protective of her team, and as far as she is concerned, I'm a total wild card. I swallow thickly and nod.

Staci runs up behind us.

"I have it!" she says gleefully, waving a heavy metal cylinder in the air. She has two injection guns clutched in her other hand.

Reilly walks over to join us, and we scoot out into a loose circle. Stocke takes the cylinder from Staci and twists it open.

"All right," Stocke says, slipping back into her usual business mode. "There are two injectors and two full doses."

Staci hands one of the injectors to Reilly and the other to me. Elise pulls off her jacket and begins kicking off her shoes.

"You can inject the brew anywhere," Stocke explains as she lifts the slender glass tubes out of the cylinder. "If the two doses don't stop him, then nothing will. Do not die in there trying to capture him. The main priority is getting all three of you out alive; second is Ryan. Is that understood?"

We all nod.

"Vaughan has a key to the room Ryan is locked in. He is going to open the door just long enough for the three of you to get inside, then shut it and lock it behind you." Stocke grabs two earpieces out of her pocket, handing one to me and Reilly. "Stay in constant communication. Elise, howl if you need out."

"Yes, ma'am," Elise says, handing her jacket to Staci, then stripping off the rest of her clothes.

Only Elise could stand buck-ass naked in front of her boss and still act like it's just another day at work. I admire her nerve.

The shift rolls over her all at once. I grit my teeth against the noise of her bones crunching and changing. Skin gives way to fur, and her face lengthens into a snout full of sharp teeth. When she's done, she shakes like a wet dog and her thick black fur ripples.

I hadn't paid much attention to her size or appearance when I saw her shifted in the last raid. There had been too much to think about, and I had been in a lot of pain. She is beautiful though. I reach over and ruffle the fur on the top of her head. The glare she gives me would be intimidating if I didn't know her. I grin unrepentantly.

Stocke hands me one of the vials. I hold it up and inspect the brew. It's dark blue; you might think it was black if you didn't look closely. Out of the corner of my eye, I can see Staci practically drooling over it. I slip it into the injection gun and lock it in place.

Stocke looks at each of us in turn, then nods. "Let's get this over with."

Staci fetches Vaughan, and the six of us go inside. The room they have the vampire trapped in is in a building attached to the back of the house by an enclosed walkway.

The vampire has been screaming off and on since we arrived, but as we get closer, it becomes almost constant. I'm not sure if it can hear us, smell us, or both. It certainly knows we're coming.

The building is a solid, windowless block that makes me think of a tomb. I shudder internally. The door is solid metal with bars on the outside.

"The door is inlaid with silver. Neither you nor Ryan will be able to damage it," Vaughan says. "I will leave the bars off while you are inside."

Vaughan lifts the two solid bars off the door.

I pull on the vampire magic inside of me without hesitation and hold it ready. I'm going to need the speed and strength that comes with it. The vampire magic is energized from Vaughan's blood, but the unsatisfied hunger for magic within me thinks Hawking smells like food. She has power coursing through her that is so different from anything I've ever taken before. My fangs push out of my gums, and I lean toward her.

"Olivia," Reilly whispers harshly, his eyes scanning my face. "Are you still with me?"

"I'm fine," I growl out. I need something to do with all of this power, or the hunger is going to overwhelm me.

The key slides into place, and the lock clicks open.

"Ready?" Vaughan asks.

Reilly nods and moves to the door, his shoulders relaxed and the injector gun held loosely at his side. He doesn't look like he's about to walk into a fight at all. I edge up behind him and take a deep breath. Elise presses against my leg, her muscles just as tense as mine.

Vaughan pulls on the door, and it slides to the right. Reilly lunges inside, and I run into the absolute darkness after him. The door bangs shut behind us, shaking the entire building. It's absolutely silent in here. The vampire stopped screaming as soon as the door started to move.

Elise is still close to me. I can hear her breathing and the subtle scratch of her claws against the concrete floor. I'm not sure where Reilly is. More importantly, I have no idea where Ryan is. My eyes are slowly adjusting to the pitch black of the room, but it seems that not even the vampire magic can compensate for the lack of light completely.

There is what looks like a table or bed near the center of the room. Directly in front of me is a long table with chairs set around it, half of them overturned. There are other shapes across the room I can't make out, but I think they might be cages. It's creepy now, but it makes sense if this is where they keep new vampires.

Quick footsteps vibrate along the floor, and I launch myself forward on instinct. A rush of displaced air rushes along my back as I dodge the first charge. I don't wait for the second, darting to the right and praying I don't trip over anything.

I slide to a stop, my eyes glued to the jerky silhouette I assume is Ryan. He's not large, maybe only three inches taller than I am.

He's slender as well, like all the other vampires in this clan I saw outside.

Just behind him, I see a low shape creeping along the floor. Ryan twitches and tilts his head back like he's sniffing. I stomp my foot on the ground, and his head whips around to me. Elise lunges and hits his back. He shrieks and I run forward, injector ready, but Reilly beats me there.

Ryan flings Elise off him, and she flies through the air as Reilly shoves the injector against his side. There is a *hiss* and *pop* as the brew is forced through his skin in a thin stream. Ryan's elbow connects with Reilly's chest, and something cracks as Reilly is sent flying as well.

Ryan doesn't pause or slow down as he charges me again. I dart to the left, away from both Elise and Reilly. Ryan is almost as fast as Reilly though, and he's not playing tag. He swipes at my back, and his nails slash through the back of my shirt, drawing blood.

I hiss in pain and duck down before pivoting and running in another direction. I pull harder on the vampire magic for a moment, just long enough to put some space between us. When I turn around, I can't see him anywhere.

My foot nudges against something damp and cold. I jerk away and swallow down a shriek. Whatever it is, it isn't moving. I crouch down, and in the dim lighting I can make out a face, eyes wide open, mouth frozen in a scream.

I scramble backward, landing on my butt in my hurry to get away. I had forgotten somehow about the necker they said had been killed in here. I hadn't been expecting a body.

Elise growls, and the sound makes all the hairs on my neck stand on end. My head jerks up, and I look for any sign of movement. Her eyes are two bright points in the darkness across the room. Something drops from the ceiling and lands right on top of her.

I run towards her, but I can't even tell who is who anymore. They tangle together, all teeth and shrieks and fur. Reilly is running from the other corner as well, but I beat him there this time.

Ryan is on top of Elise. He has her flipped on her back and is trying to swipe at her neck and belly, but she keeps him back with quick snaps of her jaw. I shove the injector against his back and pull the trigger. The brew rushes into him as the back of his hand connects with my shoulder. I hit the wall before I can react and fall hard on my side, the empty injector clattering to the floor.

I grit my teeth against the pain and scramble to my feet. Nothing is broken at least. Elise is off her back, and both she and Reilly are circling around Ryan. She darts in every few seconds, snapping at his hands and his legs. Every time he tries to get away from her, Reilly is there, blocking him. They're driving him back toward me.

"We have to kill him," Reilly shouts over the noise of Ryan's incensed shrieks.

It makes my stomach twist, but he's right. One dose of that brew should put anything to sleep. Two doses should have been enough to kill him on its own. There's no other way to stop him.

Ryan finally realizes he is being backed toward me and decides I'm the weak link. He turns and lunges for me. I don't try to dodge this time; there's no room for it, and he's too fast. I lean just far enough to the side that he won't hit me full on and throw a punch. My fist connects with his throat, and it crumples under my knuckles.

Hunger and anger overwhelm me. I lunge forward, and my teeth sink into the meat of his shoulder. I pull on his magic viciously, taking everything I can in one short rush. He is weak compared to the others I've fed on; there is barely anything to steal. His blood tastes bitter. I would spit it out if the magic inside of him wasn't so sweet.

It's over in a matter of seconds. As soon as the last bit of his magic flows into me, Ryan crumbles into ash.

CHAPTER 18

I stumble backward, spitting and coughing, but I can't get it all out of my mouth. I fall to my knees and vomit, then stay there trying to relearn how to breathe.

I wipe my hand across my mouth and realize ashy bits of Ryan are still stuck to my face. I pull up the bottom of my shirt and frantically try to wipe it away. My hands are shaking, and I feel like I might get sick all over again.

Reilly pauses next to me and brushes his hand across my shoulder. I move away from the gesture. I don't want affection or comfort from him. I wouldn't be here at all if it wasn't for him.

"Are you hurt?" he asks.

"No," I gasp out. "Is Elise hurt?"

She snorts from behind me.

I glance back. "I'll take that as a no."

Reilly walks to the door and knocks twice.

"Ryan is dead," he shouts.

I can hear some discussion from outside, then the door is pulled back and light filters in. I squint at it and realize I still have the vampire magic coursing through me like I'm still under attack.

I squeeze my eyes shut for a moment and let go of it. It makes me feel weak, and I don't like being unable to hear what Reilly is saying to Agent Stocke, but I'm already at my limits.

"What the fuck did they do to him?" I mutter to myself.

"Good question," Elise says.

I flinch. I hadn't realized she had shifted.

She is standing naked, and now slightly ashy just like I am, her hands on her hips.

"Vaughan certainly seems pleased that Ryan is dead," she says bitterly. "What a great sire."

I snort. "Yeah, he seems like a real class act."

The asshole can probably hear us. I hope he's listening.

Elise extends her hand toward me. "Come on, stand up and pull yourself together."

I accept her help and let her pull me up onto shaking legs. With the magic gone, my muscles are exhausted. We head outside, and I slip around the crowd. I need a shower, and I don't really want to talk to anyone right now.

I walk through the almost empty house and back out to the front of the property. The rest of the team is talking with someone from the local police.

My phone buzzes, and I answer it without looking at the screen.

"This is Olivia," I say tiredly.

A deep chuckle sends a chill down my spine.

"Hello," he says.

My fingers tighten on the phone, and I have to bite my tongue to keep from speaking before I get my thoughts together. I have no idea how he got this cell number. It's a JHAPI-issue phone. I haven't given it to anyone. I didn't think anyone outside of the team had it at all.

"Jason," I say, my voice tight. "It's been a while."

"Not that long," he says. "You went in after the vampire, didn't you?"

I hesitate, and he takes that as an answer.

"Of course you did. I had no doubt you would. You always charge in, even when you shouldn't. You're not very good at listening to friendly advice," he says, his voice growing more heated at the end.

"You wanted me to leave my friend to be tortured and killed in your fucking basement," I snap, my fingers squeezing my phone until it creaks. The strength of the vampire magic is still coursing through me, and the anger is only making it worse.

"I wanted you to stay out of my way. I have a mission. A calling. I thought you might understand that eventually, but you are close-minded."

"You want to destroy me and everyone like me," I growl at him.

"I want to destroy the parasites and the murderers," he says, his voice shifting back into the calm tone he had always used when I thought he was just another police officer. "Witches face a great and terrible temptation, but they can be redeemed if they just reject the magic. I gave you a chance."

I hear someone walk up behind me and turn around to see Corinne. She stops at the expression on my face.

"You didn't give me shit," I say while trying to gesture at Corinne to do something, though I don't know what. "You had me arrested, and you would have thrown me in jail to stop me."

"To protect you!" he shouts.

"You tried to kill me that night."

Understanding dawns on Corinne's face, and she pulls out her phone and begins furiously texting someone. She twirls her finger in the air, telling me to keep talking.

"You gave me no choice. You brought those parasites to us. The dogs as well. And all for what? To save a vampire that would suck you dry if ever given the chance," Jason snaps.

"You're wrong about that. You didn't break him."

"He killed Novak. I watched him." His voice is almost gleeful. I don't understand how I missed this madness. He's completely insane.

"The man who shot Novak killed him," I say quietly. The truth is that I killed Novak in the end. He wouldn't have survived the wound and Patrick draining him, but when his soul left his body, it was because I had drained him of his magic.

"You would have been an excellent warrior, Olivia," he says softly. "You walked out of that building just now without even a scratch. Not many can face a creature like that and survive, much less without being injured."

"What?" I ask, my hand shaking as I spin in a circle. Can he see me right now? Is he somewhere in the crowd gathered along the street?

"You always were so graceful. Maybe you learned that when you were dancing. I wanted to see you dance for me."

He sounds wistful and almost hopeful. When we had been in that diner, the look he had given me was pure want. My stomach twists. He still wants me. This sick fuck still wants me even though he tried to kill me.

"Where are you?"

He laughs. "Already gone, Olivia. We'll meet again, but not yet. Not quite yet."

The line goes dead. I stare at Corinne, horrified, and slowly lower the phone from my ear. My heart is racing, and I feel like I need to chase after him, but I can't. I don't know where he is.

"He saw me, Corinne. He was watching when I walked outside," I say shakily.

"Is he still here?" she asks, looking around.

"He said he is already gone, but there's no way he's out of the city yet. It's been less than ten minutes." I text Reilly, my fingers shaking as I type out the message. "I have to try to find him. Now. While we know he's still close."

"You can't, you're still injured," Corinne objects.

"I don't care. It's not going to kill me," I say, running my hands through my hair. "I have to do this. I can't let him get away again. He's going to kill people, Corinne. Every day he is free, he is hurting paranormals and helping the NWR."

She straightens her shoulders. "You can't Find him, but I can."

"We don't have a map—"

"I don't need one," she says simply.

I hesitate. "That's risky. We have time to get you a map, right? To get something."

Corinne wraps her hand around her necklace. "No, we need to Find him before he has a chance to prepare for it."

She closes her eyes, and I can feel the magic lifting off her. It laps against me in waves, burning every welt on my body as it passes by me. This is so much more raw than what I felt when she was using the map in the office that day. Her hair moves around her face in an invisible wind. The crystal is glowing in her hand, the amber light slipping out between her fingers.

I see Ivy running up behind her, Zachary close behind. They're still about ten yards away when Corinne gasps. Her eyes fly open, and I see a glimpse of fear contort her face before she screams.

The light in the crystal goes dark. Black tendrils appear on her hand, and they rush up her arm. I move without thinking and catch her before she hits the ground. Her hand is clenched tightly around the crystal. I rip each finger away one at a time. I think I break one, but I don't care. I rip the necklace off and throw the crystal away from her.

Magic is still rolling off her in waves. It's like it's being sucked out of her. I press my hands to her cheeks and pull. As soon as I do, I know it's the right choice. It's like pulling against a tidal wave. Something is trying to suck her dry, and I don't know if I can stop it.

CHAPTER 19

I shut my eyes, blocking out the hands tugging at me and the questions being shouted over and over. I reach inside and pull on her magic, letting it flow into me like a river. It's deeper than anything I've seen before. Not even Reilly has power like this. I can only hope it will be enough to save her.

Her heartbeat begins to slow and beat in an odd rhythm. I press healing magic into her. It's difficult while I'm still draining her and fighting the tug of whatever is hurting her, but I push through. It's not just her heart that's slowing down; every organ in her body seems to be dying.

I dig my nails into her skin and push and push and push. I won't let her die. I refuse. Her magic pours into me like a battery, and I push the healing magic back into her in return. The force that has been draining her is weakening.

The welts on my body are burning. It feels like fire is wrapping around my arms and creeping across my shoulders. I push the healing magic into her, doing everything I can to stall what's happening. Just enough to keep her alive.

If I wasn't taking her magic, I'd already have passed out from trying to push my healing magic like this. I need more. Her magic is deep, but everything has its limits, and she is reaching hers just as fast as I am reaching mine.

I open my eyes and see Reilly kneeling across from me.

"I need to feed. She's dying. I can't keep healing her, and she's dying," I gasp out.

"Why is she dying?" Ivy demands, her hand on her gun like she can fight whatever is happening.

"Reilly, please," I beg.

He stares at me jaw clenched.

"I'll tell you. I'll tell you everything," I say, tears slipping down my cheeks.

His face shifts, satisfaction and sadness passing through his eyes. He holds out his wrist. I bite down and moan at the sweet taste of blood pouring down my throat. His magic leaps into me. Cold. Powerful. Intoxicating.

I push it all into Corinne. There's something else inside of her that is all curled up in what's left of her magic and in her skin. It's something strange, and I can't draw it out or heal it. It's trying to eat at her magic, but I'm getting to it first. Her magic isn't completely gone, but only the barest remnants are left. The dark thing stills and curls up. Her heartbeat steadies. It is still slow, but it isn't fading anymore.

I search and search inside of her for the source of this darkness. It's oily and malevolent, like it's somehow alive. My control is slipping. I've pushed too hard for too long, and I just can't keep going, not even with Reilly's magic. I tug my teeth out of his wrist and feel the ground spinning underneath me.

Ivy is alternately shouting for an ambulance and demanding to know what's happened. I look down at Corinne. Her face is slack, her lips parted. The black veins are still on her hands. I shove her sleeve up and see that they stop just above her elbow. I don't know what would have happened if they had made it to her heart, but my gut tells me it would have killed her.

I collapse back onto my butt and wrap my arms around myself. I don't understand. This isn't anything like what happened when I tried to Find my mother. It can't be that he was just too far away. The NWR has always had their ways of hurting paranormals. But this—this feels like magic. Like a curse.

Stocke kneels in front of me and puts her hands gently on either side of my face, turning it until I'm looking her in the eye.

"Olivia, we need to know what happened," she says, using the same tone you might to talk someone out of jumping off a bridge.

"Martinez," I gasp out. "He called me. He was here. He—he saw me."

"He did this?" Stocke asks, glancing at the person beside her and nodding.

"I don't know. She tried to Find him." I bite the inside of my cheek to keep from crying. I can't break down right now. Not in front of all of these people. Not while I still have information they need.

"She tried to Find him? Out here without a map?" Stocke asks.

I nod once. "I was going to try, but she stopped me. She said she would do it and that she didn't need a map. I shouldn't have let her—"

"You're damn right you shouldn't have let her!" Ivy shouts. "That's against policy for a reason. It's common fucking sense!"

I keep staring at Stocke. Ivy is right to hate me. If I hadn't insisted on trying to Find him right then, maybe Corinne wouldn't have tried what she did. If I had just been patient, maybe this wouldn't have happened.

"Enough, Agent Andreas," Stocke snaps at Ivy. She turns back to me. There are sirens in the distance. I hope it's the ambulance. My vision is fading, and I couldn't heal Corinne anymore right now. She needs something, and I'm terrified the black thing inside of her might start growing again.

"There's something attacking her. Something magical," I say

desperately. "It's like a darkness trying to steal her light. It's hateful. I couldn't get it out."

"Magical? Like a curse?" Stocke asks, her eyes scanning my face. She shakes me gently when I don't respond right away, and I realize my eyes were slipping shut.

"I think so," I say. "It's bad. I stopped it for now, but I can't get it out."

The ambulance screeches to a stop next to us, and the paramedics run over with a stretcher.

"Anything else, Olivia? Is there anything they need to know?" Stocke asks.

I swallow, wracking my brain for anything that might make it worse. "No potions of any kind. Nothing magical until we know what's hurting her. Anything could trigger it."

Stocke stands, hurrying over to the paramedics, and I fall forward onto my hands. Zachary is comforting Ivy, and I think keeping her away from me. Reilly walks over to stand between me and everyone else and extends his hand down to me.

"Stand up," he says.

I put my hand in his and let him pull me to my feet. Everything spins, and my vision narrows to two small points, but I stay on my feet. I feel like shit, but I'm not going to pass out.

Reilly steps in close and whispers in my ear.

"We need to go, now. You aren't going to be wanted at the hospital, and if Martinez is still in this city, I don't want you exposed like this."

I nod. I don't care where I am or what I'm doing. All I can think about is the sick, dark thing that's inside of her. And that Martinez did this somehow. He taunted me, making me think he was close by. I don't know if he knows I can use Finding magic, but it feels like, maybe, this trap was meant for me.

I walk in a daze. It doesn't register that we're back in the hotel until Reilly is guiding me into our room. I head straight to the bathroom. My back still aches from the scratches Ryan left me with.

Cold water on my face helps wake me up a little bit, but I'm exhausted. Reilly is leaning against the doorjamb, arms crossed, face blank. I know what he wants, and that there is no backing out of the deal I made. I don't regret it though. There was no way I was going to let Corinne die when I had the power to save her.

I suppose he'd say she might not do the same for me. And perhaps she wouldn't, but I don't care. I made my decision about who I wanted to be after I fed off that vampire. Reilly might have no conscience. He might be okay with threats and manipulations and putting his ambition over what is *right*. My mother raised me better. I'll die before I see myself become like him.

"Maybelle helped my mother steal a spellbook," I begin.

Reilly uncrosses his arm and steps closer.

"I don't know what exactly was in it other than the spell they used, if anything. And I don't know where it is now." I stand up straight and turn to face him. "All my mother wanted was to have a baby apparently, but she had fallen in love with a vampire."

"And vampires can't have children," Reilly says.

"They can if they use this spell. Sort of," I say with a grimace. "Maybelle was waiting in another room, but she went in when she heard my mother screaming."

Talking about this makes me sick to my stomach. Reilly doesn't push. He knows I'm not going to clam up now.

"The spell killed my father. Maybelle said he turned to ash while he was still inside my mother."

Reilly's eyes widen imperceptibly. He wasn't expecting that I think, that it would kill the vampire.

"What else?" he asks.

"That's all I really know. It worked, obviously. Maybelle sold the book. My mother did her best to disappear with me." I shrug and pace back and forth in front of the bathtub. I feel like if I don't keep moving I'll fall asleep where I stand.

"So you are half-vampire, and half-witch," Reilly muses aloud. "You can steal magic, though that doesn't guarantee you can use it well."

"The healing magic was easy to control. The rest of this," I shake my head. "The rest is harder."

"You will learn though. You already are."

I shrug. "Oh, and something else. The coven that attacked the clan back in Texas, they knew what I was and how I was conceived. They were trying to recruit me. Did you know that?"

Reilly stares at me before answering. "I suspected it."

I rub my hands over my face.

"I suppose I'm lucky they didn't find me any sooner." I pause in the middle of my pacing and laugh. "Or I'm unlucky. Maybe they would have been better to work for than you. They might be insane, but they did seem very enthusiastic about the idea of training me."

"The witch council would have eaten you up," Reilly scoffs.

I turn on him. "You say that like the vampire council won't. Like *you* won't."

"I have done everything I could to make this easy for you. You could have just cooperated, but you have fought me every step of the way."

"Cooperated with what, though? You said you wanted to see my potential. If you want to know what I can do, that means you have a plan to use me somehow. I don't want to be used by anyone," I half-shout back at him.

"Tough shit, Olivia," he shouts back. "We're all getting used. We all have our part to play."

I open my mouth to argue back, but his phone rings. He turns away and answers it.

"Reilly here," he says pleasantly. I despise that he can do that, pretend he wasn't just in the middle of an argument.

I sit down on the edge of the bathtub and wait. He needs to get off the phone so I can keep yelling at him. I have to be doing something while I wait to hear about Corinne.

"He's dead?" Reilly asks, shock apparent in his tone.

I try to pull on my vampire magic so I can hear the other side of the conversation, but that makes the room swim and my skin ache, so I let it go.

"And we know for sure that he will be taking his place?"

Another pause.

"Yes. Just do it." Reilly hangs up the phone and stares out of the bathroom door, not moving.

"I would ask if everything is all right, but if someone has died, I guess it isn't," I say quietly. I can't tell if he is angry or upset. His shoulders are a tight line of tension, and his hands are white-knuckled around his phone.

"One of the council members has died. My sire is taking his place." He turns around and faces me. His jaw is clenched just as tightly as his hands.

"Who will be taking over as clan leader now?" I ask.

"His second will be doing that, I assume," Reilly says, his fingers tapping absently against the phone still gripped in his hand.

"Were you hoping for the promotion?" I ask, confused at his reaction. He seems distressed.

"I knew I was not going to be considered for the position. There is a clear hierarchy," Reilly says.

"Were you close to this council member?" I ask.

Reilly shakes his head.

"Is this bad news somehow?" I ask. I don't really care to try and comfort Reilly, but if he's this upset about whatever is happening, it could be putting me at risk as well.

"No, it's great news for our clan, and for my sire," Reilly says.

I wish I could hear his heart, because I don't believe him at all.

CHAPTER 20

It's the middle of the day, but I can't go back to sleep. Elise had texted me a couple of hours ago that Corinne is still stable, but they've been unable to wake her up. The brain scans don't show any damage, so the doctors are baffled. She also promised me that the doctors haven't used any magic or brews on her, which relaxed the knot in my stomach a little.

I sit up and shove the covers off. They don't want me at the hospital, but I have to do something. I find clean clothes and put on a little extra deodorant because I don't care to take a shower right now.

I pace the room, tangling my fingers in my hair. I feel helpless. No one else felt the thing that's inside of her. The darkness. I stop in my tracks.

No one else has felt it, but I have. I've been so frustrated that I can't draw it out of her with the healing magic that I didn't even think about a brew. I was right that the doctors shouldn't give her anything because it could react unpredictably. It was feeding on her magic, and if I hadn't been able to take the magic first, it would have consumed it.

It was sentient, but it's not a human sort of consciousness. It's more primitive, like a parasite or a weed. It just wants to take all the nutrients it can. I think it stopped because it didn't want to kill its host. She still had magic in her, just not enough for it to grow.

I race over to pull my shoes on. As her magic starts returning, the curse is going to start growing again. It has to be stopped before that, and if I can't heal it, then I have to find an antidote.

Normally, curses are irreversible. An object that has been cursed has to be destroyed. Curses that affect the body though, those can be reversed. They can be cured. The only trick to it is making the right brew. Curse-ending is somewhat of a dying art. I blame witches like Staci with their bullshit recipes. The only way to brew for a curse is to do it from scratch. Nothing but you and your magic.

Reilly's things are on his nightstand. I grab his keys and flip through his wallet, taking everything that looks like a credit card. The things I need are going to be expensive. Hopefully, he waits to kill me until after I'm done brewing.

I haven't turned on my personal phone since we left Texas. At least ten messages pop up when the screen comes on. I dismiss them all and open the map. There are dozens of brewing supply shops in the city. I click on the one most likely to have what I need and speed out of the parking garage.

I call Elise, putting it on speakerphone so I can keep an eye on the map. She answers on the second ring.

"She's still fine—" Elise begins.

"I think I know how to fix this," I interrupt. "Or at least part of it. How to get the curse out of her."

"Whoa, slow down," Elise says. "You know how to end the curse?"

Someone talking in the background, almost trying to shout over Elise.

"I think so. I felt it, and I understand it. It's like a weed almost. It wants to feed on her magic, but since I took most of it, the curse went dormant. Her magic will recover though, and then the curse will start growing again."

Elise is silent for a moment. I hear a door open and close, and the background noise cuts off.

"Olivia, you're not making sense," she says quietly. "You took her magic?"

I bite the inside of my cheek. I don't want to have to explain all of this, but these secrets aren't protecting me anymore. They're pointless.

"I wasn't born with the ability to use all these different kinds of magic. I was only born with the ability to steal it. I stole my mother's hedgewitch magic. I stole healing magic. I stole the electric magic from a detective that was killed in the NWR attack in my hometown. I stole something different from the clan leader I worked for. It changed me, but that's—that's not important right now," I say breathlessly. "I can brew something to end the curse."

"I don't—" Elise sighs. "I don't know if they'll let you."

"Then don't tell them," I say immediately. "I'm going to brew it. I'll find a way to get it to her."

"I don't know if I'm going to let you," she says quietly.

My heart drops. I hadn't expected that. I should have.

"Olivia, curse-ending is advanced magic. It's hardly done anymore; hell, curses are almost unheard of. Especially one like this. Her coven is going to find a specialist, they're already making calls. They said there's someone in Europe who might be able to help."

"There isn't time," I plead. Corinne is too powerful, her magic is probably already recovering.

"You giving her some brew you can't prove will work could kill her."

"You didn't feel it, Elise. I know I can do this."

"You thought it was a good idea to try to Find Martinez too, and look how that turned out," Elise says, all semblance of patience gone from her tone. "We're all scared, and we're all worried. You can't do something else reckless trying to fix this."

I grit my teeth. I can't talk her into agreeing with me, but I refuse to give up when Corinne's life is on the line.

"Whatever you say." I hang up the call. I should have just done this without talking to anyone about it. It's too late for that now, but I can't give up.

The first shop has the cauldron I need, but not all of the herbs. I swipe Reilly's black credit card and let out a little sigh of relief when it isn't declined. I hope it's the type that doesn't have a credit limit.

I have to visit three more shops before I get all of the ingredients I think I might need. It's hard to predict beforehand, but I'm letting my intuition guide me. This magic is something I know. It's the one thing I was trained to use, and it's always been as natural as breathing. My mother was talented, and this magic inside of me is still part of her as well.

I put the last bag in the trunk and slide into the driver's seat. I'm not sure where the best place is to brew. It has to be somewhere I won't be interrupted, so the JHAPI offices are out. I tap the card against the steering wheel. A hotel, it is.

I pull out of the parking lot and drive toward the strip. I'm sure I can find something near there. Las Vegas is not lacking in hotels, and I know some of them rent by the hour.

I stop at the first one I see with a sign out front that is blinking the number of vacancies. It's rundown, and there are people loitering in front of some of the rooms. Half are obviously prostitutes. The rest either have the cocky walk of a pimp, or they're pretending they aren't looking at the girls while unable to take their eyes off them.

I park in front of the main entrance and hurry inside. The receptionist, her name tag says Glenda in glittery pink letters, is a middle-aged woman with thinning hair and a pockmarked face. She has a cigarette hanging out of her thin lips.

"I need a room," I say, holding up the card. "Any non-smoking, by chance?"

She laughs, but it turns into a cough.

"They're all non-smoking, but nobody gives a fuck and smokes anyhow," she says, tapping her cigarette against the no smoking sign sitting on her desk.

"All right, whatever, I'll take a room anyhow."

She turns around and digs out a key attached to a little wooden handle with a number written on it.

"How long you want it for?" she asks.

"I'll take it for two days." I don't know how long this is going to take, and I don't want to have to worry about getting all my stuff out of it right away.

She raises a brow but slowly types it into her computer regardless. She takes a long drag on her cigarette and blows the smoke up toward the ceiling, then puts a card reader up on the counter. She doesn't mention a price, and I don't care how much it is. I swipe the card and sign the receipt she gives me.

She hands over the key.

"It's around back, first floor," she croaks.

"Thanks," I say, already halfway to the door.

I drive around to the back. The prostitute's eyes follow my car, but when they catch a glimpse of me inside, they turn back to the men still milling around.

Glenda was right about the room, it's definitely been smoked in recently. It takes three trips to the car, but I get everything inside. There isn't much to work with in here. There's one desk and the narrow shelf the television is sitting on.

I move the television to the floor and pull the desk closer. I set up the propane stove on the desk and begin lining up the ingredients on the shelf. I haven't wanted to admit it, but I am nervous. Elise's comments have only made that worse. I pause and take a steadying breath. There's no time for self-doubt.

I unbox the cauldron reverently. The circumstances aren't

great, but I can't help the thrill of excitement that runs through me at the chance to use this cauldron. It's something I don't think I'd ever have had the money to buy, but I've always lusted after it.

The four most common types of cauldrons are copper, pewter, iron, and steel. This cauldron, however, is made of leaded glass. The same stuff used to make those decorative crystal trinkets people buy and then don't know what to do with. I saw one of these when I was a child, and I thought the cauldron was somehow carved from a diamond. I fell in love instantly.

It's a quirky cauldron to use. You can't brew too hot with it, and you can't brew anything that's overly flammable, or you could shatter the whole thing if something went wrong.

I fold back the lids of the box and lift the cauldron out slowly. It sparkles even in the dim lighting of the motel room. It was carved with hundreds of facets on the outer edges that catch the light. They'll catch my magic too. Brewing with one of these is like watching a fireworks show.

I set it carefully on the burner and look over my ingredients one last time. I have one shot to do this right. It isn't going to take Reilly all that long to find me, and I doubt he's willing to fund another round of this. Hell, he didn't willingly fund this attempt.

I pull up music on my phone, turn up the volume as loud as it will go and drop it next to the cauldron. It's instrumental, which I would never normally listen to, but it makes me feel classy and this cauldron deserves a little class. Or as much as it can get in a pay-by-the-hour motel in Las Vegas at three in the afternoon.

I lay the cutting board on the left side of the cauldron and grab the single, large sunflower I bought. I pluck the petals carefully and set them in a pile in one corner of the cutting board. The hedgewitch magic is already tingling at my fingertips as I work. The petals perk up, taking on a kind of glow as I pluck them.

Once they are all removed, I slice each one into long slivers. I light the fire under the cauldron and grab the bottle of carbonated water. It fizzes happily as I pour it in, and it doesn't stop. I won't be able to boil anything. My magic will have to provide the heat to bind the ingredients together. The carbonation will keep it all moving.

I sprinkle the petals in, and they dance across the surface, bending and twisting and shimmering. They won't sink in just yet, I realize. They won't do that until the end.

I cut the lemon in half and squeeze each half over the cauldron. The juice runs down my wrist too, but most of it drips into the bubbling liquid. The bright, fresh scent spreads throughout the room in a rush. It reminds me of summer days on the front porch, when the only thing that could cool me down was ice cold lemonade made fresh from the lemons we grew in the back yard.

Next are the dragonfly wings. They're arranged carefully in the little plastic box I bought them in. I crack it open and lift them out. They're colorless, lacy things that could crumble at any moment. I cradle them in the palm of my hand and lower them to just above the surface of the brew before I let them slip into the cauldron. They flutter down and dissolve in a swirl of light.

The brew pulls on my magic, and I let it. I expected the magic to be bright, and it is, but it's also colorful. It pours out of every part of me. My hands, my arms, my face, my chest. Anywhere it can escape from. It bounces off the facets of the cauldron casting light all over the room like a prism.

The door crashes open with a bang that almost makes me lose my grip on the magic. I'm immediately struck by Reilly's scent, so I don't even bother turning around. He did find me sooner than I expected, but I'll deal with that in a minute.

"What the fuck are you doing?" he shouts.

I ignore him and grab the final ingredient. The most important one. This is going to carry the light, to ensure that my magic can shine inside of Corinne so brightly, the dark thing that is trying to eat her magic will have to get out of her or die.

"Olivia, do not ignore me," Reilly says with a low growl.

I glance back and hold my finger to my lips, then tip the

diamond powder into the cauldron. He sounds angry, but he looks like he's in awe as he watches the magic dancing around both of us. I'm sure he can feel it. Even a human could feel all of this.

The diamond powder hits the liquid, and the brew begins to sing. It's not audible, but I can feel it down to my bones. This is why the crystal cauldron is so beautiful. None of the metal cauldrons can sing like this. It's so perfectly clear. My magic rushes into the cauldron, and I throw my head back and raise my arms. This brew doesn't need to be stirred or prodded; it only needs my full attention and my full effort.

I feel like a conductor, and the magic is my orchestra. My fingers dance through the air, tugging on invisible strings of magic. I lean over the cauldron and watch as the bright petals twist down into the shimmering liquid one by one. Each petal makes the brew brighter until it's like looking into the sun itself.

I push the magic to its crescendo, higher and higher and higher until it's just right. I bring my hands together, and the clap thunders around the room. The brew stills instantly, but the brilliant light of the brew only grows stronger.

I'm panting like I've just run a mile, but I could keep going for hours if I needed to. I missed brewing; no other magic has ever made me feel so alive.

I turn to Reilly slowly. "Sorry, I think you asked what the fuck I was doing?"

The look of awe disappears from Reilly's face, and he clenches his jaw. "You stole my car and my credit cards and disappeared. So yes, I would like to know what the fuck you are doing."

I gesture at the cauldron. "I needed to brew this."

"And what, exactly, is that?" he demands.

"It's going to end the curse affecting Corinne," I say, crossing my arms and waiting for the inevitable objection.

Reilly stays silent though, considering. "Curse-ending is advanced magic."

"You're not the first person to tell me that today," I say, straightening my shoulders and squaring my jaw.

"Why do you think you can brew something like that?" he asks.

I drop my arms and throw my hands in the air. "Everyone misunderstands brewing. I'm sure you think most hedgewitches follow a recipe?"

Reilly nods.

"Well, that's crap. Brewing is *magic*. It's my magic. If you think about what you need, about what ingredients can give you what you're looking for, the magic will do the rest. You just have to trust your intuition and trust the magic." I point at the cauldron. "You need the right equipment, and you can't always get it. But when you have it, I mean look at this brew. You can feel it, can't you? It's perfect."

Reilly nods again, but slower.

"It is—magnificent," he says. "But that doesn't mean it can end a curse."

I rub my hands down my face. "I felt the curse. I understand it. I know this will end it. No one is going to believe that, apparently, but I know it."

Reilly stares at the cauldron for a few moments. "I'm starting to think you might be a bit unstable."

I roll my eyes and turn back to my makeshift workstation and flip off the burner. I need to get this in the vials before it cools.

"How'd you find me?" I ask as I ladle the brew into the first vial.

"My car has a GPS tracker on it. Not that I ever expected to have to use it," he says, his tone more exasperated than angry now. "What the hell were you thinking?"

"I thought I'd have more time before you found me," I say with a shrug. "Did you wake up before sunset or something?"

"Yes," Reilly says tiredly. "Something felt off."

"So, are you going to try to stop me from giving this to Corinne?" I ask.

"No."

I look up, surprised. "Really?"

He raises a brow at me. "Did you want me to?"

"No, of course not." I stopper the vial and grab the next. "You just said you didn't believe me and that I seem unstable though."

"You're most likely insane," Reilly reiterates. "But I want to see if this works."

"And you're willing to risk Corinne's life to do that?" I ask, annoyed. He's letting me get my way, and he's still finding a way to piss me off while doing it.

Reilly shrugs. "I doubt it will kill her. There's certainly a chance it will fail, but that's not the same thing."

I turn back to the cauldron and fill the final two vials. Corinne should only need one, but I'm bringing all of it just in case.

"If you want to see if this works, I might need some help getting to Corinne," I say hesitantly.

"Why? Ivy is angry with you, but you aren't banned from the hospital."

"I called Elise and told her what I was planning on doing on the way here. She said she wouldn't allow it, so I assume she has also told everyone else in case I come try," I say with a grimace.

Reilly puts his face in his hands and takes a deep breath. "You are painfully honest when you should lie, and yet you keep secrets that could get you killed."

"Does that mean you're going to help me, or not?"

CHAPTER 21

I press my back against the wall and wait, listening intently to Reilly's footsteps as he walks down the hall. It's only Cook in her room right now. I can't hear what Reilly says, but after just a few moments, both of them leave the room and the door clicks shut behind them.

I hurry to the door and open it just far enough to peek in, just in case. The room is empty except for the figure lying on the hospital bed.

Corinne is pale as death. She has a cannula under her nose and IVs in both arms. I think it's the first time I've ever seen her face without even the hint of a smile on it.

I glance down the hall one last time, which is still empty, and pull the door quietly shut behind me. I have the vial unstoppered before I reach her bed. I have to walk around to the left side because of the machine they have set up on the right by her head. I can see her steady heartbeat on the screen, which calms my nerves some.

I remove the pillow from behind her head and lower it gently onto the bed. I've given brews to dozens of unconscious neckers, so I have the technique down pat. As long as she can breathe, she can swallow. Even in her sleep. I tilt her head back, tug her mouth open, and hold it, which is a little tricky to do one-handed.

I move the vial over her mouth, letting the lip rest on her bottom teeth. I don't want to spill a single drop.

"Get the fuck away from her."

I jerk and look up, almost spilling the brew. I hadn't even heard the door open.

Ivy is standing in front of me, her gun drawn and pointed at my face. Her lips curl back, baring her teeth. She is furious.

She is also going to shoot me. There's no way around that. I pull on my vampire magic and pour the potion into Corinne's mouth. Everything goes slow. The crack of gunfire, my hand clamping over Corinne's mouth and nose to force her body to swallow, the hot pain of the bullet hitting my shoulder because I can't quite dodge it.

Corinne swallows, and I barely have time to lift my hand from her face before the magic explodes out of her in a violent, bright burst. Ivy and I are both thrown back. I hit the window and it cracks. I can't see anything but spots; I didn't shut my eyes in time.

All of my other senses swim into focus. Corinne's heart is still beating, faster now than it was before. Ivy is groaning and pulling herself back onto her feet. I press back against the window and blink rapidly, trying to see again. My left arm doesn't want to move, but the pain in my shoulder hasn't hit me yet, so I try not to think about it.

I hear something else though, something I can't identify. The hair on my arms stands on end, and I throw myself to one side away from the wall. Something slithers past me and hits the window with a wet smack. It reeks of decay and emanates a dark, oily magic.

My vision begins filtering back as I crab walk backward away from the undulating mass of darkness that is hugging close to the window. Thick snake-like protrusions are waving in the air and creeping toward me.

Gunfire cracks behind me, and I flinch, thinking for a split second that I must be the target again, but the window shatters and the black *thing* screeches in indignation as it falls onto the floor.

I scramble for another of the vials in my pocket. I don't know if my brew can completely kill this thing, but I'm hoping it can slow it down.

"Eyes!" I shout as I throw the vial at the curse. Even with my eyes shut the flare of light is painful. Magic fills the room until the air is thick with it.

I open my eyes and search the room, but I don't see the creature. I stand hesitantly, glancing at Ivy. She's searching for it as well. I pull the third vial out of my pocket and sniff carefully. The same oily scent is still there, underneath the smell of lemon and flowers.

"It's not dead yet," I whisper.

A black mass flies out from under the bed, headed straight for me. Water splashes against the creature and cuts through it like a knife. It falls to the ground in pieces, each of them writhing and flailing.

Ivy runs over and empties another container of holy water on the pieces. Each one shrivels under the assault until it dissolves into a coagulated mess.

I stumble back until I hit the wall and try to catch my breath. It's dead. I look over at Corinne. She's still unconscious, but her heartbeat is perfect, and she's breathing without struggling.

"Holy water, huh?" I ask.

"I always carry it on me. Turns out, the main threat today was just you," Ivy says angrily.

"I knew I was right," I say through gritted teeth as I slide down the wall with my hand on my bloody shoulder.

Ivy stares at me, gun still in her hand, the empty container in the other.

"I don't trust you. You are reckless. You could have been wrong today, and you could have killed her," she says coldly. "You weren't prepared to fight that—thing."

I push healing magic into my shoulder, forcing the bullet out slowly and painfully. Once it's poking out of my shoulder, I grab it and pull it the rest of the way out. It's still hot from the gun, or perhaps just from my blood.

"I don't care what you think of me," I say through the harsh breaths I'm taking. "Corinne will live."

Ivy glances at her. "She's still not waking up."

"She won't until her magic recovers more. I took almost all of it." I take a deep breath and work on healing my shoulder again. I've lost a lot of blood, and I need to stop the bleeding before I pass out and end up admitted to the hospital. The healing magic is warm and soothing, but it can't dull the pain of the wound.

Ivy finally puts her gun back in its holster and walks over to Corinne and inspects her hands and arms.

"All the black is gone," she says.

The last of my worry slips away at her confirmation. My shoulder finally stops bleeding, and I let my hand fall into my lap. It still needs healing, but that's enough for now.

The door opens, and two hospital security officers enter with their guns drawn.

Ivy raises her hands, saying something about being a federal agent. I don't bother moving, I just let my head fall back against the wall and try to appear non-threatening. They argue back and forth for a few minutes, but Stocke arrives before long and the officers are sent away.

She looks at me, obviously shot, the missing window, and Ivy, who is unrepentant with her arms crossed as she stands next to Corinne.

"What the hell happened?" Stocke demands.

CHAPTER 22

The chair I'm sitting in squeaks if I move, so I'm trying to hold very still. Stocke is pacing at the front of the conference room table. Her suit is wrinkled, and she can't seem to stop fidgeting with her hair. She pauses, opens her mouth to say something, then shuts it and begins pacing again.

The door opens, and Reilly walks in. He takes the seat to my right and folds his hands comfortably in his lap. Everyone else is still at the hospital with Corinne. Stocke had insisted they stay with her, just in case she woke up. She had dragged me back to the JHAPI building to yell at me though. Considering Ivy was still eyeing me like she was considering shooting me again, I didn't really object.

"I have worked for JHAPI since its inception," Stocke says, crossing her arms and staring out of the window. "I was the first team lead ever appointed and the first choice for this assignment. And in twenty-four hours, one person has compromised the entire thing not once, but twice."

She turns and presses her fists to the table, her eyes boring into me. I resist the urge to slump down in my chair or look away. I'll accept that the first choice, the one that got Corinne hurt, was reckless. I won't apologize for giving her the brew though. I've said all of that to Stocke already, so I keep my mouth shut.

"It's hardly compromised," Reilly says. "Your team is still intact, and we're closer to finding Martinez than ever."

Stocke glares at him. "She almost got our Finder, one of only three who work with the entire organization, killed."

"She didn't force Corinne to violate policy. That was her decision," Reilly says, leaning forward. "Olivia then saved her life, despite resistance from your other agents."

"I am going to do everything in my power to have both of you removed from this team," Stocke says, her lip curling up like an animal baring its teeth.

"You won't succeed," Reilly says, leaning back in his chair. "But I can arrange for you to be removed if you'd like."

Stocke shifts back onto her heels. I think she would kill Reilly right now if she thought she could get away with it.

"I don't think it would have mattered when Corinne tried to Find him," I say. No matter how angry she is, I need to get this out.

"Excuse me?" Stocke snaps.

"That curse was going to activate no matter who tried to find him, and no matter when," I say.

"So now you're an expert in curses? Are you an enchanter as well? Is there any branch of magic you can't use?" Stocke gets louder and louder with each question until she's shouting at me.

I stand up and shove my chair back. If she wants to shout, we can shout.

"I know you can't prevent a curse from activating unless you know what triggers it. I know a curse that doesn't require physical contact is insanely rare. It's ancient magic that has been banned for centuries because it was blood magic."

Stocke crosses her arms. "Blood magic, meaning blood sacrifice?"

I nod. "All magic, but especially enchantments, are limited by what the witch can do. I don't know how blood magic works; they don't teach anyone about it anymore for obvious reasons, but we all learned about the horrible weapons it was used to create. Those things are supposed to have been destroyed, but they weren't. Not all of them."

"So, you're suggesting that Martinez is using some kind of a cursed object to keep himself from being Found?" Stocke asks.

"Yes," I say, pulling my chair back in close and sitting down heavily.

Stocke begins pacing again.

"How many times can this curse be triggered?" Reilly asks.

"What?" I ask, turning to face him.

"Corinne tried to Find him, and she was cursed. Can this object, or whatever he has, protect him forever? Or will it eventually be used up?"

"I have no idea," I say. "It's possible it could trigger more than once, but I don't know that for sure."

"That's not something we can risk happening again," Stocke says. "Finding Martinez is off limits."

"I do think he was close by," I say quietly. "Maybe not close enough to actually see me, but he was watching somehow. I think he wants to watch me die if he can't, uh, have me."

Reilly stiffens behind me.

"Have you?" Stocke asks, brows pinching together. "Like he has a crush on you?"

I rub hands over my face. "The way he was talking to me, it was like he was flirting with me again. He said he wanted to see me dance, and he keeps trying to convince me to quit trying to stop him and join him instead."

"He knows you're a witch. Why would he try to recruit you?" Stocke asks.

"The first time, when we were in that basement, he said I could still be redeemed if I stopped using magic," I say, picking at a chip on surface of the table.

"That's odd," Reilly says thoughtfully. "I've never heard the NWR use language like that before. They've always spoken of paranormals as abominations."

I shrug. "I've never heard it before either. I think he might just be insane though."

"Who have you given that phone number to?" Stocke asks. "Your JHAPI-issue phone."

"No one," I say, shaking my head. "I've barely used the thing. I haven't even talked to anyone other than the team since I left Texas."

Stocke glances at Reilly, then back at me.

"If you are lying about this, you could be putting everyone in jeopardy."

I turn to Reilly and throw my hands up. "Tell her I'm not lying."

"She's not lying," Reilly says drily.

Stocke rolls her eyes. "You'll have to pardon me if I don't take him at his word where you are concerned."

"How else could he have gotten my number?" I ask. "Is there some kind of database? Is it public information?"

Stocke purses her lips and thinks. "There is a directory. It wouldn't be all that difficult to access if someone really wanted it."

"Well, there you go," I say sarcastically. "I have no interest in chatting with Martinez on the phone. I did not somehow secretly slip him my phone number."

Reilly taps his fingers on the table. "This is an opportunity."

"For what?" I ask.

"Martinez made a play for Olivia. He set a trap, and he almost succeeded in getting her to walk right into it," Reilly explains. "However, his failure gives us the advantage. We know what he wants most of all now."

Stocke turns to me, and I bite the inside of my cheek.

"You want to use me as bait?" I ask. He could have passed the plan by me before bringing it up in front of Stocke.

Reilly nods.

"How exactly do you suggest we do that? Should I just go outside and wave around a sign that says 'come and get me'?" I ask.

Reilly shrugs. "I don't think you need the sign, but yes, something similar to that. The plan doesn't need to be complicated."

"Why didn't he take me this afternoon? I was out in broad daylight, alone. I drove all over the city," I say, crossing my arms and leaning back in my chair.

"You weren't actually alone. I've had someone following you when you aren't with one of the agents," Reilly says. "As a matter of protection, of course. The threat from the coven that attacked the clanhouse is still high."

I dig my nails into my palm and grind my teeth together to keep from saying something because whatever might come out right now would be ugly.

"If the threat is so great that you needed to assign a protective detail to Olivia, I should have been informed of it," Stocke says, leaning forward with both hands flat on the table.

"I did mention that I believed they were still searching for her," Reilly says. "And having one bodyguard stay close is hardly a protective detail. He wouldn't have been able to stop a kidnapping most likely, but if you were taken, I would have been notified immediately."

"Maybe you should have just installed a GPS tracker in me, and then you wouldn't have had to bother having me followed," I bite out. "I can't believe you did that without telling me."

"Yet I did, and it most likely kept you from being kidnapped yesterday when you went out by yourself, despite repeated warnings about your safety. Despite the obvious threat that Martinez and the NWR pose," Reilly snaps, losing the cool he has maintained up to this point. "Stocke is right that you are reckless."

My cheeks burn, and I want to slap Reilly across the face. Electricity sparks across my fingertips where they are still curled into the palm of my hand.

"I did what I had to, and I won't apologize for it," I growl back.

"I've gathered that apologies aren't really your thing," he sneers.

"Enough," Stocke says. "Whatever lover's spat you're having can wait until you're alone."

"We are not—" I begin.

"I do not care," she reiterates, dismissing me with a wave of her hand. "Reilly, what exactly is your plan?"

"I think it's time Olivia tried to run away," he says, putting his hands behind his head and relaxing back into his chair. "Is your shoulder completely, healed by the way?"

I cover it with my hand. It isn't, but I wasn't going to say anything because I didn't want them trying to get me medical attention.

"No, but I can heal it later."

Reilly grins. "Perhaps we can explore installing a GPS tracker in you first."

My palms are sweating. I wipe them against my pants and glance over my shoulder, which still aches thanks to Reilly's stupid plan. I'm less than a block from the car rental place, but I've been walking for over an hour.

It took thirty minutes to give Reilly's tail the slip, and another fifteen to make sure he was actually gone. Both Reilly and Stocke had agreed it was necessary to make this seem real. I hadn't disagreed, but it was still a pain in the ass.

The farther I get from the Strip, the fewer pedestrians there are, which makes me breathe a little easier. I'd like to see Martinez coming if he does try to take me. I'm starting to doubt he will though. This whole thing might be a little too obvious of a trap.

I adjust my backpack again, it's awkward and heavy with all my things stuffed in it. I wonder how far Reilly will let me get before he decides this whole thing just isn't working.

I pause at the corner of the parking lot at the car rental place and scan the area. I don't think anyone is following me, and the tail Reilly had put on me is definitely gone. I head inside, and luckily, the place is dead.

There is one employee at the counter. She has a piece of gum wrapped around the tip of her finger that she's currently sucking back into her mouth. Her eyes are glued to her phone, she doesn't even look up as the door rings to alert her to my entrance.

I walk up to the counter and drop my backpack on the floor next to my feet.

"Hey," I say, but she still doesn't budge. "I need to rent a car."

She sighs and sucks the gum off her finger, finally looking up at me. "You have a reservation or anything?"

"No, and I'd like to pay cash."

"No can do," she says, popping the gum. "We've gotta have a card in case you do something stupid. Like steal the car or wreck it or whatever."

"Fine." I pull out my personal credit card. Reilly's stupid plan is going to make me broke.

She snatches the card, plops back on her stool and starts typing into the computer.

"What kinda car?" she asks.

I shrug. "Whatever is cheap."

"Uh huh," she says as she scans the screen. "We've got one compact car left. That's the cheapest."

"I'll take it."

"How many days?" she asks, popping her gum again.

"Um, three," I say, tapping my fingers against the counter impatiently.

"Will you drop it off here or somewhere else?"

"Here."

She clicks a few more things, then the printer next to her hums and prints off a couple of sheets of paperwork.

"Sign here," she says, pointing to the bottom of the first page. "There and there."

I sign both pages, agreeing to return the car with a full tank of gas and accepting the insurance. She takes a set of keys off the row of hooks behind her and hands them to me.

"It's in row D," she says, pointing toward the parking lot. "Just use the clicker to find it or whatever."

"Thanks," I say, grabbing my backpack and hurrying back outside.

The parking lot is half-empty, so it's not hard to find the car. It's tiny, but it'll do. I toss my backpack in the passenger seat as I climb inside.

I start it up and whip out of the parking spot. Stocke had suggested I drive out of the city, rather than further into it, to prevent the chance of bystanders getting hurt. I have no idea where I'm going, but I know the highway near this place leads north, and that's good enough for now.

I turn on the radio and flip through several channels before I come across a classic rock station. I don't recognize the song, but it's catchy and has a fast beat. I turn it up and speed down the highway.

About ten minutes outside of the city I notice a van behind me. I'm not sure when exactly it showed up, and there are quite a few cars on this road, but I can't help suspect it might be him. I shift uneasily in my seat, my eyes flicking to the rearview mirror every few seconds.

The van starts to slow and turns down a side road. I sigh and rub my eyes. It wasn't them. They may not come at all. This could all be a huge waste of time.

I round a turn and see something glinting on the road. I take my foot off the accelerator, but there's no time to slow down or swerve. All four of my tires blow out at once, and the car jerks violently to the right. I yank the steering wheel to the left, but I overcorrect and the car fishtails wildly. I hit the edge of the road, and the tires are jerked out onto the rough ground.

There is no shoulder, only a steep incline I can't keep the car from barreling toward. The car tips and rolls. My hands fly off the wheel. I don't know how many times it flips, but when it comes to a stop, I'm hanging awkwardly with the airbag in my face and nothing but the seatbelt keeping me from falling into the front windshield. All I can think is that I'm glad I went ahead and paid for the extra insurance.

I slap at the airbag until it deflates, then brace my knees on the steering wheel. Whatever I hit was put in the middle of the road intentionally. I don't think I have much time to get out of here. I summon some vampire strength and rip the seatbelt out of the buckle.

I catch myself awkwardly, my foot breaking the windshield further. The door is jammed shut, but two solid shoves push it open. I tumble out and see the van first, then a man I don't recognize standing a few yards away.

There's a quick pinch of pain on my arm. I flinch and look down; a dart is sticking out of my arm. I yank it out and stumble forward, but on my third step, I find myself falling forward. This wasn't part of the plan. My body is completely numb, and I can feel consciousness leaving me as everything goes black. I see a glimpse of someone else I hadn't noticed standing near the front of the car.

That was stupid, I should have looked. I should have—

CHAPTER 23

Something is rocking. My head hurts, and I don't remember why I'm lying on the floor. I rub my cheek against the rough carpet to get the itch I can't seem to move my hands to scratch. My hair keeps tickling it though. Someone brushes my hair back gently, and I hum in contentment.

"They say the devil is beautiful. I always imagined the devil was a woman too," a voice whispers. "So that she can look innocent when she comes to tempt you into giving your soul to her."

I regret waking up intensely. I try to scoot away from the hand threading through my hair, but I'm backed up against something wooden. I drag my eyelids open, but it is a struggle. I think one of them might be swollen. I'm in the back of some kind of a van. There are weapons mounted on the walls and several cases of ammo that are strapped down so they don't shift around. The back of the van must be separated from the front because it's dark back here other than the glow from a single overhead light set into the roof of the van.

"Olivia," he says. "Look at me."

Martinez crouches down in front of me. I look up at him and

bite down on the inside of my cheek to keep my face straight. He looks like something out of a nightmare. The left side of his face is red and twisted from the burns I gave him. His eye is milky white, and the skin around it is stretched down like melted candle wax.

"I don't tempt you at all, do I? Not looking like this," he whispers. "You liked me before though. I saw the way you stared at me."

I lift my head so I can see him more clearly. I let my eyes wander, I want him to have no doubt that I'm looking at the scars I left him with.

"Now the outside matches the inside," I choke out. My throat is sore and dry.

He slaps me. The smack of his hand against my cheek stings, but it's the way my face smashes back into the floor of the van that really hurts. I pull on my electric magic. I don't need my hands to kill him.

My body tenses suddenly and violently, and the metal around my wrists burns. I can't breathe. I can't even blink. Everything fades into gray, and the taste of blood fills my mouth as my teeth cut into my tongue. I don't understand what's happening, or why. I didn't think he would kill me this fast. I thought I would have more time.

The team has to be on their way, but Reilly had said it would be at least ten minutes from the moment I was taken. I don't know how long I was unconscious. I don't know if I'll last ten minutes.

There is a painful shock on my arm, and I scream, then gasp as I can suddenly breathe. I choke on the blood in my mouth and struggle to spit it out while panting. Martinez's smug face swims into view. Only the right side of his mouth seems to be able to move, while the left side is stuck.

"Did you really think I would get this close to you if I didn't have a way to stop you from flinging your magic at me?" He leans his head back and laughs loudly.

"What the fuck did you do to me?" I gasp out.

He tilts his head to the side, still grinning.

"It's what your kind did to you," he says, tapping on the shackles holding my hands behind my back. "These were made by a very talented enchanter. She made all sorts of interesting things she wasn't supposed to. All of them one of a kind, like shackles that turn a witch's magic against them."

He grins like it's all a joke. I suppose it is to him.

"There was some resistance at first to using these things after we took them from her, but I made the others understand the beauty of it." He pulls a necklace out of his shirt. A solid gold medallion hangs from the chain, and even from here I can feel the hungry, oily darkness that emanates from it. "You know what this does, don't you?"

I don't want to be anywhere near that thing.

"It was amazing to watch it take her. I had hoped it would be you, of course, but the look on your face was almost worth my trap failing."

"You weren't there. We looked," I grind out.

"I was watching from the skies," he says. "You think magic is the only way to do wondrous things. It's so easy for paranormals to forget that there's a reason humans have survived all this time, despite not having magic."

He tucks the medallion back into his shirt and pats the side of my face.

"Perhaps I'll show you the video later. I'm sure you'll make the same face again, and it will be so much more interesting in person."

I jerk away and spit at him, my saliva still tinged with blood. He glances at the stain on the sleeve of his shirt but doesn't seem bothered.

"You'll never win," I snarl at him. "People can see that paranormals aren't monsters."

He grabs my jaw, his fingers biting into my skin.

"That's where you're wrong," he hisses. "They are violent,

deviant monsters. Their true nature will be revealed soon enough. They can't hide behind their masks forever."

The van jerks to a stop, and Martinez stands up, his back still hunched because of the height of the van, and raps twice on the doors. The doors are flung open, and I blink against the sunlight. The sun is hovering just above the horizon.

Martinez steps out of the van and walks off with the other man I haven't gotten a good look at yet. We're on some kind of wide, paved road that looks familiar in a way. I push up on my elbow awkwardly, leaning against the wall behind me, then thump my head back in irritation. I'm such an idiot. That's an airstrip, not a road.

I crane my head around to get a look at the shackles that are keeping me from using my magic. They're solid black and appear to have something engraved on them, but I can't read it.

Martinez knows I'm a witch, and it seems like he knows I can steal magic, or at least that I can use offensive magic. I don't think he knows that I'm half-vampire. All that talk about redeeming myself seemed to be about me using magic as a witch.

I don't want to die here or get taken away to be tortured by the NWR, but the choice between the two is actually pretty easy. There's a chance this might work too. The witch who made these wouldn't have intended them to be used on a vampire, or they'd be silver.

I slide back down onto my shoulder and pull on the vampire magic. There's no time for the control I've been practicing. As soon as the magic spreads through me, I brace myself for the pain and tension, but nothing happens.

One of them scoffs angrily, and I focus my senses on their conversation.

"This is insanely risky," the man says. "Peterson is not pleased you decided to do this last minute without proper approval."

Martinez snorts. "The buyer has promised me eight-hundred thousand if I bring her to them alive. That is not an amount we can afford to pass up right now just because Peterson is afraid of a little risk."

Buyer? I had assumed Martinez was planning on killing me, not selling me. An engine rumbles to life, something much louder than a car.

I yank my wrists apart as hard as I can, and pain shoots through my arms, but the shackles don't even bend. At least I'm not having another magical seizure, but if I can't get out of this van before they put me on the plane, I'm still screwed.

The shackles are connected to the wall by a short chain that runs through two loops that jut out of the middle of them. It looks like a normal chain instead of the same weird black metal that the shackles are made of. If it were any thicker, I'd say there was no way I could break it, but I don't have any other options. I have to try.

I roll forward, letting my arms stretch out behind me, and begin pulling. The metal in the chain creaks and bends as the shackles bite into my skin. I'm not strong enough. It's so hard to use this magic during the day.

I grit my teeth and pull more deeply on the magic. The sunlight glaring in my face starts to burn, and my eyes ache even squeezed shut. I can deal with pain if it means surviving though. Strength flows into my body slowly, and I yank sharply on the chain. Once. Twice. Hot blood slips down between my fingers as the shackles break through my skin. I yank again with all of my strength, and the chain snaps.

I roll onto my face with no way to stop myself. I'm dizzy, but I don't wait to recover or see if Martinez heard. I struggle to my feet and launch myself from the van with all the speed and strength I have left. My feet hit the pavement, and my legs almost crumple.

Martinez shouts something, and I dart to the left. The only thing I can see in front of me is desert. To my left is a metal building attached to a long covered hangar that must be as big as three football fields with other small planes lined up inside of it. I sprint in that direction, zig-zagging to make myself less of an easy target and putting on a little burst of speed every few seconds to move vampire fast.

Gunfire cracks behind me, but nothing hits me. I hope the GPS buried in my shoulder is still working, but I know it's been way longer than the ten minutes Reilly had promised me. I have no idea if anyone is coming to rescue me, and I can't assume they will be.

I glance over my shoulder and see the van careening toward me. Martinez is hanging out of the passenger window with a gun pressed against his shoulder. I put on another burst of speed and slip behind the back corner of the metal building.

There are no doors, no way in, and nothing to hide behind. I keep running along the back of the building and skid to a stop behind one of the planes. The van skids around the corner of the building and bumps along the rough ground.

I hunch down, my arms aching from being held behind my back for so long, and scurry toward another plane. It's a hideous mustard yellow thing with a lightning bolt that extends from the nose to the tail. I crouch behind the wheel, but it doesn't hide me completely.

The van stops at the back of the hangar, a cloud of dirt kicking up around it. Martinez and the other man jump out, guns ready, as they search for me. I lean against the wheel and try not to breathe.

Their boots crunch against the rocky ground, then scrape almost silently against the concrete floor of the hangar. Martinez heads diagonally away from me, but the other guy with the mountain man beard is walking straight toward me.

I tense to run again, but a familiar noise makes me hesitate. The *whomp-whomp* of helicopter blades is unmistakable. I'm not sure if that is someone coming to help me, or if it's backup for them. Showing up in a helicopter wasn't part of the plan, but none of this was. I have no idea if the NWR has access to a helicopter, and I'm not sure why they'd use one now when they obviously have an airplane.

Mountain Man pauses, tilting his head to one side. He must hear it too. He gestures at Martinez, who jogs to the other side of the hangar and looks out at the sky.

"Time to go," Martinez shouts. Mountain Man sprints toward him, but Martinez stays where he is. I try to scoot around the wheel, but there's hardly anything between us.

Martinez lifts his gun, pointing it in my direction. I shove to the left and barely catch myself as I half-run, half-stumble. Bullets strike the plane I'm running next to. The gunfire echoes painfully against the concrete and metal all around us. I wince, my ears ringing so badly I can't even hear the helicopter anymore.

I spot the door that leads into the building attached to the hangar and put on a burst of speed. I crash through the door, little splinters of wood digging into my shoulder as the door disintegrates under the force of my body hitting it. It's dark in here, and this room is small. There is a short hall with one open door at the end that reveals a bathroom.

Another shot echoes behind me, and I duck and roll to the right. I can't go far. There isn't anywhere to hide in here, and there isn't another exit. This was a bad plan.

I grit my teeth and pull at the shackles again. I want them off. I need to be able to use my magic. The metal bites into the already sore cuts, and I have to bite down hard on the inside of my cheek to stay silent. After a few seconds of absolutely futile struggling, I realize that Martinez hasn't come in the building yet.

I press back into the corner and try to listen again, but my ears are still ringing, drowning out everything but my own labored breathing. I struggle back up to my feet and edge toward the door I busted through.

I peek out, and my eyes go wide. Hu is standing between me and Martinez, whose rifle is laying bent and half-melted in front of his feet. I'm not sure where Mountain Man is.

"You're under arrest. Get down on your knees and put your hands behind your head," Hu shouts.

Martinez grins and pulls a collapsible baton off his belt. He flings it open with a flick of his wrist, and the end sparks with electricity.

"You'll have to make me, demon."

Hu shifts his feet carefully, and fire erupts from his shoulders and chest. It wraps around him like armor, and his shirt burns away, the pieces scattering around him. His skin glistens with sweat, and the phoenix tattoo on his back glows and shifts under the magic. I've seen fire witches use their magic before, but I've never seen anything like this. Flames appear above his head, twisting into two horns.

"If it's a demon you want, I can accommodate," Hu says with a smirk.

A howl goes up, and I see Elise, fully shifted, step into the hangar a few yards behind Martinez. Following closely behind her is the last person I expected to see. Reilly's face is drawn and tired. The sun may be setting soon, but it's obvious he has been awake for a while.

Hu charges Martinez, the flames leaping out in front of him like a whip. Martinez dodges and rolls behind a plane. I dart out of the building and run toward Elise and Reilly, staying as far away from Martinez and Hu as I can. My legs are faltering, and I'm running almost human slow. I've used too much of the vampire magic, and I think the shackles might be hurting me in more ways than the obvious too. I can't keep this up.

An explosion rocks the entire hangar, and I find myself face down on the concrete. A fireball shoots up to the ceiling of the hangar, and a wave of heat rolls over me. My ears are ringing again, and the smell of smoke and burning metal fills my nose.

Elise is running toward the fight, but it takes me a moment to spot Reilly. He is headed my way, but his focus is on the fight as well. He's only a few yards away now. I struggle to my knees and get one foot on the ground. If I can just get to him, maybe he can get these shackles off me.

The other man, the one I had lost track of, steps out from behind a plane about fifteen yards away. His gun is trained on Reilly, but Reilly is focused completely on Martinez, who is shouting something at Hu I can't quite hear.

A million things fly through my head in a moment. I know the NWR have silver bullets. I know not even Reilly could survive a shot to the head at this range. The man steadies his gun, bracing it against his shoulder. I'm going to regret this.

I shove off the ground, my foot barely able to get traction. My shoulder slams into Reilly's side as the crack of the rifle reverberates through the hangar. We are both airborne for less than a second before Reilly shifts midair and wraps his arms around me, dragging me around and landing on his feet.

Reilly drops me and is standing behind the man with the rifle before he has a chance to blink. He wraps his hands and around the man's neck and twists. There is a sickening crack, and the man falls to the ground, limp.

I roll onto my stomach with a groan. That is going to leave another bruise. Reilly doesn't run to me like I expected; he runs toward the fight. I crane my neck to watch. Hu unleashes another barrage at Martinez, with Elise snarling behind him. Reilly is holding the same injector we used when we were trying to knock out Ryan.

Hu pulls the flames back, and in the same breath Reilly darts in. He is still slow with the sun up, almost human slow, and Martinez is fast. He jabs the baton into Reilly's stomach at the same time Reilly presses the injector against his neck. They drop in unison, Reilly jerking from the jolt of electricity. Martinez is absolutely still.

CHAPTER 24

I don't bother trying to get up. Hu pulls a pair of cuffs off his belt and immediately detains Martinez. Elise shifts and helps him search Martinez for any more weapons.

I feel the sun set, but it doesn't give me energy like it has been. I'm beyond exhausted. I'm starving and I'm angry and I wish I had the strength to get to Hu or Elise. I can smell the magic in them, and I want it, desperately.

Reilly sits up, dusting off the shoulders of his jacket, then standing. He looks for me and sees I'm lying exactly where he left me. There are sirens in the distance. It's about time the rest of them showed up.

One second Reilly is on the other side of the hangar, the next he is crouched next to me, helping me sit up.

"Does Martinez have a key for these?" he asks.

"I hope so," I say shakily. I hadn't even thought he might not have the key.

"Did you find any keys?" Reilly shouts.

Hu nods and holds up a key ring.

"Make sure they take the medallion off him too. It's cursed. It's what hurt Corinne," I say.

In a blink, Reilly is there and back again, keys in hand. The quick movements are making me dizzy.

"They have the medallion," he says as he rolls me onto my stomach and starts trying keys in the lock. "What are these?"

"Some enchanted bullshit," I mutter into the concrete. "Couldn't use most of my magic. It didn't stop the vampire magic, I guess it's different somehow."

"It's blocking your magic?" Reilly asks before cursing at the keys.

"No," I say, shaking my head. "It was more like it gave me a seizure. I couldn't breathe, couldn't move. It would have killed me."

There is a click, and the shackles fall off. I groan as my arms fall forward and relief floods through me. My magic is quivering inside of me, freed as well.

"Don't try to walk," he says, scooping me up.

I turn my face into his chest and take a deep breath. He smells like magic and blood and fire. I'm so hungry. There is a brief gust of wind on my face, and when I lift my head, we're outside.

There is a line of cop cars following behind the black JHAPI SUVs. They spread out. Two stop in front of the plane, which is still running, while the other heads straight for us, coming to an abrupt stop just a few yards away. Stocke leaps out, gun drawn.

"Is there anyone left?"

Reilly shakes his head. "No, there were only two of them. Martinez has been captured alive, but the other is dead."

Stocke nods and runs past us toward Elise and Hu. Cook and Ivy follow her. Reilly carries me to the SUV and sets me in the passenger seat.

I pull my knees up to my chest, but my muscles won't stop trembling. I'm so hungry, and I'm so tired.

"Olivia," Reilly says, tugging my hands away from my face. "Look at me."

I shake my head.

"You have to feed," he insists.

"No," I groan. "I don't want to hurt anybody. I don't want—"

"You won't hurt me," he says, shaking me hard once.

The movement wakes me up a little bit, and I blink at him, trying to make sense of what he is saying.

"You?" I ask.

He jerks his sleeve up and presses his wrist to my mouth. "I understand what you're taking, and I'm telling you it's all right."

"Why?" I ask, my question muffled against his arm.

"You saved my life," he says, his jaw clenched tightly. "I thought you would let me die given the opportunity."

I guess I did do him a huge favor. I'm too hungry to argue with him. I want this. My fangs slide down, and I bite into his arm. Every swallow spreads the warmth of his blood through my body. I reach inside of him and pull on his magic as well, and the trembling of my muscles slows.

I should have let him die. I could have run after that, but I hadn't thought of that when that man was lifting the gun and aiming it at his head. I had a moment of regret while I was rushing toward him, but the thought of actually letting him die makes me sick even now. I guess as much as I say I hate him, I really just hate what he has forced me into. I couldn't let him die. I wouldn't have been able to live with myself.

I swallow another delicious mouthful and sigh around his arm. Life would be so much easier without a conscience. His hand brushes a strand of hair back behind my ear, his fingers trailing along my cheek. My stomach does a flip at the touch, but I keep my eyes firmly shut and do my best to ignore it.

After another minute, Reilly tugs his wrist away from me. I lean back into the seat to keep from chasing after it, but it's a struggle. It helped, a lot, but I don't feel completely satisfied.

"Staci is here," Reilly says. "She brought healing supplies. Deal with your wounds. I need to speak with Stocke."

I nod absently. Reilly's warm presence disappears, and I let my eyes slip shut. I could sleep for days right now.

Someone clears their throat next to me. I shake off the sleepiness and sit up straight. Staci has a handful of first aid supplies she holds up for me to see.

"Thanks," I say hoarsely.

She hands me a cleansing wipe and sets a tub of healing salve on the dash for when I'm ready for it, then crosses her arms. I clean the blood off my fingers and hands, then gently dab at the area around the wound. It hurts an annoying amount.

"That brew you made for Corinne, to end the curse, how did you do it?" she asks.

I open the salve and spread it on my left wrist before I answer. Staci seems huffier than normal, like asking pains her. It's petty, but I'm going to enjoy it while it lasts.

"I felt the curse that was hurting her. With as long as I've been brewing, I've developed the ability to find the ingredients needed to enhance something, or stop it. So, I listened to my magic and simply brewed something that would cut through the darkness of the curse. It needed to be burned away," I say with a shrug.

Staci pinches her lips together. "Your intuition can't always be right. Magic is a tool. What you're talking about sounds like some kind of religious nonsense."

I laugh and start putting the salve on my other wrist.

"Your coven really did a number on you," I say with a smile. "I'm not brewing on faith. I understand what different ingredients do, and that took many hours of study. I also experimented a lot as a child. It's a skill I've cultivated because you're right, magic is a tool."

I hop off the stretcher, and she steps back. Her shoulders are hunched up, and her fingers are curled into her cardigan.

"I was looking for a recipe you know. I was going to try to help her," she says quietly.

I gnaw on the inside of my cheek and look around, hoping

someone will come interrupt what is starting to feel uncomfortably like a heart to heart.

"Um, I sure you would have found something," I say, taking a step back. "If you ever want to talk brewing theory, or try something new, let me know. I have to go—find Reilly now though."

I turn and hurry away. Reilly is standing at the corner of the hangar, deep in conversation with Agent Stocke and a man in a crisp suit I haven't seen before. There are two men, bodyguards I presume, standing a few paces behind him.

I don't want to deal with strangers, especially ones who require bodyguards. I veer off toward the van the team arrived in. Maybe it will be safer to hide in there for a little while. Elise steps into my path, her hands on her hips. She's wearing a belt buckle that looks like a mouth full of teeth, with two glinting fangs extending just past the rest.

"Hey, you," she says, eyes narrowed.

"What is up with your belt buckles?" I blurt out.

She glances down and frowns. "My mom buys them for me."

A laugh bursts out of me, and I slap my hand over my mouth, but I can't seem to stop.

Elise rolls her eyes, but she's smiling too. "They're awesome, and it would hurt her feelings if I didn't wear them."

"That's great," I say, wiping tears from my eyes.

She watches me, the smile slowly sliding from her face.

"I'm glad you didn't die today," she says. "But if you are going to stay with the team, I need you to promise me something."

All the tension the laughter momentarily erased comes back with a vengeance. I shove my hands in my pockets.

"What do you want?" I ask.

"You follow the rules. You go through Stocke for big decisions. And you don't lie about anything else, like being able to steal magic. That is important, mind-boggling shit. That's the kind of thing your team needs to know," she says, jabbing her finger at me.

"I didn't want any of this, and I'm doing the best I can," I snap, suddenly angry. I'm sick of them all blaming me for Corinne getting hurt. "I didn't force Corinne to do what she did...hell, I tried to talk her out of it."

"I'm mad at her too." Elise snaps. "And I don't care if it is your best. Do better. This is temporary for you, but the rest of us are invested in seeing this through. If you're going to run away again, just go ahead and do it."

I roll my eyes. "Now you sound like Zachary. And believe me, I would run if I could."

I brush past her. I want to be anywhere else right now. She catches my arm.

"What do you mean by that? That you would run if you could?" she demands.

I jerk my arm away. "Nothing."

I shouldn't have said that. She's perceptive, more so than the rest of the team.

"Did you forget I can hear a lie just like your vampire?" she asks.

I look over her shoulder at the person approaching and plaster a smile on my face.

"Reilly," I say. "Have they finally decided where they are taking Martinez?"

Elise stiffens and turns around slowly, stepping back so she isn't standing between us. I don't know how much he heard, or if him walking up when he did was a coincidence, but the tension is palpable.

"They have," Reilly says with a nod and a sideways glance at Elise. "They have the transport ready to take Martinez away now. It's time to go."

"Good, I need a shower and at least twelve hours of sleep," I say lightly. Elise is too busy glaring at Reilly to react.

"We'll see you back at the conference room in a couple of hours," Reilly says to Elise. "Stocke wants us all there by midnight."

I follow Reilly toward one of the SUVs. I can feel Elise's eyes on my back the entire time.

CHAPTER 25

It feels like it's been an eternity since I last sat in this room, but it's been less than twenty-four hours. I made sure to avoid the squeaky chair this time, but Ivy is stuck in it instead. She's a lot better at holding still than I am though, so you can hardly tell.

Zachary drove me here, and the rest of the team was apparently delayed in following us. Reilly had disappeared without comment after Martinez had been hauled off. I was surprised he had left me alone, and surprised he hadn't demanded answers about everything that had happened. I can still taste his blood in my mouth, and it's distracting, to say the least.

I shift uncomfortably in my chair. I have bruises all over the place, and I don't have the energy to heal them right now. I don't think I'll have the energy or the time to brew my own salves either. Maybe Staci will bring me some without too much of an attitude after our last conversation.

"What happened with the GPS, by the way? Were you guys tracking me the whole time?" I ask, rubbing my shoulder. The tracker is still in there. I'm dreading having it removed since I'll have to actually see a doctor. Growing up with a hedgewitch for a mother, and then stealing the healing magic at a young age meant I haven't had to see human doctors. I distrust them. Everything they have to do seems kind of barbaric.

"We lost the signal for about thirty minutes," Zachary answers.

"Shit, I was out for that long?" I ask.

Ivy nods. "You were gone for an hour total. By the time we regained the signal, we were behind and headed in the wrong direction."

"Well, I'm glad I got to be unconscious for all of that," I say, leaning my head against the back of the chair.

Zachary snorts. "I think we all wanted to be. It was really tense here for a while. I thought Reilly was going to tear the tech's head off."

"Leave it to Reilly to threaten random people," I say with a snort.

"He was very concerned about you," Zachary says, nudging my chair with his foot.

I shrug. "Yeah, I'm sure he was."

The door opens, and the rest of the team files in. Except for Corinne. My stomach sinks. I want to see her soon, but there hasn't been time yet, and I'm not sure if Ivy will let me anyhow.

Reilly takes the seat next to me, and I shift uncomfortably in my seat. I haven't spoken to him since he interrupted the conversation with Elise, but I'm sure I'll be questioned about it soon.

"I spoke with the hospital staff a few minutes ago," Stocke says, taking her usual place at the head of the table. "Corinne is doing well. They expect her to wake up in a couple of days. Right now, they have her sedated to allow her magic to continue recovering at a faster pace."

A murmur of relief spreads around the table. Something in my gut unclenches. Hearing she really will be okay is such a huge relief.

"Where is Martinez being taken?" Reilly asks.

"A maximum security prison back in Texas," Stocke says. "We'll continue hunting down every NWR member we can find, and continue looking for any evidence needed to build a case against him, but what we already have is solid. He's going to be locked up for three lifetimes at least."

"Are these two still on the team?" Cook asks. He doesn't look at me, or at Reilly, but his shoulders are held in a tight line, and his jaw is clenching and unclenching.

"Olivia and Reilly will be taking a week of leave to attend the Summit, where they will also be reporting on the progress we have made and ensuring that we receive the funding we need to continue," Stocke says, leaning back in her chair. "So yes, they are still on the team, and they will be rejoining us at our next location."

Cook glances back at Ivy. She keeps her expression blank, but she does nod. Cook sighs but apparently takes that as acceptance on her part.

Elise is staring at me, the same question on her face she had a few hours ago when Reilly interrupted our conversation. She's going to have to keep wondering. I shouldn't have let slip as much as I did.

"Any other questions or concerns about the future of this team and this assignment?" Stocke looks around the table, challenging anyone else to voice their objections now or shut up and deal with it.

I look down at my hands and wait. I don't know if I'm hoping someone else wants us gone or not. In some ways, it might be easier not to have to do this. I'm not sure what the alternative is though.

"All right, moving on, then," Stocke says. "We're headed to Los Angeles next. It has some of the highest NWR activity in the nation. We've known for a while that they are not only recruiting, but carrying out protests, and they have recently started attacking the local packs there."

"Openly attacking them?" Elise asks, leaning forward to rest her elbows on the table.

"Yes," Stocke says. "Ambush attacks when there are one or two of them somewhere alone. There have been four deaths so far. Basically assassinations."

"How are the pack leaders handling it?" Elise asks.

"So far, they're confining everyone to pack lands as much as possible. When they do leave, it's in groups of five at a minimum." Stocke twirls her pen in her fingers. "That's not sustainable though. These people have jobs, school, and the right to live without constant threat of being murdered."

"When do we leave?" Hu asks.

"We have early afternoon flights, so in about six hours," Stocke says. "We'll go over the rest, including case details and the NWR members we already have identified, in Los Angeles. Everyone, go pack and get a few hours of sleep if you can. It's going to be a long day."

Everyone stands and gathers their things. The adrenaline of the fight has faded, and I can tell everyone else is just as tired as I feel. One thing has been bothering me though.

"The other vampires who had gone missing, were they ever found? Or is no one looking for them now?" I ask.

Stocke sighs heavily. "Their ashes were all mailed to their respective clans."

My eyes widen. "All of them?"

"Yes," Stocke confirms. "The day after Ryan was put down."

"And the werewolves?" I ask.

"Still not officially missing. There is nothing we can do to help them, and no way to justify continuing the investigation if they aren't reported missing by their packs," Stocke says, her shoulders slumping.

I put my head in my hands. Martinez just killed them all once he decided they were no longer useful. Or maybe they died while being experimented on or whatever the hell the NWR was doing to them. If the pack leaders would just talk to JHAPI, they might be able to save their people from a similar fate, but of course they won't.

"I'll see you back at the hotel room," Reilly says, putting his hand on my shoulder and startling me out of my thoughts. "I need to speak with Stocke privately."

"All right," I say.

Zachary is already leaving the room, so I jog after him.

"Zach," I say, jogging after him. "Do you have a little bit to talk? I need a ride back to the hotel, and I want to go over that case with you one last time."

"Sure," he says. "It seems like we won't get much of a chance to work on it for the next couple of weeks."

"Yeah, that's what I'm afraid of."

I glance back in the room one last time before following Zachary. Reilly is watching me. I'm sure he overheard the conversation. I sigh; that will be yet another thing for him to question me about later.

Zachary unlocks the hotel room door, and I follow him inside. He sets his things down on the desk, and I take my usual spot on the end of Elise's bed.

"I've been thinking about the spellbook my mother stole from this coven," I say, bouncing my leg nervously. The only possible meaning I can glean from the most recent hallucination of my mother is that the book she stole might be important somehow. If there is even any meaning to it at all. Maybe it's just a nightmare my mind is creating. "Have you found anything about that in the research you've done?"

Zachary shakes his head. "The coven deals with so many magical artifacts. Nothing about a spellbook has stood out though."

"Maybelle sold it, probably for a lot of money. It had to have been to another witch or coven, right?" I ask, leaning back in my chair.

Zachary taps his pen against his mouth. "I don't know. It's possible any paranormal could have bought it. Even a human, perhaps. People are still trying out magical things, hoping if they just believe, it will work for them, and then they'll have magic too. You know, the usual romanticized bullshit people talk about."

I nod. "Still, it would be hard to keep something like that under wraps. And Maybelle managed to buy some really powerful magical items. I thought it was impossible to enchant something to change your appearance like that. The magic never slipped at all. No one had any idea she and Gerard weren't human."

"Why is the spellbook important? We might be able to find it, but that doesn't help us build a case against this coven."

"No, but it might help us lure them out. Or figure out what exactly they're trying to do. Maybe even find out who's protecting them," I say.

Zachary sighs and steeples his fingers in front of his face, his elbows resting on his knees. "Do you have any idea where to start?"

"I can try to contact Maybelle, but I don't think she's going to text back," I say with a snort.

"You might as well try."

I pull out my personal phone and realize it's dead. I haven't used it for days and apparently haven't charged it either.

"Do you have a charger?" I ask, waving the black screen at Zachary.

"I think Elise's phone uses that type of charger. It's plugged in over there by her bed," Zachary says, pointing behind me.

I walk over and plug my phone in, then plop back down on the bed to wait.

"It's still hard to believe we caught him," I say quietly. "I wish we had killed him so I'd know it's over."

"That wouldn't end this. The NWR only lost one member. The

organization isn't even crippled."

I shrug. "I know that. It's just different. The stuff that happened between me and him."

"Did you sleep with him?" Zachary blurts out. I don't have to look at him to know he's got his face buried in his hands.

"No," I say. Zachary sighs in audible relief. "But I would have. I wanted to before I knew who he was."

Admitting that out loud makes me feel dirty. I've never had great taste in men, but this was more than just being a bad judge of character.

"I'm going to have to start finger-printing guys and have you run a background check or something," I joke. "Since I seem to attract criminals."

"And vampires," Zachary says quietly.

I sit up and shoot him a look over my shoulder. "Vampires?"

Zachary raises both brows and spreads his hands. "Reilly."

"That is not a thing. I am not sleeping with him," I say vehemently. My phone is finally at five percent battery. Close enough. I hit the power button.

"Are you sure about that?" Zachary asks.

"I think I'd know if I was having sex with him," I say slowly.

"I saw the way you danced together at that club," Zachary scoffs. "Don't lie to me because you're trying to spare my feelings or something."

"What feelings?" I ask. "We're friends, sort of. If you don't hate me anymore at least. Why would I—is this what Elise was referring to? Something about how you had a crush on me when I lived with you?"

Zachary stares at me, one hand over his mouth. My phone starts buzzing in my hand from all the messages it couldn't receive while it was off. I ignore them.

"You—" He pauses and rubs his hands over his face. "You really had no idea?"

I shake my head. "You were, are, like my brother."

"Good to know," he says, standing and walking off to the bathroom.

I can't run after him to comfort him if I'm the source of his distress, so I stay perched on the side of the bed, feeling uncomfortable. I finally look down at my phone. There are six messages from Lydia. Fifteen from Patrick. I dismiss them all.

I do open the email though. There is a deposit for ten thousand dollars from Javier that hit my bank account four days ago. I toss my phone on the bed and put my head in my hands. Not that the money does me any good now. It would have been nice a few months ago, back when I thought I had a chance at a normal future.

"So," Zachary says, startling me. "I can look into the magical artifacts JHAPI has confiscated, or has any information on, just in case this spellbook has turned up somewhere. Will you contact Gerard and Maybelle?"

He's standing in the middle of the room, arms crossed, face smoothed out to his usual expression. He doesn't look upset at all, and the only sign of tension is the slight hunch of his shoulders.

"Sure," I say casually. I can definitely get on board with pretending that conversation never happened. "I've also been thinking about what you said about Reilly having connections. I still don't know if I trust him completely, but if it comes down to it, we might have to see if he can help."

"Only if you think you can trust him," Zachary agrees with a nod.

"Speaking of, what do you know about him and his sire?" I ask, picking at the comforter on the bed. "His Sire is going to be taking the council seat that just opened up. Reilly didn't seem enthused about that."

Zachary whistles under his breath.

"I'm not sure what to make of Reilly's reaction, but I know I share the sentiment." He sits down in the chair again and shakes his head. "Cesare Sangiovanni is a well-known traditionalist."

My eyes widen. "You have got to be kidding me."

"Nope," Zachary says. "I was shocked when I found out Reilly was the vampire the council sent to work with JHAPI. Sangiovanni was vocally against JHAPI's creation from the beginning, the traditionalists don't want any kind of human oversight. He has only recently shifted to supporting the organization, and then he personally pushed for this mission to take down the NWR. The other two vampires on the council are progressive, and they were thrilled to agree."

I rub my hands together. "I'm supposed to meet him at this Summit thing Reilly is dragging me to."

"Be careful," Zachary says seriously. "He is not the type of person you want to insult."

"I'm doomed," I laugh.

Zachary cracks a smile at that too. "I'll say nice things at your funeral."

There's a knock at the door, and my senses jump into overdrive. The heartbeat is familiar, and that realization is unsettling.

"I guess it's time for me to go," I mutter as I stand and walk to the door.

Reilly doesn't make any move to enter the room, but he does nod at Zachary over my shoulder.

"Are we leaving tonight or something?" I ask.

"No, tomorrow just after sunset," Reilly says. "Staci delivered some healing salves to the room, and I thought you might want them sooner rather than later."

"Oh, you brought them?" I ask, looking around for a bag or a bulge in his pocket.

"No, they're in the room. I had to come get you in person because you never got your phone back," Reilly says.

Of course he didn't bring them. That would have been too polite. I think he doesn't like me being alone with Zachary either, probably for the same reason he interrupted that conversation with Elise.

"Thanks for your help," I say, turning back to face Zachary for a moment. "I'll see you after the Summit."

Zachary nods. "Until then."

I follow Reilly into the hall and to the elevators. He's silent for a moment, but I can feel the questions brewing in his mind.

"What is Brunson helping you with?" Reilly asks.

"Why are you upset that your sire is being promoted to the council?" I counter. Reilly always wants to play the question game. If that's how it has to be, I might as well try to get whatever information I can in return.

He turns to me and steps closer and closer until I'm pressed against the wall. The elevator arrives, empty, but he ignores it.

"Why do you think I'm upset my sire will be on the council?"

"Why did you let me feed from you earlier?"

Reilly steps back with a huff. "I've told you before, you're an investment. It would be a waste if I let you die or completely lose control."

"You were obviously upset when you got that phone call. I don't think you trust or like your sire, though I don't know why. I hope it's because he's a piece of shit traditionalist and you don't agree with any of that. I wouldn't be surprised if you did though," I say, upholding my end of the bargain. He chose the easy question to answer, and so did I.

The other two questions hang between us, but instead of pressing the issue, Reilly simply turns and hits the elevator call button again. The same doors reopen, and he steps onto the elevator, holding the door for me when I hesitate to follow.

"When we get to the Summit, you will do exactly as I say without hesitation," he says quietly. "Or you'll find out for yourself why I'm not fond of my sire."

I swallow uncomfortably. For once, it sounds more like he's warning me rather than threatening me. I wonder what kind of person has the ability to scare Reilly Walsh.

CHAPTER 26

The dress is laid out on my bed like a gift. Any goodwill I might feel at the gesture curdles in my throat. Silk makes for more comfortable shackles, but that doesn't change the fact that it's just another thing I can't escape from.

I walk forward and smooth my finger across the deep red hem. The fabric is the color of fresh blood. It's garish, not something I'd ever pick for myself. I'm going to look like a walking wound. That must be what the vampires like.

My phone buzzes twice, a text flashing on the screen. It's Reilly, of course.

Be ready in an hour.

I scoff and dismiss the message. My phone buzzes again.

Or I will come dress you myself.

. . .

I throw my phone with a growl. It bounces off the headboard and slides across the bed, rumpling the top of the dress. I consider, just for a moment, ripping the dress apart with my bare hands. Instead, I turn on my heel and stomp into the bathroom. Perhaps a quick shower will cool some of my anger.

The bathroom is just as gaudy as Javier's. White marble stretches across the spacious bathroom. The glass shower takes up the entire far wall. The faucets are some shiny gold material I'm sure isn't real. The sink is an iridescent blue basin set on the white marble vanity, and it is striking. It's the only splash of color in the room. The color shifts and glimmers as I walk past it. There is a stack of plush, white towels next to the shower door on a gold tray.

I drop my clothes on the floor, leaving a trail to the shower, and step inside. The water is immediately hot, and I jump back with a yelp. It's a little too hot. I adjust the temperature and ease under the spray, turning on the other shower head so everything steams up faster.

They have full-size shampoo and conditioner; this is a classy joint after all, which I use to lather up my hair. It's unscented. I wonder if that's something Reilly requested or something they did for the Summit. It'll clean my hair either way, so I don't really care.

Some of the tension leaves my shoulders as I rinse the shampoo from my hair, but I don't feel as safe in here as I had hoped. I thought I had won something when I convinced Reilly to let me have a private room, but apparently, he still has a key. He still controls my life. I'm still about to be outed to the vampire council.

Reilly had not seemed overly thrilled to hear of his sire's imminent promotion to the council, which was unexpected. I wasn't sure what to make of his reaction. It's possible he hates his sire, but he still does everything his sire asks of him. I can't imagine someone as strong-willed as Reilly showing that kind of loyalty to someone he doesn't believe deserves it. Then again, I've been wrong about people before.

I press my forehead against the cool glass and trace my finger behind a rivulet of water. At least Martinez has been captured. Dead would be infinitely preferable, but at least if he's in jail, he won't be able to hurt anyone else. We're one step closer to seriously crippling the NWR. I sigh and push away from the shower wall and hurry to finish. As much as I don't want to do this, I don't want Reilly showing up in my room before I'm done getting ready.

I step out of the shower and wrap my hair in one of the towels, then grab another to dry my body. I leave a trail of wet footprints into the bedroom. My hairdryer is at the bottom of my bag, so half the contents end up dumped out by the time I stand triumphantly with it in my grasp. My towel starts to slip, so I re-tuck it around me and walk back into the bathroom.

There is a small vanity with a stool on the wall the bathroom shares with the bedroom. I sit down and plug in the hairdryer, then unwind my hair from its turban. A few quick strokes of the brush get rid of the remaining tangles. I sigh at the mirror, then set about making myself presentable for a ball.

I know how to do my makeup, and well. I painted it on every night for six months when I was stripping for a living, and that's just not something you forget. The makeup I wore for that isn't entirely appropriate for this event though. I go for something a little more elegant this time.

My skin is clear; I don't make all those cosmetic brews for nothing, so I keep it simple. A smoky eye, tinted brows, and a dark red lip that'll match the dress perfectly. I always tried for a sultry vibe when I was stripping, but I was young, and I tended to overdo it. I've done good tonight. I won't look out of place in the dress.

My hair, on the other hand, well, I don't have many options. Down seems too casual, so I decide to put it up. The curling iron is hot, so I begin twisting pieces around it. I only burn my fingers a few times, and the marks are easily healed. I pin the curls up, pulling a few strands down to frame my face, and drape down over my collarbone. It's not perfect, but it looks good enough. I stand and drop the towel.

The dress is still lying on the bed, taunting me. I pick up the slinky dress and unzip it, then step into it carefully. This isn't the kind of get up that allows undergarments. The silk slides sensually across my skin, reminiscent of the kind of touch I've gone so long without. I shove my feet in my heels and turn to face the tall mirror next to the bathroom door.

The dress is even more low cut than I realized. It dips down between my breasts, precariously close to reaching my belly button. The waist is tight, a piece of fabric on the bodice wraps around to the back. There is a slit on the side that comes all the way to the upper part of my thigh. The back is low as well. The zipper doesn't even reach halfway up my back.

I trace my finger over my shoulder that still has the tracker embedded in it. There isn't even a scar, thanks to my healing magic and the salves. The welts from the Finding magic are on full display like this. They look strange under the dress, like bad tattoos.

I haven't dressed up like this since...well, I guess I never have. It was never this fancy. The dresses I wore were always short. This should be a fairy tale moment, but instead it's a nightmare.

The door to my room opens behind me without so much as a knock.

"Are you—" Reilly's question dies on his lips.

I roll my eyes at his slack-jawed reflection and turn to face him.

"Am I ready? Yes, I am."

It's my turn to stare as I take in his appearance. He's wearing a sleek black tuxedo with a white bow tie that is perfectly tailored to his frame. The black fabric makes his auburn hair appear even more red. He has managed to tame it as well. He looks, dare I say it, debonair.

Reilly clears his throat, and the silent assessment ends.

"It's time to join the party," he says, extending his arm toward me.

"Grand," I say, striding past him and out the door. I have to go to this, but I don't have to take his arm. He catches up to me, and we walk in silence down the hall. A few couples of varying races step out in front of us. Reilly glances at me without turning his head.

"You look lovely, Olivia," he says quietly enough that no one else should be able to hear him.

"I look like your whore. Or a candy cane," I say, pointing at my arm.

This is the kind of get up a man puts his escort in. Not his co-worker or whatever it is we are. I didn't intend to sound so angry, but his compliment makes me want to kick him.

"An expensive whore though, at the very least," Reilly says with a smirk. "Possibly like a candy cane as well."

The elevator dings, and Reilly presses his hand to the small of my back to encourage a little haste. We slip inside just as the doors begin to close. The other guests chat amongst themselves, but I'm distracted by the line of heat from where I am pressed against Reilly. We should have waited for the next elevator. This one is cramped, and there isn't room to turn around, much less stand apart.

The elevator swoops upward, slowing to a smooth stop, and the doors open again. I step backward and turn quickly, taking a deep breath now that I can smell something other than Reilly's scent. This area of the hotel is very different from the floors with the rooms. The walls stretch up into arches at least thirty feet high. The ceiling is painted like an old cathedral, complete with clouds and fat cherubs fluttering around dimpled women who can't seem to find a shirt and men with swords.

In the alcove between each arch are statues carved from marble. They are striking. Each one conveys some extreme emotion. The one closest to me is a woman in anguish, her hand reaching out toward me as though I could save her. I pull my eyes away and quicken my pace. Reilly keeps his hand on the small of my back, and I wrestle down the impulse to shove it away. In a place like this, his presumptuousness is a claim, and that claim is protection. I'm an unknown nobody here, but based on the glances Reilly is getting, he is not.

I get a few glances of my own, but they're all lecherous. No one thinks I'm a threat. To most people here, I'm probably not. I might have learned a few new tricks hunting terrorists, but that doesn't make up for years of inexperience. I don't have the kind of control over my stolen magic someone who was born with it would have.

The hall of arches opens into the kind of ballroom I've only ever seen in movies. There is a wide staircase with a plush red carpet laid down the center. The ballroom has two levels. The bar is on the top level, while tables are on the lower level. The people milling around lean against the ornate balcony that extends around the top level. There must be five hundred people here, at least. There is room for more as well.

On the lower level, there is a clear area for dancing and a stage in the center of the far wall. There are twelve chairs on the stage, though they'd be better described as thrones. Three red for the vampires, three black for the witches, three white for the werewolves. The remaining three on the far right are a stone. They must be for the goblins.

"Would you care for a drink?" Reilly asks, his breath tickling my ear.

"God, yes," I say, not resisting as he nudges me toward the closest bar.

As we walk, I can tell the race of most of the people we pass. Another vampire with a necker, his hand around the back of her neck, his thumb brushing up and down on the vein in her neck. A pack of werewolves barking in laughter.

The goblins are the easiest to spot, of course. Their green skin stands out as inhuman. They are huddled together in small groups, keeping to the edges. Most of them look like they want to flee. A few stride around with their bulbous noses held high, daring anyone to question their presence here.

We arrive at the bar, and I lean my hip against the edge and wait for the bartender to look up so I can catch his eye. Reilly leans past me and waves him down. I roll my eyes. He's so impatient.

"What can I get for you?" the muscled, blond bartender asks Reilly.

"It's for her," Reilly says, gesturing at me.

"Do you have tequila?" I ask with a bright smile, leaning forward just far enough to almost show him the goods. Reilly frowns at me, but the bartender smiles.

"We got everything," he says, spreading his hands wide. His name tag reads 'Devan'.

"Give me a double of your best stuff, Devan," I say, setting my chin in my hand.

"With pleasure," Devan says with a wink. He grabs the bottle, spinning it around with practiced ease before tipping the spout over a sparkling glass.

"You cannot get drunk tonight," Reilly hisses in my ear.

I glare at him. "You're the one who asked me if I wanted a drink."

"A cocktail, not shots. This isn't a bar in Las Vegas."

"You worry too much."

His fingers bite into my back. "I cannot watch you every second, and these people are all dangerous. Do not let your guard down just because we're at a party."

"You almost sound like you care, Reilly," I say, patting the front of his jacket.

Devan slides the glass across the bar to me, his smile fading a little as I touch Reilly.

"Enjoy, ma'am."

"Oh, I will," I say, turning my smile up a notch. I grab the tequila and throw it back, drinking down the burning liquid with relish. I drop the empty glass back on the table with a loud thunk and spin away from the bar. "So is there going to be food, or what?"

Reilly wraps his arm tightly around my shoulders.

"Quit acting like you're incapable of being a lady. There are people I need to introduce you to. Dinner will be served in a couple of hours."

"Hours?" I gasp. My stomach growls on cue. "You could have warned me to eat a snack beforehand."

"Stop complaining."

He scans the room, and I look longingly back at the bar. I wonder if I can sneak another later when he isn't paying attention. I need something to fill my stomach if they aren't going to feed us for hours.

I spot a waiter carrying a small tray, making the rounds, and make a beeline for him. Reilly scrambles to follow me.

"What are you doing?" he demands.

"Sandwiches. Little fancy ones," I mutter, keeping my eye on the prize. He huffs out a sigh behind me but follows without further complaint.

I come up a little fast on the waiter, and he startles slightly, then extends the tray. I grab two petite sandwiches and contemplate grabbing a third, but Reilly tugs me away with a nod at the waiter who doesn't hesitate to escape.

"They're so small," I say before stuffing the first one in my mouth. A bitter taste overwhelms me, and I spit it out in my hand, trying not to vomit.

"What the fuck are you doing?" Reilly hisses, scrambling for a napkin to grab the half-chewed food out of my hand with. "When I said you needed to act like a lady, that wasn't a challenge for you to act even more ridiculous."

His eyes are snapping with genuine anger, and his jaw is clenched tight.

"Sorry, that was disgusting though, I think it's rotten or something," I say, wishing even more that I could get another drink to get that awful taste out of my mouth. My stomach is rolling.

"If you're done, I've spotted someone I need to introduce you to. Do us both a favor, and be polite. If you offend him, there is nothing I can or will do to protect you. Do you understand?"

"Yeah, yeah," I say, waving my hand at him.

He grabs it and holds it tight, grinding the bones together.

"This is not a joke."

"I understand," I say slowly, looking him in the eye.

He releases my hand, and I resist the urge to rub at the ache. He takes a deep breath, and his features smooth out to calm indifference, like a mask slipping into place. I had joked earlier about him caring, but the concern really is unexpected.

He presses his palm into my lower back and guides me down the wide staircase. We weave through the tables, passing mostly vampires in this section. A few nod at Reilly as we pass, but we don't stop.

It becomes apparent that Reilly is leading me toward a group gathered around a dining table near the stage. There are a few men who don't seem part of the group. They are facing outward, their eyes constantly scanning for anyone approaching. They tense at our approach, but visibly relax when they notice Reilly. A few people who seem to be waiting for an audience move out of our way as we step up to the table. I guess we don't have to wait in line.

Seated in one of the chairs is a man with black hair streaked at the temple with silver. There are lines around his eyes and mouth, but those are the only signs of age on his face. His eyes are sharp as steel, and the color of steel as well. He doesn't look at Reilly, only at me, taking a long breath with slightly parted lips as though he is tasting my scent. Reilly bows deeply and pushes me down into a bow as well.

The man stands, unfolding from the chair. He's taller than I expected, and while lean, every movement seems like controlled violence. He turns his cold eyes to Reilly.

"Introduce us, *passerotto mio*, or have you forgotten your manners?" the man says, his voice slipping into an accent when he uses the strange endearment. Reilly straightens, and I follow suit.

"Sire, this is Olivia Carter, the half-breed I have spoken to you about. Ms. Carter, this is Council Member Cesare Sangiovanni," Reilly says, taking my hand gently in his and extending it toward his sire.

Cesare takes it and presses cold lips to my knuckles with a short bow.

"You defy expectations, Ms. Carter. My imaginings of what you might be all revolved around a twisted creature born of some strange experiment. I am pleased to discover you are instead a beauty our Reilly here does not deserve."

I don't know how to respond. My heart is beating fast in my chest, something that won't escape Cesare's notice.

"You're too kind, though you are right. Reilly does not deserve me," I say with a smile I hope makes up for my nerves.

Cesare laughs unreservedly, throwing his head back. The people around us chuckle along. I wonder if they're obligated to, or if they just find me hilarious as well. Reilly is notably silent beside me. He's probably going to kill me later.

"I like this one Reilly," Cesare says, pointing his finger at him. "Her heart is racing like a hummingbird, but she does not cower."

"I'm not certain she knows how to cower, Sire," Reilly says in a resigned tone.

"Have a seat," Cesare says. He still has my hand, and he leads me to the seat directly to his left. I sit down hesitantly, for once comforted that Reilly will be sitting right next to me. Cesare scoots my chair in for me, and I sit stiffly in my chair, my hands in my lap.

"The two of you have had an eventful week," Cesare comments. "I must say, from the description of your injuries, I did expect you to show up looking at least a little battered."

"Healing salves work wonders," I say with a tight smile.

He reaches over and smooths his thumb across my shoulder. "There isn't a scar from the bullet wound or the GPS tracker. Whatever brews you are using must be very well made."

"The healing magic helps prevent scars as well," I say. It takes all of my willpower not to flinch away from his touch, but again, my heart is racing. I think he likes it, or perhaps he likes testing me to see at what point I'll visibly react.

"Yet these linger?" he asks, his thumb dropping down to press into a welt just hard enough to make me grit my teeth before he moves his hand back to his lap.

"Magical injuries are different, harder to heal. I'm working on it though," I say.

"Tell me," Cesare says, leaning back in his chair. "What do you feel at the point when whoever you are draining of magic dies?"

I glance at Reilly, but he is looking at his sire, his posture relaxed and his face blank. I clear my throat and twist my fingers together. Maybe this is the reaction he was hoping for.

"I'm not sure I understand what you're asking for," I say finally.

"You killed Ryan. You didn't have enough time to drain him in the few seconds you were latched onto his neck, so I assume you must have killed him by ripping away the magic that keeps him alive." He taps his fingers against the table, looking at me intently. "In that last moment, what do you feel?"

I square my shoulders.

"They become empty," I say. "With—with a witch, it's different. There's something I can't take in them, but I didn't feel that in Ryan. He just ended and turned to ash."

Cesare hums to himself, his expression turning thoughtful. I hope he's amused or whatever by that answer. I don't want to talk about it anymore, but I'm not sure I have a choice.

I grimace. Ryan turning to ash in my mouth was awful. I can still remember the bitter taste of his blood. I reach for my glass and freeze. This isn't just a memory; that same bitter taste is in my mouth right now. I stand abruptly and search the room for a waiter carrying a plate of hors d'oeuvres.

Cesare raises a brow and watches with interest.

"Olivia, what are you—" Reilly begins.

I spot a waiter and hurry toward him without waiting for Reilly to finish his sentence. He's following me, and I'm sure he is about to lecture me about being ladylike or polite again, but I don't care. I grab the waiter's arm, startling him into almost dropping the tray.

"Sorry, just, give me the tray," I say, reaching for it. The stunned waiter lets me take it.

"Would—would you like some more sandwiches?" he asks, his eyes flicking between me and I'm sure an enraged Reilly standing behind me.

"No, she would not like some more sandwiches," Reilly snaps. "You may leave."

The waiter scurries away as I lean over the tray and sniff the sandwiches, pulling on my vampire magic.

"What the fuck are you doing?" Reilly hisses in my ear.

"When I bit Ryan, his blood tasted awful," I say, sniffing at a sandwich with a cucumber poking out of it. It smells suspicious, but not bitter like the other sandwich had tasted.

"What does that have to do with sandwiches? Or with you leaving the table like that? You've embarrassed me and—"

"The sandwich I had earlier, the one I spit out, it tasted exactly the same as his blood," I snap. "There is something wrong."

"What exactly are you suggesting?" Reilly asks, brows pinching tightly together.

"Ryan lost control, and we still don't know how. We don't know why they took him, or why they let him go," I say, waving a sandwich at him. "What if it was an experiment?"

"An experiment in what?"

"A weak vampire comes back to his clan, and he's out of control. So, obviously, the more highly ranked vampires in the clan step in to try to help him regain control. But he kills one of them."

I can see the wheels turning in his head. "He shouldn't have been able to."

"It was like they sent a bomb back with him. If they hadn't been able to lock him in that room, he might have killed the entire clan, or at least a lot of them."

"It's possible the NWR did something to him to make him both lose control and become stronger, but that does not mean the sandwiches are poisoned. No one else has complained about them."

I roll my eyes.

"None of the vampires are eating them, maybe they only taste bad to me. I don't know, and I don't care. When Martinez had me in that van, he said something I didn't think was important at the time because he was rambling about so much. He said that vampire's true nature would be revealed soon. Something about taking away the mask they hide behind."

"That's propaganda speak. They say that kind of thing all the time," Reilly says.

"And they're always trying to prove it. They aren't sitting around passing out flyers. They are organized, and smart, and driven."

"What are they planning, then?"

"Dinner is being served tonight, this whole big thing," I say, looking around at the tables, all set with more forks and knives than anyone should ever need. "What are the vampires eating?"

"Everyone has brought their own neckers," Reilly says. "They're waiting in the meeting rooms on a different floor."

"Are they eating these?" I ask, shoving the tray at him.

"I don't know. I've never been concerned with what they eat," he says, eyeing the tray. He rubs his hand along his jaw, then looks at me. "You think they are somehow poisoning the neckers, and then what? The vampires feed from them and lose control?"

"It's hard to poison a vampire," I say. "It's not hard to slip something into food for neckers. No one cares about them; they're just dinner themselves."

Reilly shakes his head. "This is insane, you don't have any proof. This shouldn't even be possible."

"Stocke said she thought the stuff the NWR did in Texas was an experiment, right? That they wanted to see if they could discredit a vampire clan. It was working too."

"Yes, I remember this," he says impatiently.

"Can you imagine the shit storm if vampires at the Summit lost control and killed a necker? Or another paranormal?" I ask. "All of this, everything the NWR has been doing, has been about finding a way to make a vampire lose control. They say you are monsters, and if they can prove it to the world, they will start an all-out war."

"That all sounds terrible, but you still can't prove any of this. I can't halt this entire thing because you have a hunch," Reilly bites out.

"Ryan was a child. What happens when someone like your sire loses control? When he is three times as powerful as he is now?" I demand.

Reilly grinds his teeth together, glaring at the sandwiches like he can blame them for my insanity.

"There is an hour until dinner. Find a way to prove this by then."

I glare at him. "How am I supposed to do that?"

"That's your problem to figure out," Reilly says, leaning in close. "I have to go explain to my sire why I can't keep you under control. Let's hope neither of us fails."

CHAPTER 27

Reilly walks away, and I'm left standing with a tray of sandwiches and a huge problem. I turn and march toward the exit. I pass another waiter holding a tray and shove mine at her. She grabs it with her free hand and almost drops it, but I keep walking as fast as I can. I need to get out of here and get my phone. Maybe Zachary can help, or even Stocke if I have to talk to her.

There is a constant stream of paranormals in and out of the main room. I weave through them as quickly as I can, but I don't want to shove past anyone too roughly and start some kind of fight I don't have time to finish.

The elevator is just as busy. I manage to slip in just before the doors close, but it stops at almost every floor on the way up. I tap my foot impatiently, letting person after person slip around me to get off until it finally arrives at my floor.

I run down the hall, no longer worried about who might see me or who I might run into. My room is exactly as I left it, as is my phone. I grab it off the bed and see three missed calls, two from

Zachary and one from Elise. There is a voicemail which I tap, then put the phone to my ear.

"Olivia," Zachary voicemail starts. "Martinez transport was attacked as soon as it left this morning. He's been gone for hours. We aren't even sure when exactly he escaped. Stay at the Summit with Reilly, don't try to leave, and don't go anywhere by yourself."

My hand shakes as I lower the phone. If he has escaped, he has to be coming here. He's been a part of this experiment from the beginning. It was probably all his idea.

If I can find him, I can prove something is going on, and stop him. I look down at the welts on my arms and flex my fingers. Corinne can't help me. She's still unconscious, and Stocke wouldn't let her try to Find Martinez again anyhow. I text Zachary, telling him everything I can think of. My suspicions about the food, about where Martinez is headed, and what I'm about to do.

I turn and sprint down the hall, dialing Reilly's number with shaking fingers, but he doesn't answer. I slap my hand against the elevator call button, but it doesn't light up. I hit it again. Nothing. I stare at the elevators, panic growing in my gut. It could just be malfunctioning, but what if it's something worse?

I spin around, my dress flaring out around me, and search for the entrance to the stairs. There is a small emergency exit placard on the wall that directs me down the hall and to the left. I sprint there and hit the door at a run. It flies open, hitting the wall with a bang that echoes down the stairwell.

Magic flows through my body in a cold wave as I sprint down the stairs vampire fast. I barrel out of the stairwell onto the floor the Summit is being hosted, but I'm not anywhere near the main entrance. I don't recognize the hall I'm in. A man wearing the light blue jacket of the serving staff is standing a few paces away, looking at me with wide eyes.

"Is everything okay?" he asks hesitantly.

"No. Where are the neckers being held?" I demand as I march

toward him. He visibly shrinks back, and I realize my fangs are poking out of my mouth.

"I, uh, I'm not sure," he says, trying to back away.

I grab him by his lapels and pull him close. His face pales, and sweat beads up on his forehead.

"Then find someone who is. The NWR is about to attack this place, and I can stop them, but I need to know where the neckers are," I growl.

"O-okay. I can take you t-to my supervisor."

I spin him around and shove him forward. "Go, then."

With one last glance over his shoulder, he starts jogging down the hall. I follow, doing everything I can to push down the vampire magic so I don't waste it. His heart is racing, and he stinks of fear. He's lucky I don't crave human blood.

He leads me around two turns, then through a door marked 'Staff Only' into a huge industrial kitchen. There are chefs in their white coats creating more trays of hors d'oeuvres and dozens of waiters weaving through the chaos. He taps a woman in a crisp black suit on the shoulder. She holds up her hand to the person she was in the middle of speaking with and turns to him.

"She—terrorists in the building—the neckers," he begins to stutter out. The woman raises a brow.

I grab the waiter by the back of the collar and drag him out of the way.

"I need to know where the neckers are. Their food has been poisoned, and if the vampires feed on them, they are going to lose control and murder everyone," I say, throwing my hands wide.

The woman looks at a loss for a moment. "Who are you?"

I bite the inside of my cheek before answering. Of course, the woman needs some assurance I know what I'm talking about. It would be way easier if she didn't though.

"Olivia Carter, I've been working with JHAPI at the request of the vampire council," I say as calmly as I can. "Look, I don't have a lot of time here. Do you want to die, or are you going to help me?"

503

The woman hesitates, evaluating me, then grabs a walkie-talkie off her belt buckle.

"Delay dinner for thirty minutes. No one goes in or out of the necker holding room until I say so, all right?" She puts the walkie-talkie back on her belt and crosses her arms. "If you are with JHAPI, where are the rest of the agents?"

"My team is in a different state," I say. "But other agents are on their way. This was a last-minute tip."

My phone starts buzzing in my hand. It's Zachary.

"Give me a minute," I say, turning away from the woman and slipping back into the hall. The door swings shut behind me.

"Zach," I say with relief as I answer the call.

"Olivia, what are you doing?" he asks.

"They've poisoned the food," I say. "I ate a sandwich, and it was bitter like Ryan's blood. I think they injected him with something that made him lose control and made him stronger. They're going to do the same thing here, and all these vampires are going to lose control in the middle of the Summit."

"How do you know this?" he asks.

I pause in my pacing. "You don't believe me?"

"I'm asking how you know," he says, his tone suggesting he's trying to keep me calm.

"Martinez has escaped. All these disappearances, they've been experiments. Stocke said they were, and she's right. They were all practice runs for this," I insist. "Zach, I can't do this alone."

He sighs. "I can have them send a team over, but if you're wrong, we're going to look like idiots. The councils will be furious."

"They're only willing to delay dinner thirty minutes. Can they test the necker's blood before then? Or the food?" I ask.

"I don't know," Zachary says. "Maybe Staci can figure out a way to prove it's contaminated, but without having an idea of what it has been poisoned with, we can't test it."

I sigh and pace back and forth across the hall.

"The elevators aren't working, by the way. I don't know what else they've done, but they may have blocked the exits somehow."

Someone is talking in the background. Zachary holds his hand over the phone for a second, drowning it out.

"All of the elevators?" Zachary asks.

"I don't know. The one that led up to my room is the only one I tried," I say.

"Stocke wants you to wait for a team to get there. It will be someone local, but she'll be on the phone with them."

"What if I can prove Martinez is here?" I ask.

"Is he there?" Zachary asks.

"I think so," I say. "And I'm going to find him."

"Olivia, you can't do that—"

"Just get people here, okay?" I hang up the phone.

The door behind me swings open again, and a waiter hurries past, but my attention is captured by a snippet of conversation. The woman I spoke to is asking for security to come upstairs and remove me.

I shove my way back into the kitchen.

"What the hell are you doing?" I demand.

"I need security up here right now," she says into the walkie-talkie before looking at me with raised hands. "Ma'am, I need you to please leave."

"You cannot send those neckers into that room—"

"I spoke to our head of security, and he told me there is no threat from the NWR. There is no tip," she says calmly.

"Just because your head of security doesn't know, doesn't mean it isn't happening," I say, stepping toward her. I want to get to Martinez, but all of this is for nothing if any of the vampires feed on these neckers.

"Ma'am—"

"What is the problem here?" Cesare asks from behind me. I didn't hear him walk up.

I turn around slowly. He doesn't look angry, merely curious.

Reilly is standing a few paces behind him, as well as the two bodyguards who were at the table earlier.

"The food the neckers ate was laced with something," I say haltingly. "Their blood is poisoned now. It will make a vampire lose control."

Cesare frowns. "And how fast acting is this poison?"

"I don't know, but I don't think it takes very long to go into effect. The NWR wants everyone to lose control during the dinner."

"And you don't have a way to prove this?" Cesare asks.

"There's never been anything like this before. It's not like I can ring up a lab and have them test it in the next ten minutes," I say, glancing back at Reilly. I wish he would help.

"Reilly has assured me you are not insane and you are not simply trying to make me look like an idiot," Cesare says, extending his arm to me. "Walk with me."

I slip my hand into the crook of his arm. The magic rolling off him is intoxicating. If someone like him were to feed on one of the neckers, I don't know what would be capable of stopping him.

Cesare leads us back into the hall. I keep my eyes straight ahead and focus on putting one foot in front of the other. If I'm wrong, I have a feeling it will be the last thing I'm ever wrong about.

One of the bodyguards walks ahead of us and opens an unmarked door. We follow him inside. There must be almost a hundred neckers in here, all dressed in black. They bow in unison.

Cesare gently removes my hand from his arm and walks forward, grabbing the arm of the closest necker.

"Tony, feed from her," he says, nudging the woman toward his bodyguard.

I start to object, but a firm hand wraps around my mouth, cutting off the words. I can smell that it's Reilly. His hand stays tightly clasped over my lips as Tony leans down and bites the woman's neck. He drinks from her with long gulps while the woman goes glassy-eyed.

"That's enough," Cesare says after a couple of minutes.

Tony lowers the woman to the ground and stands up straight, awaiting his next order.

"Did she taste odd?" Cesare asks.

"No, sire. She tasted better than I've ever had," he says.

Cesare looks at his watch. "In five minutes, I'm going to give a speech accepting my position on the council. Reilly, if he loses control, put him down and come tell me Olivia was right."

Reilly lowers his hand from my mouth but stays pressed against me, his other hand wrapped tightly around my arm.

"Yes, sire," he says.

Cesare looks at me as he passes by until a strange grunt draws our attention. Tony huffs again, his fangs pushing down onto his bottom lip. A quiver passes through his body, and he looks at Cesare and growls.

"Interesting," Cesare comments.

Tony lunges toward him in a blur, arms outstretched. Reilly yanks me backward, and we slam into the wall behind us.

I don't see Cesare move. One moment he is in Tony's path, the next he's standing behind him, holding his head while Tony's body topples forward. Both crumple to ash. Cesare shakes the dust from his hands as the neckers behind him start screaming.

"Reilly, evacuate the main hall," Cesare says as he pulls out a handkerchief.

Reilly steps out from behind me and hurries out of the room. Cesare walks toward me, stopping only a foot away and carefully wiping the remains of his bodyguard from his hand.

"You have been very useful," he says, his eyes scanning my face.

"I think Martinez is here," I say shakily. "He escaped. I got a voicemail."

"Then find him if you can," Cesare says before stepping around me to address his other bodyguard. "Stay with them, make sure no one leaves. We don't want anyone feeding on one of these by mistake after this is all over."

He walks out. The neckers are all huddled as far back as they can get, their eyes on me and the bodyguard now that the others have left.

I stumble out into the hallway and take a deep breath. He just murdered one of his own men, and no one flinched. Reilly knew what was coming, and he let it happen. I press my hand to my mouth and wonder what I'm protecting. Maybe Martinez is right, maybe the mask does need to be stripped away.

Patrick's tear-streaked face flashes through my mind, and I drop my hand. Cesare might be awful, but not all vampires are. They aren't all monsters any more than all humans are. I'm going to do what I can to stop Martinez. There will be no capturing him this time. I'm going to finish it.

I look down at my shaking hands, and the Finding magic shifts inside of me. I picture Martinez, just like I did with Corinne when I was practicing this in her room. The magic moves and stretches out into the hotel, but something else moves too. I can feel *her* shift inside of me. She's always there.

I force myself to look up, and she's standing in front of me in the hallway like she's real. No mirror this time, just her.

"Mom," I say, my voice quaking.

"Olivia," she says, her face splitting into a smile. "Finally."

"Are you real?" I ask.

"I need you to find the book," she says. "I made a mistake, but you can still stop him."

"Stop who?" I ask. "Reilly?"

She shakes her head. "No, the god that is coming unbound. He wants to destroy all of us."

"What book? How is that going to stop anything?"

"Find it, Olivia," she whispers. "Only you can undo this terrible thing I did."

"Mom," I whisper, my voice shaking like I'm five years old again and waking up from a nightmare. "I don't understand."

"You were born with a burden I tried to hide from you. I'm so sorry." Her eyes fill with tears that slip down her cheeks.

"No, don't cry," I say, reaching up a trembling hand to wipe them away, but she grabs my hands and I freeze. She is real. I don't understand how this is possible.

"Find the book. Find the magic," she says urgently.

"What book?" I ask, clinging to her hands. I don't want this to end.

"Find the book. Find the magic," she repeats. "You'll need all of it."

She leans forward and wraps me in a hug, whispering the same thing over and over, but I barely hear her. I squeeze her as tightly as I can, my fingers curling into the fabric of her dress as the comforting scent of herbs surrounds me.

"You don't need me," she whispers.

"Yes, I do," I sob.

"I'm holding you back."

I shake my head viciously and squeeze her even more tightly to me. "No."

She pulls back and cradles my face in her hands.

"My girl," she says. "You can do anything. Be anything. Do what's right."

"I miss you." And I do. I miss her every day, and I'm so angry she can't be with me anymore.

She smiles, and I realize she's already fading. My fingers are sinking into her and through her. I close my eyes because I can't watch her disappear again.

"I'm so proud of you," she says.

My hands and arms tingle as the magic that was giving her form flows back into me. Some warmth I didn't realize I was missing curls back up in my chest. The constant pain that has wrapped around my arms and shoulders fades into nothing.

I blink my eyes open. I'm standing alone in the hallway, but I know where he is.

CHAPTER 28

People are pouring out of the main hall. There is a sense of restrained panic as they all attempt to walk but not run. I push through, having to use my elbows to make any progress in the opposite direction of the crowd. Martinez is somewhere in there.

I make it inside and shove my way up toward the bar. I find an empty spot along the railing and close my eyes, focusing on the magic. Images flash through my mind. The mass of people pouring out the exit. Reilly near the stage on the phone. Then a woman in a red dress, her eyes shut. I look up and see Devan staring at me.

He has a bottle of tequila in one hand and an empty glass in the other. My stomach sinks. There's no way it's him, but the magic pulling me toward him knows the truth, no matter what disguise he is wearing. There is a thick gold band on his right hand, just like the one Maybelle and Gerard both wore.

He pours a shot of the tequila and drinks it, eyes still on me, then turns and disappears through a door behind the bar. I run after him and jump over the bar, my dress dragging the glass off and shattering it. I push through the door and run in the direction I can feel him headed.

Distant gunfire echoes from somewhere downstairs. I put on a burst of speed and skid around a corner. Martinez, still looking like Devan, is standing at the end of the same hallway the neckers are on, waiting for me.

"You're always forcing me to go with Plan B," he says calmly as he tugs the ring off his hand and drops it in his pocket. The handsome facade is gone in a blink.

"Whatever you're planning, it's not going to work," I say, my hands clenched at my sides.

He takes two steps back and grins, his smile twisted gruesomely. He lifts his hand, showing me a small black box with a red switch.

Click.

An explosion rips through the room the neckers are in, and the door flies off its hinges. A fireball billows out of the room, and I stumble backward, shielding my face from the heat. There is another explosion farther away, and then another that rocks the entire building. My head is spinning, and Martinez is getting farther and farther away.

I sprint after him. Moving this fast, I don't even feel the fire as I dash through it. Anger is building in my chest, and magic is sparking at my fingertips. There were so many innocent people in that room. Hundreds more may be dead from the other explosions as well.

I round a corner and stop. He's close, but there are people running everywhere. Two shots hit the wall next to my head, and I duck down. He slams into a group of people running down a connecting hallway, and I lose sight of him again for a moment.

When he reappears, he has his arm wrapped tightly around the neck of one of the wait staff, his gun pressed firmly against her head. She screams as he drags her backward, her eyes wide and frightened.

"None of you is getting out of here alive," Martinez hisses.

"Neither are you," I growl at him. I don't think I'm fast enough to get to him before he can pull the trigger.

"You should have just walked away from it all in Texas," he shouts. "If the clan had fallen, you would have been free, and I could have shown you how to redeem yourself. We could have done this together!"

"What do I need redemption from? I'm not the one murdering innocent people!" I shout back as I take a few steps toward him. If I can close the distance a little more, I might be able to get the gun.

"I know what you did before Brunson found you. How you sold those drugs," he says, pressing the gun even harder into the girl's head. She sobs, and her feet slip as he drags her backward down the hall. "I know that vampire almost killed you. They're monsters. How can you not see that?"

"It was one vampire, and he was insane," I say through gritted teeth.

"You're just like her! Always making excuses. It's like you want to die. Why won't you let me save you?" he yells, spittle flying from his lips. "My father tried to beat it out of her, but that didn't help either."

"Let this girl go, Jason," I say, trying to calm him now. "This is between us. She doesn't have anything to do with it."

He squeezes her more tightly to him. She scrabbles at his arm, gasping for air. I take another step closer and pull on the vampire magic harshly. I need every bit of strength. I can't save anything for a counterattack; it has to be now or never.

"She let them feed from her! She's just another jezebel whore lusting after the parasites that will suck all of humanity dry!"

"You're the monster here!"

A gun goes off twice behind him, much closer than before, and for a split second his eyes leave me. It's a reflex, the kind of thing you can't help when you are startled, and it's all I need. I lunge forward and close the distance. I wrap my left hand around the gun, pushing it back into his face, and yank the girl forward, freeing her from his grasp. She runs screaming as he kicks me in the stomach.

I wrap both hands around the gun and rip it away as he pulls out the same baton he had in the hangar. I jerk almost out of reach, but he has a foot on my dress, and the end of it hits me in the stomach with a bone-aching burst of electricity. All of my muscles seize, and he punches me in the face. I fall to one knee, and he hits me again, pain from the strike and the taser burning through my arm. I roll onto my back and push electric magic in an arc from my hand to his leg. He jerks away, and I lunge forward and tackle him.

My elbow connects with his jaw, and I grab the hand with the baton and squeeze. His hand breaks, the end of the baton cracking as well, and he screams in pain. I rip it out of his hand. Rage, hunger, and pain rush through me. I sink my teeth into his neck and drink down a rush of blood. A small, stagnant pool of magic is hidden deep inside of him. I reach for it without thinking and pull it into me. He claws at my back as I rip away his pathetic magic. It's familiar and earthy, something I've stolen once before. The first kind of magic I ever took.

I rear back, my teeth ripping out of his neck, and shove off him. He lays there, twitching, as blood gurgles from the wound in his neck.

"You sick fuck," I pant, frantically trying to wipe his blood off my mouth. "You're a witch. All this time, you've been killing your own kind."

"No," he hisses, struggling to sit up, but he's too weak now that I've taken most of what little magic he had. "My mother was a hedgewitch just like you, but I rejected the magic. I am redeemed."

"You are pathetic," I growl at him.

"Take the rest of it," he says desperately, lifting his hand toward me. "Get it out of me. Get it out. I want to be clean."

I stare at his outstretched hand, then reach down and clasp it tightly with my own.

"No," I say.

I let all of the anger and betrayal and hatred burn into the electric magic that is churning inside of me. It flows out of my palm and into him like a lightning bolt. The magic crackles down his arm, searing his skin in fractured streaks. He screams, the sound tearing from his throat. The sound is inhuman and hurts my ears. Jagged cracks open across his torso and his face, light pouring out of them as the magic overwhelms his body until he bursts into flame.

I jerk my hand away and stumble backward as his body crumples forward. The sounds of the chaos around me filter back in. People are still running, trying to escape. Gunfire, which I hope is the SWAT team, is getting closer and closer.

The smell of burning flesh makes me gag. I turn away from Martinez's corpse, my vision swimming. I need to find Reilly. I need to get out of here.

I lift my hand and shut my eyes, letting the Finding magic take over. It doesn't scare me anymore, though perhaps it should. The magic spreads out of me like a net, searching for Reilly. He's not far.

I run toward the hallway I came from, but another explosion knocks me onto my back and deafens me. Plaster cracks and falls from the ceiling. I struggle to my feet and run in the other direction. The building is shaking, and smoke is pouring out of the hallway. I'm getting farther from Reilly, but there's nothing I can do about that if the building is about to collapse.

I find a door that leads into the stairwell and sprint down the stairs. Someone below me trying to get out as well, but the exit is jammed. Reilly's location shifts. He's getting closer now instead of farther away. I'm on the second floor when the door to the stairwell bursts open and Reilly runs in. He's holding the GPS tracker in his hand.

"Hurry up," he says, waving at me.

I take the last flight of stairs two at a time, and Reilly grabs my arm, yanking me through the doorway. I follow, letting him drag me as I stumble over my own feet.

"Are you okay?" he asks, looking back at me.

"Martinez is dead," I gasp out.

He stops in his tracks and turns around, grabbing me by the shoulders.

"You killed him?" he asks, inspecting me for injuries. He freezes when he sees the welts are gone. "What—"

The building shakes, something crumpling above us with a loud crash. Dust sprinkles down from the cracks in the ceiling.

Reilly reaches down and rips my dress' split even higher.

"What are you—" I begin, slapping at his hands, but he drags me onto his back and takes off at full speed.

I wrap my legs tightly around his waist and cling to the front of his jacket with my hands. The ceiling crumbles behind us, and the floor starts cracking underneath his feet. Everything turns into a blur as he charges forward faster than I thought anyone could move.

The hall is a dead end, but Reilly doesn't slow down. He sprints straight for the window, and we crash through it in a shower of glass and fire as the ceiling collapses behind us. He lands neatly on the grass but doesn't stop running. This side of the building is about to collapse completely.

Fire trucks and emergency vehicles line the street, but Reilly bypasses all of that, running along the edges of the activity. He turns down a side street that passes by the hotel and stops in front of a limo. The door opens, and Reilly sets me down, then pushes me inside, following close behind.

I collapse into the seat and wrap the pieces of my dress around my legs. Cesare is sitting opposite me, suit spotless, hands folded in his lap.

Reilly closes the door, and the limo speeds away. I look through the back window and watch as the side of the hotel crumbles, a cloud of dust and smoke billowing up from the remains.

CHAPTER 29

The clanhouse is like nothing I've ever seen before. It's not just a mansion; it's a sprawling estate that covers at least an acre. Balconies jut out of the vine-covered brick along the front of the house. The windows are all obscured except for the two on either side of the front door.

The limo stops in front of the house, and the door is opened by a vampire. I'm not sure if he is a butler, bodyguard, or both. Cesare steps out, and Reilly nudges me to follow.

The front door swings outward, and we walk inside. Directly in front of us is a wide, sloping staircase that is covered in red, plush carpet. At the end is a tall, stained glass window that is lit from the outside somehow even though it's the middle of the night. The stairs split and continue up to the second story, wrapping around on either side and lined by an intricate wrought iron railing.

Two large paintings are hung on either side of the staircase. One is of some old city, perhaps somewhere in Italy. The other is the traditional Renaissance type with a woman laid back on a settee, her hair strategically covering all the fun bits while a man kneels beside her. The clan is obviously wealthy, but the decor makes it feel like a museum and not a home.

"Freshen up, and meet me in the library in an hour," Cesare says as he walks ahead of us.

Reilly leads me up the staircase to the left. The floors up here are dark wood. There are rugs every few feet that soften our footsteps. Two women walk past us, both nodding in greeting at Reilly and ignoring me.

We pass down a long hallway, through a large open room with a high ceiling that is painted to look like the sky, then up another short flight of stairs before Reilly stops at a door and pulls out a key. He unlocks what I expect to be a room but is actually an entrance to a sort of self-contained house.

To the right is a living area. There are two couches and a love seat set around a fireplace. I can see a dining room through an open door, and to the left appears to be a kitchen.

Reilly presses his hand to my lower back. "This way, we don't have time for a tour."

"Right," I say absently, still looking around as he guides me toward his rooms.

We walk through what I assume is his bedroom, though it's decorated like it could be any other room in the house, and into a small bathroom. The walls are stone, and there is a thick rug laid in the center of the room, but it still feels more like a jail cell than a nice bathroom.

There is a claw foot tub set under the window, though the shutters are closed blocking any view you might have. The shower looks recently added. It's set in the corner, but there wasn't room to make it very large.

"Take a shower. I'll have clothes laid out on the bed for you," Reilly says, turning to leave.

"How many people died?" I ask quietly.

He pauses at the doorway. "I don't know. We may not know for a couple of days, but that's not important right now. You made a good impression on Cesare, despite everything. You need to get through this meeting with him before you worry about anything else."

I turn to face him. "What does he want from me?"

"He wants you to do as he says."

"That's not an answer," I say, shaking my head.

"Take a shower," he repeats, before shutting me in the bathroom.

I strip out of the tattered dress and avoid the mirror. I'm sure I look disgusting. I turn on the water and pick out the pins that are still holding my hair up. I toss them behind me, not caring about making a mess.

Black grime from the smoke and debris trails down my legs and into the drain as I step under the hot water. I scrub viciously at my skin, catching bruises and scrapes I don't even remember getting. I force myself to slow down and heal them. I'm not as exhausted as I could be now that I'm not being constantly drained by the Finding magic. I don't want to be in pain while talking to Cesare.

I dunk my head under the water again, and despite the temptation to linger in the shower, the imminent meeting keeps me from relaxing. I wash quickly, not bothering to condition my hair. I forgot to grab a towel, so I have to walk across the chilly room to grab one off the shelf by the bathtub.

I dry off and wrap the towel around me before padding into the bedroom. As promised, there are clothes laid out on the bed for me. They're not something I'd ever pick out though. Reilly even thought of underwear and a bra, which makes me grimace, but I'd rather have it than not.

I pull on the shirt and realize a tag is still attached. I rip it off and toss it back on the bed. My wet hair leaves wet spots on the white blouse, but I don't have anything to tie it back with. The black slacks mostly fit, but they're uncomfortably high waisted. I pull at them, but there's no making them less tight.

I glance at the full-length mirror next to the bed and sigh. I look like some kind of soccer mom on her first job interview since she had kids.

There is a single knock at the door, and Reilly walks in. His hair is also still wet, and he is dressed in one of his usual suits. It's not awkward on him like it is on me.

He stops near the end of the bed.

"You look like an adult," he says.

"I look stuffy," I retort, crossing my arms.

He walks closer and brushes a strand of wet hair back behind my ear. I keep my eyes fixed on his chest; I'm too tired to play these games with him right now.

"It would be wise for you to be able to hear and smell everything you can while we are here," Reilly says, dropping his hand.

"You make it sound like we're walking into a raid or something," I say.

"This is more dangerous," Reilly says, turning away.

"Why do you not trust your sire?" I ask, my voice just above a whisper.

Reilly stands still, his back to me and sighs. "You already know why. Let's not keep him waiting."

I furrow my brows, not sure what he means unless he did hear everything Zachary and I talked about in our last conversation. Reilly glances back and holds out his arm. I step up beside him and slip my hand into the crook of his elbow.

There is a familiar tattooed face waiting in the living room.

"Ihaka," Reilly says with a grin, removing my hand from his arm to greet his clanmate.

"It's good to see you again, brother," Ihaka says with a grin.

"And you," Reilly says as they press their foreheads together briefly. "How is Leslie?"

"Restless, but well," Ihaka says before looking over at me.

"Olivia, this is Ihaka, a longtime friend," Reilly says, waving me forward. "I'm sure you remember him from Javier's."

"Nice to officially meet you," I say as I shake Ihaka's hand.

"Our Sire waits impatiently for the two of you," Ihaka says.

Reilly nods. "We'll talk after the meeting, then."

"Yes, there is a lot to discuss," Ihaka says seriously.

"Soon," Reilly says before turning back to me. "Let's go."

I follow him back out into the winding hallways. We take so many turns, there's no way I'd be able to find my way back alone. This place is huge.

The library has two guards standing outside. The one on the right knocks on the door once. I hear Cesare's command to enter, and the guard opens the door for us.

The room is lit only by the fireplace and a tall lamp near the doorway. Cesare is sitting in a high back chair behind a desk, but he stands and walks around it as we enter. The door is shut, and locked, behind us.

"You did good today, Olivia," Cesare says. "I was not entirely convinced that allowing you and Reilly to work with JHAPI was the right call, but it has paid off quite nicely."

His voice is soft, almost pleasant. Goosebumps creep up my arms.

"I'm glad it paid off," I say hesitantly.

"Yes, I have learned to be patient throughout my life. In fact, twenty-five years ago I bought a book. Much to my chagrin, the spell I thought was within it could not be performed again for many years," he says, spreading his hands wide and shrugging. "How delightful it was to discover recently that the spell had already been cast by someone else. It was also quite interesting to discover what the witches left out of the book."

He walks closer, stopping right in front of me, the tips of his shoes only inches from mine.

"I suppose they did not consider the death of the vampire involved in the spell important enough to mention. That wasn't very polite of them, don't you agree?"

"It was kind of a dick move," I say, my voice steady even though my heart is racing. "I doubt my father appreciated it."

Cesare laughs.

"No, I doubt he did. I'm sure we can find a way around that eventually," he says, placing his cold hand on my shoulder. "All magic requires balance, a price to be paid. Sometimes you can give the spell something of equal value to avoid paying too high a price."

I look at Reilly, unable to reply. Reilly doesn't meet my eyes though; his gaze is focused on his sire's hand on my shoulder. His heart is beating faster than normal, almost like he's afraid.

"So you want to create more like me?" I ask, finding my voice again. "Half-witch, half-vampire?"

"Perhaps," Cesare says. "It's interesting what you can do. We still haven't found your limits, I think."

"I don't know about that, I seem to be able to exhaust myself pretty easily," I say, struggling to not lean away.

"Reilly said he thought your injury was limiting you, and that is gone now," he says, dragging his fingers down the outside of my arm.

"That was holding me back," I agree. "I still need to work on control though. The electric magic is new and hard to use. It's not like the rest."

"Another way JHAPI is going to be useful. Learn what you can from that fire witch," Cesare says, as he lifts his hand away, finally, and strolls toward the table. "The witch council has been angling to steal you away from us; of course, we won't let them."

"Of course," I say.

"JHAPI will eventually outgrow its usefulness as an organization, but I think it best that we continue to work with them while we still can. They not only trust us right now, they rely on us."

"We made them look good," Reilly comments.

"And we need to keep it that way," Cesare agrees. "I don't want to hear any more rumors that the team lead is attempting to have either of you removed."

"I will make sure that doesn't happen again, Sire," Reilly says, walking up to stand next to me.

Cesare sits down behind his desk and looks at the two of us over his clasped hands.

"Learn everything you can, Olivia. There will come a time when you will have to use it, and failing me will not be an option."

"Yes—sire," I say, not sure how to address him.

"Go and rejoin your team tomorrow," Cesare says, sitting down and crossing his legs. "I'll call you back when I need you, but until then, we can keep picking away at the NWR. They'll be desperate after the failure here."

Reilly tugs on my arm, and I follow him out of the room. He is silent as we walk through the clanhouse. We pass dozens of other vampires, but no one stops us.

It's not as quiet as it was when we arrived. I can hear conversations floating up from downstairs. The quiet moans of feedings as we pass by closed doors. I can even smell someone cooking, so they must house some of the neckers here.

Reilly pauses in a quiet alcove halfway back to his rooms but doesn't look directly at me.

"I'm sorry."

I stare at him, confused. Never in my wildest dreams did I expect an apology, and I'm not sure what he's apologizing for anyhow. He's not lying either. His heartbeat is still fast, but it's also steady. He means it.

"For what?" I ask, glancing over my shoulder to make sure no one is approaching.

"He touched you because he knows I want you," Reilly whispers, staring straight ahead. "He was toying with me, not you."

I open my mouth to try to respond, but I don't know what to say. I can't deny that Reilly and I have chemistry, but I didn't think it meant anything to him other than the thrill of the chase. Reilly had seemed bothered in the room, but I hadn't understood why.

"Let's not linger," Reilly says.

I shut my mouth and follow him, my head spinning from everything that has happened. The rest of the walk is silent and uncomfortable.

When we arrive back at his rooms, Reilly opens the door and ushers me in ahead of him. As the door shuts behind us all, the sounds from the rest of the house go silent. These rooms must be sound-proofed.

The Viking, whose name I still don't know, Ihaka, and a person I've been both dreading and waiting to see are in the living area. Leslie is sitting on the couch, her legs curled up underneath her, looking bustier than ever. She smiles when she sees me.

"Olivia Carter," she says. "This is some crazy shit, huh?"

I laugh. I can't help it.

"I'm glad to see you somewhat alive," I say with a smile.

"How is Javier doing without me?" she asks, tilting her head to the side.

"I'm not sure," I say, the smile slipping off my face. "I haven't spoken to him since I left a couple of weeks ago."

"Ihaka won't let me contact him at all," Leslie says with a pout. "He won't let me see anyone really."

"So I've heard," I say, walking over to sit on the couch opposite her.

"Does she know now?" Ihaka asks.

Reilly nods. "She knows enough."

"Knows enough about what?" I ask, looking at everyone in turn.

"You know about the Bound God," Reilly says. "And the coven Zachary has been investigating, off the record."

I tense, so he had overheard at least part of our conversation. "Yes, so what?"

"Cesare believes he is real," Reilly says, walking around the back of the couch to stand behind Leslie. "And he thinks that this god is the key to overthrowing the council and propelling vampires back into a place of power in the world."

"I'm sorry," I say, leaning forward to rest my elbows on my knees. "He what?"

"Whether you believe this thing is a god or not, there is something that has been held back by a spell for several centuries. The thing Aris and Izul stopped," Reilly says.

I look at Ihaka, then at the Viking, and at Leslie, but no one is laughing.

"That's not just a myth?" I ask.

"No," Ihaka says. "Though most have forgotten it is true, except for the coven that still guards it."

"The one that killed my mother." I lean back and cross my arms. "What is this thing going to do if it breaks free anyhow?"

"It wants to destroy paranormals. Anything that has or uses magic," Reilly says.

"Then why does Cesare think it can help him?"

"He wants the vampires to go into hiding once it is released. After the witches, goblins, and weres are decimated, he intends to have you kill it," Reilly explains. "After that, he believes his rise to power will be fairly easy."

I bust out laughing, but it's clear no one else thinks it's a joke.

"He thinks I can kill this thing? Aris and Izul had an army behind them if the stories are true. I'm one person, and I barely know how to use half the magic I have."

"That's why I've pushed you. If you're going to stop this thing before it wipes out half the paranormal population, you need to be stronger," Reilly says.

"Why you've pushed me?" I ask, getting angry. "You threatened me and manipulated me. You destroyed my entire life."

"This is more important than your life," Reilly says, snapping back.

"You could have told me why you wanted my help!" I shout,

jumping up to my feet. "You threatened everyone I care about. You destroyed my friendships!"

"I did what I had to do to get you to a point where you would understand what we're facing. Neither of us has any choice here. Cesare ordered me to find you and prepare you for this," Reilly says, skirting around the couch and advancing on me. His eyes are flashing with anger.

"You didn't have to do what you did. You used me. You're still using me," I say through gritted teeth.

"I found out early on that I had to use people if I was going to survive, much less succeed. Grow up," Reilly snaps.

Leslie leans around from behind Reilly's back.

"Just for the record, he wasn't going to actually follow through on his threat to wipe out the clan. If that makes you feel any better," she says with a shrug.

"What?" I ask, anger being replaced with confusion.

Reilly rubs his hands over his face. "If you find the right leverage, and you're just scary enough to be convincing, you don't ever have to follow through on your threats."

I stare at Reilly for a moment, and he stares back, jaw clenched tight. Ihaka is smiling behind him.

"Leslie makes Reilly sound like a soft-hearted man," Ihaka chuckles. "He is not, but he tries to not kill people unnecessarily."

I plop back down on the couch and put my head in my hands. "Say I trust you lunatics. What exactly are you planning?"

"We have to contact the coven without Cesare finding out and figure out how to stop this thing from being released," Reilly says, his voice tired.

I stare at the floor, the vision of my mother replaying in my mind.

"I think we might also need to steal that spellbook Cesare has," I say, looking up at Reilly.

"Why?" he asks, brows pinching together.

I lean back against the couch.

"It turns out what I thought were hallucinations were something more," I say. "I don't know exactly what she meant, but I think my mother knew this was coming."

"Your mother?" Reilly asks.

"Yeah," I say. "It turns out you can Find the dead."

Reilly sits down next to Leslie, and I take a deep breath, then start at the beginning.

CHAPTER 30

Corinne is sitting up in the hospital bed reading a book when I walk in. She looks up with a smile, and while she's still a little too pale, her eyes are bright.

"Olivia, I'm so glad you finally came to visit," she says, putting her book down.

I walk over and sit down in the chair next to her bed.

"It has been a long week," I say. "And I wasn't sure if you wanted to see me."

Corinne twists her mouth up ruefully. "Everyone has been just as angry at me as they have at you. We both know you're not to blame though."

I look down at my hands, twisting them together. "If I had been calmer, we might have waited."

"And then the same thing would have happened," Corinne says, leaning over to put her hand on my shoulder. "The trap was set, and we had no way of knowing Martinez would be using magic against us like that. It's completely unheard of. No amount of safety measures could have prevented it."

I sigh. She's right, but I still feel guilty about the whole thing.

"Honestly, if it had happened in any other way, I think I'd be dead because you might not have been there to drain my magic and stop the curse," she says.

"I'm glad you didn't die."

"Me too." She pats me on the shoulder and leans back into the pillows. "The welts on your arms are gone."

I brush my thumb over my forearm. It's almost weird to be able to wear short-sleeved shirts again.

"Yeah, I let go, like you said, but—" I hesitate.

"But what?" she prompts.

"I spoke to her. She didn't seem like a memory. She talked about things I didn't know, and she asked me to do something. It wasn't just an echo or whatever you called it," I say quietly.

"It wouldn't be the first time I've been wrong," Corinne says with a shrug. "It should be impossible, but you should be too. I believe, for what it's worth, that you Found her ghost somehow."

"It does make me feel a little less crazy to hear you say that," I say with a laugh.

"Magic never follows the rules we try to set on it," she says.

"No, it really doesn't."

"Are you staying with the team?" Corinne asks.

"Yes," I nod. "The vampire council still wants Reilly and me on this assignment, especially after the Summit attack."

"That was insane. Ivy came and filled me in on it. We're lucky there weren't more casualties," Corinne says, shaking her head.

"Just over a hundred neckers were killed. Dozens of paranormals. It feels like we lost." I put my head in my hands. "It doesn't feel like we stopped anything."

"You stopped a war," Corinne says, placing her hand on the back of my head. "If the councils had been wiped out, and the vampires had been made to look like monsters, this country would have been thrown into chaos. Thousands would have died instead of hundreds. It may not feel like enough, but you did everything you could."

"Sure," I say, staring at my hands. I clear my throat and sit up. "I shouldn't stay long, but I wanted to see how you were."

"I'll be out of here tomorrow," Corinne says as I stand. "I'm glad you came by though."

"Me too," I say with a smile. "I'll see you again soon."

"See you soon," Corinne agrees.

I leave and close the door quietly behind me. Zachary is waiting outside.

"Did it go all right?" he asks.

"Yeah." I nod.

"Are you sure you want to do this?"

I take a deep breath. "I want to find the people who killed my mother."

"And you're sure about Reilly?" he asks.

"As sure as I can be. He wants to stop Cesare, and I'm willing to help him do that if it gets me what I want," I say.

"I still don't think this god is real," Zachary says.

"I hope he isn't," I say, shaking my head. "But whatever this coven is trying to stop, Cesare is trying to release. Maybe we can take them both down at once."

Zachary nods, and I follow him down the hall. Reilly is waiting for me in the car, perhaps as an ally, perhaps still as my enemy. I'm willing to risk it if it means finally tracking down the people responsible for my mother's death. I had given up on finding them, and on finding out why she died.

I dig my nails into my palm. I know where the book is. I can get it, somehow, and I can figure out what I'm meant to do. I'll do it for her.

PART IV
FORBIDDEN MAGIC

PROLOGUE

The air is damp and cold despite the unyielding light that fills the cell. Condensation drips down the stone wall until it slips into a crack. Felix rolls up to a sitting position and scratches his unkempt beard. He hasn't had access to a razor in at least a week. He's not sure exactly how many days have passed though.

His granddaughter must be worried. Justine knows he'd never disappear like that, not willingly. And there aren't many people that could pose a threat to a witch like him.

Felix grits his teeth in anger. No matter how powerful he is, it seems he can never protect the people he cares about. The power he was born with is more of a liability than a benefit; no wonder so many of his kind are dead. He stares at his hand, wishing he could strip the magic away. If he hadn't been born with this curse, he would never have drawn Alexandra's eye.

Felix tilts his head back against the wall and closes his eyes. When he was young and stupid, Alexandra made him feel special and needed. He snorts. He was useful like all tools are. If he hadn't been so blind, perhaps he could have seen how she was using not just him, but their son as well.

Alexandra wanted one thing: power. She had traded in the colorful dresses that first caught his eye for severe black robes styled after the ancient witches she admired. Her favorite had been Aris, of course. A bloodthirsty woman who chased after power her entire, miserable existence.

Aris had led wars, massacres, and had beaten the entire magical world down until they submitted to her idea of unification. Felix sighs. The creation of the councils was good for witches and other paranormals in the end, but the cost it had required still seems too high.

These are thoughts he usually avoids, but sitting in a dark place with no sense of time has made the memories impossible to ignore. His son's wide eyes and pale face as he was killed haunt him. The sound he had made, half sob, half pleading, still rings in Felix's ears, even after half a decade. It was Alexandra's fault he had died, but she hadn't cared. She said he must have been weak.

Felix had taken his granddaughter and run that same night. He had fled to the one place Alexandra couldn't follow. He and Justine spent years flitting in and out of the shadows, hiding, training, scraping by. All it took was one mistake for a new monster to find him.

Footsteps echo down the hallway. Felix lifts his head and waits, cross-legged on the floor. The door swings open revealing a tall figure. The flickering light of the torches in the hallway cast shadows across the man's lean face.

"It's time," he says, tilting his head as he takes Felix's posture in. "Do you still intend to cooperate?"

"You haven't given me a choice," Felix rasps.

The man smiles. "It is easier to plan when the pawns have only one direction in which to move."

Felix snorts and pushes up off the floor. He pointlessly dusts off his grimy pants and follows the vampire out of the cell. Felix curls his fingers into a fist, his nails biting into his skin. If he didn't have Justine to think about he'd kill himself before he'd do this. It's wrong, like so many things he has done in his lifetime.

Then again, he's just a tool. He was always going to be used by someone, it's just bad luck this particular person got to him first.

CHAPTER 1

Five days earlier...

A cool breeze carries the smell of pine trees and the babbling of a small creek. I brush a stray hair away from my face and poke the grimy metal tooth of the bear trap with the end of my stick, flinching in anticipation of it snapping shut. Nothing happens.

Colin snorts behind me. "Are you going to set it off so we can move on, or are you scared of it?"

"I'm going to let you step in it next time," I mutter, knowing he can still hear me.

"I saw it, I wasn't going to step in it," he insists.

"Just keep telling yourself that," I say, looking back at him with a smirk.

He rolls his eyes and leans down to dig the map Agent Stocke gave us out of my backpack so he can mark the location of this trap on the grid.

I jab the stick sharply into the center of the trap. It leaps up, snapping the stick in half with a clank that hurts my ears. I flinch, just like I had for the previous three. Colin laughs but tries to turn it into a cough to cover it up.

"Go ahead and laugh it up, fur-ball," I say as I pick up the now safe trap and toss it as him.

"Fur-ball?" He asks as he catches it, still trying not to smile and drops it into his backpack. He gets to carry the heavy stuff since he is the werewolf. I might be just as strong as he is when I'm drawing on my vampire side, but I'm not going to waste all my energy on that. He was smug about it, and I let him stay that way to keep him in a good mood. Delicate male egos and all that.

"Yeah," I say, waving my hand at him. "Werewolf, fur-ball, same difference really."

"I thought JHAPI agents had sensitivity training and knew not to insult werewolves," Colin says, a smile still tugging at the corner of his mouth.

I pull on my backpack. "I'm just a consultant."

"Oh, so I didn't even get stuck with an agent, I'm stuck with a civilian." He looks up to the sky and shakes his head dramatically. "Goddess save me."

"You're lucky to have me," I say with a huff. "Now how much more do we have to cover?"

"It's only been three hours. We still have this entire area to cover," he says, pointing to the upper half of our section on the grid. There are four small x's designating where we found traps set by the NWR. They had protested Angeles National Park allowing the werewolves to run on federally owned lands for years. After the recent escalation of tension, the NWR decided to take matters into their own hands and set hundreds of traps throughout the woods.

The local packs had been trying to deal with it themselves, but after some human hikers wandered off the trails and ended up injured, one of them almost dying, they reluctantly agreed to accept JHAPI's help. That is why I'm stomping around in the woods with a werewolf trying to avoid stepping on a trap myself.

The NWR, being assholes, as usual, had laced some traps with silver making it difficult for the werewolves to touch. I get the thankless task of poking at everything first to make sure silver doesn't spew out of it and injure Colin. One of the first traps the pack had found did that. The wolf ended up with silver dust in his eyes and up his nose and he had almost suffocated.

Colin looks over the map one last time, then starts off again in the direction we had been heading before I saw the glint of metal under the pine needles and dirt the trap had been covered in. I had shoved Colin to the side just in time, despite his protestations afterward that he had seen it. Delicate male egos indeed.

My thighs protest the steady uphill trek. I adjust the straps on my backpack and keep scanning the ground despite the discomfort. I follow Colin around a tree and the ground changes from dirt and pine needles, to rock. I look up and freeze in my tracks. We're higher up than I realized, and the view is breathtaking. Tree-covered mountains stretch all the way to the horizon. Low clouds cast a haze in the distance, but the sky above us is almost cloudless.

I turn my face up to the sun, enjoying it in a way I haven't since I took the vampire magic from Javier. The hedgewitch magic inside of me sings with energy from being this close to nature. I grew up in cities, and never really left. Even living in the country I stayed inside when I wasn't in town. Maybe, when this is all over, I should get a cabin on the top of some mountain somewhere and become a hermit.

"It's a great view," Colin says, interrupting my reverie.

"Yeah," I say quietly. "I've never seen anything like this before."

"You never get used to it no matter how long you live here," he says. "I still stop and stare every time."

"Have you lived here your whole life?" I ask as we start walking again. I glance back at the view one last time before it's blocked by trees.

"Yep, born and raised in the pack," he says as jumps onto the top of a boulder that's over waist high to look around us. I lean against a tree and take a long drink of water. I'll take any break I can get.

"What do you do for a living?" I ask. Most witches work for the coven somehow. Contract work for magic goes through them, and so does your paycheck. They'll cover living expenses and give you some of it back, but it's meant to keep the witches dependent on the coven, so they don't give you much. I've always been curious if packs worked the same way.

"The pack owns a construction business. I'm a site superintendent." He hops down and starts walking again, correcting our direction slightly.

"Are all the employees pack members?" I ask.

"Nah," he says with a shrug. "The owner is, and quite a few of us are, but we hire humans and even werewolves from other packs. The business is too big to keep completely pack. It would have stunted the growth of it."

"That seems smart. I wish witches had the same thought process," I say, thinking back to all the opportunities my mother had been forced to pass on thanks to her coven.

"What coven are you with? Or is JHAPI your coven now?" He asks, glancing back at me.

"I'm not part of a coven. Haven't been since I was sixteen," I say, watching for Colin's reaction. He looks surprised but doesn't pry.

"How'd you end up working with JHAPI anyhow if you aren't an agent?" He asks instead.

"I'm working with the vampire council actually, and they insisted on having a representative on this team while they try to take down the NWR."

"They can do that?" He asks, his tone incredulous.

"Apparently." I hesitate, then decide if I'm wrong, JHAPI can deal with the mess. "I'm sure the werewolves could demand the same thing if they were interested. There is already a werewolf on the team though."

He snorts. "No self-respecting werewolf would leave their pack behind to join a government organization. Can't trust the government, and can't trust them."

I roll my eyes. "That's bullshit."

He comes to an abrupt stop and looks back at me, his jaw clenched tight. "And what the hell do you know about it? You're not a werewolf, you don't understand how a pack works."

I face him without flinching. If he wants to be all sensitive about it, that's his choice.

"JHAPI needs every type of paranormal to succeed. They need people that understand werewolves, witches, vampires. Hell, even goblins. Elise is an amazing agent and good person. What are you so worried about anyhow? That JHAPI is going to try to take something from you?"

"You should know exactly what we're worried about," he says, turning and walking away. "The council is the only authority we should have to answer to. The humans want to control us because they're afraid of us, just like the NWR. That's all JHAPI is, another way for them to find an excuse to lock us up."

I snort, which earns me another glare.

"You should pay more attention then," I say lightly. "JHAPI has done more to fight the NWR than anyone else in the last hundred years. We're making progress. Having every human agent in the organization partnered with a paranormal keeps anyone from getting away with prejudice."

"Eventually the true goal of the organization is going to become apparent. It's only a matter of time—" Colin trails off, sniffing the air.

I pull on the vampire magic sharply, and all my senses swim into focus. Blood. Werewolf. A whimper.

Colin growls and lunges into a run. I sprint after him, my backpack bouncing around as I struggle to keep up with him. He flows through the trees and around the boulders while I struggle to keep traction on the dirt and slippery pine needles. I grit my teeth and speed up. I can't let him get away from me.

The smell of blood is getting stronger, and just ahead, through the trees, I catch a glimpse of fur. A wolf is hanging by one leg from a snare trap. Unease twists in my stomach. This isn't right.

I jump forward, tackling Colin. He growls in anger, and his elbow catches the side of my head as I ride him down to the ground. He flips underneath me, eyes glowing gold. He might still be in human form, but there is nothing but wolf looking back at me right now. He's operating entirely on instinct, but I can't let him go, not when I'm sure this is a trap.

CHAPTER 2

I rear back and slap him across the face, trying to shock him into reason. He throws me off and lunges at me. I shift to the side with vampire speed and catch him in the stomach with a kick, then jump on his back and wrap my arm tightly around his throat, just like I remember Reilly doing to me in that gym.

I dig my arm in tight and squeeze. Colin struggles wildly, slamming me back against a tree. My shirt tears and my skin splits as I hit the stub of a broken branch, but I don't let go. I tighten my grip, and he sinks to his knees as his brain is deprived of oxygen and blood.

He drops forward onto his hands. I force him onto his stomach before finally loosening my hold on his neck.

"This is the second time I've saved you from walking into a trap, you asshole," I gasp.

He is shaking under me, his eyes still locked on the werewolf that is now struggling in the snare again. Blood is matted in their fur from where the snare has cut into their skin. There is also a sickening burning smell which tells me the snare is braided with silver. It's not enough to kill the wolf, but it has to hurt like a bitch.

"What—trap?" He gasps.

I unwind my arm from his neck and sit up slowly.

"I don't know, but that's one of your pack that went missing almost a week ago, right?" I ask.

"Yes," Colin growls, twisting his head to glare at me.

"Those injuries are less than a day old," I say pointing at the still wet blood on her leg. "She was hung up there recently, which means it was probably intentional. Which means it's a trap. The kind that makes a werewolf rush in without thinking."

Colin grinds his teeth together, but nods. I stand up and offer him my hand, which he takes. He looks at his pack member again and curls his hands into fists, still clearly struggling not to run to her.

"How did you keep up with me? And overpower me?" He asks. "I thought you were a witch."

It's been a secret for so long my first impulse is to lie and say I took a brew. I don't have to lie anymore though. The vampire council knows, and I'm sure the witch council has found out somehow. I want this pack to trust JHAPI, and he'll be able to hear a lie.

"I'm half witch, half vampire actually," I say cautiously. "This isn't really the time for an in-depth explanation, but I'm as strong and fast as a vampire. When I need to be at least."

"That's not possible," he says, his eyes wide.

I grin and let my fangs drop. Colin takes a step back in shock.

"Yet here I am," I say before retracting the small fangs. I'm still not used to them, they feel awkward and sharp in my mouth.

"This is insane," he says as he shakes his head and turns back to the wolf. "We can't leave her hanging like that."

She is watching us, but every few seconds she goes back to twisting and clawing at the air. She can't seem to twist up high enough to bite the cable of the snare though.

"Of course not," I say, frowning. "We're going to get her down, but we have to figure out what the trap is first so we can avoid setting it off."

Colin squats down and scans the ground carefully. I walk in a wide circle around the wolf, scenting the air for other humans, but the smell is faint. They came and went last night or this morning.

"There's no trip wire," Colin shouts.

"There has to be something else then," I yell back.

I pull my cell phone out, it'd be great to have some backup, but of course, there is no signal out here. I shove it in my backpack which I take off and set on the ground. I don't want it restricting my movements.

I turn to walk back to him when I hear the sharp ping of metal tearing. The cable hasn't snapped, but about halfway down a few strands have broken. I furrow my brows. They could have easily used a cable strong enough to hold her up there indefinitely even if it did have silver in it.

I pick up a small rock and examine at the ground directly below her. The dirt looks a little fresher, and the pine needles are damp like they were stirred around.

I toss the rock. It hits the ground underneath the wolf dragging dirt and pine needles with it as it collapses the camouflage on the wide pit underneath her. Silver tipped spikes line the sides and jut up from the bottom ready to kill her if she falls. I grit my teeth.

"Don't throw any more rocks," Colin yells urgently.

"I wasn't planning on it," I shout back as I jog over to him. "What is it?"

He points at lumps of freshly disturbed dirt that are evenly spaced in a circle around the pit.

"I don't know what those are, but I don't think we want to find out," he says.

"They went to a lot of trouble here," I say, running my hands through my hair and taking a deep breath.

"Keri getting taken was a huge embarrassment for the pack

politically," Colin says through gritted teeth. "If it looks like we just lost her in the woods, it'll be even worse."

"Well, for right now we just need to figure out how to get to her," I step back and scan the area, trying to decide how close we can get. "That cable isn't going to hold much longer, especially if she keeps moving. Can you talk to her? Try to calm her down?"

"I can try, but she's completely out of it. If she's been shifted this whole time, she won't be thinking anymore. The human side of us goes to sleep after a while," Colin says.

"Just try," I say. "I'm going to try to figure out how we can get to her without touching the ground."

Colin turns to Keri and walks as close as he dares. He kneels down and howls. The sound is soft, sad. She pauses in her wriggling and twists her head to stare at him. He starts talking then, a slow, but constant stream of chatter. He has her attention for a moment, but she growls and starts fighting the snare again.

Colin looks back at me.

"Just keep trying."

I jog over to my backpack and open the pocket I stuffed my brews into. I brought two that can knock a human unconscious for over an hour. On a werewolf, it'll last maybe fifteen minutes. I pick the vial up and look back at Colin. He's still talking to her, but it's not working. Another two strands of the cable snap and curl up with a twang. She has to stop moving, or we're going to be out of time.

"Colin," I say, holding up the vial where he can see. "I can knock her out, but I'm not going to do it unless you agree."

Colin's lip curls up into a growl. He looks back at Keri who is still struggling wildly and rolls his shoulders.

"What is it exactly?" He demands.

"A knock-out brew. She'll just fall asleep for about fifteen or twenty minutes," I explain, holding the vial loosely between my fingers.

Colin looks unhappy, but he finally nods. I stand and throw the vial. It hits her side and breaks, the brew sinking into her fur and skin. She growls and snaps, then goes still.

"Now what?" He asks.

"I think I have an idea, but it involves trusting me some more," I say, crossing my arms.

He narrows his eyes at me. "Explain."

Colin's control is hanging on by a thread. One word answers, the growls, the tense line of his shoulders all betray the struggle. I know weres are protective of pack members, but this seems like more than that. It worries me.

"We can't walk up to her, and the cable will snap if we try to pull her up, so the only option left is to try a jump and grab," I say, tapping my fingers nervously against my arm. "And I have to be the one to jump because I can break the cable, but you probably can't since it is braided with silver."

"You may be fast, but there's no way you can jump that distance and land on the other side once you have her weight," Colin says, shaking his head.

"It's our only option," I say, dropping my arms. "I'm doing it."

I start toward Keri, but Colin grabs my arm. "You're going to get both of you killed."

"I'm not going to stand here and watch her fall into a pit of spikes and die. I'm not asking you to risk your life, I'm doing this. Let me," I say, yanking my arm out of his grasp.

"Fine. Prove me wrong then," he says.

I walk the perimeter until I find a gap in the trees on both sides. I'll have to be quick. I'll need to loop my right arm around her waist and reach overhead and break the cable with my left hand while somehow not losing any momentum. The landing is going to be a bitch.

I pull ruthlessly on the vampire magic. I've only got one shot at this. Now is not the time to ration my magic. Strength courses through my limbs and my fangs push out of my gums. I crouch down, my eyes locked on the cable and sprint forward. Step. Step. Leap.

For a half a second I'm flying through the air, then I hit the wolf. I wrap my right arm tightly around her, my fingers grasping at fur. We swing forward, and I yank on the cable with my left hand as I push white-hot electricity into the metal. It stretches and cuts into my hand before it finally snaps.

She's heavier than I expected and my eyes go wide as I realize we won't make it. Not by a long shot. Instead of flying, we're falling now. My feet hit the dirt, and I squeeze my eyes shut, expecting an explosion. Colin's racing heart pounds in my ears, but that's it. I tentatively open my eyes.

Maybe six inches in front of me is one of those potentially deadly lumps of dirt. I look down at my feet and breathe out a sigh of relief. By sheer dumb luck, I managed to land in a clear spot. The bad news is that I'm still at least six feet from safety holding an upside down, passed out werewolf. She's getting heavier by the second too.

Colin skids to a stop in the gap between trees in front of me and pants heavily, looking between me and the distance that separates her.

"Now what?" He shouts.

"Now we play catch," I shout back.

"You have got to be kidding me," he mutters.

I can hear it as clearly as if he had shouted it with how much magic is surging through me right now.

"Come on, I'm getting tired. Just be ready to catch her," I say as I attempt to adjust my grip without moving. I glance over my shoulder, and sure enough, there's another lump behind me that's even closer.

"Your plans haven't really worked out that well so far," he says, but he braces himself and holds his arms open.

I shift my left hand to her good leg and take a deep breath. I have to be fast, but it's too far to just toss her. If I can pivot without stepping on anything I think I can get enough momentum swinging her around me to throw her to Colin.

I wrap my right hand around her bad leg below the worst of the injury and nod at Colin to let him know I'm ready. I twist, swinging her around me in a wide arc. Her head gets perilously close to the ground.

I rotate back around to Colin and let her go, stumbling forward half a step before catching myself. She flies toward him, tongue flapping in the wind, and hits him in the chest. Colin topples backward and hits the ground with an armful of unconscious wolf.

My hands are shaking from the effort of maintaining the vampire magic for so long. I can't keep this up indefinitely. I pull harder on the sluggish magic and crouch down slightly. This is going to be a hard jump since I can't get a running start.

"Come on," Colin says, lifting Keri and moving out of the way.

I shake off the fear and leap. I get so close, but I'm more tired than I thought. I hit the dirt again three-quarters of the way there, my foot landing on one of those lumps this time. I hear a click and sprint forward. Screw jumping again.

Colin is running too, Keri clutched tightly to his chest. Everything feels slow as I run, even the rabbit-fast beating of my heart. I dive behind a boulder just as I hear something erupt from the ground. The explosion deafens my sensitive hearing. I curl into a ball as shrapnel flies overhead and hits the trees all around me.

The explosion set off another mine, and then another. I press back against the boulder and press my hands to my ears, letting go of the vampire magic in a rush.

After a few seconds of silence, I hesitantly lower my hands and look around. Thick silver balls are embedded in the trees all around me.

"Colin?" I shout, my voice sounding odd inside my head. My ears are still ringing. Dirt that was thrown up in the air is still on the wind making everything feel gritty. It smells like smoke and hot metal.

"Olivia, are you hurt?" Colin shouts back.

I struggle to my feet and glance down at my body just to make sure. "No, I'm not."

I spot Colin. He'd had the same idea, but he had found a bigger boulder thankfully. He's covered in dirt, and if he looks like that, I must be a mess too. I can feel the grit on my face, but I resist the urge to wipe it away since my hands are even dirtier.

"I told you there was no way you'd make that jump while holding her," he says smugly.

I roll my eyes. "You're welcome, fur-ball."

"She's hurt bad. I can still smell silver in her along with something else I've never smelled before," Colin says looking down at the still unconscious Keri.

I hurry over. The snare is twisted into the flesh of her leg. I dig into the wound, thankful she's still asleep, and free the cable. I drop it on the ground and run my hand over her flank, sending my healing magic flowing into her.

"I can heal her a bit, enough to make sure she survives the trip down the mountain," I say as I try to sort out all her injuries.

"You're a healer?" He asks, surprise overwriting the concern on his face for a moment.

I shrug. "A lousy one, but it'll be enough."

The silver is easiest to purge. I can feel the small particles dripping out of the wound on her leg. The snare had cut all the way through her skin and muscle, scraping and gouging the bone itself. I send the bulk of my healing magic there, encouraging the bone to heal and the muscle to begin stitching together from the inside out.

Werewolves heal extremely quickly, but injuries caused by silver can heal human slow. Giving it a jumpstart should encourage her own magic to kick in and take over. I can feel it trying, but something is interfering.

I spread my magic throughout her body and find it stuttering over a strange, foreign substance. It's some kind of chemical, and it feels foul even to my magic. I let my magic eat at it, but it's slippery, and there's a lot of it. When my head starts to spin, I untangle my fingers from her fur and step back unsteadily.

"Sorry," I say breathlessly. "That's all I can do."

The unwelcome but familiar hunger makes my stomach twist. Colin isn't as powerful as Elise, but right now even his magic is tempting. I can almost smell it. I bite down on my tongue and take another couple of steps back.

"Are you okay?" Colin asks, his brows pinched tightly together in concern.

"I'll be fine. We need to get her to some kind of doctor as soon as possible," I say, shaking my head to clear it.

Colin nods then tilts his head back and howls. It sounds utterly inhuman, loud and clear and haunting. It echoes throughout the forest until he stops. His eyes are glowing lightly again, and the wolf peers out at me.

There is an answering howl. Colin grins.

"They'll be ready for us," he says, turning and starting down the mountain.

CHAPTER 3

The view might be nice, but I refuse to step foot on a mountain ever again. My thighs are burning and shaking, and I'm not sure how much farther we have to go before we reach the bottom. Overusing my magic wore me out, and with no one to feed on, I'm running on empty.

I pause and lean against a tree for a second to catch my breath. I'm tempted to take my backpack off and leave it here, but the brews are too expensive to leave behind. Colin pauses about ten feet ahead of me and looks back.

"Do I need to carry you too?" He asks, amused.

"Shut up," I mutter, envious of Keri even if she does look ridiculous with her tongue hanging out of her mouth like that. Wolves are normally regal creatures, but I guess everything can look stupid in the right circumstances.

I shove off the tree and head down to where Colin is waiting. He starts walking again as soon as I step beside him.

"We're almost there, less than a quarter mile now," he says, answering the question I didn't want to ask.

I let out a sigh of relief. "Finally."

Keri twitches in his arms, a whiny growl escaping her lips. Her eyelids flutter halfway open and she huffs groggily.

"I'm surprised that didn't wear off sooner," I say with a sigh. "Do you think she'll try to hurt you when she wakes up?"

"Perhaps. The Alpha is close; I can smell him," Colin says with a shrug. "He will be able to calm her if needed."

"Ian Grzeski, right?" I ask. I read his name in the file when Stocke had been laying out the plan for this, but I hadn't seen him when we arrived. Stocke had simply introduced me to Colin, and we had headed up the mountain. There was a large area to cover and not much time. The full moon was in four days and the pack wanted to know they could run without risking life and limb.

"Yes," Colin nods. "He has been the Alpha since he was nineteen years old. The youngest Alpha in over two hundred years to maintain control of a pack for this long."

"He's also one of the most influential Alphas, isn't he?" I ask. He may not be on the council himself, but his aunt is, and they have a close relationship. The werewolf council works a bit differently from the vampire council. The three werewolf council members each oversee a region of the country. If there is unrest, crime, or some kind of disaster in their region, it reflects badly on them. They are intended to mentor and help the Alphas in their region though, not control them.

They have small packs of their own, but they are limited to only five pack members to prevent any council member from amassing too much power. The werewolves believe that centralization of power is a threat to freedom. Packs should thrive or fail on their own merits as long as they don't put other packs at risk through irresponsible decisions.

"Yes, our aunt is on the council. Ian is well-respected, as he should be," Colin says, pride apparent in his voice. There's something more though. I hesitate to call it fondness, but that's what it is. He isn't smugly proud of how powerful the pack is, he is proud that his Alpha has done well like a brother might be. I've never heard a witch talk about their coven like that, other than Corinne I suppose.

"Our aunt? Are you related to Ian?" I ask, surprised.

"He's my brother," Colin says with a nod.

A man with dark blond hair and thick beard tinged with red appears from seemingly out of nowhere ahead of us. He stalks toward us silently. He isn't that tall, or bulky, but his lean form is all muscle and all power. He glances at me, but his focus is on the twitching werewolf in Colin's arms.

"Why is she unconscious?" Ian asks in a deep voice as he comes to a stop in front of Colin. He brushes his hand over Keri's neck soothingly and her twitching slows.

"A knock-out brew," I explain. "She was struggling in a snare that was breaking and if she hadn't stopped, she would have fallen into a pit of stakes and died."

Ian's eyes flick toward me and his mouth turns down in irritation. He clearly wasn't asking me, but I'm not going to let him act like I don't exist. It was my decision to dose her anyhow.

"She wasn't able to hear me," Colin says. "There is a lot to explain. The trap we found her in was more elaborate than anything else we've found so far. You heard the explosions?"

Ian nods. "Even the humans heard. Agent Stocke has been very uneasy since then."

As if on cue my JHAPI-issue phone begins buzzing with missed calls and messages. I pull it out and turn it to silent. We're almost back, it can wait until then.

"I'll carry her," Ian says, gently lifting Keri from Colin's arms. Colin bows his head in acceptance and helps Ian move her into a better position.

"The NWR injected her with something," I say as we start walking again. "I did what I could to get it out, but there was too much for me fix completely. I don't know for sure, but I think it might be keeping her from shifting back."

Ian glances at me again, still suspicious.

"Olivia saved Keri's life, got the silver out of her leg, and started to heal the wound from the snare trap," Colin explains. He's trying to convince Ian to trust me.

"I'm sure Agent Carter is dedicated to doing her job," Ian says plainly.

The comment feels like an insult. This guy is determined to dislike me; though it might be more accurate to say he's determined to dislike JHAPI.

"Not an agent, just a consultant on loan from the vampire council," I correct. If he wants to be dismissive, he can at least get his details correct. Ian, of course, ignores me.

The steep, downward slope of the mountain begins to even out. The tall pine trees get farther apart and the shrubby bushes common in this part of California become more prevalent. The sunlight that I appreciated earlier is beating down on my back and threatening to put me to sleep.

Colin and Ian easily leap over a small, rocky creek with ankle deep water while I splash through it. My shoes will dry. Just ahead I can see the semicircle of JHAPI vehicles parked in front of the small cabin that is being used as the base of operations for this effort.

Agent Stocke is standing, arms crossed, in the center of it waiting for us. Her shoulders slump in relief when she spots me and Colin. She walks toward us, shoving her phone in the pocket of her pants.

"What the hell happened?" She asks as she falls into step beside Ian.

"The NWR set a different kind of trap," I say with a yawn. "They had Keri strung up in a snare over a pit of stakes and surrounded by land mines of some kind."

"Bouncing Betty's," Colin interjects, shaking his head in disbelief.

I wave my hand in acknowledgment. "I might have accidentally set a couple off, but luckily we avoided getting hit by the shrapnel. Cleaning up all those bits of silver is going to be a bitch though."

"Olivia stopped me from running into the trap," Colin says, ducking his head. "When I smelled Keri, and then the blood, I rushed in on instinct."

Ian gives Colin a disappointed look as he stops next to one of the vans.

"Open it," he demands. "I want to lay her inside rather than on the ground."

Colin nods and pulls the sliding door open. Ian sets Keri down carefully and Colin grabs a mostly empty backpack and gently places it under her head.

Ian run his hands over Keri, feeling for injuries he can't see, then inspects her leg thoroughly. The fur has all been rubbed off, and it's still matted with blood, but the pink-ish healing skin is visible. I did a good job on that at least.

Ian looks back at me. "You healed this?"

"I started too, but I ran out of juice," I say with a wan smile, wiggling my fingers.

"You said she was in a snare over a trap," Stocke says. "How exactly did you get her down?"

"Jump and grab," Colin says, trying to suppress a grin as he gestures for them to ask me.

"The snare line was breaking, and the NWR doesn't make mistakes like that. If the snare was intended to break, there had to be a reason. I tossed a rock underneath Keri and the camouflage covering the pit collapsed. Colin spotted the landmines. The only option was just to jump over the trap, grabbing her on the way." I cross my arms, ready for criticism. I'd dare any of them to come up with a better idea, especially in the limited time we had.

"She almost made it too," Colin adds.

I turn a glare on him. "She was heavy. And I made it far enough."

Stocke pinches the bridge of her nose between thumb and forefinger and takes a deep breath.

"It's a miracle you manage to stay alive," she mutters. "I've called the rest of the teams in, I don't want anyone out there with explosive devices we aren't prepared to disarm."

"So you've given up on helping us already?" Ian asks, his calm tone belying the tension in his shoulders.

Colin raises a brow at me as if to say, *See, I told you JHAPI couldn't be trusted.*

I smirk at him, they don't know JHAPI or Agent Stocke.

"Hardly," Stocke scoffs. "But I'm going to get agents qualified to handle disarming bombs. This is worse than we thought. I'll have people out here by tomorrow morning."

Stocke and Ian begin discussing logistics, but I can't focus on their conversation. I walk around to the front of the van and plop down on the ground leaning my head back against the grill and letting my eyes slip shut.

"You alright?" Colin asks, nudging me with his foot.

I shake myself and blink at him. "Yeah, just tired. Using that much magic wears me out."

The rumble of a diesel engine draws my eyes to the rough, gravel road that leads to the trail we had just walked down. A jacked-up, red truck with tires way bigger than necessary bounces its way toward us.

"There's the doctor, finally," Colin says.

"Seriously?" I ask, staring at the flashy truck.

Colin shrugs. "Jimmy is a good doctor."

"Is he pack?" I ask.

"Yes, but he's a witch, and a healer. He married into the pack but declined the bite, for obvious reasons."

"Your pack has a legitimate healer on call? That's insane," I say, sticking my hand up toward Colin who takes the hint and pulls me up to my feet.

"He was definitely a welcome addition to the pack," Colin agrees.

The truck skids to a stop a few feet away and Jimmy drops down from the driver seat. He hurries around the front of the truck and heads straight for Keri.

"Ian," Jimmy says, greeting the Alpha as he approaches Keri. Jimmy kneels by the side of the van and buries his fingers in her fur.

I remember the last healer I met in person. He was dressed in a white suit like he thought he was some kind of angel. Most angels don't charge hundreds of thousands of dollars to save a life though.

The healer was insanely powerful. I had only been able to touch him for a second before my mother dragged me away with profuse apologies but his magic had felt endless. I hadn't stolen enough of it for him to feel the loss, but even the little bit I did manage to get has made my life easier.

My mother had been furious and had forbidden me from using the magic. I hadn't ever listened though. I've never been able to watch a person suffer without helping. Reilly was right about that being my weakness. I tuck my hands in my pants and watch Jimmy work.

Keri's body shudders slightly as his magic works its way through her. It smells clean, like rain and fresh cut grass. The wound on her leg fills in from the inside out, and the flesh flows closed in a wave. New fur sprouts out of her skin, growing until you can't tell she was ever hurt.

My eyes go wide. I always knew my healing magic was stunted, I just never realized the extent of it. This is wondrous.

Keri wakes up with a start, her lips curling back into a snarl. Ian immediately leans over her and grabs the back of her neck roughly. She goes limp and rolls onto her back, showing him her stomach. He stares at her for a moment, their eyes locked, then releases his hand and steps back. Keri watches Jimmy warily but doesn't make any other aggressive moves toward him.

"What in the hell was she injected with?" Jimmy asks, frowning.

"We don't know," Ian replies. He pauses, looking at me, then back at Jimmy. "Olivia said she thought it was keeping Keri from shifting back to her human form."

Jimmy nods. "It is, but it's not clear how. I've never felt anything like this before."

"Will you be able to fix it?" Ian asks, his brows pinched in concern.

"Of course, what do you think I am? A human doctor?" Jimmy scoffs. "It's just going to take time. I want to work on her at my clinic. I think I have few brews there that will help too."

"Whatever you need to do," Ian agrees.

Jimmy steps back and Ian scoops Keri up. The backseat of the truck has a stretcher they strap Keri onto. She noses at the straps, but Ian flicks her nose and she lays her head down with a huff.

"I'll update you in a couple of hours unless something terrible happens," Jimmy says, clapping a hand on Ian's shoulder.

Ian nods and Jimmy heads around the truck to climb up into the driver seat. The diesel engine roars to life and he takes off, driving faster than seems safe.

"Finally," Stocke says.

I turn to face the direction she is looking and see Ivy and the werewolf she was partnered with walking toward us. Not far behind them are Elise, Zachary, and another wolf in Ian's pack.

"Do you want to rinse off?" Colin asks, gesturing at my face and hands. We're both still smeared with dirt.

"Absolutely." I follow him to the small cabin behind us. It's a quaint structure with only one room and one bathroom. The floors are rough-hewn planks covered by a worn rug tossed down in the middle of the room. A threadbare couch is shoved against a wall out of the way and the center of the room is dominated by a folding table Stocke had brought in. Maps are set out in neatly organized piles along with a checklist of everyone involved in the search.

"Ladies first," Colin says, sweeping his hand toward the bathroom door with an exaggerated bow.

"Oh, so now you have manners?" I ask, raising my brow at him as I take him up on his offer.

"I'm a gentleman," he says, leaning against the door jamb and crossing his arms.

The hot water tap does nothing when I turn it on but the cold water tap sputters out icy water. I scrub at my hands with my fingernails to get the worst of the grime off then coat my hands with soap and rub them together vigorously. Once they're clean enough to be passable, I start on my face.

"Ian will come around, I think," Colin says quietly.

I squint back at him, water dripping into my eyes. "He seems pretty determined to prove we're not trustworthy."

"He's the first Alpha that has ever willingly worked with JHAPI. He has to be cautious," Colin insists.

I shrug and splash more water on my face. Colin hands me a towel and I dry off, having to chase rivulets of water that are dripping down my neck.

"Cautious is fine, I get that. I just hope that Ian is being honest with us," I toss the towel back at Colin. "We had to leave behind at least five werewolves we know were captured by the NWR in Las Vegas without even attempting to find them because the packs wouldn't admit some of their people had been taken."

"My brother wouldn't do that," Colin says, his jaw clenched tight.

"Let's hope not," I say before brushing past him and leaving the bathroom. Colin lets me go without a word.

I step back out into the sunshine and glare up at it.

"I thought those explosions had to be your doing," Elise says. Her belt buckle is a black, hissing cat today. This one seems like a statement piece. The pack was more uncomfortable with Elise being here than any of the other agents. After talking to Colin I understand a little better why, but it's still bullshit.

"Yeah, I seem to have that kind of luck," I say tentatively. She hadn't spoken to me more than was absolutely necessary since I left for the Summit. I'm surprised she's approaching me now.

Elise smiles and snorts. "I've never met anyone with worse."

"How did you and your little group do?" I ask.

"Found a few traps, nothing exciting though," she says with a shrug. "Glad to see you're alright though. Zachary was about ready to race across the mountain."

Colin steps out of the doorway behind me and I move out of his way. He pauses, looking at Elise, then purses his lips and sticks his hand out.

"Colin Grzeski," he says, introducing himself.

"Agent Elise Hawking," Elise replies, glancing at me with a slight air of disbelief. The pack had treated her like a leper as soon as we had arrived. The werewolf assigned to her team had looked like he was being punished somehow.

Colin stands stiffly, the two of them eyeing each other, both waiting to see what the other might do or say.

"Olivia has a reckless streak," Colin says finally.

"You have no idea," Elise agrees, raising one brow.

"You're not allowed to bond over my character flaws," I mutter, picking at some dirt still under one of my nails.

Colin grins and starts to say something else, but a shout from Ian interrupts.

"Sorry, gotta run. See you around," he says, deliberately looking at both of us. He jogs away toward Ian who is watching me with an unreadable expression.

"That was interesting," Elise says quietly, turning to stand next to me.

"Felt like progress," I say, nudging her shoulder.

"Yeah, it did," she agrees with a smile and something in my chest loosens. Maybe we can be something like friends again.

CHAPTER 4

I park in the underground garage of the hotel. This is a nicer place than the last one we stayed at. Reilly even sprung for a suite with separate bedrooms, which was a relief. I guess he's less worried about keeping an eye on me now that we're more like allies and less jailer and prisoner.

I let my head fall back against the headrest. I'm tired, still grimy from where I couldn't wash the dirt away, and the hunger is making me feel weak. My personal phone buzzes in the seat next to me. I stare at it grumpily. I've been getting messages and calls at least three times a day since I turned it back on. I unbuckle my seatbelt and grab the phone, my finger hovering over the unlock button.

With a huff, I unlock the phone and open the messages. There are a few from Lydia, but most are from Patrick. It looks like he's been texting me every day since about a week after I left. There is a gap right after the incident at the Summit, but only a few days.

November 9 09:34 pm: Are you okay? Were you hurt?

November 9 09:42 pm: Olivia, please just let me know you're okay...

November 12 02:06 am: I'm just going to keep trying.
November 12 03:12 am: I'm sorry.

November 13 08:23 pm: Mr. Muffins peed on Emilio's pillow. He was furious. Muffins is smug.

Tears prick at my eyes, and I press my hand to my mouth. I miss that stupid cat so much. If I can't be there to harass Emilio, I'm glad she's still giving him hell.

I take a deep breath and text back a quick reply praising Mr. Muffins and letting Patrick know I'm fine. Most of the anger toward the clan, and especially Patrick, has faded. Things with Reilly, on the other hand, are getting increasingly more awkward.

My phone buzzes again, and Patrick's excited reply flashes across the screen. I climb out of the car and head toward the elevators that take me to the main floor of the hotel. I keep my responses to Patrick short. Part of me wants everything to go back to normal, but normal went out the window a long time ago. I'll stop ignoring him, but I don't think I can go back to the easy friendship we had. At least not yet.

I'm sharing a suite with Reilly, but I haven't actually been to the room. We checked in early this morning before sunrise, and I had left right away to meet with the team.

A spacious elevator carries me up to the twelfth floor. I step out, and a small placard on the wall points me in the direction of room 1289. The room is near the end of the hall. I unlock the door and slip inside, shutting it softly behind me. The sun hasn't set yet, but it's habit to stay quiet when I know someone is asleep. Even if that person is *dead* asleep.

I tiptoe through the open sitting area. Recessed lighting is cycling from blue to purple to red and back again giving the whole room a strange vibe. Two couches face each other in the center of the room underneath a chandelier. The bright pieces of glass twinkle in the shifting light.

On the other side of the couches are two thick double doors. One is open, revealing a glimpse of the bathroom and a large jacuzzi set up on a marble pedestal. That looks like my next stop after I grab a change of clothes. I still feel gritty from where dirt and debris made it down my shirt.

To my left is a closed door, and to my right, I can see into a bedroom. Reilly's bare foot is sticking out of the covers. I guess the other room is mine.

I open the door to my room and flip on the lights. My bags are all piled on the king-sized bed, but it's what lines the wall to my left that catches my eye.

There is a long, wooden table and on it, neatly organized, is my wet dream come to life. There are four cauldrons; one in pewter, copper, iron, and the crystal one I bought in Vegas. A gas stove with two large burners takes up one end of the table, the chrome gleaming invitingly. On the opposite end is a shelf stacked with ingredients. Herbs. Little vials of shimmering liquids. A set of sharp knives.

I walk forward, mesmerized, and open the drawers at the bottom of the shelf. They are filled with crystals of varying sizes. Many of them I had never been able to afford before. There is one drawer with four sections, each containing pure gold in different forms. Powdered, rough nuggets, cubes, and slivers.

I pick up a bundle of lavender and inhale deeply. It's potent and as fresh as dried herbs can be. The ingredients are all vibrant and eager to be used.

I had complained most of the way from Cesare's clanhouse in Portland to Los Angeles about how I needed to be able to brew. I had spent at least an hour expounding on all the things I wish I had, and the best ingredients, and the best tools. Apparently, Reilly had been listening and not ignoring me like I thought.

I check the time. It's almost sunset. I walk back to the sitting area and pause a few steps away from the door to Reilly's room. His toes twitch and his breathing changes, growing deeper and faster.

My fingers itch with a need to brew. Since I have all of this, I want to try something new. Reilly sits up abruptly, his eyes going straight to me. The sun sets completely; the vampire magic inside of me stirs, happy that it's gone.

"You're filthy," Reilly says as he steps out bed, unconcerned that he's only wearing those stupid silky boxers he favors.

I avert my eyes from his bare chest. Just because we're roommates doesn't mean he gets to wander around half naked in front of me. He could give a girl ideas. Very bad ideas.

"There was an incident with a small explosion," I say, shrugging.

He's standing in front of me in a flash. I take a half step back, but he catches me by my shoulders and searches me for injuries.

"I'm fine," I say, shoving at him. "And put on some clothes. This isn't a nudist colony."

"That's too bad," he says with a grin, glancing down at my body.

I roll my eyes. "Not gonna happen."

"So you keep saying." He turns away and heads back into his room. I had forgotten about the raised, white scars that crisscross his back. I've never seen a vampire with scars before, hell, I had no idea they even *could* scar.

I plop down on one of the white couches, dirt from my clothes rubbing into the fabric.

"What exactly happened?" He asks from the other room.

"The NWR set out one of the missing pack members a bait. I had to navigate some land mines to rescue her," I explain, for the third time. "Just read the report tomorrow, I don't feel like rehashing it right now."

Reilly walks out of his bedroom buttoning his shirt. He's wearing his usual black slacks, but he still hasn't put on shoes.

"We were told the only thing in those woods were bear traps," Reilly comments.

"Yeah, Stocke wasn't pleased. She's calling in a bomb squad or something, and she isn't going to let the team back out there."

Reilly nods. "Good."

I tap my fingers against my thigh and gnaw on my lip for a second. "Thanks for the brewing equipment."

He finishes the last button and looks up. "Of course. You need more brews than JHAPI will issue you. Make what you need and then some. I think we're going to need everything you can brew to deal with Cesare and whatever this Bound God turns out to be."

"Sure thing, I'll just skip sleeping for the next couple of weeks," I sigh. That's Reilly, always practical. I can't complain though, he gave me everything I asked for. I do want to brew everything I can. Despite my shiny new magic, there's something about having a brew in my pocket that makes me feel ten times safer.

"Speaking of, I have arranged a meeting in a few days with someone who should be able to get us the information we need. You have to come," Reilly continues.

"Then Zachary is coming," I say. If he gets to hand out orders, I do too.

"We need to keep this small. The more people that know, the higher the risk of Cesare finding out," Reilly says, adjusting the cuff of his sleeve.

"We can trust Zachary. He's been secretly investigating the coven on his own already. You don't get to cut him out. You have your clan mates, and I have my friends."

Reilly's nostrils flare in frustration.

"I liked you better when you were scared of me," he mutters.

"I was never scared of you," I say, narrowing my eyes at him.

"Lie," Reilly says smugly, his cheeks dimpling as he smiles.

I roll my eyes and stand up. It takes more effort than it should. "I'm going to—"

"You're exhausted," he interrupts. "You need to feed."

"If you'd let me finish a sentence," I say sarcastically, "I was going to tell you that I'm going to brew something to help with that. I need to do it now while I'm hungry so I can test it."

He frowns. "I've never heard of anything that could curb a vampire's appetite."

"Well, I'm not a vampire," I say walking around the opposite end of the couch toward my room.

"You're half vampire," Reilly insists, following me.

I stop and turn to face him. "Look, I'm good at this. I may not get it right the first time, but I'm going to figure it out. I've been doing this since I was five years old and there has yet to be anything I haven't been able to brew."

"It's still a risk," Reilly says, his mouth pulling down into a frown. "If you're hungry, you can feed. You shouldn't risk hurting yourself just because you don't like that you need blood and magic."

"I'm trying to make myself stronger," I insist. "If I'm in the middle of a fight, and I get exhausted like this, I can't stop and feed. I need something that can help when feeding isn't an option."

"I don't believe that's what this is about," Reilly says, crossing his arms.

"Believe what you want," I say, turning away and walking up to the worktable.

"I'm staying in case this goes horribly wrong," Reilly says from behind me.

I wave my hand at him dismissively. I don't care what he does as long as he stays out of my way. I examine the cauldrons I have to choose from. The cauldron is the base of the brew. I run my fingers over the iron cauldron and frown. That one isn't quite right. The pewter, however, warms under my hand.

I move the cauldron to the gas stove and turn on the burner, then hesitate, and turn it back off. Not until later, I think. The heat should come in at the end once the magic has already had its way with the ingredients.

A hesitant thrum of magic grows in my chest as I pick out the ingredients. My hands aren't as sure as they usually are when I'm doing this. I pick up two crystals and stare at them, neither is perfect, but perhaps the garnet will work. Bat wings are one of those ingredients I hardly use, but I lay it out with a smile. A creature of the night feels right.

Some of the hesitancy fades as I begin preparing each ingredient. The cinnamon bark grinds into a coarse powder. I sneeze, and it billows up like a cloud.

"Are you sure you know what you're doing?" Reilly asks.

"Shush," I say, shooting him a glare. "Don't interrupt." I turn back to the workstation and carefully slice, chop, and crush each ingredient. I add a few more things as they come to mind, but when I'm ready to brew, it still feels incomplete. I frown and fill the cauldron with cold water; it'll come to me.

Deep-red magic sparks out of my chest and flutters around the cauldron. I grab the cinnamon and sprinkle it into the water. The sparks chase it down, and the water glows red and warm even though I still haven't lit the fire. Steam curls off the surface and I hurry to add the bat wings. The brew darkens and begins to churn.

I twirl my finger over the surface and the bubbling liquid beings to spin. More magic pours in; my fingers shake slightly. I curl them into a fist to hide it. I've brewed tired before; it isn't going to stop me. Gritting my teeth, I let my magic flow.

The crystal goes in whole, followed by a handful of gold. Something rich to complement the color. I turn away from the cauldron and dig through the drawers until I find a bar of dark chocolate. I break off a piece and hold it over the cauldron. It melts in my fingers and drips into the brew.

The red sparks dance in, over, and around the cauldron. A warm glow emanates from the cauldron as well, growing in steady beats that match my heart. I stir the brew gently. The brew clings to the rod as I lift it out, then plops back down in the cauldron.

I still need…oh. Of course. I grab the knife I chopped with and prick my finger. Sparks gather around the wound and carry the blood straight into the brew.

"That is odd," Reilly says quietly.

I ignore him but smile to myself. It is odd, but also strangely cute. My magic is straining to give me what I want. It can feel the need, but it still isn't sure how to do it. Whatever this does, it won't be perfect. I can only hope it helps.

The lighter on the gas stove clicks twice, then a flame erupts from the burner. I crank it up to high and watch the brew intently. The red grows darker and darker until it's closer to purple. I stir it quickly; the thumping beat of the magic grows faster. My heart races right along with it.

My heart pounds painfully like it might explode, once, twice; then magic vanishes into the brew with a loud clap. The flame goes out.

I lean against the workbench trying to catch my breath. The brew smells like blood. I'm not sure if that's a good sign or not. I grab a small vial and dip it in the brew making sure I don't touch it.

"Be careful," Reilly warns.

"I've got you here to rescue me." I grin and toast him with the vial.

Taking one last deep breath, I throw it back like a shot. The thick liquid coats my tongue and burns its way down my throat. Too much cinnamon. I grimace and resist the urge to spit it out.

A sharp cramp tears through my stomach. I double over and wrap my arms around my middle, the empty vial bouncing on the carpet and rolling under the table.

"I think I'm going to be sick," I gasp out. I turn and run for the bathroom, my legs shaking under me. Halfway to the toilet, I collapse on the cold bathroom floor.

I curl into a ball, pressing my hands to my stomach. The brew backfired. I'm not nauseous, I'm hungry. I've never been this hungry. Fangs punch out of my gums and dig into my bottom lip as I blink back angry tears. I've never failed at a brew this badly before. This shouldn't have happened. It shouldn't be possible.

Reilly kneels next to me, but his face is blurry. I blink and realize he's shouting at me.

"Olivia," he repeats, giving me a hard shake. "What do I do?"

I jerk upright and sink my teeth into his neck. Blood. Magic. Power. I need it. He goes still as I crawl into his lap and push my hands into his hair to make sure he can't get away.

I moan around the blood pouring down my throat and pull on his magic greedily. I've been so hungry. I don't know why I haven't been doing this every day. I should take all of it.

"Olivia, that's enough," Reilly whispers. He smooths back the hair draped over my face.

I growl and dig my teeth into the meat of his neck. He hisses and tries to jerk away, but I'm wrapped tightly around him. Reilly stands with a muttered curse, slipping his arms under my thighs to support me. He's walking, but I don't care, not while I can still feed.

Icy cold water pours over my head, and I jerk back in shock, my teeth tearing loose. Reilly pushes me against the wall of the shower and shoves his arm into my throat. Sense trickles back into my brain. I untwist my fingers from his hair, spluttering at the cold water still pouring over my face.

"Shit," I gasp hoarsely.

Reilly's eyes flash with anger, and he grinds his teeth together. He looks truly dangerous like this.

"You are not testing that on yourself again," he growls.

"No kidding," I say. "That shouldn't have happened. I don't understand."

He slowly releases his hold on me, watching warily to see if I attack again. I close my eyes and slide out of the spray of water. He stands in front of me in his soaking wet suit, feet still bare.

"I'm sorry I attacked you," I say, feeling like an asshole.

He shrugs, unconcerned. "What went wrong?"

"I don't know," I say, shaking my head. "I've never fucked up a brew that bad before. I didn't think it was possible."

"No one is infallible," Reilly says. "You're not doing this again."

He turns and walks out of the shower, leaving wet footprints on the bathroom floor.

I smack my hand against the tap and turn the water off, then sink to the floor as I wipe my hand across my mouth. It comes away streaked with Reilly's blood.

I let my head fall back and shut my eyes. I don't like giving up, but I can't be stupid either. I can't risk losing control like that again. My only choice right now is to feed.

I can't sleep. All I can think about is the taste of Reilly's blood. It hasn't ever been like that before. I enjoyed sitting in his lap a little too much. I roll over with a groan and crawl out of bed. It's time for another bath. Maybe the hot water will relax me enough that I'll actually be able to sleep. I have training tomorrow afternoon, and I can't afford to be up all night.

Reilly's door is closed. I tip-toe to the bathroom and shut the door behind me as quietly as I can. Hot water pours out of the tap as soon as I turn it on, steam curling into the air. I drop my clothes in a pile and climb into the huge bathtub. It really is big enough for at least six people.

The hotel has supplied bubble bath in several scents. I grab the vanilla and lavender and dump some in. Too much judging by the volume of bubbles it's already creating.

I shrug and slip down into the rising water. The crackle of bubbles popping and the rush of the hot water is soothing. I lean my head back against the edge of the tub and stretch my legs out in front of me.

The door opens, and I freeze as my senses jump into high alert on instinct. Reilly's warm scent flows over me. I turn my head slowly. He prowls toward me. His shirt is hanging open over his slacks and his abs ripple as he walks.

"Wh-what are you doing?" I ask, stuttering over my words. My mouth is suddenly parched.

"Something I should have done a long time ago," he says as he comes to a stop right next to the bathtub.

I stare at him with wide eyes as he kneels down next to me and traces his finger down the side of my neck, then further down until his hand disappears into the bubbles. My breath catches.

"You want this," he says, sure of himself.

"No, I don't," I say weakly.

He leans in closer. "Lie."

My heart pounds in my chest as the last of my self-control vanishes.

"I hate you a little," I say breathlessly as I push him back. He goes unwillingly, pulling his hand out of the water as he moves back to his feet.

I stand up slowly, letting water and bubbles slide down my body. Reilly watches with heavy-lidded eyes, then wraps his hand around the back of my neck and pulls me into a kiss. It's everything I had dared hope it would be.

He pulls away from my mouth and kisses down the side of my neck, lips and teeth grazing my skin. He reaches up and twists his fingers in my hair, holding me as tightly as he can like he's afraid I might run away. My lips part as his breath sends goosebumps down my back.

He presses the tips of his fangs against my skin. His tongue darts out, tasting my pulse before he bites down hard on my neck. I moan and dig my nails into his back. He pulls me out of the tub, and I wrap my legs around his waist. He holds me tightly, and carries me out of the bathroom with long, purposeful strides. His lips and teeth never leaving my neck.

We walk into his bedroom and he pulls away, his tongue catching a drip of blood clinging to his lower lip. He throws me down on his bed. I bounce once on the soft mattress and watch with hungry eyes as he strips out of his shirt, then slowly pulls off his belt.

I want him to touch me everywhere. I've been holding this back for too long. Hell, it's just plain been too long. I have needs, and Reilly with his dimples and muscles is going to fill every one of them.

He drops the belt on the floor and unbuttons his pants. He shoves them down and I see his hard, thick—

I shoot up straight, panting and sweaty. My arms flail out into the dark room searching for warm skin, but I'm alone. Fuck. Stupid, shitty, unnecessary dreams. I drop my head into my heads and groan in frustration. Sexual frustration. I'm torn between relief and the overwhelming desire for that to be real.

Then again, it would be a disaster if it was. I don't trust Reilly, certainly not enough for that to be more than a fling. The fact that I'm attracted to Reilly at all is a mark against him. My track record with men is unlucky, to say the least.

I throw the covers back and swing my legs over the side of the bed. I need a cold shower. I slip out of my room silently and head toward the bathroom. The door to Reilly's room is standing wide open unlike in the dream. I pause in the center of the sitting area and watch the slow rise of his chest.

The last time I barged in on him sleeping, he was laying in the bed on top of the covers in ridiculous silky boxers. My cheeks heat at the memory. I turn and walk resolutely into the bathroom, dumping my clothes in the middle of the floor.

Cold water hisses out of the shower head and I step underneath it, gritting my teeth against the shock of the change in temperature. I brace my hands against the shower wall and shove my head under the flow, trying to think of anything to distract myself.

Brews. That's what I need. More knock-out brews. Healing brews. Literally anything. If I can't sleep, I can be productive. Hedgewitch magic was the first I ever stole, and I know I can always come back to it when I need it. It's reliable. Unlike men.

CHAPTER 5

It's just past one pm when I turn down the long driveway that leads to JHAPI headquarters. In the distance is a sprawling ten-story building, one of several structures on the hundred acre property. Hu had told me they had buildings meant for training with magic that were built with special materials that were impervious to some of the more destructive elements, like fire and electricity. I'm eager to test that out.

I stop at the white line that is drawn a few feet in front of a tall wedge barrier with yellow and black reflective stripes painted across the front of the steel, just in case you missed it. They are serious about preventing anyone from driving in here without permission.

A man in uniform with a badge pinned to his chest and a gun belt around his waist steps out of the guardhouse and approaches my car. I roll down my window and hold out the paperwork Stocke had given me yesterday.

"I'll need to see your license too," the guard says as he takes the paperwork and scans through it.

I dig my license out of my wallet and hand that over as well. He looks between the license and the paperwork, then nods and hands it all back to me.

"Park on the ground level in the parking garage, then go straight inside to get your security badge."

"Will do," I say with a smile.

He nods and waves me forward. The barrier sinks down into the pavement until all that's visible is a patch of concrete slightly lighter than the rest. I drive forward.

The driveway continues for a quarter of a mile before you reach the parking lot, and the garage is on the back side of that. I drive around in circles before I finally find an empty spot. I park with a sigh of relief and text Hu that I'm here.

I grab the duffel bag that has my spare clothes out of the backseat. The only other people walking through the parking garage are wearing the standard black suit of JHAPI agents. I look down at my purple tank top and black leggings and shrug. Hopefully, they'll let me in the door.

A covered walkway extends from the parking garage to the entrance I think I'm supposed to be using. I follow behind the other agents, taking in the scenery as I walk. A huge concrete dome is just visible past the far corner of the main building. A group of six people jog along a paved trail that circles the entire back half of the property.

Stocke had mentioned that the second half of the training process to become a JHAPI agent was conducted here at the headquarters. They weeded out the weak and untrustworthy on the other side of the country, then shipped them here to finish.

I push open the glass door etched with the JHAPI logo and step into the cold, but bright building. It's bustling with activity. Chatter and the quick footsteps of people walking with purpose echoes off the tile floor. A glass elevator zips upward, disappearing into the tall ceiling of the atrium about five floors up. Every other floor is lined with a balcony. The entire space is brightly lit from the glass front of the building which starts out wide at the bottom and narrows to a point at the top.

Access to the elevators and the doors that lead farther into the building are blocked by metal detectors and guards. Every person that passes scans their badge and waits for the guard to wave them through. The lines are moving efficiently with no more than two or three people waiting at a time.

I stop gawking and head toward the information desk. Hu said he'd meet me here, but I'll need to get the security badge before we can go anywhere. There's no line, so I approach the closest person behind the desk and set my paperwork on the counter.

"Hey," I say, getting their attention, "I need to get a security badge."

They glance at my outfit, but take the offered paperwork and start checking it against something on their computer.

"ID please."

I hand that over as well and lean against the counter, taking in the room again. Hu waves at me from behind one of the barriers and slips out the exit behind another agent. I wave back with a smile. Hu, despite being scary as fuck when he needs to be, always seems to be in a good mood.

"Here is your security badge," the woman at the desk says, drawing back my attention. "It is valid for two months, and you'll need to swipe it at every checkpoint. It will work for every area you have access to. If it doesn't work, assume you aren't cleared to access whatever is behind that door."

"Thanks," I say, accepting the rectangular badge. The picture is from my driver's license, which is a huge improvement over the last picture I was forced to wear around. I pull the lanyard over my head and pick up my duffel.

"We need to head back out the direction you came in," Hu says, arriving in front of me. Thankfully, he's already dressed in gym clothes as well, so I don't feel quite as out of place anymore.

"Lead the way," I say, adjusting the duffel bag on my shoulder.

We head back outside and follow the sidewalk that wraps around the building. As we pass the corner, the rest of the facility becomes visible. There isn't just one concrete dome; there are at least six that I can see.

"What are those things?" I ask.

"The training facilities JHAPI built for the paranormal agents. They're concrete, so you can't set it on fire or melt it with electricity," Hu explains. "Each one is divided up into sections on the inside. I reserved two for us so that we have more room to move around."

"Why aren't they enclosed?" There are high arched openings every few feet.

"For air witches mostly, but also to keep things cool when the fire witches get started. It keeps the air fresh inside too," Hu says as we pause to let a group of joggers pass over the sidewalk in front of us. The jogging trail winds throughout everything back here.

"I've never seen anything like this," I say, a little awed by the extent of the facility.

"In that direction," Hu points to the left past the domes, "they have obstacle courses meant to wear out vampires and werewolves. They made sure there was something for every type of paranormal when they built all of this."

"I can see why funding is such a big deal to them," I say. All of this must have cost millions upon millions to build.

"Have you been practicing the basics we went over the last time we trained?" Hu asks.

"Yes, every spare moment," I say, lifting my hand with a grin. The electric magic crackles into a twitchy sphere in the palm of my hand. It took days to get to the point I could contain it at all, but after that, shaping it became surprisingly simple. The magic wanted to be controlled. I had simply needed to find the focus it required.

"That's great!" Hu says, stopping to examine it.

"That's not even the best part." I flick my wrist and twirl the magic around my hand in a slow figure eight, grinning in satisfaction as Hu's eyes widen.

"We're going to get to work on more than I planned today," Hu says, straightening back up. "I'm glad I asked Elise to come help."

"Oh, she's going to be here?" I ask, surprised.

"Yes, she'll be joining us a little late, but I wanted you to be able to work on dealing with multiple attackers."

"Sounds good," I say flexing my fingers. "I'm excited to get to really use the electric magic. It behaves so differently from the rest."

"Elemental magic can be temperamental like that," Hu agrees. "Each kind has its unique issues."

"I thought that since I've used elemental type magic for so long that it would be easier to control," I say with a sigh.

"I've never met anyone with more than one type of magic before, of course, but I think you could provide some fascinating insights into magical theory. It's too bad you don't have magic of each type. There are so many experiments I'd like to run," Hu says, a wistful look in his eyes.

"That would be a lot of magic to steal," I say, raising my brow at him.

"Oh, I don't mean literally every possible magic. I just meant one of each of the four types. Physical, mental, elemental, and the odd one: space-time." Hu glances at me, slightly embarrassed. "I studied magical theory in college."

"Space and time?" I ask raising a brow. "No witch can time travel."

"No, but some do have the talent of foretelling, or my least favorite, psychometry," he says with a shudder. "It's so creepy. And, of course, that's just a loose set of categories. Impervs clearly use physical magic, however, hedgewitches, who technically use earth elemental magic, create brews that cause both physical and mental changes. My Professor insisted they fell into all three categories because of that."

I come to a stop, taking in all this information. "I have so many questions."

Hu laughs. "Sorry, I love magical theory, so I get kind of carried away when I talk about it."

"Foretelling can show the future, and psychometry can show the past, but neither of those affect space," I say gesturing around us.

Hu grins and leans in eagerly. "There is an old branch of magic that some people believe completely died out after the Great War led by Aris and Izul. They were called shadow walkers."

"Shadow walkers?" I interrupt with a laugh. "That sounds dramatic."

"That's the basic translation," Hu says, waving away my gibe. "It comes from the Latin phrase *nocte viator*, which literally translates to *night traveler*, but over the years it became shadow walker."

"What can they do, exactly?" I ask.

"That is the interesting part," Hu says, his eyes bright. "There are different theories. One claims they can travel from shadow to shadow, basically invisible. Another says that there is a realm that mirrors this one that the shadow walkers created, and can return to at will. A place where it is always night and magic doesn't work."

"So, basically, a witch's version of a scary fairy tale," I say, biting down on a smile. Hu is passionate about this, I don't want it to seem like I'm laughing at him. I'm just laughing at these theories.

"There is historical evidence they existed. For some reason, during the Great War, they started being killed off. With rarer magics, especially back then, it wouldn't have been that hard to completely stamp out an entire magical talent from the world."

"I wonder how many we've lost," I comment as we start walking again.

"Probably dozens. There was a branch of physical magic that involved manipulation of gravity that was ended sometime in the early fifteenth century. Some argue there used to be witches that could manipulate ice as an element as well."

We pass one of the domes. It seems even bigger when you're standing right next to it. A flash of light startles me, and a wave of heat blows past us. A fire witch and an air witch are dancing around each other, flinging magic back and forth with friendly taunts.

Hu keeps walking. I drag myself after him, but I wish I could stay and watch. I've never seen magic used like that outside of a fight where I could appreciate it.

We walk into the second dome, marked by a sign as Training Area B. The concrete floor is divided into four equal sections. Hu reserved the two sections on the left giving us almost a football field worth of space to work with. We drop our things on a concrete bench.

Hu strips off his shirt, folds it and lays it on top of his bag. He stretches and the thick muscles of his shoulders and back ripple under the bright tattoo.

"Alright," Hu says, rubbing his hands together. "Now that you can control your magic the key is thinking about how you should direct it. My fire can be used to strike and to protect."

He holds his arms out and the fire flares around him like it had at the airport outside of Vegas. It flows around his chest, ready to lash out with barely contained energy. His hair moves as if he's caught in a breeze as the air around him shifts from the heat.

"If you were to hit me with any sort of offensive magic, even one of your brews, the fire around my chest would try to consume it," Hu explains. "It won't be perfect, but everything I can do to give myself an edge is beneficial."

I flex my fingers, thinking. "Back at Javier's clanhouse when the coven attacked the electric magic spread out like a net when it came up against the other witch's magic."

Hu nods. "That's good. How long did it hold up?"

"Not long," I say, remembering the recoil as my magic collapsed, and I was thrown back onto the floor. "It was two against one. I was up against an air witch using wind to feed the magic of a fire witch."

"Mistake number one," Hu says. "Never let them work together like that. You don't want to be stuck between them, but you want to keep them from supporting each other as well."

"Easier said than done," I say with a shrug.

"We aren't here for easy," he says, crouching slightly. "Dodge or block what I'm about to throw at you. Your choice."

"What—"

Hu lifts his hand and a stream of fire spirals toward me. My eyes go wide and I pull on the vampire magic, leaping to my left just in time to feel the fire shriek past me. Sweat beads up on the back of my neck from the intense heat. I skid to a stop a few feet to Hu's left.

He doesn't give me a chance to think, just twists toward me and casts his magic again. I flee, feeling like I've forgotten every bit of magic I practiced over the last few weeks. Before Hu can cast again, I use the vampire magic to move as quickly as I can toward his back, then come to an abrupt stop and lift my hand. Electricity rushes out of my raised palm and spreads out into a crackling net between us.

He's faster than I thought was possible for a witch and his magic crashes into mine in a shower of sparks. The collision rattles me and I grab my wrist with my opposite hand to keep my arm steady. Fire pushes against the bright, white electricity, each of us pushing more and more magic as it becomes a contest of sheer power.

I grit my teeth against the effort and try to think. It's becoming increasingly obvious I'm going to lose this battle. Hu takes a step forward and my eyes go wide as I'm physically pushed back, my feet sliding across the rough concrete.

I twist my arm and snap my hand closed. The net of electricity crashes around the fire, bright white drowning out the red-hot flames. The crush of magic on magic explodes and Hu and I are flung apart. I twist mid-air, using my vampire magic to land on my feet and sprint forward, throwing a quick bolt of lightning that forces him to stay on the defensive.

A growl makes the hair on the back of my neck prickle, but it's too late. Huge paws hit my shoulders and I'm crushed down onto the concrete, just barely catching myself with my forearms to prevent my face from taking the brunt of the fall.

I lay underneath Elise, who teasingly nips my ear, and try to catch my breath.

"Fucking cheaters," I pant.

Hu is laughing so hard he can barely breathe.

Elise steps off of me and sits back on her haunches, tongue lolling out of her mouth as she does her best impersonation of a friendly dog who didn't just tackle someone in the middle of winning a sparring session.

I sit up with a groan and glare at them both. Smug assholes.

Hu walks over, still grinning. "You did great, Olivia. However, make sure you counter-attack faster next time. And don't waste as long pushing back in a contest of strength."

Elise huffs in agreement, her tail thumping against the ground as is to emphasize his point.

"You really go for realism in training," I say as I struggle to my feet. My forearms are scraped from the impact, but I have a feeling I'm only going to end up with more scrapes and bruises before we're done.

"No other way to do it," Hu says.

"And here I thought you were the nice one on the team," I say with a grin. I'd still be lost without Hu's help, and honestly, I find this kind of training exhilarating. "I guess the other lesson is to pay attention to my surroundings and threats that may show up after the fight has started?"

Hu nods and lifts his hands for a high five which I deliver with a resounding smack. "There's hope for you yet."

Two hours later I'm laying on the concrete with a burn across my scraped forearm, a bite mark on my ass, and a grumpy, singed werewolf ripping my tennis shoe apart.

"You literally bit me on the ass, Elise," I shout across the open space. "I have a right to defend myself."

She looks up from the shoe and turns her tail toward me as if to rub the damage in my face. Hu is laying a few feet away, just as exhausted as I am, but somehow still able to laugh hysterically.

"I don't have another pair of shoes with me you vindictive puppy," I mutter.

Elise rips the sole of the shoe completely off and looks at me smugly.

"Oh my gosh, I'll heal it, alright?"

She snorts and begins her shift back to human. The electric burn begins to heal as she shifts, but an oozing pink slash that stretches from her lower back to her left thigh remains once she's back on two feet.

"That hurt worse than silver," she announces as she strides toward me, naked and unconcerned.

"I got burned and bitten, stop whining," I say as I stand up.

She reaches me and holds her arm out haughtily. I roll my eyes and grab it, sending my healing magic coursing through her. With her already accelerated healing, it's almost effortless to heal the burn. I tug her forward so I can examine the skin. The mark is completely gone, and her ass is back to its usual, spectacularly muscled self.

"Good as new," I say, dropping her arm.

She twists around to inspect it and nods in approval.

"We've got that meeting in a couple of hours," Hu says as he walks past us. "I don't know about you two, but I want a shower and dinner beforehand."

"Absolutely," Elise agrees. She looks back at me. "Come on, I'll show you where the showers are."

All my injuries ache, but I'll wait to heal them until I'm in the shower. I need to take a few brews and healing myself is easier with fewer distractions. I grab my duffel bag, and Elise pulls on a bathrobe laying on top of her backpack.

"JHAPI frowns on its agents walking around naked in all areas not designated for training," Elise says, answering my unasked question. "I forgot once and almost got suspended."

"I'm sure you made somebody's day though," I say with a laugh.

"Why do you think I didn't get suspended?" She says with a wink.

The showers are attached to a traditional gym. We walk past the humans and paranormals lifting weights and running on treadmills. Most are wearing PT uniforms with their names on the back.

"Agents in training?" I ask.

Elise nods. "Most actual agents don't have time to work out, so you won't see many of them in here at once."

The women's bathroom is empty as we head back to the shower area. I dig a healing brew out of the duffel bag and drink it. It warms me from the inside out. The aches vanish, and the scrapes fade to pink. A nudge from my healing magic and the burn is fixed as well.

"So, you made it out of the den of the vampires alive," Elise says as she brushes past me.

"Barely," I agree with a laugh. I toss my bag down on a bench and start stripping out of my workout clothes.

Elise faces me, hands on hips. "What the hell is actually going on with Reilly? And don't lie to me."

I freeze with my shirt in my hand. I had hoped to avoid this conversation, but Elise was bound to get me alone eventually.

"It's...complicated," I say.

"I will bite you on the ass again if you don't give me a straight answer," Elise growls.

"Okay, okay," I say, lifting my hands in surrender. Everything has changed. If Elise had cornered me like this a few weeks ago, I would have thrown Reilly under the bus and hoped for the best. "Until the Summit I didn't trust Reilly at all. He drug me out of Texas and threatened to kill the clan I had worked for if I ran."

Elise's face shifts from determined to furious. "I'll arrest him right now."

"He was bluffing," I say, sitting down on the bench heavily. "I thought I was the pawn in his political games, but it turns out Reilly is just as much a pawn as I am. His sire is the one pulling all the strings on all this."

"I still might arrest him," Elise says, crossing her arms. "What does his sire want with either of you?"

"You know all that stuff Zachary has been investigating? The crazy coven?"

Elise nods.

"Cesare is a traditionalist. He wants vampires to enslave humans, and to do that, he has to take out anyone that could stop him. Cesare believes that the god they have trapped somewhere is real, and he wants to release it so that it can destroy the other paranormals races; witches, werewolves, goblins." I shake my head. "For some reason, he thinks I can kill it once it has weakened the other races enough. He forced Reilly to find me and start preparing me."

"No offense, but I don't see you killing a god anytime soon," Elise says with a raised brow.

"I don't either," I say with a shrug, looking down at my hands. "I can steal magic, but the more I steal, the more I need. It takes time to learn how to control it, and I don't know how much time I have."

"So, what's the plan?" Elise asks.

"The plan?" I ask.

"For stopping Cesare," Elise says, crossing her arms. "You're not just going to let him get away with it. I know you better than that."

"No, of course not," I say, looking up sharply. "We're going to stop him. We just have to figure out if this god is even real and where it is."

Elise stares at me for a moment, her lips pursed as she considers something.

"I'm not convinced on this whole god thing, but you clearly need help," she says as she turns away and steps into one of the shower stalls. She turns on the water and steps under the spray. "If Zachary is involved in all this, then so am I."

"You don't have to help with this," I say.

"Oh, I know," she says, sticking her now wet head out of the stall. "And you're welcome."

I huff out a laugh and finish undressing. I am grateful, but this task still feels too big. Sometimes I wish I could just walk away from all the crap with Cesare and focus on finding the coven that killed my mother. My mother thought I was a part of all this though, and I can't walk away from something she asked me to stop.

I stand up and step into the shower stall next to Elise. The water sprays down over my head I let it drown out the worry, just for a moment.

CHAPTER 6

Elise is glaring at Reilly. And not in a subtle way. It's a full-on, about-to-start-a-fight kind of glare, and I'm stuck in between them. I kick her shin under the table, but she doesn't waver. I should have lied to her.

"And then Elise tore up her shoe," Hu says, finishing up his dramatic re-telling of my training session with tears of laughter streaming down his face.

Reilly is laughing as well. His shoulders are relaxed, and he looks completely free of worry. He glances at me, his dimples deepening as he smiles. I want to lick his face.

I shift in my seat and turn away from Reilly. That dream has damaged my mind. It was easy to ignore the attraction when he was still threatening me.

"Glad to hear you're learning," Reilly says. His eyes flick toward Elise, but he continues to ignore the glaring.

I shrug. "Hu is a good teacher."

Hu smiles at me. "I was worried you might end up hating me. Some people don't take well to being pushed like that."

"I could never hate you," I say waving my hand at him dismissively. "You're too nice."

"You've never tried to wake him up in the morning then," says Aaron Cook, his partner, as he walks into the room. Zachary follows closely behind him. Elise finally turns toward the table and drops the evil look. "He turns into the grumpiest person you'll ever meet."

"Not everyone wants to wake up and go for a run at five am," Hu grumbles as Cook sits down next to him.

Ivy and Corinne arrive next, and it's a relief to see that Corinne looks healthy again. The color is back in her cheeks, and she has a healthy tan.

"How much longer are you stuck on desk duty?" Cook asks as she takes the seat next to him.

"Ugh," Corinne groans. "I have a doctor's appointment tomorrow afternoon, and they should clear me then. I'm *better*."

"Only because I have been keeping you from trying to use your magic again too soon," Ivy says punching Corinne's shoulder lightly.

I can't even imagine how hard it would be to go so long without using any magic at all. They would have had to sedate me.

"Desk duty is terrible," Corinne says, sighing. "I have a new appreciation for Staci's patience. I don't know how she manages to stay sane doing all the paperwork."

"She's a nerd. She likes it," Cook says with a snort.

Corinne and Hu smack him at the same time. Cook flinches, and I bite down on a laugh. He hasn't been as combative toward me; I don't want to start anything today.

"Don't be an ass," Corinne says. "She's a good agent."

Cook holds up his hands in surrender. "Never said she wasn't. We'd be lost without her."

I relax back in my chair as the rest of the team trickles in. Despite the explosions, everyone seems to be in good spirits after working with Ian's pack to clean up those traps. Having Corinne back is even better. She is the glue that holds the team together with her ability to befriend anyone.

Agent Stocke and Staci walk in last, along with the analyst that briefed us on the issues in Los Angeles when we first arrived. Agent Tomlinson is a thin man with wire-framed glasses and a sharp intelligence. He sets the folders he is holding down on the table and clears his throat. The conversations die down, and everyone turns their attention to him.

"Per Agent Stocke's request, agents equipped to handle explosives were dispatched to the Grzeski pack lands yesterday. They found two more areas with hidden explosive devices and will continue their search tomorrow," Tomlinson says, starting the meeting. "The werewolf council reached out yesterday with their appreciation, which is unprecedented to put it lightly."

"They actually used the word thank you?" Elise asks leaning forward.

"They did indeed," Tomlinson says with a small smile. "They also requested that your team meet with Ian Grzeski tomorrow afternoon to establish an ongoing relationship with JHAPI to eliminate the NWR in this area."

Elise sits back in her chair, shocked.

"Can we bring the entire team?" Stocke asks.

Tomlinson nods.

"The only stipulation was that Olivia Carter attends the meeting," he says, looking straight at me. "You made quite the impression."

Ivy stares at me, her brows knit together like she's not sure how to feel about me receiving praise for helping JHAPI.

"Who knew Olivia would end up a diplomat," Zachary says, amused. He gets a few laughs; I send him a good-natured glare and shrink back into my seat.

"Ian Grzeski has very close ties to the werewolf council. Whatever happens tomorrow, will set a precedent for how other packs deal with JHAPI across the country," Tomlinson continues. "The JHAPI Director will be personally following up with the team on this and has given Agent Stocke the authority to negotiate on behalf of the organization to cement cooperation with the werewolves."

Tomlinson sits down, and Stocke stands from her seat at the head of the table.

"I have more good news," Stocke says, looking proudly at the team. "During the attack on the Summit, and subsequent raids, several NWR members were captured. One of them has been identified as the third highest ranking member of the NWR, Evan Peterson."

That name is familiar. I remember Martinez and arguing with the other man about someone called Peterson while I was chained up in the van.

"Peterson is being transferred to a higher security facility here in Los Angeles. We will be given access to interrogate him tomorrow evening," Stocke says.

"What are the odds he makes it here without a repeat of what happened with Martinez?" I ask, still bitter that he managed to escape.

"That was a disaster," Ivy says.

I'm surprised she's willing to agree with me, out loud no less. Corinne winks at me from across the table.

Stocke purses her lips and gives me a withering glance. "We learn from our mistakes. He is being brought in by plane, and they have tripled security."

"Do we have permission to test the new truth potion?" Staci asks eagerly.

My stomach twists. Surely they wouldn't interrogate the prisoners like that.

"Tomlinson?" Stocke asks.

He taps his pen against his notepad. "There has to be a

recorded test proving it will cause no harm to the person that takes it. Truth potions have a very bad reputation."

Staci sits back in her chair and nods, resigned. She had to have expected that response though. I'm all for using half-tested brews on people, but the truth potion is dangerous.

"I can hear if Peterson speaks a lie," Reilly offers. "As can Agent Hawking."

"I'd like you in the room then," Agent Stocke nods. She looks over at Elise. "There is another NWR member that I'd like you to interrogate. Zachary, you'll be her second."

Zachary nods in acknowledgment.

"Alright, I'll see you all tomorrow at one pm," Stocke says, wrapping up the meeting.

Everyone stands, and I trail out behind the group. Reilly pauses at the doorway and waits for me to catch up.

"What exactly did you tell Elise?" Reilly asks as he falls into step beside me.

"The truth. She wanted to arrest you," I say, smirking.

"Arrest me? I should be given a medal for putting up with you," Reilly snorts.

"Putting up with me?" I say, raising a brow. "I'm pretty sure you're the one that's difficult to handle."

"Someone definitely needed to handle you," Reilly says with a grin.

I roll my eyes.

"Are you hungry?" Reilly asks.

I curl my hand into a fist and take a deep breath before responding. "Yes. I tried to not overdo it in training, but I couldn't hold back. Hu would have roasted me."

"I'll feed you when we get back to the hotel," Reilly says, not taunting me for once.

"I know I need to feed, but I can't keep weakening you like this," I say, guilt twisting in my gut.

"We'll figure something out," Reilly says with a shrug.

I keep my mouth shut, but I don't want Reilly to turn up with some random vampire. I have to try to brew something to help again. I'll be more careful this time. My hedgewitch magic hasn't failed me yet. I always find a way. Eventually.

CHAPTER 7

"That is not just Ian's pack," Elise comments as Zachary parks the car in a paved area on the side of Ian's sprawling house.

"Who else is it?" Ivy asks, trying to peer around her head from the backseat. Corinne and I are crammed in the back of Zachary's sedan with her. It's just big enough for three adults to sit, but not comfortably.

"No idea," Elise says. We pile out of the car just as Agent Stocke parks.

There are at least twenty werewolves milling around outside Ian's house. I recognize Colin and a few other familiar faces from the day we spent trying to clear traps from the forest. However, there are four distinct groups. They must be different packs with the way they are watching each other with almost as much wariness as they are watching us.

Ian steps out of the crowd and waits as we cross the lawn.

"Agent Stocke," he says in greeting, shaking her hand. "Thank you for agreeing to meet with us on such short notice."

Stocke nods. "It's our pleasure. I am surprised to see so many packs here today. We were only expecting to get the honor of speaking with yours."

"I invited the other Alphas in Los Angeles to join us since whatever we decide also affects them," Ian explains.

"Well, we're certainly glad they're here. Do you mind introducing me before we get started?" Stocke asks.

"Of course, please come with me," Ian says.

Two men and one woman approach our group. I hear an odd noise and glance back at the house. A little face peers out of the blinds, but disappears in a flash when they realize they've been spotted.

"Agent Stocke, this is Alpha Pollard, Alpha Renner, and Alpha Costa," Ian says pointing to each of them in turn. Alpha Costa, the woman, is the only one that steps forward to shake Stocke's hand. The two men nod impassively.

"I am not convinced this meeting is a good idea," Costa says. "In the past, the government has tended to shoot first and ask questions later, especially when a wolf has lost control. However, your agent saved the life of one of Grzeski's pack without causing her harm, and at great personal risk. If nothing else, I am willing to hear you out."

Alpha Renner scoffs quietly behind her. Apparently, my great personal risk doesn't mean much to him.

"I'd like you and Olivia to join us inside," Ian says to Agent Stocke. "The rest of your team can wait with my pack."

I glance at Agent Stocke, but she takes Ian's demands in stride and nods to the rest of the team. They head towards the rest of the werewolves to wait. Elise looks back at me, and I can tell she's frustrated. I'm still not sure why they want to talk to me specifically, and it's making me nervous.

I follow the small group into the house. The tile floors are spotless, and the walls are decorated with pictures of pack members and a few paintings of men and women that must have been the previous alphas.

Ian leads us to an open study with a window that looks out into the backyard. The walls are lined with built-in bookshelves. There is a round table with eight chairs near the middle of the room. We all sit down, but with only six of us, the werewolves manage to leave a chair on either side of Stocke and me, segregating us from the group. I guess this is going to be us against them.

"Thank-you again for meeting with us," Stocke says, leaning back in her chair with one hand comfortably on the table. "The werewolf council expressed interest in a more formal relationship between JHAPI and the werewolves. Of course, they don't have the power to mandate that for your packs. Are any of you interested in our help?"

With that, Stocke takes control of the meeting. Instead of the two of us being interrogated by them, it feels like they're the ones being interviewed.

"Is that what you're actually offering?" Renner sneers. "Help?"

"Yes," Stocke replies, tilting her head. "JHAPI was created to protect, first and foremost. They knew the best way to do that was with an organization that was not just human. We leave human crime to the FBI, and we focus on threats to the paranormal community."

"Sounds like an excuse to police us even more," Renner mutters.

"Note that I said threats to the paranormal community, not threats from them," Stocke says raising a brow. "My team was the first created specifically to eliminate the NWR. Recently, JHAPI has created two more teams like ours so that we can respond to more threats, more quickly. Having the support of the werewolves across the country would only help us in achieving that goal."

"Are you trying to recruit more werewolves to your agency?" Ian asks. He's the only one that doesn't seem angry or suspicious today, which is a big change from the first time I met him.

"Yes, along with other paranormals," Stocke says. "However, the first priority is just gaining the support of the packs."

"It seems like you care more about what the vampire council has to say," Pollard says, speaking up for the first time. He is older than the others, his hair and beard both dark gray. "They have dumped millions into your organization, and you have one of their own on your team."

"We don't know what she is," Renner says, turning his steely eyes to me. "Only what she told Ian's beta, which could have been a lie."

The table is silent a moment while they all stare at me. I hold their gazes steadily, all the nerves gone.

"Well? You aren't going to answer?" Renner snaps.

"I haven't been asked a question," I say, leaning forward to rest my elbows on the table.

Ian smirks and asks the question for Renner. "Are you a vampire or a witch?"

"Both, apparently," I say. The table is still as they all listen carefully to my heartbeat. "My mother was a witch, and my father a vampire."

Renner sniffs unhappily and leans back in his seat. "I don't like it."

"My name is Olivia, not It," I say sarcastically.

The gets a laugh out of Costa and a smile out of Ian. Only Pollard stares at me impassively. He must not have a sense of humor.

"You've never cared about the were's input," Renner argues. "JHAPI is happy to let the witches and vampires keep pulling the strings."

"Ever since the organization was founded, we have done everything possible to gain the input of the werewolf council," Stocke says, looking directly at Renner in challenge. "It has been the choice of the werewolves to rebut every offer of cooperation. This is just another example of that. We are fighting the same enemy you are, and we are doing it better, yet you still don't want to work with us."

Renner's hands curl into fists on the table.

"What are you implying?" He demands.

"I'm not implying anything," Stocke says. "I'm stating a fact. The werewolves have let their paranoia and suspicion hold them back. You could be the driving force behind JHAPI, but instead, you're left in the dark while the rest of the country forges on without you."

Renner growls, the sound reverberating around the room. I glance at Stocke, shocked at how plainly she's speaking. It's like she's trying to piss them off.

"Did you come here just to insult us?" Pollard asks, putting both hands on the table like he's ready to stand up and walk out. Costa, however, is watching the exchange with a thoughtful expression.

"No," Stocke says. "I came here to be honest. I'm not going to dance around the issues to save your pride. Has anything I have said been less than truthful? Has it been in any way wrong?"

"You're making us out to be paranoid conspiracy theorists," Pollard says unhappily.

"Is she wrong though?" Costa asks, looking around her. "It's in our nature to mistrust anyone outside of our pack. I don't agree that this has held us back nearly as much as she implies; caution is not a fault. However, it might be time for us to consider what they have to offer."

"Perhaps the decision will be easier to make when we know what JHAPI wants from us, and what they are willing to do for us," Ian says. He doesn't seem bothered by Stocke's comments. Or perhaps he just has a very good poker face.

"We want your honesty and cooperation when agents need to communicate with a pack. We need you to report when your pack members go missing, and we would like to be able to speak with pack members that might be witnesses," Stocke says. "We would also like to be involved in more joint operations like the one to clean up Angeles National Forest."

"I am willing to consider this," Costa says, leaning forward. "However, I have some questions."

"I'll answer anything you care to ask," Stocke says.

The meeting drags on for another half hour. Stocke rises every challenge the alphas throw at her. Ian asks a few pointed questions, but I get the impression he's trying to help us more than hinder us. Renner never stops being angry and paranoid, but even if we only win over two of them, it's still progress.

My stomach is rumbling by the time we all head back outside. The other alphas make a beeline for their packs, but Ian hangs back with us for a moment.

"I would like to invite you and your team to have dinner with my pack on the night of the full moon," Ian says. "It's a good time for them to get to know you as people. That will go farther toward changing minds than any of these meetings."

"We'll be there," Stocke says. "Reilly Walsh, the other representative will be with us as well. I trust that won't be an issue?"

Ian shakes his head. "We have no issues with the vampires so long as they have no issues with us."

CHAPTER 8

I open the door to the hotel room, then pause. There's someone in here, and it's not Reilly. I grab a knock-out brew from my pocket and pull on the vampire magic. Smells and sounds rush to my senses. This particular scent is familiar and particularly unwelcome.

I slip inside. Bodyguards are standing on either side of the doorway to my room with their hands folded in front of them. Their eyes are focused on the brew I'm holding, but they don't make a move to take it away.

Cesare is standing in front of the workspace Reilly had set up for me holding the vial of my most recent failure. He sniffs it, then grimaces and sets it back down.

"I assume that was ineffective?" He asks without looking at me. He flips through my notes and picks up a small vial of my blood. I curl my hand into a fist to resist the urge to snatch it away from him.

"Yes," I say as evenly as I can. "Didn't hurt or help."

Cesare looks at me and sets the vial down. He stalks forward, his eyes cataloging my outfit and the brew clasped in my right hand.

"Reilly tells me your training is going well," Cesare says. "You are finally getting control over the elemental magic you stole."

"Yes," I repeat. I know, logically, that Reilly is still keeping up the pretense of reporting back to Cesare, but it makes my gut twist with a feeling of betrayal. I don't want Cesare to know anything about me.

"Let's sit," Cesare says, waving at the couches.

I follow him reluctantly and sit on the couch across from him. One of the bodyguards takes a position by the front door while the other stands behind me. My skin prickles with unease. I can't see him, and I doubt I could move fast enough to avoid a strike. The move feels calculated. Cesare wants me to feel unsafe.

"How is Javier Moreno?" Cesare asks.

"I don't know. We haven't spoken since I left Texas," I say.

"Perhaps I can arrange a visit," Cesare says. "You should stay in touch with your friends. After all, they do mean a lot to you."

"I'm sure Javier is busy, but I'll call him soon," I say, curling my hands into a fist on my legs. I don't want Cesare doing anything with Javier, not even arranging a visit.

"How often do you feed from Reilly?" Cesare asks.

"Not often," I say.

"Still," Cesare says, tapping one long finger against his chin. "Find someone else. If you can't, I'll have someone sent to you. I don't like the idea of you weakening him if you were to take too much. Reilly is useful to me."

"I'll find someone," I say, trying not to sound too desperate. My pulse is picking up despite my best efforts to stay calm. I am angry and worried, and I don't know how to hide it if he can hear my heart beating.

Cesare flicks his finger toward the vampire standing behind me. I flinch when a hand appears next to my face.

"Feed now," Cesare says. "I'd like to see it, and it's best if you stay well fed."

"I fed last night," I say, making no move to take the hand.

"And you're going to feed again," Cesare says, his voice slipping into irritation. "Don't be petulant about it."

I grit my teeth and take the vampire's hand. My fangs push out of my gums painfully slow. I hesitate before biting down, but I don't have a choice. I don't want to find out what Cesare would do if I refused.

I sink my fangs into the meat of the vampire's wrist and pull lightly. He is powerful, but nothing like Reilly. I feed as slowly, taking the smallest amounts of blood and magic possible. The vampire's hand twitches slightly, and I take that as an excuse to pull away.

"You took so little," Cesare comments.

"I took enough," I say, and I did. The hunger is always there, but I fed from Reilly just last night.

Cesare flicks his finger at the bodyguard who removes his hand and joins the other vampire at the door to the room.

"I suspect you don't view Reilly as a true threat, not any longer," Cesare says, leaning forward and looking me in the eye. "Don't for a second make that mistake with me. Like any other tool, you are replaceable."

His voice is velvety smooth, but his words cut like a knife. I stare at him for a few breaths, then nod.

"Don't worry, I won't forget," I say sharply.

He grins, his fangs glistening in his mouth.

"I'll see you again soon, Olivia." He stands and then is gone along with his bodyguards. The door slams shut behind them.

I stay perched on the couch, staring forward. If he wanted to scare me, he succeeded, but I doubt it had the desired effect. I dig my nails into my palm. I'm going to make sure Cesare doesn't succeed, even if I have to find a way to kill him myself.

The door opens again, and I stand up, electric magic at my

fingertips and all my senses rushing to high alert. Reilly pauses in the entryway, taking in my stance and the lingering scent of Cesare at the same time. His jaw clenches tightly, and he looks around as if he's expecting to see Cesare still in the room.

"He's gone," I say, forcing my hands to relax.

Reilly looks me over. "What did he do?"

"Threatened me, mostly," I say, plopping back down on the couch. "He doesn't want me feeding from you anymore, and I guess he knows I'm not scared of you. He made some not-so-veiled threats against Javier intended to keep me in line."

"I smell blood," Reilly says, walking toward me slowly.

I wipe my hand across my mouth, but it's clean. Reilly pinches his brows together, and I sigh heavily.

"He insisted I feed while he was here. He really doesn't want me feeding from you," I explain.

Reilly growls and kicks the other couch in a violent outburst that has me jerking back onto my feet. The couch cracks in half and smashes against the wall with a loud smash.

"What the fuck?" I shout. Reilly faces the now dented hotel room wall, his shoulders heaving.

"He's never checked up on me unannounced like this before," Reilly says, his voice rough with anger. "He suspects something."

"Did you really think you would be able to do any of this without him getting at least a little suspicious?" I ask, incredulous. "He has no reason to trust me, and you said yourself that he knows you're attracted to me...or whatever."

I look down at my feet, uncomfortable. We hadn't talked about that since his apology. I don't trust Reilly enough to let anything happen, and he had gone back to his meaningless flirtations.

Reilly sighs and drags his fingers through his hair.

"This was a message meant for me," he says tiredly. "Threatening you was secondary."

"Why do you think that?" I ask. There's something he's not telling me.

"He came when I wasn't here, something he wouldn't have known unless he was watching my movements," Reilly says, finally turning to face me. "Cesare doesn't do anything by accident. Every word, every action, is deliberate."

"So, he didn't want to see you?" I ask, confused.

"No," Reilly says shaking his head. "He wanted to remind me that he could get to you at any time, and there's nothing I can do to stop him. It's a lesson I learned a long time ago but had apparently forgotten."

"I don't understand. Does he really mistrust you that much? Wouldn't he make you bring me back to the clanhouse if he did?" I ask.

"No, I wouldn't be useful to him there. If it got to that point, he would just kill me and be done with it," Reilly seethes. "Cesare finds whatever weakness you have that he can leverage, and he makes sure you never forget that he knows what it is."

"I thought you didn't have any weaknesses," I say, half-joking, but Reilly's face darkens.

"Only monsters without a conscience can claim that," he grinds out.

"Cesare can threaten all he wants," I say squaring my shoulders. "He's not going to try to kill me until after this Bound God is dead, and we're going to stop him before that happens."

Reilly looks at me, old grief showing in his eyes as he laughs humorlessly. "You sound just like her."

"Like who?" I ask, confused.

"It doesn't matter," he says, turning away again. "We're going to get the answers we need tomorrow night."

Reilly walks into his room and shuts the door, leaving me with a broken couch and more questions than answers.

CHAPTER 9

The sun is still up, but I'm already awake. I've been laying in the oversized bathtub long enough for the water to get cold and my fingers and toes to go all pruny. My phone buzzes loudly on the tile. I grab it, dripping water all over the floor and the screen.

For once, it's good news. Corinne was just cleared for active duty. I text back congratulations and accept the offer to meet her and Ivy for dinner before the interrogations later tonight. I dry off and get dressed quickly. They want to meet me there in about twenty minutes.

Since the restaurant is close by, I decide to walk rather than take the time to go down to the parking garage and then get the car out. The streets are crowded with pedestrians. Everyone must have had a similar thought since the weather is perfect. Sunny and seventy degrees even though it's early December.

Bob's Burger Barn looks like the kind of place a guy would have taken a girl he was going steady with back in the fifties. The booths are shiny red vinyl, not a crack in sight. The waitresses are all wearing full skirts and white blouses with collars. A perky redhead greets me with a smile, and since I don't see Ivy or Corinne yet, I let her lead me to a booth near the window.

She lays out three menus, and I sit back to people watch while I wait. It's mostly families here. They might know about vampires and werewolves, but none of them understand the turmoil that's going on so close them. They've never heard of the Bound God. They don't get almost blown up on a regular basis. A little girl with brown hair is pouting because her mother won't buy her a milkshake. If only that was the worst of my problems. Being an adult sucks.

The door tinkles and Ivy walks in alone. I wave to get her attention even though I wish Corinne had arrived first. I doubt Ivy really wants to sit and chat with me.

"Corinne is running a few minutes late," Ivy says in lieu of a greeting as she sits down across from me. She takes one of the menus and flips through it.

I shift in my seat, but the vinyl squeaks and causes Ivy to glance at me.

"I hate vinyl," Ivy says, looking down at her side of the booth accusingly. "It's uncomfortable and always feels sticky."

"Yeah, it's pretty terrible," I agree. We lapse into silence again. Neither of us is good at small talk

Ivy smacks her menu down on the table, and I jerk in surprise. She looks at me and folds her hands together.

"I think Corinne did this on purpose," Ivy says. "She wants me to apologize."

"For what?" I ask, drawing my brows together.

"For shooting you," Ivy says with a huff. "I still think it was justified, but she keeps going on about my trust issues and how my perception of you as an outsider made me behave irrationally toward you."

"That sounds like Corinne," I say, biting back a smile.

"You risked your life to fix your mistake," Ivy says after a pause, "and I can respect that."

"Uh, thanks," I say, grabbing a roll of silverware to have something to fidget with. I don't like receiving compliments or apologies, a mix of the two is almost unbearable.

"I still don't like that your personal need for revenge or whatever else might affect the team again," Ivy says. She looks up at me, face serious. "We all have our shit, but you can't let it put anyone in danger."

"I didn't ask for Martinez to become obsessed with me," I reply. "And I'll never put the team in harm's way. I'd leave before I would do that."

Ivy nods and looks back down at her menu. "I guess all they serve here is burgers. Even their salad has a burger on it."

"They serve milkshakes too," I say with a smile. Thank heavens that talk is over.

Corinne appears at the edge of the booth, smiling a little smugly, and Ivy scoots over to give her more room. She winks at me as she sits down.

"I can't believe I'm finally cleared," Corinne says. "It's been an eternity."

"We're all glad to have you back," Ivy agrees with a rare smile.

It's terrifying to think how close Corrine came to dying. Death seems so far off until it touches you. I push the morbid thoughts aside and grab one of the menus. There is food to be eaten.

Maximum security is no joke. The prison is a fortress. I feel a little violated from all the pat downs by the time we get inside the place.

Armed guards pace the long halls, always in groups of two or more. The walls and floor are all the same shade of dreary gray. There are no windows; there are cameras though, every five feet at least. There is not a single spot in this entire place that is not being monitored twenty-four seven by someone.

The interrogation rooms are high tech as well. They have the traditional one-way mirror, but there are also large screens set above it that show different angles of the room. Another screen shows a thermal scan of the room. I guess we'll literally be able to watch Peterson sweat.

Cook and Hu are in a neighboring room watching Elise and Zachary's interrogation. Reilly and Stocke are still in the viewing area with Staci, Corinne, Ivy and me.

I take a seat next to Staci and observe Peterson. He's unassuming. Not tall, but not really short either. His hair is brown and average length. He isn't ugly or handsome. He is someone you simply wouldn't ever look twice at. Until you see his eyes.

Peterson is staring straight ahead, his gaze is filled with hate. He doesn't know who is on the other side of the glass, but that doesn't seem to matter.

Stocke is staring back at Peterson, tapping the thick file she is holding against her arm.

"He's going to react badly to your presence I think," Stocke says.

"Good," Reilly says with a toothy grin. There's no way to mistake him for human even without the fangs showing.

"We do need to get some information out of him," Stocke says, exasperated.

"Angry means talkative," Reilly says. "He won't be thinking straight after he realizes what I am."

"How long has he been waiting?" Stocke asks the guard standing in the doorway behind us.

"Forty-five minutes, ma'am," he replies.

"Alright, he's stewed long enough. Let's do this," Stocke says.

She and Reilly put on the tiny earpieces that will let us speak to them if needed and leave the room. A minute later, the door to the interrogation room opens and they walk inside. Peterson pretends to ignore them, but he can't hide the subtle twitch of his hands.

Stocke walks around to the front of the table and looks at Peterson. Reilly stays behind him. Peterson tries to look over his shoulder, but his arms are shackled to the chair and he can't turn far enough to see who it is.

"That's going to unnerve him," Ivy comments with a grin.

"Evan Peterson," Stocke says, her voice is clear through the speaker overhead. She opens the file and reads it with pursed lips.

Peterson looks up at her, stoic.

"Charges of terrorism, hate crimes, murder, attempted murder, property damage, vandalism. The list goes on and on," she says, dropping the open file on the table with a thunk. "You're not exactly an upstanding citizen."

His mouth twists into an expression of disgust and he snorts.

"Oh, you disagree?" Stocke asks. "You think you're a good guy?"

Peterson grinds his teeth together, the muscles in his jaw clenching and unclenching.

Reilly steps closer, his shoes making a clear sound against the concrete floor. Peterson's hands curl into fists and the muscles in his neck stand out with the effort of not trying to look behind himself again. The thermal camera shows Peterson's face getting warmer and warmer.

"They have to be careful not to make him too angry," Corinne says, concerned.

"I don't see how they're going to get anything out of him other than how much he hates paranormals," I say, leaning back in my chair.

Stocke leans forward and braces both of her hands on the table. "What are you, Peterson? Come on, I know you have something to say."

"I am a warrior of the light," he snaps, baring his teeth. "I don't sell my women to vampires like cattle. I fight the war no one else is willing to fight."

"That's a start," Stocke straightens, raising both brows and nodding slightly. "Do you mind answering a few questions?"

Peterson scoffs and shakes his head.

"I'll take that as an enthusiastic yes," she says as she walks around to the side of the table. She leans her hip against it and crosses her arms. "Did you know Martinez was a witch?"

"I suspected," Peterson spits out, enraged once again. "No one believed me, but I was right. We should have known with the way he always slithered back from even the most dangerous missions still alive while good men were left behind."

Reilly nods, confirming for Stocke that Peterson told the truth.

"It's a little ironic that your best man was one of us," Reilly says, speaking for the first time. "I guess humans really are the weaker species."

Peterson stiffens, his face going red.

"Get that thing out of here," he demands. "Or are you planning on feeding me to it?"

Stocke laughs. "Man, I wish. However, legally, that's not allowed."

"They take and kill humans every day. And what do you do? You arrest *me* and not them," Peterson says stretching forward as far as he can go.

"Let's play a game," Stocke says, pulling out the chair across from Peterson and sitting down.

"What?" Peterson growls out.

"I'm going to guess where important people or stockpiles in your organization are, and you are going to tell me if I'm right or wrong," Stocke explains.

Peterson scoffs and leans back. "I'm not going to tell you anything."

"You won't be able to stop yourself," Reilly whispers directly into Peterson's ear. "You can't keep me out of your mind."

Peterson jerks away, yanking against the restraints that hold him in the chair with a shout.

"Get the fuck away from me parasite!" He rages.

Reilly laughs and walks around the table to stand next to Stocke.

Stocke picks up the thick folder and flips through it before settling on a page. "Here's a good place to start. I'm going to guess the location of your stockpile of silver. Think about it real hard for me."

Peterson grunts and jerks at the restraints again, unable to tear his eyes off of Reilly.

"The stockpile is in Raleigh, North Carolina," Stocke says definitively. The slightest movement of Reilly's head indicates a negative.

"It's in Indianapolis," Stocke tries again.

Reilly tilts his head. Not quite right, but Peterson is getting nervous. The thermal camera shows his face heating even more.

Stocke lowers the folder and looks him in the eye. "Chicago."

Reilly smiles. "That's it."

Peterson growls and spits at Reilly. "Get out of my head abomination! Get out!"

Stocke adjusts the folder and settles in to list off the other places they want to confirm. Peterson continues his struggle.

"He really thinks Reilly can read his mind," I say in surprise and amusement.

"They're using his own worst fears against him," Ivy says, nodding in approval. "It's a brilliant tactic. Stocke is good at getting into people's heads like that."

"Zachary's father was like that too," I comment.

"You knew his father?" Ivy asks, her brows pinching together.

I shift in my seat. I hadn't realized that wasn't common knowledge. "Yeah, I was kind of half adopted by his family way back when. I hadn't seen Zachary in years before he showed up in Texas though."

"Oh," Corinne says, realization forming on her face. "That's why Cook has always been so rude to you."

Ivy laughs. "That makes so much more sense."

I cross my arms and intensely regret speaking up.

"Zachary recovered from the heartbreak just fine," I mutter. "Did he tell everyone about that?"

Corinne pats me on the shoulder. "He sure did," she says pityingly.

I turn my attention back to Peterson, who is getting angrier as the interrogation goes on. Each time Reilly can detect the way his heart speeds up as Stocke guesses a location correctly, he becomes more convinced Reilly is somehow reading his mind.

The other team crowds into the viewing room as Stocke and Reilly are wrapping up.

"What the hell did they do to this guy?" Cook asks as he watches Peterson let loose a stream of curses at Reilly.

Ivy launches into an explanation. I move to the back of the room, ready to be out of this place. It was satisfying to see Peterson break like that, but all the information they got just reminds me how much more there is, and always will be, for JHAPI to do. It's exhausting.

"That was genius," Corinne exclaims as Reilly and Stocke walk back in the room.

"We'll see," Stocke says, shaking her head. "Everything we got in there could be highly inaccurate."

"You got him angry enough to be honest," Ivy says. "He was scared. You got something right at least."

A guard comes to return Peterson to his room. He tries to fight the guards, but his movements are too restricted to be effective.

The team files out of the room and I trail behind. Reilly waits for me.

"Are we still going to talk to your mysterious contact tonight?" I ask.

Reilly nods. "Yes, Zachary said he would meet us in the hotel parking garage around eleven pm."

"Where are we going, exactly?" I ask.

"My contact owns a bar downtown," Reilly says, looking me up and down critically. "Wear something nice."

"Only if you promise me tequila," I say.

Reilly shakes his head with a sigh. "I promise," he says, resigned.

CHAPTER 10

Reilly parks the car in a dimly lit parking lot overshadowed by an ornate building. I'm not sure if it's gothic, or just gaudy. Flowering vines grow up the stone walls of the castle-like structure. A giant, neon sign spells out FANGERS, flashing brightly with red light.

"What the hell is this place?" I ask as I step out of the car and adjust my tight dress.

"An eye-sore," Zachary mutters.

"The most popular nightclub in Los Angeles," Reilly says, ignoring Zachary, and nodding toward the line that wraps around the building. "It caters to vampires, so of course, the humans want in too."

"Are we even going to get in?" I ask, incredulous. I've never seen that many people lined up for a nightclub before. And, if I'm honest, judging by the outside, I don't really get it.

"We're on the list," Reilly says, adjusting his cuffs. "Did you really think I'd bring you two here just to stand in line?"

I snort. "You like showing up places unannounced."

Reilly leads us to the front of the line. A few people give us the stink-eye, but most of them are staring at us eagerly. They must be assuming we're all vampires.

"Reilly Walsh," Reilly tells the bouncer in a bored tone. The hulking man looks over his list and nods once. Another employee behind him lifts the rope and lets us past.

The red carpet leads into a dark tunnel. The stone around us is cold and damp. We're walking up a fairly steep incline. Zachary stumbles behind me and reaches out to steady himself on my back.

"Sorry," he says quietly. "It's ridiculously dark in here."

"They're going overboard on the creepy vampire vibes," I say, pulling him up to walk beside me. I keep a hand on his arm to make sure he doesn't walk into a wall. Until Zachary had tripped, I hadn't realized that I was relying on the vampire magic to see.

The tunnel turns sharply left and right several times before we finally reach a section that is lit. Red light shines from tinted bulbs hanging from the ceiling. The thump of music echoes toward us. The beat is loud enough to feel in my gut.

The tunnel ends abruptly at a short staircase. Another bouncer sits in front of the heavy, wooden door, but he doesn't request ID or anything else; he opens the door without comment.

Music pounds out of the central area of the nightclub. We walk inside, and I look around in awe, it's a spectacle. While the outside was gaudy and kitschy, the inside is whatever everyone always hopes a nightclub will be.

Hot guys and hot women are grinding underneath the flashing lights. Dancers hang from the ceiling in cages and from long silk scarves performing elegant acrobatics. The bartenders are flashy, spinning the bottles as they pour. A DJ stands on a platform raised above the rest of the room with flashing lights dancing behind him.

"What now?" I lean over and shout at Reilly.

He grabs my arm and leads Zachary and me toward a staircase I hadn't noticed in the back of the room. It leads down.

The heavy pounding of the music fades into the background as we descend to the lower level. The flashing lights give way to flickering firelight simulated by wide screens built into the walls. There is no dancing down here, but there are couches and private nooks where couples, and small groups, are flirting and feeding. The entire atmosphere is more intimate and dark.

"Do you want a drink?" Reilly asks.

I nod. "Absolutely."

We weave our way over to the bar. Reilly and Zachary both get leered at on the way over. I have to tug Zachary along when a particularly busty woman with big, blue eyes winks at him.

"You're no fun," Zachary complains.

"She would eat you for breakfast," I say, laughing at him.

"I'd let her," Zachary says wistfully.

Reilly orders me a shot of tequila at the bar then wanders off into the crowd. I lean back against the bar to wait for my drink. The mix of people down here is fascinating. It's mostly vampires and humans, but a few are definitely werewolves. A witch here and there, but not many of those.

"You don't find places like this in Dallas, Texas," Zachary comments.

"No kidding," I agree, shaking my head.

A vampire leans into a necker next to me, knocking my elbow. I glare at them and turn back to the bar. The woman looks a little peaky to me already. I narrow my eyes. I doubt she should be fed on anymore.

The necker's eyes glaze over and a light sheen of sweat forms on her brow. I frown and pick up the shot the bartender sets in front of me, but I'm too distracted to drink it. That vampire has to stop feeding from her soon, or she's going to end up passed out in the parking lot from blood loss.

Her cheeks lose their color, and her lips follow. I smack my drink down on the bar. The vampire isn't paying any attention to me though, his eyes are shut as he slurps down the necker's blood.

I reach out of flick him on the nose. Electricity leaps from my finger and leaves a bright red mark all the way up his forehead.

"You've gotta leave some blood for her, asshole," I snap as I yank the necker toward me. She collapses onto my chest, her head flopping around. She can't even stand.

The vampire hisses, his fangs still bloody, and swings at me. I duck under the fast but clumsy attack and shove the necker at Zachary who catches her and pulls her back into the crowd. With her out of the way, I face the now furious vampire.

"Who the fuck do you think you are?" He demands.

I grab the shot and toss it back, then slam the glass down on the table. "The lady about to kick your ass."

He growls and lunges, but he doesn't have Reilly's speed or finesse. Hell, he couldn't even keep up with Hu. I step to the side and kick him in the balls as hard as I can.

The fight has drawn attention now. Two vampires appear behind the guy I just kicked. One of them helps him up while the other takes a step toward me.

"Enough," Reilly says from behind me. He looks at the three vampires and gives a short bow. "Apologies for the—"

"You are not apologizing for shit," I interrupt as I shoot a glare at Reilly.

Reilly grinds his teeth together and grabs my arm roughly, attempting to drag me away from the group, but I jerk out of his grasp.

"We are not here for this," Reilly hisses quietly.

"I think you should let him apologize, you dumb bitch," one of the vampires shouts at us.

"I think you should kiss my ass," I shout back, stepping in front of Reilly.

A crowd has formed around us, leaving only the space between me and the vampires empty. The one I kicked struggles to his feet, his face crimson with anger and embarrassment.

"I think the lady is right," a smooth voice says, cutting through the chatter. The entire bar goes silent. A vampire with long, blond hair and a face that you can't help but stare at walks up to the edge of the circle, the crowd flowing around him like they're afraid to touch him.

The three vampires step back, each bowing their head slightly.

"She attacked me, completely unprovoked," the first one explains.

"You were about to embarrass yourself, Gerard," the blond vampire purrs. "And me. Do you know how long it has been since someone drained a necker in my bar?"

Gerard shrinks back, shaking his head.

In a flash of movement I can't follow the blond vampire is standing over Gerard. He wrenches back Gerard's head with a handful of hair and bends down close to his face.

"Literally fucking never," the blond vampire growls. He yanks Gerard forward, sending him sprawling across the floor of the bar. "Get out, your clan is no longer welcome here."

The crowd parts again as the disgraced vampires scurry away, and the blond vampire turns to me with a smile that sends a chill down my spine.

"Olivia Carter, you make quite the entrance," he says with a grin. He approaches, eyes flicking to Reilly for a moment before he stops in front of me and grabs both of my hands. "My name is Adrian, I'm sure you were dying to know."

"I was getting curious," I admit, taken aback by the hand holding and the fact that he knows who I am.

"Olivia," Zachary says urgently. "Shouldn't she be waking up by now?"

I pull my hands away from Adrian and hurry over to the necker Zachary is still holding. Her neck is still bleeding sluggishly, and her breathing is unsteady.

"Shit," I say, pressing my hands to her neck. I don't have any of my blood replenishing brews with me. I came prepared for a fight, not this. I push healing magic into her, trying to restore the damage to her neck at least.

Adrian appears at my shoulder holding a small vial.

"This might be useful," he says as he tips it into her mouth. The brew rushes through her body, warming it as it restores her blood.

"I've never seen a bar keep that on hand before," I comment as lower my hands. The necker is beginning to stir, but she's going to have a hell of a headache.

Adrian smiles and tosses the empty vial over his shoulder. A man in a black suit deftly catches it and slips it into his pocket.

"People dying gets messy," Adrian turns to his bodyguard. "Get her back home."

Zachary hands the groggy woman off and adjusts his blazer.

"And who might you be?" Adrian asks, leaning toward Zachary. I can't be sure, but it looks like he's smelling him.

"Zachary Brunson," Zachary says, extending his hand.

Adrian takes it and kisses his knuckles before turning and pulling Zachary's arm into his. Adrian slips his arm into mine as well and begins leading us toward the VIP section we had been barred from earlier. I glance back at Reilly who is watching us with a frown on his face.

"Come along, Reilly," Adrian says in a sing-song voice. "I haven't forgotten about you."

Reilly rolls his eyes but follows.

Adrian leads us past the thick, red velvet curtains that hide the VIP section from view. The music is quieter back here, but the beat of the bass is more intense. The flashing lights are replaced with a dim red glow that doesn't quite reach the dark corners of the room.

There are couches scattered around the space and narrow walls that turn the room into a maze. A woman is suspended from the ceiling by a set of aerial silks. She undulates and rolls upward, her long legs moving with effortless precision.

At the very back of the room, on a raised pedestal, sits what can only be described as a throne. It's made of plush black velvet and twisted iron that extends several feet high. Adrian releases our arms and moves ahead of us at vampire speed, his long hair trailing behind him. He turns and sits down on his throne, crossing his legs and leaning back to take in the three of us.

His bodyguards move a couch in front of the throne and motion for us to sit. Zachary and Reilly each take an end, leaving me to sit in the center. I cross my legs uncomfortably and stare up at Adrian.

"Now, I think I already know what you want," Adrian begins, "but I do love hearing people ask for my help. So, indulge me," he says, spreading his hands wide in invitation.

We had already agreed to start with the most important question. Reilly shifts and leans forward slightly.

"What is the prophecy of the Day of Breaking?" Reilly asks.

"Ah, a history lesson. Let's see this one was prophesied by Allaghar the Prolific," Adrian sighs, his lips pulling down into a frown. He clears this throat, then begins to recite.

"Bound will be unbound
   God will fight God
   Filled with the blood of the weak
   The Key must be found
   Lest Chaos consume
   And magic be lost
   The Key must return to ash
   What was born of it

"It's a bit long winded if you ask me, but it gets the point across," he says with a shrug. "The old goblin languages don't really translate well."

"The prophecy is from a goblin?" I ask. Maybelle had scoffed at Gerard's premonitions, but I always wondered how he knew so much.

"Of course, all the great prophets have been goblins," Adrian says, waving my question away. He twirls a lock of hair around his finger and his eyes stray to one of the dancing girls. I have a feeling we can't afford to lose his attention.

"What is the key to the prophecy?" I ask.

Adrian turns his focus back to me. "That's the question everyone has been asking for two millennia. I'm sure I'll figure it out eventually."

"Is the Bound God even real?" Zachary asks, doubt evident in his voice.

"Many powerful people certainly think so," Adrian says, tilting his head to the side. "Do you doubt the prophecy, Zachary?"

"Yes," Zachary says, crossing his arms. "It's been two millennia like you said. He hasn't made an appearance in all that time."

I glance at Zachary. He has been unconvinced that this god exists since the beginning, but the prophecy makes my skin itch. There has to be something to it. Cesare is evil and power hungry, but I don't think he is gullible.

"Hmm," Adrian taps his finger against his lips. "I suppose we can't all be believers."

"How do you kill the Bound God?" Reilly asks.

Adrian sits up, eyes bright with interest. "Now we're on the right track. However, what might you need to know before you kill someone?"

Reilly sighs, grinding his teeth together in annoyance before he responds. "Where is the Bound God?"

"Bingo!" Adrian exclaims, pointing at Reilly. "Though, the answer to that is interesting."

WITCH'S BITE

He leans forward and snaps his fingers at a shot girl walking through the section with a tray of drinks. She hurries over.

"Bring me a drink," he says before looking at us. "Would you like anything?"

We all shake our heads, and I wonder what exactly he is going to be drinking. Reilly always turned his nose up at human foods. I really hope it's not a goblet of blood.

"Now," Adrian says as the girl hurries away. "Location is an interesting thing if you think about it. For example, if someone is dead, their rotting corpse sits in a grave. But," he smacks his hand down on the armrest, "that's hardly where *they* are."

"Are you saying the Bound God is dead?" Reilly asks, his brows pinching together.

"No, of course not," Adrian says dismissively. "I'm saying there are places outside of the physical realm. Places I can't point out on a map. The legends claim this alleged god is trapped in just such a place, and the Praesidio coven guards the entrance to this realm."

I stiffen at the mention of the coven. We hadn't been able to find out their name before.

"The Praesidio coven," Zachary says. "Where are they?"

"They stay close to the source of power," Adrian says, eyes flicking from Zachary to me, "since they control the witch council."

"Who is the coven leader?" I demand, leaning forward and bracing my hands on my knees. I want to run up onto the pedestal and shake the answers out of Adrian, but I have a feeling he could kick my ass if I tried.

"A witch named Alexandra Hunt," Adrian says.

The shot girl interrupts my next question, and I have to suppress a groan. It's a goblet of blood. I press my lips together in disgust. It smells inviting, which only makes my stomach turn more. There's just something about drinking it out of a glass that makes me want to gag.

"Now, I'm sure you're going to want to walk out of here and

629

Find her," Adrian says, emphasizing the word find. "But you should know that's a very bad idea."

"Why?" I ask, curling my fingers into my palms. He's going to have to give a damn good reason to dissuade me from doing just that.

"The NWR is an organization of humans, yet your fellow agent was hurt trying to Find one of them." Adrian lifts the goblet to his mouth and takes a long drink, his eyes closing in bliss. He swallows, then continues. "Alexandra is old, crafty, and meaner than Jason Martinez. Do you really think she would leave herself vulnerable?"

I sit back and close my eyes for a moment as the memory of Corinne's face when the curse attacked her flashes through my mind.

Zachary shakes his head, frustrated. "How do you know anything about that?"

"I know everything," Adrian says, taking another sip. "Almost."

"Who is blocking my investigation?" Zachary challenges. "Since you know so much about JHAPI."

"Who isn't, would be quicker to answer," Adrian says with a laugh.

Reilly smirks, but Zachary is unamused.

"Oh, come now," Adrian says, seeing Zachary's irritation. "It should be obvious at this point. The witch council is protecting their own. Cesare Sangiovanni seeks to hide his scheming. The human politicians just want their organization to succeed. Your one-man battle against the system is futile."

Zachary crosses his arms, but Adrian is right, it should have been obvious. We're not here because we're trying to go through the proper channels though. We're here to get answers no one else has.

Find the book. Find the magic.

. . .

My mother's words echo in my mind.

"My mother stole a spell book from a powerful coven years ago, and created me," I say, searching Adrian's face for recognition. He nods, encouraging me to continue.

"Cesare has it now. What's in it?" I ask.

"I suppose only Cesare and your mother know that," Adrian says, raising his brow. "I can tell you that it is very old. It was written by Izul himself."

Reilly looks up sharply. "Is Izul the one that trapped this god?"

Adrian swirls the remnants of blood in his goblet. "Another answer that is most likely hidden in Cesare's lair."

"Does the coven know what Cesare is planning?" I ask.

Adrian downs the rest of the blood and sets the goblet on the arm. He stands and walks down the two short steps coming to a stop in front of me. I look up into Adrian's blue-gray eyes.

"Yes, but that's not the question burning in the back of your mind though, is it, Miss Carter?" He asks, his voice low as though the question is only meant for me.

I have been struggling with the brew I need to free myself from this dependency on other people's magic for days. It's starting to seem impossible. Adrian may not be a hedgewitch, but he did to claim to know everything. Almost.

"Has anyone ever cured a vampire?" I ask.

Adrian's eyes go wide.

"Oh, now that I didn't expect," he says. "Cured is an interesting choice of words."

"It almost a curse," I say. "The price you pay for speed, strength, and a long life is very high. I imagine someone has regretted the trade-off."

"Still, you're hinting at something you aren't asking outright," Adrian insists, crossing his arms.

I huff and tap my fingers against my thigh. "If I don't feed, I get weak. I've been trying to brew something that will satisfy the hunger, or at least diminish it."

Adrian gives me a pitying smile.

"Darling, that is simply the price you pay for your heritage. Vampires hunger. You can't take all that power and expect that to be the end of it." He reaches down and takes my hands, holding them between his own. "The more you have taken, the hungrier you've gotten?"

I grit my teeth and nod.

"It will always be that way. Accept it, and you can control it. I can smell the hunger on you right now, and it smells like weakness." He releases my hand. "I want to speak to Olivia privately."

"Why?" Reilly demands, his voice bordering on a growl.

Adrian turns cold eyes on him, his face shifting from playful to deadly in the space of a breath. "I'll ask whatever price I want, Reilly Walsh. I answered your questions without demanding payment in advance."

The two bodyguards appear on either side of the couch, and Reilly stands stiffly. Zachary hesitates, looking at me for confirmation. I nod. Adrian is eccentric, but I don't feel threatened.

Reilly and Zachary follow the guards toward the exit, but Reilly pauses near the curtain and looks back at me before speaking directly to Adrian. "Hurt her, and I'll kill you."

"You could try," Adrian says with a wide grin that looks anything but friendly.

I stand and make a shooing motion at Reilly. His dramatic offers of vengeance are kind of appreciated, but I don't think antagonizing Adrian is going to make whatever he wants from me better. Reilly gives me a stony look but finally leaves.

Adrian faces me and the music around us fades. I glance around and realize the room is empty. Even the dancers are gone. I'm not sure when they left.

"You are unique," Adrian says, stepping in close to me. "And it makes me curious."

"What do you want?" I ask hesitantly.

"I want to know what it feels like when you feed from someone," he says, his eyes straying to my lips. "And I want to know what you taste like."

My mouth goes dry. The only vampire I've ever willingly let feed from me was Reilly, and those were different circumstances. He was also dead sleep at the time.

"That's it?" I ask warily.

"Yes," Adrian says. His fangs descend slowly. "But me first."

He traces my cheekbone, then slides his hand into my hair and tugs me forward, gentle enough that it feels like a question. I shut my eyes and go with the movement. He pauses with his mouth near my neck and inhales deeply. I twitch and clench my hands to keep from jerking away. Neckers do this all the time. It's no big deal. Maybe if I repeat that enough, it will feel true.

Adrian leans in even closer, his breath tickling my ear, then licks a stripe across my neck. He steps back with a shit-eating grin. I stumble forward at the abrupt loss of support.

"Delicious," he says, smacking his lips.

I look at him, incredulous.

"You just wanted to lick me?" I demand, wiping at the smear of saliva on my skin.

He shuts his eyes and shakes his head.

"Hardly. I want to drink until there isn't a drop of blood left inside of you," he opens his eyes, "but I learned to resist such urges hundreds of years ago."

I stare at him confused.

"I drink my blood from goblet now. I feed because I must, but I don't let the hunger control me. Do you understand?" He asks.

I drop my hand to my side. "Yes, but I can't get people to pour their magic into a goblet."

"No, but you can take a little from many people," Adrian says seriously. "Reilly found you one donor, and however unwilling you might think he was, you didn't really hurt him. Quit fighting him on it and start finding a solution."

"Why do you care?" I ask.

"Because I believe the prophecy," Adrian whispers, a sad smile crossing his face.

"What does that have to do with me?" I ask, even though the answer has been pressing in on me for weeks.

"Don't be willfully ignorant," Adrian says with an unimpressed look.

My mother has said I was born with a burden, but it can't be this. I don't want to be part of a prophecy. Hell, I don't even think I buy into the idea of it.

"Now," he says, holding out his hand. "I want to feel it. And don't stop until I tell you to."

I take his hand carefully. "I won't take enough to seriously weaken you."

"You'll take as much as I want you to take," Adrian says with a frown.

"You don't understand—"

"I understand enough. I want to *feel* and I want to *know*," Adrian interrupts. "Do what I ask or I really will feed from you."

I lift his wrist to my mouth and bite down angrily. I hate being threatened. His blood rushes into my mouth and I pull on his magic sharply. My eyes close involuntarily. This is power unlike any I have felt before. Adrian must be ancient. Strength flows into me like a river, but I wonder if I would even be capable of taking all of it.

"I thought it might hurt," Adrian gasps.

I look up. His eyes are wide, and his lips parted. He almost looks like he is enjoying it.

"But this is something else. It is indescribable."

I hum in agreement and continue feeding. I feel so warm. The hunger is both desperate and for the first time, completely satisfied. I want more because it is so good, not because I feel weak.

A slight tremor shakes down Adrian's arm. His brows are pinched together now, and the strange blissful look is gone. I slow the pull on his magic. Despite his insistence that I do not stop until he says to I don't want to hurt him.

He looks at me, and his eyes seem tired. I try to pull off his wrist, but he grabs the back of my neck and holds me still.

"No," he says firmly. "Not until I say."

I grind down with my teeth and growl around his wrist. Despite wondering if I could take all of his magic, I can already feel the strain from what I have taken. He hasn't been this weak in centuries.

He grits his teeth, breathing faster and faster until he's panting harshly. I reach inside of him, as deep as I can, and pull hard on the magic remaining, then jerk out of his grip.

Adrian falls to his knees but glares up at me.

"I said—"

"No," I snap. "I'm not killing you, and I'm not leaving you defenseless."

He huffs but lifts his hand toward me. "Help an old man up."

I roll my eyes and pull him to his feet. He stands in front of me, pale and shaking, and satisfied.

"You're insane," I say, shaking my head.

"I'm not the one that talks to ghosts," Adrian says.

I feel the blood drain from my face. No matter how much Adrian claims to know, he shouldn't know that.

"What...how?" I ask.

"You've been touched by the dead," he says. "I can see it on you."

"You're a vampire, you can't see something like that. No one can," I say, confused and frustrated.

"You of all people should know it's never that clear-cut," Adrian whispers. He tucks my hair behind my ear and for a moment my nose fills with the scent of familiar herbs. "She is still watching even though she can't be with you, she always will be."

I bite the inside of my cheek to keep from visibly reacting.

Adrian smiles and sweeps past me. "I'm sure Reilly is terribly worried I'm molesting you in here. You should rejoin your friends before he tries to do something heroic."

I remain frozen in place. Despite all logic, I believe him. Perhaps just because I want to.

The curtain opens with a swish and Reilly soundlessly appears in front of me.

"Olivia," Reilly says quietly, concern etched on his face. "What did he do to you?"

"Nothing," I say, shaking myself and taking a deep breath. "Let's go."

He grabs my arm as I turn away. "I will kill him if—"

"Reilly, I'm fine," I say firmly. "He didn't hurt me, at all. Stop acting like you're some kind of knight in shining armor. You spent months threatening me and everyone I care about. You of all people should know I don't scare easy."

I turn and walk away, leaving Reilly to follow. Ever since the Summit, he has acted like I'm breakable. It's confusing, and I don't trust it.

CHAPTER 11

"I don't trust this," Elise says, interrupting my thoughts as she parks the car. "There's something they aren't telling us."

I haven't been paying attention to the conversation going on around me. Everything Adrian said last night has been weighing on me. The prophecy. Memories of my mother.

Dealing with the NWR isn't a waste of time, but I'm itching to do something else. We have to get the spell book from Cesare soon. Reilly had told me earlier this evening that the clan members he can trust are meeting with us tomorrow night. Tonight can't go by fast enough.

"Stocke was suspicious as well," Reilly agrees.

"We know the NWR is planning something for the full moon," Zachary says. "Keeping the packs out of the forest should keep them safe."

"We'll see," I say, patting the pockets of my jacket. They clink, stuffed full of brews.

"How many did you bring?" Zachary asks, incredulous.

"As many as I could fit," I say with a grin.

STEPHANIE FOXE

He shakes his head and opens the door to the car. We climb out and head up the front porch steps. Last time I only saw one small area in the back of the house, I'm curious what the rest will be like.

Elise knocks firmly and a few seconds later the door swings open. Colin welcomes us with a grin.

"Welcome to the Grzeski pack house," Colin says as he waves us inside. His eyes land on Reilly and his nose twitches.

The front of the house is even nicer and cozier than the back. The entryway is stately with dark wood floors and a high ceiling that extends up to the second floor. The staircase curves up to a balcony that overlooks the open space. I can see the back of a couch. It must be set up as another sitting area.

A small head pops up from the back of the couch, then two more. I wink at them and hear a squeal. The heads disappear. Colin looks up as well and smiles.

"Ian's daughter and my other nieces and nephews," he explains.

"I think I saw them last time I was here," I say as we walk farther into the house. Whatever they cooked for dinner smells delicious, and meaty.

"They are hard to contain, so that's not surprising," Colin laughs.

Reilly, Elise, and Zachary head into the dining room to greet everyone, but I tap on Colin's arm.

"Could you show me where the bathroom is?" I ask.

"Sure," he says. He leads me down the hall and around a turn. "Just down there. The door on your left."

"Thanks," I say over my shoulder as I head in the direction he pointed.

The bathroom is sleek and roomy, especially for a guest bathroom. I wash my hands and wipe away a smudge of mascara under my eye, then lean against the sink with a sigh. I've spent all my time recently working for JHAPI I can't stop thinking about what happened at the Summit. About what my mother said.

Every time I look in a mirror I hope to see her standing behind me again, but she never is. I rub my arm absently. Sometimes my skin still aches a little, but it's a phantom pain. The welts are gone and so is she.

I open the door and almost step on a little girl that was apparently trying to peek under the door. I freeze with one foot in the air as she scrambles backward. She sits back on her bottom and looks up at me with a determined expression.

"I wanna see your fangs," she exclaims before clamping her hands over her mouth like she's shocked she managed to say it out loud.

Impressed at her nerve, I grin and pop my fangs out. Her eyes go wide, and her jaw drops.

"Wicked," she says in an awed whisper.

"You should see Reilly's," I say. "They're even bigger."

"Whoa," she says, a new plan already forming on her face.

She turns her head down the hall, hearing something I can't, then scrambles to her feet and runs away. She slips around the corner just before Ian appears at the end of the hallway.

"I see you've met my youngest," he says, motioning in the direction the girl just disappeared.

"Apparently," I say, shoving my hands in my pockets. "What's her name?"

"Eliza," Ian says, coming to a stop in front of me and blocking the hallway.

"I'm sure she's a handful," I comment, not sure why Ian is striking up a conversation with me alone. "She seems fearless. Those are always the kids getting into trouble."

"That is very true," Ian agrees with a laugh. He looks at me contemplatively, sliding his hands into his pockets.

"Did you have a question?" I prompt, trying not to sound rude. I'm not going to stand here all evening while he sorts out his thoughts.

"You said that you are half witch, and half vampire," Ian says finally. "However, that doesn't explain how you can use different types of magic."

I shrug. "I'm unique, I guess."

"Can you use every type of magic?" He presses.

"No," I tilt my head, considering how much to explain before deciding on blunt honesty. "Only the types of magic I've stolen from other paranormals."

His mouth thins as my words sink in. "You steal it?"

"Borrow might be a better word," I say thoughtfully. "Or copy? They don't lose their magic permanently. Depending on how much I take they can recover in a day or a couple of weeks. I keep what I take though."

He grinds his teeth together. "And how many people have you stolen magic from?"

I shake my head and sigh, then try to walk past him, but he grabs my arm. I look down at the fingers clamped around my arm, then slowly back up to his face.

"Let go of me," I say, letting some anger leak into my tone. "Or do you want to see how it works?"

He releases my arm, but his lips curl into a sneer. "Is that a threat?" he growls

"I haven't taken magic from anyone that didn't deserve it, or give the magic to me willingly," I bite out. "But I'm not here to be interrogated."

"I don't know if I trust you," he says, his voice low and dangerous.

"And I'm sure I don't trust you," I say. "Are you going to tell us the real reason you asked the entire team to come to dinner?"

His face closes off and his eyes go hard. "I don't know what you're talking about."

I tilt my head to the side and tap my ear. "Lie."

Ian steps to the side, out of my way. "Perhaps it's best if you rejoin your team."

"No kidding," I mutter as I brush past him and walk down the hall. I round the corner and almost walk into Reilly, who was walking in the opposite direction. Reilly stops and looks back over my shoulder at Ian, something passing between them.

"It's fine," I say, just above a whisper.

Reilly nods, then follows me toward the dining room.

The dining room table is actually two huge tables set end to end. It's set with plates and silverware, but the food is laid out buffet style in the adjoining room. The pack is still milling around and chatting.

Corinne has managed to include herself in a small circle of women and is talking animatedly about something. Ivy is hovering close by, but like most of the rest of the team, the pack just walks around her without a word. Stocke has also found someone to talk to, but they don't look happy about it.

"What a warm welcome," I murmur to Reilly.

"Everyone is on edge," he replies just as quietly. "They're not just suspicious of the team, there is something else going on."

Colin walks in holding a huge tray of freshly grilled burgers. He carries them through the crowd toward where the rest of the food is laid out. A couple of people try to grab a piece of meat as he passes them, but he dodges the attempts.

"Dinner is ready," Ian announces. "Please, let our guests get their food first."

I reluctantly grab a plate and while Reilly sits down at the table. The wolves look at him and whisper among themselves. I fall into step beside Elise. She is looking particularly bitchy.

"What was that all about?" Elise asks, nodding her head toward the hallway.

"No clue," I reply.

We near a small group of werewolves standing near the entrance to the kitchen.

"Traitor," one of them whispers as Elise walks past.

She doesn't flinch or acknowledge him in any way. I stop and glare at him.

"You want to try that again?" I hiss. First Ian, and now this. If these assholes are going to ask us here, without even telling us the truth about the situation, they can at least try to be polite.

The werewolf looks me up and down and turns away dismissively. My fingers twitch with the urge to zap him, but I feel a presence at my elbow.

"You aren't going to pass on one of my famous burgers are you, Olivia?" Colin asks, squeezing my elbow gently.

Colin is lucky I like him. I tear my eyes away from the asshole that insulted Elise and shake my head. "No way, I'm starving."

"Come on then," Colin says, guiding me away with a relieved sigh.

I rejoin Elise in the line. She's staring straight ahead with a blank expression, but I can tell she's furious. I pull on my vampire magic, and all the chatter grows in volume. I can pick out what she's hearing, and can't turn off. The word traitor is used a lot, along with other less flattering terms. I don't know how she isn't shifting and ripping them all apart.

We move through the line quickly and take our seats. Reilly frowns at my plate of food, but the burger smells amazing. I tap my fingers impatiently against the table as we wait for the rest of the pack to get their food. Elise had warned us that it was an unspoken rule to not eat until everyone was seated. Personally, I think it's a dumb rule. My burger is getting cold.

Colin sits down across from me and Reilly with his own plate of food.

"Where are you from originally, Agent Hawking?" Colin asks, drawing her attention.

"New York," Elise says, "but not the city. My pack is in the north-eastern part of the state."

A slender woman with dirty blonde hair sits down next to Colin and beams at me.

"Hi, I'm Keri," she says, extending her hand across the table. "We sort of met."

"Oh," I say, leaning over to shake her hand. "Nice to officially meet you."

"My memories of the whole thing are really fuzzy," she says, still smiling. "You seemed so menacing out in the woods, but I wasn't really thinking straight. All I remember is that you tackled Colin. I thought you were trying to kill us both."

Colin lays his arm over the back of her chair and looks at her fondly. That explains a lot. He hadn't mentioned she was his girlfriend, or at least that he wanted her to be.

"You were pretty drugged up," I say with a polite smile.

Ian stands at the end of the table, and the conversation quiets. "I want to thank the JHAPI agents for joining us today on such short notice," he says, nodding toward Agent Stocke. "I hope that they can one day be our trusted allies, and not—"

A sharp, urgent howl interrupts his speech. Several of the weres jump to their feet and Ian's face shifts into a growl.

"Secure the perimeter, go now!" Ian shouts.

"What is going on?" Stocke demands, jumping to her feet as well.

An explosion rattles the windows and shakes the entire house. Ian tilts his head back and howls.

CHAPTER 12

Fucking werewolves and their stupid secrets. I leap to my feet and grab a brew from my pocket. The room is filled with the sounds of bones shifting and the angry growls of wolves. Stocke is shouting at Ian, but he is not listening.

Ian shifts from man to wolf in one fluid motion and bolts out of the room.

"Spread out, but stay with your partner," Stocke shouts over the chaos.

Staci draws a small gun from her waistband and follows Stocke out of the room.

"Ian," Reilly growls at me.

I nod, and we run out of the room, everything else fading into slow motion as we move. I can barely keep up with Reilly as I navigate the tight turns of the hallway.

Gunfire cuts across our path, shattering the windows at the front of the house. I drop down into a crouch a few feet from Reilly who is kneeling behind a sofa. He peeks up over the back and holds up five fingers. There's five of them.

A howl comes from directly outside.

"Shit," Reilly says, jumping to his feet and lunging toward the broken windows.

I follow him, but a child's scream from overhead brings me to a halt. Gunfire cracks in the back of the house, but all my senses are focused on the sounds of a fight upstairs. I turn and sprint up the stairs following the rabbit-fast heartbeat of Eliza.

The open area on the balcony is empty. Something heavy crashes into a wall at the end of the hallway. I run toward the furious growls and sounds of cursing.

A man, half-shifted, lies dead in the doorway. Past him, two men dressed in black with guns slung over their shoulders advance on the children. I don't know how they got in here so fast, but I can only imagine what they would do if they managed to kidnap the pack leader's kid.

The man on the left has a net that crackles with electricity when it brushes against the floor. The other has one of those poles with a loop on the end meant to catch dogs. Eliza dodges a throw of the net but takes a hit from the pole, protecting the two smaller children clinging to each other behind her.

Rage fills me. All the power I took from Adrian courses through my muscles and magic sparks on my fingertips. The man with the pole looks back and goes for his gun, but he doesn't have time to reach for it before I grab his head and twist. His neck cracks and he falls to the ground, limp.

The other man lifts his gun and shoots, but too slow. I lunge to the side, the bullets striking the wall, and dart behind him. I kick him square in the back, and he flies into the dresser with a thud, his head hitting a corner with a loud crack. Not taking any chances, I stomp down on the back of his neck, killing him as well.

Eliza is watching with wide, glowing eyes. Her tiny body is shaking with a power she can't control yet. Her hands are half shifted into claws and fur lines her face. Werewolves can't fully shift until puberty. I'm shocked she's even gotten this far. The other two children begin to cry as I approach. Eliza turns to try to reassure them.

"Eliza, on my back," I command as I scoop the other two children up, putting one on each hip. Terrified of me, they struggle, kicking and biting, but I don't care. I can't leave them here.

Eliza climbs up on my back and wraps her legs and arms around me.

"Hang on tight as you can. We're going to go fast," I say, adjusting my grip on the other two.

"Okay," she whispers in a scared voice. She tightens her grip more than a human child would be capable of.

I run. The sounds of fighting are still concentrated toward the front of the house. I leap from the balcony, not bothering with the stairs, and land in the entrance to the hallway. Eliza whimpers but maintains her grip on me.

The faint scent of Colin and Keri floods my nose. They're nearby.

"Colin!" I shout, running toward the scent.

Keri appears from around a corner and runs toward me, relief clear on her face.

"Colin is out back looking for kids. We couldn't find them," she says grabbing one of the kids that reaches for her with a sob. "They were supposed to be downstairs. This way."

We slip into one of the rooms and shut the door behind us. Keri pulls a rug back and opens a hidden trapdoor.

"There's a tunnel that leads to a safe house down here," Keri explains as she drops the first kid in. I hand her the other kid, and then Eliza, who begins to cry at being separated from me.

"I have to stay with them," Keri says.

"Go," I nod. "I'll cover this back up."

She drops down after the kids. I lower the trapdoor and press it shut. The sounds of crying abruptly stops. Soundproof. I put the rug back in position, then hurry back to the door and listen for any sounds of movement outside. I need to get back to Reilly.

Stocke had wanted us to stay with our partners, and I don't want to leave him on his own, but I don't know where he is now.

Another explosion rocks the house, closer this time. I stop hesitating and rip the door open, running toward the last place I saw Reilly and Ian. Outside, light from the full moon illuminates the corpses that litter the front lawn. Both human and wolf, but thankfully mostly humans dressed in black. A fireball erupts behind me, billowing over the top of the house, but oddly it has a face. I grin, it must be Hu.

A body goes flying through the air from the corner of the house I'm facing; I run toward it. As I round the corner, I see where the fight is. Reilly is moving almost too fast to see leaving bodies in his wake. Ian clamps his jaws around a man's throat and drags him backward with vicious shakes. A dozen werewolves are spread out around him working in groups of three or four.

The NWR are advancing in small groups toward the side and back of the house. One person in front is holding a large black shield that stretches up above their heads and extends down to their feet. A small window allows them to see where they are going. The men behind him lean around, firing steadily as they walk.

Most of my team have taken up positions inside the house, leaning out to shoot then retreating to safety. The bullets dent the shield and slow their progress, but they can't penetrate the armor. The NWR is keeping up a constant barrage of gunfire; it's almost impossible for the team to retaliate.

I grab a brew out of my pocket and throw it at the closest group of terrorists. The vial breaks against one of them, and their hands fly to their throats as the oxygen is sucked out of the air. The man with the shield drops it. Bullets strike his chest, knocking him down. Two wolves jump into the midst of them, finishing what I started.

I flex my fingers and sprint into the battlefield. Electric magic flows down my arm and stretches out like a whip. Hu had shown me how to hold on to the magic and control it. Now, it's time to test it out.

I'm run at another group of three from the side where they're vulnerable. The closest terrorist is firing steadily as he follows the man holding the heavy shield. I flick my wrist toward him; the whip of electricity cracks against his side and the gun. His screams and curses as all the muscles in his body contract at once. I strike again, pumping electricity through him until he drops. A curl of smoke rises from his corpse.

The other shooter switches angles to face me, but I'm already swinging the magic toward him. It smacks him in the face, an arc of bright white lightning jumping from him to the man holding the shield. They both fall, spasming violently. I strike one last time, killing them both.

A gunshot cracks behind me. I duck and lunge to the side on instinct, hearing an enraged growl behind me. Elise has the shooter by the arm. She drags him to the ground and pounces on him.

"Dammit," I mutter, realizing I let an attacker sneak up on me just like in training. There are so many sounds and smells, it's impossible to keep track of everything even with heightened senses.

A loud pop and the smell of gasoline draws my attention back to the fighting. My eyes widen in horror. Near the back of the house, a terrorist wields a flamethrower, fire spewing out almost a hundred feet in front of him. Ian is in the path of a wide stream of fire, but he isn't moving fast enough. The flames swing toward Ian as he charges the group in front of him, completely unaware.

Reilly appears behind the man with the flamethrower, but he is not fast enough. Ian is engulfed in flames as Reilly tackles the man. Reilly rips his throat out with his teeth, blood spraying through the air like a fountain. Ian howls in pain, writhing on the ground in an attempt to put out the flames.

I run toward Ian, everything around me seeming to slow as I

move faster than humanly possible. Reilly beats me to Ian, jumps on him, and rolls. The flames envelop them both, and the smell of burning flesh permeates the air. I don't know how Reilly can stand the pain, but he doesn't let go.

I get within reach of them and smash a deoxygenation potion down on Reilly's back. The flames go out as the air is stripped of oxygen. I hate the feeling, but grit my teeth against the discomfort and pull Reilly away from Ian's blackened body, pumping healing magic into him in the brief moment I'm touching him. Reilly's face and chest are burned, but it's already healing thanks to him being a vampire. Reilly doesn't even pause. Instead, he turns and leaps toward a terrorist that lifts his gun in our direction.

Ian jerks and whimpers, but can't get to his feet. The fur has been burned almost completely off on one side and his eyes are swollen shut. Vampire magic surges through me, giving me strength. I scoop Ian up and race inside the house away from the fighting. I jump through a broken window and search for a spot out of sight to set Ian down. Cook and Staci are on the other side of the room shooting out of a different window.

"Is he going to live?" Staci shouts over her shoulder.

"I hope so," I shout back.

"Take this," she yells as she tosses a bright green vial at me. I snatch it out of the air. "Healing brew."

I pour the brew over the wounds then wrap my hands around his head and push magic into him. There is so much damage. He is covered in burns on the outside, and his lungs are scorched.

I start with the worst of it, healing his lungs first as the brew seeps into his skin. His body heaves as he regains the ability to breathe and begins to struggle. I lay down on top of him to keep him from getting away. He growls and tries to bite me.

"Ian," I snap. "Let me heal you dammit."

He continues to growl but stops fighting me. I push more magic into him, and his accelerated ability to heal allows my magic to work better and faster. The burns change from black to red.

They are still oozing, and disgusting to look at, but he's isn't in as much pain anymore.

I have used more magic in the last twenty minutes than I ever have before. If I hadn't fed from Adrian the night before, I'd be passed out on the floor right now. Even so, my healing magic is weak, and I'm running out of energy. I can't risk exhausting myself and becoming defenseless. My hands start to shake and I pull away from Ian.

He rolls up onto his feet, huffing in pain.

"That's all I can do," I pant as I stand. "Stay in here until you've healed more."

He lets out a noise that implies I must be stupid and runs toward the exit. I grit my teeth and follow. I guess I can't blame him for being unwilling to let his pack fight without him. Two wolves flank Ian, protecting their injured Alpha as he fights. Despite the still-healing burns he is still moving as fast as ever.

I grab a brew with each hand. It's time for me to go back to the basics. I lean out of the window and throw the first one. It shatters against a tall black shield. Green flame crawls over the top, dripping down like liquid. It will burn through that shield eventually no matter what it's made of. Based on the screaming, it's also burning through whoever is holding it.

I run over to where Staci and Cook are still crouched and stand just behind Staci's shoulder. As they lean out to fire, I step forward and throw another green fire brew. My aim is off and it hits the ground, but the liquid fire still splashes up someone's leg.

Stocke shouts something I can't quite understand over the noise. Ian howls and the wolves immediately cease attacking as they run for the house leaping through windows and open doors. I peek around the corner and realize why they retreated.

A spray of bullets takes out three of the five remaining groups of terrorists. The other two swivel to face the new threat, but the shields can't hold up against whatever is shooting at them now. An armored vehicle rounds the corner, a gun mounted on the roof that is firing in rapid succession.

From the other direction, I hear a roar. A wall of flame morphs into the snapping jaws of a dragon made entirely of fire. It surges toward the terrorists, blocking them in. The terrorists make no move to surrender, and likewise, they are shown no mercy. When the last man falls, the pounding gunfire finally ceases.

CHAPTER 13

Stocke steps out of an open doorway, gun still held at her side, and waves at the armored vehicle. The door opens, and two SWAT team members jump down. They keep their guns at the ready and scan the area for threats as a third man hops down. He removes his helmet and looks around, then walks toward Stocke, trusting his men to cover him.

"We have the front of the house cleared," he shouts across the lawn. "Everyone needs to go through here," he points at the space between the truck and the house, "and stay on the front lawn. Anyone wandering around could trigger an explosive."

"Got it," Stocke shouts back. "Everyone move."

I follow Staci and Cook around to the front of the house. Ian, still in wolf form, limps along just ahead of us. He stumbles; the wolf next to him crouches down to catch him. The wolf lets Ian lean on him, and they continue walking slower than before.

The pack collapses on the front lawn; many of them are injured. My hands itch with the desire to heal them, but I can't help them all no matter how much I want to.

Staci runs to her car and opens the trunk. She pulls out a bag and shouts for Cook and Stocke to help her. They pull out vials of healing brews and hurry over to the injured. Relief floods through me. Staci came prepared.

Hu, Brunson, and Ivy walk over to Stocke. Hu glances at me, and I give him a thumbs up. That fire magic was impressive. He grins in acknowledgment then turns back to the conversation with Stocke.

A red truck appears at the end of the driveway, rumbling toward us with its big diesel engine. The SWAT team responds immediately, aiming their guns at the truck, but Stocke runs over and explains that it's a pack member. Jimmy parks on the grass and pops out of the truck. His usual, carefree expression is gone as he surveys the pack.

He goes to Ian first, but Ian snaps at him then begins to shift. It's slow and looks painful. The burns stretch and crack as fur gives way to skin. He is healing from the shift, but he's still in bad shape. The shift completes, but Ian remains on his knees.

"Heal the others first," he demands, looking at Jimmy.

Jimmy shakes his head but hurries over to the wolf that looks the worst off.

A pack member runs out of the front door, frantic. "Ian," he shouts. "Luke is dead, and the kids are gone."

Ian growls, the sound resonating through everyone. Ears perk up all around us as the pack goes back on alert.

"Everyone spread out. Find their trail—"

"They're with Keri," I say, interrupting before Ian sends the pack running all over the property. "In the tunnels under the trap door in that room."

"You saw them?" Ian bites out.

"The NWR got in the house and trapped them upstairs where they killed Luke. They were trying to capture the kids, but I got there in time to stop them. Eliza had been fending them off," I explain. "She was very brave."

Ian nods and motions at the werewolf that ran out of the house. "With me," he says before sprinting back in the house.

"Are you hurt?" Reilly asks from behind me.

I turn around and flinch at his appearance. "I think I should be asking you that," I say, reaching up to touch the still reddened flesh visible through his shirt. It was burned almost entirely off when he saved Ian.

"It's healing on its own," Reilly says, grabbing my hand before I can touch it. "Don't waste your energy on me."

"At least get a brew from Staci," I say. "That's going to take a long time for you to heal completely."

"I will later," Reilly says. "Do you need to feed?"

"No, but I need a drink," I say, heading toward the house.

"You're going to steal their tequila?" Reilly asks with a smirk. "At a time like this?"

I roll my eyes. "Water, jackass."

Glass crunches under my feet as we walk inside. The once nice house now looks like a battlefield. A whimper draws my attention. Eliza is clinging to Ian in the hallway. He rubs her back soothingly, whispering something reassuring in her ear. If she had been taken, he would have been devastated.

Ian looks up and nods at me. I nod back, then continue on to the kitchen, not wanting to intrude in the private moment any longer.

The kitchen is almost untouched other than a tray of food that was knocked onto the ground. I step around the mess and dig through the cabinets until I find the cups.

"Stocke should not have agreed to this," Reilly comments. "And we shouldn't have come."

I fill the cup with water before responding. "Ian should have been honest."

Ian steps into the kitchen and crosses his arms.

"You knew I hadn't told you everything," Ian says. "Just like you knew I was listening right then; yet you all came tonight."

I shrug and take a long drink. "We suspected we were being used."

"Then why did you come?" Ian asks, tilting his head.

"JHAPI wants to stop the NWR. They want to do the right thing, so they had no problem being used. We all came prepared for a fight tonight." I hesitate, not sure how far I should push. "If we had known exactly what the threat was, we might have been able to stop them from getting in the house."

Ian clenches his jaw tightly, his eyes flashing with anger.

I spread my hands and shrug. "I'm just being honest. It would have been a fight and people would have died, no matter what. But the more JHAPI knows, the more they can help you."

Ian shoves his hands in his pockets. "I will take that into consideration in the future."

I bite my tongue to keep from calling him out on his bullshit. For someone as proud as Ian, even saying that must have been difficult.

"You saved my life," Ian says, looking at Reilly, then me. "Both of you."

"I was in the right place at the right time," Reilly says with a shrug.

"You still risked your own well-being to protect me. That is something I would never expect from anyone other than a pack member," Ian insists. He pauses then approaches me. "You saved my daughter's life," he says gruffly.

I lower my eyes, not liking the lump that forms in my throat when I see the fear in his. "I'm glad I got there in time," I say quietly.

"I repay my debts," Ian says, looking at each of us in turn. "If either of you needs my assistance, I will come."

A pleased expression spreads across Reilly's face. "That debt may be called in sooner than you think."

CHAPTER 14

I bounce my leg impatiently. Reilly said his clanmates would be here right after of sundown. It's been almost two hours and I'm still waiting. Reilly, however, is unconcerned and has been taking a ridiculously long shower.

Reilly exits the bathroom with damp hair. The scent of his shampoo drifts toward me. He's not wearing a suit like he normally does; instead, he has on...jeans. And a *t-shirt*. What the hell. It's black of course.

"They're late. Have they been kidnapped or murdered?" I ask, narrowing my eyes at him. "Also, I had no idea you even owned jeans."

"I prefer to wear a suit when I'm working," Reilly says, ignoring my question.

"You're always wearing a suit," I say.

"I'm always working," he replies with a grin. "And if they've been murdered, then it was either a ghost or their murderer that just texted me to say they are parking and will be up shortly."

"Ha. Ha," I say, not amused at his mockery.

He clears his throat and rubs his hand around his wrist like he misses the sleeves. "A few more people will be joining us this evening as well," he says. His heartbeat ticks up almost imperceptibly. He's hiding something.

"Other than Zachary and Elise?" I ask, suspicious.

"They'll definitely be here," Reilly says.

I sit up to press the issue, but a knock at the door interrupts. Reilly hurries over and opens the door wide. Ihaka steps inside first, grabbing Reilly's hand and pulling him in to press their foreheads together. Reilly claps him on the back and steps aside.

"Welcome to Los Angeles," Reilly says.

Ihaka walks inside with a bag slung over his shoulder. Viking follows. Rolf is his actual name, as I learned at Cesare's, but Viking suits him better.

Leslie walks in next, and she looks even better than the last time I saw her. She was always busty, but everything is particularly perky, and she has a new haircut that suits her well.

"Olivia!" She exclaims, opening her arms for a hug. I stand reluctantly and let her pull me into an embrace. She smells a little like Reilly's magic and a little like citrus from her shampoo.

"Has Reilly still been keeping you confined to his rooms?" I ask.

"Yes," Leslie groans. "However, it's kept Cesare from paying any attention to me, so it's all for the best."

Rolf settles on the far couch, resting his hands in his lap. Ihaka looks around the room, even pulling aside the thick curtains to check out the view.

Leslie glances at Reilly. "Have you been keeping him in line?" she asks me.

I laugh aloud. "As if that's possible."

Ihaka snorts from his position at the window and shakes his head in agreement.

Leslie grins. "I guess you have a point."

"Such disrespect for your sire," Reilly teases Leslie. He joins Ihaka at the window and they launch into a quiet discussion about something to do with the clan. Another knock at the door inter-

WITCH'S BITE

rupts my eavesdropping. I walk over and open it, expecting Elise and Zachary. That is *not* who is standing in front of me.

"Surprise," Patrick says, boyish grin on his face as he leans around Javier's shoulder.

"What," I say as a statement instead of a question.

Patrick's smile fades slightly, the worry that I'll kick them both out showing on his face.

"I invited them," Reilly says from behind me. I turn to him, confused and surprised. Reilly winks at me and Javier and Patrick walk inside. Javier tugs the door out of my hand and closes it behind them.

"Has she gone mute?" Javier asks Reilly teasingly.

I try to glare at him, but my face isn't cooperating. Patrick stands in front of me and looks at me warily, then leans in and wraps me in a tight hug. I stiffen, but my arms go around him automatically. The familiar smell of his hair gel and the tight grip of his arms cuts through the resentment and shock. I melt into the hug and squeeze him back. I really did miss him.

Over Patrick's shoulder, I can see Reilly watching me. My heart twists. He did this for me. He may not have said *sorry* out loud, but this is better than that word could ever be. Reilly drops his gaze and turns away.

Javier is wrapped up in Leslie. She is clinging to him with tears running down her cheeks. When I first started working for Javier, I was convinced he was just another mercenary vampire, but it's obvious he missed Leslie. Javier isn't an angel, but he's not all bad either.

I step back out of the hug and punch Patrick on the shoulder as hard as I can. Almost. I don't want to actually damage him. Patrick yelps and grabs his hurt arm.

"Dammit, you punch way harder now," he complains.

"Good, you deserved it," I say, brushing past him and plopping down on the couch. That's enough mushy stuff for now.

"Glad to see the two of you have made up," Javier says, pulling away from Leslie. "Patrick has been in a terrible mood since you left."

Patrick follows me to the couch and sits down on my left, wrapping his arm around my shoulders.

"No one else will come out with me to the bars and line dance," Patrick complains. "And it's terrible to line dance alone."

"Olivia? Line dancing?" Reilly asks with a grin. "That sounds fascinating."

I shoot him a glare. "I'm a fantastic dancer."

"I know," he agrees, his grin widening and his dimples growing more pronounced. I look away as I remember the heat of his body when we danced in that club in Vegas.

Leslie drops down on the couch and wraps Patrick in a hug. He hugs back, pulling her halfway into his lap.

"So you're a big, bad vampire now," Patrick says. "Is feeding on humans better than being fed from?"

"Mostly," Leslie says with a laugh. "I still miss it sometimes, but I think it's mostly nostalgic, you know?"

Patrick nods. "Yeah, I get it."

There is another knock at the door; I look back to see Reilly ushering Elise and Zachary inside. Elise looks around, sniffing subtly as she scopes out the group.

Javier approaches first, extending his hand to Zachary.

"Agent Brunson," he says in greeting. "It's good to see you again."

"Mr. Moreno," Zachary says shaking his hand firmly. "Likewise."

"I didn't expect to see the two of you here," Elise says, shaking his hand as well.

Javier glances at Reilly. "The invitation was a surprise to me too. I'm curious what the purpose of this gathering is."

"You haven't even told them yet?" I ask Reilly.

"Told us what?" Patrick asks, leaning around me to look at Reilly too.

Reilly walks over and stands at the end of the couches. "Cesare Sangiovanni was recently appointed to the vampire council. This was just one of several moves he has made to himself in a position where he can force a change. He is a traditionalist, and he wants to go back to the days when vampires killed freely, and humans were seen as food."

"It's not exactly news that Cesare is a traditionalist," Javier says, walking around the other side of the couches to face Reilly.

"No," Reilly agrees. "However, Cesare thinks he has found a way to rise to power. There is something that has been trapped for centuries that, if released, would attempt to destroy every paranormal. Some call it a God, and I have been trying to confirm its existence for a while. I doubted that it could be real for years, but there are too many powerful people struggling to control it to doubt the existence of the Bound God any longer."

Javier taps his fingers against his leg. Patrick watches him, waiting to see what his reaction will be. If Javier walks out, I know Patrick will follow.

"There's also a prophecy," Zachary says from behind me. "We talked to one of Reilly's contacts night before last and discovered more about it. I'm still skeptical, but that doesn't make what Cesare is doing any less of a threat."

I shift in my seat at the mention of the prophecy and Reilly glances at me before returning his attention to Javier.

"You don't have to help us. I'm planning on killing Cesare, to put it simply," Reilly explains. "If I succeed, the clan will be mine, as will his seat on the council according to the old laws, which are still in effect."

I look up, surprised. I knew we were going to have to kill Cesare to succeed, but I had no idea it was going to catapult Reilly to such a powerful position. Maybe I should have suspected something like that was at play. Reilly is always thinking two or three steps ahead.

Javier tilts his head, considering. If he helps, the entire clan is in danger, but the reward if they succeed is huge. Part of me hopes he'll take Patrick and leave.

"Well, we can't let Cesare take us back to the Dark Ages," Javier says. "I will help however I can."

I shut my eyes and take a deep breath. Javier wants to do the right thing. I should be happy.

"Assuming we survive, I won't forget your loyalty," Reilly says seriously.

Ihaka approaches Javier and puts his hand on his shoulder. "Welcome to the family."

"What now?" Elise asks. "Defeating evil is great and all, but is there a plan?"

"Ihaka and Rolf have been watching and listening to everything that has been going on at the clanhouse," Reilly explains. "We need to know what exactly Cesare is doing, and when he is going to make his move. Rolf, please explain what you discovered."

Rolf leans forward, his bulky muscles flexing under his shirt. "There are rumors of someone being brought to the clanhouse unwillingly."

"Were you able to find out who?" Reilly asks.

Rolf shakes his head. "I was lucky to have overheard that. Everything that is happening is not part of the usual gossip."

"They might have been killed," Leslie says. "One of the neckers said he saw Cesare's bodyguard carrying something out to the trunk of his car. He thought it was a body, but it was wrapped up."

"It could have been a necker," Reilly says thoughtfully, crossing his arms. "Those deaths are always covered up to avoid issues with the council and public relations."

"He has been calling back vampires he sired that have more independence, and clans of their own," Ihaka says. "They don't often stay long, but it used to be rare for him to order one of them to return home once he allowed them to move away."

"If Cesare is planning on releasing this Bound God soon he may be preparing them to go into hiding," Reilly says, tapping his fingers against his arm restlessly. "We need to try to stay ahead of him. There is a coven that has been guarding this Bound God for centuries. We need to contact them. We need them as allies."

"Absolutely not," I bite out. How could Reilly even suggest that knowing what they've done?

"We can't take Cesare down with only the people in this room," Reilly argues. He barely glances at me before turning back to Javier like the issue is settled.

"Then we find someone else," I snap back. "The coven will betray us, and they will try to control me. You heard what Adrian said. Alexandra Hunt is a mean, crafty, power-hungry old witch. They're no better than Cesare."

"The enemy of my enemy is my friend," Reilly insists. "We have to be practical."

"I won't work with them," I say, standing up from the couch. So much for his apology. It was all calculated. He tried to soften me up so he could manipulate me. The t-shirt and jeans were probably all part of the act too. Fucking asshole vampire.

"The decision isn't up to you," Reilly bites out. "You will do as I say or—"

"Or what?" I demand, taking a step toward him. "Are you going to threaten to kill Javier and Patrick again? Or will it be someone else this time?"

Reilly clenches his jaw, and the muscles of his neck stand out. "No, but you will be dooming us all if you don't cooperate."

I scoff and shake my head. "We don't need them. If you tried, you could find another way."

I turn and walk away. Zachary is staring at his hands frustrated, but Elise nods her head at me. She has my back at least. My car keys and jacket are on the little table in the entryway. I grab them and yank the door open, slamming it into the wall.

"Go with her," Javier says to someone else.

"Reilly, they killed her mother, you can't expect her to work with them," Zachary argues. The door shuts behind me, and I tune out the rest of their conversation.

Patrick catches up to me in the hall and wraps his arm around my tight shoulders. "Fuck that guy, right?"

"I want to shove him off a bridge," I snap.

"How about we find someplace with tequila so you can cope with all this pent-up rage?" Patricks suggests with a grin.

"You're a bad influence. Shouldn't you be telling me to cope with my problems like an adult?" I ask with a raised brow.

Patrick pouts. "I would never."

I relax a little and let him guide down to the parking garage. He takes the keys; I climb into the passenger seat.

"I found this awesome country-western bar online," he says with a mischievous look. "We're gonna get our groove on."

I laugh, but my thoughts are still back in that hotel room where Reilly is continuing his plans without me. He's wrong about the coven. They're going to stab him in the back and fuck me over. I don't understand why he's refusing to see that.

CHAPTER 15

I peek one dry eye open, and sure enough, the knocking is not part of my dream. With a grunt, I push up into a sitting position and swing my legs over the edge of the bed. My pants are laying on the floor in the middle of the room where I pulled them off and dropped them the night before.

I shuffle over and pull them on. The knocking increases in urgency and I smooth my hair down as I hurry toward the door. Through the peephole I see a young, slender guy wearing an actual cape. There's no doubt in my mind Adrian sent him. I pull the door open.

"What?" I demand, my head still aching from last night's drinking and the rude awakening.

The boy bows and holds out the rectangular, black velvet pillow in his hands toward me. Perched on the top of the pillow is a blood-red envelope, my full name written in calligraphy on the front, and a single white rose.

Adrian certainly has style. I pick up the envelope and the rose. The boy stands abruptly and walks away without uttering a single word.

"So weird," I mutter as I shut the door.

The envelope shimmers as I examine it. The back is sealed in black wax that is stamped with a rose. I dig my nail under the wax and open it. It's stuffed full with a thick letter. Adrian must be as talkative in letters as he is in real life.

I plop down on the sofa in the sitting area and pull out the thick parchment. As I unfold it another piece of paper falls out. I set it aside and read Adrian's letter first.

Dearest Olivia,

You are the key…

I do love the drama of that statement.

I can practically hear Adrian's voice, purring with excitement at his own flair. Still, my fingers dent the paper as the reminder of my place in all of this sinks in. Adrian had said he cared because he believed the prophecy. Somehow he already knew, or at least suspected, I was the key before we came to Fangers.

The only way to kill a god is with another god. Of course, the Bound God is not really a god, and neither are you. I think you'll find the enclosed photocopy of Izul's diary particularly enlightening, as I did.
Also, you may find it interesting that your dear friend, Reilly Walsh, came back to visit me last night with some additional questions. I did not expect you to be willing to ally with the coven that caused your mother's death, and since I am rarely wrong, I must assume you know nothing of this. I do love a good betrayal, but I like you more than Reilly. You have a day's head start. Use it wisely.

All my love,
Adrian Cormer, Master of Intrigue and Information

PS. The book won't be the only thing worth taking from Sangiovanni. Do be thorough when you next visit him.

I drop the letter in my lap and grind my teeth together. Reilly. Fucking. Walsh. I should have known he'd go behind my back as soon as I didn't fall in line with what he wanted. Did he really think that if the coven showed up, I wouldn't try to kill that bitch, Alexandra? This is all going to be so much harder if I can't work with Reilly, but he's making it impossible.

I grab the photocopy Adrian enclosed with the letter. He might enjoy the drama of announcing that I am the key to the prophecy, but I need an explanation. On one side is a scan of some kind of book with messy handwriting. Only a few of the letters are recognizable, and none of the words look like any language I've seen before. Thankfully, on the opposite side is a translation.

...a mistake. Aris lust for power has created a monster that cannot be controlled. I should have listened to the goblin prophet Allaghar, but I believed in Aris' vision. Cadriel was a normal child, but as he grew in age and power, he began to rival Aris in his need to control everything around him. Aris cannot share power, and neither can he.
He killed the fire witch that came to offer him her talent. We covered it up. It was stupid to believe that it was an accident, or that it was the first witch he had killed by taking too much of their magic.
They call him a God now. No witch was ever meant to wield all the talents, so perhaps he is a God. He borders on invincible, and this war has gone on for too long already. I worry that witches may be wiped off the

face of the earth. We only have one hope left, the only magic Cadriel has not been able to steal. I go tonight to beg the nocte viator for their help.

Nocte viator. Stealing magic. My hands begin to shake. He's not a god, but he is like me. I can imagine all the things I could do if I stole and mastered every type of magic. A fire witch that was Impervious would be strong enough to take on an entire coven. If the witch could also heal? Find? Had the speed and strength of a vampire? Their only limits would be how often they could feed. I glance down at the translation again. If Cadriel was killing openly, he wouldn't have the same misgivings I do about feeding off the unwilling.

I set aside the page and put my head in my hands. Reilly thought he could test me and prepare me for this fight, but he was wrong. Even Cesare was wrong. If Cadriel is released from wherever he is, I won't be able to kill him.

I pick up the next page. Izul stopped him somehow, I can only hope he wrote down some instructions.

Cadriel is trapped for now in the shadow realm. However, Allaghar warns us of the Day of Breaking. It was too much to hope that Cadriel could be bound forever.
Aris is dead, so the task of killing Cadriel falls on me. Coven Praesidio has sworn to protect the secret of his location and search for the key to killing him no matter how many generations it takes. Cadriel was born from the ashes of a vampire, and to ash, he must return.

Not helpful. Not helpful at all. A note in Adrian's handwriting is scribbled on the bottom of this page.

The rest is in the book. Cesare has everything you need.

My mother really didn't have any idea what she stole all those years ago. I refold the letter and the translations of Izul's writing, then rub my hands tiredly down my face. I have to get the book back like I promised my mother I would, but I will not betray her by working with the coven to do that.

Whatever that coven started out as they are just a bunch of fanatical psychos now. They hurt Leslie and Patrick, and they would have killed the entire clan just to get to me. People like that can't be trusted. Eventually, they would create someone else like me, and seek to control them just like Aris tried to do.

Reilly had kept me in line for a while with threats he hadn't intended to carry out. I have no doubt Alexandra Hunt would follow through on her threats, just like Cesare will if he finds out what I'm planning.

I can't do this alone, and I'm hoping I don't have to. I stand up and walk to my room. It's time to pack my bags and then see if there is anyone I can trust.

Zachary hands the letters back to Elise.

"You really buy this prophecy stuff?" He asks.

I take a deep breath, steadying myself to explain. "Those welts I had, they were from an accident when I tried to Find my mother, back when Reilly first showed up in Texas."

Zachary's face shifts to alarm. "You tried to Find someone that is dead?"

"I wasn't sure," I say. "Before your dad was killed, he found out that her death certificate was faked. All of it was. Reilly told me that he hid it from me."

Zachary scratches his chin and frowns. "I'm sure he meant well."

I smile at him sadly. "I know he did. I've never doubted that. Searching for her was an obsession for me back then. I would have done anything to track her down, and that wasn't healthy."

I sit down on the edge of the bed. "Anyhow, Reilly made me think there might be a chance she was still alive. I didn't know what I was doing, but when I searched for her, I didn't come up empty-handed. I somehow Found her ghost or soul, whatever you want to call it. I saw her everywhere for a while, and she spoke to me. She told me about the Bound God, and she said I had to stop him."

Elise drops the letters on the bed. "And you believed what this hallucination told you?"

"Yes," I insist. "It was her. Believe me or don't, but I'm sure of it."

"Ok," Elise says, shrugging. "Does the prophecy give any hints to how you're supposed to take down this god?"

"The Key must be found, lest Chaos consume and magic be lost, the Key must return to ash what was born of it," I recite with a sigh. "So, not really. But, I do know that I need to get the spell book my mother stole back from Cesare. Along with whatever Adrian was hinting at in that letter."

Elise snorts. "Cesare is not going to just hand it over."

"No, which is why I'm going to Find Maybelle and ask for her help," I say.

"What? Why?" Zachary asks.

"She helped my mother steal it last time. She stole it from the coven no less," I explain. "If anyone can help me, it's her."

"Will she help you though?" Zachary asks, his face showing his skepticism. "She did disappear when the coven was hunting you down."

"I think so," I say, twisting my hands together. "I have a feeling Gerard will help me convince her to."

"Reilly could probably get you into Cesare's without raising suspicion," Elise says.

"No," I say firmly.

Zachary sighs. "I know you're angry, but we might need him."

"I won't let him hand the spell book, or me, over to the coven," I say.

"Do you really think he would?" Elise asks.

"Yes," I nod. "If Reilly thinks it would help stop Cesare, he would do it without hesitation. He doesn't care that they would try to control me. He can't see that the coven is just as bad as Cesare."

"And they killed your mother," Zachary says, staring at the floor as he taps his hand restlessly against the desk.

"And that," I agree quietly.

"So, your plan is, run off and find Maybelle, then rob Cesare?" Elise asks.

"That's the short version," I confirm with a frustrated groan.

"You shouldn't go alone," Elise says, crossing her arms.

"I have to—"

"No, you don't. I'm going with you," Elise interrupts.

"You have your job here. Stocke will ask questions if you disappear," I insist.

"I'll handle it," Zachary says. "Stocke will accept my explanation. Elise is right, you shouldn't do this alone."

I bounce my leg, anxious about Elise coming with me even though I need her.

"What we'll be doing is technically illegal too," I warn even though I can see from her face that her mind is already made up.

"It's the right thing to do," Elise says. "Stop trying to talk me out of it. I'm not letting you do this alone. You're part of this team, and you need help."

"Ivy is going to kill me for dragging the team into my personal shit," I say, putting my head in my hands.

Elise laughs. "She'll understand. She might seem like a stickler for the rules, but she would break them in a second if she knew what was going on."

I drop my hands and up look up, squaring my shoulders. I can worry about what's going to happen after all this once I survive it.

"Do you have a map in here?" I ask Zachary. "I need to Find Maybelle before we leave."

"Yeah, I'll grab it," Zachary nods. He digs through the paper on the desk until he finds a map of the country. "Here you go."

"Thanks," I say taking it and unfolding it across the bed.

"When do we leave?" Elise asks.

"As soon as you have your bags packed. Mine are already in the car," I say, cracking my knuckles before spreading my hands over the surface of the map. I close my eyes and let the magic fall from my fingertips, searching for Maybelle.

CHAPTER 16

I nudge Elise. She blinks up at me groggily from the passenger seat.

"Wake up, we're almost there," I say as I pull into the gas station.

She sits up and wipes a line of drool from her cheek. "I'm hungry."

"You're always hungry. This place says it sells hot dogs," I say, pointing to the sign in the window.

"I'm going to die of food poisoning," Elise grumbles as she climbs out of the car.

"You can't, you're a werewolf," I shout over my shoulder as she heads inside. She flips me off.

I pump the gas, leaning against the dusty car. Maybelle is somewhere deep in the goblin reservation. We're going to have to sneak in and find her without getting caught. Somehow.

I rub my fingers across my forehead. The goblins are very private, and they don't take well to trespassers. They also don't accept visitors or pass along messages.

Elise returns as I finish pumping the gas with a dried out

looking hotdog. She scarfs it down in three bites, glaring at me the whole time. I shake my head and smile as I pull back out onto the road.

As we draw closer to the reservation, warning signs appear every mile suggesting we turn back now; the final one says **DEAD END**. The road ends less than a quarter mile later. I wrap both hands around the wheel as we bump over the uneven ground.

A large yellow sign marks the location of the entrance. It's impossible to miss, but not in the least bit inviting.

NO TRESPASSERS
NO SOLICITATION
UNAUTHORIZED ENTRY MAY RESULT
IN DEATH OR SEVERE INJURY

"Friendly bunch," Elise comments as she ties her hair back into a tight ponytail.

"No kidding," I say. "This should be an interesting trip."

We climb out of the car, and I look back over my shoulder at the setting sun. Reilly will be awake soon. And pissed.

The door to the underground tunnel isn't locked. It creaks loudly, rust falling from the hinges as we pry it open. It hasn't been used in ages.

There are no stairs or ladder. It's just a straight drop down; I can't see the bottom.

"How far do you think we're going to get before they find us?" Elise asks, hands on her hips as she stares down into the inky darkness.

"Hopefully we make it to Maybelle," I say. "I'm not sure I want to consider the alternative."

I crouch down by the hole and pull on the vampire magic. My

eyes adjust to the lack of light, and I can just barely make out something at the bottom of the pit.

There is a handful of small rocks scattered around in the sand. I grab one and drop it down the hole. It hits the ground in a little puff of dust after about a second.

"Can't be that far down then, right?" I ask, glancing at Elise.

She shrugs. "I can't actually calculate the distance by the time it takes for a rock to fall to the bottom of a hole, but sure."

"I should have brought Staci. I bet she could," I say, looking down the hole with a sigh. There's no other option, one of us just has to go down there and see. I sit down and swing my legs over the side. "I'll go down first just in case there's no way out of this hole."

"I don't have anything to pull you out," Elise says.

"Let's hope you don't need it." I twist around and slowly lower myself down until I'm hanging on by just my fingertips. I kick my legs out and hit dirt. I really hope the drop isn't too far.

I let go. My stomach climbs into my throat as the wind rushes past me. My feet hit the ground. I try to roll with the impact but collide with something big and hard.

"Motherfucker," I mutter, stuck upside down with an aching foot.

"Are you dying?" Elise shouts down the hole.

"No, but whoever designed this entrance should be shot," I shout back. I untwist myself and get upright. The hole doesn't lead exactly straight down, it curves at a bit of an angle. There is a small area to land in, but it's surrounded by an uneven wall of boulders, which is what I rolled into. This isn't a dead end, but the way forward isn't exactly clear.

"There are five tunnels leading out of this one," I yell up to Elise.

"Shit, which one do we take?" She asks.

I gnaw on the inside of my cheek. "Give me a minute."

I don't have a map, but the Finding magic is tugging me toward

Maybelle. The problem is that just because I know which direction she's in doesn't mean that tunnel will lead me to her.

I shut my eyes and extend my hands. Finding magic is dynamic. It isn't just about maps and straight lines. When I trained with Corinne, I was able to see her. The magic courses through me and drips from my fingertips, searching through the empty space for what I need.

I send the magic toward each of the tunnels and almost fall over as I get a dizzying vision of five different things at once. My eyes twitch, but I keep them squeezed shut and push the magic farther. I have to Find her. We've come this far and have risked everything for this chance.

The magic searches, showing me glimpses of rock and dirt. One of the strands of magic snaps back into me, and I grit my teeth. That's one tunnel eliminated. Vague images flash through my mind. Goblins. Caverns. Darkness. Another strand of magic snaps back, then another, and I drop to one knee. The last two strands wind farther and farther down the tunnels.

My arms shake with the effort of pushing the Finding magic farther than I ever have before. My right arm is wrenched forward. I get a bright glimpse of Maybelle's face. She looks over her shoulder, brows knitting together. Her lips move, but I can't hear what she says.

"Olivia!" Elise shouts. Her hand connects with my cheek, and I jerk awake with a gasp.

"Shit," I say, rolling up into a sitting position and holding my aching head in my hands.

"What the hell did you do?" She demands.

"I found the right tunnel," I say. "Wait, you jumped down here?"

"You made a really disturbing noise then went silent," she says, holding out a hand to help me up. "You wouldn't respond to anything."

I take her hand and she hauls me to my feet. "That took more out of me than I expected, but I know which tunnel we need to take."

The urge to get to Maybelle burns in my gut. I want to take off at a run, but that would be a sure way to get caught and executed or whatever the goblins do to trespassers.

Elise adjusts her ponytail and nods. "Lead the way."

"Remind me to buy you a beer after this is all over," I say, climbing over the boulder to my left.

"You're going to buy me a whole dinner at the restaurant of my choice and give me a foot rub," Elise says.

I laugh. "You are not getting a foot rub."

She grins as we walk into the narrow tunnel. "Maybe I'll let Patrick give me the foot rub instead."

I look back and raise a brow. "Patrick?"

She nods unapologetically.

"He seems like fun," she says, her eyes going distant.

I shudder and make a gagging noise. "Gross."

The tunnel goes down at a steady pace. After fifteen minutes of walking, we come to another sharp drop, though this one isn't as far as the drop into the tunnels. The ceiling is lower here. Neither of us has to duck, but Reilly wouldn't be able to stand upright here.

I keep my vampire magic close to the surface. I can smell no one has come this way in ages, but we can't risk walking into some kind of goblin patrol. Elise sniffs behind me every minute or so.

"It smells like dirt and magic down here," she says finally.

"Yeah, it's a strange combination," I agree.

I come to a halt. The tunnel splits, heading off in two opposite directions.

"Please tell me you know which way to go," Elise says.

"I think so," I say hesitantly. I take a step toward the tunnel on my right, but the magic halts me. I turn to the left instead.

We walk down the narrow passage quietly. We must be hundreds of feet underground now. It's getting cooler the farther down we go. I stop walking, and Elise almost runs into my back.

"Did you hear that?" I whisper. Something is moving in the distance. The sound is hushed but steady.

"Yeah," Elise says, leaning her head back and inhaling deeply. "I think it might be water."

We walk closer, taking care to be as quiet as possible just in case it isn't water making the noise. The sound grows louder as we approach until the rush of rapids is unmistakable.

The tunnel curves to the right and ends abruptly, dumping us out onto a small ledge with a long drop into a roaring river. A light spray of water hits my feet and legs.

"How far across is this thing?" Elise says, having to raise her voice to be heard.

I squint my eyes and peer across. There's absolutely no light down here, so even my vampire side is struggling to see very far.

"Too far to jump," I say.

"We can't swim in that," Elise says, bracing her hand against the wall to look over the edge and downstream. The ledge we're on is narrow and barely wide enough for three people to stand shoulder to shoulder.

"We might have to," I say, scooting toward the edge as well. My foot slips as a piece of rock breaks free. Elise grabs my arm, dragging me backward.

"Be careful," she snaps.

"Wait, did you hear that?" I ask.

"Hear what?"

"Exactly," I say, crouching down. "The rocks didn't hit the water."

I get on my knees and look directly down. The edge of something is bobbing in the water. I slide my hand down and feel that the ledge we're standing on curves back underneath us. I touch something that tickles my wrist and jerk back with a yelp. Elise yanks me backward.

"Sorry, sorry!" I say, rubbing my hand and shaking off the goosebumps. "It surprised me, but I think it was just a rope."

Elise huffs at me. "You're trying to give me a heart attack between the passing out and the almost falling and now the screaming."

"Shut up, it's creepy when you can't see what you're touching," I say as I lean back over the edge. Elise keeps a hand on my shoulder. I pat around until I find the rope again and tug on it. I can feel some resistance, but whatever is attached to the end slowly moves toward me.

I look down over the edge and see a small boat attached to the end of the rope. I look back up at Elise.

"How do you feel about whitewater rafting?" I ask with a grin.

"I will say again, that this is a bad idea," Elise says.

"Just get in the boat," I repeat. The wood is digging into my knees, and the bouncing motion is becoming unsettling. I want to get this over with.

Elise sighs, but slides down and drops into the boat in front of me. The entire thing wobbles and I dig my fingers into the sides and grit my teeth. I hate boats.

"Give me the paddle," she says, reaching her hand back while the other is latched onto the front of the boat.

I shove the paddle up toward her. She grabs it, holding onto it like a lifeline.

"It's easier to see down here," I say, my voice shaking just a little.

"Yeah, but all I can see is rapids and boulders," she mutters.

"Fantastic. I'm going to untie the rope now," I say.

Elise nods, and I twist around to untie us from the ledge. The goblins helpfully used a quick-release carabiner to attach the rope to the boat. I push the latch in, and as soon as I release the carabiner, the fast-moving water rushes us away. I scramble for my paddle as the choppy river tips us forward and backward.

"Go left!" Elise shouts, paddling as hard as she can.

I plunge my paddle into the water on the right side of the boat and paddle with her. We move to left just in time to barrel around a huge boulder sticking up out of the water. The current swirls around it and the boat turns sideways as we pass it. Elise jabs the boulder with her paddle and pushes us back straight.

"This is not how I planned on dying," she shouts.

"We're not going to die!" I shout back.

"Shit," she says. "There's a drop!"

I widen my knees and crouch down, hoping that might keep me from falling out. The rushing of the water grows louder. The front end of the boat tilts down. Elise leans back so far she's practically laying in my lap, and I'm doing the same. There's no time to scream before water is splashing over us.

The boat rocks violently and we are thrown in a circle. I paddle as hard as possible, but I can barely tell which direction we're headed in. The boat smacks into a boulder. The wood cracks and water pours over the side as the water traps us against the rock.

I shove against it with my paddle like Elise had done earlier. The boat creaks as we slide, then the current grabs us again. We're slung sideways, bouncing over the rough waves.

We ride the rapids, using our paddles like poles to fend off rocks jutting out of the water. There isn't time to think, only act. We're both drenched, and the onslaught is endless. My hands are almost numb from gripping the paddle so tightly.

"Not again," Elise moans.

The roar of water is even louder than before. There is no way to stop from going over this drop though.

"I can't see over the edge," Elise shouts, scooting backward. My heart pounds in my chest as we hurtle forward.

The nose of the boat goes over the edge, and my heart leaps into my throat. This drop is twice as far as the one before. It's longer than the boat.

We're falling. My knees raise off the rough wood, and I grab the edge with my free hand, desperate not to be flung into the rapids. The boat smacks into the water as it lurches violently, and the spray blinds me. I'm thrown forward, and my hands hit the bow. There's no one in front of me.

"Elise!" I scream, searching the white froth for her. A head bobs up ahead of me. I drop my paddle and scramble forward, leaning over the side and grabbing her as she goes back under.

I drag her up to the side of the boat, but the pull of the current keeps me from pulling her all the way in. She scrabbles at my arms, but we're both wet, and she's slipping away. I push the vampire magic into my arms, giving myself a surge of strength, and drag her back into the boat. She lands on top of me, coughing up water.

The boat bangs against something and cracks loudly. Elise pushes upright and grabs the only remaining paddle. She has a scrape across her chin that is dripping blood.

She shoves us away from the next boulder and the next. I sit behind her, panting and shaky. I wish I hadn't dropped my paddle, but there hadn't been time to do anything else.

"The water is calming down," Elise says, collapsing back onto her butt.

I sigh in relief and slump backward. "Some people do this for fun. They're idiots."

Elise snorts in agreement.

The rocking of the boat ceases, but the speed of the current doesn't slow down.

"I really hope there isn't a massive, deadly waterfall at the end of this," Elise says, staring up at the ceiling of the tunnel that is at least thirty feet overhead.

I kick her leg. "Don't even say that."

Elise grabs the bottom of her shirt and uses it to wipe away the blood on her chin. The scrape is already healing. I could heal it faster, but I can't risk wasting magic like that. Elise doesn't seem concerned about it anyhow.

"Are we still headed in the right direction at least?" Elise asks.

"Yes, we're getting close." Light flickers in the distance and I sit up. "Shit."

"What?" Elise asks, jerking upright. She spots the lights as well and picks up the paddle. "I don't see anywhere to get out of the water."

"Me neither," I say, scanning the river in the distance. The walls of the tunnel grow smoother. The light gets closer and closer. I let out a sigh of relief. "Just torches."

They line the walls with one every five or so feet. They don't use fire. I peer at the odd contraptions curiously. I wonder how they keep them burning. It doesn't seem like this river is traveled very often.

"I guess we're approaching civilization," Elise comments.

The river curves and widens. I notice the water isn't moving quite as fast here. A small wooden dock sticks out of a large, square tunnel opening. Elise paddles toward it, but the river is still moving quickly enough that we're being swept past it faster than she can paddle sideways.

"We have to go down that tunnel," I say frantically. The tug in my gut demands it.

"Then we have to swim," Elise says, still paddling as hard as she can. She's right though, with only one paddle she can't move the boat there.

"Let's do it then," I say.

She drops the paddle, and we both leap into the water at the same time. It's icy cold, freezing my lungs in my chest. I have a sudden fear that there might be some kind of mythological sea creature lurking in the murky green depths.

I paddle hard against the current, kicking my legs as fast as I can. It's slow moving, but we make better progress than we did in the boat. A human would have no hope of making it, lucky for us, neither of us is human.

Elise reaches the dock first and reaches back to drag me to it as well. We climb onto the rough wooden boards and flop over, panting and exhausted.

"You always get into the craziest shit," Elise pants.

"I blame the prophecy," I say, breathing just as hard.

Elise snorts and bursts into laughter. I laugh right along with her, it's infectious. Something about being alive after that insanity makes all the worries of the past few weeks seem surreal.

I roll onto my knees and look down the tunnel in front of us. It's different from the others. This one is more well-used and is goblin-made rather than natural like the ones we came through. It's also lit.

"We're going to start running into goblins soon," I say.

"We'll be able to smell them coming," Elise says, tapping the side of her nose.

"Doesn't mean we'll have anywhere to hide," I say.

She shrugs. "That is a problem for future us."

We stand, and I ring out my shirt. The weight of water is threatening to drag my jeans down my hips.

"I did not dress with swimming in mind," I mutter.

"No kidding," Elise says, shaking water off her pistol. "It's good Glocks don't mind a little dirty water."

My hands fly to my jacket pockets, and I'm relieved to find there are at least a few vials still there. I take the remaining ones out to see which I lost. I hadn't even thought about it when we first got in the boat.

"Ready?" Elise asks.

"Yeah," I say, slipping the vials back in my jacket. "Let's get this over with."

CHAPTER 17

A rush of wind blows across my face. I stop in my tracks. I didn't think there could be wind in caves.

"Did you feel that?" I ask, looking back at Elise. She nods.

I hurry forward and hear an odd noise, like someone is blowing across the top of a bottle. There is an opening in the wall of the tunnel. It's barely a foot tall, but it's twice as wide. Elise and I have to lean over to look through it.

"Holy shit," I whisper reverently.

The sight that stretches out beneath us is breathtaking. The city is massive, lights twinkling in the twisting spires as far as I can see. Thick support pillars extend from the floor of the cavern all the way to the ceiling. They must be a thousand feet tall.

There are squat, sturdy buildings and narrow ones that twist upward so far I'm not sure how they don't snap off. A perfect grid of streets is laid out among the buildings. Small patches of color lit by warm light appear to be gardens.

An enormous lake that takes up a full third of the cavern is fed by a waterfall from the river. Boats, much bigger than the canoe we were in, dot the still surface of the lake. Steam puffs out of a large industrial building near the edge of the lake.

This is more than a city. There's an entire self-contained civilization down there.

"No wonder they haven't been in a rush to join the rest of society," Elise whispers.

The steady tap of footsteps interrupts our admiration. We jump back from the window and look around for any way to hide, but the smooth tunnel walls don't provide any options.

I grab Elise and drag her back the way we came. We go around the turn and press our backs against the wall, trying to breathe quietly.

The footsteps get closer and closer. Then they stop. I keep my eyes on the curve of the tunnel, sure that a goblin is going to appear any second.

"All clear on Skywalk," a gravelly voice says. He smells like metal and stone.

The footsteps start again but heading in the opposite direction. My shoulders slump in relief.

Elise nods in the direction of the goblin, and I nod back. We creep after him silently. Far enough behind the guard that we can't see him, but close enough to hear him.

The tunnel becomes more complicated, splitting off multiple times. The torches shift into odd little lanterns that glow softly. I keep mistaking it for daylight even though it can't be. The floors are smooth and well-traveled.

Every so often an opening appears with stairs leading down. I pause near one of the doorways, the tug in my gut pulling my attention toward as I try to walk past.

I point down the stairway and Elise nods. I feel jittery leaving our guard behind. It's easier when you know where the person you are hiding from is located. It's terrifying when they might appear in front of you at any moment and there is nowhere to hide.

The stairwell ends in a somewhat open room. Pillars, delicately carved with alternating patterns, support the ceiling.

New footsteps echo behind us. Elise and I rush toward the opening on the opposite side of the room. It's not until we're three steps down that I realize guards are coming from this direction too.

I skid to a halt and Elise tumbles into my back, but it's too late. Two goblins wearing leather vests and red linen pants appear in front of us.

"Trespassers!" One shouts. The other lifts his hand toward us and the ground beneath our feet groans and moves.

Elise drags me back up the stairs, and we sprint across the open room. Another pair of guards run out of the other stairwell.

I fall flat on my face as something bites into my legs. The stone floor is sucking me down like it's quicksand.

"Olivia!" Elise shouts, scrambling back to my side. Her hands and knees sink into the stone.

"I'm here to see a friend!" I shout at the guards, no longer trying to struggle. I can't break the stone. "She's one of you. She's a goblin, her name is Maybelle. It's about the Day of Breaking!"

One of the guards flinches at the mention of the prophecy.

"I know what the key to the prophecy is," I press on. "I have to talk to her, please!"

The guards stand in a circle around us. One of them, the only one wearing a cape, steps up in front of me.

"What would a human know of the prophecy?" He demands, looking down at me with cold violet eyes.

"I'm not human," I say, smiling at him with a mouth full of fangs.

He hisses and lifts his hand. The stone tightens around my legs.

"Wait, wait!" I shout. "I'm not a vampire either. Let me show you. I'm a witch."

"That is not possible," he growls, anger darkening his face.

"Don't freak out," I say. I lift my free hand and push the electric magic into a small sphere. It crackles brightly. The goblins all take a step back. I close my hand, and the magic is snuffed out.

The goblin in charge narrows his eyes.

"They have come to assassinate the king!" One of them exclaims, pointing a bony finger in my direction.

Elise rolls her eyes. "I'm a JHAPI agent, not an assassin. We are here because we need to speak with Olivia's friend. Cesare Sangiovanni intends on releasing the Bound God."

A quiet gasp travels through the group.

"The vampire council would allow this?" The goblin leader asks, crossing his arms.

"They don't know about it," I explain.

"Bind them," the goblin says.

The other guards move around us, clapping thick cuffs around our wrists. The stone flows away from my feet and smooths back into the ground like it never happened. I had no idea goblins had magic like that.

We are put in the middle of the guards and led down the stairwell. The tug in my gut says we're headed in the right direction. The nasty looks we're getting from the goblins don't exactly fill me with confidence though.

"This is a disaster," Elise says, leaning her head back against the stone wall. She's being held in a separate cell across from me.

"Could be worse," I say, stretching my legs out in front of me. "We could have drowned."

She snorts out a laugh. "Right."

"I hope this wasn't a huge mistake," I whisper.

"You had to try," Elise says with a shrug.

"I can practically feel Reilly raging at me right now."

"I bet they're all throwing a fit. Poor Zachary," Elise laughs. "He's an angel for volunteering to stay behind."

"Or just smart," I say, nudging at a loose pebble with my finger. "Maybe he knew we were doomed."

"They may not execute us," Elise says thoughtfully. "They may just keep us in these cells until we're old and frail."

"Yeah right," I scoff. "By the time the guards got us back here, they seemed convinced we were assassins. Shitty assassins, but definitely up to no good."

There's a crash from the direction of the guards. I scramble over to the iron bars attempt to peer down the hallway, but the cells are slightly recessed. I can't see anything.

Quick footsteps head toward us, and a squat goblin appears, panting. His face looks strangely familiar.

"Gerard?" I demand in shock.

"You're later than I expected," he says.

Another goblin with curly red hair held up by a lime green scarf and light scars on her green face appears behind him.

"You really got yourself in trouble this time," Maybelle says with a fond smile.

My eyes go wide, and a smile spreads across my face.

"Maybelle! How did you even know we were down here?" I ask as Gerard kneels in front of my cell and begins fiddling with the lock.

"I've been keeping an ear out," Gerard explains. The lock opens with a pop, and the door swings outward. "I knew you'd be here soon."

"Who is this?" Maybelle asks suspiciously as she points at Elise.

"Agent Elise Hawking, she's-"

"Agent?" Maybelle barks angrily. "You brought one of them into this?"

"She's my friend, and she's trustworthy. She understands what's at stake," I snap back. "Get her out too."

Maybelle groans in frustration but nods at Gerard, who seems to be waiting for her approval. He kneels down and works on the lock to Elise's cell.

"Hurry," Maybelle hisses.

"I am," Gerard growls at her. The lock clicks open, and Elise hurries out of her cell.

"What now?" I ask.

Maybelle lifts her hand and a wave of magic splashes against my skin. I stumble with an embarrassing squeak. My arms are green, and my fingers are long and delicate.

"What the actual fuck?" I exclaim, looking at Maybelle in horror.

"It's just an illusion. I disguised you as guards," she says. "Now, come on."

I look down and see that I am wearing the red pants and leather vest we saw on the other guards. The goblin version of Elise looks at me, her face reflecting exactly how I feel. This is creepy. I want my body back.

We walk down the hallway. Two guards lay unconscious on the floor. Maybelle was not gentle with them. A short stairway leads back up to what is basically the ground level of the city.

I look around, nervous that we'll be spotted.

"Just act normal," Maybelle says, elbowing me in the side.

I straighten my back and try to look like I belong. Ahead near the doorway are two guards, but they're lounging in wooden chairs sipping on something hot. They nod absently as we pass by and I can barely restrain my sigh of relief.

We climb several more stairways before finally being released out into the city. It's louder down here. The rumble of engines in the distance competes with the rush of the huge waterfall that pours into the lake. I can't stop myself from gawking.

Maybelle takes my elbow and drags me along at a quick pace. The neat grid of the roadways that we saw from the skywalk was deceiving. Only the main roads are aligned in orderly grids. The streets that connect them are winding and confusing.

We pass one of the towering spires. There is a constant stream of goblins going in and out of the arched doorway. The base of the structure is bigger than I expected. They looked so delicate from above.

Gerard stops at a small house set amidst a huddle of larger buildings and unlocks the front door. We're ushered into a small sitting room, and the door is locked behind us. Maybelle waves her hand; the illusions fall away.

Another goblin, younger than Maybelle and Gerard, is sitting at a small table in the middle of the room flipping a knife end over end.

"Welcome to Donheim," he says with a mischievous grin.

CHAPTER 18

"This is Kabs, my nephew," Maybelle says, pointing at the goblin with the knife.

Kabs grins and nods at us, his short black mohawk bobbing with the motion.

The small room we're in has stone floors and a small fireplace built into the wall near the door. A fire is crackling merrily inside it, but there isn't the slightest hint of smoke in the room. To my right, a narrow staircase leads to an upper level.

There's a teal couch across from the table with bright red pillows. It's good to see Maybelle's love of color hasn't changed just because her appearance has.

"How did you know we were coming?" I ask, turning to Gerard.

Gerard smiles showing slightly sharp white teeth. "The same way I knew we'd find you in Pecan Grove. I have the gift of foretelling. It's minor and short-sighted, but it helps when it can."

"You're a prophet? Like the one that prophesied about the Day of Breaking?" I ask, trying to understand.

Gerard waves away my suggestion. "A distant ancestor. There

are others that still have his power. I'm not one of those favored families."

"And you," I say pointing at Maybelle. "You turned us into goblins."

"A simple illusion," Maybelle says, shrugging.

"Is that how you made it seem like you were a human for so long?" I ask.

"I worked with an enchanter to create a more powerful version of my magic, but that isn't important right now. What the hell were you thinking trying to sneak in here? Donheim is well guarded, and there are constant patrols. Honestly, I don't know how you survived the trip down the river," she rants. The tone of her voice is so similar to the times she chastised me for trying to date men who weren't good enough for me that I can't help but smile.

"I missed you too," I say fondly, pulling her into another hug that muffles her complaints.

"You came here for a reason. What do you need?" Gerard asks, interrupting our reunion.

I turn to Maybelle. "Cesare Sangiovanni has the spell book you and my mother stole. I need it, and I can't steal it from him on my own."

"Why?" Maybelle asks, eyes widening in horror. "That thing has brought nothing but trouble."

"Cesare wants to release the Bound God. That book has something to do with it," I explain. "I don't know what, all I know is that I have to get it."

"The Bound God," Kabs asks with an incredulous laugh. "You actually believe in that crap?"

"Hush," Maybelle snaps at him.

Kabs stills and his face pinches together and looks at all of us. "You're serious."

"I'm the key to the prophecy, aren't I?" I ask Gerard.

He nods solemnly.

"How long have you known?" I ask, anger churning in my gut. He could have told me.

"I suspected," Gerard says unapologetically. "I've only known for sure since I dreamed that you were coming here for Maybelle's help."

"You don't have to do any of this," Maybelle says, crossing her arms. "Stay down here with us. You could sell your healing salves. I could make you look like a goblin when you need to go out."

"I can't Maybelle," I say, surprised at her. "I can't let everyone I care about get slaughtered. And if this god gets released, Donheim won't be any safer than anywhere else."

Maybelle turns away, pacing the room in agitation.

Elise looks at me with concern. I shrug. I knew convincing Maybelle wouldn't be easy, but I hoped she would come around once I mentioned the Bound God.

Gerard sighs and rubs his fingers over his eyes. "She's right, Maybelle. You can't hide from this any more than she can. You've known that for a long time."

"I don't believe in fate," Maybelle growls at him. "I make my own way, always have."

"This isn't about fate," Gerard growls back. "You set things in motion when you stole that book, and these are the consequences."

Maybelle continues to pace, her hands clenched into fists at her side.

"Come on, Auntie," Kabs pipes up. "It's not like you to back down from a challenge. Stealing from a vampire sounds like a good time."

Maybelle shoots Kabs a glare before turning back to face me and crossing her arms.

"You'll do as I say without question," Maybelle says, finally agreeing to help us. "There will be no unnecessary heroics. No stealing anything else. And we are not going to try to kill Cesare."

I nod quickly. "I just want the book. None of us have a hope of killing Cesare on our own."

"I want to help," Kabs says, twirling the knife around and slipping it back into the sheath at his waist. "You'll need me anyhow."

Maybelle presses her lips together in disapproval. "I don't want you mixed up in this."

Kabs rolls his eyes dramatically. "Where have I heard that before?"

"Let Kabs go," Gerard says, his eyes distant. His words feel heavy like they mean something.

Maybelle looks at his expression and deflates. "Fine. Let's all rush headlong into danger and certain death."

"Do you really think we don't have a chance of doing this successfully?" I ask, sinking down into a chair by the table.

Maybelle sighs and shakes her head. "If we're careful, and if you all listen to me, we can do it. Probably."

"What's the plan then?" I ask, leaning forward.

"How well do you know the layout of the clanhouse?" Maybelle asks.

"Fairly well," I say, thinking back to the multi-storied mansion. "It's fairly straightforward. I saw the spellbook in Cesare's study."

"We'll go in during the day," Maybelle says.

Gerard shuffles around the furnace, swinging a pot over the fire. The smell of some kind of herby soup fills the lower level as Maybelle goes through the details of her plan. My stomach growls. I have no idea how long we were wandering in the tunnels before we made it here, or how long they had us in those cells.

With the planning complete, Gerard dishes up bowls of a thick, creamy soup. Elise sniffs it suspiciously before eating, but I shovel it in my mouth without question. I'm too hungry to be picky. It's weird, but not really bad.

"You work with JHAPI?" Kabs asks, looking at Elise and me.

Elise nods. "I've been with the agency for five years."

"Maybelle and Gerard won't talk about their time on the surface," Kabs says, leaning forward. "What are humans like? Scared of everything?"

"Have you never been out of Donheim?" I ask, stirring the hot soup to cool it down.

He shakes his head. "No one really leaves Donheim," Kabs explains. "And if they do, they never come back. Except for these two idiots."

Maybelle rolls her eyes. "It's no better or worse than Donheim."

I smile as the two continue to bicker. Maybelle seems fond of Kabs.

After dinner, Maybelle shows me and Elise the small room we'll be sharing tonight. Or today. I pause, realizing I can't quite feel if the sun is up or not.

Elise heads back to the living room to take Kabs up on his challenge to a game of chess. Maybelle gets two glasses of red juice that smells like strawberries and plums and leads me out to a small balcony, leaving the door open behind us. I sit down beside her and stare in awe at the view. It's dark on the lake, but the water is dotted by the lights of fishing boats. The bright points bob and move around the lake like slow-moving stars.

"It's beautiful," I say.

She nods. "I suppose it is. I haven't appreciated it in years."

"Why?" I ask.

"The closer you are to the lake, the less you matter here. Humans value waterside properties, but goblins don't view it the same. Fishermen are not necessarily poor, but the work they do isn't really respected. Being near the lake is either a necessity or all you can afford," she says with a sigh. "Let's just say I've lived by the lake for a long time."

"What have you been doing here since you got back?" I ask.

"Getting people what they need," Maybelle says with a wan smile. "Gerard and I have always been good at that."

The cafe back in Pecan Grove was the most popular restaurant in town. If the apothecary had opened, it would have been just as successful. Maybelle had been universally loved by the townspeople.

"I'm sure you're the toast of the town," I say taking a swig of my red juice.

She snorts. "Hardly. We came back here out of desperation. We're surviving, but no one was happy to see us."

"Except Kabs?" I ask, looking back over my shoulder. He's laughing at the table with Elise, apparently winning the game of chess.

Maybelle shakes her head. "He ended up in the same rough spot I did at his age. The family kicked him out; I was glad to take him in. He's bright and motivated, he just doesn't always use his head before he acts." She takes a drink then looks at me slyly. "Like someone else I know."

I huff out a laugh. "I've gotten better at that."

She raises her brows.

"I have!" I exclaim. "I've been handling my problems like an adult."

"Says the woman that snuck in here with no plan and now wants to rob a vampire," Maybelle says. "Again, with no plan."

"It worked out," I say, grinning. "And you came up with a plan."

Maybelle shakes her head, and we fall silent as we look out over the lake. The twinkling lights of the boats bobbing across the surface make it look like the night sky is at our feet.

"We can do this, right?" I ask quietly. "We can stop him?"

Maybelle is silent for a moment before responding. "Of course."

CHAPTER 19

The sun has been up for an hour. I tap my fingers against my thigh impatiently. The mossy ground beneath my feet is slightly damp. Elise is much better at waiting than I am. She is relaxed and leaning against a tree.

We're on a hill overlooking the clanhouse. The house is huge, but the estate it sits on is even bigger.

"How much longer?" I ask.

Maybelle lowers her strange, silvery binoculars (though I was informed earlier that they are *not* binoculars, they are a feat of goblin artistry) and gives me a look. "I can't summon neckers out of the house with my mind. We wait until someone leaves, then we intercept them. You know the plan."

Elise stands up straight. "I heard a door."

Maybelle scans the house, then nods. "I see them. There are five, more than enough."

Our small group follows Maybelle down the hill. She moves like someone much younger, and unexpectedly fast considering she's barely four feet tall. Kabs takes up the rear.

The neckers are walking towards an SUV parked around the

back of the house; laughing and joking around if looking a little tired. They don't see us coming.

Elise kicks the first person in the side of the face then grabs the next closest one by the shoulder and jerks him around to face her, cracking him across the jaw. They both fall to the ground in a heap. Maybelle has a stranglehold on one of them, her hand tight over their mouth. Kabs has managed to wrestle the fourth to the ground and is punching them enthusiastically.

I grab the third from behind, pouring a thin line of knockout brew onto their face. She slumps in my arms, and I lower her to the ground. I quickly dose the rest of them lightly. They're humans, and they've been fed on; it doesn't take much to knock them out. They'll be out for at least an hour. If that's not long enough, then something has gone terribly wrong.

We drag the unconscious neckers into the garden behind the house and stuff them in a hedge.

"Come here," Maybelle whispers to Kabs. She focuses on one necker and puts her hand on Kabs shoulder. He morphs into a perfect doppelgänger of the man Elise knocked out. Maybelle repeats the process, making each of us look like a different necker.

My body doesn't feel different, and if I stare at my hand hard enough, I can see my real body beneath the illusion. That takes away some of the creep-factor. Maybelle's magic hasn't actually changed me. It really is just an illusion.

"So, we just walk in?" Elise asks.

"Yep," I reply. "We look like we belong. It shouldn't raise any suspicion."

"Just don't talk to anyone," Maybelle says before brushing past us and starting toward the house.

I follow her, Kabs and Elise hurrying after us. Maybelle walks up to the door the neckers exited and opens it. I hold my breath as we go inside. This is insane. We're walking into Cesare's clan-house, where he is probably sleeping right now, to steal something from his personal study. My mother would be so proud. I smirk to myself. The best part is that she actually would be.

I move up beside Maybelle and lead the group through the somewhat familiar house. I didn't spend any time wandering around while I was here, but I learned the basic layout. The ground level is feeding rooms, a kitchen, and a small medical area with brews for emergencies. The second level has more feeding rooms and a lounge with televisions and games. The rooms are all off in the different wings that are set aside for the older vampires that Cesare sired. Cesare's study is on the top floor. Of course.

I lead us up the sloping staircase and past the stained glass. Maybelle has to drag Kabs away from some of the art. Based on the whispers I'm overhearing, I think he wants to steal it.

Laughter rings out ahead, and my heart pounds in my chest. I'm irrationally afraid the illusions are going to fail as the two women round the corner. They stop laughing when they see us and look coldly at Elise. Well, at whoever they think Elise is.

We don't see anyone on the next level which gives the house a creepy, deserted feel. I know they're all just sleeping, but it makes me antsy. We walk up the final flight of stairs and I hesitate. This place all looks the same after a while.

"This way," I whisper, turning to the left. The hallway grows darker as we approach the study. The door lacks the guards it had last time, but I know it's the right one.

I point out the door. Maybelle walks over and looks around, then crouches in front of it, deftly pulling a small lock-picking kit from her pocket. She picks the lock before I can ask how long it's going to take and the door swings inward. It's dark in the study; the fireplace is not lit this time. I walk in first, barely daring to breathe as I scan the room. It's empty, but I feel watched being in Cesare's area of the house.

Maybelle and Elise follow me inside while Kabs stays by the door and watches the hall.

"Where is it?" Elise whispers.

"I don't know," I whisper back as I pull on the vampire magic to increase my sense of smell. There is a lingering scent of old leather and magic in the room. I walk to Cesare's desk and begin poking around.

Elise and Maybelle spread out in the room moving books around and looking behind picture frames. I run my hand on the bottom of his desk. My fingers hit a bump. I drop to my knees and inspect it. The wood is slightly worn just behind the knot; I push on it firmly, and it slides backward. A soft click emanates from the desk as a panel cracks open.

"There's a safe," Maybelle says, rushing to the side of the desk.

The entire side panel swings open. Inside is a small black safe, an old one with a bronze dial and handle.

"Can you get it open?" I ask. "Or do we need to break it?"

Maybelle gives me a look. "Can I get it open? Of course, I can." She leans down and presses her ear to black metal, then begins to turn the dial slowly.

Kabs looks back and waves at us urgently. I run over to his side and peer out of the crack in the door. A man in a black suit with a gun clearly visible is walking down the hall. I shut the door, keeping the handle turned until it's fully closed, then releasing it slowly to avoid a click.

I turn toward Elise and Maybelle and press my fingers to my lips, then lean against the door and listen. The guard walks closer and pauses in front of the door. I hold my breath. His shoes squeak on the hardwood floor, then his footsteps lead away again.

I slump in relief and wait until he's headed back down the stairs to crack the door open again. Kabs nods at me and takes up position to watch the hall once again.

"I've got it," Maybelle says.

I hurry over to her side as she opens the door to the safe. There are a couple of odd trinkets inside, but the only thing I care about it the creased, leather-bound book inside. It smells so strongly of magic that my nose twitches.

I reach my hand inside and pick it up, careful to not brush against anything else in the safe. It's heavier than I expected. A strange symbol is engraved on the outside.

"That's it," Maybelle confirms.

"Let's get out of here," I whisper. Adrian had hinted there was something else for me to find at Cesare's, but without any idea what it is, I can't risk wandering around looking for it.

"Wait," Maybelle says. She grabs a book off the shelf from the other side of the room and hurries back over to me. The book morphs into an exact copy of the spell book I'm holding.

"How long will it last?" I ask.

"Until he opens it and realizes it's a fake," Maybelle says, setting the copy back in the safe and closing it. "Knowing it's fake will shatter an illusion like this one."

Kabs looks back at us. "Still clear, we should go now."

We file out of the study, shutting the door behind us. My stomach twists with the urgency to get out of here. It's hard to walk when all my instincts are telling me to run.

A door opens ahead of us, and a bleary-eyed necker stumbles out. His hair is sticking up in every direction and dried blood is flaking off his neck. He scratches his stomach and glances at our group, then pads past us. Hopefully on his way to take a shower.

"Katie!" A man says sharply behind us. Shit. I was distracted by the necker in front of us and didn't hear him. We all come to a stop and I hesitantly turn around. The man is walking toward us with a puzzled expression on his face. He's looking right at me. Dammit. I deftly move the spell book behind my back as I turn to face the necker.

"Yes?" I ask with a tense smile, hoping he is actually talking to me.

"What are you doing here? I thought you were going into the city today," he says, suspicious.

"Change of plans," I say with a shrug.

He throws his hands up and rolls his eyes. "Then I need your help downstairs. I let you have the day off for your errands, not so you could wander the house."

"My bad," I say, wiggling the spell book behind me. If I'm going to have to go with this guy, I can't keep it with me. Elise takes it and I try to look appropriately apologetic. "What did you need help with again?"

His irritation shifts into anger. "Don't be stupid. Come on," he says, turning and heading away from the group.

I look back over my shoulder. Elise is watching me tensely. I mouth *just go*. Elise tries to follow me anyhow, but Maybelle grabs her elbow. She pushes Kabs after me instead, her touch morphing him into a replica of the man I'm following.

I nod and hurry after the man. My heart is pounding out of my chest. Elise has the book. She can get it out. That's the most important thing.

The man leads me to a massive industrial style kitchen and shoves a tray into my hands. "Get the meal ready."

The meal. Right. There are three refrigerators and a pantry big enough to hold a party in.

"Is a sandwich okay?" I ask hesitantly.

The man looks at me like I'm crazy. "You can give him a plate full of mustard for all I care. We just have to keep him alive."

What the fuck.

"Yeah, of course," I say, opening the closest refrigerator. The amount of food is overwhelming. I grab an apple and string cheese and put it on the plate. The necker is busy working on something else, so I grab a single serve bag of baby carrots. It's a balanced meal for whoever they have. Sort of. It doesn't sound like they treat him all that well.

Kabs steps around the corner into the kitchen, hidden by the refrigerator door, but I shake my head and mouth, *wait*. I want to know who they are keeping prisoner, and why.

"You done?" He asks.

I nod and point at the tray. "Yep."

Kabs slinks back around the corner and I shut the refrigerator door.

He gives me another look. "You're acting really weird."

"Sorry," I say, drooping my shoulders so that I look a little tired. "Got a little carried away last night, then didn't sleep well." I really need him to buy this act and stop being suspicious.

"Right," he says slowly. "Whatever, let's get this over with."

He picks up a bucket of water from the sink and leads me out of the kitchen. We go down a staircase I hadn't seen last time I was here. It's narrow and dark. The stairs aren't museum quality like the rest of the house, they're rough-hewn wooden planks. Kabs creeps quietly behind us, something the human necker wouldn't be able to hear. At least I have backup.

The clean walls of the upper levels give way to cold stone. I look around curiously as we descend two more levels of stairs. We reach an open area and I stop in my tracks. This is a dungeon. There are six cells carved right into the stone with dull metal bars. It would be pitch black down here if it wasn't for the bright light coming from one of the cells.

The necker walks up to the cell and I hurry to catch up.

"Bucket," he says to whoever is in the cell.

The prisoner, a rough looking man with the beginnings of a beard and jet black hair, walks up to the cell door with an empty bucket. The necker pours the fresh water into the bucket then waves me forward. There is a small space at the bottom of the bars to slide the tray.

I meet the man's eyes and the strength of his magic almost overwhelms me. It's dark, almost smoky, and intoxicating. I want to drink it down. Understanding clicks in my brain. This is what Adrian meant in his letter. The other thing worth finding.

With a sharp, quick motion I smack the tray into the base of the necker's skull and he drops like a bag of rocks. The prisoner freezes, looking at me in surprise.

"What the hell are you doing, Olivia?" Kabs asks from behind me, still looking like a perfect copy of the necker I just knocked out.

The prisoner looks at the man on the floor, then back up at Kabs, clearly confused.

"We have to get him out," I say to Kabs.

"No," the prisoner says, speaking for the first time. "You're not taking me anywhere."

"Are you seriously refusing to be rescued?" I ask, incredulous.

The prisoner crosses his arms and plants his feet. "Yes."

"Why?" I demand, stepping up to the bars.

"None of your business," the man hisses. "Now get out!"

I narrow my eyes. "No. I don't know why, but I need you. You're coming with us."

"You don't even know who I am, why do you think you need me?" He asks, taking a few steps back.

"What do you know about the prophecy of the Day of Breaking?" I ask.

He laughs. "Plenty. Too much in fact."

"I'm the key to the prophecy," I say, trying not to sound pretentious.

The man's face shifts, then he shakes his head. "It doesn't matter."

"What are you talking about? Of course it matters. I can still stop Cesare," I insist, smacking my hand against the bars.

"It doesn't matter," he says, walking back up to the bars until he is inches from my faces, "because the Bound God has already been released."

CHAPTER 20

"What? How? When?" I ask, all the color draining from my face.

"Which question do you want me to answer first?" He responds sarcastically.

"When?" I ask again, my voice edging into a growl.

"The night of the full moon," he says.

Four days ago? I pinch my brows together. Nothing has happened. The world hasn't ended, at least it hadn't before Elise and I got to the goblin city.

"Why hasn't he brought about the apocalypse yet?" I ask.

"I don't know, you'll have to ask him," the prisoner mocks, snorting in derision.

"How was he released?" I ask, gritting my teeth.

"I set him free," the prisoner says, turning away. He rolls his shoulders like he's trying to work out tension. "I did it."

I step back, stunned. "Why?"

"So many questions," the prisoner says. "None of this matters. It's done. Run far away from here and try to survive whatever comes next."

"No," I growl out. "I'm not running. If the god has been released, I'll just have to kill him."

"And how do you think you're going to do that?" The prisoner asks.

"I'll figure it out." I pull a knockout brew from my pocket and throw it at him. It breaks against his chest despite his attempt to dodge it. He falls flat on his face. "Get the cell open, Kabs. I'm bringing him with us."

"Maybelle is going to kill both of us," Kabs says as he runs up to the cell. He presses his hands against the stone wall. It moves under his hand, creating an opening.

I run into the cell and pick the prisoner up, throwing him over my shoulder with a grunt. "Let's get out of here."

We creep back upstairs and through the silent halls. This place is dead in the early mornings. Most neckers will sleep until two or three in the afternoon at least. That doesn't mean no one is awake though.

A shout from above us has me stopping in my tracks.

"Wake Cesare up! Two neckers have the prisoner!"

Shit. "Kabs, run," I hiss. They must have had security cameras down there.

We sprint, skidding around a corner in the kitchen. The backdoor is locked, a silent alarm flashing in red above the doorway. I take a half step back, then kick it firmly. The door cracks but doesn't open, so I kick it again. It breaks in half and I force my way out.

We run across the back lawn. I can smell that Maybelle and Elise passed this way recently. I risk a glance behind us; the men are just now exiting the house.

Kabs disappears into the trees ahead of me and I run faster to catch up to him, letting the sluggish vampire magic give me more strength. Maybelle and Elise appear in front of us and I skid to a halt.

"I specifically said no heroics!" Maybelle hisses at me.

"I need him," I say firmly.

"Why is he unconscious?" Elise asks, pulling her gun.

"I had to knock him out," I say uncomfortably.

"He didn't want to be rescued," Kabs explains. "Refused our help and tried to make us leave."

"You..." Maybelle throws her hands up in exasperation. "You *kidnapped* some necker—"

"He's a witch," I interrupt. "I don't know what kind. I've never felt anything like him before, but he's powerful."

"Well, there's no going back now," Elise says. "Let's get out of here."

"Elise, you take Kabs," I say. "Maybelle, get on my back. Elise and I can run faster than either of you."

Maybelle looks skeptical, but she climbs on my back, wrapping her arms around the unconscious witch instead of my neck. It's awkward, but it'll have to work.

Elise runs ahead of me, Kabs gleefully clinging to her back. I'm glad someone is having fun. The sound of our human pursuers fades as we quickly outstrip them. Our car is parked over two miles away. I won't be able to keep this pace up the entire way.

"Elise, slow down," I gasp. She slows to a jog and I catch up to run beside her. "I can't hear them anymore, can you?"

"No," Elise says, not out of breath at all. "We'll make it back to the car."

We run the rest of the way in silence, both of us listening intently for any sign that they're catching up. Roots stick out of the uneven ground, threatening to trip me with every step I take.

The car is parked on a deserted, dead-end road that winds through the forest. Maybelle climbs down from my back and Kabs hops off Elise.

"Looks alright," Maybelle says uneasily.

"I don't smell anyone," Elise comments.

We hurry over to the car and pile inside. The witch is stuffed in the backseat between Elise and Kabs while Maybelle claims shotgun. I crank the engine and peel out.

The prisoner is tied to a chair, still unconscious. Elise and Kabs have gone to get us food and phone chargers since both of our phones are dead. Maybelle is pacing the motel room floor.

I have read and re-read the translation of the same passage in the spell book at least five times. It's wrong to call it a spell book. It's half spell book, half Izul's diary. He was a brilliant man, but he let Aris influence him to use that intelligence in terrible ways.

We captured Cadriel, but to really kill him, he must be drained of his magic. The idea that we must create another abomination to kill the first one is unthinkable. I will keep the knowledge for now, just in case we must use this last resort.

"We might have had a couple of days without Cesare looking for us if you hadn't taken him," Maybelle says, interrupting my thoughts.

I close the book with a sigh. "I know, but I couldn't leave him there."

Maybelle rubs her bony fingers down her face then looks at me. "What's done is done."

Guilt at dragging Maybelle into this mess settles in the pit of my stomach. I grab my wallet and pull out the shiny black credit card I never gave back to Reilly.

"Go back to Donheim," I say, holding out Reilly's credit card to her. "This will get a rental car and whatever else you and Kabs want to take back with you."

"No," Maybelle says pushing my hand away. "I'm seeing this through."

There is a quick rap on the door then Elise and Kabs walk in. The smell of delicious, fried food hits me. My stomach rumbles.

"He's still out?" Elise asks.

"Yep, but he should be waking up any minute now," I say as she hands me a bag of food.

Elise unpacks the chargers and plugs in our phones. "Find anything else in that book?"

"Nothing I haven't already shown you," I say, tapping my fingers against it.

A groan draws my attention to the prisoner. He twitches and I watch him impatiently. Waking up after being hit with a knock-out brew is a slow process. Your brain wants to stay asleep, but your body is hopped up on adrenaline as it tries to fight off the effects of the brew.

His eyes snap open and he tries to move, but we bound him tightly to the chair. He isn't going anywhere.

"Wha...th...fu..." He slurs.

"Finally," I mutter. I walk over to stand right in front of him, grabbing his face to get him to focus. "Hey, what is your name?"

He jerks his face out of my grip and he looks around the dirty motel room. "None of your fucking business," he snaps in anger. "You have no idea what you've done."

"Fill me in then," I say, spreading my hands wide. "All I do know is that you, supposedly, released the Bound God even though you know about the prophecy. So far, you sound like an asshole."

He bares his teeth at me. "You sound like an idiot."

"Oh no, now my feelings are hurt," I say sarcastically. "Are you going to insult me or give me answers?"

Elise flicks her claws out behind me, shifting just enough for her hands and teeth to begin to change. "Answers would be good," she agrees with a threatening grin.

The prisoner snorts and rolls his eyes. "You don't scare me."

Elise sighs. "I told you this wasn't going to work."

"Maybe Staci will want to test her new truth potion on this guy," I say, gritting my teeth.

"If what he's saying it true, we don't have that kind of time," Elise says, shaking her head. "We have to contact JHAPI soon and we can't sit around in this motel room waiting for him to come to his senses."

"Fine, call Zachary if the phone is charged enough," I say. "We should warn them at least."

"Let me go," the prisoner growls.

"No," Elise and I say in unison.

"You have no reason to keep me," he insists.

"Explain to me why you let the god loose, and I'll consider letting you go," I say, leaning down to speak to him at eye level.

"Cesare would have killed me if I hadn't," he spits out.

"Lie," I say, crossing my arms.

"What are you?" he asks, narrowing his eyes. "You aren't a werewolf like that one," he says jerking his chin toward Elise. "You can't hear my heartbeat."

"Give me your name and I'll tell you," I say.

He stares at me, still furious. "Felix Rust."

I don't recognize that name. Maybe Zachary or Reilly will. "I'm half witch, half vampire," I tell him, holding up my end of the bargain.

His eyes go wide. "You're like him," he whispers.

I snort. "Yeah, an abomination according to Izul. Key to the prophecy has a better ring to it though."

"The prophecy is just meant to comfort foolish people that don't want to understand how the world works," Felix sneers. "I don't care about it. I only want to protect—" He trails off without finishing his sentence and shakes his head.

"How can you say you don't care about the prophecy? It came

true. You caused the Day of Breaking," I say, throwing my hands in the air.

"Of course the prophecy came true," Felix sneers. "You trap someone powerful, eventually they are going to get loose. It was the inevitability of failure, not fate."

"What are you trying to protect if you don't care about stopping Cadriel?" I demand.

"My granddaughter," Felix bites out. "Justine. After Cesare captured me he told me I could either help, or he would kill her. If Cesare could get to me, then I have no doubt he could get to her too."

I rub my temples. "It still doesn't make sense. If Cadriel has been loose for days why didn't he immediately attack?"

Felix sighs. "He was weak. He couldn't even stand when he first re-entered this world."

"Why? And what do you mean he re-entered this world?"

"Ignorant children," Felix mutters before responding. "What do you know about the nocte viator? The shadow walkers."

"That they died out a long time ago and they could travel in shadows or something," I say, trying to remember exactly what Hu had said about them.

"Wrong and wrong," Felix says with a sigh. "The shadow walkers while in the cover of darkness manipulates space and time to travel to a realm that is outside of both. Time passes differently there; sometimes slower and sometimes faster. If you travel in that realm you could end up somewhere completely unintended in the physical realm if you don't know what you're doing."

That explains the bright light Cesare had on this guy in that prison cell. The blinds are all open and the late evening sunlight is still pouring into the room, but the sun will be setting soon. Felix has just been buying time and waiting for the sun to set. He knew we couldn't keep him here.

"And Cadriel was trapped there?" I ask.

Felix nods. "A shadow walker can bring anyone and anything into the realm if they are strong enough."

"But that person can't get out unless they can use that type of magic?" I ask. It's starting to make sense.

"Correct," Felix says.

"Let me guess, you and Justine are the last two shadow walkers left in the world?" I ask.

"Most likely," Felix says, his eyes distant. "Cadriel began hunting the shadow walkers hundreds of years ago trying to steal the magic. After he failed, and we trapped him in the shadow realm, Izul tried to finish the job. He thought that if the magic died out, then Cadriel would be as good as dead. Some of my ancestors hid in the shadow realm for years in order to avoid being slaughtered, and so, we survived. Unfortunately."

"You really think it would have been better for Izul to have succeeded?" I ask, horrified.

"This magic is a curse," Felix snaps. "Even to this day we are hunted, not to be slaughtered, but to be *used*. Cesare isn't the first, and he won't be the last."

"Look," I say, rubbing my hands down my face. "We can't keep you here. I know you're gone as soon as the sun sets, but if there is anything you know that might help me kill Cadriel, please tell me."

"There is no way you can win," Felix says. "Just run and hope for the best."

I grit my teeth and turn my back on him. "Let's call Zachary."

Elise turns her phone on and it immediately buzzes with missed calls and messages. "Zachary has called nine time," Elise says, looking worried.

She dials his number and puts the phone on speaker. It rings twice.

"Elise?" Zachary asks, sounding somewhat frantic.

"Yes, what's going on?" She asks.

"The witch council was attacked last night. It was a massacre, only one of the council members survived. No one knows who is responsible, and the witches are refusing to let JHAPI inside." he says. "Whatever is in there has them terrified."

"Shit," I say, sitting down heavily on the bed.

"Zach, the Bound God has already been released," Elise says, glaring at Felix. "It must have been him that attacked the council."

"You and Olivia need to get back here as soon as you can," Zachary says, fear evident in his voice. "Reilly has been…angry since Olivia left. We talked him out of trying to work with the coven, but I don't know if that will last."

"If the coven shows up, I'm killing Alexandra Hunt," I spit out angrily. "If Reilly tries to stop me, I'll kill him too."

"We'll have your back, but I hope it doesn't come to that," Zachary says with a sigh.

Felix looks at me curiously. "What do you have against Alexandra Hunt?" he asks.

"She killed my mother," I say before turning back to the phone. "Zachary, as soon as the sun sets Cesare is going to know that he was robbed. Tell Reilly and make sure no one goes back the clanhouse."

"What do we do now that this thing is loose?" Zachary asks.

I look down at my hands and spread my palms wide. There is only one choice. "I'm going to Find him, and I'm going to kill him."

"Do you have any idea how to?" Elise asks.

I look up. "The spell book says he has to be drained of magic to have a chance of killing him. That's something I can do if I can get close enough. I have to try."

"You won't be able to just walk up to him," Felix scoffs.

I turn on him, furious. "No shit," I snap. "If you don't have anything helpful to add you can shut up or I'll knock you out again."

"If you want to have a chance of killing Cadriel, you'll have to trap him in the shadow realm again," Felix snaps back.

"And are you volunteering to do this?" I demand.

"No," he says, his face shifting as he decides something. "Can you take someone's magic without killing them?"

"Yes, it just depends on how much I take. If I take all of it, they will die," I explain. "Why?"

"I don't want Cadriel or Cesare to take over the world, but I'm not willing to fight. I'm done being used. Let me find my granddaughter and ensure her safety. After that you can take my magic and do what you want with it," Felix says. "Either way, I'm leaving as soon as the sun sets."

"Why are you offering to help now?" I ask, suspicious of this sudden change in heart.

"Hunt killed my son," Felix says gruffly. "I feel more inclined to help someone that hates her just as much as I do."

"It's a deal then," I say. "How long will it take you to find Justine?"

Felix shrugs. "There is a safe house she is supposed to go to if something every happened to me. If she's there, I'll be back soon."

"And if she isn't?" I ask, narrowing my eyes.

"Then I don't know how long it will take," he says, unconcerned with my desperation. "Wait here for no more than three hours. If I'm not back before then, assume I'm dead and all hope is lost."

"If you can't show me how to use the magic, it will be pointless though," I say, frustrated. "I don't automatically know how to use magic I take."

Felix snorts. "That shouldn't be a problem. I can teach you."

"Can you teach me in a couple of hours?" I ask.

"Were you not listening to the part where I can manipulate space and time?" Felix retorts sarcastically. "When we enter the shadow realm, I can make sure time is slowed for us."

I cross my arms. "Then it's a deal."

"I'll call you back, Zachary," Elise says.

"Fine, but as soon as Reilly wakes up Olivia's phone is going to be ringing off the hook. She should probably talk to him soon," Zachary says.

"Oh, so now he wants to hear what I have to say?" I mutter sarcastically.

Elise smirks and hangs up. I look out the window, the sun is half set already. I can feel it in my bones, and I suspect Felix can too. Grabbing the knife on the bed, I lean over and cut the ropes that bind him to the chair.

He nods gratefully and rubs his wrist. The sun sinks below the horizon, and the air Felix shakes. Smoky magic curls around his extremities. I meet his eyes as the deep purple magic wraps around him. His body fades into the smoke, then is gone.

I stare at the spot he once occupied and curl my hand into a fist.

"Do you think he's coming back?" Elise asks.

"I really hope so."

CHAPTER 21

I stop pacing and scuff the weird stain on the carpet with the toe of my shoe.

"It's been three hours," Maybelle says. Again.

"I know," I admit. "I'm going to wait just a little longer." I can't give up yet. Felix hadn't been lying when he said he would return, and he did say time passed oddly in the shadow realm. He's not that late. Yet. My phone buzzes in my hand and I glare at the caller ID. It's Reilly again.

The temperature of the air drops almost imperceptibly and the smell of magic fills my nose. I step back as the air in front of me shimmers, then splits open. Dark, smoky magic pours out like fog and pools on the floor. Felix slowly comes into view along with a woman behind him. When he had said granddaughter I thought she must be a child, but Justine is my age. Judging by the sneer on her face she is not happy to be here.

"You're late," I say, tension making me sound angry.

"Yet, you're still here," Felix says with a shrug.

"I still don't think you should do this," Justine says to Felix, though her glare is fixed on me.

"My decision is made," Felix says calmly.

Justine takes a step forward, her long black ponytail swinging behind her. "If you kill him, I will make you suffer."

"I don't need you to threaten me in order to avoid doing that," I say calmly before turning to Elise and asking, "Ready?"

"Yes, we'll go back to the team as planned," Elise agrees, her lips are pressed tightly together in disapproval. "Will I need to come back here to pick you up tomorrow at sunset?"

"No, if Olivia can't find you by the time we are done training her, then she might as well not show up for the fight," Felix answers for me. He thrusts his hand out. "Take everything you can without killing me. There's no point in giving this to you if you end up weak."

I nod and wrap my hand around his wrist. The first pull is always so satisfying. Hunger stirs in my gut, eager for more.

Felix's magic is strange. It's obvious he is powerful, but it doesn't feel anything like the cold, deep magic of a vampire. The magic has no weight to it. As I take it, I feel lighter. The smoky magic seeps into every corner of my body.

Felix shudders as he begins to feel the drain. Justine grabs his arm to support him and looks at me with undisguised hatred. I pull on his magic faster. I don't want to draw this out.

His hand twitches and his arm shakes as he struggles to remain standing. Just a little more, he's almost at his limits. Felix's knees give out and I drop his arm. Justine catches him and lowers him to the ground. The unfamiliar magic drifts inside of me.

Felix looks up at me. "That was unpleasant," he says in a rough voice.

"So I've heard," I agree.

"I can still feel the magic, you didn't take as much as you could have," Felix accuses.

"If I take the absolute most I can without killing you, you'll be unconscious for a long time," I say. "I need you to train me still."

Felix nods in understanding, but he doesn't look pleased. "Justine will take us into the shadow realm where we can begin teaching you."

Elise grabs the keys off the table. "How long will she be gone?"

"Until tomorrow after sunset," Felix says, struggling to his feet. "That will give us five times that long in the shadow realm. It will have to be long enough."

"Don't do anything stupid, Olivia," Elise says.

I grin. "I would never."

Justine rolls her eyes and stretches her hand out to her side, magic rolling out from her body. The purple magic creeps upward and the air itself splits open, revealing absolute darkness. Felix walks into it without hesitation and disappears into the inky black hole.

"Go," Justine says, "I'm not holding the portal open forever."

I walk up and tentatively reach my hand into the darkness. It vibrates along with the magic I just took from Felix, but it's cold. Taking a deep breath, I plunge through the opening.

The room doesn't fade from sight like I expected. I can still see and hear. A strange current tugs at my legs. My hair waves around my head, being pulled in one direction as though it's caught in a wind.

I turn in a circle and see Maybelle watching silently, arms crossed, face concerned. Kabs looks eager, about ready to follow me through the portal. Elise's heart is pounding in her chest as she stares at me, but it's like she's looking straight through me.

"We're no longer in the physical realm," Felix says.

I jump and stumble backward with a scream. I thought I was alone.

Felix chuckles. "However, we're not completely in the shadow realm either. She will fade from sight soon."

Justine appears in the darkness. The cold seeps through my jacket as the motel room becomes blurry, like I'm looking at it through gauze.

For a brief second I feel like I'm falling, then a new world starts filtering into view. My feet slip slightly and I look down. There's sand under my feet. It's silver and glows faintly. A steady, cool breeze blows it across my feet. The sand is heaped into dunes all around us and scattered with silvery trees and shrubs bent from the constant wind.

Something wriggles under my foot and I jerk away. A strange, glowing worm pokes its head out of the sand, then sinks back in and disappears.

"What was that?"

Justine shrugs. "I call them glow worms, but no one has bothered to learn much about them. Look up," she says. "That's where it gets good."

I do as she says and stop breathing. The sky looks close enough to touch. I've never seen an aurora borealis in person but I don't think it could compare to this. Every color I can imagine is streaked across the sky in constant motion. Bright flashes of lightning cut through the colors every few seconds. It's like some kind of cosmic storm.

"It's beautiful," I say reverently.

A fist appears in my peripheral vision and I duck on instinct, stumbling backward to avoid the next strike. Felix sits off to the side watching, unconcerned, as Justine shifts her stance and prepares to attack me again.

"What the hell are you doing?" I demand.

Justine charges, pulling a thin stick off her back. I duck under the first swing and slam my fist into her stomach. Justine wheezes as she's thrown back half a step. She tosses the stick to her other hand and swings again, striking from a different direction this time. I catch the stick and kick, but she checks the kick and shoves me back.

"She's not completely hopeless," Justine comments, looking at me critically.

Electric magic sparks from my fingertips as I keep a safe

distance between us. "You're supposed to be training me, not trying to kill me," I snap.

"If you use magic in this realm, you will attract some unwanted guests," Felix warns looking suspiciously at the sand dune to our left.

"Unwanted guests?" I ask, looking around. "People live here?"

"Not people," Justine says. "The shadow creatures. They feed on magic. If they smell it, they come running; and they are vicious. They might show up regardless, but using magic is like lighting a beacon."

"You can't fight them off with magic either," Felix explains. "Anything you throw at them they simply absorb and grow stronger from it."

"And bigger," Justine says with a shudder.

"How am I supposed to train here if I can't use magic?" I demand.

"You need to learn how to control the shadow walker magic. That is the one type of magic that you can use here. The shadow creatures hate it for some reason," Felix says. "It can't hurt them, so I've never been sure why. They run from it though."

"And is Justine going to keep randomly attacking me?" I ask, glancing at her.

"Perhaps," Justine replies with a grin.

"The best way to learn, is to do. Come sit down and I will explain the basics," he says, pointing to the ground in front of him, "then the real training will begin."

I walk toward him while keeping a close eye on Justine. Felix sits down cross-legged, and I drop to the sand in front of him.

"Now, in order to bring more than two or three people into this realm, a portal must be open. With enough focus and magic, you can create a portal that will stay open for minutes, or even hours. But when you fight Cadriel, what you want is speed; creating the portal is slow. Besides, you don't want to leave an exit he can just stroll out of if he kills you," Felix explains. "There is a faster way to move while you are in this realm."

Justine runs toward me and I jump to my feet, but a wave of the dark shadow magic swallows her up. I freeze, looking at the spot she was just standing. A kick sweeps my legs out from underneath me. My back hits the sand; Justine looks down at me with a grin.

"You can slip into the in-between to travel faster and avoid an attack," Felix says.

"Or catch someone by surprise with an attack of your own," Justine finishes with a sly grin.

She's way too happy about getting to knock me down. This training is going to be even tougher than Hu's.

CHAPTER 22

"You can break into arguably the most well-protected clanhouse in the continental US, but you can't manage to avoid walking face first into a kick? Good to know," Felix snaps sarcastically.

Justine snorts, the first thing I've seen resembling a smile pulling at her lips.

I spit a glob of blood out onto the silvery sand and press my hand against my cheek. It's swelling and probably already showing a bruise. My legs shake as I push back up to my feet.

Justine is already moving again. I slip backward into the in-between, the place between realms. The magic carries me as I push through the current that tugs at my legs; Justine's hazy silhouette follows me. I push back into the shadow realm, putting on a burst of speed, and charge the place I think she is going to end up.

Training without being able to use the new offensive magic I have stolen is difficult, but necessary. I used to be able to take on anyone with nothing but a few brews in my pocket. The electric magic has become a crutch and my weakness at the same time. I can use it better now, thanks to Hu; but it still tends to exhaust me.

I haven't wanted to risk using the vampire magic either. Justine is faster and stronger than I am without it.

Even though I want to quit, I could do this for hours if I had to. The shadow magic doesn't drain me as quickly as the others. It moves through me, in and out, like I'm breathing. It's almost inexhaustible.

Justine appears in front of me and I dart to the side but trip. Sands gets in my eye as I tumble down the short hill.

"Did I give you my magic so you could run around like a damn chicken with your head cut off?" He shouts, his face red. "Use your brain! Think ahead!"

I scramble to my feet and dodge Justine's strike. She advances, twirling that stupid stick like a baton. I want to rip it out of her hands and beat her with it, but I'm lucky if I can dodge a few blows. I'm completely on the defensive here. Even when I was training with Reilly, it wasn't this bad. That asshole must have been going easy on me.

Again and again, I slip out of the way just in the nick of time. As I duck under another swing I realize I've been missing something obvious. I keep using the shadow magic to move myself into the in-between, but that's not the only way I can use it. Gritting my teeth, I push the magic out underneath Justine's feet and open the ground beneath her.

She falls; the stick slips from her hand as the current sucks her down. I run forward, concerned for a split second, but a kick against the back of my legs stops that in its tracks. My legs fly out from under me. All the air is knocked from my lungs as my back hits the ground.

"Finally," Justine says, standing over me with her hands on her hips. "I thought you'd never think of it."

"You could have just told me," I say, exhausted.

Felix appears over me as well, still pale. "Then you would not be learning to think for yourself. Cadriel will be neither slow nor stupid. You have to be able to think outside the box, and faster, if you are going to survive a fight against him."

"Fair point." I take a deep breath, then push up into a sitting position. "Why am I not thirsty?" I ask, still trying to catch my breath. I should be dying of thirst after the time we've spent exerting ourselves.

"Because this isn't real," Justine says. "You don't need to eat or sleep here."

"This place is fucking weird," I say under my breath. "Why are you helping, by the way?"

She seems to hate me, but she's putting out a lot of effort to help.

Justine looks away. "Felix said Alexandra killed your mother."

I nod.

"She killed my parents as well," Justine explains. "My dad believed in all this prophecy shit. I don't, but he would have wanted me to help. So I am."

"How do either of you know about the prophecy?" I ask. "It isn't exactly common knowledge."

"We were part of Alexandra's coven. The Praesidio," Justine says.

I swallow uncomfortably. I suspected as much, but hearing it said out loud still makes me sick to my stomach. They seem to hate the coven as much as I do at least.

"Get up," Felix barks at me. "There's no time for this."

The hours blend together and I lose all sense of how long we've been here. My arms and legs have become a mass of bruises, but I can't risk using the healing magic. After a particularly brutal knockdown, Felix finally allows me a break since I can no longer stand.

"How much longer?" I ask. I won't quit, but I can't deny I'm hoping this is almost over.

"It's been about six hours, I suppose," he says, squinting at the horizon. "We still have what will feel like days before it will be night again in the physical realm."

I shut my eyes and shove down the urge to flee back to the real world.

"You can go after him now; you will fail, and he will continue. What use is that?" Felix asks calmly, sensing my frustration.

"I know," I bite out. "I'm not giving up."

"You are learning more quickly than I expected," Felix says, offering the first compliment I've heard him utter. "You'll keep getting faster."

Justine walks over and holds her hand out to help me up. I take it despite wanting to lay down for a while longer. She looks me over, pursing her lips.

"Do you have a healing brew in your jacket?" She asks.

"I think so," I say.

"That shouldn't attract the creatures," she says. "Use it and let's get back to work."

I down the healing brew and the aches fade.

Justine tosses me her staff. "You should learn to use this too."

I wrap both hands around the smooth wood and brace myself for her next attack.

A warm trail of blood slides from my nose over my lips. I wipe it away with the back of my hand and regret using that last healing brew hours ago. My left leg ache from a strike Justine got in. I think it might have split the skin. She holds the staff loosely and watches me, waiting for me to make the next move. She took the staff back a little while ago after she decided I had gotten the hang of it.

I step backwards into the in-between. My feet slip in the current and I fall. I can't breathe and I grasp at the air uselessly. Gritting my teeth, I force myself to stop panicking and let the shadow magic lift me back up. I fall out of the in-between and hit the sand. Justine is a few strides away, giving me time to jump back up to my feet and face her.

"Enough," Felix interrupts, "it's time to return." He points at the edge of the horizon where a red moon is beginning to rise in odd, jerky movements. Once second it's just peeking over the horizon, then I blink and it's halfway into the sky. It feels like I've been here for a week.

Justine puts her short staff on her back and nods at me. "Good luck," she says. It actually seems like she means it.

"Do you think I'm ready?" I ask Felix, staring out at the blood red moon that hovers dully against the backdrop of the brilliant sky.

"No, not at all," he crosses his arms and sighs. "Maybe if you had five or six years of focused training and few more types of offensive magic, but—" He trails off into silence, simply staring straight ahead.

The ever-present wind blows sand over my bare feet. I wiggle my toes, trying to remind myself this isn't just a nightmare. This is my new, and possibly brief, reality.

"Is he really as powerful as a god?" I ask. The question has been weighing on me. A god sounds invincible. Then again, so did the Witch Council, but they're all dead now.

"I don't know," Felix says, rubbing his hand over the scratchy stubble that has almost grown into a full beard since his imprisonment. "I hope not."

I turn my head just enough to see his reaction to my next question.

"You and Justine aren't coming with me, are you?"

He looks down, his face drawn and tired. "No, we aren't."

"Can't blame you, I'm not even sure why I'm going sometimes," I say with a sharp laugh.

He claps his hand on my shoulder, giving me a tight, unhappy smile. "Wouldn't want to waste all this training, now would you?" He asks.

"Definitely not," he agrees. "Use your Finding magic and let it guide you to your friends like we talked about. Just remember, it will draw the shadow creature to you, so move quickly."

Felix claps my shoulder one more time, as if he's trying to reassure himself, then steps away. His footsteps fade away, the swish of the sand blending into the rush of the wind in my ears. Justine's magic vibrates behind me as she carries them into the in-between.

I face the vast, rolling dunes, and for a moment I feel overwhelmingly lonely. This place is beautiful, but desolate. I turn away from the view. Whether I'm ready or not, and whether I succeed or not, it's time to go do everything I can to fulfill my mother's last request.

I'm doing the *right* thing, and, despite how much I wish Felix and Justine were coming with me, I won't have to do this alone.

CHAPTER 23

Sand falls over my feet as I climb up the steep sand dune. The Finding magic tugs me forward like a guide. Nothing looks familiar here, but I'm almost there. Reilly is close, well, as close as he can be when I'm in a place that isn't even real.

A weird, yipping noise breaks the silence. I turn around slowly. Dark shapes watch me from the bottom of the hill. I step back and the creatures break into a run, heading straight for me. Shit. I turn and run in the direction the magic is pulling me. I crest the hill and it immediately slopes downward. Half-slipping, half-running, I careen down the sharp incline.

The yips turn to pained-sounding howls. I slide to a stop and lift my hands. The shadow magic begins swallowing me. The creatures reach the top of the hill and sprint toward me. Justine was not kidding about their size. They're larger than wolves with teeth like lions.

If I can get Cadriel back into the shadow realm, he may not want to risk using magic, which would give me an advantage with my brews. If he does use magic…there has to be some way to turn that to my advantage too.

The creatures and the silvery sand fade into shadow, and the current of the in-between tugs at my feet. I manage to keep upright, but it's a struggle. The soft white of the hotel room shimmers in front of me. I'm shaking from fear and the exhaustion. My leg is killing me.

Shadow magic pushes me forward and I stumble into the midst of a crowd of people.

"Olivia!" Elise cries in relief. She catches me as I slump forward.

"How did she do that?" Someone asks in the background.

"Nocte viator," Hu answers, his voice reverent.

I nod. "Yes, Cesare had captured one of the last shadow walkers. That was how he released Cadriel."

"What the hell did Felix do to you?" Elise asks.

"Training," I say with a dry throat. It seems like all the thirst I hadn't felt in the shadow realm is making itself known now. I look up and realize the entire JHAPI team is here along with Reilly, his clanmates. The only people missing are Javier and Patrick.

Maybelle and Kabs are watching a few steps away from the rest of the group. Maybelle looks uneasy, but she gives me a small smile and nods in greeting.

"And I thought we were hard on you," Elise says, shaking her head. "Someone bring her a healing brew."

Reilly is standing behind everyone else, his arms crossed, glaring at me. He's furious. I expect him to come yell at me but he turns and walks into his room. Ihaka follows him.

"I couldn't use magic in the shadow realm," I explain to Elise. "And I ran out of healing brews."

Staci hurries over with a healing brew.

"Thanks," I say before swallowing it down. The relief is immediate.

"Where are Patrick and Javier?" I ask.

"They went back to Texas to get the rest of the clan that is going to join the fight," Elise says. "I guess you learned how to use the shadow walker magic?"

"Well enough," I confirm with a nod.

Stocke steps forward. "I understand that you and Reilly have disagreed on how to move forward. However, while you were gone, the team filled me in and, after the attack on the council, I have been able to persuade JHAPI to throw their full support behind this mission," Stocke says. "Did you learn how to kill this Bound God?"

"Maybe. I have an idea at least," I say, my mind still whirring with all the possibilities. "I need to get Cadriel back into the shadow realm where it's not safe to use magic. The creatures that live there feed on it, and if you use anything but shadow walker magic, they come running. That will either keep him from using magic at all, or make it harder on him the more he uses."

"And if it doesn't?" Zachary asks, always the skeptic.

"If he kills me, then he's trapped again," I say with a shrug. "It's a win-win."

"You can't go fight him alone," Elise says, shaking her head firmly. "That's just a suicide mission."

"It might be suicide for whoever joins me," I protest.

"No," Zachary says. "I agree with Elise. You have to take backup. I'm going with you."

"I'm going too," Elise says. "Partners stick together."

I look at her with wide eyes, but there isn't a trace of hesitation on her face. I don't want to get either of them killed; this is my burden not theirs.

"I'm in as well," Hu says as he steps forward and puts a hand on my shoulder. "I want to see the shadow realm."

"If that's the only reason I can just take you there right now," I say, frowning at him.

"That's not even close to the only reason," Hu says, nudging me. "I'm going."

"And I came to finish this," Maybelle says, walking over to stand beside me. "I want to see this creature killed. My illusions will help you."

Kabs pops up beside her and crosses his arms. "Where she goes, I go."

Maybelle doesn't argue, so they must have talked about this already.

"Don't even think about arguing," Elise says.

"No one else," I say firmly.

Stocke nods in agreement. "The rest of the team can back you up from outside. What supplies do you need?" Stocke asks.

"Some basic brews, maybe," I say, thinking through the possibilities. "There isn't much that can help me fight Cadriel."

"Cesare has to know we're planning something," Stocke says, looking around the room at our small group. "JHAPI will do everything they can to stop him while you take on Cadriel, but we could use some more backup."

"There's someone I can call," I say. Ian said he owed me and Reilly a favor. This is a big one, but I'm calling it in. "Do you know where Cesare is?"

"Cesare has been seen near the witch council, and we think Cadriel is there as well. As far as we can tell, he never left after storming inside and killing half the council. Do you have the strength to Find Cadriel?" Stocke asks, looking at me skeptically. "We need to be sure before we charge in there with no idea what we're up against."

"I think so. I'm not magically exhausted, just physically," I explain.

"I can help her Find him," Corinne says, stepping forward. "It'll be easier if we do it together. I have the experience, and Olivia is surprisingly powerful."

I look down at my clothes. "I'm just going to go change real quick," I say.

Corinne nods and I hurry to my room. I strip out of my sandy jeans and jacket. Justine managed to tear a hole in the arm. My door opens and I look up to yell at whoever just walked in, but shut my mouth when I see that it's Reilly. He closes the door behind him.

"What do you want?" I ask as I turn away and strip off my shirt. If he wants to barge in while I'm changing then he can deal with seeing me half-dressed. I don't care.

"You could have been killed," he says in a tense, quiet voice.

"I could be killed tomorrow, too." I grab a clean pair of jeans and step into them. "Hell, I could be killed in the next twenty minutes. I'm not exactly living a risk-free life right now." I snatch a wrinkled t-shirt out of a pile of clean clothes and turn around to face him. "And it's not like I failed. If I hadn't gone when I did, we'd all be fucked."

"You jeopardized everything without even warning me," Reilly snaps, the anger finally surfacing. He stalks toward me, his jaw clenched tightly.

"You wouldn't even consider not working with the coven," I argue as he stops right in front of me. "I know Adrian told you how to contact them. Did you go behind my back and talk to them yet?"

Reilly leans in close. "I will not fail at this. Cesare must be stopped."

"No shit," I snap. "That's what I'm trying to do."

"Don't get in my way again," he hisses.

"Take your own advice," I say, shoving him away from me. "Don't get in *my* way. I'm going to kill Cadriel with, or without, your help. And I will kill Alexandra Hunt if I have to."

There's a single knock and the door opens. Corinne pops her head in. "You done, Olivia?" She asks congenially, ignoring that we're in the middle of an argument.

"Yep," I say, brushing past Reilly. "Definitely done." His angry heartbeat thunders in my ears as I walk out of the room.

The rest of the team is standing around the edge of the room, and one of the couches has been shoved out of the way. A large map of Washington state is rolled out on the floor.

"I'm going to guide the magic," Corinne explains, hands on her hips as she checks to make sure the map is smooth. She looks up at me. "You'll have to trust me, and it will feel a little odd, but it's much less risky than even a normal Finding."

Reilly walks past us, nods at Ihaka, and the two leave the hotel room. I tear my eyes away from the door and focus on Corinne.

I nod. "Okay. Is there anything I need to do?"

Corinne holds out her hand. "Link your hand with mine and stretch the other out over the map."

I put my hand in hers and extend my arm over the map as instructed. Her magic flows out around us in a wave that tingles along my skin. I push my magic out. It rushes toward the map, eager to Find our target.

A gentle tug slows it down and the magic pulses. Everything sways and I hear our heartbeats like an echo around us.

"That's it," Corinne whispers.

I look down. The map is covered in delicate, bright red tendrils of magic; more than either of us could have done on our own. The magic filters down until there is one strand remaining.

"Found him," we say in unison. Corinne releases my hand and with the final beat, my magic snaps back into me. I know where he is now. Nothing can stop us from killing him.

"He's definitely still at the witch council," Corinne says, turning to face Stocke. "We'll know if he leaves."

"Great work," Stocke says, nodding her head in approval. "I have the blueprints for the council building. Let's go over it and decide the best way to enter."

No one is paying attention to me for the first time since I made my dramatic entrance. I gladly slip into my room and close the door behind me, taking a deep breath. There hasn't been a moment to relax in days, and there isn't one now, but a few minutes alone is better than nothing.

I dial Ian's number. The phone rings, and I stare at the gleaming brewing equipment. It taunts me with a reminder of

Reilly's manipulations. I pace the room, tempted to throw the cauldrons out the window, when a thought sparks at the edges of my mind.

Stopping in my tracks, I stare at the remnants of the last disastrous brew. I've been trying to find a way to cure my hunger. What if I've been going about it all wrong? What if...*oh*. This could change everything.

"Ian Grzeski," he says, answering the phone gruffly.

"Ian, it's Olivia," I say. "It's a lot sooner than I expected to have to make this call, but I need your help."

I step back and the smoky purple magic fades, taking the failed brew with it. It's clear what's missing from the brew now. Getting the final ingredient will be tricky though. My door opens and I jump, startled at nearly being caught.

"Ihaka?" I say, surprised he has come to talk to me.

He closes the door and sniffs the air. "It smells odd in here."

I point at the workbench. "Just trying something new," I say. It's not a lie, and my heartbeat stays fast, but steady. "Can I help you?"

"Did Reilly ever tell you about Ava?" Ihaka asks.

"No," I say questioningly. "Who is she?"

"The first vampire he sired. He turned her around two-hundred years ago," Ihaka says, walking farther into the room. "Perhaps you should ask him about her sometime."

"Why?" I ask.

Ihaka crosses his arms. "You do not understand him," he says. "And until you do, you will not be able to convince him when he is being stupid."

I snort. "Can anyone do that?"

Ihaka shrugs. "You might be able to, if you care to learn how. There is a reason that Reilly is so angry with you for leaving like you did."

"And? What is it?" I ask.

"That is his story to tell," Ihaka says cryptically.

"I really don't have time to dissect whatever trauma has caused him to be a manipulative asshole right now," I say, walking toward the door. I need to talk to Maybelle, but I don't want to leave Ihaka alone in my room either. "Do you mind?" I ask, opening the door.

He walks over. "It is important that you understand, and talk to him," Ihaka says. "But it's up to you."

"Thanks for the tip," I say, opening the door and waving him ahead of me.

He nods and leaves. I follow, but stop in the doorway. Maybelle is standing in a corner watching Kabs talk with Elise and Patrick.

I catch her eye and subtly motion for her to join me. She looks at Kabs one last time and shakes her head, then heads over. I shut the door behind us.

"I still don't like that vampire," Maybelle says quietly, glaring at the door like he might be standing right behind it.

"We agree on a guy for once," I say.

She narrows her eyes. "You haven't—"

"No," I say, cutting off her question. "Definitely not. I don't trust him."

"That hasn't stopped you in the past," she says slyly.

"I'm learning from my mistakes," I say, crossing my arms.

"What did you call me in here for?" Maybelle asks.

"I have a plan, but I need your help," I say.

She narrows her eyes. "Explain."

"Felix was right; Cadriel's escape from the shadow realm wasn't fate, it was just inevitable. We have to kill Cadriel. Trapping him again isn't enough, it will only ensure that eventually he will get out again, and the next time Cadriel might succeed," I say.

Maybelle nods. "I agree."

"I think I've found something in the shadow realm that gives me a way to level the playing field between us, but I need your help to make it work," I say.

"My help?" Maybelle asks.

I nod. "I need to hide something from Cadriel until the last moment."

"What are you hiding? Some kind of trap?"

"Sort of," I say. "It's a brew. I haven't been able to make it work yet, but I've figured out the last ingredient I need."

CHAPTER 24

"Please put your seats in the upright position as we prepare for landing," the pilot announces over the speaker.

The flight from Los Angeles to Seattle is shorter than I expected; we made it just three hours after sunset. My fingers dig into the armrest. Cadriel is close. I glance at Corinne and she grimaces; she can feel it too.

Patrick peers out of the window, then puts his hand on my knee. "Don't die, okay?" he says quietly.

"I'm not planning on it," I say, linking my fingers with his and squeezing his hand. He squeezes back. I'm grateful he's here, even though I'd prefer it if he wasn't going to be part of this fight.

The private jet Reilly hired for the team circles the city once before descending toward a small airstrip. The tires bump once as plane lands on the runway.

Everyone gathers their things, not that anyone brought much. I have a small satchel full of brews slung over my shoulder, but there was no point in bringing anything else.

Patrick joins Javier, Emilio, and the rest of their clan. Leslie is with them as well. Emilio doesn't look pleased to be here, but I don't think I've ever seen him look pleased to be anywhere. He's wearing his usual suit with the lace cuffs despite the impending battle. I shake my head, amused.

Maybelle slips in front of me as the group hurries off the plane. "Stay close to me," she says quietly, glancing back to make sure I heard.

I nod. Reilly has been quiet for most of the flight. It makes me nervous.

We walk down the narrow staircase that unfolds from the jet. The airstrip is dark apart from the lights that mark the runway. Stocke and Corinne fall into step beside me.

"Do you have Cadriel's location pin-pointed?" Stocke asks, looking at the two of us.

"I can feel him," I say. "He's still at the witch council."

Corinne nods in agreement, confirming his position.

"Our backup is meeting us in a few minutes," Stocke says, nodding in approval. "And Ian's pack is almost ready. We're fortunate they agreed to work with us."

Maybelle stops abruptly in front of me. "Reilly," she growls.

People in black robes spread out from the dark hangar. My blood runs cold. I look at Reilly as he walks up behind us, disbelieving even though part of me expected this. I thought he would try to convince me one last time. I thought I'd have more warning.

"What did you do?" I demand.

"The coven will help us," Reilly says, his face set.

Maybelle steps up behind me and put her hand on my elbow. I curl my fingers into a fist and prepare to pull on the shadow walker magic. I can't risk being trapped here in some kind of fight while Cadriel is out there, free to kill.

"This isn't going to go how you think it is," I say coldly.

Stocke steps forward, angry. "This was not what the group agreed to," she says, sweeping her arm toward the coven.

Reilly clenches his jaw tightly as Ihaka and Viking step up on his other side. "You do not dictate who I choose to ally with, Agent Stocke."

"I can't believe you lied to her again," Patrick hisses from behind us.

I glance back. Patrick is furious, and Javier doesn't look much happier.

"You promised us honesty when we joined you, Reilly," Javier says coldly.

"I promised I would do everything I could to ensure we succeed," Reilly retorts.

"What a rag-tag little group you have put together, Reilly," a woman says, her deep voice booming across the empty space. She is wearing a fitted black robe and her gray hair is twisted up into a severe bun.

"Ms. Hunt, we discussed that you would come alone," Reilly says, gesturing to the ten witches behind her.

She steps slightly forward from the group and purses her lips. "I changed my mind," she says, settling with her hands on her hips. Her eyes find mine and she smiles. "Olivia Carter, we should have met long ago."

"I'm not sorry we didn't," I say, grinding my teeth together.

Alexandra turns her attention back to Reilly. "Reilly, be a good boy and bring Olivia to me. We need to go after Cadriel soon, but she will need time to adjust."

"You swore to me that you would fight alongside us." Reilly says, his posture changing subtly. "What are you doing?"

My fingers twitch. I want to pull her into the shadow realm right now and end this, but Reilly is hesitating. We need him on our side. If there's even the slightest chance he'll come to his senses, I need that to happen. I watch him from the corner of my eye, ready to disappear if he tries to grab me.

"She is a weapon. Someone needs to take control, aim, and fire. Otherwise, she is useless," Alexandra says, looking me up and down disdainfully. She pulls a glinting, silver collar from the pocket of her robe and presses her hand to the pendant hanging around her neck. "This is what will allow us to defeat Cadriel, and Cesare."

I stare at the collar, understanding and horror creeping over me simultaneously. "Those were supposed to all have been destroyed," I bite out.

The device is horrifying. It strips away the free will of whoever wears the collar, turning them into a zombie controlled by the witch that wears the matching pendant.

Stocke pulls her gun and aims it at Reilly. The rest of the team follows suit, half of them aiming at the coven as well.

"If that's what I think it is," Stocke begins. "Then you will have to go through us to get to Olivia."

"I thought I was going to have to hunt down my dear Felix, but using you will be much better," Alexandra continues, unconcerned by the guns pointed at her.

"You know Felix?" I ask, hesitating in my confusion. He never mentioned that he knew her personally. All Justine had said was that Alexandra killed her father.

She laughs and cocks her head. "He's my husband. Didn't he tell you?"

Husband. Not even ex-husband. He's still married to her. I look at the collar and Felix's words about being used come back to me. She probably put that *thing* on him, and she killed their son in her pursuit of power. She's a monster.

"Don't do this," I whisper, taking a half step back from Reilly. "You know it's wrong."

He clenches his jaw and looks at me, then looks back at Alexandra. His heart is racing almost as fast as mine. At least this isn't easy for him.

"This wasn't part of the deal," Reilly says, clenching his hands into fists.

"There is no deal," Alexandra shouts, anger contorting her face. "Hand her over, now."

"You're not taking her," Reilly insists, his voice shifting into a growl as his fangs extend.

"Do you really think you have a say in this?" Alexandra asks, sneering. "You made it easier for us to find Olivia, but I was always going to take her when the time came."

Reilly growls and shifts his stance. "You're exactly like Cesare."

"I'm nothing like that coward," she scoffs. "The vampires have proven they aren't fit to be in power. I am going to use Olivia to kill Cadriel, then the witches are going to govern paranormals once again."

Stocke shifts and points her gun at the coven instead. "You aren't taking anyone, and you sure as hell won't be ruling anything."

"Stupid human," Alexandra spits, rage shattering her haughty composure. "As if you could stop me."

Dark, smoky magic drifts from behind the witches. I force myself to keep my eyes fixed on Alexandra, but I almost look down when the magic disappears. My nose tingles as the smell of Maybelle's illusion magic drifts toward me. She's hiding it.

Alexandra lifts her hand to the witches behind her and says, "Bring me Olivia."

The witches behind her fan out, preparing to attack. We outnumber them, but I still don't like our odds.

"Get out of here with whoever you can," Stocke whispers, looking back at me. "Get to Cadriel without us."

"Only if I have to," I whisper back. I won't leave my friends to face the coven alone, and I refuse to let Alexandra Hunt take anyone else that I care about from me.

The air splits open behind the line of witches and several fall into the dark fog that pours out. Justine appears out of the darkness and races toward Alexandra, a sword held in both hands.

Stocke opens fire, and the group splits apart. Reilly attempts to get in front of me, but I run to the side and lift my hands. Lightning erupts from my palms and collides with the stream of fire two witches are sending toward the team. I close my hands and crush their magic inside of mine, snuffing it out.

Hu runs forward and lifts a wall of flame between the group and the remaining witches. As the fire rushes by, I catch a glimpse of Justine advancing on Alexandra, who waits patiently for her next attack. Justine won't be able to kill her alone.

A rush of water breaks through the wall of fire and I sprint through the gap, moving vampire fast.

"Olivia, no!" Reilly shouts from behind me. I ignore him.

Justine swings her sword, but Alexandra waves her hand and a burst of water deflects the blow.

I catch Justine's gaze for a half-second and hope she knows what I'm thinking; we can do it just like training. Shadow magic envelops me as I step sideways into the shadow realm, just far enough to disappear from sight. I run toward Alexandra's shadowy silhouette.

"You idiot!" Alexandra shouts, her angry voice echoing through to me. "The coven's time is now, and you are working against us! You could have been my heir!"

"That's all you ever cared about!" Justine shouts back. "You let your own son die for this pointless shit!"

Justine dodges a wave of water and pours shadow magic into the ground right next to her feet, then drops the sword. It falls through the realms, but not in the direction it seems gravity would dictate.

I raise my hand and catch it by the hilt. The current tugs at my feet as I step back into the physical realm, already swinging the sword.

"This is for my father, you bitch," Justine growls.

Alexandra tries to turn toward me but the sword connects with her neck. The impact vibrates painfully up my arms as the blade cuts through bone. Alexandra falls, her head separating from her body.

Justine and I lock eyes, and for a moment, share a common

sense of grief. Alexandra is dead, but that won't bring back either of our parents.

I look back at the others. A few witches are fleeing now that Alexandra is dead. The others are all dead, or unconscious. Viking is drenched in blood. He grabs a limp witch by the back of the neck and sniffs them carefully, then tosses their body aside.

Stocke is shouting at Reilly, he listens to her stoically. Ihaka is watching me. He shakes his head and turns away. I curl my hand into a fist. In the end, Reilly was on my side, but the betrayal stings. He was so easily blinded by his own ambition.

I toss the sword back to Justine. "How did you find us?"

"Felix told me you were concerned about the coven showing up to stop you. I followed you after I took Felix back to the safe-house and I overheard that vampire talking about Alexandra," Justine says, glaring at Reilly. "I knew I'd never have a better shot at killing her."

"Thank you for helping," I say.

"I didn't do it for you," she says dismissively, already stepping back into the shadows.

"I'm still grateful," I say.

"Don't waste my grandfather's gift," she says, her voice muffled as she disappears.

I take a deep breath and walk toward the group. And Reilly. Justine's fight may be over, but mine isn't.

CHAPTER 25

"Can you give us a couple of minutes?" I ask, interrupting Stocke's rant.

She nods sharply. "I'm going to go make sure no one was hurt," Stocke says, turning away angrily.

I walk toward the hangar. This isn't a conversation I want to have in front of everyone else. Reilly follows me into the small waiting area attached to the office. I turn around abruptly.

"Don't *ever* do that again," I say, stepping in close and shoving my finger in his face. "I was starting to think I could trust you, and then you betrayed all of us."

"I couldn't risk failing," Reilly says, his eyes flashing with anger even as guilt bunches up his shoulders.

"Try again," I bite out.

Reilly turns away and drags a hand down his face. "I was trying to protect you. I thought that if we had more powerful people on our side that you would have a better chance of beating Cadriel. I didn't know she had that collar." He turns back, his face drawn, and looks me in the eye, "I'm sorry." He reaches out and drags the back of his hand down my arm, "Please, Olivia."

I grit my teeth. His heartbeat is steady, just like it was throughout his apology. He means it.

"If you pull something like this again, I won't wait to see if you come to your senses," I say firmly. People make mistakes. I know that better than most, but I also know that I won't keep someone in my life that lies to me. Ihaka's comments from the night before come back to me and I bite the inside of my cheek. "Who is Ava?"

Reilly looks up, his eyes wide. "Who told you that name?" He asks angrily.

"Just answer the question. Or are you going to try to insist on a question for a question like we used to do?" I sneer.

He looks away and sighs. He is silent long enough that I start to think he isn't going to answer me.

"The first person I turned was a woman; her name was Ava. She was a woman born before her time. Feisty, opinionated, brave," Reilly says, looking up at me with a pointed raise of his brow as if to say *just like you*. "She hated Cesare, and she convinced me to help her overthrow him. She said we could take over the clan and shape the future into something better. We could stop killing humans to feed. We could have peace with the other paranormal races."

Reilly shakes his head. "Cesare caught her. She managed to convince Cesare that I wasn't involved. He killed her and a few others. I escaped death, but not punishment," Reilly says, his hand reaching up to his shoulder. "Cesare expects betrayal I think. He rules by fear, not respect."

"The scars?" I ask quietly.

"Yes," he nods. "Whip a vampire long enough with a silver-dipped cat-o'-nine-tails, pour holy water over the wounds, and even we will scar."

I stare at him, horrified. The agony he must have gone through is hard to imagine.

"How could you stand to stay with him after that?" I ask.

"Surviving has always been the most important thing," Reilly says, finally looking up and meeting my gaze. "I could have struck out in anger that day, but then I would be dead and no one would be trying to stop Cesare now. It was only a matter of time before he did something like this. I had to stay close and wait for the right time, and for the right people, to try again."

Ihaka was right. I could never have convinced Reilly not to work with the coven without knowing how desperate he is to kill Cesare. This is personal for him; it's not about ambition. I couldn't have done what Reilly did. I don't have that kind of patience. Then again, I probably would have just run away.

"Back when Cesare showed up at the hotel, you said I sounded like someone," I say quietly. "You meant her, didn't you?"

"Yes, you always have. Tough, determined, brash. You have more patience than she did though." He steps forward, watching me carefully.

My brain tells me to run far away, but as Reilly leans in close, our breath mingling, I find I don't want to. Just as I'm about to turn away, he shuts his eyes and pulls back.

"Elise is coming," he whispers.

I step away, relieved and disappointed.

Elise pushes the door open and approaches, eyeing Reilly warily. "Ian and his pack are ready for us."

"Took them long enough," I say.

"Are we going ahead with the original plan?" Elise asks as we walk back outside, the door swinging shut behind us.

"Yes, I'm sure Cesare is wondering where we are," I say, a smirk tugging at my lips. He has no idea what's coming.

CHAPTER 26

The doors to the stately building lay broken in the midst of other rubble. Yellow police tape flutters in the gap left behind. Our footsteps echo through the ominously quiet atrium as we enter the former seat of the witch council.

The marble floors lead us straight ahead. On either side of the wide corridor are pictures of previous council members. Many of the portraits are burnt, some were ripped from the wall and lay shredded on the ground. Cadriel must have been angry when he came through here.

The corridor ends with a tall arch leading into an open room. Broken pews, once used for meetings, litter the floor between us and the raised stage the council would have given their announcements from. There is only one chair remaining. Cesare sits in it, his arm propped comfortably on the armrest as he waits.

"Reilly, I suspected you were not completely loyal, but this? Recruiting other clans to join your little mutiny?" Cesare gestures at Javier and the other vampires he brought with him, shaking his head in disapproval. "It reeks of desperation."

"You released something that has been bound for almost a

thousand years, that you cannot control, just to kill the witches," Reilly says, his voice resonating through the room. He steps away from the group, putting himself between Cesare and everyone else. "Yet, you accuse me of desperation? That's weak, Cesare."

"Olivia will kill Cadriel for me, or return him to his shadowy prison," Cesare says, sitting up straight and waving his hand dismissively. "And after that, she will do whatever I tell her to do in order to spare the lives of everyone gathered here tonight. That is the difference between you and me, Reilly," Cesare continues. "I am willing to do what it takes. I knew you weren't the day you watched me kill Ava and didn't nothing to stop me."

Reilly growls at the mention of her name. "Today, you will be the one who dies."

Cesare laughs and snaps his fingers. Vampires stream into the room behind him. "You think you can kill me with a small JHAPI team and a weak clan?" Cesare asks, gesturing toward his clan. There are at least thirty of them.

Reilly smirks. "Did you really believe this was all of us?"

Cesare's smile fades and he narrows his eyes. "The coven didn't join you," he says, irritation slipping into this voice. "I have already been informed of how that fight went."

A long howl raises the hair on the back of my neck as it echoes through the entire building. It's impossible to tell what direction it's coming from as the rest of Ian's pack joins in. They got here almost an hour before us, just as planned. Cesare's fingers dig into the armrest. He wasn't expecting that at all.

A man with long blond hair slips out from one of the doorways almost unnoticed. I make eye contact, confused to see Adrian here, and on Cesare's side of things. He winks at me.

"I've got this. Go take care of Cadriel," Reilly says, drawing my attention away from Adrian. He is looking back at me with determination burning in his eyes.

"Kill Cesare, for Ava," I whisper.

Reilly nods, flashing me a smile.

Cesare stands from his makeshift throne. "I will make you suffer," he growls.

Reilly turns back to face him. "Come down here and face me then," Reilly shouts.

Cesare moves in a blur, the vampires charging after him. Gunfire booms as fire flares up between the team and Cesare's clan. Werewolves stream into the room from every direction. Adrian kicks the throne into two vampires that make it past the fire, then leaps after it, a grin on his face.

Reilly and Cesare collide in the center of the room, exchanging blows too fast for me to see. They break apart and Reilly wipes a thin line of blood from the corner of his mouth.

I crouch down and press my hands to the floor. Streaks of lightning race toward two vampires. They jump away from the magic, but it arcs up and strikes their legs. They fall to the ground, convulsing.

Patrick and Leslie grab a vampire that leaps toward Corinne and Ivy. Corinne lifts her gun and shoots him in the face with a silver bullet, killing him instantly. Emilio has some kind of rapier. He moves gracefully through the fight, running the sword through a vampire's heart, then jerking it free. The vampire crumbles into dust.

"Olivia, we have to go!" Elise shouts.

I run back over to her, but a sickening crunch jerks my attention back to the fight in the center of the room. Adrian is between Cesare and Reilly. The broken leg of the chair is jutting out of his stomach, blood flowing freely from the wound.

"You chose the wrong side," Cesare taunts, twisting the wood.

"I always did want to die gloriously," Adrian gasps, smiling despite the pain. He kicks Cesare, forcing him back and rips the piece of chair out of his gut.

"They'll be fine, Olivia," Elise says, jerking me forward. "Let's go."

Maybelle and Kabs are waiting for us in the shadow realm. I

can't leave them there, vulnerable, for any longer than necessary. I force myself to turn away. We'll all die if Cadriel isn't killed. I have to believe that Reilly and Adrian can take care of themselves.

Elise, Zachary, Hu, and I sprint into the fray. Fire surges around us, forming a tunnel that protects the group. The Finding magic pulls me insistently forward. I know exactly which door will take us down to Cadriel.

The stairwell is steep and dark. My eyes water at the scent of decay which grows stronger as we descend. A scream rips through the air and I sprint ahead. Only Elise is able to keep up as I move vampire fast.

The door at the bottom of the stairwell is open, but a body blocks the path. I leap over the corpse and skid to a stop in a wide room. The ceiling is low and the lighting is dim, making the entire area feel claustrophobic.

A man with shaggy brown hair lifts his face from where it's buried in a witch's neck. He drops her and turns to face us, blood smeared in the corner of his mouth.

Cadriel isn't tall, or muscled, but the sheer amount of magic held inside of him seems to have its own gravity. I can see why they called him a god. Fear curls in my gut as he looks directly at me.

"Did Cesare send me more food?" Cadriel asks, scanning the group curiously.

"Run!" A man screams from behind Cadriel, banging his hand against the iron bars he is trapped behind. "You will only make him stronger!"

I hadn't even noticed the cages behind Cadriel. At least a dozen witches are crammed inside the small space.

"Cesare didn't send us," I say, keeping an eye on Cadriel. "Your old friend Izul did."

WITCH'S BITE

The words have their desired effect. Cadriel's face goes red with anger and he hisses at me like a wild animal. I need him angry and unfocused for as long as possible. The group spreads out. We have to time this perfectly. I'll only get one shot to get Cadriel back in the shadow realm.

"Izul is dead!" Cadriel shrieks, his skin turning gray as he draws on imperv magic. "He is dead and I will kill the rest of the witches after I take their magic for myself!"

Zachary lifts his gun and fires at Cadriel several times in rapid succession. The bullets thud against Cadriel, but they can't penetrate his skin. Nothing can. Cadriel waves his hand absently and a gust of wind knocks Zachary to the ground.

The air around us shakes with his rage. Cadriel steps forward and lifts his hand. Fire erupts from his palms and rushes toward us, but Hu's fire magic collides with it, stopping it in its tracks. Hu falls to one knee. His arms shake as he desperately pushes back against the overwhelming power of Cadriel.

I run forward and send my electric magic racing over Hu's. The crackling, white light wraps around the fire like a net. Two against one, we slowly force Cadriel back.

Hu struggles to his feet and claps his hands together. His fire magic erupts, seeming to double in power. The three magics twist together, then collapse with a sharp crack.

Elise, already shifted, runs past Cadriel and nips at his heels, drawing his attention to give me a chance to create the portal. Magic pours from my hands, and the shadowy magic twists in the air. It is much more difficult to create a portal to the shadow realm that will last as long as I need, but Maybelle and Kabs have to have an escape route in case I'm killed.

I grind my teeth together. I'm almost done. Elise just needs to keep distracting Cadriel for a few more seconds. A faint step is all the warning I get before someone charges me from behind. Vampire magic rushes through my limbs giving me the speed to dodge their swing.

Zachary shoots the vampire attacking me, the bullet searing him all the way through with silver. I kick him, sending a surge of electricity down my foot and into his chest. The vampire drops, but there are five more running into the room.

"Hu!" I shout.

He turns and blocks them with a wave of fire. One of them runs toward the wall and kicks off of it, vaulting over the fire. Hu flings a fiery whip at him, but the vampire dodges that as well.

Zachary fires three rapid shots at the trapped vampires. The third hits its target.

"Just go!" Hu shouts. "We can hold them off!"

As much as I need Hu for this, I can't wait for him, and Zachary can't hold off the vampires alone. I grit my teeth and run straight at Cadriel.

Elise is darting back and forth, barely able to keep ahead of Cadriel. He isn't as fast as Reilly, but like me, he is almost as fast as a vampire. Elise spots me and leads Cadriel toward the hidden portal.

I charge him, pushing my speed to the limits. With one last push, shadow magic rushes out of me and the portal stabilizes.

A vampire swipes at Elise. She dodges the attack and darts to the side, away from the portal. Cadriel skids to a stop, unable to change directions as quickly as she can. I leap toward Cadriel. He turns halfway, his dark eyes locking with mine as we collide, and fall into the shadows.

CHAPTER 27

We hit sand as Cadriel's fingers bite into my arm. Maybelle, who has been waiting for our arrival, waves her hand. The portal disappears behind an illusion, along with the cauldron I placed here the night before. Kabs presses his palms against the sand and pours his magic into it. I need the shadow creatures to come as soon as possible, and the best way to draw them in by using all the magic we can.

"I won't be trapped here again!" Cadriel roars as his magic plunges into me and yanks on the power inside of me. I fight back, reaching deep inside of him. Our magic slides together like nails on a chalkboard.

He shoves me away in shock. "What are you?" he demands.

"I'm just like you. A half-breed," I say, panting a few feet away from him. A strange, new magic prickles uncomfortably inside of me. My skin shifts to gray, becoming invulnerable. I didn't manage to get much, though, and the magic feels weak. It won't hold up against an attack for very long.

Kabs and Maybelle watch us uneasily as they wait for the shadow creatures to appear, or Cadriel to attack.

Cadriel's face splits into a crazed grin. "Izul told me the knowledge to make another like me was lost," he says gleefully, reaching his hand out toward me. "No one could stop us if you join me. We are gods compared to them!"

I sneer at him. "Gods? Hardly. How many witches do you have to drain just to satisfy the hunger?" I demand. "I know the more you steal, the hungrier you get. And I just felt how much stolen magic you have inside of you."

Cadriel cackles. "Who cares?" he dismisses. "The power should be ours."

"You're nothing but a parasite," I snap angrily, then charge him.

Cadriel doesn't try to dodge my attack. We collide, rolling down the short hill we landed on, and the tug-of-war over the magic begins again. Cadriel's magic is harder to grab than a normal witch. My own magic spasms inside of me as he tries to steal it. I struggle to resist the pull while still trying to rip away every bit of magic I can from him.

The electric magic twitches inside of me, then begins to flow into him with a rush. I grab a brew from my pocket and flick the cork out with my thumb, but he smacks my hand away. The vial flies out of my hand, spilling the knock out brew onto the sand. I grit my teeth and reach deeper inside of Cadriel, ripping away a hot, powerful magic from him in return.

Magic and anger churns inside of me. I smack my hand to his chest and release a burst of fire. He jumps away, and wind rushes past me, blowing the flames to the side. He hits the sand a few feet away and slides further down the hill.

"You are going to kill us both using magic in this place," Cadriel shouts, scrambling to his feet; looking at the hills in fear.

"As long as I take you with me!" I yell, lifting my hands again. Heat surges through my body, and fire erupts from my palms. Cadriel had stolen so much of it, and now the powerful fire magic is inside of me. Struggling to control the fire, it pours out of me and surges around Cadriel. I'm using too much, too fast, but it won't be reigned in. A wall of water splashes through the fire, dousing half of it. I drop to one knee as the magic snaps back into me.

"Look out!" Kabs shouts.

Hulking black shapes swarm over the crest of the hill and surge toward us like a river. The shadow creatures yip and howl, a bone-chilling noise that echoes around us.

"I warned you!" Cadriel yells.

The pack of shadow creatures race toward us, but Kabs sends his magic into the ground. A churning wave of sand shoots up, blocking their path. One of them falls from the crest and tumbles gracelessly down. Maybelle runs forward, spear held high and stabs down viciously on the back of its neck. It twitches once, then goes still. Others race down after it, only slowed by the obstacle Kabs put in their way.

Another small pack is charging in from the opposite direction. Kabs and Maybelle will barely be able to hold off the first pack, they can't stop this one as well. A shadow creature leaps at Cadriel and he kicks it, sending the thing flying. It hits the ground, claws scrambling for purchase as it slides a short way down the hill. Another charges him. He catches it by the neck and slams it onto the sand, but three more pounce on his back.

I run for the cauldron I left here the night before. Maybelle has it hidden, disguised as one of the many twisted shrubs that dot the sand. When I get close enough, I stretch my left hand out and channel pure magic into the cauldron, starting the brew.

I may be a vampire, and I may be able to steal magic, but I'll always be a hedgewitch first. Brewing was the first thing I learned. It's the one thing I have left from my mother, and it's a part of me now. Herbs and crystals are my usual ingredients, but they can't do what I need today.

My hair whips around my face and the ground vibrates under my feet. Grains of sand float up, hovering around my legs like stardust. Deafening thunder cracks through the sky overhead. The magic draws the attention of the shadow creatures. A few break away from the group, heading straight for me and the magic I'm wielding.

I pull the short staff off my back and race toward the next creature before it can attack me. It lunges, massive jaws opening wide. I swing low, catching it in the throat, then bring the staff down on its back. The creature stumbles. I kick back and catch another in the face, noticing it just barely in time. Lifting my hand, I send shadow magic toward the two standing close together, opening the ground under their feet. They are swallowed up by darkness and disappear.

Cadriel shouts in the distance, enraged, and lightning cracks through the air in a bright flash. The magic strikes one of the creatures, but it doesn't falter. It grows. Electricity crackles through its thick black fur as it doubles in size. The monster jumps at Cadriel, but he meets it head on, striking it as the imperv magic rolls over his skin.

Another creature creeps toward me, growling menacingly. Its muscles bunch as it prepares to leap. I take a step back and let the magic flow into the brew once more. Watching the creature closely, I grab the small knife from my waistband, switching to hold the staff one-handed. It leaps toward me, its teeth gleaming in the silvery light of the shadow realm. I deflect the attack with the staff and slash the knife across its stomach. Mottled black blood drips out of the creature, coating the knife.

I step back into the in-between. I have to do this while Cadriel is distracted, and I may not get another chance. Slipping back into the shadow realm, I duck down behind the shrub that hides the cauldron. This part is going to suck, but I can't risk using too little. Before I can over think it, I dig the point of the knife into my wrist. Blood streams out, but it doesn't drip on the sand, it flows into the cauldron in front of me. I scrape the bloody knife on the edge of the cauldron and the black blood of the shadow creature sinks into the brew as well. It churns, the color changing from green to black.

I don't know what the shadow creatures are, exactly, but I know they devour magic. I'll never be able to kill Cadriel while he has all of his. My blood mixed with the blood of the shadow creatures will be able to drain every last drop of magic from him and destroy it. I stir the brew with the knife. The contents of the cauldron twist and swirl together, changing into something powerful and terrifying.

I dart away from the cauldron. Cadriel is still distracted but he won't be for much longer. The shadow creature I cut attempts to charge me again. I bring the staff down on its head, then kick it under the jaw. It flies backward, unconscious and bleeding out.

A bolt of electricity flies toward me. I drop the staff and the knife, barely getting my hands up in time to counter Cadriel's attack. Lightning smashes into fire. The opposing magics twist together, electricity striking the sand in blinding flashes. The fire magic is almost uncontrollable, but the sheer power of it allows me to hold Cadriel off.

"Kabs!" Maybelle screams.

My focus wavers for a split second. Two creatures are running at him from behind. Kabs turns, and sand rushes up to block them just in time. Cadriel pushes forward, overwhelming my magic. I'm thrown back and tumble down the hill.

I jump to my feet but Cadriel doesn't run after me. He's staring at Maybelle, and at the spot where the portal is hidden. She kicks a shadow creature's head as it snaps at Kabs, then runs it through with her spear. The illusion flickers, barely enough to show the portal we came through, but he *knows*.

Cadriel looks down at me. "You shouldn't have tried to trap me here again," he spits out. He lifts his hand toward Maybelle, a dark and angry expression on his face.

"No!" I scream as I sprint toward her, slipping through the shadows to get there faster.

I move as fast as I can, the vampire magic pumping through my shaking limbs. The lightning is faster. It streaks past me, and straight into Maybelle.

The magic hits her as I leap from the shadows less than a foot away. She turns toward me; her eyes wide and fearful. The electricity jaggedly sears her skin, and she screams. White light pours out of the wounds as the magic rips through her.

She seems to fall in slow motion. My heart stutters as I reach for her, thinking that if I can just catch her, maybe I can save her. She hits the sand, and the bright electricity fades into nothing.

"Maybelle!" Kabs cries. The sand rises up around him, swallowing the last of the shadow creatures. He runs toward her.

I drop to the sand beside Maybelle and drag her into my lap. Every ounce of healing magic I have rushes into her. Her scarred face is locked in a silent scream of pain, and her eyes are still wide with terror. The magic flutters through her, useless. It's too late. She takes one last shuddering breath, then goes still. She's gone.

I look up at Cadriel, rage unlike any I have felt before filling me. She was the closest thing to a mother I had left, and he killed her. He took her from me. The illusions Maybelle created shatter, the magic falling away like ash.

Cadriel runs toward the now visible portal. I roll into the shadows, letting Maybelle's body slip from my arms. As he reaches the portal, I step out of the shadows and lunge toward him.

"You're dead, you piece of shit," I scream as I wrap my arm around his neck, keeping him from taking the final step.

"I will not die here," he hisses, desperation giving him strength. He drags me forward, stepping halfway into the portal. Our feet slip from sand to the rushing current of the in-between.

In front of us, the air twists, revealing the underground room we came from. Behind us, is the dim light of the shadow realm. If he gets back to the physical realm, then all of this was for nothing. I bite Cadriel's neck, my teeth digging into the taut flesh. His blood fills my mouth, making my stomach twist in revulsion. I wrench magic and strength away from him. His steps falter as he is forced to fight back against the pull on his magic.

I drag him away from the physical realm. We fall and the current sweeps us downstream toward the cauldron. Cadriel elbows me in the cheek, catching my eye and knocking me aside. The skin splits; blood drips down my face. He pulls away, scrambling to his feet. I leap onto his back, clawing at his face and neck. Anything I can grab. He stumbles and I force us back into the shadow realm. I wrench his head to the side and drop my feet down to the sand for leverage. I just need to reach the brew. I only need a drop.

Kabs runs toward us with a battle yell, his hands outstretched. The sand under our feet rolls upward and we both fall. My back hits the iron cauldron. The brew erupts around us as it shatters. The black liquid falls on us like rain, seeping into our skin.

Magic drains out of both of us like a sieve. It feels like my soul is being ripped from my body. I never understood how much this hurt.

Cadriel shrieks in pain and anger. The warmth of the fire magic bleeds out of me, followed quickly by the shadow magic. The vampire magic is ripped away and my body grows weak. Cadriel pulls out of my grip and rolls away from me. Bright trails of magic flow out of him and into the brew. It hovers where the cauldron used to be; now a twisted mass of pure magical energy.

The last bits of magic I stole from Novak drain away, sparking at the tips of my fingers as it disappears. My body shakes as I struggle against it instinctively. Cadriel convulses, spit foaming at the corners of his mouth. Every muscle in his body strains against the brew.

The warm healing magic fades quickly. There was so little; it's easy for the brew to consume it. Tears gather in my eyes as the hedgewitch magic begins to drain out of me. Pain cuts through every cell in my body. It's the only thing I had left from my mother. I didn't think I would have to lose this too. I didn't think I would have to sacrifice everything to kill Cadriel.

The last bit of my magic seeps away. I'm empty. There's nothing left but loss and rage.

"What have you done?" Cadriel demands, baring his teeth at me like a wild animal. The portal is shaking unsteadily. It won't hold for much longer. He tries to stand, but his legs collapse underneath him. He crawls forward on hands and knees.

Howls erupt behind us and I hear the rush of sand as Kabs shouts a warning. I force myself to move. I have to end this. Every limb shakes as I lunge for Cadriel. My nails claw into his back, slowing his retreat. He grabs my hair and jerks me off his back.

He killed Maybelle. I won't let him get away with it. I grab his leg, clinging to it as he kicks back trying to hit me in the face. I push my feet into the sand and jump toward him. He twists unexpectedly, gets a hand around my throat, and forces me onto my back.

I grab a handful of his hair with one hand and yank him closer, then force my thumb into his eye. He screams as I crush it into his skull. Blood drips down my hand. I get a knee between us and push him off of me.

"No," he moans. "I won't stay here!" He turns away and drags himself toward the portal on his stomach, fingers digging into the sand.

A spear lands next to me. "Take it!" Kabs yells.

I grab the weapon and drive it into his leg. Cadriel howls in pain. I jerk it free then plunge it into his back. The spear hits bone, jarring my arm painfully. He wheezes as I stab him again and again. Maybelle's face as she fell is all I can see. I hate him.

"Just die!" I scream, my face contorted in rage as I plunge the spear into him again.

He claws at the ground, still trying to drag himself away. I grab his hair, wrenching his head back, and drag the blade across his throat. Blood sprays over the silvery sand, coating it with red.

Cadriel gasps for breath, coughing as his lungs fill with blood. Slowly, his body goes limp, then cracks. He collapses into dust.

I scoot away and fall back onto the sand; tears streaming down my face. My fingers tighten around the spear. He's dead, but Maybelle is gone and nothing will bring her back.

"Olivia!" Kabs shouts.

I force myself upright. Kabs swallows up the last two of the creatures in a wave of sand, but there are more cresting over the top of the hill. We're about to be overrun.

"Run!" I scream. The portal behind me is shaky. I don't know how much longer it will last, and I can't remake it.

CHAPTER 28

"Kabs we have to go!" I shout.

"I won't leave her!" Kabs yells back, sobbing. He tries to pick her up, but she's as tall as he is, and he can't seem to get back to his feet.

I grit my teeth and jog toward him. Her body is cold and limp. My muscles strains as I lift her. She isn't very heavy, but I'm exhausted.

"Let's go," I beg.

Kabs nods and we run toward the portal. It's shrinking.

"Faster!" I yell. I pick up the pace, my legs and arms burning with the exertion. The portal shrinks even further, but we duck down and leap through together. The magic shudders as we pass through, then collapses and spits us out onto concrete.

"Stay down!" Zachary shouts.

Fire rushes overhead. Sweat drips down my forehead from the suffocating heat. The magic dissipates; I push up to my knees and hand Maybelle to Kabs.

"Stay with her," I say hoarsely. He nods and crawls closer to her.

Hu is still facing off with the same vampires. It's like we were only gone for a minute, instead of what felt like an hour. A wall of fire swirls around him, lashing out when one of them gets close.

Zachary fires twice and his gun locks back on empty. He scrambles for another magazine, but the vampire he shot is still running at him. Elise jumps, colliding mid-air with the vampire. She latches onto his throat and bites down hard, dragging him to the floor.

The ground beneath the other vampires churns and they sink into the stone like its quicksand. I look back at Kabs. The tears are gone, replaced with determination.

Hu shoves both hands forward and the wall of fire flares out. I choke down bile as the smell of burning flesh fills the room. Zachary shoots the trapped vampires, putting them out of their misery. When all that's left is dust, Hu lowers his hands and steps back.

"Is Cadriel dead?" Hu shouts across the room.

I nod once and Hu slumps in relief.

"Are they still fighting Cesare?" I ask as I glance back at Kabs. He is kneeling by Maybelle again, head bowed.

Elise woofs once, then sprints toward the stairs. That must mean yes. Hu runs after her. I try to follow, but I'm slow. I might as well be human now. There isn't a drop of magic left in me.

"Are you hurt?" Zachary asks, looking me over.

"Not badly enough to care," I say. "But my magic is gone." I look down at my hands. They're shaking. It feels like someone carved out all my guts. I can't fight like this.

"Gone?" He asks, his brows pulling together in concern.

"Yes, but there's no time to explain right now," I say, shaking my head.

"We'll get you a gun then," he says. "Come on."

I shake off the fear and jog after him. As we near the top of the stairs, the sounds of fighting grow louder and louder. There is a steady rap of gunfire in the background.

Zachary peers around the corner, then waves me forward.

Stocke is behind a short wall with an AR-15 against her shoulder. She pulls the trigger every couple of seconds, her aim steady. Ian's pack has forced the vampires back, allowing JHAPI to pick them off from a distance.

Staci is crouched next to her reloading her weapon. She sees us and waves us over, kicking a backpack in our direction.

"There's more ammo in there, Zachary," she shouts over the racket.

"Olivia needs a gun," Zachary shouts back, digging through the backpack.

"Olivia, try the purple one," Staci says.

Zachary pulls out two magazines that fit his pistol then tosses me a purple gun with a large cylinder set on top.

"Is this a paintball gun?" I ask, confused.

Staci grins and nods. "Yeah, sorry it's all I have. I got some empty paintballs and figured out a way to inject them with brews."

"That's fucking genius," I say, lifting the gun and firing over the wall. The paintball splats against a vampire and she drops like a stone. At least I can still do this.

"Knock-out brews," Staci says, answering my unasked question. "I brought a non-lethal option just in case."

It's better than nothing. I fire steadily, dropping vampires when I don't miss. I'm more consistent when I'm throwing a vial but I have to be much closer for that, and vampires are fast.

Viking flies through the air and lands on his back, sliding toward us. A vampire that I recognize from Cesare's friendly little visit runs toward him.

"Shit." I leap over the wall and fire twice, but miss. I run toward Viking. The bodyguard reaches him first and rears back for a strike. I fire again and the paintball hits the bodyguard in the neck. He falls forward.

I shove the unconscious vampire off of Viking. He's dazed and his stomach is bleeding sluggishly, but he doesn't look like he's going to die.

A chuckle makes me look up. Cesare stands in front of me. His suit jacket is torn and there is blood on his teeth.

"I am going to enjoy killing you," Cesare taunts.

I don't see him move before I'm shoved back. Viking drags me away from Cesare. Reilly is standing between us, having blocked the attack.

The two vampires strike and dodge, each of them moving so fast my eyes can't follow. Viking keeps a firm grip on me, half shielding me from what's happening.

"Let go of me!" I yell. "Go help him instead!"

"If you are vulnerable Cesare will attack you again," Viking says, holding me a little tighter just in case I try to flee. "That will distract Reilly."

Ihaka and Ian, in wolf form, charge in from opposite sides. Ihaka is holding a short wooden spear.

"Cadriel is dead," I shout, still straining against Viking's grip. "You hear me Cesare? He's dead! Your plan failed!"

Reilly takes a kick to the chest and flies a few feet backward. He skids to a stop, one knee and one hand on the ground.

"You will join Cadriel in death," Cesare hisses at me.

"You first," Reilly shouts.

He charges and Ihaka throws the spear. Ian jumps forward and lands on Cesare's back, grabbing the back of his neck with his jaws. Cesare growls and stumbles backward, trying to reach for Ian, who leaps away.

Reilly catches the spear in mid-air and plunges it into Cesare's chest. It pierces him through the heart, the bloody end jutting out of his back. Cesare falls to his knees, a sneer still on his face, and disintegrates into dust.

CHAPTER 29

It's over.

I'm sitting in a van with a shock blanket wrapped around my shoulders. I'm not sure what the purpose of it is, but it's warm and I'm shivering from exhaustion. Most of the team is milling around aimlessly. A few people dressed in uniforms are walking with purpose carrying stretchers.

Zachary and Elise walk up. Zachary steps in front of me, his expression full of concern.

"Olivia, are you all right?" he asks.

"Yes," I whisper. "Is everyone okay?"

"Ivy is pretty banged up, but she'll live," Elise says, her lips pressed into a thin line.

I shut my eyes and bury my face in my hands, relieved. I couldn't have taken another death. "That's good."

"I'm sorry about Maybelle," Zachary says. "I know she meant a lot to you."

I nod, not wanting to speak about her death so soon.

"How did you do it?" he asks. "It seemed like you were only gone for a few minutes."

"A brew," I say, dragging my hands down my face. "I realized how to make it work after failing to find a way to cure the hunger I've been struggling with. I found the last thing I needed in the shadow realm. A way to destroy magic."

"I guess that was the key the prophecy mentioned," Zachary says. "I didn't believe it until now, but it was true."

"Yeah," I agree. "Adrian thought I was the key. He was both right and wrong."

"Is your magic really gone?" Zachary asks.

"Yes," I say, looking down. Pain from the reminder of the loss twists in my chest. "I can't even brew now."

He puts his hand on my shoulder and squeezes it sympathetically. "You're going to be okay without it," he says quietly.

"Eventually," I agree, trying to smile, and failing. I can feel a distant echo of the hunger inside of me that I lived with for so long. I could steal magic again, but I don't want to be like Cadriel. I won't be a monster.

"You always manage to survive the craziest shit," Elise says. "You'll get through this too."

Adrian walks up, looking angelic despite leather pants. There is a bloody hole in his previously white shirt. He stops in front of me and smiles, his teeth stained with blood. "How does it feel to fulfill a prophecy?"

"Terrible," I say with a harsh laugh. "How'd you manage to survive getting skewered?"

He scoffs. "I'm not that easy to kill."

I shake my head and smile. "I'm glad you aren't."

"It appears you aren't either," he says, tilting his head.

"Just dumb luck," I say.

"Be proud of what you have accomplished," he says, putting a cold hand under my chin and lifting my face up to his. He leans in and kisses me soundly on the cheek.

I cringe and wipe the side of my face, smearing the lip-shaped imprint of blood.

"I'll see you again," he says. "Hopefully." Adrian turns and walks away.

Zachary shakes his head. "He is so odd."

"You are not wrong," I agree. I spot Reilly walking toward us. "Can you give us a minute?" I ask.

"Sure," Zachary says, shoving off the side of the van. He and Elise head in the same direction Adrian went.

Reilly's shirt is torn and stained red. His suit jacket is gone. Even his hair is mussed. He stops in front of me, his hand brushing lightly against mine.

"Fancy meeting you here," I say lightly. After everything that's happened today, I'm just glad Reilly is alive. I'm glad I'm alive. Any worry about tomorrow can wait until then.

Reilly wipes away the blood Adrian left on my cheek. "You killed a god," he whispers.

"And you killed Cesare," I say looking up into his eyes. I don't need to be able to hear his heartbeat to know he wants me right now, not when he is looking at me like that.

In some ways, I'm still not sure if I can completely trust Reilly. But there hasn't been a single person in my life, not even my mother or Brunson, that hadn't lied to me at some point. Reilly is beginning to feel worth the risk.

I lift my hand slowly, watching for his reaction, and wrap it around the back of his neck. His eyes drop to my lips and I pull him forward, taking the kiss I've been wanting for so long. It's better than my dreams.

One of his hands tangles in my hair and the other slips down to my lower back as he pulls me closer. I memorize the feel of his lips against mine. The warmth of his fingertips through my shirt. The hard press of his chest against mine. It all reminds me that I am *alive*.

CHAPTER 30

The newly formed witch council sits at the table with the Director of JHAPI, the two official vampire council members, and the werewolf council. The team is briefing the councils on everything we just went through and reassuring them that the Bound God is dead.

Giving my testimony to the hearing was miserable, but it's over at least. JHAPI and the werewolves thanked me for my sacrifices. The witches were less appreciative, one of them even hinting that I must be part of some kind of conspiracy to cripple them. I'll never really be accepted by the witches. It shouldn't bother me, but it does. Especially since I've lost all my magic.

Most of the world will never know exactly what happened with Cadriel. The official press release says there was an explosion. Maybelle is receiving a medal for bravery posthumously. It's not enough, but there isn't really a way to thank someone who gave up everything like that.

The only good to come out of this is that the werewolf council is finally convinced JHAPI is not out to get them. Ian had a lot to do with that. It isn't perfect, but at least things are changing for the better.

The vampires have been shamed for almost letting one of their own get away with a crazed plot to take over the world. Reilly is hopeful that he can improve things for the vampires though. He certainly has his work cut out for him.

Agent Stocke finally finishes her testimony and the Director of JHAPI leans forward, clasping his hands together. "Agent Stocke, I commend you and your team for the personal risk you undertook in order to stop a madman," he says, glancing back at me and nodding in thanks. "I am appointing you as the lead liaison between JHAPI and the councils. Is there an agent that you would like take over your position as team lead?"

Stocke only hesitates for a moment before replying, "Yes sir. Agent Ivy Andreas has a healthy respect for the rules and a natural instinct for leadership. She will lead the team well if you give her the chance."

The director nods. "Thank you all for your efforts. This briefing is adjourned," he says.

I sigh in relief. It took several hours, but at least it's over. I'm the first one out of my seat, and I hurry toward the exit. The rest of the team is taking this opportunity to shake hands with the director and speak with the councils; I'm not interested in any of that.

The halls are packed with people today. I weave through the crowds until I reach the break room. There's a vending machine inside and I'm dying of thirst.

I cover a yawn and feed the dollar bill into the slot. It doesn't have tequila, unfortunately, but I'll take water over nothing. The bottle tumbles down and I grab it from the take out port.

"Olivia, I'm glad you're still here," Staci says, walking up from behind me. "I want to talk to you about something."

I jump, easily startled now that I can't hear people coming. I hadn't appreciated how much the vampire magic enhanced my senses until I lost it. "Sure, what did you need?" I ask.

"Stocke just approved my vacation request. Two weeks off," Staci says, crossing her arms like she's getting ready to argue.

"That's nice," I say, confused. "Are you going to visit family or something?"

"You lost all your magic, even the hedgewitch magic. I want you to take mine to replace it," she insists. "As much as you can without killing me."

I step back. "You don't know what you're asking—"

"Yes, I do," Staci says, closing the gap between us. "You love brewing. It's your life. I want to do this for you, it's not like I'm giving up my magic forever, it'll just be a couple of weeks before I can brew again. You killed Cadriel for us, it's the least I can do."

I stare at Staci with my heart in my throat. She has her jaw set stubbornly; she won't let this go until I agree. It's not like this is an offer I am going to turn down anyhow. She's offering me my life back.

"Okay," I say, my hand tightening around the cold bottle.

She lifts her chin and nods once, satisfied. "Let's go, Stocke is waiting for us."

"Right now?" I ask.

"Of course," Staci says, turning and heading down the hallway.

I follow, my heart pounding in anticipation. Staci walks into the same room we used for our team meetings and sits down in the closest chair. Zachary, Elise, and Stocke are the only people there.

Zachary nods and smiles at me.

"Take it," Staci says, holding out her arm.

"Are you sure?" I ask her again, trying to give her every chance to back out.

"Yes," she says, shaking her hand at me insistently.

There is no doubt in her eyes. No fear. I walk forward and take her hand. Her magic is warm and familiar. I ache to have that again.

"Thank you," I whisper.

She nods, squeezing my hand gently. I reach into her, and the magic I love the most begins to fill all the empty space inside of me.

CHAPTER 31

Two weeks later...

"Are you nervous?" I ask.

"No," Reilly says, shaking his head slightly. "The ceremony is going to be boring. Besides, the council is lucky to have me."

I raise my brow at him. "You think very highly of yourself."

He grins, showing off his dimples. "I defeated a god and the most powerful vampire on this side of the world."

"Excuse you," I say, crossing my arms. "I'm the one that killed a god."

"I helped," he insists.

"You weren't even there!" I protest.

He grins mischievously. A knock at the door interrupts our argument and Javier walks in, followed by Lydia.

"Javier," Reilly says with a welcoming smile. "I'm glad you could make it. There are quite a few clans I want to introduce you to."

Lydia walks over to me. "Olivia, it's been a while," she says politely. Her greeting isn't exactly cold, but she seems uneasy.

"It has," I agree. "A lot has happened since the last time I saw you." An uncomfortable silence stretches between us. "Javier is finally getting everything he wanted. Recognition from the council," I say finally.

Lydia nods. "Yes, it's good to see him rising through the ranks. We've worked toward that for years."

"I'm glad it's Javier," I say, trying to reassure her a little. "He's a decent vampire."

She smiles proudly. "Yes, he is."

Ihaka opens the door and sticks his head into the room. "I hate to interrupt, but you are needed, sire," he says.

"Thank you, Ihaka," Reilly says before turning back to Javier. "We'll finish up this discussion soon, Javier. I promise."

I follow the group outside. Reilly waits for me by the door.

"Ava would have loved this," he says quietly.

"The boring ceremony? Or knowing that Cesare is completely defeated?" I ask, looking up at him.

"The latter," he says with a smile.

"Go make her proud," I say as we separate. Reilly continues on toward the stage and I slip out into the hallway to find my way to my seat in the audience. Stocke is waiting for me near the back.

"Agent Stocke, I thought you might be here today," I say, greeting her with a smile.

"Of course, I can't miss the appointment of the newest council member. I did need to talk to you though," she says.

"What's up?" I ask.

"You aren't obligated to work with Reilly Walsh anymore," Stocke comments.

"No, I'm not," I reply. No one else has mentioned it, but I have been thinking about it. It's strange to have my future so open again. It feels foreign.

"I'd like to formally offer you a position with the agency. You'd have to go through the second phase of training, and then you'd be assigned—"

"Sorry to interrupt, but the answer is no," I say, cutting her off.

Stocke looks surprised. "Can I ask why? I thought you'd at least consider it," she says.

"I have considered it. I thought the offer might come after everything, and since I'm special," I say with a rueful smile. "But I know what I want to do."

"You aren't going to be joining Reilly's clan are you?" She asks, looking toward the raised stage the council is walking out onto skeptically.

I laugh. "God no. I'm going to do what I wanted to do in the first place; open an apothecary." The laughter dies in my throat and I stare down at my hands, white-knuckled where they are clasped in front of me. I had wanted to do it with Maybelle. Hopefully, I can make her proud.

"We can help with that then. As a thank-you," Stocke says. "It was already put in motion in order to offer you the job; your record is being wiped clean."

Shock colors my face. "What?"

"Your felony," she explains. "It's being wiped from your record. You'll be able to apply for all the certifications you need to join that healer's guild or whatever it's called."

A weight I've been carrying since I was eighteen is lifted from my shoulders. I made mistakes, and paid the consequences, but having that follow me around for life was depressing.

Stocke claps her hand on my shoulder. "If you ever miss the excitement, let me know. The position is yours if you want it."

I nod, still unable to speak around the lump in my throat. Stocke smiles and walks away to find a seat. I look at Reilly standing with the vampire council. He's so young compared to the rest of them, but he's right where he belongs. We all are, finally.

Leslie is going back to live with Patrick and Javier for a while, despite Reilly being her sire. Kabs is back in Donheim though I suspect he won't stay there long. He is volunteering to be one of the first goblins to live openly in a human city.

And I'm going home. I don't know when Pecan Grove became home, but it has.

CHAPTER 32

The old house has a new coat of paint. My mother had painted it bright yellow when we first moved in. It was a total eyesore, but she loved it. The new owners apparently did not. I can't really blame them.

The door opens and squat, middle-aged woman walks out with a sunhat shielding her face. She pulls on some worn out gloves and starts pulling weeds. I smile, glad someone is taking care of the place. The commercial on the radio ends and an upbeat song starts playing. I put the car in drive and pull away from the curb.

Every street I pass has its own memories. Walking to school. Playing with friends, not that I had many. I take a left and pass the hospital. It's huge now; updated with gleaming windows and a parking garage. When I used to go with my mother, it was dingy. At the time it was one of the smaller hospitals in the area. Everyone that couldn't really afford to go to the hospital ended up there. My mother brought healing brews every Sunday and helped everyone she could.

I tried to help too, in my own way, when I stole that healing magic. I hadn't realized it meant we'd have to stop going there completely. The old twinge of regret twists in my stomach. There were so many people that we missed out on helping. I can fix that now though. I don't have to hide anymore, and if my apothecary takes off, I'm going to start the volunteer work again.

After the hospital, the houses get farther apart. It's not quite out of the city, but it's not really in the suburbs either. The parking lot is just past the simple, iron gate that leads into the cemetery. There's no one here but me.

Thunder rumbles overhead as I climb out of the car and walk around to the passenger side to get the flowers. Looking down at my hoodie and wrinkled t-shirt, I have an overwhelming feeling of being underdressed. I take a deep breath. It doesn't matter. They can't see me…most likely.

The gate creaks as I push it open and step into the cemetery. It swings shut behind me and I wind my way through the grave plots until I find what I came here for. The Brunson's are buried in a single grave, one on top of the other.

I stand at the foot of the gravesite and stare at the headstone. I'll always regret not seeing Debra again before she passed. Some selfish choices you don't get a chance to make up for and running away like I did is one of them.

I nervously adjust the flowers in the vase, then set them by the headstone. They're sunflowers. Her favorite.

"Zachary is doing good," I say quietly. "And I found my mom. I don't think I would have if the two of you hadn't taken me in when you did. So thanks." I shove my hands in my pocket. I'm not good at this, but I hope that wherever they are they can hear me, and they know I mean it.

The wind picks up and the first drops of rain hit my face. I pull my hood up and turn away from the grave. This was my last goodbye. The rain beats down harder, but I turn my face to the sky. The sun is breaking through the clouds illuminating everything. I smile despite the tears slipping out of my eyes.

CHAPTER 33

The glass window gleams in the light of the street lamps. My feet are sore, and while my body is tired, my mind is still whirring from the excitement of opening day. Customers actually came, and better yet, they bought things.

Patricks holds out his hand for a high five and I slap my hand against it with a satisfying smack.

"I make a great salesperson," he says, leaning back against the counter with a pleased grin.

"You make a great flirt," I retort, smiling at him. He was actually helpful this evening. He strolled in a little after sunset and managed to sell as much as I had during the entire day. He kept winking at old ladies every time they picked up a salve.

Mr. Muffins winds between my legs and meows loudly.

"You were not helpful at all," I tell her, hands on my hips. "But if you're nicer to the customers tomorrow, I'll give you extra tuna."

She flops down onto her back and purrs loudly, acting like she's innocent.

"You're not fooling anyone," I mutter.

"Well, I'm going to head out," Patrick says, something off in his tone.

I narrow my eyes at him. "Why?"

The bell rings and I look up.

"Reilly?" I ask. He's wearing a black button down shirt over jeans. It's almost casual. My eyes wander past him to the three bodyguards right standing outside. "What are you doing here?"

"I couldn't miss opening day," he says with a grin.

Patrick hurries to the door, nodding politely at Reilly. He looks back over his shoulder and winks at me before hurrying out of the store.

I shake my head, but I can't hide the pleased smile. "What are you really in the area for? I know you didn't fly all the way from Seattle just to see me."

Reilly ignores my question and wanders down an aisle, pausing to pick up whatever catches his eye. I step over Mr. Muffins and follow him.

"You've been busy," he comments, gesturing at the shelves lined with brews and salves. He crouches down and inspects a little jar of cosmetic cream on the bottom shelf.

"Between brewing and still taking care of Javier's neckers, yeah, busy is one way to put it," I agree with a shrug.

"I was surprised to hear you were still doing that," he says, glancing up at me.

"They still need healing, and the brews can take care of that well enough. Javier asked for a few of the neckers to volunteer as part-time workers here, at his expense, in addition to my normal pay. He said to consider it a raise," I snort. "I think he just doesn't want to lose me."

"I can't blame him," Reilly says, standing up slowly.

I look down at my feet. He's not here for me. Thinking he is, is only going to get me hurt.

"You know it's strange," Reilly comments as he prods a vial of shimmery liquid. "We haven't actually been on a date yet."

I look up sharply, my stomach doing flip-flops. I open my mouth, but no words come out.

"I have reservations at a restaurant in Dallas. Supposedly, they have the best steak you'll ever eat." He holds out his hand. "Will you come with me?"

"Dallas is two hours away," I protest.

"I have a helicopter," he says with a grin.

I slip my hand into his. He twines our fingers and pulls me in close, wrapping his arms around me. Standing in my own store, with everything I thought I'd never get, is surreal. There are no more secrets, and no more prophecies. I close my eyes and bury my face in his chest. This is it. This is what it means to be free.

Can't get enough Olivia? *Sign up to the newsletter to get the short story prequel UNSTEADY MAGIC.*

A BIG THANK YOU

Thank you for choosing to read this series. I can't express how much it means to me to know that readers are sharing in the stories I have created.

Forbidden Magic is a special book for me since it marks the completion of my first series. Two years ago I didn't think I would ever finish a book. One year ago writing an entire series felt equally impossible. But here we are :) With a little elbow grease and a lot of sleep deprivation, I did it.

It's not over though! Olivia's story is complete, but I have more stories to tell, and I hope that you'll enjoy the next series just as much.

I received an email last night as I was putting the finishing touches on this story. Thank you, Corrie. It had been a long day (a long month really), and I was exhausted. Hearing from a reader reminded me why I love writing. It was exactly what I needed :)

A BIG THANK YOU

Never hesitate to contact me! You can always email me or shoot me a message on Facebook. I check the Facebook group regularly as well. If you post there, I'll see it!

MAKE A DIFFERENCE

Reviews are very important, and sometimes hard for an independently published author to get. A big publisher has a massive advertising budget and can send out hundreds of review copies.

I, however, am lucky to have loyal and enthusiastic readers. And I think that's much more valuable.

Leaving an honest review helps me tremendously. It shows other readers why they should give me a try.

If you've enjoyed reading this book, I would appreciate, very much, if you took the time to leave a review. Whether you write one sentence, or three paragraphs, it's equally helpful.

Thank you :)

Follow Me

Thank you so much for buying my book. I really hope you have enjoyed the story as much as I did writing it. Being an author is not an easy task, so your support means a lot to me. I do my best to make sure books come out error free. However, if you found any errors, please feel free to reach out to me so I can correct them!

If you loved this book, the best way to find out about new releases and updates is to join my Facebook group, The Foxehole. Amazon does a very poor job about notifying readers of new book releases. Joining the group can be an alternative to newsletters if you feel your inbox is getting a little crowded.

Facebook Group:
https://www.facebook.com/groups/TheFoxehole
Newsletter:
https://stephaniefoxe.com/#Follow-Me
Goodreads:
http://goodreads.com/Stephanie_Foxe
BookBub:
https://www.bookbub.com/authors/stephanie-foxe

MORE BY STEPHANIE FOXE

Misfit Pack is the first book in a new series by Stephanie Foxe –

Not all survive the bite, her twin brother didn't.
Your neighbor is just as likely to be a vampire as they are to be a troll, human, elf, or a werewolf. Amber's Parents never forgave her after her brother died. They were young and careless, but Amber left all that guilt in Texas when she fled to the pacific northwest to be a nurse. But when she decides to play hero, her life as a nurse is cut short. Newly turned wolves aren't easily trusted.

If you crave fast-paced, action-packed urban fantasy with romance kept on the lighter side, then you'll be wrapped up in Amber's pack tighter than your coziest reading blanket.

Buy this book now and become apart of Amber's pack where you'll feel their pain, sadness, and empathy, all while being warmed by their determination, growth, and triumphs.

Stephanie Foxe also writes with her husband as Alex Steele. In The Chaos Mages Series you will meet Logan Blackwell and Lexi Swift as they solve crimes in a world full of magic and myths, much like in Misfit Pack.

Vampires don't rob banks. Werewolves don't bust into jewelry

stores. And Detective Logan Blackwell doesn't work with a partner.

Too bad all three of those things happened in one day. Supernaturals are getting possessed, wreaking havoc, then turning up dead. Blackwell has been tasked with finding out who is responsible and stopping them before they kill again.

After a series of unfortunate incidents that include blowing up part of the Met, Blackwell's boss is fed up. He sticks Blackwell with a partner who has issues that only complicate his life.

Assassination attempts threaten both their lives, but no one will tell him who is trying to kill Detective Lexi Swift, or why. He's already lost one partner, and he's not willing to see another die. It's a good thing she's tough and wields magic almost as chaotic as his.

Old enemies, new threats, and more destruction than his boss can handle are bad enough, but sometimes our inner demons are the most dangerous. When they find the person responsible, Blackwell will face a fight he never expected, and one he may not win.

But most importantly, will the pink ever get out of his hair? He should never have taken that bet...

www.StephanieFoxe.com
www.AlexSteele.net

facebook.com/StephanieFoxeAuthor
goodreads.com/Stephanie_Foxe

Printed in Poland
by Amazon Fulfillment
Poland Sp. z o.o., Wrocław